Hunky

The Immigrant Experience

by

Nicholas Stevensson Karas

Published by 1stBooks 2/4/2009

1stBooks
1663 Liberty Drive, Suite 200
Bloomington, IN 47403

ISBN: 978-1-4140-3038-8 (e)
ISBN: 978-1-4140-3037-1 (sc)

Library of Congress Control Number: 2003099292

Printed in the United States of America
Bloomington, Indiana

This book is printed on acid-free paper.

All inquiries should be addressed to:
1stBooks
1663 Liberty Drive, Suite 200
Bloomington, IN 47403

HUNKY By Nicholas Stevensson Karas
History, biography, autobiography and fiction

From the collection of the Historical and Genealogical Society of
Somerset County at the Somerset Historical Center, Somerset, Pa.

Photograph courtesy of the Winber Coal Heritage Center archives, Winber, Pa.

Photography of S.S. Patricia of 1899 ©, courtesy of Mystic Seaport, Mystic, Ct.

*"...one
who does not honor one's past
has no future."*

This book is dedicated to

Vasyl Najda
Kateryna Mynko
Andrij Karas
Zuzanna Ivanco

who had the courage to leave Europe,

and
Anna Najda-Karas,
who molded my character through her sacrifices,

and the millions of other immigrants whose
stories are not much different from mine.

Acknowledgements

It would be difficult, if not impossible, to write a book of such scope without the help of many other people. To the following, I am especially grateful and indebted:

Jeanie Custer, Rose Ann Nider-Custer, Michael R. Dixon. Rev. Stephan Dutko, Rev. Donald Duza, Mary Maruschak-Eret, Elaine Evans, Stella Nider-Fisher, Jim Flatness, Stephan Karabin, Ivan Karas, Rev. Michael A. Karas, Stephen Karas, Lois Kepes, Toni Kiss, Ted Koast, Laurance Krupnak , Michael Kundrat, Rev. Dan Loya, Walter Maksimovich, Robin Pinko-Van Mechelen, Steve Nemeth, Andrew Nider, Charles Nider, Martha Nider-Nedrow, Mary Holovka-Nider, Michael Nider, John Phillip, Catherine Nider-Ralston, Carol Bitsko-Roehn, Margaret Romans, Susan Seese, Malina Spierings, Kasia Strzalkowska, Sandra Studebaker, Rev. Paul Suda, Andrew Syka, Jaroslav Trunecek, George Warholic, David Wecht and Joan Young.

Preface......

This book contains two stories.

One is that of two families whose modern origins are in the eastern portion of the Carpathian Mountains, in east-central Europe. Their small mountain villages are only 24 miles apart. One family lives on the southern and the other on the northern slope of the continental divide, separated by the forested "green border." And, though they basically are the same people, they are worlds apart. However, they come together not in any of the alpine passes that could join them, but in the factories of 20th century America.

While this is the story of two unique families, it is also the story of hundreds of thousands of other peoples from east-central Europe who came to America in the late 1800s and early 1900s. The individuals who composed these two families are not that different from the thousands of other peasants who also were looking for a way to escape their life of drudgery, toil, oppression, bondage, and most of all, poverty. They longed for the emancipation that had been denied them both as a nation and as individuals for almost a millennium. While most of Europe was preparing for life in the 20th century, their lives had changed little in nearly a thousand years. To do so, they had to move. Everyone in this mobile horde of humanity, whose descendents today live in America, has experienced similar circumstances, events and even unusual personalities among their kin.

It was fascinating to witness, through research and experience, through recorded history, how these people developed similar, almost identical communities to one another in the United States even though they were often physically separated by hundreds of miles. This attests to the sameness of the characteristics they held in common and their origins. What is singular about these two families is how they addressed the obstacles they found before them and how they overcame them to eventually find dilution and acceptance in this nation's great melting pot.

These families are typical of a large group of people who possessed a strong ethnic identity and a nearly common language and were able to survive as an entity without a country of their own for the last 700 years. This is the second story. Their origins date back to the Kyivian Rus, a branch of the Slavic Family, better known today by the modern term Ukrainians. Initially, these people inhabited only the Pryp'yat (Prypit) Marshes at the headwaters of the Dnieper River between today's Ukraine and Byelorussia during the second century.

From here, as their populations burgeoned, Slavs spread in all directions. One group moved southwest. Eventually, their leading edge reached the Adriatic Sea but left remnant populations behind to inhabit the Carpathian Mountains. In these mountains, an eastward extension of the Alps, conquering nations later overran and politically separated these people from the main body of Rus. Later in history, the continental divide became the physical and political separation between Poland and Hungary. In 1772, the border temporarily disappeared. They all became part of the multi-ethnic Austro-Hungarian Empire.

These Rus in the Carpathians, who identified themselves as Rusnaks and, more recently by others, as Lemkos, Boykos and Hutzals, and some more recently as Rusyns, and exhibiting slightly different dialects, became prisoners--in every sense of the word--in their own land. Time, distance and political isolation further separated them from the Rus of today. Because of this, Rusnaks, whether in Europe or America, are still a people trying to establish an ethnic identity.

The Moscovy Russians, a.k.a. the Red Russians, after occupying other Rus lands, referred to them as Little Russians. Still others lumped them with the White Russians (Byelorussia). They were the Rus of two pre-Russia provinces Halych, or Galicia and Volhynia. Both provinces were lost to the Poles and Moscovy Russians. When Lithuania rose to prominence in the 12th century, and was united with Poland through a royal marriage, their western portions were made a part of Poland. The remaining eastern portions were absorbed into a growing Moscovy that would become Russia.

This lasted until retribution set in, when the Austrians, in the third quarter of the 18ᵗʰ century, together with Prussia and Russia, conquered and trisected Poland out of existence.

When my grandparents were born a hundred years later, the Europe they came to know was a much different place than it is today. East-central Europe, across the tops of the Carpathian Mountains, was acknowledged as the most backward region of the continent, especially the new lands now occupied by the Austro-Hungarian Empire. Their abject poverty was complete, irrefutably primitive, and of no concern to the Austrians, Poles or Russians who controlled every aspect of their lives.

The entry for *Ruthenian* in the 1911 edition *of Encyclopedia Britannica* succinctly describes the state of Rusnaks in Europe:

> *"The Ruthenians number some three million in Galicia, Bukovina, and in the Carpathians along the edges of Hungary from the 21ˢᵗ meridian eastwards. Throughout Galicia the Poles formed the aristocracy, though in two-thirds of it the Ruthenians formed the bulk of the population, while the middle class is Jewish (German). The Ruthenians are therefore under an alien yoke both politically and economically. Their intellectual centre is Lemberg, L'viv or Lwow, where some lectures in the university are given in their language, and they are agitating for it to have equal rights with Polish."*

It wasn't until the late 1800s, after centuries of religious persecution, economic deprivation and political subjugation, that the Rusnaks and other peoples of the Carpathians sought relief by emigrating to the United States and Canada. However, only a very few of these 1.5 million people lived to find what they sought. Time-consuming labor and pervasively low incomes, that barely allowed them to meet their ability to live, kept them shackled to their work in steel mills and coal mines, and seemingly forever, to their low-income status.

While it wasn't they who benefited by their emigration from the Old to the New Country, it was their children who were able to begin the climb. However, even most first-generation descendents of these "Hunkies," as they were called by outsiders, who did find political and religious freedom, did not climb very high up the social or financial ladders of America. Instead, it was their grandchildren who eventually reaped the fruits of their migration, labor and dreams. However, today, it is impossible to find a living Hunky among them.

Nicholas Stevensson Karas
Orient Point, New York
Winter 2009

Part I CREATING HUNKIES

Chapter 1   Half of the Beginning

It is mid-November in the year 1887.

The place is the ancient Rus province of *Halychyna*, in east-central Europe and hard against the northern slope of the Carpathian Mountains. Snow caps the range's higher peaks but now falls as light, misty rain at lower elevations on the still-verdant foothills. Wisps of fog fill the mountains upper ravines and give the landscape a dark, moody, foreboding countenance, as if it is a huge, frowning, angry face.

Weeks earlier, a frost had turned the surrounding beech forests a golden yellow. Now, when water gathers on their leaves, it weighs them and eventually loosens their hold on the twigs. Whenever the slightest wind blows they, with a silent flutter, fall with the rain.

A solemn procession of mourners—men, women and children—twenty-two in all, treks up the shallow valley floor. They follow a muddy footpath, along the edge of a small stream, to a burial ground on the edge of the small village. In front of the burial ground, in a scattered rectangle, are large stones, remnants of the foundation of a long-forgotten church. It had been destroyed centuries ago by a Tatar horde that pillaged the village, killed its men and carried off many of its women and children.

Protisne (Pro-tis-neh) could hardly be called a village. At various times in its history it was administered as part of Smil'nyk (Shmil-nik), a village with thrice the number of people and located on a hill on the opposite side of the Sian, a river that fully separates them. Archeologists believe that it is older that Smil'nyk because of its riverbank location. Smil'nyk at one time had a water-driven sawmill on the bank opposite Protisne. Three years ago, it was washed away by a spring flood and remains in ruin. A mill for grinding flour still stands on Smil'nyk Brook, where it enters the Sian, across from Protisne. Because of its importance, it was rebuilt soon after the flood. The people of Protisne share the same church in Smil'nyk, but not the same graveyard.

Protisne has no center like most other European villages. It is composed of a collection of 43 thatch-covered log houses built side-by-side in two rows separated by the small stream. The stream is really just a creek that flows into the Sian. Villagers call it *Hluboki* or Deep Creek, but it is deep only where it enters the much larger Sian. There is no road through the center of the village. The stream is its center. Only a dirt footpath connects each house on each side of the stream.

Their paths gradually widen the farther downstream the houses are located until they reach the road on the right bank of the Sian River. A half-mile upstream on the Sian the main road ends in a ford. During most times of the year, the Sian here is seldom more than ankle deep. A casual footbridge, that is no more than a series of long planks set on the tops of exposed large stones, allows for a dry crossing. The two villages are considered "poor villages" and its people too poor to afford more than one church and too poor to afford the building of a real bridge. Horses, oxen, cattle, sheep and wagons must slosh through the river between the villages. All villages in these mountains are considered "poor villages."

The hills that create the 3-mile hollow with Protisne in its lower reaches, are split almost equally by the creek, and rise 200 to 300 feet on each side of the stream. Houses stretch halfway up the length of the creek, and small, cultivated fields spread up each hillside from the back of each house to the tops of the hills. A forest of beech, pine, tamarack and spruce trees cover the upper half of the hollow and the tops of the hills.

Protisne has no post office, nor inn or tavern. It has one store and a collection of houses in which 382 people live–244 Rusnaks, no Poles or Gypsies, but 35 Jews. It does have, however, on the far side of the ford, a distillery run by the Jew Ihor Zellman. He operates it for the Polish count who owns this village as well as several other villages on the surrounding land.

There is a tavern, *korchma* in Rusnak, just outside the village on the road to Stuposiany the next village south of Protisne. It is located a kilometer upstream from Protisne where the Wolosatka

(Vo-lo-sat-ka) River meets the Sian. It is a wooden building that has always been in need of repair. However, its clients don't seem to mind its shabby state. The tavern is run by the Jew Jakub Jablonski and, like the distillery, is also owned by the Count Cuzinski. The count also owns several mills in the area, and these, too, are run for him by Jews. By 1900, Jews were finally allowed to own land and the count's estates were bought by the German Jew Mojzesz Feld.

Despite its diminutive size, all these features are enough to justify a name for the settlement. Protisne is a Ukrainian word that means, "to clear an opening in the forest." It is an old village that was settled nearly 700 years ago when the first migrating Rus used the Sian as a path into the mountains from the lowland plains of Halychyna. They followed the upriver course into these gentle mountain foothills looking for new grazing land for their sheep and a few cattle.

* * * * * * * * * * *

Grass is still green along the edges of the path the mourners trod. Where the path steepens, some had stepped on it to avoid slipping. The mournful sound of a *pochorna*, the funeral trembita, rises softly into the damp, cold air and reverberates off the hills. It comes from the cluster of thatched houses below, from outside the house of Yurko Najda (Ni-da). It had been blown every evening at dusk as he lay dead inside his house. In happier times, the 10-foot horn is used by shepherds to talk to one another from hilltop to hilltop or to call their sheep. Now, it plays a more solemn role.

Silently, slowly, the people follow a bearded priest toward an elongated pile of yellow-brown dirt and stones, and an open grave. Yurko's three brothers had dug the grave that morning. The superstitious older people of the village believe that it is bad to leave a grave open during the night because evil spirits will inhabit it. This will bode ill when a body was lowered into it. Immediately behind the priest, four, darkly-clad men, carry, on their shoulders, a simple wooden coffin. Everyone, even the priest, is dressed in dark, somber clothing. It is tradition. It is the way of all Slavic peasants in these mountains.

Four days earlier, Yurko (George) Najda lay on his deathbed. Relatives and friends had gathered around him and spoke only occasionally and in low whispers. They all knew he was dying, that the end for him was near. All work around his farmstead was stopped. Three of his four young sons Ivan, Andrij (pronounced An-dree) and Vasyl, stood vigilantly behind the bed and watched as grieving relatives and friends came to bid him good-bye. His sons were still too young to fully comprehend what was going on. They were still grieving the loss of their mother who had died but a year earlier.

Kateryna Antonishak-Najda had died while giving birth to their youngest brother Hryec. Vasyl, 7, thought it was a heroic gesture when all her relatives and friends, who had recently borne children, took turns breastfeeding Hryec (Harry). They did so until he was able to eat on his own. They had saved his life. It wasn't so much heroics, as it was just another way of Rusnaks and other Slavs when events like this occur.

As the priest was giving him his last rites, Yurko Najda died without uttering a single word or contraction of his body. Only his crossed hands, as they slid to his sides, announced that the end had come. As is tradition, someone went into the kitchen, reached the clock on the wall above the stove, and stopped its pendulum. The clock had been their only wedding gift. Marysha (Ma-resh-a), the wife of Yurko's brother Andrij, found two towels on a shelf next to the stove and draped one over each of two small mirrors. The old people are very superstitious and believe this must be done as soon as someone dies or the spirit of the dead person might look into the mirror, believe it was still alive, and linger about the household.

Soon after the last breath escaped Yurko, and the emotions of those around him subsided, his body was moved to the kitchen. Male relatives, his brothers, washed and shaved him, then dressed him in clean clothes. When a woman dies, her female relatives wash and dress her. Then, on a long bench covered by a white sheet, with straw beneath it, they placed his body in front of the kitchen table. Marysha stood back and looked at the body of her brother-in-law. Emotions rose within her and tears began to fill her already reddened eyes as she silently wept. Then, the church bell in Smil'nyk began to ring.

Two candles and a table-cross were brought from St. Michael's Church in Smil'nyk, that served the people of both villages. The candles would remain lighted until the body left the house. That, too, was tradition. The next day, a carpenter from Litowyschce (Lutowiska) came and measured Yurko's body.

For three days, every morning and every evening, the bell at the church rang in honor of Yurko Najda. Each evening relatives and neighbors came to the house to pray for his soul. On the second evening, a Polish official from Lisko (Lesko) came, looked at him for a few minutes, filled out a certificate, tucked it under one candle holder, then left without blessing himself or saying a word.

In the light rain, the priest begins the *panakhida*, the service for the dead, and takes the smoking, brass *kadilo* from the cantor. Methodically, while chanting, he swings it over the coffin. As it sways back and forth, it releases bursts of pungent, aromatic frankincense. In the damp air, the smoke seems to hang momentarily over the wooden box. As he sings, his rich baritone voice floods between the narrowing hills and into the village below. The cantor responds, echoing the priest's chant.

More people arrive as the *sluzhba*, the service, continues and form around the grave, their heads constantly bowed in respect, whispering only in the lowest of voices. One woman cries openly, but most, like the men about them, are silent, stern-faced, and resolute. Death is nothing new to them. It is a part of living. Only their *babushkas* (kerchiefs) shield their heads from the light rain. None of the male family members have worn hats since Yurko died. This, too, is tradition. The men, with heads bare, and hands crossed at their waists, tolerate the rain. It runs down their faces, off their chins and down the length of their short coats. None wear the traditional white sheepskin capes that would shield them from the rain.

Immediately to the right of the open grave, a simple, hand-made wooden cross leans off-center. It has cracked and weathered from only a season of exposure to rain and snow. The excessively cold winters and barely tolerably hot summers in the continent's interior are hard on everything exposed. The cross looks fragile, as if it could be toppled by even a gentle breeze. There are no flowers on Kateryna Najda's grave. The grass is tall, gone to seed many months ago, and stands resolutely, unwaveringly against the impending winter winds.

Yurko Najda had not been to his wife's grave since early spring. He had been too sick to climb even the small hill to the burying ground. That year, many in the two villages had become ill. Influenza had overcome them. For a while, they feared it might be the cholera that was sweeping all of northern Europe. Some said

7

it was the Jews who had brought it from Russia as they escaped the Tsar's pogroms. If not the Jews, then the Gypsies. They had to blame someone or something for what they could not understand. They were not stupid people. Their guilt was being uneducated. They lived in a foreign society that had abandoned them. Only a few had ever been exposed to the ways of the world outside their small, isolated mountain villages. The flatlanders called them *horyschani*, mountain people.

Few gravesites in the small, hillside cemetery behind the church ruins had seen the sickle that year. It looked dilapidated, overgrown, abandoned, with small, hand-made wooden crosses rising in a scattered scheme above the tops of the tall grasses.

Rusnaks in the village could not afford stone monuments. It was a luxury only for the wealthier Poles and a few Jews. Though serfdom in the Austro-Hungarian Empire had been eliminated forty years earlier, these villagers were still captives on their own land. But now, they were economic rather than political serfs and life seemed so much harder. They were trapped, tied to the land as strongly as if God had planted their feet in it and forbade them to leave. But word had filtered north across the boarder that Czechs and Slovaks to the south were beginning to leave. Many highlanders thought their time, too, to leave was drawing near. Their loyalty to a land that was fruitless, unrewarding, was drawing to an end. In a thousand years of husbanding it, the land had never yielded a bounty.

During the preceding spring and summer, most villagers recovered from the unusually virulent flu but not Yurko. Physically, he was never a very strong person and the drudgery of working his field six days a week, from sunrise to sunset, had taxed him of all the strength he did possess. Most of the land surrounding the village was not productive as farmland and grew more stones than rye or barley. While summers here were hot, they were too short to grow the coveted wheat the lowlanders grew farther north.

One of the community's best fields, emanating north of the village, not far from the Sian, had been the Najda's since anyone could remember. For untold generations, since the early 1200s, it had been passed down from father to the oldest son. It was a small patch of rich bottomland that each spring received more soil after the flooded Sian River retreated to within its banks. It was said in the village, that the Najda's had been among the first to follow the Sian upriver toward Halytsych Mountain. And, because they were among the first, they were able to take the best land that was next to the river.

While the field was returned to them to toil when serfdom was abolished, they were still not its real owners. All the fields belong to the Polish count. It had been bigger but Yurko's father Mykola (Nicholas), before he died, divided it equally between him and his brothers Andrij, Ivan and Mykola. He had the right to do so. The parcel with the homestead was given to Yurko because he was the first born. And, as is the customary right, he inherited the farm. Besides, Andrij already had a house. Andrij's father-in-law had no sons so he moved into his wife's house when he married Marysha Sarenkova. Mykola, Yurko's youngest brother, never liked farming. He sold his parcel of land to Yurko and moved to Sianok where he worked for a Jew as a butcher.

Life had been easier for Yurko when he first married Kateryna Antonishak. There were several Antonishak families in Protisne; even more were living in Smil'nyk and nearby Stuposiany. She was from Smil'nyk. Kateryna had shared the burdens of harvesting their field with the help of a hired hand. From the beginning of their marriage, they, like most others in the village, had planned to have a large family so their children could eventually help in the fields.

As fall approached, his health worsened. Yurko's brothers would help. But Andrij and Ivan had their own fields to tend and Mykola seldom returned to Protisne. The farm was too much work for Yurko's two older sons--who weren't much older than Vasyl-- and sister alone. Fortunately they were able to hire Simon Pavuk, an older cousin, who was able to do most of the heavy work.

Now, Vasyl stood at the edge of the grave between two uncles, occasionally grabbing Uncle Andrij's hand when he understood something that was said in the ancient Church Slavonic canticle for the dead. On the other side of Uncle Andrij, were Vasyl's brother Ivan (John), five years older, and Andrij, three years older. They stood silently by themselves. Tears filled Ivan's eyes as he glanced toward his younger brother Hryec, who was on the opposite side of the grave, in the arms of Uncle Mykola's wife Oksana.

But where was his sister Marysha? Vasyl thought. She was 14 and two years ago had moved to Lisko to work in a cousin's house. The mother had been ill and needed help raising three young children. They had been back once, during the summer, so she could see her sick father.

9

But where was she now? Surely someone had been able to tell her that father had died. Why didn't she come with Uncle Mykola?

Tears filled his eyes as he thought of his father.

"Cry," Uncle Andrij whispered as he glanced down at his weeping nephew. "Don't be afraid to cry. It makes life easier to bear. What is done is God's will. Who are we to question it?"

Tears streamed from his pale blue eyes, down the sides of his sharp nose and ruddy cheeks, and mixed with the light rain. His light brown, almost blond, hair was disheveled and stood in contrast to all the drab colors that surrounded him. He watched helplessly as sliding ropes slowly lowered his father's wooden casket into the crudely-dug grave. It was then that he realized his father's house would be empty that night. He and his brothers would be all alone. They were orphaned.

There were no flowers to place on Yurko Najda's simple wooden casket. Instead, as each mourner passed, they grabbed a handful of dirt from the nearby pile and gently cast it onto the lowered coffin, then blessed themselves. The priest replaced the *kadilo* with a water-filled *kropilo* and blessed the grave continuously as the mourners passed. They, too, blessed themselves incessantly every time he made the sign of the cross.

The lucidity of my grandfather Vasyl Najda's description to me, at the age of 7, of his father's burial is as clear and crisp as if I had been there to witness it myself. Maybe it is because of the uncanny similarities of his father's burial to those of my father's burial 40 years later. Though I was only three when my father died I can still clearly recall every detail. It must be the gravity, the intensity of such an event that registers so profoundly on a youngster's mind. When in later years, my grandfather described his father's burial, it seemed as if it was the burial of my father. And, it was he who held my hand as they lowered my father's coffin.

The Najda's were the last to leave the graveyard.

"Come with me Vasylij, Ivanko," his Aunt Marysha said as she grabbed Vasyl's hand. He still stared into the open grave. "You and your brother will spend the night with us. Andrij will go with Uncle Mykola. Your house is no place to be alone tonight."

*   *   *   *   *   *   *   *   *   *   *

The next morning...

"Wake up Vasylij. Do you want to sleep the entire day?" yelled his aunt. "The cow must be taken to the pasture and chickens fed. Your brother is already there. Life goes on. I will go with you to help."

The Najda house and farm were on the lower end of the village, no more than 300 yards below Uncle Andrij's house. Their farms were on the left side, the east side of the deep creek, the sunny side in the morning. It didn't look much different from the other houses that lined the dirt path with the last house, a half-kilometer farther upstream. All the houses were made of fir logs, split level on two opposite sides so they would flatly abut each other. They were locked at their corners with simple dovetail joints. Moss was placed between the logs and in the joints as they were being laid together. The joints were further chinked with river clay that turned white after it dried. Before it dried thoroughly, red-painted slats were pressed in and the clay held them firmly. In Lisko County, the strips were always painted red.

All houses were rectangular in shape with the proximal side facing the stream and the distal half facing the orchard, gardens and fields that led up the hillsides, much like spokes emanating from a wheel's hub. A few houses had wooden floors but most were earthen. Some houses had only one room but a few had two, small bedrooms, usually located between the kitchen and barn. A hallway led from the kitchen, with a bedroom on each side, to a door that opened into the barn. These rooms had wooden ceilings with a trapdoor that opened to a large storage space above them and under the roof. All roofs were highly pitched to shed rain and snow and heavily thatched with straw, reeds, or whatever materials were available. They were, however, in constant need of attention.

The last house built in the village had been erected more than fifty years ago. Few remember when the others were built; it seems they had always been there. Three of the houses in the village had been empty for the past few years. Their owners had gone to America. They said, as they departed, that they would return...but none had. There was no need to build new ones.

The back half of the house was the barn and harbored three cows, an oxen, a horse and several sheep and goats, as well as a hayloft. While its roof was contiguous with the living quarters it was separated from them by a wall with a door to the barn. If the owner could afford it, a separate barn was built behind the house

11

to hold the animals, but only a few houses had barns. The Najda house did. It contained the chickens, a few geese and ducks and a pigpen with a sow and six sucklings.

A stylized sun was on the top portion of the front door and simple, colorfully-painted, stylized flower patterns ran along its edges. Dominating the center of the door was the "tree of life" depicted here as a large flower in bloom with radiating petals on top and symmetrical branches coming off the main, vertical stem. There were seven branches, depicting the seven Najdas who had once lived in the house. There was room left on the bottom for more additions but that was never to happen.

Vasyl's mother loved flowers. To have their beauty around her during the long winter months in the Beskids, as this part of the Carpathians was called, she painted their images about the door and windows. When Yurko had been well, he built two flower boxes and mounted them under two front windows. Now, the boxes were filled with weeds and old, dead flower stalks. Nothing had been planted in them since her death.

The living quarters consisted of a kitchen and two bedrooms. The kitchen was the largest room and the front door opened into it. The inside walls had been covered in a stucco-like finish made of sand, clay and mortar and painted with a whitewash made of lime, water, chalk and glue. The windows were small and divided into four panes. The white finish created more light inside the room. In the far corner was a large stove that filled a fifth of the room. It was made of cement, bricks, mortar and clay. Part of the stove had removable plates above the firebox and most of the cooking was done on these. The clay oven was next to it and was built as part of the stove and reached almost to the low ceiling. Along one side, still a part of this rambling stove, was a masonry bench that doubled as a bed in the evening and behind, and above it, was a masonry shelf where dried foods were stored. A small stack of chopped wood was in a bin on one side. If more wood was needed, it was kept in a larger bin just inside the barn. The stove was the house's only source of heat.

To one side was a dryboard against the bottom of one of three kitchen windows. The clay-covered, whitewashed walls were nearly a foot thick and acted as natural insulation that kept the house warm in winter and cool in summer. A large, rectangular table occupied the center of the room and was constructed of rough-hewn planks. Benches were on both sides of it and two homemade chairs were on each end. There was also a backless chair near the dry sink that held a pail of water with a dipper in it. Next to it, on the wall, was a washbasin that hung on a thin, wooden peg that was driven into the wall above the sink.

A narrow hall that led to the barn separated the small bedrooms. The bedrooms were small and ceilings low. The bed frame sat directly on the floor. In lieu of springs there were a series of ropes that were woven back and forth within the frame. They had to be tightened regularly. There were wooden floors in the two bedrooms but the floor in the kitchen was earthen. A series of boards were mounted flat against the whitewashed masonry walls and pegs for hanging clothes protruded from them at regular intervals. There was a 9-pane window in each bedroom.

Because their field was the richest in the village, it was coveted by all. Ihor Zellman, who ran the distillery across the Sian and a *sklep*, the only store in the village, out of the front of his house, had coveted Yurko's house. He had offered to buy Najda's field when he realized how ill Yurko had become.

"He wants it for nothing," Vasyl remembered his father's exact words. "I would sell it," he said that summer as he lay ill in bed, "but I will not **give** it to him! He knows we are on hard times. He is like a vulture waiting for me to die. Don't ever sell it to him," he said to his sons.

"What is that?" Marysha Najda said in an alarming voice, as she and Vasyl approached the front door.

Tacked onto the door was an official-looking notice.

"It must be trouble," she said aloud as she took it down. Below what was a signature, was a seal stamped on the bottom. Even if she could read she would not have understood it. It was written in Polish. She knew it was official and in Polish because of the white eagle in one corner and the red and white flag in the other. If it was Austrian, the eagle would have two heads, she thought.

"Hurry Vasylij!" she yelled. "We must find the priest to read this for us."

Like most Rusnak villages, the entire population of Protisne, except for the priest, was illiterate. They ran down to the Sian and over the boards to the other side, then climbed the hill to the church in the middle of Smil'nyk.

13

Uncle Andrij had joined them as they watched every movement in Father Stefan's face for a hint of what it might contain as he read the paper. Octagonal-shaped glasses, simple magnifiers, sat on the end of his long nose. He unconsciously stroked his graying beard as his brown eyes moved back to the top of the paper and read it again.

"This is not so! It cannot be! It is not fair!" he finally said, looking first at Marysha and then at Vasyl. "This cannot be. I knew your father well. He was not like other men in our villages. He did not drink the Pole's vodka!"

The first invasion of the province of Galicia by the Mongol/ Tatars occurred in 1240. They destroyed all its cities and villages and either killed many of the Rus inhabitants or carried them off to Asia as slaves. A few years later the Black Death, the Bubonic Plague, reached deeply into the Carpathian Mountains and Rusnak villages. At times the entire population of a village was destroyed. A hundred years later, Galicia was a land still depopulated, devastated and ripe for conquest. With a desire to expand his realm eastward because of pressure from the German princes and their *Drang Nach Esten,* (Drive to the East) the Polish king Casimir, united his army with Lithuanian forces, and together conquered Kyivian Rus and Moscovy.

In Galicia, Casimir systematically replaced the remaining Rus nobility with his own. He did this in two ways, by giving them the option to convert to Catholicism and identify themselves as Catholics and Poles, or flee beyond their reach to avoid outright slaughter. It revealed a flaw in the Rus nobility that would haunt its people for centuries to come. Most took the first offer. For those who wouldn't convert and escaped, he confiscated their lands, estates and homes and castles and turned them over to his loyal royal followers who aided him in the war. It was these escapees who would eventually form the basis of the Cossacks.

As justification for his move against fellow Slavs, he first sought and was granted a Papal edict...."to bring Christianity to the Rus." He meant the Roman version because they already were Christians. In return, Pope Clement IV expected Casimir to force the conversion of the Rus to Roman Catholicism in exchange for the edict.

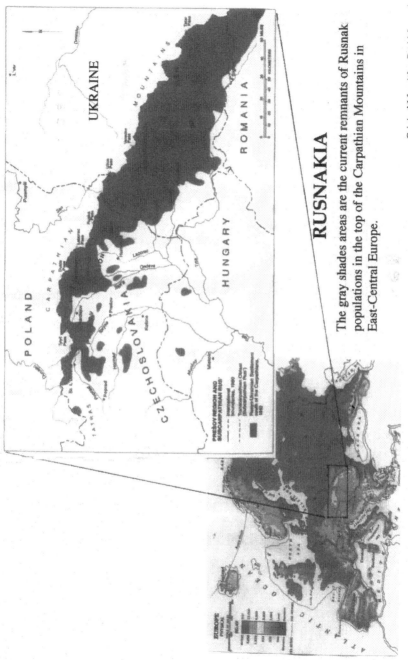

Original Map After Paul Magosci

RUSNAKIA

The gray shades areas are the current remnants of Rusnak populations in the top of the Carpathian Mountains in East-Central Europe.

Polish gentry then moved into the country, in the role of feudal lords, occupying the lands assigned them by Casimir. They brought with them German Jews from Poland to Galicia to act as their administrators. The nobles and magnates resorted to the hated practice of *arenda,* or leasing, in which leaseholders agreed that anything they could squeeze out of the peasants, above a set figure that went to the *pan* (master*),* was their profit. Initially forbidden to own land, but allowed to lease it, Jews often became leaseholders by paying the nobles. By 1600 there were more than 4,000 Jewish leaseholders in Galicia. Because they had to make good their investment--leases ran only two to three years--they mercilessly exploited the peasants. It was not uncommon for a leaseholder to demand six or seven days of labor from the peasants and, with the help of the noble's minions, to drive them into the fields to work, even on Sundays.

Another form of arenda was the leasing out of an estate's monopoly on the production of alcohol and tobacco to the leaseholder, who then charged peasants whatever price he wished for these prized commodities. Needless to say, the practice did not make Jews popular with the Rusnak or Ukrainian population.

According to historians, Jewish participation in the oppressive arenda practices of the Polish nobility/Jewish alliance provided the single most important cause of the terrible retribution, which would descend upon Jews on several occasions in the future.

In 1772, Austria defeated an internally weak and divided Poland. It was then, bit-by-bit, trisected between Prussia, Russia and Austria. By 1795, Poland disappeared from the map of Europe. Austria received Galicia but Poles petitioned the emperor and they were allowed to administer the province for the empire. This continued until the end of WW I. Instead of levying a tax, each Rusnak family was required to buy monthly a set amount of Polish-made vodka at the local magazine (store) or *sklep.* This was owned by the count but run by Jews in his service, who thus became their tax collectors. And who loves a tax collector?

"NOTICE," the priest read aloud as if he was delivering the dictum in the village center to a gathering of serfs.

"Be it known that Yurko Najda and his heirs have forfeited this property in the Village of Procisne (Protisne), County of Lesko, Province of Polish Galicia, in lieu of failing to pay the vodka tax. The property has been purchased for back taxes by Ihor and Rebekah Zellman."

It was signed: Dr. Józef Zdun, owner of Procisne, for Count Stanislaus Joseph Cuzinski, 21 Nov. 1887 *anno Domini*.

"This cannot stand!" exclaimed Andrij Najda. "We will appeal to the authorities."

"What appeal? What authorities?" asked the priest.

"The Count is the authority here. He doesn't care who owns the house as long as he gets paid for the vodka. There is no appeal in this land."

"We'll appeal to Vienna. The Austrians are more reasonable than the Poles," said Marysha.

"That, too, is useless," responded the priest. "The doctor pays the Count and the Count pays the Austrians his annual stipend. The Austrians are fighting rebellions among all their conquered peoples. That is the fate of empires built by force. The Bohemians and Magyars want to be free from the Austrians and are now agitating for their liberty. Even the Slovaks want freedom. Less money from the Polish Count would not be popular. Adjust to what we have left or we may lose that, too."

"Don't feel it is just your family that is being taken advantage of," said Mytro Timko, a village elder with whom Andrij had stopped to talk a few days later in Smil'nyk. "There was the Bihun Family in Pryslip, a little town on the other side of Caryn, above Dvernyk. Oh, you know where it is."

"Yes," said Andrij, "I know people there. I have been there."

"Well, one day, a Polish Jew, Izaak Kornfeldow and his wife Sura, came into Pryslip looking for a place to live. They came from Caryn a few kilometers below Pryslip. They were so poor that even the poorest Rusnak was better off than they were, if you can imagine that. It was just before Passover and they had but one egg with which to celebrate. You know, you cannot make matzo balls with but one egg. Word of their sad state got out in the village and Ivan Bihun's wife Oksana felt sorry for them. She gave them a few more eggs.

"As it always seems to happen with Jews, life then turned better for them in Pryslip than in Caryn. The village was owned by Marie Weissenfeld and Joanna Karlowitz and that didn't hurt their chances of bettering themselves. Somehow, he became the factor in the tavern there that was owned by Weissenfeld. They eventually made so much money that they were able to buy a shingled house. And, they, too, became landowners because of the stupidly of the local Rusnak peasants.

"The *duraks* (dumbbells) drank so much, far more than they could afford, and the Jew willingly and with forethought, gave them credit and recorded every drink. They owed Kornfeldow so much koruna that when the Jew demanded payment, and they had none, they lost their lands. He got several farms this way before the idiots finally saw the light. The others finally got smart. All the peasants then refused to drink at the inn. The owners became upset with Kornfeldow because he couldn't pay his lease. First he sold his farms and finally his shingled house. It got so bad that they were again down to one egg and then they left Pryslip."

"Where did they go? Andrij asked.

"I don't know," said Timko. "Maybe they changed their names and are here in Smil'nyk."

"Maybe that was the same reason they left Caryn, with only one egg. But that doesn't explain how my brother lost his farm..... he never drank."

"There are more ways than one to skin a cat," Timko said as they parted company. "We have nothing or no one to blame for our miseries but ourselves. Maybe, if we were educated, our lot would be better."

On owning villages...

It seems difficult for most Americans to understand how someone could own a village either today or in the past. Archeological evidence supports the fact that the Rus began moving into the Carpathian Mountains during the 7th and 8th centuries, with smaller numbers at least a century earlier. They followed the rivers, then streams and finally rivulets west and then south into the mountains. Where they decided to stay, they immediately began cutting swaths, or *protisnij*, out of the forests for their settlements and grazing land for their sheep.

The next band that followed moved farther upriver and did the same when they came to a site that looked good. In this way, their settlements looked like long strip malls, with no real center except where a church was eventually built. Their settlements usually straddled both sides of a stream if they were shallow and easily crossed. If that was not the case, then one side became dominant and the houses were connected by a path that eventually became a road. Thus these mountain villages were always water oriented.

These migrants were herders first and farmers second. Farming was used primarily as a subsistence source of food for the families. At first, they came in small bands, extended families and clans. The inhabitants they met in the highlands at that time were Kelts, who for centuries, occupied most of Europe but, whose numbers were rapidly declining as new ethnic groups migrated westward from beyond the Steppes. In the mountains, the Kelts were few in numbers and continued to live there as Slavs moved in among them. Eventually, they were assimilated by the Slavs.

In the 13th century Galician Rus was conquered by an army composed of Poles and Swedes, then Poles and Lithuanians who, through marriages of royalty, temporarily joined their houses and their countries. With the Rus royalty destroyed, or convinced to become a part of Polish nobility in order to survive, most of the highlands remained ungoverned. For a while the peasants who survived had little or no administration. The king's followers and supporters were given these lands for their loyalty. It wasn't until the 15th century that they developed enough interest in them to move in and make them pay in terms of lumber and other natural resources, and sheep and farm goods.

The first move in organizing their domains was to grant all serfs they found on their estates a 24-year freedom from taxation. Thereafter, they had to pay taxes, in one form or another, to the landed Polish gentry. The lands were passed down from one heir to another, or bought and sold. The peasants became serfs and remained with the lands and were the owner's property. They were Carpathian slaves in every meaning of the word. They were there to do the owner's bidding and work the land. At first, they were required to work two or three days for the lord. This was gradually expanded to six days for the owner, and then the lesees, and the seventh for themselves.

The word slave is an interesting word. Most linguists believe its basis is an Arabic word. In the centuries before Christ, Greek entrepreneurs developed a slave trade with the Arabs. The Arabs had a fascination with blonde blue-eyed women and children and would pay premium prices for them in Baghdad and other Arab centers. Jews entered the business and while they believe Jews should not be made slaves they had no compunction about trading other peoples in slavery. Eventually, the Jews were displaced by

Vikings who also profited in selling slaves and was one of the reasons they moved east and took their captives south down the Dnieper River to slave markets. The Arabic base word for slaves became the word that today describes the Slavs.

Living conditions for peasants in now Polish-administered Galicia and Ukraine steadily worsened under the control of the Polish nobility. It had been a traditional right among peasants here, when they were under Rus rule, to be able to leave their lord's land and look for better conditions elsewhere. The Poles were quick to end this practice. At first, if peasants wanted to leave, they were able to do so but only at a certain time of the year, at Christmas. And, could do so, only if they paid an exit tax and found someone to replace them. In 1496, this right was further limited to but one peasant family per village per year.

In 1505, the Polish *sejm* (parliament) forbade any peasants to leave a lord's land without his permission. "Unable to move, deprived of personal rights, exploited at will, the peasants now became serfs, little better than a slave of his nobleman landlord." Poles did not hesitate to re-employ this practice of serfdom at a time when in Western Europe, in Britain, France, German and Austria, it was rapidly dying out. As Engels further put it, "... it emerged as a particularly oppressive form in Eastern Europe and Ukraine. It was this condition that finally gave rise to the Cossacks whose initial revolt took place against the Poles."

To increase productivity and profits, the owners encouraged villages to form--especially around stores, inns, distilleries, and grain and lumber mills, which they also owned or controlled. In this way, the gentry could pay support to the next royal title above their station until the king finally received his tithe. It was this gentry that supported the king with money and men when a war arose.

Most of the written history of the hundreds of villages across southeast Poland began about the mid-1500s when these towns were organized by their new owners and given, you might say, patents for their existence. As an example, Protisne's written history begins in 1565 and the owners were two Poles, Barbara and Herburtow Kmitowa. However, ownership changed often as relatives inherited the villages or they were sold and bought by new owners. From 1565 to 1937 Protisne was transferred 18 times. It was not unusual for the original estates, as they were called, to own as many as a dozen villages. Somewhere among these villages, the owners would usually build a manor house or two.

Some Polish historians have tried to foist the idea into history that these lands were always Polish. They claimed, that through purely benevolent actions, they encouraged the Rusnaks to move to the towns they created and offered them the chance to live on the land they selected for a 24-year grace period. However the ethnology of the village names tells a different story. *Protis* is the root word for the village of Protisne, Procisne is Polish. *Protis* is a Rus or Ukrainian word that means "to clear a passage [in the woods]," or "to cut out the woods." It attests to the ethnic identity of the first settlers as precursors of present day Ukrainians.

Chapter 2   The Other Half of the Beginning

Saturday, June 6, 1891 — It was a pleasant late spring morning in the isolated mountain village of Vilag, a perfect day for a wedding. From the woods above Andrij Karas's *(Karasz in Hungarian)* village, the mournful dual-note lament of a cuckoo flowed down the pasture and over the hundred or so high-pitched, thatched-roof houses.

Andrij had just walked through the back of his house, through the door that led to the barn, and threw open its large, wooden doors. Sun flooded in as he stood in its midst. He looked outward and drew a deep breath, savored it for a few moments, then swore to himself that the air smelled green and wet.

His parent's house, No. 105, was one of the highest in the small village. The sprawling hamlet was built on a long, gradual slope and straddled both sides of a small stream. As he looked over the rooftops he drew a certain sense of security and belonging from what he saw. Andrij knew, as his eyes scanned over their thatched peaks, that a dozen of these houses belonged to other Karases. He felt a certain comfort, a satisfaction that he was surrounded by so many of his kin. And, that twice as many more were filled with close relatives…aunts, uncles and endless numbers of cousins.

The village was nestled in a large bowl near the very top of the Carpathian Mountains, just 24 miles as the raven flies, southwest of Protisne and Vasyl Najda, but on the south side of the continental divide. It was in a realm that had been under Hungarian rule for almost a thousand years. Its inhabitants, however, were all Rusnaks and not Hungarians, and never were Magyars.

The lands on both sides, one under Polish domination and the other under Hungarian, were now united under the rule of the

23

dual monarchy, the Austrian-Hungarian Empire. For the last 200 years, the invisible "green" border along the crest of the divide, that once separated both dominions, had been eliminated. And Rusnaks living on both sides easily passed back and forth through the low alpine passes as they had a for countless centuries earlier. However, the two families had never met, but one day they would.

Andrij Karas, a 23-year old, was a Rusnak like the Najdas on the north side of the divide. He spoke the same dialect and practiced the same religion as they did and was about to get married. He wasn't very tall, 5 –1/2 feet and weighed no more than 150 pounds. He was lean and sinewy. With blond hair and blue eyes, he was typical of other men and women in this region. His wife-to-be was 17-year-old Zuzanna Ivanco (*Ivanczo-Hungarian, pronounced Ee-vant-so*). All week long, Zuzanna, in House No. 69, had fretted about the horrible weather that had engulfed their village. She complained uselessly about it to her mother Maria. It had rained almost every day that week.

"Don't worry so much," said her older, married sister Maria, chiding her the night before, "it will turn out nice when the time comes for the wedding; it always does."

"I wish Simeon (*Sam*) could be here to see me get married," said Zuzanna. "I miss him so much."

Zuzanna was the youngest of seven children of Peter and Maria-Polivka Ivanco. Fifteen years ago, her father died of tuberculosis two years after she was born. Her older brothers had often filled his role for her as they grew. But Simeon had been the closest to her. The year before (*1890*), in February, he had married Olena (Helen) Sejka (*Syka*) just before they left for America. He now worked in the steel mills in Allegheny City, in Pennsylvania. They left to escape the poverty of the Carpathians.

For the young people of Vilag, as for many who lived in the surrounding mountain villages, this seemed a time for change, for them to marry and to escape the fruitless life these mountains offered. Andrij's youngest sister Anna, earlier that year, in February, married Ivan Ivanczo (John Evans), a third cousin to his bride. A few weeks after they were married, they emigrated to America and lived almost next door to Sam and Helen Evans. It was a time for change for all of these Rusnaks.

In spring and summer, it rains often in the tops of the Carpathian Mountains. The peaks seem to catch passing clouds and drain them of their water-laden lode. It did make the hillsides lush and green. By the morning of Zuzanna's wedding day, as her sister had predicted, the sky dawned clear of clouds. The warmth the sun exuded finally engulfed the slight valley in which their village was centered. It had been a cool, almost cold spring, and this was the first, really warm day that year.

Like all young people in love, Zuzanna's and Andrij's lives were filled with hope even though he had no money, no job, no future except for tilling the little bit of land around his father's home and herding the small flock of sheep they owned. Life had been difficult for decades for everyone in these mountain villages. To them it had always been that way. Few seemed to question why it was so.

Several days after the wedding---Andrij, along with a handful of other village men, most about his age, a few older, as old as his father Mykola---went south looking for work. They had hoped to find employment on the farms owned by Hungarians on the fertile plains below their mountains. To their dismay, they discovered that there was little work available. What few jobs there might have been that summer had quickly been taken by Slovaks, among whom the Hungarians, and a few Austrians, had built their farms.

It became a hot, dry summer that saw the crops Andrij planted in his father's fields wither and die. Even the garden by the house bore only small potatoes and turnips. To compound their misery, the summer and fall was followed by a severe winter. Their first year of their marriage had been filled with despair. All their dreams, their plans had been thwarted and had been put aside. Though they had talked of having children Zuzanna and Andrij agreed that it was not the time nor the place to think of bring children into the world. They could barely feed themselves, let alone, another mouth. The knowledge that in her family, before she was born, a sister and brother had died during infancy because of malnutrition. Zuzanna didn't want that to happen to her children. No house was free of malnutrition. Before Andrew was born, his parents lost a son John to the same malady.

The following spring, even earlier than the year before, and alone, Andrij again went looking for work among the Hungarians. He found nothing. In desperation, he later attended a meeting of several men in Vilag. Some had brothers and fathers who had, in the past few years, trekked to America and found work, and began sending home a few dollars. Times were becoming progressively difficult and the men in the village, as well as surrounding villages, began leaving for America in increasing numbers. They readily found work in steel mills or in coal mines. The little money they were able to send back was all that kept their families from starvation. It was just barely enough.

That night, after the meeting, as he gathered around the kitchen table with his wife, father and mother, and sister Maria and brother Michael, Andrij reluctantly announced his decision. "If Zuza and I are to have a family, I think I must go to America," he said. "There is no hope, no possible way I can find work here. Even the Magyar, Medveki, cannot afford to hire me for a few days to work in his forests. The call for lumber is slow.

"There was a man at the meeting tonight, a man from Medzilaborce, who has been to America. He now represents the steel mills. He told the others he would help them with the passage to get to America. There are four or five who said they are going. I think that I, too, must go. Otherwise, we will starve and die here soon after we have eaten our last sheep. At best, we live from day-to-day.

"Zuzanna, I will send for you as soon as I make enough money for your ship ticket. Maybe in America, we can start a family. Maybe."

Andrij's frustration was felt by everyone in Vilag. Everyone in the surrounding villages; everyone who was a Rusnak in the Carpathian highlands felt it even though they had never known another way, a life any better, any different. They had become an anomaly in the modern world, a people without leaders, a people without a literati, a people without an intelligentsia. And most frightening of all, a people without a future. Through assimilation, they were becoming extinct. Education had been denied them for centuries, denied them as a means to keep them bound to their slave-like status. They had been intentionally kept this way ever since the first aggressive Magyar tribes swept over their lands in the 10th century and separated them from their brethren to the south. It had been this way since the first Polish armies, in the 15th century, moved east across these mountains and separated them from their kin to the north.

Because of the subjugation, and because they could neither read nor write, they gradually, imperceptibly at first, became a people without an identity, a people who had lost their past, their history. They were a people now without a royalty that often could produce such leaders. When would-be leaders did rise from among the proletariat, usually as priests because education was limited to them, they were restricted, imprisoned or eliminated. Only in the latter half of the 19th century were these leaders able to, at times, set aside their dedication to religion, and look to other needs of their people. It was they who, in these mountain Slavs, began to develop an awareness of the possibility of a different life for them.

Andrij Karas and his wife Zuzanna would become two such people even though they didn't know it when they were married. But they both sensed, both knew that something had to change and that change could not take place for them in Catholic Hungary.

Control by the state—in Poland, Hungary and Russia—was so exact that Rusnaks could not find the way nor the means to rise above their pitiful station...other than by emigrating. But, in the New World, they were about to find another despot in the form of Andrew Carnegie, a man with the power of a king who would use them as industrial serfs. Even so, he would help set them free. But few Hunkies, however, would ever look at him as their emancipator. Despite his personal ambitions, to them he was a *defacto* Lincoln in disguise. But, there was a difference. In America they didn't have to do what their father, grandfathers and those before them had done. They could, if they had the will and any innate intelligence, rise above their stations.

Emigrating was the first step, though few at that time knew it.

Chapter 3 Life in Verner/Woods Run in 1892

The Allegheny River begins in western New York and takes a twisting, turning, winding course south through ancient hogback ridges as it works its way toward Pittsburgh. The Monongahela, of almost equal size, begins in West Virginia and flows north through southwestern Pennsylvania, through a similarly tortuous land, and joins the Allegheny in Pittsburgh. From their confluence, they flow west as the Ohio River until it meets the Mississippi where it, too, loses its identity.

It can be said, that along the shores where these three rivers meet in Pittsburgh, in the mid-19th century, is where America began its rise to prominence as an industrialized nation built on a foundation of iron and steel. The industrial revolution in America was inevitable. But if any one person could be credited as being the principal catalyst, it would be a 12-year-old uneducated, fatherless Scottish immigrant. Andrew Carnegie and his mother came to the United States in 1848 and joined a colony of Scottish relatives and friends in Allegheny City, then still a city separate from Pittsburgh. He soon realized that his future would evolve among these once verdant hills and burgeoning industries and immediately set about its beginning.

By the age of 30, employed by the Pennsylvania Railroad, Carnegie was buying steel rails for the company from England. Because of their short longevity, American-made iron rails were inferior and constantly had to be replaced. Being naturally frugal, he balked at the high price of English rails and the added cost of shipping. However, England at that time was the only source and took advantage of it. Carnegie believed he could make steel rails

29

as good, if not better, in Pittsburgh, and at a cheaper price. Therein began his rise in the steel industry. He eventually left the railroad and formed the Carnegie Steel Company where, on the flood plains of the Ohio River, he achieved success beyond even his egocentric expectations. However, he was ruthless in business, and success was achieved over the bones of many people.

Suddenly, in this period (the Iron Age) of history, everything durable in the world had to be made from iron or steel. Scores of allied industries sprang up among the blast furnaces that dotted the flatlands between the rivers and their embracing hills. In later years, after Carnegie sold the company, he became especially benevolent, as if to make amends to his past employees. For most it was too late and for those who could neither read nor write, it was for their descendents to appreciate. It did, however, bode well for his legacy.

The Scam...

"Sam is at work," Helen Evans said to Andrij the evening he arrived in Verner from Europe. She hugged him for the longest time, then stood back to better view him. "You do look like a greenhorn," she giggled lightly as she stared at Andrij in his Old Country garb. "He is working the night turn this week. "

As did other Ivancos who came to America, for convenience, Sam (*Simeon*) changed his last name to Evans and Olena or Olenka became Helen. Evans' name now sounded thoroughly English. In Rusnak, John is Ivan and Ivanco is Johnson, with the I pronounced as a long E, with the accent on –van, thus E-van. The jump from Ivanco (Ee-vant-so) to Evans was easy and made life in America, especially when dealing with Americans, a bit easier.

Andrij was a bit startled when he first saw his sister-in-law's face. The picture in his mind of her was the way she had looked the day she and Sam left for America. It had been only a year-and-a-half but he could see a change. She seemed to have grown older in that short time.

Helen was now 19, of solid build but not overweight, and just over 5 feet tall. Her hair was blonde and straight because she was preparing for bed when Andrij arrived. Its color seemed to accentuate the blueness of her eyes and they showed brightly even in the yellow light from the single kerosene lamp.

"He will be home at 6 tomorrow morning, eat breakfast and then go to bed," she said as she closed the door behind Andrij. "He will take you to the mill late tomorrow afternoon when he returns to work. You will stay with us. Follow me. We have boarders but there is an empty bed. We have been expecting you.

"Have you eaten? Would you like a cup of coffee?" Without waiting for an answer she filled the coffee pot with water from a bucket next to the dry sink.

"Tell me," she asked, "has life gotten any better in Vilag since we left? My mother's letters are always asking for money. I guess you don't have to answer that. Did you see them before you left? Are they in good health? How is your mother, and father? How is Zuzanna? Have you any children yet? We, too, are holding off. All our extra money has gone into buying beds for more boarders, or a few dollars that we send home. It is only with boarders that you can make enough to put aside. Tell me, how was your crossing?"

The next morning, an excited Andrij was already up when Sam returned from the mill. A weary and tired Sam Evans walked through the door and dropped his lunch pail into the dry sink. He didn't notice his brother-in-law, whose back was to him, eating eggs, fried potatoes and bacon that Helen had just prepared. At first, he thought he was one of the boarders working the day turn and wondered why he wasn't already in the mill. Immediately behind Sam were two of their boarders who also worked the night turn at the same mill but were not on the same gang.

Andrij turned around and jumped up from the bench as soon as he saw it was Sam. They embraced in a bear hug and kissed each other on the cheeks. The two had been good friends in Vilag and only three houses separated their homes. And, there was a long history of marriages between the two families that went back well beyond what anyone living could remember.

He introduced him to the two boarders, George Pinko and Vasyl Kundrat. They, too, were from Vilag and though they were a few years older than Andrij, he had known them. Everyone in Vilag knows everyone else. The village is that small.

"It doesn't look like hard work has done you any harm," Andrij said as he stepped back to get a better look at his brother-in-law.

"Wait Andruska, your turn will come. You, too, will learn what hard work is really like. You will earn every cent you make here. But, how is my sister? Is she with child yet? And how did my mother and my brothers Mihailo and Andrij look. And, is my sister Maria still having babies? Is life any easier in Vilag than it was a year ago?"

It was the same, piercing question his wife had asked last night. These were the questions asked every "greenhorn" as soon as they arrived in America. And when Sam let up Pinko and Kundrat added their questions.

"We can talk while I eat. I am starved and thirsty.

"I talked with George Hrenko a few weeks ago after I got the letter from the priest saying you were coming," Sam spoke as he wolfed down four eggs and flushed them with a mug of hot, black coffee. Coffee was a luxury they had not known in Vilag. There, it was served sparingly and only to pregnant women in the belief that it helped the development of the baby within.

"He said he thinks he can get you a job. But, he said that jobs are scarce right now. We are just going back to work. The union was trying to organize us again and the company closed down the plant for two weeks. There is an opening in the cinder pit gang that works on the heater next to his. He knows the foreman and will talk to him on your behalf."

"Why can't I talk to the foreman? I thought there were lots of jobs here, just for the asking," Andrij said.

"There are but that's not how things are done in America," Sam answered. "You cannot go to the foreman for several reasons. First, you do not speak English. He is a big Irishman and does not like Hunkies."

"What is a Hunky?"

"You will learn soon enough.

"Second, you must work through a second man, Hrenko. That's the way I got my job. That's the way you must do it to get your job.

"Tonight, you come with me to the mill and I will introduce you to Hrenko. He is a Rusnak like us. He can be trusted; he is from Presov, farther west of Vilag. He will tell you what to do and help you get a job. Otherwise, it could take weeks if you tried to do it on your own. Hrenko has been here for six years and knows his way around. He can speak enough English to get you in."

"Sam, you look tired," Andrij said.

"Twelve hours a turn in the mill makes anyone look tired," he answered. "Sometimes it is the heavy work but most of all it is the intense heat in the cinder pit that wears you down. It is like working in Hell."

"What is the cinder pit?"

"Don't worry. Soon enough you will find out. It is the only place the Irish and the Americans will let us work. It is the worst possible job in the mill. It is fit for Hunkies, as they say."

Late that afternoon, it took Sam and Andrij less than five minutes to walk to the mill. The Evanses lived within three blocks of the mill entrance. The guard let Andrij in after Sam got him to understand that his friend had just come over on the boat and was looking for a job. Sam was a few minutes earlier than he normally would have been and looked for Yurko (George) Hrenko in the locker room. Men working the day turn had already showered and washed and the room was filled with steam, like a Turkish bath.

Hrenko was a short man, just over 5 feet tall and not especially muscular. Andrij immediately wondered how he was able to work in a place that looked so physically demanding. His face was thin and his high cheekbones seemed to accentuate the dark brown eyes that glowered from under heavy eyebrows. A large, handlebar moustache covered his entire upper lip and his thin, lower lip was almost non-existent.

Hrenko had the habit of always trying to project an air of superiority when among other Slavs. Few fell for the façade. When Sam introduced him to Andrij, Hrenko smiled and showed a row of teeth that were in desperate need of help. Even his handshake was weak, almost like shaking hands with a woman, Andrij thought. Instantly, there was something about him that Andrij didn't like.

They spoke in their native language and Andrij sensed that some of his words were slightly different, maybe more Slovak than Rusnak.

"Sam tells me you need a job," he said. "Can you read or write?

"Were you a farmer in Vilag?

"Well, there are no sheep or cows in Pittsburgh, but if you have a strong back and arms, there is work for you. I will talk to Mike Gallagher on the turn tonight. If he agrees, I will tell Sam and he can tell you if you get the job and when to start.

"Do you have the money?"

"What money?" Andrij asked in surprise.

"What money? I thought Sam told you."

"He didn't tell me anything about money?

"Well, I'll tell you."

The right side of Hrenko's face sporadically twitched as he spoke and it caught Andrij's attention. He is having trouble telling me this, Andrij thought. It must be wrong what he is saying, what he is doing. I must not trust him.

"If you want a job in the mill you must pay the foreman and then he agrees to hire you. That is the way things are done in this mill and all other mills around Pittsburgh. That is the way you get a job in America."

"How much must I pay to get a job?"

"Gallagher is an okay guy. You pay only once, up front. He is better than are most other foremen. For them, you must give a small part of your pay every two weeks. That is when you are paid here, every two weeks, on the first and middle of the month."

"How much must I pay Gallagher to get the job?"

"Twenty-five dollars."

"That is more than two week's pay. I don't have $25. I have less than $1 in my pocket.

"That's too bad, because you won't get a job."

"Can you lend me the money?" Andrij asked as he turned to Sam.

"I have no money saved," Sam said. "We are still paying Gottlieb for the two beds we got for two new boarders."

"Look," Hrenko said when he thought the deal was about to slip past him. "I'm not sure Gallagher will go for this but if I interceded for you, tell him you used all your money to get here, maybe he will let you pay it off a little each week. But, I know what he is going to say. It will cost you more if you do it that way. Instead of $25 it will probably be $35. I'll see if I can get him down to $30. He is a friend of mine and I am a friend of yours. Okay?"

Son-of-a-bitch, Andrij thought to himself. He turned to Sam and Sam rolled his eyes and turned his head away as if saying, What can I do?

"Okay," Andrij said after a few moments of hesitation.

The six o'clock whistle blew as Sam and Hrenko quickly departed for their respective gangs.

"I'll see you in the morning," Sam said to Andrij as he walked away. "Can you find your way out of here and home?"

"Mike," said George Hrenko, "I just captured another greenhorn for you. He is so new I can still smell the salt on his jacket. He wants a job. I told him $25, cash up front, like always. But he has no money, he used it all to get here. So, I told him that maybe I could get you to agree to installments. But if that's the way then you want $35, but maybe I could get you down to $30."

"Look you fuckin' Hunky," Gallagher said as he grabbed Hrenko by the collar and effortlessly pulled him to within a few inches of his face. Gallagher was a big man who had came from Ireland as a 14-year old kid. Like all immigrants, even 20 years ago, he started work in the cinder pits. He worked his way up quickly and became lead foreman on three blast furnaces because he was an aggressive "pusher." The mill's management used the term for all their lower echelon personnel because their job was to constantly push the laborers to increase the output of steel tonnage every month and set new records. Push was the word that constantly came down from the very top and was pronounced with a Scottish accent.

"You're a greedy little bastard. If I ever finds out you been getting more fer a job and cheating me out of it, you won't lose just your job, you'll disappear, become a part of a pig iron ingot. No one will miss another damned Hunky. Furstay?"

"Come on Mike," Hrenko answered after he broke free of Gallagher's grip. He was a bit shaken from the handling Gallagher had just treated him to. He looked around to see if any Hunkies had seen the incident. However, he wasn't surprised. Gallagher was an unpredictable man and he had seen him blow up before.

"Maybe he just got chewed out by someone above him," Hrenko thought to himself.

Hrenko was a greedy bastard. He would sell out anyone, even a fellow Rusnak for money. He had no conscience; some thought he had no soul. He had never been seen in church and his reputation was well known. Because of his dealings, he had no friends and lived as a boarder with one of the few Irish families still in Verner. No decent Rusnak woman wanted him as a boarder regardless of how much he was willing to pay. Hrenko hated the Irish as much as they disliked him but he put up with the abuse and degradation because he now wanted to go back to Europe.

When he first came to America, he had been loose with his money and developed a taste for whiskey. A few years ago he realized that he would never get out of the cinder pits, never rise above the menial task he daily dreaded. It was then he decided to begin saving. He was trying to earn the coveted thousand dollars goal every immigrant believed was enough to set them up in Europe as better than most farmers. However, whiskey was still keeping him from reaching his objective at the pace he would have liked.

"Haven't I always been good in getting you greenhorns," he said to Gallagher? "Hell, most of the men in your three cinder pit gangs, I got for you. And what do I get, a lousy $3 for all my effort. And, I'm taking a chance. What do you think they would do to me if they ever found out?"

"Okay," Gallagher said. "Thirty dollars. But you get your cut from his last payment. I want it in six payments, $5 each on time. I don't want it drawn out too long or you'll pay me out of your envelope."

"Good," said Hrenko. "I'm going over to his friend's gang on Number 9 to tell him it's okay. When do you want him here?"

"Two days from today. And don't forget you still work here. Don't take all night getting back."

While Gallagher was the king of graft on the night turn at his furnaces, George Hrenko was his faithful knave.

Chapter 4   City of Iron--Men of Gristle

More than 80,000 men were involved in the making of steel in the Pittsburgh area when Andrij Karas arrived in the Summer of '92. In the previous 30 years, iron making in America had grown from what was almost a cottage industry into a Goliath that consumed enormous amounts of raw materials, energy and had an insatiable thirst for men. It was an industry built on brawn. Even though mechanization, at every turn in the process, was constantly being developed to alleviate some of the physical effort and thus increase tonnage, there was still a great need for strong, unskilled labor at all entry-level positions.

Of the vast horde of men involved in making steel, only 5 percent were classified as skilled workers. Most of these were Germans or English immigrants who had been here for a decade or two. Semi-skilled workers, often their sons or later immigrants from Ireland and Scandinavian countries, comprised about 20 percent of the work force. That left an army of nearly 60,000 men whose contributions were their arms, their backs, their legs, their brawn, and too often, their lives. And, of these, nearly three-quarters or 45,000, were immigrants of which Slavs had now become the majority.

After the Civil War, the iron and steel industry began expanding at a rapid rate, and a cheap labor force was needed so it could turn a profit. Carnegie was counting on it. The Irish Potato Famine, that had supplied soldiers for both armies, now stood ready to supply a cheap labor force in almost unlimited numbers for the iron and steel industry. And, because there was now good money to be made in America, they were joined by hordes of Scots, Welsh and English, and Scandinavians.

But the demands of making steel--12-hour shifts, seven days a week, and every day of the year, and low wages at the beginning jobs — gradually caused these people who entered the industry in the cinder pits to become disenchanted. They began to look elsewhere. If they were not able to rise within the industry to semi-skilled and skilled jobs in order to find better working conditions and higher pay they would leave steel making for other industries. This created a expanding bottom void that began to be felt in the late 1880s and early 1890s.

There were many uneducated young American men in Pittsburgh who could have found employment in the mills. And, during the early 1890s, many of them did. However, as Slavic immigrants, peasants and serfs by any standard, began to flood into the furnaces and hearths as common day laborers, those Americans working side-by-side with them began to develop a resentment toward these new foreigners.

The immigrants, however, accustomed to generations of forced obedience to authority, usually an ethnically different authority, readily accepted what they were told to do, at what wages the mill's owners thought they could least pay and under what conditions they would work. The Americans among them began to develop a dislike of the immigrants and their subservient attitude. It was contrary to the democratic ideals they had been taught and exercised.

Maybe even more important was the inability of Americans to communicate with the immigrants. The immigrants naturally kept to themselves and Americans in the cinder-pit gangs isolated themselves from what was becoming a majority in their ranks. After a while, they refused to work with the Slavs.

American day laborers stood in startling contrast to Slavs for several reasons. Slavs were intrinsically stolid individuals who revealed little or no emotion or sensibility. "An impassive lot," as one foreman described them. There is a common saying among other Europeans that Slavs are easy to bend but impossible to break. Americans who worked with Slavs, especially single, or married men whose wives were in Europe, resented them because they were willing to live in unsanitary conditions in company housing without complaining.

This reflected the crude standards of sanitation in village life in the Old Country. But, there it was tolerable, counter-balanced by space, a modicum of people, and unlimited clean air---a rare commodity in Pittsburgh. Americans also disliked the way the Slavs hoarded their money, to spend it only on immediate necessities, while young Americans found it difficult to save anything. To them, Hunky became a term of opprobrium as well a place of origin. In the end, they felt it was degrading for them to work among Slavs and refused jobs like those in the cinder pits.

Steve Boone was a 24-year old West Virginia coal miner who was lured to Pittsburgh in 1898 by stories his cousin Martin Crowley had told him of the high wages paid semi- and skilled workers in the Allegheny mills, the kind where Andrij worked. One day Boone showed up at the employment office with his cousin and was being interviewed for a job. The interviewer told them that Boone could not start at any of those positions without experience or a trade. He could, however, work his way up to them in a few years if he was capable. But he had to start in the mill at the bottom.

"There are jobs open in the cinder pit," he told the pair.

"Yeah," agreed Crowley, "I knows of one or two helper's jobs on my shift dat's open. It's a good think to know if you wants to learn the iron game."

"No," said the interviewer, "I mean in the cinder pit itself."

"Hell no," he said and turned to his cousin. "You don't wants to work dere. Onlys Hunkies works in dem jobs. Dere too damn hot and too dam dirty for a 'white' man."

He didn't take the job.

As they walked across the yard from the employment office Crowley put his arm over his cousin's shoulder and said, "Dere are a few of dem dam Hunkies dat's all right, but a dam few. If'n I had my way, I'da shipped de whole damn lot back to where dey come from. Bein' a cinder-snapper's no kinda job fer an American."

While mechanization of the industry at the upper ends of the process now demanded fewer and fewer skilled and semi-skilled workers, beginning jobs still required an extensive labor force. The slow departure of the first British immigrants from the steel industry created a growing scarcity of men who would work long shifts, endure the strenuous requirements and be satisfied with pay that didn't allow one to live comfortably in the United States, even at the lowest levels.

Mill owners were facing a dilemma as the initial European labor force began to dry up until the industry discovered a huge number of desperate people in east-central Europe. They were easy targets because these people had been disenfranchised for centuries. They had been treated as serfs, then peasants, and were intimately familiar with hard work and minimal incomes. Even better, they could neither read nor write in their own language, let alone speak English. They were the perfect fodder for the cannons of the mills.

To get them to come, the mills and mine owners sent emissaries into east-central Europe to lure them to "the good life and high wages" available in the coal fields and steel mills in America. First they scoured the western Carpathian Mountain region for Hungarians and Bohemians. Comparatively few in number, these were quickly swallowed up by the industry and more were needed. The agents continually moved farther east and recruited large numbers of Slovaks, then Rusnaks. Then, they headed south to gather up Serbs, Slovenes and Croats, all from lands controlled by Austria and Hungary. Their thirst still went unsatisfied and they moved down the northern slopes of the Carpathians and signed up horde upon horde of Galician Rusnaks, then added Poles and even ventured into Russia and came back with Ukrainians.

They all were the ideal day-labor force for the mills and mines of America. Unlike most other immigrants, these men came not out of any desire for religious or political freedom but primarily to make money. They wanted to better their lives and realized that this was impossible to do in Europe. Few had any initial intention of staying in America. Most set goals of working five, maybe ten years, and to save every cent possible so they could return and buy land and live in a semi-affluent state. To do this, most were young, single men, who would tolerate the most basic living conditions to save as much as possible and thus shorten the time to return home. They would live as cheaply as possible--six and eight to a single room, feed on the most basic foods and deny themselves anything that cost money or the social pleasures of young men. They felt they could tolerate anything, work the most menial jobs, take wages lower than other ethnic groups would tolerate, all this and more as long as in the end they could return to their homelands as "wealthy" persons.

All this was to the mill and mine owner's advantage, to capitalize upon, and was made possible because these were very unsophisticated, isolated people, men whose ancestors had been kept at the poverty level in their homelands while the rest of Europe was moving into the 20th century. They were men uneducated, even in their own languages, men who lived close to the land under conditions that would have been considered primitive by others and whose entire daily struggle was to put food on their tables. They had no time for frivolities like music, theater, art or even politics--and least of all schools, which were usually unavailable or often intentionally denied them. Their only relief in Europe was found in religion, and in America, too often in the saloons.

It was this polyglot that greeted Andrij Karas when he first stepped off the train in Verner. However, he could feel at home, among his own kind in Verner and nearby Woods Run, because most of the people living and working there at that time were Rusnaks from Austria and Polish-occupied Galicia. Other communities in the Pittsburgh area had their own ethnic concentrations. Towns like Homestead were filled almost exclusively with Slovaks, McKeesport was heavily Hungarian, and so on. It was the way they immigrated; "string immigration" anthropologists called it, when one group of men follows another. Oftentimes entire villages from a surrounding area would settle in one town in America.

The initial immigrants who filled the company houses and apartment buildings in Verner and Woods Run were Irish. But, as the century waned, they found work in other industries or moved up the skilled-labor ladder. They first moved out of Verner, then Woods Run, and farther up the surrounding hills and away from the noise and dirt of the mills. They did leave behind a few Irish proprietors, however, who operated saloons or bars on almost every corner, especially along Cass and Preble streets.

The next morning at breakfast, Sam told Andrij of George Hrenko's deal with Gallagher. "It is not so good," he added, "but it is work. If you don't go for it, it can take weeks to find an opening. And then you will probably face the same situation; all this before you make your first dollar."

Reluctantly, Andrij agreed.

"But you cannot wear those clothes in the cinder pit, they are too good. I have some old clothes you can have. You don't start work until tomorrow. Helen and my sister will take you later to a store on Preble Street that sells good used clothes. You need to get a good pair of shoes, ones with thick soles, and a pair of gloves. You cannot work unless you have heavy leather gloves. If you do not have enough money for them, Helen will rob the jar and lend you enough for that.

"You can wear your good clothes to the lockers and change there. At the end of a shift, your work cloths stay in the locker until you can stand them no more, then you bring them home and let Helen wash them. But, don't ever leave your gloves or shoes in the locker until you can afford a good lock. *Rozsumish?*"

"I understand," answered Andrij.

"Hrenko said that Ghallagher can put you in a cinder pit gang and you start tomorrow night. You will go with me."

Chapter 5   Into the Furnace

Andrij followed Sam out the door. The half-dozen boarders who lived with them and who also worked the day turn were immediately behind him. There was no wind and the air seemed especially stifling for the end of June. It would be another hot day... even hotter once they were inside the furnace sheds.

Sam paused for a minute on the bottom step before stepping onto the sidewalk to let a string of solemn mill workers pass. Sam and his entourage stepped into an opening and quickly became part of a long undulating line of near-silent men heading toward the mill's chain-link gate two blocks away. Others came down Spruce Street and were joined by those who lived on Cass Street. In all, there were more than 200 men all heading toward one point. Some, in smaller groups, walked in the street because there was no traffic. Andrij heard them talking among themselves in low tones. He couldn't make out their language but it was familiar; it was one of a half-dozen Slavic tongues spoken by this horde of mill workers from east-central Europe. It was a mass of humanity, a sea of darkly-clad individuals that moved almost in unison, toward a drudgery they undertook willingly but disliked intensely. It was an uninspired walk and Andrij sensed that there was no joy in their stride nor their minds. They were resolute to a man.

It was not like working back home, Andrij though. There his labor had been hard but it was outside, in the mountains where the air was clear and clean, the grass green and the fields surrounded by trees. There was the ever-present sound of life—birds, cattle, dogs as well as people—awakening to the day. All this seemed to make his work there almost pleasant.

Hrenko was already at the lockers waiting for Andrij and Sam when they arrived at the mill.

"I'm glad you agreed," Hrenko said. "Gallagher is a good man and said that $30 would be okay. I had a hard time convincing him but he finally agreed. He said you could pay me $5 a payday, every two weeks, for six paydays.

"Okay?"

"Okay," Andrij said and reluctantly shook the hand Hrenko offered.

"Follow me and I will take you to Furnace 9."

As they walked from the lockers across the open mill yard, Andrij was awestruck by what he saw. The size of the huge blast furnace close-up startled him. He had difficulty comprehending that men could build something so massive, so complicated. It seemed almost alive, breathing as it spewed fire and smoke, and hissed steam. They walked the length of one of two sets of small-gauge railroad tracks that disappeared into the huge shed made of sheets of corrugated metal that housed the furnace. The blast furnace rose from the back of the shed, through its roof, and towered a hundred feet above the ground.

To the left of the tower, he could see small, iron buckets linked together every 20 feet by a heavy chain that moved slowly, continuously up a track on an inclined hoist. They clanked and clamored as they rose. As they moved they seemed to loudly complain about being dragged to the top. The bottom of the hoist was buried in a bin that received alternate loads of iron ore, coke and limestone. With a thunderous crash, that Andrij felt through his feet as they walked toward the shed, three railroad cars at a time released their loads of ore into the bin through doors on their bottoms. The slack from the ore billowed high into the air and momentarily obliterated the blast furnace. It didn't last long.

The tops of the bins were wide enough so that three cars could be dumped at one time before the next trio of cars moved in. The top of the hoist ended just above the blast furnace. As each bucket was pulled over the top, it rolled upside down and dumped its load into a large funnel atop the furnace. Inside, the ore and its ingredients formed layers that temporarily floated on the molten iron until they, too, melted. The intense heat liquefied each successive layer until they reached the bottom in a molten state. It was so hot inside that Andrij could almost smell the heat.

Instinctively, he raised his arm in front of his face as if to ward off the radiant heat that emanated from the furnace.

Hrenko saw his response and laughed. "You'll get used to that after a few days in the pits," he yelled.

The noises inside the shed were so loud that you had to yell if you wanted to be heard. That took extra energy and after a while you spoke only when it was something important. That didn't bother Andrij who was by nature a reticent person. However, it made you see things about you with greater intensity because this was a dangerous place to be. And, in a very real way, your eyes replaced your ears.

The great heat needed to melt the ore came from four cylindrical stoves that looked like huge farm silos and were about the same size. The stoves burn natural gas, which in turn heats the air that is then forced by turbo-blowers into pipes that run into the blast furnace.

"Once they start the fire in that thing," Hrenko said to Andrij in an authoritative voice and gestured toward the towering furnace as they approached the shed's large, open doors, "it runs all the time for three or four years; sometimes more. It stops only when the bricks begin to burn up. The inside of the furnace is lined with clay bricks but after a while even they break apart from the heat because it is so intense."

Andrij walked slightly behind Hrenko as they approach the furnaces. As Hrenko spoke and gestured, Andrij saw the muscles on the sides of Hrenko's thin neck flex and strain against a red bandanna. It was obviously tied too tightly, Andrej thought. Besides, it looks silly on him. It makes him look feminine.

Inside the shed Andrij could see the bottom of the furnace. From one hole on its left, a steady stream of molten iron poured through a trough lined with clay. It coursed out the left side of the building to waiting ladle cars. When a car was full, it was rushed to an open area, exposed to all the elements, behind the shed were it would be poured into a channel leading to the numerous molds. Here, the iron was left to cool naturally into ingots. They were called pig iron because the trough that led to them had a series of parallel channels that fed each mold and together they resembled a series of piglets, side-by-side, feeding off a sow lying on her side.

"The burned coke and other 'junk' in the ore is lighter than iron and floats on top," said Hrenko as they approached a group of workers wielding shovels. "When it gets too much junk floating on the iron, the foreman gives the order and blows off the coke cinders into one of two pits outside the furnace," he pointed to one as he spoke. "And when the slag in one pit is cool enough to handle, you and your buddies go in and shovel it onto the platform. You have to be able to throw it far back on the platform or it will slide back into the pit. From there a tractor pushes it off the edge of the platform where it is dumped into small cars. The cars are on rails that will take it to the slag heap."

The blow-off ran through channel runners similar to the molten iron channels but had a gate that could direct the molten slag to one of two pits dug into the ground below the lowest level of the blast furnace. The pits were about 20-feet square and 3 to 4 feet deep, with upward sloping sides. Slag, as the burned cinders and other impurities are called, was air cooled but occasionally helped with a water hose when air inside the shed was too warm to make a difference. A steam-driven tractor, much like today's front-loaders, moves into the pit with an arm-like hammer that brakes up the "clinkers" or big pieces of slag. When the operator is finished a gang of cinder-pit laborers move in with shovels. The slag heap was outside, behind the shed. When one cinder pit was being poured, the other was being "dug."

Water is used sparingly on the slag to hasten cooling it down to the temperature at which it can be handled. As it cools, layers are "peeled off" by the "cinder-snappers." Usually, only the pit boss would hose it down. If he uses too much water, the molten slag inside could become a bomb. "Cooling off" was considered an art and seldom trusted to "....dumb Hunkies."

Working in the pits was a hot, miserable job and no one escaped burned holes in their clothing or welts on their arms and legs where they were burned when the hot slag "popped." To keep their shoes from burning, men made their own sandals with thick wooden soles into which they slipped their shoes. Without them, a pair of shoes wouldn't last through "one turn," as the men called a 12-hour shift.

"This is Boris Spivak," Hrenko said to Andrij. "He is head of this cinder pit gang. He is in charge of you and five others, but he works just like you. You do as he says. He also directs the clinker breaker. Watch out for the clinker breaker. He is not a Hunky and likes to bother us. He knows only one Rusnak word, *chekai*, and when he yells jump, jump out of the way."

Andrij shook hands with Spivak. They nodded without speaking to one another. Andrij immediately sensed that Spivak resented Hrenko. Hrenko was acting like a foreman and was nothing but a cinder pit member. But, he knew of his covert relationship with Gallagher and only for that reason tolerated him.

"But first, come with me," Hrenko said. "I want you to meet one of three assistant foremen who work on Number 9.

"Bob," he said to a tall man with pure white hair who was checking the color of the flame in the furnace. "This is Andy, a new man for the pit. Gallagher asked me to bring him over here."

Robert Ryan was prematurely gray for his age. He was probably no more than 35 and stood a head above the men who were working the furnace in front of him. He had large, bushy eyebrows that were still coal black in color and intensified his ruddy complexion. Ryan looked at Andrij for a moment and then back at the furnace, studying the color of the flame. Then he looked back at Andrij. Andrij offered him his hand but Ryan didn't move.

"When the hell are they going to send me some real men?" he said. "Get him a shovel and show him where to work. And you, get your ass back to your pit. Your gang is falling behind without you."

Ryan walked away turning his back on Andrij and Hrenko.

"He's a busy man," Hrenko said apologetically. "If you have a problem, go to Spivak, not him. The less you have to do with the Irish the better."

When Andrij got back to the pit Spivak and four other men were temporarily resting on their shovels. They had just finished cleaning a pit and the slag from the last blowoff was still too hot to handle.

"This is Big John, a Russian," said Spivak as he introduced him to the gang.

"I am not Russian," he immediately answered, "I am Ukrainian. Originally from L'viv. Recently from Odessa. My passport is all the Russian I am."

"That is Harry," Spivak continued. "And next to him is John, both Rusnaks like you. You are a Rusnak, aren't you?

"Yes," said Andrij. "You are a Bohemian, yes?"

"Yes, I am. But the Americans think we're all the same. To them, we are all Hunkies. All except Tony, there. He is not a Hunky but a Wopp."

47

Tony was the only one who came over to Andrij and shook hands. "I am not Wopp. I am Italian. From Sicily."

"Why do they call you Wopp?" Andrij asked.

"Because we have no American consulate in Palermo. When *Siciliano* come to Ellis Island, without papers, Americans stamp his entry certificate with W.O.P.P."

"What is W.O.P.P. mean?"

"With Out Pass Port. The *Napolitani* make fun of us and call us Wopps. Now all Americans, and even Hunkies, call us Wopps."

"Men," said Spivak. "This is Andy the fish."

"Why you call me fish?" Andrij asked.

"Because that is what Karas means. Didn't you know that?

"No, I didn't.

"What kind of fish"

"Does it matter?

"Let's go to work, the slag is cool enough. "Captain" Bob will be on our asses if he turns this way. He doesn't need an excuse to yell at us. To him, we are all no good, lazy Hunkies.

"If we are so no good, why do their hire us?" Andrij asked.

"Because we come cheap!"

The term Hunky seems to have originated in the steel mills of Pittsburgh and first came into use in the late 1870s as the first Hungarian immigrant laborers began arriving in the mills. The term was coined by Irish immigrants who were still working in the cinder pits and who had not yet begun their climb up the work ladder.

They shortened the name Hungarians to "Hungies" and somewhere in their varied brogue it was further refined and became Hunkies and Hunky. Mixed with the first Hungarian immigrants were Bohemians or Czechs and to differentiate between the two ethic groups they were called Bohunks, a combination of Bohemian-Hungarians. The Irish saw no difference between them and the Slovaks who then followed in a massive wave of immigration that dwarfed the number of Czechs and Hungarians working here.

After all, weren't they all citizens of Austro-Hungary? Hunky, they believed, was an appropriate term for all of them. Following the Slovaks in even greater numbers were Rusnaks from eastern Slovakia and Galicia, and Poles. It didn't matter to the Irish, English, Welsh or Germans, or the American workers who picked up the term, that the Galicians and Poles were ethnically different from the Czechs and Hungarians because they, too, were all a part of the Austrian Empire. The term quickly spread to the coal fields of western then eastern Pennsylvania and foreign miners, as well, became Hunkies.

Andy, as the men in the pit called him, picking up they name Hrenko had used, moved into the cinder pit with the others and took his first shovel of slag and tossed it onto the platform that had just been cleared by the tractor. He was surprised at how light it was. He thought it would be heavy like iron. Little did he realize that that was the first of what would eventually be millions of shovelsful before he put it away for good.

"Someday," Andrij thought to himself as he lifted the next load of slag," this shovel will set me free. Maybe."

There was always an informal contest going on among some of the men in his gang. It was the same in all the cinder-pit gangs. It was a macho thing. Each time a shovel of slag was tossed it became a contest to see who could throw it the farthest back on the platform. It was good training for a shot-putter.

Andrij worked well into his second hour as a pitman before he began to feel different. He sensed something was overcoming him but he didn't know what it was. His face was flushed from the proximity to the intense heat and his forehead was covered in beads of sweat. The heat was so intense that Andrij felt he could smell it; even taste it. He had never experienced such heat. It seemed to sear the inside of his nostrils and he now regularly flared them attempting for some kind of relief. He had started work with his sleeves rolled up but now took a moment to roll them down and button them at his wrists. It was some protection from the heat, but not much. At times the cinders were almost as hot as the nearby blast furnace and as he bent down to load a shovel he now automatically turned his face to one side to avoid the heat rising from the cinders.

Spivak was a good gang boss and knew he had to watch Andrij, to see how he reacted to the heat. He could sense that his newest man was having difficulty adjusting to the heat and worked his way to him.

"Go back on the platform to the water machine and get a drink," he ordered. "You are dehydrating."

Andrij looked quizzically at him and Spivak realized he didn't understand what he said.

"You are loosing your water. Over there," he pointed. "Go get a drink and splash some on your face. It will help. Take one of the white pills from the bottle next to the water. It is salt. You are also loosing salt. Take but one. No more than three on a turn and never all at once."

Andrij welcomed the change. The water on the face seemed to help the most. In a few minutes, he was back and shoveling with renewed vigor. With bent arms and back Andrij worked silently with the other men until the whistle blew at 6:00 a.m. Men from the day turn were already waiting behind them. As they left their holes in the slag, the cinder pits were filled by men who looked just like they did, clones, most mustachioed, just over 5 feet tall, slender, light-brown- or blond-haired, light complexions, all tired-looking even before they lifted their first shovel of slag.

Andy had never showered before or been naked in front of other men. For a few moments he was hesitant about taking off his soiled, sweaty cloths. He was so tired that he stopped thinking and undressed. It didn't matter and he quickly overcame any reluctance. One thing the mill company was generous with was soap and hot water. He lingered in it, almost falling asleep, until Sam Evans yelled for him to come out.

"I don't think I will eat breakfast," he said to Sam as they walked home. "I think I will go right to bed." He did eat breakfast. He couldn't resist the smell of frying eggs and bacon. It seemed that he had just fallen asleep when Helen was shaking his shoulder.

"Get up. You have just enough time to eat and get to work. It is nearly five and you must be there by 6:00."

To him, it seemed that he had never left the pit as he waited for a free shovel from a day-turn man. His muscles ached and his back was sore, but only for a few minutes. After a dozen shovels of cinders, he was again loose and limber.

"There is enough time between now and the next hour," Spivak said about 1 a.m., "to eat lunch."

The pail Helen had prepared contained two pork chops, a small loaf of white bread, three hard-boiled eggs and several dill pickles. The container on the bottom was filled with black coffee.

Andy sat on a turned-over wheelbarrow. When The Russian saw him, he came over and sat next to him.

"How long have you worked here?" Andrij asked after they sat silently together for a few minutes.

"Let me see," he thought for a while before answering. "Eight, maybe nine years, I think. I have written down somewhere but that no use to me."

"Why?"

"I cannot read. Can you?"

"How long have the others worked here?"

"Spivak is longest. Twelve years. Wopp is next, 11 years, I think. You Rusnaks are new here, maybe 2 years, maybe 3."

"How can you do this, 12 hours on then 12 ours off, for every day of the year? How do you get ahead, to get a better job?

"If you are Hunky, you not get ahead. Pit is beginning and end for you. There is nowhere for you to go but here, or home to Old Country, or to wooden box."

"Sometime they make you second helper for foreman, and maybe first helper, when times are good. But when there are bad, cutbacks, you go backwards if you are Hunky. It is like being part of beehive. Once they make you a cinder-snapper, it is like being drone; you not do anything else.

"Maybe if you could read and write, even in Rusnak, you might have chance, but very, very small chance," he said as he pinched two fingers together and squinted to show what "small chance" might look like.

"See man over there? Old man with gray hair who limp. He is Ivan Skyba, from Smerek, in Galicia. He still insists he be called Ivan instead John. But that not his story. He looks 60, maybe 65 years old. No? He is 45, maybe 40. He be in cinder pits for 20 years, when there no strikes. Maybe first man ever come here. He has son, Alex. Alex very smart young man. He go university, here, in Pittsburgh. He became chemist. He graduate with honors and his father think Alex would get good job. He came to mill to get job in laboratory.

"When they asked him his name, he say Skyba. Then they say, oh no, you can no work here, you must start in cinder pit and learn business. What has cinder pit to do with chemistry of steel? Slag is slag and you not need fancy paper to understand that. Anyway, he listened to them and do as they say. He do that for year. For one year. Then he go superintendent and asked for transfer. Super asked him his name and then say, no, we need your kind in cinder pit.

"He quit and went across river, to McKee's Rocks, to three plants there and could not get lab job. He go New York City looking for job. They send him some place name Albany. He get job with company called General Electric. He send for father and mother but his father not go. He said there was no work in Albany for Hunkies. He make so much money his father not need work. But Ivan stay here. Now you know what means 'Dumb Hunky'."

"Besides, why you want get better job? The $1.65 a day you make here is three, four times what you get back in Vilag, if you could find job there. You are like all of us here, except maybe Tony. You came here to make *tysiach dolyary*, 1,000 dollars. That is every Hunky's goal, to make $1,000. That is enough money so you can go home and buy farm and live off it from what you make here. You want live like *bohatch*, no?

"How long you plan to stay here before you go back?"

"Five years," Andrij said.

"You have wife here or Old Country?

"In Old Country. But I will bring her here."

"Andy, lissen me. It take you 10 years if you lucky to save $1,000, even if there be no strikes. And, if you live like dog you can save $1,000. Think your wife like live like dog for that long? I don't think so. That's why I leave my *zenna* home."

"You guys going to bullshit all day?" Spivak yelled at them. "Get your shovels and get to work."

Chapter 6   A Daring Passage

Sam Evans had obtained a job for Andrij when he first arrived in America, at the Allegheny Iron Works in Verner, owned by Lewis, Oliver & Phillips. Even though Andrij immediately began to work, the amount of money he made was not what he had been led to believe. It was nine months before he was able to save fifty dollars to send home. His wife and family were in dire need of help but Andrij was obligated to first pay back the loan he was given for his passage. Somehow they managed

Andrij found it impossible, at first, to put money aside. The mills were wrought with labor problems. Carnegie was determined to break the hold unions had bitterly gained on the steel mills and on his workers. To break them he caused strikes and lockouts that constantly interrupted Andrij's ability to save. And, Andrij had immediate living costs--room, board and clothing--that had to be met before a surplus could be built. His life was one of bare existence. It was almost inhuman. Despite this, for two years, it was his intermittent dollars that kept his family alive and that of his wife's, even though Sam also sent money home.

It wasn't until October, in 1896, that he finally amassed enough money to buy a ticket for Zuzanna. He bought a steamship ticket at a local bank and Helen sent it, along with a train ticket and a few dollars. Zuzanna then had the priest at St. Dimitri write a letter to Helen, asking her to find a place for her and Andrij to live once she arrived in Verner. Andrij had been boarding with her brother Sam and his wife Helen since he arrived in Verner. Zuzanna received Helen's answer just a few days before she departed Vilag. Because of the uncertainty of the exact day she would arrive in New

York, Helen gave her instructions of how they could be found after she arrived in Pittsburgh.

Helen instructed her to take a local train from Union Station once she arrived in Pittsburgh. "Ask the conductor before you get off the train from New York," she wrote, "where you can catch the train to Woods Run. It is in Allegheny City, just across the river from Pittsburgh. Get off at Woods Run Station. It is only 3-1/2 miles or 5-1/2 kilometers from Pittsburgh.

"When you arrive in Woods Run, walk two blocks down Ketchum Street, toward the Ohio River, to St. Alexander Nevsky Church. You can see the church and its Russian cross from the train station. It is the only 'Russian' church in all of Pittsburgh. The priest there will send someone to Verner to get me or Andrij."

Zuzanna Karasz (Karas), now 21, and alone, boarded the steel-hulled British ocean liner *S.S. Friesland* in Antwerp, Belgium in early December. She was Number 355, had an upper bunk on Level II, with other emigrants, had two pieces of luggage and her final destination on the ship's manifest was listed as Pittsburgh.

December 17, 1896---The New York harbor pilot, now in command of the large passenger ship, stood on the wing of the flying bridge with its captain. A fresh, cold breeze from the southwest snapped the pants of his uniform and forced him to hold the cap on his head with his left hand while the other grasped the cold, metal railing. The captain relayed each of the pilot's orders to his first mate who was standing just inside the hatch in the wheelhouse. The officer then repeated them to the coxswain who tightly gripped the huge, stainless steel wheel of the vessel.

The *S.S. Friesland* was built for the Red Star Line in Glasgow just seven years ago but sailed under a Belgian Flag. It was fully loaded with 600 Third Class passengers. After the anchors were hauled aboard, at the pilot's command, her triple-expansion steam engine was engaged. Before entering the overnight quarantine anchorage off Staten Island, the captain lowered the sails on four masts. The next morning, the 437-foot vessel, aided now only by her single engine, slowly began to move from the quarantine area deeper into New York Harbor.

For the benefit of the passengers, the pilot took the ship close to Bedlose Island and the statue they had all heard about. Zuzanna, alone, leaned on the port railing to watch the island sweep past.

Her mind was not on the unknown events she knew she was soon to encounter, but momentarily flitted to those of her husband Andrij. He was somewhere to the west, in a place called Allegheny City. She wondered how much he might have changed since she last saw him. It had been three-and-one-half years since he left Vilag. Her life had been put on hold ever since the day they made that decision.

Suddenly, Zuzanna stood erect as the statue came into view. A spontaneous roar arose from the people on deck. The ship seemed to list a bit to port after everyone rushed to get a look at the huge lady with the torch in her hand. Many openly wept, some blessed themselves and others fell to their knees in prayer.

Zuzanna, however, stood resolute, tightly gripping the ship's cold railing and stared into the blank eyes of the statue of a woman as the boat slowly passed the island. She suddenly felt overcome by a sense of accomplishment and pride. She had just completed what she thought she could never have done, crossing to American by herself. It was a novel feat for a slight, young woman, uneducated, from an isolated mountain village, and who had never been required or even allowed to make a decision on her own.

But ever since the day she and Andrij decided to postpone having children, even to herself, she seemed a changed person. Her idle moments were consumed in planning their future. She never regretted Andrij's decision to leave Vilag and go to America because she knew it was their only way to escape the servitude, the vassalage to a land and a society that had her trapped in those verdant, beautiful but retarding mountains. All she would be if she remained there would be a vehicle for raising children and continuing the centuries of commitment to a life without hope. Maybe, in America, she would not entirely escape it, but surely her children would break the bonds.

For weeks before her departure, women from the village would find some excuse to come to Mykola Karas's house, or her mother's house when she visited home, and warn her of the dangers of crossing. It was dangerous, they said, even if you crossed with others you knew, and the pitfalls of doing it by herself were numerous. One reminded her of the ship, filled with thousands of emigrants, that was lost at sea just a few years ago. Or, why couldn't she wait until summer because the ocean was always more dangerous to cross in December. And, the sea was filled with icebergs.

"What would you do if the ship sprang a leak? One woman asked. "At least wooden boats float...sometimes."

There was more envy in what they were saying rather than concern for her safety. Covertly, they, too, wanted to escape their lives in this land.

And one told her of the stories she heard of unaccompanied women who were raped by men who shared the third class steerage with them. Worst of all, they said, were members of the ship's crew who lured them into their cabins and had their way with women.

"You know stories of sailors and how they act, don't you?"

They told her of women who had gotten as far as Praha (Prague) and were never heard from again, either by people she was to meet in America or those in Praha. Don't go. Don't be stupid. Make your husband come back here and take you if he wants you to live with him in Pittsburgh.

I'm sure these stories would have held back many ordinary women from traveling alone, but my grandmother was not an ordinary woman. I'm also sure that every grandson would feel the same way. But it was her accomplishments that eventually would set her apart from other women of her era. She was just 21 at the time and what she had just accomplished was rare for any woman in her day. A decade later, it would be a bit more commonplace, but not in 1896. She had revealed a strength of character that was unique and would carry her and her family through two world wars, until she encountered the *Schutzstaffel,* the *SS.*

The *Friesland* didn't go to Ellis Island, as most immigrants expected, but continued north in the Hudson River and made for the docks in Manhattan. The *Friesland* continued past the lower tip of Manhattan, skirting dozens of long piers that reached into the river. At the 23rd Street Pier, the three tugs that had waited for her slowly began the approach, two on the port and one on the vessel's starboard side. Slowly, the two on the port side pushed against her bow and turned her toward Manhattan and then nudged her into the open space. As she approached the pier on her starboard side, dockhands on the pier began throwing "monkey fists" to deck hands on the ship. The ship's crew caught them and quickly fed these light lines through the ship's hawsepipes. Then they pulled the heavy hawsers, attached to the light lines, through the pipes and made them fast to huge cleats on the ship's deck.

Immigrants were barred from going to the gangway that was being raised into place on the dockside of the vessel. The ship's crew, now in full uniform, held back the crowds that were building along the lateral passageways on deck.

"Only first and second class disembark now," a man with a megaphone kept repeating. "Steerage class go to lighters on the port side. You will be taken to Ellis Island for processing."

Zuzanna Karas knew this. She had been told earlier by her steerage-section steward what was going to happen and where to go. She was at the top of the ladder that led down along the outside hull to a stern lighter that had come alongside and was waiting for passengers. When the broad-decked government lighter was secured to the *Friesland*, a man at the bottom yelled an okay and waved the people to come down.

"Stay together when you go through the inspections," yelled their steward. "It will be easier and faster if you do." He waved and people on the lighter waved back at him.

It took the Bureau of Immigration lighter just a few minutes to slip back on an ebbing tide, to Ellis Island. En route down the Hudson they passed other government lighters headed for more immigrants on the *Friesland*.

As Zuzanna watched Manhattan flit past she felt a sudden sense of uneasiness, of apprehension, flood over her. She discounted it and turned to a Slovak woman who had befriended her during the crossing. She also was to join her husband and had a young child in hand.

"I cannot believe we are here," Zuzanna said to her. "Just two weeks ago we were in Antwerp. And two weeks before that I was still in Vilag. Maybe I should have stayed in the Old Country. I'm afraid of what awaits me."

"I hope it is a better life than what we left behind," the woman said.

"I think anything would be better," Zuzanna said.

While Zuzanna was offloading from the lighter, there was a small crowd of immigrants outside the building, from another passenger ship, waiting to go inside. Through its many windows, she could see that the building inside was packed with more immigrants. By the time the government boat tied up, the crowd had disappeared inside and Zuzanna and the others were released.

Blue uniformed guards on the dock yelled for them to hurry and guided them, like traffic policemen, with their arms outstretched, toward the doors. The din inside was ear shattering. Without incident, she passed the first doctors who casually scrutinized her. Beyond the doctors, two uniformed guards caused Zuzanna and others to pass between them and each hurriedly added a number to the card pinned on the immigrant's outside garments. Then another guard directed her to a pen defined by white-painted pipes that, inside, had rows of long wooden benches with curved backs. He told her to sit there.

A few minutes later, another person in a somewhat different blue uniform approached the distal end of the bench where she sat. At first he spoke to her in English, then German, Italian, Polish and finally Russian. When Zuzanna recognized *tvoja meno, tvoja imja,* she answered "Zuzanna Karasova."

"This batch is for you, Wasco," he said as he turned to one of several other men behind him and dressed similarly.

As Zuzanna approached Wasco, he asked, *"Kak ti?"*

*"Ne rozumiu, "*she answered.

"They're not Russians," Wasco yelled to the man who assigned him this group. "They're Rusnaks from Galicia."

"Hungary," she corrected him. *"Ne Halycyna."*

"What's the difference?" the other immigration officer yelled back. "Can you talk to them?"

"No problem, Mike."

"What's your name?" he asked Zuzanna.

"Are you married?

"How old are you?

"Can you read or write?

"Have you been sick lately?

"Do you have any money?

"Let me see it?

"That's interesting. Where did you get American dollars? Did someone send it to you?

"Are you skilled? I mean what kind of work do you do?

"Do you have any relatives here to meet you?

"Where are you going?

Seeming satisfied with her answers, Wasco passed her.

"You're finished. Go ahead. Go! The next man will give you your entry permit."

My God! What do I do? Where do I go? she suddenly asked herself in an utter state of confusion. I wish Andrij was here to meet me.

Zuzanna made it to a set of three doors on the far side of the building. Before each one was a man in uniform who was helping immigrants leave in the right direction. On a piece of paper Helen had scribbled a name. She could not read it but she knew what it said, PITTSBURGH. When one of the mean saw it he pointed to a door with a sign over it: PENNSYLVANIA AND WEST.

"Do you have a ticket?"

Zuzanna had the envelope ready in which Helen had sent the ship's ticket and a prepaid train ticket.

He opened the envelope, looked inside and said, "Good. Go through that door and someone will help you onto the right train."

She didn't know what he said but followed where he pointed.

A black man, the first she had ever seen, in a porter's uniform saw her approach, read her ticket then took the heaviest of her two bags. She resisted letting go at first but when she saw him point with his free hand to a waiting train, she relented.

"Do you all have all your bags?" he asked as he led her to a train.

"Lordy, is that all you have?

"The train to Woods Run and Pittsburgh leaves in half-an-hour," he said as he stored her bags on shelves with nets above the seats. The train leaves at 5:14."

He waited a few moments with his white gloved hand for a tip. Realizing she didn't understand the custom, he parted. As he did, he sighed aloud, "Welcome to America."

The 5:14 to Pittsburgh started exactly at 5:14.

"Don't take off your card," said the conductor who punched her ticket as the train began to move. On it was printed PITTSBURGH. "Wear it all the time so the other conductors knows when to tell you to get off. You're lucky, there are no transfers for you to make. Just stay on to Pittsburgh. That's the end of this run and you must get off. The train is scheduled to get there tomorrow at 9 o'clock in the morning."

She had no idea what he was saying.

"Welcome to America," she heard him also say as he headed for the next passenger. The phrase sounded familiar.

Chapter 7   Welcome to America

Sam Evans was startled when he heard someone knocking, then pounding on his door. He had difficulty waking because his sleep was so deep. He looked at the clock beside his bed and saw it was just 10:30. He looked at his wife. She wasn't around. He had been especially tired when he finally got to bed. The foreman had instructions to set a new tonnage record for that week and everyone was mercilessly pushed.

He was slow to open the door as the knocking continued. He was startled when he saw Father Nedzilnitsky, the priest from Woods Run, standing at the door. At first he thought the priest was the bearer of bad news. Then he saw his sister standing behind the priest. He turned and yelled, "Helen! Andrij, get up! Your wife is here.

"*Durak*," Helen called her husband as she came out of the kitchen with flour on her hands and approached the door. By then, Father Nedzilnitsky and Zuzanna were inside. Zuzanna squealed with delight as she embraced her brother and then her sister-in-law.

"Andrij is working the day turn," Helen said as she broke free of Zuzanna's arms to look at her. He won't be home until after 6:00, about 6:15. Oh what a surprise he will have."

After a few minutes, an exhausted Sam went back to bed, but his wife and Zuzanna talked about the Old Country until mid-afternoon. Helen brought her baby from their bedroom. She was just a little over a year old, and nursed her as they talked.

"Sam insisted that we name her Susan, just like you.

"That was also the name of our first sister," Zuzanna said. "She died in childbirth. I guess my mother really wanted to have a daughter named Zuzanna and also gave me that name."

"It is a popular name now in Europe for girls," Helen said. "Remember, I, too, have a sister named Zuzanna."

"You must be tired," Helen finally said to her sister-in-law. "I could never sleep on trains. Why don't you take a nap. I must finish making bread and then I have to get supper started for the men. I have an army to feed. There is a small bed in our bedroom. You can sleep there. But, as you might remember, your brother snores terribly, especially when he is so tired.

Zuzanna heard the alarm go off at 4:30 in the next room where several boarders were asleep. She too, got up, straightened her clothes, and began helping Helen make supper for the men who would be leaving soon and for those who would be returning.

"My God!" Zuzanna exclaimed as she rushed to greet her husband as he walked through the door. "What has happened to you in four years? You have lost weight. I can see it in your face. You didn't tell me you had grown a mustache. How long have you had that?"

"It's a surprise. Like it?"

"No!"

If Andrij had any fat on his body when he left Vilag, he quickly lost it after but a few weeks in the heat and strenuous work in the cinder pits. He was lean and wiry. Zuzanna could feel the hardness of his muscles as she continued to hug him. And even though he was just 27, a few gray hairs were now evident on his temples. The mills quickly change anyone who works there, even for a short length of time.

"I must work again tomorrow," he said as he ate supper, "and I won't be home tomorrow evening because I must work a double turn."

"What is that?" Zuzanna asked.

"He must work 24 hours straight and then he works for a week during the night," Helen interrupted. Andrij continued eating.

"But I will have the day off after that," he said.

"It's not a bad house," Helen said two days later, as she led Zuzanna and Andrij on a tour, "but you cannot rent the entire house.

The mill where Andrij works owns it. The two rooms upstairs are made into an apartment and they are available. Another Rusnak family, the Rusinkos, I think, from Ol'sinkov, live downstairs."

Helen looked much like her sister-in-law Zuzanna. They had been friends even before she married her brother. She was a Sejka, but one could see that similar genetic controls were very evident in both women. She was just a year older than Zuska, as she called Zuzanna, and maybe an inch taller. She wore her blonde hair in a bun, and always under a *babushka* when she went outside. She hated the slack. Unlike Zuzanna, who was usually reserved, almost reticent, Helen always seemed to be talking, bubbling over with enthusiasm, and always was the center of activity when they got together. She was, however, "good of heart" as Zuzanna told her husband when he commented that her sister-in-law talked too much.

All the mill houses were small and cramped but they were made affordable for the beginning laborers. It was part of the trap which the company had created and into which the uneducated immigrant fell. It was an insurance policy for the mill owner's against strikes and their workers wandering elsewhere. A renting worker would be less likely to go on strike against his landlord or leave his job because it meant he would lose his house or flat. And because almost all of these Hunkies could not speak English, nor read and write even their own language, they were less likely to leave.

The trio entered the front door and a small vestibule. Inside, a door on the left led into the first-floor apartment, also composed of only two rooms. The door at the top of the stairs led into the second floor flat. It looked like the house was originally designed for one family and the door in the vestibule was an add-on to make two apartments possible.

"There are only two rooms," Helen apologized, but they are big. That is important because you and Andrij could not afford to live here alone, especially if you decide to have children. The rent is $14 a month. And with the cost of food and other things, you will just about break even, maybe put one or two dollars in the tea can. Andrij will get about $24 or $25 every two weeks. If you want to save money it must come from keeping boarders. With boarders, you can make ends meet and then put a little aside. The rooms are big enough for eight bunk beds, one on top of the other, like on the ship, and their trunks. Sam and I, sleep in the kitchen. That is the way most people here do. We have four boarders but just got two more bunk beds and will have six. Of course, we'll soon be losing Andrij. But, boarders are not hard to find. Men from the Old Country are always looking for rooms. They hate to cook for themselves."

The front room, as was expected, was bare of furniture and the walls and woodwork were badly in need of paint. However, it was cheerier than most similar apartments on Benton Street because it was a corner house and there were windows in front as well as on the side overlooking Spruce Street. Nails poked out of the wall in an irregular pattern where pictures must once have hung. A single gas light fixture dropped from the ceiling in the center of the room. The company buys natural gas in such huge quantities for their mills that it is able to include it in the price of the rent at no additional charge. On one wall in the front room, just above the floor, was a gas outlet and valve. It was there for the occupants to hook up a small, portable gas heater.

A half-paneled door, with a bare glass pane, separated the front from the back room. On it, you could see where the previous occupants, seeking some degree of privacy, had left the rods and hooks for a café curtain. The back room was laid out the same as the front room but in reverse, with a back door opening onto a small, wooden, second-storey porch. The flat included a gas kitchen stove with four burners, an oven and a cylindrical water tank that was an intrinsic part of the back of the stove. A small, built-in heater was a part of the water tank next to the oven. It provided the only heat for that room.

The water closet on the stove had to be manually filled with water obtained from the fire hydrant in the back yard. A faucet had been secured to one of the ports on the hydrant. There was no running water inside any of the houses or apartments. A dry-sink with a drain board was off to one side of the stove and a drain and short pipe emptied into a bucket. It was probably most often emptied simply by throwing its contents off the back porch, hopefully when no one was underneath. Another gas lighting fixture, a duplicate of the one in the front room, hung from the center of the kitchen ceiling and another gaslight poked out of the wall between two dirty, single-paned windows. Beneath it was probably where the kitchen table would go. Immediately under the light was a series of shallow shelves, fixed to the wall, where dinnerware could be stored.

The kitchen walls were bare except for a large calendar that had been left behind. It was a lithograph of Christ on the cross. Underneath the picture was the calendar part that showed two months at a time. Above the calendar was an advertisement for a funeral parlor. The writing was in Cyrillic but you didn't have to be able to read it to know what they were selling. Besides, it was doubtful that anyone who occupied the apartment could read regardless of the language. On both outside edges of the months were grave monuments with Russian Orthodox crosses. Andrij commented that the people who had lived here must also have been Rusnaks.

"There is one Italian family three houses away," said Helen, "but most people here are our own.... Rusnaks, and a few Slovaks. Last year, the Horvath family came here. You know him, Stefan Horvath, he is also from Vilag. He's much older but his wife Anna is only 30. They brought their two children with them. He sold everything in Vilag so he could bring everyone here at once. Also, I hear, his nephew Josef sent him money to come. $170. They live right behind this house. There are so many of us here that Americans and Irish call Woods Run "Hunky Town." Actually this is Verner Station. Woods Run Station is where we go to church and where the school is for children. That is where Zuska got off the train. But, you don't have to worry about school, not yet, do you? Both are just five blocks away, short blocks, and opposite each other on Ketchum Street. But you already know where the church is," she said as she turned to Zuzanna.

"Your street name....in case you get lost, tell someone that you want Benton Street. Number 4. Sam and I live on the next block behind you, next to the Horvath's, on Cass Avenue. It is sometimes called Preble Street and runs all the way to Woods Run. There is an alley, Mill Alley, that separates the blocks. In front of our house we have the railroad tracks. There are always trains running, day or night. We should move. It is too noisy and Sam sometimes has trouble sleeping during the day when he works the night turn.

"Maybe soon."

Slack...

Zuzanna Karas never got a real look at the three river valleys until months after she arrived. If she had, she might have immediately changed her mind and returned to Europe. Even on bright sunny days, the skies above the rivers and Pittsburgh, and Allegheny City on the north side of the Ohio, were filled with dark, acrid smoke. At times, the sun fails to show for days on end even though the sky above is clear. The overcast is caused by smoke pouring from hundreds of smokestacks. It spews continuously, by day and by night, day after day, with no pause because making steel is a never-ending process. It consumes all 24 hours in a day, seven days a week and 52 weeks a year.

At the turn of the 19th century, there were more than 50 mills in the Greater Pittsburgh area. Mill after mill populated the river flats. Their smokestacks often stood in straight lines, row upon row, disappearing in an infinity of haze and smoke. Furnaces and coke ovens added their smoke and belched their flames into the sky. At night they set the hillsides aglow with their red, orange and yellow flames. In a way, it was pretty, very pretty, and you sensed the city never slept, was always alive, and that somewhere something was always happening.

Iron ore arrived in long lines on railroad cars that had been off-loaded from mammoth ore boats that moved continuously across the Great Lakes. The ore began on the shores of Lake Superior in the world's largest open pit mine, the Mesaba Range, and floated its way to the south shore of Lake Erie.

Mesaba ore covered all of Pittsburgh like a wet blanket. Not a single thing escaped its touch. Most newcomers don't notice it at first but after a week or two one suddenly realized that it was everywhere, on everything. There was no freedom from it. It is called slack and is a fine metallic powder, the residue of countless piles of Mesaba ore that were unloaded and stored in the open everywhere there was a furnace. The ore is the beginning stage of iron making. Slack is blown off huge pyramids of ore every time there is a gust of wind. Seemingly weightless, it is put into motion and stays airborne until the wind hesitates, wafts then dies.

Slack also emanates from smokestacks as a fine, crystalline dust that is caught up in the heat that rises with increasing speed up the length of the chimneys. Periodically, the mills "blow their stacks" and for the next hour or two the sun downwind of the plant, is obliterated. It lands on the housewife's clotheslines. It lands on the streets and sidewalks. It is pulled into the house by drafts or on a person's shoes and carried into saloons and even the churches on a wafting wind. It is just one of the concessions to a healthy life made by those who work and live among the three rivers. It justifies Pittsburgh's one-time moniker of "Smoke City."

It falls heaviest on the immigrant laborers because they live in the cheapest housing that is always located closest to the mills. The farther from a mill a house is located the more expensive is its rent. Laborers also live closest to their work because they cannot afford trolley or carfare to commute. Thus, their economic status is directly reflected by where they live. Those who progress in the mills, up the ladder from laborer, to semi-skilled to skilled workers, move from the tenements and company houses on the flats next to the mills and up the sides of the valleys to the tops of the hills. It is said that one can easily tell a man's position in the mill by how far up the hillside he and his family live.

Then, there are the noises produced by the mills. The Lewis, Oliver & Philips steel mill, in which Andrij and Sam worked, was just a block from Benton Street. The heavy, ponderous machinery never rests. It is constantly at work, day and night, night and day. Women often marvel at the ability of their men to sleep so closely to their machines. It is only because of fatigue that they are able to do so. They come home so tired after a 12-hour turn that they can sleep anywhere. But the same is not true of their wives and children, if the men have families. It does affect them in ways that do not manifest themselves until they grow older or notice differences in their personalities after they leave the area of the mills.

James Verner was the great grandson of Fritz Werner, a Hussein mercenary who stayed in America after the Revolution and who went west instead of back to Germany. Land use along the Pittsburgh rivers at that time was primarily agricultural and comparatively cheap because it was on a flood plain. Periodically, the rivers each spring would flood, engulfing the land to the base of the hills. When it receded it usually left rich bottom land on the plains, eroded from other parts of this huge watershed. It was ideal farm land.

With his mustering-out pay from the British, Verner was able to buy a fair-sized farm on the flats between the Ohio River and the rising hillside. The bottomland was rich and productive. As he prospered, he wisely bought more and more land that surrounded his farm. James eventually inherited it from his father, nearly 500 acres, but never farmed it. For the last 20 years, he had been selling it in small acreages to various mills that began to establish themselves in the area and needed access to the river to build shipping docks.

Verner was wise not to sell all the land at once because as land grew scarce, the value of his remaining land rapidly multiplied. Overnight, he became a wealthy realtor. He subdivided some of the land he still held into building lots with several small streets. He laid out Verner, as it was called, in a six-block development with 12 to 24 building lots in each rectangular block. He then sold them piecemeal to individuals. The mills also bought lots as they needed them and built houses for immigrant workers who didn't mind living next to a rolling mill or blast furnace. When Zuzanna arrived in Verner, the entire block between Benton Street and the mill to the east, was vacant except for four houses on the corner of Benton and Porter streets.

The complex was located between the mills on the river's edge and the railroad tracks hard against the hills. It was then on the edge of Allegheny City and the train stop there became known as Verner Station, or simply Verner, as the immigrants knew it. A few thousand yards closer to the center of the city was a second local train stop called Woods Run Station. Woods Run or Woods Creek, was the name of a small stream that came down from the hills and entered the Ohio River. Over thousands of years, it had eroded a huge gorge into the flood plain.

By the turn of the century, Verner Station would expand into a community of ten small blocks. It was now wedged between the Pittsburgh Forge Iron Works on the north, the Rolling Mill and the Allegheny Iron Works on the south, the Ohio River on the west and on the east by the railroad tracks of the Pittsburgh, Fort Wayne & Chicago Rail Road and the high banks of the ancient river.

Because all of the Rusnak's non-work activities--the church, the stores and school--were directed toward Woods Run, immigrants in Verner would more closely identified themselves with Woods Run. When Sam and Helen Evans arrived in American, Woods Run was still populated primarily by Irish immigrants. But, in Verner, Slavic immigrants were already the primary residents. That was in the process of quickly changing in Woods Run. As the Irish moved out to better locations and the swelling numbers of Slavs overflowed Verner, they moved in to replace the Irish.

That distance between the two stops on the trolley line was really no more than 2,000 yards. They were located on the western edge of Allegheny City that in 1907 would be incorporated into the

City of Pittsburgh. A rolling mill and an oil refinery separated the two communities. The stream, Woods Run, further accentuated the division between the two communities.

In Woods Run, just beyond the mouth of the stream, was Ferry Street. It ran from Beaver Street, the main street, down to the river. There were no bridges crossing the Ohio River at that time, other than the Ohio Connecting Rail Road Bridge. Midway in the Ohio River, off Woods Run, was Brunots Island. It served as a place to anchor the middle spans of the railway bridge. The ferry from Woods Run was the only way to get to McKees Rocks on the south side of the Ohio River. In the early years of the great influx of immigrants, during the last decade of the 19th century, all Slavs, either Rusnaks, Slovaks, Croatians, Serbs, Slovenes, Poles or Czechs who lived on the south side of the river, and who had that day off on Sunday, took the ferry to Woods Run, to attend the area's only Slavic church. It was also one of the first Orthodox Churches built in America. The 9th Ward Public School was also on Ferry Street.

The bigger portion of Hunky Town was centered around Alexander Nevsky Church. Some would dispute this and claim that the center was the saloon in the Hartman's Hotel on Kerr and Beaver streets. The church was one block east of Refuge House, a boy's reform school that eventually would become the Western Pennsylvania Penitentiary. It was not the greatest environment in which to live or raise a family. But, most of the immigrants looked at it as a temporary stop.

The Courtyard...

Living in Verner or Woods Run was not expensive but not as cheap as Sam and Helen's letters had led Andrij to believe. The small, two-storey wood-frame house, they looked at was built by the mill in the 1860s. It was a clone to a dozen others on Benton Street and Cass Avenue. The house immediately next to it on Spruce directly abutted against it with no space between. One could almost jump from one porch to the next. The house to the right on Benton was built with only a two-foot walking space separating them. This alley was the entry into the rear courtyard. The house extended back the same length as Andrij and Zuzanna's and each floor also contained only two rooms. The house next to it, however, was longer and contained three rooms on two floors. Together they formed the three sides of the courtyard. On Mill Alley, behind the three houses

69

were another three houses that formed a similar courtyard opposite theirs. One was Sam and Helen's house.

This was the typical housing pattern not only in Verner and Woods Run but also in almost every company-housing complex in the dozen or so towns that sprang up along the rivers in Allegheny City and Pittsburgh. The dual courtyards became the primary outside living space for the inhabitants of six houses and the playground for their children. Once they grew older and walked to school, the streets expanded their recreation area.

It was this view of the courtyard behind the house that sickened Zuzanna with her initial look. In the center of each courtyard was a six-sided, enclosed gazebo-like structure. Each side had a door. Most were closed but one was unfettered and exposed a privy. It was the one that belonged to "4 Benton, Upstairs," and had the address scrawled on it in chalk. Ten feet away was the fire hydrant with a polished brass spigot. Some one, probably a youngster who had been playing with it, left the water running. The water formed a puddle that was lightly covered with skim ice that extended back to the privy. Three blond, blue-eyed children, the oldest about 5, were playing in the frozen mud and took delight in cracking the ice with their feet.

The kitchen door opened onto a small, second-floor wooden porch that creaked loudly as Zuzanna and Helen walked onto it. It startled a woman in the courtyard below who had been washing clothes in a galvanized tub that sat atop a large wooden crate. Wisps of steam rose from its hot water into the chilled air. She looked up and, for a moment, stared directly into Zuzanna's eyes. Zuzanna in turned looked down and into her eyes. They, too, were blue but seemed sunken into her head. Her long, blond hair was falling from the bun in which most of it had been tied. She looked tired, worn and weary. She was probably no more than 21, maybe 22, probably the same age as Zuzanna. Her eyes seemed to be saying something to Zuzanna, almost pleading, as if to say, Run, run away now before you, too, become trapped as I am. There is no way out.

Zuzanna automatically smiled, then offered a slight wave with her fingers.

The woman didn't return the smile but nodded her head in recognition and returned to plunging her hands deep in the tub of clothes and hot water.

"I think her name is Rusinko," Helen said. "They are from O'sinkov, just a few kilometers west of Vilag , a small village against the Polish border."

A sudden gust of cold, December wind spun the dirty snow in one corner of the yard into a tight cyclone. It rose a dozen feet above the frozen packed clay that made up the courtyard's floor. It caught up leaves, papers and trash carelessly discarded by those who lived there. The corners of the courtyard were filled with rubbish…a bedspring that was broken, porcelain pots with holes in them and scores of empty whiskey bottles.

In stark contrast, a small patch of green, no more than 5 feet square, stood out as if to make a statement. Somehow it survived the frost that had come especially late that year to western Pennsylvanian. Several tomato plants, heavy with small, frozen fruit, clung to their stalks. Next to them were a row of lettuce, turned brown a long time ago, and a row of radishes that had gone to seed. Chances are that every one of the 12 families who occupied both sides of the courtyard had started life as farmers. But only one, the owner of the "garden," protested their current fortunes.

The woman straightened up from her wash tub and momentarily grabbed the small of her back as if to ease the pain. It was then that Zuzanna saw that she was fat with child. Then she began transferring the wet clothes to a bushel basket.

"Vasyl," she called without looking into the house.

A young man in his early 20s came out and lifted the tub, carrying it toward the privy. He dumped the water onto an iron grid that covered a drain a few feet from the toilets. Wash water was the only way the privies were flushed. He disappeared into the house and a few minutes later returned with a galvanized pail and filled it with water from the hydrant.

"What will we do for furniture?" Zuzanna asked after she returned to the kitchen. "We need a bed, table and chairs. I used almost all the money you sent me," she said as she turned to Andrij, "to get here."

"Don't worry," interrupted Helen. "Later we will go to Preble Street, in Woods Run. There is a Jew from Humenné who sells new and used furniture. He will give it to you on credit as long as your husband has a job. If you buy all you need, he will even deliver it free of charge. He is a fair man and his prices are not bad. Sam and I go to him when we need things.

"See there," Helen pointed across the two open courtyards that backed onto each other, to the far side. "That is my flat, on the first floor."

That afternoon, while Sam slept, Andrij went with Helen and Zuzanna to Gottlieb's New & Used furniture store and helped them pick out a bed, a few chairs, a slightly-chipped porcelain-topped kitchen table and a portable gas heater. All, used furniture.

"As soon as you get the okay for the flat," Gottlieb said in perfect Rusnak, "let me know and I will have the furniture delivered."

"It was an excellent table," Helen said as they walked home, "because it had leaves on each end that could be expanded for more table space."

Helen was worried that they dallied too long at Gottlieb's so they walked home at a brisk pace. She was concerned about getting supper done on time for her two boarders who were working the day turn. They got back at about 5:00 that afternoon, just as Sam awoke.

During the first six months, Zuzanna took in three boarders. I say **she** took in three boarders rather than my grandfather because they were my grandmother's responsibility. It seems that she was created specifically for the role that was now thrust upon her. She was a fiercely independent person and meticulous beyond belief, at times, a hampering characteristic. This was surpassed only by her fastidiousness. Her constant nemesis was the slack and she held it at bay only by continual attention. It was she who really ran the house and did all that was necessary to support the boarders. She prepared their breakfasts and suppers, packed their lunch pails and daily hauled the necessary food from the grocery and bakery stores, and the butcher shops. It was also she who washed and ironed their clothes and repaired them when necessary.

Can you imagine casting that kind of responsibility upon a 21-year-old woman today? However, her task at that time was really no different from the thousands of other wives of steel workers or coal miners who performed the same role. It was she, who in the end made the extra money that was saved for their return to Europe.

Two of the first boarders were from Vilag and one from the nearby village of Zvala. Income from them paid the rent and the extra food to feed them and left a few dollars that might be saved. They could have taken in one more but Zuska was just learning to run a house and she was hesitant to board anyone whom she didn't know or was not from nearby villages. That had to change or it would take them a decade to earn their thousand dollars.

On the north side of Spruce Street, just around the corner from Benton, the company had built three, five-storey tenement buildings for its workers and another one, three stories high, on the opposite end of Benton Street on the Allegheny Iron Works property. They were more like dormitories than apartments. These were occupied by single men who rented a room and shared it with one or two others. They all took their meals and had their lunches made at two nearby restaurants; one on Cass and one on Preble streets, and run by Greek immigrants. The tenements were always a ready source for more boarders if they were needed.

Zuska saw less of Andrij than she would have liked but was so involved in keeping house--cooking and washing for the boarders and her husband--that she had little time to fret about their relationship. She, too, looked at it as a sacrifice to be endured until they returned to Europe. The 12-hour shifts, with no weekends off, were brutal on them, both physically and mentally. Nor was the pay in the mills as good as the mill's agents in Europe had led them to believe. Zuzanna figured that after six months they would have paid off Gallagher, the three boarder's beds and household furnishings, and used clothes for Andrij. Though it seemed to them that they just made ends meet but they never wanted for anything.

"If you watch how you spend your money," Sam would frequently say, "you could slowly build a nest egg." Sam had been in America a year ahead of Andrij. It was his letters that convinced him to make the move.

Andrij, in turn would ask, "Sam, how much have you saved?"

"Not much, but we have a child now."

"Maybe you better take in more boarders," he would say sarcastically." That was always Evans's answer when more money was needed.

Despite the times, Andrij and Zuska had been able to save a few dollars out of each manila pay envelope. When they had accumulated 20 or more dollars, they would send it home, dividing it between both families. And, there was always a dollar or two that found its way into Zuzanna's "tea box." However, they lived "close to the bone," as Andrij's father Mykola was wont to say.

Zuska, however, after the anniversary of her first year in America, began to miss her mother and girl friends. However, she kept these thoughts to herself, not wanting to burden her husband with her problems. Several girls from Vilag were already living in Pittsburgh, across the river. When she first got to America, she saw them a few times. This was when they came to church in Woods Run. Because it seemed that Andrij was always working she never felt confident to take the ferry to McKees Rocks by herself or travel as far away as Homestead where others lived. She did it once with Helen. But Helen was burdened with little Susan. Travel out of Verner, even to Woods Run, became rare.

"American is too big a place for me," Zuzanna would say as an excuse when Andrij told her to go visit her girlfriends.

Andrij, too, felt the loss of not seeing his parents, his sister Maria and his older brother Paul and younger brother Michael. But he would never tell Zuska because he believed she would use it to berate him for taking her away from her family. Mary had married Stefan Dancsi and they struggled in Vilag with two daughters. Paul living with his wife in the old homestead, had a daughter and two sons. By the end of her second year, Zuzanna somehow had saved nearly $100 even though they were still sending small amounts back to Vilag. When the apartment next door suddenly became available, Sam tried to convince him to move into it. It was longer and had three instead of two rooms.

"It would be a wise investment if you bought four more beds for the third bedroom. Eight boarders isn't that much more work than four," Sam said one night when he and Helen came for a visit.

"What do you know about feeding and washing clothes for eight men?" Zuzanna unexpectedly exploded and angrily shot back at her brother.

It was a hot, sultry evening in July in the year 1898. They sat on the back porch because it was too hot inside. They could only socialize like that when their men were both on the day turn.

"At times, boarders are like children," she continued. "And when they drink too much who will clean up their mess? Not you. Not Andrij. It is always me. I am getting tired of running a hotel. Andrij, give me some cognac."

"Do you think that is wise in your condition?" Helen asked.

"What condition?" Andrij immediately asked.

"I wasn't sure," Zuzanna said as she suddenly changed the tone of her voice and became demure. "I wanted to wait one more month before I said something. I think we are going to have a baby."

Andrij was suddenly filled with delight. He had never really thought of himself as a father. Now he had to change his way of thinking about many things.

Fortunately, the cognac bottle was almost empty and there would be no celebrating. Besides, tomorrow was another workday. Few mill workers, regardless of their physique, could over-indulge in alcohol and work the next day. The mill was too demanding for that. Every greenhorn quickly realized that once they began working 12-hour shifts, there was also the safety factor. The mills were always a dangerous place to work and there were accidents almost every day.

The question of more boarders was resolved a week after the conversation by a letter from Vilag. Father Bohdan wrote that Andrij's father Mykola was hurt in a fall from a wagon a few months ago and couldn't get around. His family needed help. His brother and sister had their own families to feed and had no surplus to help their father. The burden fell upon Andrij. They sent home all the money they had accumulated. That set them back almost to the beginning.

When the three-room apartment next door was vacated, they moved in. It had been rented by a couple from Slovenia and before they left, they told Zuzanna they had enough of life in America. They had been here almost 12 years and had accumulated their $1,000 and decided to return to Zagreb. Surprisingly, it was Zuska who lobbied Andrij to make the move to the bigger apartment.

"It is the only way we can make enough money to return home," she said the next morning at breakfast.

"Maybe Sam is right, eight boarders may not be that much more work than four."

"But the baby," Andrij said.

"What about the baby? Aren't Hunky women supposed to be strong? Aren't we able to deliver a child in the field in the morning then go back to the plow that afternoon? Am I not a good Hunky woman?"

Later that day, Andrij asked the foreman to put his name in for the bigger apartment. A few days later, he got the approval.

They bought two beds from the Slovenes and retained two of their boarders. With the aid of their four boarders and Sam, they made the move in a few hours. There really wasn't that much to move. It did give Andrij and Zuska a room to themselves; at least until they added more boarders, which was now their goal.

"We do it slowly," Zuska suggested. "We still have time. The baby isn't due until March. The following day Zuska went to Gottlieb's New & Used Furniture on Preble Avenue, and bought two more beds, bunk beds. Now she could keep eight boarders in the largest room in front. The middle room was theirs alone, but not for long. They got a second table for the kitchen and bought two long benches. She added another boarder before the end of the month and one the next month, and had a full complement.

"They eat like horses," Zuska complained. "Every day, they want steak or pork chops for breakfast and *holubki* (pigs-in-the-blanket*)* for dinner. They won't settle for chicken that is cheaper, or goulash. And they expect *perrohi* (flitters) two, three times a week. I know they work hard but they expect to eat like *pans* (lords) all the time. How can we ever save enough money to return home?"

"Do like we all do," said Helen. "Give them what they want but keep a book on each man. Tell him that if he wants something extra, he can have it. You buy it and at the end of the month you add that extra to his bill. This way, everyone is happy. Otherwise, the single men will just spend it on whiskey at O'Brien's Saloon."

When Zuzanna decided to come to America, she planned on not having children until they returned to Europe. They were successful for a while until Zuska began believing that she was getting old, maybe too old to have children. That was nonsense but Andrij thought that maybe a child would give her something different to think about. When Zuzanna disclosed she was pregnant, he wasn't too disappointed. But, he worried that the child and now eight boarders would be too much for her to cope with. For several months after Andrij learned of her pregnancy, had thought of the mounting dilemma that would soon become a reality.

"Before the child is born," Andrij said to Zuska one morning in late January," I think we should get someone in to help you make the meals and the washing. Maybe next month. You are getting so fat I can see you are having trouble going up and down the stairs, even getting around here."

"We cannot afford someone," she said. "Get that thought out of your mind. It would take from what we are putting away each pay day."

"It would hurt us even more," he said, "if something should happen to you or the baby. It is a good idea to get help for you now and not risk your life later, or the baby's. Don't the Horvaths have a girl who is 14 or 15? She could help you around here. Especially when the baby comes. Go see them today and see what they would ask for pay."

At first, Zuska resisted the idea of finding a helper and silently pondered what alternatives she had. There were none. Andrij was right. She needed help. A house full of boarders was a lot of work and a child would hamper her for a while. Suddenly, her mind flipped back to the first day she and Andrij looked at their old apartment, to the time on the porch when she looked down at the woman washing clothes; the woman that was almost her age, the pregnant woman. It was only now that she could fully realized what the woman's eyes had been telling her. But it was too late. There was no escape. What had she gotten herself into? Was all this worth the effort. Would life really be different for them when they went back to Vilag with a thousand dollars? Was that enough money to make them free? For the first time, she doubted it.

The Horvaths lived on the ground floor, next to Sam and Helen's house, and on the opposite side of their courtyard. Emily Horvath had just turned 16. Ironically, her father said that she had been going to school long enough and that it was time that she should help the family. Besides, it would be one less mouth for him to feed. "There is no need to send a girl to school," he once said. "What will school do for her, find a rich husband?"

So it was a willing audience that greeted a very pregnant Zuzanna Karas when she walked across the courtyards to talk to Anna Horvath. Emily had no particular liking for school and she was more than willing to go live with the Karases. It was just 300 feet from her house and it wasn't really like leaving home. Zuska bought another single bed and Emily shared the bedroom with Andrij and Zuzanna. Zuzanna quickly realized just how much help Emily could be.

Fortunately, Andrij that week was working the day turn and that night was asleep in bed when Zuzanna shook him.

"Andrij, it is time. Wake Emily and tell her to get Helen. You go get Mrs. Dohanych. I have been having cramps off and on all day. They are steady, more often now. Go! I don't know how much time there is."

Almost every immigrant woman has helped deliver a baby or two at one time or another in her lifetime. And, every village in Europe has one or two women who do it professionally. In Verner and Woods Run, there were several European midwives who also made it a business. Mrs. Dohanych was one and was reputed to be the best. She even had eight of her own children as proof of her empathy. Most Slavic women actually preferred a woman midwife rather than a doctor because they believed she related better to what a pregnant woman was undergoing. Mrs. Dohanych had been a midwife in the Old Country and had been trained and certified there by a hospital in Humenné. She had delivered more than 200 children both in Europe and in Pennsylvania. When she arrived in America, she immediately attended a clinic course, despite the language barrier, at St. John's General Hospital in Allegheny City. The teachers there immediately recognized her ability, one gained through experience, and this transcended the language barrier. She immediately received her State Certificate.

In this era, seldom were pregnant women, immigrants or not, taken to hospitals for delivery. Almost all were delivered at home. Only in instances when complications occurred did they go to hospitals. Occasionally, doctors would make house calls to deliver children in Verner but the vast majority, Rusnaks or others, had midwives perform the task.

Just before breakfast Andrew Andrievych Karas was born. He was a healthy 7-pounder. After the event, the night turn workers trooped through the bedroom to their bunks after breakfast and hardly noticed the baby being breast fed. March 15, 1899 was the only day Andrij Karas ever missed work. At that time, Mrs. Dohanych had only one other newborn to attend that week so each day she stopped in to advise Zuzanna on the tasks of motherhood and even helped Emily make meals and lunches for Andrij and the boarders. That was an expected part of midwife services. On her last day, Andrij slipped her a $10 bill. Five dollars was the customary fee.

Midway through her third year in America (1899), just when they were thinking of going to the Ohio Valley Bank and opening a savings account, the union tried to organize workers at Oliver Brothers & Phillips Allegheny Iron Works. Most German and Irish immigrants in the mill and their first-generation descendants had been agitating for higher wages for months before the union sent in their organizers.

In response, the company, with lightning speed, shut down the plant, brought in their own armed detectives, and locked out the strikers. The union's men became violent and three workers were killed by company "detectives." The state police were finally brought in to restore order but their sympathies lay with the owners and they bullied the strikers outside the plant and even near their homes. Ironically, most of the strikers lived up the hill, on the east side of the railroad tracks. Only Hunkies lived in Verner and Woods Run and really didn't want to go on strike. Because they lived around the mill, they bore the brunt of the police harassment. City, County and State Police all supported the mill owners. It was common knowledge that the company was always very generous at police fund-raising events. When the owners felt they had broken the strikers and decided to reopen the mill, the returning workers had to pass through a police cordon to enter the plant.

The Slavs and Italians didn't hesitate to return and most first-generation Germans entered with them. It was the "old-timer Germans," the skilled laborers, who refused to work. Eventually, most lost their jobs. A week before the company reopened the plant; it sent representatives to Louisiana looking for black laborers. They had no difficulty locating as many as they wanted. To transport them *en mass*, they hired a boat that came up the Mississippi then Ohio rivers and tied up at the company's dock on the Ohio River in Verner. They had gathered nearly 50 black men and the company decided to temporarily turn the sternwheeler into a hotel to house them.

The lockout lasted only two months but Andrij and Zuzanna had to again dip into their savings. Rent still had to be paid. Several of the younger boarders had no savings but lived from one pay envelope to the next. Zuzanna had to carry them and that temporarily consumed what little they had saved. Most people living in the company's houses felt relieved that they hadn't been evicted. The mill's management was smart enough to realize that strikers who were allowed to live in their houses would return to work when the strike was ended. They needed these men to begin production as soon as possible. Andrij was among a half-dozen

Rusnaks in the mill who suddenly found themselves as gang bosses on a shift that now answered directly to the shift foreman. It also meant a nickel an hour more, or $4.20 more a week in their pay. He also had a black man in his cinder pit crew. Spivak was made the first Slav assistant-foreman the mill had ever had. Fortunately, he was Andrij's superior.

In June the next year (1900), Helen gave birth to their first son. Andrij and others kidded Sam, that the baby should have been named Strike instead of Peter, because they figured he was conceived during the strike period, when Sam was idle at home. But then again, maybe he wasn't so idle.

Stefan, the Karas's second son, and my father, was born March 5th, during Zuzanna's fifth (1901) year in America. Andrij's base pay in the steel mill increased slightly during that time, from 13 to 15 cents and hour. Even with the added nickel as a gang boss he made only 20¢ an hour. Working 12 hours a day and seven days a week produced less than $17 a week. And, the added cost of the two boys began to consume some of it. Life was a struggle in America... the picture calendars the mill agents had given the villagers while they were soliciting workers in Europe had lied.

Then there was the baptismal party Zuska insisted upon for Stefan. They hadn't had one for Andrij so she felt they should make up for it with Stefan's party. It cost them more than they expected. They had never seen so much whiskey consumed at one time.

"He who has produced two sons in a row, should celebrate," said Andrew Kachur, Stefan's godfather, a émigré from Vilag.

"That would be all right if we were still in Vilag, and on a farm where boys can work," added Mary Czyuk, one of Zuska's girl friends from the Old Country, and Stefan's godmother, "but not here, not in America. It seems we make just enough to get by and now Zuska has another mouth to feed and body to clothe.

"Be grateful that he is healthy," answered Kachur. "Money you can always find. Besides, they are not Hunkies. They are Americans because they were born here. Maybe they will get better jobs in the mills than we have."

That statement momentarily grabbed Zuska's thoughts. "Maybe our family is already on the way to breaking with the past," she pondered. But how will that matter if we take our sons back to Vilag. Will they be expected to be herdsmen, farmers like their grandfathers?

Kachur's concern for the child's health was serious. Among Slavic families producing children in the mill housing, the death rate was appalling. One child out of three died before it reached the age of two. Among English-speaking Europeans, it was one out of seven. Health investigators were alarmed at this statistic and attributed it to malnutrition of the child as well as mother, and overcrowding.

"The mothers (keeping boarders) are too poor, too busy, too ignorant to prepare food properly," Health Department officials said "Rooms are over-tenanted, and backyard courts too confining to give the fresh air essential for the physical development of children."

Though invitations to the christening party were never issued, people who knew the Karases knew another son had arrived. Andrij was surprised to see Hrenko walk into his house. He carried one arm in a cast, in a sling. His left, free hand was on a cane and he limped badly as he walked across the threshold. His head was bandaged and one eye was covered. His mustache had been shaved. When he smiled and extended his left hand to congratulate Andrij, he could see that several of his upper front teeth were missing.

"My god," Andrij said as he shook hands. "What happened to you?"

Zuzanna, standing next to Andrij, quickly blessed herself.

"It was the damned State Police, during the lock-out," Hrenko answered. "I was standing in front of my house watching them moving a bunch of kids from the street. They ordered me to get inside.

"When one yelled, 'Get inside you damned ignorant Hunky bastard,' I spit on the ground before his horse. He beat me with his nightstick. He should not call me a damned Hunky bastard!"

Without hesitation, Hrenko moved inside when he saw the table with several whiskey bottles and glasses, and a washtub filled with ice and beer.

"That's bullshit! It wasn't the State Police," Sam whispered as he leaned toward Andrij. He had been standing near Andrij when Hrenko walked into the house. "I don't know who it was but someone told one of the union men that he had to pay $40 to get a job when he first came here. And, that Hrenko was the one he paid it to for a foreman. The union man talked to another organizer and they were furious. They told the man that it was against the law but they couldn't get his money back. However, they would make things even. Other Hunkies were there at that time. They told him that they, too, had paid Hrenko.

"That son-of-a-bitch Hrenko has some balls just to show up here.

"Did Helen tell your wife?
"Tell her what?
"That our third child is on the way.
"My God Sam, when do you find the time?

Like most Rusnaks, Andrij and Zuska were deeply religious. Before traveling to America, they witnessed the beginnings of the return of the Orthodox Church of their ancestors to Vilag and other villages across Carpathia. The movement was also alive in America, especially in Allegheny City and Pittsburgh, where many Carpatho-Rusnaks had come to work. However, they needed a church in America and Andrij became instrumental as one of ten men to begin building a new St. Alexander Nevsky Church in Woods Run. The present building had been a Protestant Church before they took it over. They needed a new building because the growing number of Orthodox reconversions was growing so rapidly that the old building could no longer house the congregation. Each single member was assessed $15 and a family $25. But, that was only the beginning. It, too, shifted money from their savings.

Chapter 8   The Rumors

After Stefan was born, Zuzanna's desire to return to Vilag increased rather than abated. The most immediate effect on her psyche in coming to America was to realize the inferior status in which Northern and Western Europeans in the United States placed her and her fellow Rusnaks. In Vilag, she was aware of the subservient role assigned her by Hungarians and Poles, and to a lesser degree, Slovaks. But in America, she experienced an entire society denigrating her and her people. On the other hand, she knew that if she and Andrij were to elevate their status, or at least that of their two sons, it was possible in American but not in returning to the old ways in Europe. Zuzanna was having difficulty reconciling her attitude between this and a more primary desire to see her mother, sister and brothers, and for them to see her two sons, to see her home and her friends.

It also began to put doubts in Andrij's mind about forming a real life here but he kept those thoughts to himself. If they were to return to Vilag as they had always planned, he asked himself, what would he do to feed a growing family? They left Vilag because of poverty. And in the years they had been away life in their village hadn't improved. But, as rumors revealed, it had worsened. The Hungarians were becoming even more oppressive.

Despite the setbacks that always seemed to occur just as they were getting ahead, they did manage to save money. They had accumulated nearly $1,000. It was not as much as Andrij wanted. He thought that a few more years of work in America was all they needed to reach their goal. He knew that farming wouldn't pay because the soil was so poor and the growing season so short. But, he had another idea.

Andrij hoped it would be enough to buy most of the woods he once coveted on the south side of Vysoky Grün and at the top of the bowl above the village. Maybe he could timber some of it, he often said to Zuska, and buy the rest with what he made, or maybe he could owe it to Medveki. Zoltan Medveki had been a reasonable man in the past. From time-to-time, Andrij worked for him and in doing so had developed some idea of the lumber business. Medveki had not been like many of the Magyars whom the Rusnaks believed had usurped what was once their land a thousand years ago and then made them their serfs. Andrij hoped he had enough to buy all of Medveki's woods, but he really didn't know how much it would cost, or even if he would sell. He moved on an innate feeling, a conviction that Medveki wanted out of lumbering.

When Andrij became tired of the day-in, day-out monotonous, demanding heavy work in the cinder pit and wanted to quit, it was only the image of the green woods above his father's field that would sustain him. They had no real life in America. It was all consumed by work. Life for them, and thousands of others, was put on hold.

Andrij was on his back porch looking into the courtyard when he saw Sam walk out of his back door and wave to him.

"Come over," he yelled, "Bring my sister. I have a surprise."

"What, is Helen pregnant again?" Andrij said jokingly as he entered the kitchen behind his wife.

"As a matter of fact, I am," said Helen, who was in the kitchen with Sam and several others.

"Did you call me over to have a drink, to celebrate?

"No, I want you to meet two people.

"I'm surprised you don't recognize them...even though it is probably ten years since you saw them.

"I recognized them immediately," said Andrij "I'm dumbstruck," he said as he rushed across the room to hug his youngest sister.

Zuska rushed past the others to embrace Anna, who from all appearances, could easily have been her sister instead of sister-in-law.

"Anna, how are you? "

"And who are these children?" Zuzanna asked.

"They are Maria and Simeon," she said. "We lost two, Andrij a few years ago. But you knew that. You were still waiting to join my brother. And just recently, we lost Anna. They are the reason we decided to leave Vilag. John cannot earn enough to feed the family and we cannot grow food in the little garden."

Oh my God! Zuzanna fleetingly thought to herself. And I want to go back to Vilag. I must be crazy.

The silence weighed heavily on everyone for a few minutes.

"But where are my two nephews?" Anna asked. "I cannot wait to see them."

Sam turned to Andrij to introduce Anna's husband. "This is Ivan Ivanco (John Evans).You must remember him. We share the same great-great grandfather. We are cousins of a sort. It looks like we are all kind of related to each other, in one way or another."

"I do," said Andrij as the shook hands and embraced. "But, it has been almost ten years since I saw John. Besides, all the Ivancos seem to look alike."

"The Karases are no different," quipped John.

John and Anna Evans settled first in Verner and went to work beside Andrij and Sam. But after two years, he found a better job in a pipe-making mill in McKees Rocks and they moved across the river.

Mary Evans, Sam and Helen Evans' fourth child was born in early 1903.

Also in 1903, the union again attempted to form at Oliver & Phillips and this time the entire work force seemed to support it. When they called a strike, everyone walked out. It happened all too quickly. It looked like it would be a long strike because of the union's strength and growth in other mills in Pittsburgh. When John Baranskij, a rare Hunky foreman at Superior Rolling Mill on the other side of Woods Run, saw Andrij in church, he told him there was an opening for an assistant foreman job at Superior. Andrij jumped at the chance and got it. He never thought he would rise from a pit boss to a second assistant foreman. However, it was at a few cents an hour less than he had been making as the pit boss, and a long walk away. There was the trolley that ran the length of Preble Avenue, as Cass Street was now called, from Verner to Superior Station. It cost 5¢ in either direction. Still, it was better than no work at all.

It created a new routine in their household. Every morning Andrij had to rise at 4:45 a.m. Zuska was already up making breakfast and packing lunches for him and the boarders who still worked. By 5:30, to save money, he would walked the ten blocks, if it was a nice day, from Benton Street, along the railroad tracks, down Preble Avenue to Superior Rolling Mill & Iron Company. It was owned by Harbough, Mathias & Owens, a company notorious for paying less than other mills. But, it was work. The shift started at 6:00 a.m. He and the others worked until 6:00 p.m., again a 12-hour shift. Most times they ate lunch between loading the furnaces.

On the last day of a turn, he worked a double shift, 24 continuous hours, and didn't get off until 6:00 a.m. the second day. Then, for the next seven days they would work from 6:00 p.m. to 6:00 a.m. The only day off Andrew Carnegie gave them for the entire year was on the Fourth of July. Of course, it was without pay.

Andrij's job was to grab, with long, heavy pincers, the hot sheets of steel after their final reduction in thickness and pull them around a slight turn onto rollers where they would cool for three hours. Even though he was now a second assistant foreman, he was expected to work side by side with any of the gangs under his aegis. At times, he moved to the cold-rolling table where he pulled the sheets into a feeder that moved them back and forth, under extreme pressure, between rollers. Each time the position was reversed, a man on the controls, usually an old German, would spin the knobs and almost infinitesimally reduce the thickness of the steel sheet.

Working in the mills was extremely arduous and compounded by the intense heat. It was always hot, even in winter. It was as hot as working among the blast furnaces and in the cinder pits. In winter, at the end of each shift, he and the others could walk halfway home before they had to don their jackets. It was just three blocks from the mill to the Black Bear Saloon in Hartman's Hotel where he took an obligatory drink. This was not social drinking among the workers, but a ritual. Everyone, Hunky or not, stopped in for a shot and a beer. It was an act that ended the workday for them. As the men lined up at the bar, nearly a dozen at a time, the bartender, always an Irishman, who needed no direction, was pouring shot glasses and immediately behind it filling mugs with beer.

The men felt they had earned a drink after 12 hours of work. The whiskey was supposed to clear the ever-present dust from their throats and the beer washed down the whiskey and settled their stomachs. As soon as the beer was finished, usually without stopping, the bartender cleared the glasses and began setting up another round. Almost in unison, as if choreographed, the men wiped their mustaches, bent down, grabbed their lunch buckets and walked out the door. Waiting behind them to step up to the bar were another dozen men and the procedure was repeated. This went on until the shift was cleared and no more men appeared.

Of late, Andrij and a few of the men in his gang would move to the tables and have another drink. After a few beers, the mill was temporarily forgotten, but it now seemed to take more than one or two to forget their drudgery. Most married men felt pangs of conscience and eventually made their way home. But for the single men, who comprised the majority of immigrant laborers, the bar, and often lodges associated with their churches, formed social centers for them. It was not unusual for a man to spend $20 a night, on a payday. There was a lot of drinking in progress, especially when beer was 5¢ a glass and a shot 25¢. Ownership of bars and saloons turned over quickly because it took but four or five years for its owner to make enough money, if it was wisely invested. If he wanted to, he could move elsewhere and find another business.

Zuzanna became increasingly worried as the months passed with Andrij's now all-too-frequent stops at the Black Bear Saloon or the Men's Bar at the Ukrainian Social Club. It was the Friday night just before New Year's eve in 1906 that was the turning point. He started drinking with his friends Nick Kachur and Simeon Evans, but an Evans not immediately related to his brother-in-law Sam Evans. After work and a short stop at the Black Bear they all ended up at the Men's Club. Andrij became so drunk that he passed out. His friends were in no better shape and unknowingly abandoned him as he sat on the floor in the Men's Room.

It was well after midnight when a deeply-concerned Zuzanna took the trolley to Woods Run. She got to the Black Bear just as it was closing. The bartender told her that Andrij had been there earlier in the evening. When he wouldn't serve him and his friends any more brandy, he said they left for the Men's Club.

"I never saw him leave," said Wasco Chunko, one of two bartenders cleaning up and about to close the club. "Look around for him. Maybe he is still here."

Just as she turned and was about to look in the club's poolroom, the door to the men's toilet banged open. Andrij, disheveled, drunk and smelling of vomit stood leaning against the door jam.

"Zuska, take me home," he slurred.

"Andrij," she said to him the next morning, "I have never seen you this way. I have never seen you drunk, maybe tipsy, but never drunk. What is happening to you?"

It took him several minutes for him to gather himself, to muster a response he didn't want to realize.

"I lost my job," he said.

"You lost your job? Oh *Bozé miy.*"

"The super wanted to cut my pay by 5 cents. I refused. He said either that or get out. He didn't even let me answer, but fired me because I was searching for words in English.

"You're out," he said. "Clean your locker. You damned Hunkies are all alike. Try and give you a break and you suddenly think you're too good to work. Get out!"

"Andrij, what will we do? Phillip's is still shut down."

"I will see Sam tonight. I think Pressed Car might have a job."

As soon as workers had struck Allegheny Iron Works, the company shut down the blast furnaces and the rest of the mill. The sale of steel and steel products had been declining for the past three years and Phillips had been in financial trouble. They were on the verge of doing it themselves. The union and its workers were now an excuse for them to do it and the company blamed them for the move. The Schoen Steel Wheel Company of McKees Port, just across the river, made wheels for railroad cars. Despite setbacks in other areas, the demand for railroad cars was still good, even growing as American railroads expanded their western lines.

Schoen saw the faltering Phillips' mill as a chance to expand their own facilities and begin producing entire railroad cars. Phillips, in turn, was glad to get the plant off their hands. Schoen immediately began retooling the Verner plant as the Pressed Steel Car Company. They rehired many of the unskilled, old workers where they could fit them into new assembly jobs. Sam Evans was one of the first to go back.

"Things don't look as good here as everyone is saying," Sam said. "Orders slowed down last month, just as they were getting ready to open all the lines. It is amazing how quickly things can change. It isn't just Pressed Car but the whole steel business. The big bosses are talking about a recession. And here, they're suddenly talking of layoffs. But, I will try on Monday. If you do find a job there, at least it is again close to home."

On Monday afternoon, Andrij was at his brother-in-laws house waiting for Sam to return from work.

"You're lucky. We lost a man in an accident on Friday. My foreman said you could come in tomorrow. Are you ready to go to work?"

Andrij got the job but rumors abounded in the big plant. The workers grumbled incessantly and talked constantly of the plant shutting down. It seemed it could happen almost any day. The men were dissatisfied with the low pay but working an eight-hour day was a new experience for them. Also, they couldn't make nearly as much money as when they worked in a blast furnace.

Then in the middle of these distressing events, they heard of the Carnegie steel mills in Braddock, near Homestead, reopening. Some suggested moving there if they could get a job. The Braddock mill had settled a 10-month strike, giving its workers a 10-hour day and 6-day work-week and a 4-cents-an-hour increase. It seemed an impossible concession in the face of an industry-wide recession that was forcing other mills in Pittsburgh to either drastically cut back or close. It turned out that the mill had received a unique order from a Japanese shipbuilder for a large amount of quarter-inch steel plates. The Japanese were going to modernize their fleet, victorious after the recently-ended war with Russia.

"I don't know how long this job will last," Andrij told Zuska in late January. "We are working week-to-week. We must save every penny because I think we will soon be going to Vilag. There are rumors, new rumors every day, that the banks in New York are tightening credit. New orders for cars have stopped. Something is about to happen in America, something we have never experienced and it frightens me."

It frightened Zuzanna even more, but she was surprised about her husband's first serious talk about going home. She knew the work situation was serious but didn't imagine it could suddenly become this bad. This was the first time in nearly ten years that Andrij had ever said they were going back. That alone was alarming enough.

Chapter 9   The Panic of 1907

Wall Street has always been moved by rumors but not as much in this period as they are today. Even in 1907 day-to-day or week-to-week swings were common and expected. However, rumors that began early in that year of an impending collapse in the financial security of lending banks were too persistent not to be seriously regarded. When it was discovered in May that Knickerbocker Trust, New York's and the nation's leading bank at that time, was having financial problems—too many loans and repayments too slow—it triggered a run on all the banks in Manhattan. In turn, bank stocks elsewhere fell and they pulled down all stocks on the New York Stock Exchange. At that time, the Panic of 1907 was the most severe financial crisis the nation had ever faced.

Stoppages in all branches of manufacturing began almost as soon as the word was out. By mid-May, on a payday, the last payday he would ever know, half of Andrij's mill was shut down. He was one of 650 men let go. It was just the beginning. Almost all were Slavs, except for a few Italians, Syrians and Hungarians. He buttoned the manila envelope in a shirt pocket, went back to the showers. After an exceptionally long shower, he cleaned out his locker and then began the walk home. Instead of taking Preble Street, he crossed the numerous railroad tracks and climbed the high embankment on the west side. There, he found a ledge where he could sit. He had always wanted to see the mills from the hill. He was dog-tired after a long night and long week. The climb sapped the last of his strength. But he had to do it. As a note of thanks, the mill stuffed a single HavaTampa cigar into each envelope along with the bills and change.

Andrij took it out. Lit it. Then let the smoke curl upwards from his mouth and over his face, causing him to momentarily close his eyes. When he opened them he saw a clear blue sky. It was an unusual day in Pittsburgh and there seemed to be a certain irony in that. A spring storm during the night had poured copious amounts of water on the city of dust. Now, for a few hours, it seemed sanitized, cleaned, like Andrij had never seen it before. The sun was just rising and caught the golden cupola of St. Alexander Nevsky Church turning it into a mini-clone of itself. Andrij sighed. He had not been able to attend church as often as he would have liked. He had only one Sunday morning free a month between the change from night to day turns.

The mills were still pouring out their rivers of smoke into the sky but on this day the winds were from the northwest, a clearing wind that was accompanied by a chill in the air. It seemed cold for mid-May, too cold. The smoke spread over the Ohio River and capped Brunots Island, Branford, Esplen and Crafton. McKees Rocks was engulfed in the smoke and he wondered how his sister Anna and her husband John were doing. He hadn't seen them in six months, since at the funeral of their second child that died since they had been in America.

Below, he caught the sun glittering off dozens of rails and noted places where they bifurcated with spur lines running to each mill. Subconsciously, he named each mill.

To the left, the boys' reform school loomed ominously on the banks of the river just beyond the church. Its red bricks were dulled by constant exposure to smoke. The only real color was the lawns in front of the prison that were beginning to show green even though remnants of gray-colored snowdrifts, insulated from the spring air by a layer of slack, still hid in the shadows of the north and east walls. It had been a winter of much snow and cold.

In more than a decade of intimate living among these corrugated steel sheds, smokestacks, railroad tracks, cluttered houses and piles of ore and drifts of slack and dirt, he never had the opportunity to sit back and look at them all at once or even at the place where he had lived. He glanced toward the southwest to Verner and tried to pick out his house. It was difficult at first because they all looked alike. Then he recognized the corner of his building. Zuska and his sons were there, he thought. His oldest son was probably getting ready to go to school. He glanced back toward Woods Run and followed Preble Avenue to its end on Westhall

Street. There was his son's school, Woods Run Public School. In a little while, 9-year old Andy would be walking the length of Preble to his classroom. He stared at the ornate three-storey building and felt the pangs of his conscience rising within his thoughts.

It was then that Andrij was suddenly overcome with an epiphany that would evolve into a credo, an answer to the emancipation of his sons and his people. Education! He suddenly realized that what separated him from the Poles, Hungarians and Russians, all those who controlled the lives and destiny of Rusnaks, was education. We cannot escape as a nation, as an entire people, but we can as individuals, he reasoned. That is how I will escape the bonds that have embraced me and my ancestors. Education is our way out of serfdom, out of a slavery we have known for a thousand years.

As he thought to himself, another part of his mind, on another level, was being confronted by contradictions. But what is to become of this movement, it said to him, if we leave America and return to the Old Country, the old ways, the old limitations? How will I continue the education of my two sons, of myself and my wife? He came up with no immediate answer.

I will have to resolve this in another way, at another time, and in another place, he thought. Right now, I must figure out how to escape the dilemma we are in. But, is returning to Europe the answer? There it was again. Am I placing too much faith in obtaining a forest with my money? Time will tell me if I am right or wrong in what I am doing, in what I have done. If we cannot survive in Europe, we can always come back to Pennsylvania. Others have made the crossing and re-crossing again and again, he rationalized. We have that option, maybe.

His mind snapped back to reality as he spotted his brother-in-law's house. Sam had become like a real brother to him. They and his sister Anna and her husband were the only people, he belved he would miss when they left this place. The money was not worth it.

"To hell with the money," he yelled out loud and even startled himself when he heard what he had just said. "I cannot live like this. I have given too many years of life to the mills."

The winds stopped blowing for a moment and allowed the billowing smoke to rise straight into the sky. It obliterated the sun and stopped Andrij from his day dreaming. He threw away the cigar butt, then picked his way down the steep, Hryec hill to the tracks. He crossed them between trains moving in opposite directions and was back on Preble Street. As he walked home a scant smile was on his face. He had suddenly discovered a way out. It might not help him but it would help his children. As soon as he got home and told her of the plant closing, he began telling her about the revelation he had experienced while sitting on the hill.

"It is time to go home," he said. She agreed with him. "But, if life there is too difficult, we will return. Maybe not here, but to America."

During the next few days, Zuzanna went around the neighborhood selling their household furnishings. If she sold them all, it might cover the ship's tickets.

"I have one regret in leaving," Andrij said a week later as they waited in Union Station for the train to New York.

"I don't think Andy and Steve will get as good an education in Vilag as they were getting at the Woods Run school. Education would have helped them become something. I saw what it was doing for some of the people who were here before us. Their sons didn't have to work in the mill when they came of age. Maybe we can return when things get better here. Maybe there is now a school in Vilag. Someone said the Hungarians were opening schools for everyone. We have crossed the ocean once. It is not as big as I once believed. It would be easier the second time. If life in Vilag again becomes unbearable we could come back. And, maybe by then, things in the mills here will have changed."

Andrij was still tying to come to terms with himself to solve contradictions that still ran rampant in his mind.

Their forced decision to leave had really come at an opportune time. Within the next six months, the steel industry in the United States almost collapsed. Strikes also collapsed as mill after mill began shutting down. Those that remained open did so with vastly reduced manpower. In almost every mill that was operating a downshifting in positions occurred. Skilled workers were offered semi-skilled jobs and semi-skilled were returned to the day-labor force. Those who wouldn't work as laborers went into other fields. The immigrant day-laborers at the bottom of the pile, were let go *en masse*.

Sam Evans was let go but unlike many decided not to return to Europe. Andrij and his wife spent their last evening in the United States at their house. John and Anna had also taken the ferry across from McKees Rocks to say good-bye.

"Sam," said Andrij after they finished what remained of an almost empty whiskey bottle, "why don't you come back to Vilag with us. You have no idea when the plant will reopen. It could be six months, a year, even two years. Can your savings hold out that long? And then, it will be like the first day you and Helen came to America...all over again. Come with us."

"I don't plan to go back to work at Pressed Steel Car if they open up again. And, I don't want to go back to work in a mill. I have had enough of that. Helen and I have some money saved. Besides, we have too many children to go back. We have five. You know, at Pressed Steel, I began to work more and more as a mechanic , helping the maintenance crew fix the machines and the new fleet of trucks. And, there are more and more cars now on the streets. I have a way with fixing things that my boss said I was a natural. I hear that the American Bridge Company, downriver at Economy, is expanding their plant. They are building the Panama Canal and have lots of work. I think I will take the train there and see how things look."

"How is your plant doing...are you still making pipe?" Andrij turned to John and asked.

"We are still operating" he said, "but it is only a matter of weeks, maybe days, until the contracts are filled. There have been no new orders and we all expect that every Friday will be our last."

"Are you ready to go back?

"Back to what? First, there is nothing to go back to. Second, we have not been here long enough to save but a few hundred dollars. And that will be eaten as soon as I get my cigar in the envelope. Besides, I don't like mill work. I never minded working outside, on a farm, no matter how hard it was. But here, hard work gets you almost no where.

"When I was young, I worked from time to time for the Jew who ran the *sklep* in Vilag. I liked that kind or work. I liked working with people, across a counter and saw how he made money. I think I can do the same.

"I think I will open a grocery store with a butcher shop on one side. There is a store vacant on Preble Street in Woods Run, a few doors this side of Bednar's Saloon. I have always wanted to go into business for myself and this may be the time to make a move. Anna can do some baking and we will have a bakery part in one corner of the store. You know that no one can resist her *kolachki*. Oh,

95

I forgot to tell you. I got a letter two days ago from Vilag, from my cousin Mitro."

"You mean Dimitri, Dimitri Ivanco?" Andrij asked.

"Yes. Mitro is what his younger sister used to call him when they were little. She couldn't pronounce Dimitri so he's been known as Mitro ever since.

"Things there have been turned upside down. He is planning on coming over in a few weeks. You know he is a butcher. It's not a good time to come to America but he is determined. Maybe we will go into business as partners."

"We will move," said Sam. "I think we will like living in Woods Run. It is closer to church and to the school for the children. We don't like to see what is happening to the houses here in Verner. The company has no money to fix them and has let them go. They are falling apart. We were thinking of moving, even before the plant shut down. Besides, almost everyone in Woods Run is a Rusnak. It will be almost like living again in a Carpathian village."

"No it won't," Andrij said. "But anyway...good luck!"

It was the large immigrant population that was hit the hardest by the recession. With no work in the near or even distant future for them, many were forced to return to Europe with what little they saved. For most, their dreams of getting rich in America were shattered. Ironically, maybe those who could not afford the cost of ship's passage remained in America and took jobs wherever they could find them, were better off than those who returned. The recession deepened as the months went on. Many sought out the mines but here, too, the recession was in effect. It was the wrong time to be adrift in a country whose language you couldn't speak.

If it wasn't for his dream of buying the woods and making a living as a lumberman, I don't think my grandfather would have returned. There was no way for him, or others who did return, to anticipate just what affect a worsening political situation in Europe could and would eventually have on their lives. Like some say, the worst part of taking a chance is not taking it.

Chapter 10   Life In the Mountains Moves As It Has For A Millennium

Sixteen years after Yurko Najda's death, the summer of 1903... Orphaned, the four Najda brothers and their sister spent the next years of their lives being shuffled from one relative to the next, from one neighboring village to the next, and working from one farm to the next....when, as they grew older, to find work.

It wasn't, however, until my maternal grandfather Vasyl decided to break the routine, that their lives would undergo a drastic change. It wasn't done, however, of his own volition.

All of east-central Europe was being caught up in change. At first, it had been slow to cross north over the continental divide. The Najdas, their relatives and friends, had heard about opportunities in America. The word filtered north through several low, alpine passages in the mountains that had been thoroughfares for centuries. They were reopened for the last 200 years because both Poland and Hungary were now a part of the multinational Austrian Empire. And some, with relatives on the south side, in Hungary, had sons and fathers who left these mountains and made the crossing to America. It was inevitable that they would be next.

Andrij, Vasyl's second oldest brother had married two years ago and now lived with his wife's family in Stuposiany. It is another small village, a half-mile farther up the road, or up the Wolosatka River, from Protisne. The Wolosatka enters the Sian just above Protisne. This river, and most of the length of the road, lead almost to the very top of the mountains. Ivan, his oldest brother, the year before, went to live with his mother's sister Helena and her husband Mytro Andrushak in Dvernyk, two miles down the Sian River valley from Protisne. They have only daughters and Ivan was needed to help work the farm. Hryec, *(Harry)*, now 16 has grown up with Uncle Mykola in Lisko. His sister Mary, four years ago, married a man from Sianok and now lives there. Only occasionally, on holidays, does she return to Protisne. Contact with her brothers has grown progressively less. Vasyl hasn't seen her since Easter.

Summers are usually warm, sometimes hot, but always beautiful in the rolling hills of Carpathia and this July was especially warm. The vista of the surrounding land is alive with small clusters of men, women and children who dot the open fields making hay. Life, for a while, is pleasant. Only occasionally does a cooling breeze waft up the hill from the village and small stream. Vasyl, now 23, and three young men are haying what is now Zellman's field. For the past five years, he has worked what once had been his and his father's field. Two days ago, with well-worn scythes, they had cut the tall grasses in this field and let them lay where they had fallen, to be dried by the sun.

"They will leave us alone today," Michael Boburchak, 23, said, referring to the Zellmans, "because it is their Sabbath."

"And tomorrow, Mykhailo," Vasyl answered him, "we will leave them alone because it is ours."

Though they were basically from the same ethnic stock, and probably somewhere in the near distant past their genetic gene pools had been merged, they didn't look at all alike. The only similarity was their fair complexions. Mykhailo, as Vasyl called him, was almost cherubic in appearance. His rosy cheeks seemed only to exaggerate his deep, brown eyes and straight, brown hair. He was tending on the portly side and nearly 6 feet tall, an exception for people whose primary foods were potatoes, cabbage, turnips and bread, with the occasional chicken and very rarely a piece of beef or mutton. He was the epitome of a gentle Carpathian bear. But beneath this benevolent facade was hidden a belligerent young man who despised his status and those who controlled him. Occasionally, his frustrations boiled over and he candidly blurted out his feelings, regardless of who was within earshot. Vasyl was always quick to quiet him.

Mykhail and Vasyl had grown up together and were the closest of friends. It was only natural that Mykhail's attitude should have influenced him. Or, was it the other way around? Their feelings were mutual but those of Vasyl were not revealed as readily. They could not remember when they first met; it just seemed to them that they had always been together since they became cognizant of each other's presence. The Boburchak house, and their field behind their house, was next to the Najda's and the second one up the creek from its confluence with the Sian River.

Stefan Pavuk, the second young man haying, was two years younger but they treated him like a much younger brother. It was Stefan's and not their fault. It was his constant, inquisitive nature that may have contributed to this relationship. He was always asking their advice, their opinion on matters and seldom making up his own mind. He was forever a sophomore. His physical stature was somewhere between Vasyl's and Mykhail's but he walked with a slight limp. As a youngster he had broken his leg in a fall from a haycart. It was never properly reset. His house was next up the creek to the Boburchak farm. And when they were not working their father's farms, they would hire out to Zellman because Zellman did not work in the fields. Zellman once arrogantly told them he worked with his brain and not his hands. That he was smart enough to get others to work for him. He had no children who could work for him. His work was in the sklep.

Paul Turko, the third man, was two years older than Vasyl. His family's house was the highest up the valley in the village, near the end of the dirt road and close to Deep Creek that divided the village. His was a large family with four brothers, all older, and four sisters. Because of the continental senioriate system of inheritance, there was no future for him in these mountains as a farmer or herder. Like most Rusnaks in these foothills, Paul had grown up on a limited diet, mostly carbohydrates, which kept them from reaching their full genetic stature. He was 5 feet 4 inches tall, lean and lanky; sinewy would be a better word. His body had been honed by a decade of hard work in the surrounding fields. His gray-blue eyes were deeply set and gave him the appearance of constantly frowning. Nor did his wryly-shaped mouth distract from this image. But such was not the fact. Paul had been Vasyl's brother Ivan's best friend and contemporary. After Ivan moved to Dvernyk, Vasyl filled the void and together they had become best friends and itinerant farm hands.

Since his father's death, Vasyl had grown into manhood and his shoulders were broad and bulky. He looked as if there was still room for him to fill out. His face was oval in shape as opposed to most Rusnaks in these hills who featured round faces and round heads. It was offset by high cheekbones and his light skin tanned easily in the summer sun. He was a picture of health. His light-brown hair, almost blond, and light-blue eyes were his most salient features. They were the first things one would recognize if he approached you on a path. The next would be his smile.

By any standard, my grandfather was a handsome young man. Despite his road-in-life, he always seemed to have a smile on his face and inside, a positive attitude. He blamed no one for the tragedies in his life. He often said it was God's will and he never doubted it.

Vasyl was the most reticent of the haymakers, and of his brothers as well. Probably because of his age at the time his father's death, it seemed to make a deeper impression on him than his two older brothers. The sight of his father's simple wooden casket being lowered into the ground was a picture he would carry with him throughout his life. He felt he had been betrayed by his father's early death, robbed of a legacy, a relationship his brothers knew but was only hinted at for him because of his young age. It made him hold back his emotions, especially when he found himself among strangers. In a conversation, he often did not willingly contribute unless he was asked. Conversely, this reticence did seem to give him a sense of respect, a lack of frivolity. It did, in the end, project an aura of masculinity of which young girls, as well as male contemporaries in his sphere, seemed to be aware.

Every haymaker had a metal *kozivka* hanging from a leather thong on his belt. Vasyl's had been forged by Volodymyr Salabaj, his father's uncle, and it had been his father's. The short, sheath-like scabbard in which it was kept was usually filled with water and contained an *osevka,* a honing stone that was periodically used to sharpen the scythe's blade.

That Saturday, the four young men continued to cut hay as the coolness of the morning segued in a hot, sultry day. Midway down the edge of the field, they stopped to sharpen their scythes and take a drink. A jar of water had been hidden in the wet grass early in the morning before they started. Most of the water's coolness had disappeared but it was wet. Vasyl removed his cap and wiped the sweat from his brow on the back of his arm. His untanned forehead, under the cap's brim, made him look strange. He drank deeply from the jar then handed it to Stefan.

"I think we have cut enough hay," Vasyl said as the others lay resting on the ground. "We must turn over yesterday's hay or Zellman will scream at us."

"It is not so much Zellman," said Turko. "It is his wife. She must be a witch. I would hate to live with her. I think she hates us because we are not Jews."

"She hates anyone who is not a Jew," said Vasyl. "That is sad, more for her than for us. It is her cross to bear and not ours."

Vasyl set the scythe against a tree and from behind it took a pitchfork that he would use for the rest of the day. He leaned momentarily on its long handle, as if to gain his breath. The pitchfork was used to turn over the hay they had cut the day before to now expose its greener underside to the sun.

He stared first down the slope at the house where he was born, then his eyes swept past the weathered barn and finally over the river. He concentrated on the cluster of thatched houses on the opposite hill. Three crosses on the church, that stood on the peak of the hill, rose well above the cottages. In the distance, he could see others working hay in several fields that fell away from both sides of the church in Smil'nyk (Shmeel-nick).

"Some day," he said to his friends, who were slowly getting on their feet, " I will again have a field of my own, a house, a barn, a horse, cows and chickens, pigs and geese. Here my great grandfather was a farmer. My grandfather and my father were farmers. That is all I ever want to be, a farmer, like they were. I know God will not deny me this."

A deeply religious person, he blessed himself with his thumb and two fingers, first touching his forehead, then chest, and then his right shoulder. Like many of his peers, he had been caught up in the return to Orthodoxy, the religion of his ancestors that was beginning to sweep across these mountains. It was one of the few ways they could express their disdain for the Poles who dominated their lives for centuries and the Catholic Church's hierarchy they brought with them to be forced upon the Rusnaks. They were only partially successful.

He became silent for a while, then again turned and looked across the Sian (Shan), toward Smil'nyk, to the opposite hill. Dark green Carpathian beech trees, unique to this part of the world, framed the edges of the fields the haymakers were working. Along the fields' bottom edges, tall pines and larch finished framing the picture. Smil'nyk lay in its center.

"It makes a beautiful picture, doesn't it?" Vasyl said.

"It does," Boburchak answered, "but that is not all you see. I know what you are thinking about. And, it is not only a farm. It is a woman to put into your dream house. I can see the glimmer in your eyes. It is Kateryna Mynkova."

"Do you think she will be at the wedding party tonight?" asked Vasyl.

"It's her cousin who got married today," answered Paul. "What kind of relative would she be if she wasn't part of the wedding. I know she is in the wedding party.

"Will you be there?"

"What else is there to do in Protisne or Smil'nyk on a Saturday night?"

"Let's finish the field before sundown or Zellman will have us working on Sunday.

Chapter 11   Saturday Night in Smil'nyk

If you traveled the dirt road and forded the Sian at its customary crossing, the church in Smil'nyk is a quarter-mile from ruins in Protisne. If you took the raven's path, as did all young men, it was half that distance. Smil'nyk was larger than Protisne. It had more than 350 Rusnaks, several Poles, no resident Gypsy's or Germans, but a smattering of Jews.

Vasyl had always been curious as to why so many Jews lived in his village and almost none in Smil'nyk. Smil'nyk was located on the north side of the Sian, but away from the river, unlike other Rusnak villages in the area that were always built immediately along a river's banks. This made getting the daily buckets of drinking water a less difficult chore. Historians believe that this hilltop site was selected in the early 9th century because it was easy to defend. And, that the settlement began as a fort where two trade routes, along the rivers, crossed.

Volodymyr Salabaj was the village's blacksmith. In fact, he was the only blacksmith in the four villages that clustered here about the Sian River. If it was made of metal, and if it was broken, it was said that Salabaj could fix it.

His talents were always in demand, even by the few Polish families who had moved to Smil'nyk two or three generations ago. They were directly related to the Polish gentry, the *pan* whose estate house was located outside the village, toward Dvernyk. While they were considered a lesser royalty, and lived as farmers in land they were given, they were still royalty and the beneficiaries of special privileges that were endowed them.

Nor did Salabaj owe anything to Jakub Kohn, or his brother Jozef, the wealthy Jewish lawyers from Lisko who bought the lands from the Polish count, and who now owned their villages, because he didn't use their land as did others in Smil'nyk. Salabaj was as independent as anyone could be in an occupied region in the latter days of the 19th century in central Europe.

Volodymyr had four daughters and a son, but Olenka, his youngest, was his pride and joy. He and her mother Sonja had planned the wedding for months. Sonja and Olenka's sisters Anna and Olha had even traveled to Uzhorod, on the recently-finished railroad, to buy material for her wedding aprons. For weeks, she, her sisters and cousins embroidered aprons, blouses and corsets for the maids-of-honor, in the traditional style of their village.

Festivities in the big barn behind Salabaj's house were well underway by the time Vasyl, Stefan and Mykhail arrived early Saturday evening. The *ryadoviy*, or bridal dance, had just been completed. The itinerant Gypsy musicians, the *hudaki*, had the guests in a frenzy on a wooden floor Volodymyr had built especially for the event. Salabaj normally used the barn to store wagons and often the hay that most farmers used to pay him for his work. Money was seldom exchanged in these villages. He occasionally boarded horses for others, but had no horses or cows of his own. He sold or traded the hay to those who could not gather enough from their land. He was considered the wealthiest Rusnak in these villages. Now, all the equipment had been moved outside. Where the hard-packed earthen floor was exposed, it was swept clean.

As they walked past the wedding table, Vasyl and Mykhail tipped their round felt hats with their small upturned brims and whiskbroom-like feathers to the bride and groom and the array of wedding guests behind the table. The ushers wore the traditional wooden Cossack sabers in their belts, a relic from the Rusnak's past. Married women wore green aprons while unmarried girls wore white.

Spotting several of their friends, and his brother Ivan, standing in the far corner of the barn, the trio made their way toward them. On the opposite side, Kateryna Mynkova had left the wedding party to join her girl friends and chatted and giggled as they watched Vasyl, Stefan and Mykhail enter the barn. She occasionally stole glances toward Vasyl.

"Vasylko," Ivan said to his younger brother as he embraced and kissed him, "how have you been? It has been several months since I last saw you."

"I am fine," Vasyl answered. "Hard work always makes one feel good. But it is weddings that make one feel better. I didn't know you would be here."

"I did," interrupted Paul Turko as he, too, embraced Ivan. "I've known for some time, your brother has had his eye on Fenja Salabaj. Don't look now, but I bet she is staring at him from the wedding table."

Vasyl couldn't resist. Fenja was leaning over, talking to one of her sisters, with her hand over her mouth as if to hide the discussion. Vasyl gave her a quick wave and she responded.

"How long has this been going on?" he asked Ivan.

"Not long. But she is ready to get married. I think she fears becoming an old maid. They say she is 20 and has never known a man."

"Tell us, Ivan?" asked Turko, "is that true?"

Ivan didn't answer...just smiled.

"One more dance," said the Gypsy musician, "before we take a break."

Goaded by Mykhail and his friends, Vasyl finally mustered the courage to leave them and walk down the side of the dance floor, past the wedding party, to where the young girls had gathered. He felt unsteady on his feet as he approached Kateryna. The chardash had started and couples were already on the floor before he got to her.

Even in the light of the kerosene lanterns she was a sight to behold. She wasn't tall, maybe 5 feet, like most of the women and girls in the villages. He hair was so blond, so light that it looked almost silver. Instead of braiding it into a bun on the back of her head, she wore it straight, in a ponytail, with just a single, black, velvet ribbon holding it together. A garland of flowers adorned her head, revealing she was one of the bride's maids and multicolored ribbons danced from them onto her back. He'd never forget that sight.

He extended his hand and asked, "May I?"

They had casually known each other for more than a year, but only in passing. The first time they met was in church in Smil'nyk. He knew he must have seen her before but never noticed her. He had gone there just before Christmas because his Aunt Mary, with whom he lived, wanted to visit her sister. She asked him to come along to carry some of the baking she had done. Their eyes seemed to merge as they stood opposite each other in the pewless church. He stared at her but she also stared at him. Not a word passed between them. None had to. It was an out-of-character reaction for Vasyl.

His aunt told him that she was a Mynko. She, and her older brother Ivan, were orphans, like he was. Their mother died when Kateryna was but five years old. For the past ten years they have been shunted between uncles and aunts, mostly Pavuks, on her mother's side. They were now living with her aunt, Zuzanna Salabaj, who had helped deliver her when she was born.

Then again, at Easter, his aunt used the same excuse to get him to go to Smil'nyk. Was this a part of a plan, he remembered thinking to himself as he walked with her up the steep, sandy path to the village ? It was during the blessing of the *paskas,* outside the church, that he saw her long, flaxen hair unfurled for the first time in sunlight. He'd never forget that, too. A garland of early spring flowers crowned her head, and a single red ribbon dangled from each side.

They danced the first minute without saying a word. Vasyl recognized Kateryna's brother Ivan playing his violin with the Gypsies. Vasyl was about to say something about her brother when Kateryna spoke. She was younger than he was, he thought. She is just a teenager. Only 17. I am not taking her seriously. But maybe, in a few years, it will be different. She should have let him speak first. She was fresh."

"You are Vasyl, Vasyl Yurkovych, are you not?" she asked pointedly.

She knew he was. Before he could answer, she spoke again.

"Your Aunt Marysha tells me you are good with your hands, that you work wood like an artist. That you can build anything you want. Is that true?"

"That might be," Vasyl finally answered, still stunned by her beauty.

"Then you should talk to my Uncle Volodymyr."

"He is my uncle too, but my great uncle," Vasyl interrupted.

"He is the head of a committee from our villages," she continued as if he had not spoken, "that plans to build a new church. It will be at the bottom of the hill exactly between our villages so no one must walk farther than the other. The church here is in need of repairs…and is too small. He is looking for young men to help. A mastercarpenter, Hrehory, **(Gregory)** is coming from Lisko to apprentice new men. It is a chance to learn. A chance to better yourself. Don't you want that? It is better than being a farmer. Besides, you don't even have your own farm."

"I will someday," Vasyl answered.

"How much money do you have? Have you saved any?"

"Zellman doesn't pay me enough so that I can save."

"Then why do you work for him? Why do you work for nothing?"

"There is nothing else here I can do."

"Yes there is. You can become a carpenter."

As Vasyl and his friends walked home that evening, Paul Turko made a startling revelation. "I have signed up with a mining agent to go to America," he said. "I have been thinking of it for a long time. There already are several men in America from our villages. There is nothing here for me, no way to make a living. I am a burden on my family. I must go. I leave in a week with three others from Litowyschce"

"Maybe we should go with you," said Mykhail Boburchak. "We are no better off than you. Still, it is difficult to leave what is so familiar."

They walked him home, up the creek, to say goodbye. All took turns embracing Paul in front of his house.

Maybe I will never see him again, Vasyl said to himself as he walked back to his house. That's too bad. He has been a good friend and I will miss him.

Chapter 12   September in the Carpathians

Vasyl, Mykhail Boburchak, and six other men are raising timbers for a new church. Even though it was September, they could already feel the chill of a freshening north wind on their backs. They are not far from the river, just a few hundred yards from the fording place. All of the 16- by 16-inch foundation timbers are in place, set on a layer of large, flat stones gathered from the nearby Sian. All of the vertical members also are in place with temporary supports. Master Carpenter Hrehory Ivanovych directs them as they attach block and tackle to what will be one of 24 huge beams that will form a vaulted ceiling. But only one beam is finished and ready to be lifted. Farther up the field, on a hill capped with huge spruce trees, Volodymyr is seen leading a team of horses, skidding a recently-cut log to the church site where it will be peeled and shaped with adzes into a square beam.

In the opposite direction, from Stuposiany, two men on horseback have just forded the river and are slowly approaching, watching the construction activity. Eventually, they stop a hundred feet away to view the work.

"They are strangers," Vasyl says to Mykhail as he hauls on the block and tackle, lifting a 12- by 12-inch by 20-foot beam onto the crosspieces. As he does, out of the corner of his eye, he catches them staring at him.

"They are not from here," he says in a low voice to Mykhail who is but a few feet away." Their clothing is strange. I have never seen pants like theirs, or high leather boots with laces."

"Maybe they're from Warsaw," Mykhail answers. "Or Kyiv."

"Have you ever been to Kyiv?" Vasyl asks.

"No!"

"Then how do you know how wealthy people dress in Kyiv?"

The two horsemen draw nearer but do not dismount.

"What are you building?" the bigger one asks.

"A church," answers Mykhail.

"It doesn't look like a church, not yet anyway," says the stranger. "It has no real foundation, no basement."

"Yes it does" Vasyl, uncharacteristically blurts loudly. "We are its foundation!

"It is not a brick or stone church like the pope tells Poles and Slovaks to build.

"It's not a cement church the kind Uniates now build because they are not as rich as Poles, but not as poor as we.

"Its foundation is the people who support it. And, because we support it, it is our church, our building. It is a *pravo-slavna tserkva,* an Orthodox Church, a wooden church that is built by the people who own it. It is built with their hearts, their sweat and their love. It is not a state church, nor a Rome church, but their church and no one else's. It is a wooden Rusnak Church. It is both very old and it is very new. It is being built in the old style, as our ancestors did before the Jesuits forced our people to change."

"My God!" exclaimed Mykhail as he turns at and looks directly at Vasyl. "I suspected but I never thought you had all this in you. You truly are my brother, at least, in mind."

"Who are you people?" the stranger asks. "Are you not Poles? Is this not Poland?"

Mykhail then quickly turns and addresses the stranger, "We are not Poles. We are not Slovaks. Some say we are White Croats, but I don't think so. We are neither Russians nor Ukrainians. We are Rusnaks. We are the Rus of the mountains, the Rus whose brothers have abandoned us."

Volodymyr arrives, listens for a while and then interrupts the conversation he has been hearing.

"Do you really want to know who we are?" he asks turning to the two strangers and then Mykhail and Vasyl.

"We are people who are broke! That is who we are.

"We have no money to buy more logs from Count Cuzinski. If we would say we are Catholic, he would freely give us the logs. Nor do we have any nails left. Our saws and axes are dull. I can sharpen them but there is already too little metal left on them.

"Hrehory says he will go back to Lisko," now addressing the other workers, "unless he is paid today. He will teach you no longer. So, he goes back to Lisko and we go home. Maybe by next spring we will find more money to finish our church."

"You guys are in a real predicament," the horseman says as Volodymyr departs, leading the borrowed horses up the road toward Smil'nyk. "But we can help you out. Come work for us and we will pay you enough so that you can buy all the logs you need and build all the churches you want.....wooden, or stone ."

"Who are you?" Mykhail asks.

"We are representatives of Consolidated Coal Company and we need miners. We need hundreds of miners to dig coal out of Pennsylvania."

"Where is Pennsylvania?" Mykhail asks.

"I know where it is," interrupts Vasyl. "That's where Paul Turko is now. He sent us a calendar with your name on it. I know you. I remember seeing you. You came here a year ago looking for men to work in your coal mines. You must have seen our friend Turko. He went with you, didn't he?"

"Yes, I remember him."

"Pennsylvania is in America, where all your dreams can come true," the stranger answered, disregarding what Vasyl had just said. He spoke as if he had said it many times. "We don't care who you are or what you do, what your father did, or what is your nationality or religion. We need your strength, your backs and your work, because we are building a new country. And this new country needs coal to feed its furnaces.

"We don't ask you to do it for nothing. We will pay you well. In America we have built company houses and a store near the mines. There, you can live and eat cheaply enough so that you can save money. You can send it home or you can build yourself a new home in America. Land is cheap and the pay is good.

"We'll even help you get there. We will advance you money to buy your passage, your *Schiffkarte* from Hamburg to New York.

"We already have signed 10 men from Litowysi, Zatwarnyts, Stuposiany and Smil'nyk, but we need more. Are you ready to go?"

"Maybe my farm lies in America," Vasyl says to Mykhail. "Maybe it does."

Chapter 13   The Journey Begins

Lower New York Harbor..._Friday, Nov. 20, 1903_---Twenty-three-year old Vasyl Najda leaned on the port railing of the third-class promenade of the _S.S. Patricia_ and gazed at the huge metallic statue of a woman with a light in her upraised right arm. A low-lying, wispy fog was scattered over most of the harbor and on Bedloe's Island (Liberty Island), and engulfed the feet of the massive monument. Since the ship passed Montauk Point, on Long Island, just after sunset the day before, he had been almost alone on this part of the deck. It was cold and the wind cut through the gray blanket in which he had wrapped himself.

He could no longer stand the stench of vomit, garlic and tobacco in steerage, or the constant crying of children and the incessant babble of so many different languages that were foreign to his ears. It had been that way for most of the two weeks the crossing had taken. At times, it was so bad that he spent nights topside, huddled against the warm exhaust tubes, when it wasn't raining or snowing. The North Atlantic in late November is no place for a pleasure cruise. During the voyage, he often wondered why he had ever left the clean air and green fields of his beloved Carpathian Mountains. There was another reason he was on deck. He was too excited to sleep and wondered what lay ahead for him and his companions.

In less than a month I will be 24 years old, he said to himself. What do I have to show so far for my life? Callused hands, sore muscles and a body of bones. I have no wife, no children, no house, and no farm. I have nothing. But that is not true, he contradicted himself. I do have one thing, I have hope, and that is why I am doing this. I have a future, and with God's help, I will survive. At least here, no one will care who were my father or grandfather or what they did to live. The slate is clean.

Vasyl had been fascinated by his first glimpse of America, even though it was only a lighthouse in a darkening sky. He was entranced by the way the beacon revolved around the tower in the crystal clear night and stared at it until it was just a speck on the horizon astern of the ship. He had never before seen one lighted. Fourteen days earlier, after they left the docks at Hamburg, Mykhail Boburchak had pointed out a lighthouse on the south side of the Lower Elbe River, at Cuxhaven. Vasyl hadn't been impressed by it. But it was mid-morning and it wasn't lighted.

Dawn was still under the horizon when the *S.S. Patricia* passed Ambrose Light Ship, slipped through The Narrows, then dropped anchor off Clifton, on the northeast corner of Staten Island. The ship was close enough to the island to see that its bluffs were covered with snow. In the distance, he could see the numerous lights of lower Manhattan dancing in the chilled, waning darkness. The *Patricia* was in the quarantine area where all ships must first anchor before being allowed to pass to the docks on Manhattan. Soon, immigration inspectors would be coming alongside to take the ship's manifest from the bursar and do a cursory check of first and second class passengers. However, they would spend most of their time with third class passengers in steerage.

Just then, Mykhail jumped out of the hatch that led down into steerage and joined him along the railing. He saw Vasyl staring at the statue and paused for a few minutes before finally speaking.

"There were times when I wasn't sure we would get here," Mykhail said. "There were times when I wanted to turn back. What is on your mind now, Vasylij? What do you see?"

Vasyl hesitated for a few moments.

"I see my farm," was all he said at first, paused for a while, then continued.

"I, too, still cannot believe what we have seen in the last four weeks, sights we never imagined existed, people who dress and talk so differently."

"Yes, I see that, too," responded Mykhail, "but I also see a lot of hard work ahead. We've come a long way in a short time, both in distance and time."

The start...

As they stood there together, mesmerized by the twinkling lights on shore, Vasyl's mind recalled the September meeting at the Jew's tavern in Stuposiany with Brian McDonald. As he did, his hand automatically slipped into his right pant's pocket. He felt the bundle of 25 U.S. one-dollar bills he had wrapped in a handkerchief. They were still there.

Anyone interested in going to America was invited to attend that meeting. Also, the word was out that McDonald would buy anyone who attended a beer or two. Vasyl was surprised at the number of men who packed into the grubby little tavern. He didn't know there were that many men willing, or even able, to go to America. It was the free beer that brought some, he surmised. But he also knew that other men were leaving Galicia in droves. Some villages, to the foothills in the west, already looked abandoned.

"I want all you men to be sure you completely understand what I am saying through my translator Yurko," McDonald said that night.

McDonald was not a tall man, an inch or two under 6 feet. But when compared to the Rusnaks to whom he was talking he was half-a-head above them all except Mykhail. Some of it was his hair. He wore no hat and his reddish-blond hair was in disarray. He was a first generation Irish-American who would also have stood above his kinsmen. His face was ruddy but pleasant and though he was only in his mid-twenties, about the same as most of the men to whom he spoke, he looked older. Nearly 10 years in the mines, before given this position, had aged him. His American boss said he had a better gift for gab than for digging coal. As he spoke, he placed his right arm across the shoulders of Yurko Korenko.

"You all know him, he is one of you. He is from Rabeh just a few miles north of here and has been to American several times. If you don't understand me or what I am telling you, ask him and I will repeat it again.

"As I have told you before, I am here to recruit men to work for the Consolidated Coal Company that has mines in Maryland and Pennsylvania. Last year, our geologists discovered a new vein of soft coal in Somerset County, south of Johnstown, near a small town called Pine Hill. That is southeast of Pittsburgh. Many of you have probably heard of Pittsburgh. Some of you must have relatives working there in the steel mills.

"So far, the vein is not deep, maybe a hundred feet under the surface. We have several mines in Pennsylvania but they are all working at their maximum so we cannot shift men to work in the Pine Hill Mine. That is why I am here, to encourage you to come to Pennsylvania. We will pay you well.

"How much money you make will depend upon how hard you work. Consolidated will pay you about 22 cents for each car you fill with coal. If you work with a partner, you will get 11 cents. Most men can fill four to five cars a shift. You work by weight. Five cars can make a ton and a ton is worth $1.25. A shift is 10 hours long. That comes to about a dollar a day. In Pine Hill, at the general store, a loaf of bread costs 5 cents, but just 3 cents at the company store. We are now building new company houses next to the mine site. Single men pay $5 a month for room and board, and that includes three meals a day.

"In order to get past U.S. immigration officials, you must have $25 or the equivalent in your pocket so that you don't become a ward of the state or country. It can be in Shillings, Marks, Zlotys or Rubles.

"There are several ships a month leaving for New York from Hamburg. We have reservations for 15 to 20 men on the *S.S. Patricia* that sails on November 6th. The *Schiffkarte* for passage on the German-American liner *Patricia* costs $32.25. The railroad fare from Sianok to Hamburg is $3.25. Sianok is 24 miles from here. How you get there is up to you. This gentleman is Hans Gruber. He is with the Austrian Federal Transportation Office. He will help you get on the train."

Gruber was off to one side, sitting at a table, with a paper pad before him and a pencil in his right hand. He stood up, smiled, bowed slightly from his hips, looked around at everyone, and then sat down. He was neatness beyond perfection and even wore a tie under a green *Jägerfleid* jacket, though it is doubtful he had ever hunted. He was a small man whose entire adult life had been dedicated to accounting. He wore horn-rimmed glasses that seemed to perch precariously near the end of his sharply-defined nose. Under the nose was a short, handlebar mustache that showed signs of gray. It was his thin lips, however, that revealed his true disposition.

"If, in the past few days, you told Yurko that you wanted to go to America, he placed your name on Gruber's list. If you want to go but didn't tell Yurko, tell him now and he will add you to the list.

Gruber has an office in Sianok and if he has your name on the list he will give you your train ticket when you get there. He will see that you get on the train. On the other end, there will be someone to greet you in Hamburg and take you to Emigrant Village. You will stay there until your ship leaves.

"I will be in Hamburg and meet you before you are taken to the ship. Before boarding, I will give you the *Schiffkarte* and the money, if you need it. I will not be on the ship when it leaves but someone from Consolidated will be at the exit gate at Ellis Island, in New York, to greet you when you have passed through immigration and customs. He will get you to the train that will take you to Johnstown and the wagon to Pine Hill. All these costs will be borne by Consolidated.

"If you have $60.50 or the equivalent in shillings, you will not need help from Consolidated to get to America. If you do not have $60.50, to pay for your passage and the cash needed to enter the United States, we will lend it to you. Once you begin work, after the first month, Consolidated will dock your pay at the rate of $1 a week until it is fully paid. If you agree, each man is expected to sign a paper here, tonight.

"Are there any questions?"

There were hundreds of questions but no one dared ask them.

"Then, form a line in front of the table. Tell Yurko your name and Hans will make sure it is on his list. After you have signed, we can see how good is the Czech Pilsner. C'mon. I'm buying."

"Here," Yurko said to Vasyl who was standing closest to Gruber's table, "sign your name there." He pointed to a line on a sheet of printed English words.

"Yurko, what does it say? You know I cannot read," asked Vasyl.

"It is in English, Vasylij. I cannot read it either. Just sign and move on."

"I cannot sign my name. I cannot write," Vasyl answered.

"Then just put your mark, any kind of mark and Gruber will witness it."

Vasyl took the pen Yurko was holding and put the point on the paper, then stopped. He thought for a moment then drew a small vertical line under the printed word. Near the top of the line he drew a small horizontal line that crossed it at right angles. Just beneath it, he unsteadily drew a second though longer line, parallel to the top line. Beneath that, he drew another small line that crossed the vertical line on a downward angle.

"Was heisen Sie?" Hans asked without thinking, then paused.

"What are you called?" he said.

"Vasyl Najda," Vasyl answered

"Vasyl. Vasyl Nider," said Gruber

"No, not Nider. Najda," corrected Vasyl.

Hans thought for a moment about how to spell this Slavic name, then wrote "Wasil Nida." It was still incorrect. In German, a W is pronounced as a V.

"Next."

When everyone who was going signed, McDonald, with a stein of beer in his hand, again addressed the crowd.

"Today is Thursday, October 1, 1903," McDonald, said to the line of aspiring coal miners while Yurko translated. "As I said, the *S.S. Patricia* leaves Hamburg on November 6th. You must be in Hamburg at least three days before she sails to clear emigration. But, you will also need two days for examinations in Hamburg before you can board the ship. Maybe three. You cannot board it before November 5th. The train ride from Sianok to Hamburg takes four days if you make all your connections. You must spend one night in Berlin because of connections. You have three weeks to get ready. I suggest you get there ahead of time. There are ten of you. I think it would be wise for you stay together and travel as a group."

"So, you do not want to be a carpenter," said Kateryna Mynkova. "Now you want to be a coal miner."

"No," answered Vasyl. "I want to be a farmer. But I must first be a coal miner before I can be a farmer. I am almost 24 years old and I do not have a *Groschen* to my name. How can I ask you to marry me if I cannot even afford a tunic."

For a moment, what Vasyl said startled Kateryna.

"What makes you think I would marry you? I'm too young to get married. I may never marry," she answered in a girlish, coquettish way.

"I know you would marry a farmer," answered Vasyl. "That is one reason I want to be a farmer. I cannot be a farmer here. But I can be one in America."

"Look after my cousin Stefan," said Kateryna. "He's younger than you or Mykhail. I don't know why, but he looks up to you two."

"Stefan is your cousin? I didn't know that," said Vasyl.

"Well, he's really my second cousin. My mother was a Pavuk who married a Mynko."

As they parted, he held onto her hand for a moment and then she suddenly pulled herself closer to him and daringly, kissed him on the cheek. Even she was not that forward to kiss him on the lips.

Tears were in Marysha Najda's eyes (Thurs, Oct. 22) as Vasyl packed his few belongings into a homemade canvas bag. His brothers Ivan and Andrij, and their wives Juliana and Marysha, were in the kitchen. They had come the night before and crowded the house to see their brother-in-law leave for America. This was the first time he had seen Ivan's wife since their wedding three months ago. He had always believed Ivan would marry Fenja Salabaj and his sudden decision to marry a girl from Litowyschce was unexpected. When he saw Juliana's growing stomach, he knew why.

"I think going to America is the right thing to do," said Andrij. "There is nothing here for any of us. You have no farm, or even a girlfriend. Why should you stay? You have no wife or family to keep you here. If I didn't have a wife and a child, I would go with you."

"Europe has become a crazy place to live," added Ivan. "People are crazy, doing strange things to each other like I have never heard before. There is hunger everywhere and madness. In June, the crazy military killed the King and Queen of Serbia. In August, the Turks massacred more than 15,000 Bulgarians, all Slavs, like we are. I tell you, Europe is not a safe place to be.

"And, the Magyars on the other side, are getting stronger, weakening their alliance with Austria. If they break away, the Poles will soon follow. The Poles are already treating us Rusnaks as if they were again the authority over our lands and us. And the Austrians are not doing anything about it."

"These are troubled times," added Uncle Andrij. "Already the Russians and Germans are talking of war. You know, if Germany goes to war, the Austrians will be pulled in. And the Turks will be on their side.

"But enough of this talk of war," said Uncle Andrij.

"Don't cry Marysha," he said to his wife. "He will be back with us after he makes his fortune in America. Maybe by then the times will change and our life will be better. What do you think Vasylij Vasylko?"

Ever since his father died, except for three years, Vasyl had lived with Marysha and his Uncle Andrij. Childless, he quickly became their son in every sense of the word. Vasyl stood up to go. It was time. She hugged him and then Uncle Andrij hugged him and kissed him on the lips as Rusnak men are prone to do to their sons. His two brothers and their wives followed suit and everyone had tears in their eyes.

Four men, including Stefan Pavuk, had already gathered at the church in Dvernyk as the sun rose above Vysoky Grün. Vasyl had often wondered what was on the other side of the high peak but never had free time to climb to the top or go through Ruske Pass on the peak's east side. When he had time, it was winter and no one in their right mind would do it then.

"Where are the others?" he asked Boburchak as he arrived in Dvernyk. "We are three short."

"They are not leaving until tomorrow. Maxim Pavuk must get some legal papers signed in Lisko and is taking them that far in his wagon. There is room only for four in his wagon."

"Let us begin," answered Vasyl. "We have a long walk and must get as far as Solina tonight. Mykola Kushnevski has relatives there and thinks we can sleep in their barn."

Fortunately for walkers, the road to Solina, then Lisko and eventually Sianok beyond, is all downhill, though hardly noticeable at times, because it closely parallels the Sian River. It is in its best condition in late summer and is little more than the width of a wagon. Unless it rains, its ruts are filled with sand and easy walking. In many places, the road narrows to little more than a footpath that parallels the river.

None of the young men have been farther away than two or three villages from Dvernyk, Protisne or Smil'nyk. They never had a reason nor the time. From the beginning, a new world now lay before them. Vasyl and Mykhail walked side by side. Stefan Pavuk opted not to ride with his uncle and was behind Vasyl with Mytro Danko from Smil'nyk. Within the hour, they reached Chmil and Volodymyr Kretchko was sitting on the side of the road waiting for them. He was older than most of the others; about 35, and spoke very little. Andrij saw that his eyes were red and knew why. He didn't bother to engage him in small talk.

The road crosses the Sian just before Zatwarnyts. There was no bridge, just a ford. The river was higher than usual for late October. The men removed their pants, rolled up the bottoms of their shirts and waded across. The water was cold because it came down from the mountains. Snow had sporadically topped the higher peaks but continually melted, to the chagrin of the waders. On the other side, in Zatwarnyts, Boris Hayko was waiting for them. The entourage now numbered seven.

The day was sunny but the weather brisk as they walked at a steady pace. Their loads were light, only small handbags that were tied by ropes and slung over one shoulder, or light, home-made rucksacks on their backs that contained all their worldly possessions. By noon the day had warmed and their pace slackened somewhat. Along the road, near Krywe, they found a cluster of four farmhouses on one side and a community well. They stopped there and ate boiled eggs, bread and *kobasi* they carried in their duffels.

An old woman, looking out a small window in the nearest house, saw them and after a few minutes walked out.

"Are you going to America?" she asked. "I wish I were young enough to go with you. It seems almost every day there are young men like you stopping here to drink. They are all going to America. Soon, there will be nothing but women left in Galicia."

Under her arm she carried something wrapped in a cloth.

"Here," she said and thrust it at Stefan.

He opened it and saw a round loaf of rye bread. It was still warm and had been baked just a half-hour ago.

"It won't last long," she said, "but it may give you strength to make your journey. God be with you." She blessed herself, turned, and slowly walked back into the house and quietly closed the door.

Stefan's eyes moistened and he turned his head so the others could not see him as he made room in his bag for the bread.

"She reminds me of my *Baba* (grandmother)," he said.

The sun had already set but ahead, through trees, they saw on their left the shimmering reflection of the Solinka River. The village was just ahead, where the Solinka and Sian met.

"My uncle's house is just on the other side of the bridge," said Kushnevski.

"*Dobré vechir*," Kushnevski greeted a man who was unloading hay from a two-wheeled cart.

The man turned around, stunned for a moment because the light was fading and he could not at first make out who had greeted him. He was startled to suddenly see so many young men in his yard.

"Mykola, is that you?"

"Yes Uncle Stefan," answered Kushnevski. "It is me."

"What are you doing here?"

"I am on my way to America. My friends and I need a place to sleep. We must catch the train tomorrow in Sianok. May we use the barn?"

"Of course, you are welcomed....if there is room."

"What do you mean, 'if there is room'?"

"There are four Russian Jews in it. They asked to sleep there.

"But Mykola, you can stay inside, with me and your aunt and cousins. We have room."

"No," Mykola answered. "I began this journey with my friends and will stay with them."

"As you wish.

"But come eat something with us. I cannot feed all your friends, but I will have Anna put on a big pot of water for tea. Come with me and I will give you a lantern. Come inside. Come. Come."

There was plenty of room in the barn. Kushnevski's three cows were in the barnyard and the sheep were in a field.

"Luckily for the Jews," Mykhail said as they entered the barn, "that he keeps no pigs.

"*Dobré Vechir*," Vasyl addressed four Jews (*Thursday night, 22 Oct. 1903*) huddled in one corner of the hayloft. "*Yak se mash?*"

At first, no one answered.

"*Ochin horoshaw*," one finally said.

"What language are they speaking?" Stefan asked Mykhail.

"Didn't Mykola's uncle say they were Russian?"

"Are you not Russian, too?" asked one of the Jews who overheard Stefan.

"No, we are Rusnaks," said Mykhail. "But we understand most of your words."

Mykola then came into the barn with them. His uncle was immediately behind him carrying a big pot of tea and a varied array of cups of different sizes and shapes.

Others in the emigrant party were sitting on and around an empty four-wheeled wagon that had been drawn into the barn, and from small cloths, began unwrapping food— bread, cheese and pieces of smoked *kobasi*. Several began cracking boiled eggs as Mykola poured steaming hot tea from the big pot.

Vasyl turned to the Jews and asked, "Have you eaten?"

"No."

"Then come and join us. We do not have much but will share it with you."

"We cannot."

"Why not?"

"Your food has not been blessed by a rabbi."

"But, it was blessed by a priest, an Orthodox priest. Won't that do?"

"The *kobasi* is made with pork. We cannot eat pork. It is against our religion. Your food is not kosher. No, but thank you."

"Whatever you wish.

"Why are you here?" Vasyl asks.

"We are going to America."

"So are we," added Stefan.

"Are you going there to work in the mines?" he asked. It wasn't as absurd a question as one might consider. The four Jews were not dressed much differently from any of the men around them. They wore peasant clothing and could well have been farmers. But maybe their shoes were better.

"Are you farmers?" Vasyl asked.

"Two of my friends are. The other is a tailor. I am a lawyer."

"You aren't dressed like a lawyer."

"It is easier these days to travel dressed like a farmer rather than a lawyer," Smolensky said.

"Why are you going to America?" Stefan asked.

"The pogroms have become too much. We fear for our lives. We are most recently from Zhytomyr."

"But Zhytomyr is in Ukraine, not Russia," said Vasyl

"Everything that is not Prussian or Austrian today is Russian. Ukraine is Russian, believe me," said the one who was a lawyer and seemed to be their spokesman.

"We lived outside Moscow for most of our lives. Then the Tsar sent his Cossacks to drive us out. Life has become intolerable there for Jews. We feared that if we stayed much longer we would not be alive. We have friends in Kyiv and Zhytomyr, but they could do only so much."

"We were going to leave from Odessa," again said the most outspoken of the three. "But the route was too close to Kishinev. Did you hear what happened there?"

"No."

"It was the worst attack on Jews in a hundred years. The city is equally divided between Christians and Jews, and tension had been running high. A Christian girl was killed on Easter eve and some blamed it on the Jews. They said we had killed the girl to make *Passover matzo*. That is stupid. How can anyone make flat bread from a human being? The Christians went crazy. Dozens of Jews were killed and many more wounded. Living conditions for Jews in Russia have become intolerable, intolerable. So, we walked here instead of to Odessa. That route is too close to Kishinev."

"You are, like it says in the *Bible,* you truly are wandering Jews," said Vasyl. "Where do you go from here?"

"To Sianok," said one of the Jews as he stood up, "and then by train to Hamburg where we will take a ship to New York."

The boisterous call of a rooster, that obviously had had a good night's sleep, awakened the men in the barn. In the house, Stefan Kushnevski had been up long before the rooster and, as the men gathered themselves for the second leg of their trip, he came through the door from the house with another pot of boiling water.

"At least you can have some tea before you start," he said. "And my wife offers you these loaves of bread and some butter."

Several of the young Rusnaks had gathered in a corner of the barn and were on their knees reciting morning prayers. It was then that Vasyl realized that the four Jews were gone. It wasn't until mid-morning, just outside the small village of Srednya, that they caught up with the Jews. As they approached the village, they saw a commotion in progress at one of the houses. In the center, several villagers had surrounded the four Jews. The young men hurried their pace to see what was happening.

"They came into our yard to steal a chicken," screamed an old woman. On the ground behind her were several hens with their broods pecking away at the dirt. She seemed panic stricken as she pointed at the tallest of the four Jews. He was obviously the older of the quartet. His gaunt appearance, dark skin, long, black beard and aquiline nose made him look somewhat different from the other three.

Nor did he look like Ihor Zellman, Vasyl noted to himself. Vasyl hadn't noticed his features the night before because it was too dark even in the lantern's light to see very well. It was the first time Vasyl had a good look at them.

"He came here to steal," she yelled, "search him. He's hiding something under his coat."

"Stop yelling," Mykhail finally shouted at the women.

"Let her see what you have so we can shut her up."

"I stole nothing. I came here only to the well for water. We have been on the road for three hours without water. Surely it is the code of anyone with a wayside home to offer water to a traveler."

"The coat. Under the coat," she yelled. "Let us see what you have there."

Finally, he unbuttoned his great coat and an arba kanfot unfolded and stopped at his knees. The many knots on his small prayer shawl swung back and forth as he stood there motionless, exposed. It was as if all his clothing had suddenly been torn off and he stood naked before the crowd.

"Oh my God," the women said in disbelief. "He is only a Jew! I thought he was a Gypsy."

"Stupid women," Vasyl said in anger. "Have you never seen a Jew before? Half the people in your village are Jews. Where do you live....in the woods?"

"He doesn't look like other Jews," she yelled as if to justify her fright. "He looks more like a Gypsy."

"Come with us," Vasyl said to the Jew and his companions. Let us get out of here. We all still have a way to walk before we reach Sianok."

A few hundred yards away from the well, Vasyl turned sideways and spoke to the accused Jew.

"She is right," Vasyl said to him. "You do not look like your companions or other Jews who live around us. Why"

"It is because I am a Sephardic Jew. My ancestors came from Spain and Portugal 400 years ago, to escape the Inquisition. Now we Jews are escaping another inquisition.....a pogrom. My companions are Ashkenazi Jews who lived in Poland, and Ukraine, when it was a Polish province."

In early afternoon, just as they were about to enter Lisko, the county seat, the seven Rusnaks and their four new traveling companions were overtaken by Maxim Pavuk and the others bound for Pennsylvania.

"Lisko is not a big place," said Maxim. "You are about 15 minutes from the center of the town and the municipal office, by the fountain. I will leave your companions there." After he finished speaking, he drove off and disappeared in a cloud of dust.

Lisko may not have been a big town according to Maxim Pavuk but it was the largest accumulation of people these men had ever seen. At that time, its population was nearly 10,000 and more than half were Jews, a quarter Polish and the rest made up of Rusnaks (Rusyns), Gypsies, Greeks, Germans and Armenians. In contrast, most of the people in the countryside were Rusnaks, a few Poles and the odd Jew who preferred to farm rather than run a business in town.

Lisko was typical of many Central-Eastern European towns under the influence of Austrians, Poles or Hungarians. Its main street was 20 feet wide, dirt, (usually mud) and ran in a straight line through the center of town where it opened into a triangular market area about two acres in size. Whenever it rained, it became a rutted quagmire. The center of town had always been a commercial site since the village was formally organized by Poland in the late 1400s. More than likely, it had been founded 400 years earlier as a Kyivian Rus outpost. Now, it is where farmers from outlying areas, almost all Rusnaks, on Friday mornings brought the surplus food they grew to sell or barter. Here they would exchange for money or the things they needed that they could neither grow nor make themselves.

On each side of the main road, and the roads that surrounded and defined the triangular commercial center, were shallow trenches or gutters that functioned as sewers. They paralleled each street and were only clean after a rain. On the far side of each ditch, inside the triangle, were numerous shanties, quickly constructed shacks, where their owners displayed products for sale or barter. Almost to a man, they were operated by Jews and a few Greeks. It was one reason the Jewish population was so large in Lisko. The other was because Lisko was also the seat for Lisko County and even then a haven for Polish and Jewish lawyers.

Newly-installed electric utility poles ran the length of the roads, next to the ditches. To cross from the road to the shops, at broken intervals, numerous boards straddled the ditches. Intermittently, flat bridges made of heavier boards crossed the ditches to allow farmers with wagons entry into the center of the triangle where they tied their horses or oxen for the day.

Like many small cities or towns in this region, Lisko was unique in some of its architecture. It was settled by waves of Sephardic Jews who escaped the Inquisition in Spain in the last decade of the 15th century. They brought with them long-instilled concepts of living and housing, and many of their homes revealed a distinct Spanish-influenced architecture.

Surrounding the center of Lisko, outside the ditches, were several municipal buildings, three small hotels and several taverns. These were constructed of stone or bricks and were one and two stories high. Dominating the vista, on a slight hillock behind the state buildings, was a two-towered Roman Catholic Church that served the Poles who had taken administrative control of this village in the 14th century. On the opposite side of the triangle, two blocks away, was a Jewish synagogue. There was no Orthodox Church in Lisko for Rusyns, nor a Greek Catholic (Uniate) church for those Rusnaks who had been coerced into converting to the Roman brand of Christianity.

The sight in the square was one of mass confusion for Vasyl and his companions. They were able to smell it even before they saw it. There were more people walking about, talking and arguing with shopkeepers than all the people in Dvernyk, Smil'nyk and Protisne together. And there were more horses and wagons in the tie-up than they imagine existed.

"People here must be very wealthy," Stefan said, "to own so many horses."

"There they are, the others," Mykhail said to his group, "at the fountain. We can stop a few minutes to cool our feet." Maxim had deposited the three others where he said he would, and they greeted each other as they joined forces.

"I must visit my uncle to say good-bye while we are here," Vasyl said to Mykhail and Stefan. "I will be back in a few minutes."

Aunt Marysha had told him that the shop was on the far side of the triangle and that it would be easy to find. "Look for a sign, with the head of a pig and a bull, hung above the door," she said.

It was easy to find. It was no more than a hundred yards from the fountain. Inside, hanging upside down on hooks that lined the shop were live chickens and ducks; their feet tied together. Beneath them were several crates filled with more live chickens, ducks and even a few geese. The waist-high counter was made of several thick, roughly-hewn oak boards mortised together. On the lateral sides, were several wide-mouth bottles and crock jars of various condiments. On the floor, on each side of the counter, were two large wooden barrels. One was filled with pickles in brine and the other with herring, also in brine.

Behind the counter, hanging from the ceiling, were three sets of block and tackle. From one hung a beef hindquarter. From the other, on a double hook, hung a side of pork and a side of mutton. From the third, hung a skinned, whole, headless calf. The floor both in front and behind the counter was covered by an inch or more of rough-cut sawdust. Standing immediately behind the counter at two butcher blocks were two men. One man was unfamiliar to Vasyl but the other was his Uncle Mykola.

Mykola looked up and immediately recognized his nephew.

"Vasylij," he blurted out. "Come here. Come around the side. Let me see you."

Vasyl moved around one corner of the counter and his uncle came forward and embraced him in a bear hug. He smelled of mutton and his bloodstained apron rubbed against Vasyl's vest. He was stronger than his other uncle, Vasyl thought, probably because of lifting so much heavy meat.

"I hear you are going to America," he said. "Your cousin was here a few days ago. I was hoping you'd stop and see me. It has been a few months since I saw you last. It is a brave thing you are doing. You really don't have much choice. Do you? There is nothing here for you. If I were younger, I would go with you.

"Natasha," he said as he turned to a young woman who was sweeping more sawdust under the hanging quarters to catch the dripping blood. "Go get Hryec. Tell him that his brother is here. Go. Go quickly!"

"Here, come with me. I have something for you for your long journey."

As he led Vasyl through the shop and out a back door, Vasyl asked his uncle who was the other butcher.

"Oh him. He is the Jew who used to own the shop. Now he works for me. He owed me so much back pay, he thought he could get away without paying me, that a few weeks ago I went to a lawyer here to see what he could do to help me. Because the Jew couldn't pay me the Polish judge gave me the shop instead. Can you imagine a Pole doing that for a Rusnak?"

"I don't think he had a choice," said Vasyl. "I think it is the law."

They walked a rickety catwalk to a small shed. Vasyl immediately recognized it as a smokehouse. He could see the fragrant blue-colored smoke rolling through a pipe on the roof and through open slats between the roof and its sides. His uncle opened the poorly-fitted door and pulled down a three-foot length of smoked sausage.

"Here, put this in your bag. Maybe when you chew on it, you will remember your Uncle Mykola." He then embraced him again and kissed him on the lips. "Good luck, my nephew."

Harry, as Hryec was called in America, was six years younger than Vasyl, and had been working in the horse corral inside the triangle. The town had hired him and two other Rusnaks to clean behind the horses and pick up all the debris from each shop that was usually piled behind each shanty. They had a horse and two-wheeled wagon and periodically hauled their gatherings to a dump outside of town.

Vasyl almost didn't recognize his brother. He had seen him only once in the last year when Mykola and his family had come to Protisne for a wedding.

"You have really grown, brother," Vasyl said. "I believe you are taller than me. And, you have put on some weight. I think Uncle Mykola feeds you better that Uncle Andrij fed me. I am glad for you."

Indeed, Harry was taller than Vasyl but only by an inch or two. His hair was darker in color but they shared the same blue eyes, high cheekbones, thin lips and fair complexion. He sported a neatly-trimmed brush mustache.

They hugged longer than they might have at other meetings. Because they lived apart since their father died, they had never really had the chance to develop a typical brother relationship.

"I wish I were going with you," Hryec, said as they separated to arm's length from each other. "Have you heard from Paul Turko? Does he like America?"

"Not once," answered Vasyl. "Not even has his family heard. But he hasn't been there that long. We aren't even sure he is alive. He may have drowned in the ocean for all we know. I had our priest write him a letter saying I was coming to Pine Hill. I never heard back."

"Good-bye, Hryec," Vasyl said. "I wish we could have lived closer together so I could have gotten to know you better. Maybe someday. I must go. My friends are waiting for me. I will have someone write to Uncle Andrij after I get there and let you know how the crossing was."

They embraced again and kissed each other on alternating cheeks.

Vasyl hurried back to the fountain and rejoined his companions. A few minutes later, Stefan, who was sitting on the rim of the fountain pool, stood up and looked at Vasyl.

"Is that what I think I smell?" he said.

Vasyl looked at him and smiled in agreement.

"I could eat some now," said Stefan.

"No. Later. Maybe tonight."

The four Jews were older than all except one of the Rusnaks and reached the center of town a half-hour behind them. The older one, the lawyer approached Vasyl and spoke.

"We must leave you here because we dare not go any farther."

"Why not?" asked Vasyl. "You can travel with us."

"Today is Friday. Tomorrow is our Sabbath. Our religion demands that we be inside before sundown. We cannot walk as fast as you young men. I fear we will not make Sianok before then. Besides, we have friends here and can stay with them until Sunday.

"However, I thank you for letting us travel with you. Maybe our paths someday will cross again."

"What is your name?" Vasyl asked.

"It is Simon. Simon Smolensky of Brody. And yours?"

"Vasyl Yurkovych Najda."

"God be with you, Vasyl. You are a good man."

The four Jews disappeared into the horde of people while the Rusnaks at the fountain gathered their strength for the last leg of their journey to Sianok.

"I don't know why you are so friendly to Jews," Mykhail said to Vasyl. "Didn't Zellman rob you and your brothers of your inheritance? Have you forgotten so easily?"

"What good would it do to remember?" said Vasyl. "Would it bring back my father or the farm if I treated them ill? They are humans like we. Don't we pray to the same God? Was not Christ a Jew?

"That is all in the past. The future lies ahead, down that road."

Vasyl turned his head toward the road to Sianok. "Let's find Gruber. Let us go!"

The population of Jews living in the Carpathian Mountains at the end of the 19th century (and their foothills) was vast and numbered more than 200,000. They could be found in every settlement, from cities down to the smallest village. They preferred to live in or near the towns because these were essential to their kinds of businesses. For centuries social isolation and insecurity made Jews strive to better their economic position. And, in the midst of a primitive and somewhat carefree and easy Slavic community, their shrewdness, their capacity for work and their doggedness were bound to tell.

However, wealth is a relative term. Because Rusnakia and its people were so poor, Jews living among them could hardly be considered wealthy. In every village, regardless of size, where there was almost always an inn. The owner, or an operator working for Polish *pan*, was always a Jew. The liquor he sold was cheap, often made from wheat rather than potatoes and terrible to the taste. Because of their plight, peasants sought its relief, though it was only temporary; alcoholism was a pervasive problem. Money was seldom available and peasants paid for it by the food they grew. If the crops were not in, or if surplus was unavailable, the Jewish tavern keeper was always willing to put their purchases on credit. However, he always made sure the bill was paid one way or another.

In this way, the innkeeper eventually accumulated a surfeit of timber, eggs, poultry, or sheep which he took to the nearest town to sell. With this money he bought salt, flour and some cheap necessities of life which he sold or bartered for more local produce. He may also have owned the local *sklep* (store). In the mountain villages, even though his trade was scant, because it was a surplus he eventually came to own most of what there was to be owned in a village. And because he had money he was also a *de facto* banker and would lend money that was backed up by good security, usually the peasant's small patch of land. He practiced usury to its fullest extent and many a drinking peasant eventually became a renter.

Whether poor or wealthy, the Jews of Carpathia and their foothills formed one of the most compact and distinctive communities of its kind in Europe. Many lived traditionally in accordance with the ancient Mosaic Law and kept strictly to themselves. Their caftans of black alpaca (wool) reaching down to their heels, their wide-brimmed hats of velour or felt, their long ringlets hanging down both sides of their faces as demanded by customs or law, the luxurious patriarchal beards of the older men, made them conspicuous figures. These Orthodox Jews were strongly opposed to any new ideas or habits and faithfully preserved the spirit of the Middle Ages. Their status, like that of their serf/peasants neighbors, had hardly changed in the last 400 years.

Sorrow and pride of race welded all these diverse Jewish elements into one closely-knit community. Generally, in a somewhat symbiotic relationship, Jews easily fitted in with the Rusnaks, and most fulfilled a needed function within the Rusnaks' primitive peasant society. While Jews formed most of the middle class in the 19th century possessions of Austria and Hungary, they were divided into two sub-groups. The lower class supplied craftsmanship and business acumen. In the larger villages and towns, Jews participated in many trades. They made and repaired shoes, clothes and watches. Most traditional peasant costumes and lambskin coats were made by Jewish tailors. Others copied and produced the local pottery. Souvenirs for tourists, such as the ornamented sticks called *tshakans,* were often carved by Jewish craftsmen.

In contrast, the upper portion of this middle class group was composed of wealthier and better-educated Jews. They controlled the higher commercial life and the law courts and their intellectuals dominated public life. They were the doctors, lawyers, journalists, musicians and artists. It was this group that dominated life in Lisko.

Ironically, most Rusnaks did not begrudge Jews their positions in their villages. Anti-Semitism was not pronounced in the mountains. This explains, to some degree, why my grandfather felt no qualms when he decided to help Simon Smolensky. And, it is why the people of my paternal grandfather's village, on the south slope of the Carpathian Mountains, saved more than 600 Jews from the *SS*. But that part of the story comes later.

It was near sunset when they reached Sianok. They were right, Vasyl thought to himself. They would never have made it before sunset.

Sianok, on the Sian River, was a much larger town than Lisko, with nearly 25,000 inhabitants in 1903. Even the river here is much wider, deeper and moves more swiftly. As they were instructed, they found the train tracks on the edge of town and followed them to the station. Gruber's office was opposite the train station.

"How many of you are here?" asked Hans Gruber.

"There are still ten," answered Boburchak.

"Good," said Gruber. "When I call your names answer yes."

"Wasyl Nider!"

Vasyl interrupted when his name was called and handed him a small piece of paper. "It is Vasyl Najda. Here it is written by my priest."

"Oh! Yes," Gruber said and was slightly embarrassed for being corrected by a peasant. "It doesn't matter, you are here."

When he completed his roll call he addressed the men.

"Tomorrow's train will take you to Berlin," Gruber instructed the group. "Your first stop will be in Rzeszow. You will all stay on the train all the time. Do not get off when it stops along the way because you might miss getting back on. Stay on the train until it gets to Berlin. The train will stop at the border in Slubice for about an hour. There a German locomotive will be exchanged for the Polish engine. While this is happening German customs officers will board the train. They will ask you where you are from and where you are going. Tell them you are from Austria. I have written you names on your tickets. If you do not understand the officers, just show them your train ticket. They have been through this before and will let you pass.

"You will also be checked by HAPAG (*Hamburg Amerikanische Packetfahrt Aktien-Gesellschaft*) doctors at the border crossing to make sure you are free of cholera. Russian Jews have been blamed for bringing the disease to Hamburg. You have nothing to fear because you are not from Russia and have not been exposed to any Russian Jews."

Someone in the group moaned.

"When you get to the *Banhoff* in Berlin, there will be someone there to meet you. He will be carrying a sign with CONSOLIDATED MINING printed on it. Show him your ticket and follow him. He will take you to your accommodations for the night because the train for Hamburg does not leave until 9:00 the following morning. You will not have to pay for the rooms. In the morning, he will call for you at 7:00 a.m. and take you back to the *Banhoff*. I suggest you do not find somewhere to eat breakfast, but wait until you get to the station. There are several convenient kiosks there where you can get tea, coffee and rolls, depending upon what money you have. You should arrive in Hamburg in mid-afternoon. There, another Consolidated representative will meet you.

"Tonight, you can stay here, at the bureau. There are enough bunks in the back room for all and toilet facilities. I will see you in the morning.

"*Dobré vechir!*"

Gruber's attention to a full count of recruits was not entirely attributable to what is often recognized in the character of most Teutonics as deutsche Ordnung, a uniquely German dedication to a sense of order. That he was Austrian rather than German would have made no difference. There was, however, a more profound reason. Many steamship lines, like Cunard and German-American, actually paid the Austro-Hungarian government an annual emolument on the condition that they deliver to German continental ports 20,000 emigrants a year. This was the practice during most of the first decade of the 20th century.

Steamship lines, whose vessels crossed the Atlantic between Europe and the United States and Canada, became extremely competitive and vied for the lucrative market these emigrant passengers had created. But it wasn't the first and second class passengers who earned them the most money. During the period from 1890 to 1914, third class, sometimes designated as 4th class passengers, but always considered steerage, composed more than three-quarters of their fares and most of their profits.

This arrangement eventually caused its own demise and, along with the impending war, ended the mass migration of east-central Europeans to America. The extreme competition that arose between government agents, like Gruber, who were given quotas for areas, caused them literally to capture numerous undesirables along with those willing to work and endure the hardships until success was achieved.

The motivation to gather everyone and anyone and ship them to the United States and Canada was not only money. It was also a move by some governments to search out thousands of unwanted people, often criminals and those dependent upon the state for subsistence, and rid themselves of them by shipping them abroad. The program backfired when American officials started returning large numbers of such immigrants to Germany, along with those who had medical problems. To strengthen this practice, the United States made the shipping lines responsible for the costs of returning passengers. Compounding this for the Germans, many of those after being deported flooded the streets of Bremen and Hamburg. To say the least, the citizens were enraged.

The zenith in passenger numbers peaked during 1907, when in one year, 1,200,000 emigrants were admitted to the United States. During this decade almost half of the ship owners' incomes were derived from steerage passengers.

"If we lost our steerage passengers, we would be out of business within a week," said Albert Ballin, managing director of HAPAG.

The next day *(Saturday 24 Oct.),* with great intrepidity, ten Rusnak would-be coal miners, stepped aboard the imposing railroad car. None had ever even seen a picture of these things, let alone gotten near or boarded one. Now they were going inside one, as if into the belly of a monster. The noise of the steam engine was enough to dissuade all but the most fearless. Boburchak didn't hesitate and Vasyl followed.

When the last one took a seat, Gruber, at the end of the car, smiled without showing his teeth, handed out one train ticket to each man after calling out his name. When that was done, he gave them a snappy salute. He bowed slightly, then clicked his heels and escaped out the door, down the car's short steps and onto the pavement.

As the train slowly rolled away, Gruber felt assured he had done his part. He walked toward his bureau office and stopped for a moment with one hand on the door handle. He smiled to himself as he glanced over his shoulder and looked down the railroad tracks as if he was searching for another line of men. He momentarily wondered how many McDonald would have in the next batch.

"How long did Gruber say it would take to get to Rzeszow?" Mykhail asked Vasyl.

"One hour," Stefan said.

"No," Vasyl corrected Stefan. "That is how long he said it would take to get through the border. He didn't say how long the ride was."

"How far is it?" Mykhail asked.

No one answered. No one knew. It didn't matter. Nothing they could do would either shorten or lengthen the time it took to get to the German border. It was just their uneasiness about what they were doing, what lay ahead that made them engage in small, unimportant, frivolous conversation. That eventually ended as each man became absorbed in thinking about what his future might hold.

Vasyl was sitting next to the window and stared out, unfocused, absorbed in thought as the landscape swept past at unbelievable speeds. He, too, was nervous. He had never before moved this fast. The fastest he had ever traveled, he recalled, was once when Volodymyr wasn't around and he raced one of the borrowed horses back to the barn. He had no idea how fast he was traveling.

"How fast are we going?" he turned as he asked Mykhail.

"Probably 40, maybe 50 kilometers per hour," he answered.

"How do you know that?" asked Stefan. "Have you ever ridden this fast?"

"No. But I heard Yurko say that's how fast these Polish trains travel. He said the German trains were even faster. But, he said the Pennsylvania Rail Road trains in America are the fastest. And the biggest. I hope we will ride one of them."

"We will," said Vasyl. "Don't you remember McDonald telling us that? That is how we will get to Johnstown, Pennsylvania."

Just then a conductor entered the car from the forward door and began working his way back to where the Rusnaks sat.

"Tickets," he yelled. "Have your tickets ready," he said in Polish. "Have your tickets ready," he repeated in German.

"What does he want?" Stefan asked.

"Your ticket. Get your ticket out, I think," Mykhail said. "That's what those up front are doing."

When the conductor approached the seat where the trio sat, Mykhail asked him how fast the train was traveling.

"Speak Polish," the conductor said as he grabbed all three tickets and punched holes in them for the first leg of their journey.

"You're in Poland," he added, "speak Polish."

"We are not in Poland," Vasyl retorted. "This is Galicia. Galicia has always been a part of the Rus lands. Speak Rusnak."

"Stupid, dumb Russian peasants," the conductor responded.

"Actually," said Mykhail. "We are not Russians so you cannot call us Ruskie. Although we are citizens of Austro-Hungary, just like you, we are not Austrians nor Hungarians. Don't you know you are not Polish? There is no Poland today."

"Don't count on it," the conductor said as he was about to pass through the sliding door to the next car, "there will be."

"Who will give it to you?" Mykhail yelled, as the door slammed shut.

After a few minutes Stefan sat up in his seat, turned to Mykhail, and asked, "Why do the Poles think they are better than us? Why did the conductor call us dumb? Are Rusnaks really dumber than Polaks or other people? Why do the Poles have a president and a king and we have neither? Why is it the Poles and Austrians who tell us what to do?

It took a while for Mykhail to formulate a response.

"I don't know the right answers," he finally said. "I do know that we, as a people, are not dumb. The answers are complicated."

"There is a simple answer," interrupted Vasyl after Mykhail was silent for a while.

"What is it? Stefan asked because he was unable to wait for Vasyl's response.

"We are not dumb, we are uneducated. Just think....there are ten of us and not one of us can write his name or read it if someone else wrote it for us. We have no one to teach us to write and read in

Rusnak. Even our priests are not well educated. It is because we are uneducated that we must do as others want us to do. If we are to become equals to Poles, Austrians, and even Jews, we must become educated or remain their slaves throughout our lives."

"What is it you want out of life?
Vasyl asked Stefan.

"And you Mykhailo, what do you want? Why are you on this train? Why are **we** on this train? Where are we going?"

"We are going to America to make money," Stefan finally said. "We are going there to get rich. We are going there so you can make money and come back and buy a farm."

"No my trusting friend. That is not why we are on this train," Vasyl said.

"I'll tell you where we are going," Vasyl answered his own question. "We are going to find our future, our destiny, and most of all, to find out what we can do; what we as individuals are capable of doing or as a people if given the chance; what we can become.

"For nearly a thousand years we have been little more than slaves in our own land. First it was the Magyars, then the Tatars and the Mongols who came from the east. Before that it was Vikings who captured our people and sold them to Greeks and Jews who in turn sold them to the Arabs. The very word Slav comes from the Arab word for slaves."

"Vasyli, I have never seen you so worked up," said Mykhailo. "Where did you learn all this? Have you been to the Jew's tavern drinking without me?"

"No. I listened to the new priest who was hired last year. He is not like some of the others we have had....most were just a step above the serfs he serves. This one is smart. He told me he studied at the university, in L'viv. He spoke a lot of sense. I believed him.

"Why do you think we have no leaders, no learned people? It was because our princes and nobles were all killed off by the Poles and the Hungarians. The few who survived accepted their offers, to become Poles and Magyars, to become Catholics...or die.

"We are the last people in Europe to enter the 20th century. We have been held back just to work the land as modern slaves. But I plan to change that, for myself, at least...and for my children and their children. I can do that in America and so can you. All you need is to want to be freed from your past. That is why I am going to America."

The ride seemed endless as the train drove onward into the night. It seemed that just as it reached its fastest speed it began to slow, then come to its first stop, Rzeszow. Then it continued on to Tarnov, Krakou, Katowice, Opole, Wroclav and Legnica. It was dark when the train turned north, and after three hours approached the border town of Slubice. Then, it began to slow and finally came to a full stop.

After a few minutes, those who were awake heard the engine's sharp, high-pitched whistle blow, then someone outside, in the rear of the car, shouted. The train lurched a few feet in reverse before it again abruptly stopped. Outside, there was the clang of heavy metal and men shouting as the train moved forward again, but only a few feet. Then, they again heard the smashing of heavy metal upon metal and felt the reverberating jolt throughout the train and into their bodies.

This time, the train didn't stop but moved ahead at a snail's pace. It traveled no more than a hundred yards and seemed to glide almost effortlessly over a bridge, its wheels clicking as it ran over breaks in the rails, and crossed a wide river. Then, another jolting stop. The engineer seemed to blow the locomotive's high-pitched whistle much longer than before. And, it seemed to have a different pitch. Unknowingly, they had just crossed the border into Germany and were now in Frankfort a. d. O., (*an der Oder*), on-the-Oder River, and came to a stop.

Half an hour passed. In the dim light of the kerosene lamps, the ten men sat silently, seemingly terrified of what might happen next. They heard the clamoring of men opening and closing metal doors as they passed between cars. Suddenly, the sliding door in the front of their car opened with a bang and a uniformed man moved through, followed by a second in a different uniform. The Polish conductor followed behind them.

"*Fahrcarte, Fahrkarte und Ihren Ausweiss, seine kennkarta!*" (your ticket and ID) the lead man said. Then he repeated himself in Polish and finally Rusnak.

"The German is probably the customs man," Mykhail said to Vasyl and Stefan. He speaks *po nashomu*. "He wants our tickets and identification."

"We have no identification papers," Stefan said in panic.

"Don't worry, Gruber said all we need is the train ticket," Mykhail said and handed the first man his ticket.

"*Danke,*" he said. He looked at it for a moment and saw where Gruber had printed a name. He then withdrew a booklet from under his left arm and, under the heading *Vorübergehend* (transient) he wrote Mykhail Boburchak. He then handed the ticket back to the man behind him. He took it and punched a hole next to the one that the Polish conductor had punched in Sianok.

"*Danke,*" said the German conductor and handed it back to Mykhail.

In the meantime, Stefan and Vasyl had handed their tickets to the customs man. When their names were registered and tickets punched the customs official turned to the other side of the isle and asked three Rusnaks there for their tickets. It took more than an hour for customs to clear the entire train. There were six cars and other customs officials had worked from the front backwards. Vasyl's car had been the last to be checked. As the three men walked back through their car to the exit, the Polish conductor stopped for a moment and glared at Mykhail. He said nothing, then moved ahead. The German conductor, instead of getting off, took the last seat as the customs official and the Polish conductor stepped down from the train.

They waited there another 15 minutes before the front door to the car slid open. A bearded man in a white smock entered. His white crew-cut hair seemed to stand out in the dim light. The Rusnaks had never seen such a hairstyle. Around his neck hung a stethoscope and his breast pocket was filled with wooden tongue depressors. Behind him, a women in a dark blue uniform with red crosses on her lapels followed, carrying in one hand a small kerosene lantern with a highly-polished reflector and a deep, tin cup in the other.

Another German conductor was behind them as they entered but they stopped to let him take the lead. He asked the passengers to again show their tickets. Two Jewish families filled the first four seats. The men all had heavy beards and the women *babushkas* and heavy, blanket-like shawls that reached to their knees, overlaying skirts that reached their ankles. The children sat as if frozen.

"*Russich,*" the conductor said after a quick glance at their tickets. The doctor pointed to one man, asked him to stand, and the nurse shown the light in his face. He depressed the man's tongue, then pulled down the eyelids and asked him if he has pains in his stomach and when was the last time he went to the toilet.

These were medical personnel sent to the eastern border by HAPAG to check emigrants from the East who might have cholera. They didn't want them spreading the disease onboard the boats or in the embarkation center. Also, Hamburg was in the middle of another cholera scare and the people there blamed the shipping lines for bringing in so many foreigners, especially from Russia, where the epidemic was rampant. Anyone suspicious was put into quarantine for up to two weeks before being allowed to travel to Hamburg.

The doctor seemingly satisfied, dropped the depressor into the tin cup the nurse held, and went on to the next man, then the woman and finally the children.

"Gut," was all he said and moved to the next group.

When they came to the Rusnaks, the conductor turned around and said to the doctor that they were Austrian citizens. He again said good and skipped them and then departed through the rear door of the car.

It was another 15 minutes before someone outside blew on a high-pitched, handheld whistle and the train engineer responded with the locomotive's whistle. The train lurched ahead, almost stopped, then slowly began to move, steadily picking up speed. In no time, the clicking of the train's wheels on the rails created a mesmerizing timbre. One by one, the Rusnaks fell asleep and in the Stygian darkness traveled across Germany. However, it was a restless sleep and though the night was short, it seemed endless.

Stefan was awake first and watched Vasyl slowly come alive as the train continually swayed from side to side.

"It's getting light," he said and Vasyl's eyes sprang open. He sat up in the uncomfortable bench seat.

"Where are we?" he asked.

"God only knows," answered Stefan. "I wish I was back in Smil'nyk. I wonder what my sister and mother are doing right now."

"The same as they have always done at daybreak," interrupted Mykhail. He spoke while his eyes were still shut and seemed to be trying to eke out a bit more sleep. That was impossible.

"Your father has already taken the cow from the barn and released her in the field," he continued, "and your sister is probably on her second cup of tea."

"Anyway," answered Stefan, "I wish I was still at home."

"What is there at home for you?" asked Vasyl.

141

"Work, work and more work," Mykhail answered for Stefan. "And what do you get for it? You get nothing but tired and older and more tired. Your father is a farmer. Your grandfather and great-grandfathers were farmers. The best you can hope to do, if the Jews and Polaks don't swindle you out of your farm, is to become a farmer; to farm land that yields almost nothing. It grows stones better than potatoes. Why in the world would you want to be back home?"

No one answered. They all knew there was no future at home for any of them. All that was there was the past. And that was not a very happy one.

"And what would **you** do if **you** were home," Stefan asked Vasyl.

"I would be getting ready for church. Have you forgotten, today is Sunday."

Since daybreak and after the first stop at what looked like nothing more than a few houses and a crossroad, the train was running considerably slower. It was but a half-hour before the train stopped again. Mykhail got up and walked to the platform between the cars. As the train started again, he reappeared in the doorway and as he took his seat he said, "They have taken on cans of milk. I guess were are gathering up all the milk so Berliners can have it with their oatmeal."

"Have you any food left?" Stefan asked Mykhail.

He shook his head no as Vasyl retrieved his canvas bag from under the seat. Without speaking, he pulled a small bundle from the bag and unwrapped the cloth. It contained two pieces of dark bread and lots of crumbs. He handed the smaller piece to Stefan and then broke the large piece in half, giving part to Mykhail. There was nothing more, but they were accustomed to going without.

Chapter 14   Berlin

It was near noon when the train slowed on its approach to Berlin. Suddenly, it was inside a large barn with an arched, glass ceiling that hovered above them like a large, transparent cloud. It was the largest barn any of the men had ever seen. It was made almost entirely of glass and metal frames. The sun filtered down in bursts of rays through sooty glass panes. It reminded Vasyl of holy pictures with the long sunbeams emanating from a central point somewhere in the sky.

We're in heaven, he thought. There were at least two dozen tracks that paralleled their train and several trains were already stopped at their platforms.

"Berlin! Berlin!" yelled the conductor as he moved forward through the car. "Everyone off. Everyone gets off here. This is the end."

As he passed the group of Rusnaks, he motioned for them to get up and pointed toward the rear door.

The platform outside was crowded with disembarking passengers. Vasyl had never seen so many people in one place at one time. There were even more people here than all he seen back in Sianok. It suddenly all seemed too confusing to him, a mountain man. He looked into the moving crowd for someone carrying a placard with CONSOLIDATED on it. There was no one. The ten men grouped together with their hand baggage like frightened school children on their first day in school.

The noises were deafening. Locomotives on arriving trains released steam pressure and the clanging of steel and spinning of huge wheels on steel tracks intensified the din as other trains began to depart. It was compounded by the strange language that was the most confusing. Vasyl had never heard so many different tongues. Most were German. In the din he recognized some Polish words. They came from a group of people from the car behind them. They cursed at the Rusnaks for not moving as they squeezed past them on the platform. There were uniformed Germans, train personnel, on the platform giving orders and directions to the throng of people. There was a multitude of tongues that were totally unfamiliar to the Rusnaks.

Their German conductor saw the Rusnaks huddled like cattle on the platform and returned to give them directions.

"Go. Go to the gate," he kept repeating in German and pointing to the far end. No one knew what he was saying. In frustration, he threw his hands into the air, gave up and disappeared into the throng.

"McDonald," said Vasyl, "said we were to wait on the platform until someone with a sign came to get us. We must wait."

Almost like a pool of water pouring down a drain, the people from the trains moved down their platforms and disappeared through the numerous gates. In a matter of minutes, the platform was abandoned except for the Rusnaks and a few baggage handlers.

"What will we do if no one comes?" asked Stefan.

"Don't worry little brother, someone will come," comforted Mykhail.

"But what if..."

"Don't worry," Vasyl said. "I promised Kateryna I would look after you and I will. We all will."

A half-hour passed since the train arrived but still no one had shown.

"Maybe we should walk to the gate," suggested Mykhail.

No one answered but no one disagreed so they began following him. Those with rucksacks on their backs began to move down the platform. The others picked up their bags and followed.

Suddenly, at the gate, a frenzied-looking man appeared. In his hand was the placard they all wanted to see and he ran to them.

"Are you the group from Galicia?" he asked in Polish.

"We are from Halychyna," Mykhail answered.

Then the man began speaking rapidly in Polish.

"*Ne rozumiu,*" Vasyl interrupted.

"You are not Polish?" he questioned.

"No," several men answered almost in unison.

Then the man spoke in Slovak. More words were familiar to them.

"I'm sorry I am late," he apologized. "There was a breakdown in the street car. I had to wait for the next one to come along."

As he spoke, Vasyl smelled alcohol on his breath.

"Come, follow me," said Pavel Kuchera.

The main center inside the train station was noisy, crowded and filled with strange smells and more foreign voices. "Stay close together," Pavel said as he looked back to see if they all were coming. Satisfied, he turned around and led the line of Rusnaks to the opposite side of the giant hall, then through a pair of large opened doors. Suddenly, they were in Berlin, the only real city any of them had ever experienced. In front was a large square jammed with trolley cars, horse and carriages, and noisy automobiles that all seemed to be going in different directions. It appeared as mass confusion to the farmers and left them speechless.

After taking a head count, Pavel quickly crossed the square to a slightly raised island-curb that was already filled with a cluster of waiting people. As each of the Rusnaks jumped onto the elevated walk, Pavel handed them a 5-pfennig coin. "That's for the trolley," he said to each one as he dispensed coins. "Do as I do when it arrives."

Within a few minutes an electric trolley approached with its contact arms arcing and crackling, like thunder and lightening, as its main arm regularly lost and again made contact with numerous overhead wires. Pavel jumped onto the trolley when his turn came and dropped the coin into a four-sided glass box. The Rusnaks did the same.

"Don't sit," he ordered, "stand. The hotel is just a few minutes away."

The trolley scooted them away, down a narrow street that looked like a narrow river gorge. On each side, buildings came almost to the edge of the roadway and rose three and four storeys. They had never seen anything like them.

The trolley hardly slowed at a sharp turn and the men swayed out with it, holding onto the overhead straps or the vertical poles that occurred every fourth seat. It seemed that they just got started when Pavel pulled a cord above one of the windows and a bell responded, clanging violently. Within a few feet, the trolley came to an abrupt stop.

"Out. Get out here," he yelled at the men and led them onto the cobblestone roadway.

GÄSTHAUS HEINRICH, read the sign above a pair of swinging, windowed doors that led into a small hotel. The windows looked like they had not been washed since the hotel was built, probably more than 50 years ago. There were no handles or doorknobs and the inside edges of the doors were worn, filthy, greasy-looking, where thousands of hands over the years must have pushed and pulled on them. Just inside was another set of doors that were wedged open Later on, in winter, they would be closed to form an anteroom.

Pavel saw the men looking into the hotel and quickly got their attention.

"Not yet," he addressed the group. "We go across the street to the restaurant. It is time for *Mittagessen, obid,* **lunch.** This one is on Consolidated, as well as your supper tonight. We do not want you to arrive in Pennsylvania looking skinny."

He led the men into a dingy-looking restaurant. Despite the fact that it was not yet one o'clock, it had only a half-dozen customers.

"Take a seat!" he ordered. "I doubt any of you have ever been in a restaurant before."

Pavel walked over to the counter, leaned over it as he spoke softly, quietly to a barrel-chested man who emerged out of the kitchen. The waist-high counter, with an opening in the middle, lined most of the left side of the dining room. Behind it were two doorways. Both doors were jammed open. It was easy to see beyond, into the kitchen, where another man and several women worked preparing food over stoves and work tables.

On the right side of the dining room, in rows parallel to each other, and perpendicular to the outside wall, were a dozen tables that seated six persons each. It looked like a mess hall in a military barracks or a prison. All the right ends of each table abutted against the bottom of a windowsill that looked out onto the street. Each window was covered with a diaphanous half-curtain that filtered the sunlight through gauze and dust. The windows were no cleaner than those at the entrance. Flies frantically buzzed against the glass in vain attempts to get outside. Those that did it long enough eventually died and fell to the sill where they lay on their backs, most with their feet in the air.

The walls were plastered and painted a color that once was white. They were bare except for the rear wall that sported a colorful beer advertisement. The lithograph showed a man in a Tyrolean hat lifting a glass of yellow beer to his lips. In the background, a blonde-headed girl, in heavy braids, smiling unnaturally, seemed to be romping up a green mountainside pasture toward a dark blue sky. Underneath, were a few words in German. You didn't have to be a linguist to understand the meaning of the poster.

The men slowly shuffled in, taking seats on either side of the tables until most of the first three were filled. They dropped their bags under the table or on empty seats. As they did, one aproned woman entered the room from behind the counter with an armful of large soup bowls. She left six on the end of each table as another woman following behind her unloaded a fistful of large spoons next to the bowls. Behind her, a third, also a portly women, and also with a white apron that approached her ankles, brought in a large, green, ceramic tureen, sculptured to look like a head of cabbage, filled to its brim with steaming stew.

"*Goulash*," she said as she made her way to the middle of the table and placed it there. The woman with the spoons came back and placed a ladle on each table. The other women returned with two more tureens and added them to the other tables. The first women returned with four large, round loaves of dark bread and four long knives. Each table got one of each.

"What, no butter?" Mykhail asked jokingly.

"No butter," said Pavel, who was seated at the first table.

A man came out of the kitchen and passed between the counters with eight opened bottles of beer, their necks held between the fingers of his large, fat hands. He placed four on each table and the men passed them down. Then he returned to get eight more.

Vasyl passed his on to Mykhail and asked the man, "Can I have milk?"

"*Kein Milch*," said the German. "*Pilsner oder Wasser?*"

"*Woda*," he answered.

For the first time since Pavel arrived, the men began talking among themselves. It was their first realization that they truly had left Carpathia behind, that there was no turning back.

"Not bad soup," said Mytro Danko. Danko, whom they discovered *en route*, was the oldest man in the group, near 40, and was born in Smil'nyk but grew up in Litowyschce, a few miles north of Smil'nyk. He had not known Vasyl nor Mykhail. He sat next to Pavel and across from Vasyl and Mykhail. "It does taste different than when my wife makes it."

"Have you ever had it with meat?" asked Pavel. "Germans eat lots of meat, especially pork. What do you eat at home?" he asked Mytro.

"Why do you ask him that?" questioned Mykhail.

"Do you do it to embarrass him? You know what he eats at home. He eats potatoes and cabbage. On Sunday, he may have a chicken. Maybe once a year they kill a pig, if they have one. His home is probably no different from your home in Slovakia. Have you forgotten what life was like there? Or do Slovaks eat better at home because their country is closer to the Germans?"

Just then, a neatly-dressed couple walked into the restaurant. The woman stopped short, just inside the doorway, and began to survey the patrons. She stared at the group of Rusnaks at the first tables and lifted her chin as if to get a better perspective of them. Their clothes immediately identified them as peasants, farmers who barely eked out a living and had little money to spend on clothes. She noticed the shabby jackets on Vasyl and Stefan and their unkempt, unruly hair. Then she caught sight of two rucksacks on the empty chairs. As she did, Mykhail, who saw her scanning his table, purposely slurped the last of the *goulash* as he drank it from the lip of his bowl.

One man in the kitchen spotted the couple and rushed through the doorway, drying his hands on a hand towel stuffed in his apron strings. He tried to seat them. As he approached them, bowing slightly, the woman spun on her heels and said in a low voice to her companion, *"Nicht hier! Komm Fritz.*

"There are four beds in each room," Pavel addressed the men as they gathered about him in the shabby lobby of the run-down *pension*. A scruffy-looking clerk leaned across the counter, as Pavel spoke, and handed him three skeleton keys that all looked the same.

"I wonder how many times before Pavel had said this to a group of men?" Vasyl said quietly to Mykhail.

"Divide yourselves into groups of four. One room has only two beds. Here is one key for each room. There are no facilities in the rooms. There is, at the end of the hall, a bathtub and a toilet. There is no pot in the commode to be emptied. Do what you have to do in this toilet. Just pull the chain on the tank, that is on the wall near the ceiling, and water will flush the bowl. There is one gas light in the toilet. Don't light it! The clerk will come up to do that when it gets dark and light it for you.

"I don't know how well you slept on the train. I can never get any rest when I make the trip. I suspect you all may be tired. I suggest you get some sleep. Also, I suggest you use the bathtub. I can tell that most of you should use it. I also suggest that you stay in the hotel until I come to get you for supper. Berlin is not a safe place for hillbillies.

"I will be back here at 7:00. We will go across the street to eat. Are there any questions?"

Calling it a room was gratuitous.

The escalating need for rooms for transient emigrants in Berlin was taxing all of the existing hotels. Any hotel, regardless of quality was cashing in on the unsatisfied demand. What they saw was more like a monk's cell and never intended for more than one bed. It was 9 feet wide and 8 feet long. The door opened in one end. Opposite of it was a small window. A heavy curtain was pulled off to one side and was to be drawn to the other side when someone wanted to darken the room.

There were no beds. Instead there were two double bunks against the far corners on each side of the window. In the opposite corners, near the door, were two wire-framed chairs that looked like they had once been part of a sidewalk cafe's ensemble. On one chair were four thin, course-material towels and one small bar of yellow soap that smelled like kerosene.

Under the window was a corresponding wire-framed table with a battered wooden top. It showed signs of cigarette burns and stains of beer and food. On it, in a tin dish that looked like it had held sardines at one time, was another bar of decaying yellow soap that the room's last occupants had not taken with them. Next to it, in a heavy, glass, chipped ashtray, was a half-burned candle. Next to it was another that had not been used. Dropping from the ceiling was the base of what had once been a gas light. It was broken just beyond the shut-off valve.

Mykhail had taken one key. Vasyl and Stefan joined him along with Mytro Danko.

"Which do you prefer?" Mykhail asked as he dropped his bag on the empty chair.

Vasyl sat on one of the bottom bunks and bounced gently. "This one will do," he said. "It is hard," he added. "Maybe it has too much straw."

"Germans don't use straw," Mykhail answered.

"Germans don't sleep here," Vasyl retorted.

Pavel again was late. It was 7:30 before he got to the hotel. And again, his breath smelled of alcohol. The Rusnaks, hungry, were milling about in the lobby waiting for him. They all sensed that Pavel was a person who didn't deserve their respect. He was thin, gaunt, and probably weighed no more than 130 pounds. The color of his skin was pale, almost yellowish. He face always seemed flushed in contrast to the pallor of the rest of his skin. His hair was blond but stringy and unkempt. His blue eyes sank into a head that showed most of its bones. Large, blue veins on his temples showed through his skin. It was obvious that he was an alcoholic. And that, coupled with a constant cigarette in his mouth, made him look unhealthy. He was the extreme opposite of these "hillbillies."

"Are you all here?" He asked and then began counting. "Ten, good." He didn't want to loose anyone before he got them all aboard tomorrow's train to Hamburg.

As the men passed single file through the one narrow doorway out of Gästhaus Heinrich, the line suddenly stopped to let in a woman. Her perfume preceded her and her cherry red lips and darkened eyes were an unfamiliar sight to the Rusnaks. Her red satin dress matched her lips. As she squeezed by, her heavy breasts seemed to be purposely rubbed against the two men in the doorway. In one hand she held a black patent leather pocketbook and in the other she held on tightly to the hand of a man whom she seemed to be dragging through the portal.

"It must be Sunday," Mykhail said as he followed Pavel into the restaurant and saw their tables already set.

"Of course it is. Why do you ask?" Pavel turned as he walked and answered.

"Look," Mykhail said as he and the others took seats around the table, "the Germans are just like Rusnaks. They, too, eat chicken on Sundays."

"He has a problem," Pavel said to Vasyl as he leaned over to speak to him.

"We all have a problem," was all that Vasyl said.

Anticipating their arrival, the tables had been prepared before the men arrived. A large roast chicken sat in the middle of each table. On each side were bowls of steaming boiled potatoes adorned with parsley. On the end of each table were stacked six plates and as many knives and forks. Next to them was a pot of steaming coffee and six cups. As each man passed in, he took a plate, knife and fork. Next to the chicken was a pitcher of water.

After supper, as they crossed the street back to the hotel entrance. The man they had seen being dragged in scurried out the door by himself and quickly walked away while avoiding to look directly at any of the men. Inside, the woman in red with whom he had come was leaning against the counter talking to the clerk. She opened her purse and handed him several crinkled Deutsche marks.

"*Bis später,*" she said to the clerk as she turned and walked past the column of entering men. She smiled broadly at them, trying to make eye contact with anyone who would respond.

"What was that all about?" Stefan asked Pavel.

"That is something which you really don't want to know about," he said. "Let me give you all some good advice. Berlin is not a place familiar to you. There are good Berliners and there are bad Berliners. Outside, there are a lot of bad Berliners. I don't know if you have any money with you. If you do, keep it on you at all times. If you must leave the room, even to go to the toilet, take your money with you.

"Life looks and smells good outside the hotel but it isn't. The prostitutes will take all your money. Often, they have a boyfriend who will visit you while you are busy with her, or drinking in the saloon down the street. Before you know it, she has all your money and is gone. If you catch her, her pimp is there to stop you. And, sometimes you, too, are gone. Last spring, there was another group of Rusnaks here. I lost two and no one has ever heard of them since. Maybe they wound up in the Spree as food for the carp.

"Maybe it was Turko," Mykhail said jokingly.

"Could be" answered Vasyl. "No one has heard from him since he left."

"Tomorrow morning, I will be here at 7:00 sharp," Pavel continued. "We will catch the trolley to the train station. As you know it is just a few minutes away. Make sure you have the rest of your train ticket with you and all your belongings. There will be no time here for *Früstück*, but I will give you all enough small change so you can get coffee and a bun on the train platform. The train for Hamburg leaves at 7:55.

"I can tell that some of you have not taken my suggestion to use the bathtub. Sometime tomorrow afternoon, the shipping line's doctors will check you. I suggest you leave behind what Carpathia you may be holding onto. Do not embarrass yourselves.

"Dobré Noch!"

"She did smell good," said Mykhail as they climbed the single flight of stairs to their room.

"Did you ever see such big tits?" added Mytro Danko. "Maybe we can go outside the hotel door...just to look. I've never seen women like that before."

"You mean there are no *kurvi in Litowysi*," kidded Mykhail.

"There was a Gypsy girl, but my mother interrupted us. I think she knew."

"Did you get back your money?"

"It wasn't money involved. It was a chicken."

They all laughed as they entered the room but stopped immediately. Their rucksacks were haphazardly tossed on the floor and their contents littered on the beds. Vasyl's canvas bag was not to be seen. Then he spotted it on the floor, far back under the bed, thrown there by someone who obviously was disappointed. He quickly looked through it and found his father's ancient pipe and gently unwrapped it from the cloth he had used to protect it. It was okay.

The men rummaged through their bags, gathering up what was theirs.

"Has anyone lost anything?" Vasyl asked.

"What is there too lose? It seems we didn't have anything they wanted."

"I wonder who has been in our room?" Stefan asked.

"Probably the desk clerk," Danko said. "He has all the keys."

"What does it mater," said Mykhail. "The keys are all the same. It could have been someone from another room."

"Does anyone have any money?" asked Mykhail.

"I have a few zloty," said Danko. "Why?"

"I have a few Groschen that Kateryna gave me," said Stefan.

"I have a few Groschen, too, but the most they would buy here is a loaf of bread," said Vasyl.

"That is what I have," said Mykhail. "Fortunately, McDonald said he would make us a loan just before we got on the ship. What will you do now?"

"I'm heading for the toilet," answered Vasyl.

It was near midnight when they heard the pounding.

"Who's there?" yelled Mykhail. The pounding continued. He asked again.

"It is not the door, stupid," said Vasyl.

"Who's in the room next to us? Are they our brothers?"

"No," said Mytro, as they lay silent, listening.

Then they heard a woman's voice and the steady thumping began again.

The next time they heard the pounding it was on their door. The clerk was holding reveille.

"Get up," he yelled. "Get up now or you will miss the train. You have 15 minutes to be down stairs. Don't make Pavel mad."

Pavel was on time as the last men scurried down the stairs.

"Good," he said. "That's ten. Follow me."

The morning air was cool, even for the last days of October. It had rained during the night and the streets were still wet. Dying yellow leaves on the linden trees that lined the street were still dripping. Farther down the cobbled street, they could see a stopped trolley car. As it started, a bell clanged to warn pedestrians to get out of the way. It was automatic. There were no pedestrians at this time of day.

As it pulled away, a second trolley moved in to take its place and the Rusnaks filed onboard. At first, they chatted among themselves, as the trolley started, then suddenly grew silent as

153

it entered the huge municipal square and began to slow. In the square's center, the tracks passed close to a huge, weathered bronze statute of a helmeted, heavily-bearded man in chain male sitting on the back of a ferocious-looking horse. The horse had reared up on its hind legs as the man was leaning down from the right side. His left hand was on the reins, tightly pulling back the horse's head into a sharp, exaggerated curve. The eyes on the horse bulged, its nostril flared and it mouth was agape showing its teeth and the bit. In his right hand was a raised battle-ax, about to strike.

At the horse's feet was a mélange of writhing bodies lying on the ground. Some looked dead. Vasyl studied them and wondered who they were. One, with a short stabbing sword in his right hand, was raising his forebody above the ground. The left hand was pointing to the horseman, with his arm outstretched and his fingers open, as if pleading for mercy. On his head was a different kind of helmet, askance, slipping off to one side. Across its top was a short, decorative horsehair crest that evidenced his rank as a Roman Centurion. To Vasyl, it looked like a cock's comb.

"Let's hurry," Pavel yelled back as he jumped from the almost stopped trolley. The men piled off the open streetcar like a scene of duck diving into a pond.

"Follow me," he said and quickly crossed under the vaulted rotunda of the train station. Hundreds of people filled the vast arena looking for the gates with the appropriate sign that signified their destination. There were two that read HAMBURG. Some of the men started for the right gate but Pavel stopped them.

"No," he said, "that leads to the first-class platform. "You go to the one on the left. Follow me!"

Pavel stopped at the gate to let the men catch up to him, then passed a guard who tipped his hat to him.

"How many are there today?" he asked Pavel.

"Ten."

Then he turned to the line of Rusnaks behind him and told them to get their tickets out and show them to the guard.

"There is a kiosk on the platform. I will get you something there to eat."

All the doors on the left side of the train were closed as first class passengers entered their individual compartments from the other side, through doors that opened directly onto the platform. After passing a dozen cars, they came to the first open door. Inside, instead of compartments, they entered the car from the back and parallel seats ran its length.

"Stop here," Pavel said at the kiosk. In German, he said something to the woman inside the enclosure. A second woman, who had been sitting down, out of sight, suddenly rose, dropped a newspaper she had been reading, and appeared at the window.

"Take a bun or roll and tell the woman if you want coffee or tea. *Wieviel?*" he asked the first woman. She answered and he dug into one pocket to match some coins with the bill in his hand.

"The price has gone up since last week," he complained to her.

"Don't tell me," she quipped back. "I don't set the price. I only work here. And, my pay hasn't gone up. If you don't like it, tell it to the Kaiser." She handed him two brass coins in change.

"Go inside the train after you get what you want," Pavel said to the men and disappeared ahead of them into the car. The car was empty. As the Rusnaks filed in Pavel directed them to take the first, then second and third rows of seats.

He watched as they maneuvered their coffee, rolls and hand luggage. "Put your bags in the overhead racks and you will have more room for your feet.

Ten, he said to himself.

"Look for a man with a Consolidated sign," he addressed the men. "Hamburg is the end of this line so that is where you must get off. You should get there about noon. Good-bye, Rusnaks," he said.

Without waiting for a reply, he disappeared out the door.

Vasyl again had the window seat with Stefan between himself and Mykhail. Mytro Danko, in the seat in front of them, turned around and was talking to Mykhail when the conductor boarded the train. He had been outside talking with Pavel. From a back pocket, he pulled out his hole puncher as he said, "*Guten Morgen. Fahrkarte, bitte.*"

When he realized they didn't understand, he tried it in English. "Good morning. Ticket's please." Then he stopped for a moment and addressed Danko. "Do you want to face your friends? Get up," he said to Danko and motioned appropriately with his free hand to the two sitting next to Danko. He then pulled the back of their chair forward and suddenly the seat was facing backwards.

Danko giggled and then thanked him.

"Don't thank me," he said. "Thank German ingenuity. Tickets please."

At 7:55 the train to Hamburg began to move.

Does he think we Slavs are so stupid that we could never have thought of such a seat? Vasyl said to himself as he stared out the window, his forehead resting on the glass and feeling the vibrations of the tracks being transmitted to his head and body.

Maybe we are. Look at us. We are being herded around like cattle. Since we left Lisko we have been told what to eat, where to sleep, when to get up, where to sit, where not to go, where to shit and when to wash. Are we children? Maybe we are a stupid people and this is our place in life. It seems as if it always has been this way. Did we ever have men with swords to defend us? Did we ever have swords to defend ourselves? Did we ever have leaders like the man in the statue? All we have is a history of working for someone else. Who are we?

The clacking of the train's wheels on the iron tracks, coupled with the gentle side-to-side cadence-like swaying of the car lulled most passengers into closing their eyes if not into falling off to sleep. In a half-stupor, Vasyl, from time to time, heard the conductor call off the names of cities and towns he had never before heard. He didn't remember how many times the train had stopped, maybe a half-dozen. It didn't matter until he heard Hamburg announced. He bolted up in his seat and felt the train begin to slow.

"You must really have been tired to sleep so much," a wide-awake Mykhail said. "You didn't sneak out on us last night and find a *Fräulein*, did you?

"Don't be stupid," Vasyl answered. "Even if I had money I wouldn't."

"Don't be so serious. I was only joking," said Mykhail.

"I know," Vasyl answered. "I'm hungry. One *bulka* isn't enough."

Chapter 15   Hamburg

Ever so slowly, the train pulled in between two platforms under a large overhead roof. The building's sides were opened and had glass windows only near the top, not at all like the station in Berlin. There were more than a dozen tracks leading into the terminal but not as many as in Berlin

"Hamburg! Hamburg! Hamburg!" the conductor kept saying as he walked to the back of the car. "Everybody off! Everybody off! Hamburg!"

"Now we must look for someone with the Consolidated sign," said Vasyl. "Let me see the paper that Gruber gave you so I, too, can look for it."

"We don't have to," said Stefan as he peered out the window and struggled to get his arms through the straps on his rucksack. The train hadn't quite stopped and still moved slowly deeper into the station. "I see his red hair. It is Brian McDonald. He is here, like he said he would be. And with him is Yurko Korenko."

It was almost like seeing an old friend, a countryman, as the men gathered around the Irish-American on the platform.

"Welcome to Hamburg," he said as he began counting. "Who is missing? I count only nine."

Just then Danko popped out of the train door, still fumbling with the buttons on his fly. "Sorry," he said. "I got so excited that I had to go to the toilet."

The men followed McDonald down the platform and through the gate into the terminal building. Vasyl caught up to him and asked him what to do with the ticket.

"It's all used up. It isn't good for anything now. But keep it as a souvenir. Maybe some day you will want to look back at it and remind you of this trip."

Vasyl stuck it into a vest pocket.

Outside, a horse-drawn wagon was waiting for them on the far side of the square. McDonald waved to the driver. He didn't see the wave. McDonald whistled and the high, shrill call caught his attention. The driver jumped to his feet in the wagon, looking around, then saw McDonald waving. He snapped the reins in his hands on the backs of a pair of horses. He brought the wagon around to the curb and McDonald jumped onto the long bench with the driver.

It wasn't a large wagon and the men had trouble getting themselves and even their scant amount of hand baggage onto it.

"Here!" McDonald yelled to Vasyl who was the last to try to get onto the wagon. "There is room here. Come sit with us."

Vasyl threw his canvas bag to Mykhail, ran around the side of the wagon and joined McDonald.

"We have a lengthy ride to Veddel, to 'Emigrant Village'," he said. "It is on the other side of the city and next to the docks." The driver snapped the rains on the backs of the horses and they began to move. He turned them back sharply, in the direction where he had been waiting, and the metal-rimmed, wooden wheels set up a clamor on the square's cobblestone surface. Once out of the square, the cobblestones disappeared.

The few apartment buildings that surrounded the square and the streets leading to it soon faded, replaced by factories and warehouses. As they crossed over a large bridge, Vasyl could see huge cranes beyond the warehouses. The smokestacks at one factory they passed belched dark, acrid smoke into the air. It seemed to settle in layers above the buildings on this windless day.

"You and your friends are lucky," McDonald said. "You will not have to stay with the hundreds of people who arrive here every day. Normally, you would stay in one of the dirty, flea- and roach-ridden hotels along the docks and have to wait a week, sometimes more, to be cleared by the health authorities and customs officials. But HAPAG is building, what they call, Emigrant Village to house their customers before their ships sail.

"There are so many emigrants now that the Germans are beginning to build a railroad spur from the main train station direct to the Village but it won't be operating for another year.

And, because your group is associated with Consolidated, and not escaping pogroms, you will not have to stay in the barracks with the others. The original Village is only a few years old and is already overcrowded. HAPAG has constructed two new buildings, and has four more underway. For our people going to America, Consolidated has worked out a special arrangement with the ship line. God only knows, they need more space to hold the emigrants before they can be shipped.

"Oh yes, there's another bit of good news for you. Normally, immigrants must be quarantined in the 'Clean Side' for two weeks after they have passed the medical examinations. That is to make sure that steerage on the ship does not become contaminated and there will fewer rejections in New York. You have already been examined once so your initial medical examination here should only take the better part of two or three days and the doctors here assure us that you are disease free. After that, you can board the ship.

"You will be the first to stay in the newest barracks that are being built by Albert Ballin, head of HAPAG's passenger service division. If you arrived last week, I would have had to put you with the other emigrants and you would have to wait during the normal quarantine. They are not as nice. Consolidated is taking care of you."

"Why would Ballin do this for us and others like us?" Vasyl asked McDonald.

"Ballin was an emigrant just like you. He is a Jew who came to Hamburg from Denmark with his father when he was just a boy. True, he didn't have a long journey, but he came to know the plight of people like you and the hundreds of thousands of Jews who are now leaving Russia, Rumania and Austro-Hungary."

"That may be true," said a chronically skeptical Mykhail to Vasyl and Stefan, "but I think it is also money."

Albert Ballin's father established a small, unprofitable travel agency at Hamburg's waterfront that specialized in helping mainly Jewish emigrants. However, he died young. Albert, at 17, was the only one of his seven children willing take over the business. He turned out to be a better businessman than his father. With a partner who owned two small vessels, they began shipping only passengers, emigrants, to America. In 1881, he transported 4,000 and the next year 11,000. In 1883, with two additional ships, he moved more than 18,000 people from Hamburg to New York. It made the officers of the much larger Hamburg-Amerika Line sit up and take notice. They viewed him as rising competition so they bought him out and made him one of their officers. In 1899 he did so well that he was made managing director of the line.

During this period, the hundreds of emigrants, who arrived almost daily at the Hamburg docks were victimized in every manner possible, even by unscrupulous company officials. Seeing how badly they were being treated Ballin started to build his Emigrant Village, a place where they could safely stay before boarding HAPAG ships. Their accommodations were ideal and word was quickly spread among Jews and other groups. This in turn persuaded many emigrants who might have sailed from Bremen, the larger port at one time, to choose Ballin's Hamburg. Located on the south side of the Elbe River in Veddel, the initial phase of the Village was completed in 1900. Food and accommodations were good and reasonably priced, almost subsidized, and the emigrants were protected from the strange, inhospitable outside world by guards and a high brick wall.

"All the barracks won't be completed for another year or two, but you are the first to try out the two that have been," McDonald said. "Ballin may be generous," McDonald started speaking again after a few minutes, "but he is also smart. More than half the passengers on his ships nowadays are emigrants. He hopes that those who travel on his line, and have a good experience, will tell their relatives who are still in Europe about how well they were treated on a HAPAG ship."

Ballin's Emigrant Village was rising almost on the docks on the tidal river's edge. He had planned it to be as far away as possible from the center of Hamburg, to remove it from those who would take advantage of his fares. In the near distance, hundreds of construction workers created a bustle of activity as the transfer wagon with the Rusnaks pulled to a stop at a large iron gate. A man, in what looked like a police uniform, with clipboard in hand, approached the driver. The gate controlled an opening in a 10-foot high red brick wall that was in the initial stages of construction. Dozens of masons and their helpers worked to extend the edges of the wall that would eventually surround the entire 15 acres of the village.

As the driver spoke to the guard, McDonald leaned toward Vasyl and whispered in his ear, "Looks a lot like a prison, doesn't it?"

"I don't know. I've never seen a prison."

Just inside the gate was a completed two-storey brick building and as they approached, a man before them, in a white smock, disappeared through a door in its front. Both levels seemed to have more windows than walls. Above the door, that obviously was the main entrance, was a sign in German and a large red cross. Only two of the barracks-like dormitories were completed but more were in various stages of construction. These, too, were made of red bricks, like the wall at the gate. Even foundations of more buildings were under construction beyond these. A high, chainlink fence, which started at the back of the two-storey building, ran between the two finished buildings and continued down the line, also separating the other buildings under construction. Beyond them was a completed part of the complex and another masonry building with a three-storey clock tower. No matter where you were in Ballin's Emigrant Village, you could always know the time.

Why the fence? Vasyl thought to himself, then quickly disposed of the thought. The area and the cacophony of sounds reminded him of an army of ants diligently working as horse-drawn wagons with bricks, sand and lumber moved through the complex. Men shouted as they loaded dirt, dug by hand from the foundations, onto wagons.

The driver pulled up to the entrance of the dormitory. As the men unloaded from the wagon, a woman, in a white smock and strange-looking hat emerged from the door. She, too, had a clipboard in her hand. The men had already come to realize that a clipboard was a sign of authority. She recognized McDonald and walked toward him.

Without acknowledging him, in an abrupt manner, she asked, "Do you have a manifest?"

He fumbled inside his jacket and pulled out a folded list. While he did, she quickly counted the Rusnaks.

"There is a discrepancy here," she addressed McDonald after looking over the list he had given her.

"There are 11 men here and your list names only ten."

For a moment, McDonald was puzzled, then a smile spread across his face.

"Don't count Yurko," he said, "he is not going to America, but back to Poland with me."

"You mean Galicia, in Austria, don't you?" she said.

"Whatever you call it nowadays," McDonald answered.

"Listen to me," she said as she turned and addressed the men.

"My name is Hilda Schwartz. "I am your hostess while you are here. If there are any problems, or if there is something you do not understand, contact me. My office is just inside the door in this, the medical building. I am here to help you.

"This afternoon you will be deloused and sanitized. As you enter the dormitory, you will see two doors. The one on the right is for men. There are no women in this group so don't concern yourself about the other door. Go through that door and you will see many hooks on the wall and benches. Take off all your clothes and hang them on the hooks, put your shoes and boots against the wall. Open your bags and lay everything open on the floor. If you have any food, throw it into the can marked Abfall (Garbage). You will be fed here and have no need for other foods.

"Then, go through the door on the opposite side of that room. It is marked *Sturzbad* (showers). Go in there and wash. There is plenty of soap and towels. Do not come back out this way but go through the door on the opposite side of the showers. There, a doctor is waiting to examine you. If you are modest, wrap yourself in a towel. When you are finished with the doctor, he will tell you which door to go through. In the next room you will find all your clothing and baggage. It will have been fumigated. Someone will be in that room to direct you to the lounge.

"Are there any questions?

"Good. Now go inside. Stay in one line."

"Men," said McDonald. "Yurko and I will be waiting for you in the lounge. Good luck!"

"Why did he wish us good luck," Stefan asked Mykhail.

"I was talking to Yurko as we rode here in the wagon," Mykhail said. "He said that we will be examined today, tomorrow and Tuesday," by nurses and doctors.

"That is kind of them to do that," Stefan answered.

"Kindness has nothing to do with it," Mykhail said. "They are looking out for their own interests. When we get to America, we will be examined again, very thoroughly, by American doctors. If we have diseases, they will not let us into the country but return us to Europe. The return cost is borne by the ship company. The Germans have found that it is cheaper to weed out the sick here and save the money it costs to send people back."

The most difficult part of the examination for the Rusnaks was the embarrassment of undressing before all the other men. Most had never before seen a nude male, other than maybe a younger brother. The doctor's initial examination was only cursory and all ten entered the room with their now-fumigated clothing and dressed. Mykhail checked his bag and found everything there.

"Is yours okay?" he asked Stefan and Vasyl.

"What would they have taken?" Vasyl said. "Even the few, worthless *groschen* were still in my boots."

"I'm glad to see that you all passed the first examination," McDonald said as the last of the men entered the lounge. You are in good hands now. Yurko and I will see you tomorrow afternoon. Is there anything you need?"

"Tobacco," said Danko.

"I'll talk to Hilda on the way out," he said and left.

An hour later, Hilda returned to the barracks with three small packages of pipe tobacco in her hands.

"Who asked for tobacco?" she asked.

Danko came forward and so did Vasyl.

"How much do we owe you?" Vasyl asked.

"McDonald paid for it," she said. "It was nothing. I hope it is the kind you like. It is the brand my father smokes."

Several new, stuffed chairs were on the far side of the lounge. Against the right wall were several more chairs with cane seats and backs, and more that were neatly arranged around three small card tables. On the tables were new packs of cards and sets of checkers. In one corner of the lounge was a small sink and next to it a table. On the table were a gas hotplate, a box of wooden matches, a large coffeepot and a smaller teapot, and two dozen white, heavy ceramic mugs. Alongside the pots were three tin cans marked KAFFEE, TEE, and ZUCKER (COFFEE, TEA and SUGAR). Next to the cans were a half-dozen spoons. Everything was new, unused.

As they milled around for the moment, looking through the numerous glass windows, the woman who spoke to them as they got off the wagon entered the lounge.

"There are things in here that many of you have probably never seen," she said. "I will show you how they work. We even have electric lights in these newer buildings. To make a light go on, just pull gently on the string. She did so as she spoke and a bare, clear light bulb on the lounge ceiling sprang to life.

She then walked over to the sink. A single spigot came off a large board painted white that was mounted on the wall behind the sink. Beneath it was a small enameled sink with a drain that disappeared into the floor. "Turn this round handle to the left, counter-clockwise," she said, "and you have water. To shut it off, turn it to the right. There are similar spigots in the toilet, in the other room.

"This is a gas stove. The gas burns when it is lighted. They are not dangerous if you light them correctly. First, you light the match," she did so as she spoke. "Then you hold it to the edge of the circle of holes on the stove. As you do, with your other hand, turn this valve slowly to the left, not right, and the gas will light." It did. "Turn the valve more to the left and the flame will get bigger. It will boil water faster than you have ever seen. When the water is finished, you turn off the gas, to the right. Do not turn it too tightly or you will strip the brass inside. But do turn it until it stops and maybe a little more pressure, then stop.

"If you want coffee or tea, you must make it yourself! There is a box of matches near the stove.

"Follow me," she said as she first entered the dormitory. "Here, in this little room," she spoke, "is the toilet. The flush water is in the tank near the ceiling. To make it flush, pull this chain." She did and water gushed down into the bowl. "Do not use too much paper to wipe yourself or you will block the toilet and you will have a mess in here."

She walked out the bathroom towards the beds, and heard someone flush the toilet. It labored.

"She turned around and addressed the men following her. "You must wait until the tank is again filled, when the water stops running, before you can flush it another time."

She turned and walked into the dormitory.

The room was 150 feet long and 25 feet wide. It was well lighted with double windows 5 feet apart, on both walls. The only door was the one through which they entered. Two rows of single, iron-framed beds ran down each side of the room. There were 50 beds in a row for a total of a hundred in the dormitory. Each bed had a small pillow, a mattress bag that encompassed the mattress, a sheet and a gray blanket. Eventually, these would be replaced by bunk beds that doubled the capacity of the dorm.

"This will be your home only for tonight." Then she added, "I hope. If you pass the doctor's examinations tomorrow, you will move to the other building," she said as she pointed, out a window, through the fence, toward the other completed dormitory. "It is exactly like this one. This is the 'Unclean Side.' That building, on the other side of the fence, is the 'Clean Side.' You will stay there until you embark on your ship. I understand that the *Patricia* is departing on Friday. Once you are over there, you must never cross back here or you will have to go through the delousing and fumigation again. Beyond that building is The Portal. It is through there that you will pass to get to America."

"Don't Rusnaks eat breakfast?" Hilda Schwartz yelled the following morning in a high voice as she stood in the doorway leading into the dormitory's sleeping section.

"Get up! It is 7 o'clock. I will be back in 15 minutes to gather you and take you to the mess hall. After you are done eating, we will return here and you will wait until the doctor calls for the examinations."

It was a simple meal. Oatmeal, boiled eggs, bread and jam and coffee or tea. The mess hall was a huge building, almost the size of a football field and only partially completed. They ate in a corner of the kitchen, behind huge sheets of hanging canvas. On the other side, workmen were noisily tending to their jobs. In less than a half-hour they finished breakfast. Schwartz gathered her wards and marched them the hundred yards from the mess hall back to their barracks. Before she left the kitchen, she grabbed a huge metal pitcher filled with steaming coffee and carried it to the barracks where she dropped it on the table in the corner of the lounge.

It wasn't until late in the morning that she returned and announced that the doctors were ready. "Get all your belongings and follow me. Do not leave anything behind because most of you will not be coming back here." She led them out the door and into the medical building, bypassing the showers, and into the examination room. There were two doctors sitting at separate desks, a nurse standing by a set of scales and a male clerk at another nearby desk.

"There are benches and hooks over there," she pointed as she spoke. "Take off all your clothes, except your underwear. Then form a single line behind this red line." Schwartz pointed to a red line painted on the hardwood floor near the middle of the room.

"If you do not have underwear, there are towels on the benches. The doctors will call you one at a time. When you are done, the clerk will tell you where to go. There are two doors in the back. Good luck!" That was the last they would ever see of Hilda Schwartz.

The clerk came over to the men as they undressed and began to line up. He asked them their names and checked them off on a list he had on the clipboard. The examinations were thorough. For the next three hours, the ten Rusnaks were probed and prodded in places even they didn't know existed on their bodies. The nurse drew blood from each man as they waited in line and added the individual samples to a bucket with ice. When she had blood from all ten men she covered the bucket and returned to a table near the back of the room. There, she pressed a buzzer on the wall and in a few minutes the door opened and a man, also in a white jacket, took the bucket, turned and disappeared behind the door.

When the first doctor had finished with a man, he sent him to the second doctor with a reflective mirror with a hole in its center, mounted on a strap on his forehead. He looked in their mouths, up their nostrils, in the ears and in their eyes. It was their eyes in which he seemed most interested. He rolled back their eyelids and examined every nook and cranny. When he was satisfied, the clerk checked off their names and then told them to go out *Tür 1* and get dressed.

Mytro Danko was the first man to go through *Tür 1*. It opened into a small waiting room filled with chairs. One by one the Rusnaks who had passed the examinations came through the door. Danko would mentally count them as they entered. Vasyl Najda was Number Nine.

"Who is not here?" they asked him.

"That fellow from Zatwarnyts, or was it Litowyschce?" he said. "Andrij Butchko. The second doctor was about to examine him when I left."

"It takes only 15 minutes to be examined by him," Danko said. "I am worried. No one has come through that door for more than an hour since Vasyl. There must be something wrong. Maybe he has the disease of the eyes. Yurko said that if someone had it, they would not be allowed in the United States."

"He was coughing a lot," someone said. "Maybe he has the Jewish disease."

"What is the Jewish Disease?" Stefan asked just as the door bolted open.

It was not Butchko but the clerk. He heard Stefan's question.

"It is tuberculosis," she said, "and you don't have to be Jewish to get it."

"Is he coming with us," Stefan asked.

"No!" answered the clerk.

"All of you, follow me," he said and led them out another door. It opened on the far side of the fence to the other completed dormitory. Inside the dormitory, a woman in a white smock, who had been sitting in the lounge reading a newspaper stood up quickly when she saw the men arrive and greeted them.

"I am Gerta, Gerta Rubinsky," she said. "I am Hilda Schwartz's counterpart on the Clean Side. You all have passed the first part of the medical examination. The blood tests will be completed by Thursday. If you are ok, you will be allowed on the ship. The Patricia is now in the river. It draws too much water to come to the dock so a ferry will be outside The Portal to take you to her. You will stay here tonight and tomorrow. Friday, after dinner, you will be allowed to board the lighter and then the ship. Until then, you will stay here, on this side of the fence. There is a canteen where you can get something to eat. I understand that Mr. McDonald will be here later to talk to you.

"There is a church in the older section of the Village, but it is still under construction. My office is just inside the front door, in the lounge. I stay here all night and will help you with any problems you might have."

"What will happen to Butchko?" Stefan asked.

"I'm not sure," she answered. "That will be up to McDonald."

It was late in the afternoon when McDonald arrived at the Clean Side dormitory.

"I'm sorry to hear about Butchko," he said as he entered the lounge. Men who had been lying on their beds heard McDonald arrive and gathered in the lounge to hear what he had to say.

"What will happen to him?" Vasyl asked.

"I wish we could have spotted his coughing at our first meeting," McDonald said, "It would have saved a lot of disappointment. He will have to go back to Zatwarnyts, unless he wants to stay here. But, there is nothing for him here and German workers in Hamburg do not want him. There already is a glut of unskilled workers here. There are too many emigrants now flooding Hamburg who have been rejected and more will be here for different reasons. It is best he return home. HAPAG and Consolidated will share the cost of his return train ticket. There is nothing more for us to do. I will see you off tomorrow instead of Friday because I must go back to Galicia. Consolidated still needs more miners. I will take Butchko back with me.

"You can eat at the canteen. Your food is paid for by the company. You don't have to go to the big mess hall in the Village where all the other immigrants eat. You are the only emigrants in the new section for the moment, so all you need to do is tell them you are with the Consolidated group. They are expecting you and will charge it to my account.

"On Friday, Gerta will take you to the main mess hall for dinner. That one is on HAPAG because you will be boarding too late to eat on the ship. After that, you will return here, gather all your belongings, and wait for her to take you to the lighter. If you look past the red building on the dock, you can see your ship. The *Patricia* came in yesterday and is anchored in the river. And, because there are so many immigrants on this trip, they will use a ferryboat instead of a lighter. There are many other passengers who will be joining you in steerage, or third class, as many as 1,000, so I suggest you always stay together.

"Yurko has an envelope with your name on it and he will give it to you in a few minutes. It contains your *Schiffkarte* and 25 new, one dollar United States bills. Your name should be on the ticket. Open the envelope to make sure the ticket is there and count the bills to make sure there are 25. At Ellis Island, before you are allowed to pass through immigration and off the island, you must show them proof that you are not dependent upon them. The $25 is that proof. If you loose it, they may not let you into the country.

"Once you clear immigration in America, and it will probably take most of the day, you will go outside. Try to stay together if at all possible. On the other side you will meet another Consolidated man. He will be carrying a big sign with CONSOLIDATED on it. He will get you to the train and to Johnstown, Pennsylvania. His name is William Johnson. Sounds almost like Johnstown, doesn't it? You can trust him.

"What you do with the $25 after you leave Ellis Island is up to you. It is your money. It is being loaned to you by the company.

It is a lot of money. It is more than what you would earn for a whole year of work in Sianok or Lisko. If you are wise, it will help you get started in a new life in America. It is your 'seed' money and your future. Don't loose it on the ship, in New York City, or in Pennsylvania. Good luck."

After they got back to the dorm, Stefan slowly approached Vasyl who was sitting on his bunk. He looked troubled and was fumbling around for words. He was about to speak to Vasyl when Mykhail, sitting on the bed next to Vasyl spoke first.

"What's wrong Little Brother? You look like something is bothering you. What is it?"

"I don't know how to say this. I am ashamed," Stefan said as he turned to Mykhail. "I cannot count. Will you count the dollars McDonald gave me to be sure the amount is correct?"

"It was the first time Vasyl had ever seen Mykhail speechless."

The silence was long and deafening; too long.

Suddenly, a grin crept across Vasyl's face. It turned broad and then he began to laugh. Not loud enough to attract the attention of others in their group but enough to make a frown spread across his friend's face.

"Stefan," Vasyl finally said. "Don't be embarrassed. Mykhail cannot count either. Here, give them to me, I will count them for you."

"They're all here," Vasyl said when he counted aloud to 25. "Don't be embarrassed," he said to them. "If it were not for the priest, when I was an altar boy, I, too, would be dumb like you two. One time, he sent me to get a dozen candles from a box in his house. When I returned with ten, he realized that I didn't know how to count. He then taught me."

They all chuckled after that.

There wasn't much reason for anyone in their villages to know how to count because few ever gathered enough coins to be aware of their value, or owned more than a few cows or sheep. Maybe chickens, but it was always their *Baba* who tended them.

"This is the first time in my life that I have spent an entire day doing nothing, absolutely nothing, other than getting up from this bed to take a piss," Mykhail said.

"Are you hungry?" asked Vasyl who was lying on the bed next to him, his arms behind his head and staring at the ceiling.

"A little," Mykhail answered. "Is it already time for supper?

"It is," interrupted Stefan. He was standing next to the window and looking toward the clock tower a thousand yards away. "I can already see large numbers of people going to the mess hall and a few returning.

"It could not have taken the Germans long to build those newer barracks," he said. "They are framed out with wood and then cemented in between. I wonder if they have forgotten how to make houses from logs."

"What logs?" asked Vasyl. "Don't you remember the countryside as we left Berlin. There were fields, plenty of fields. But there were no forests. Without forests, you must make your house from sand and stone."

"And their roofs are not thatch, like ours," added Mykhail as he lay in his bed. "They are metal and metal does not burn. It is a much safer house."

"Metal does rust," said Vasyl.

"Enough of this idle talk. Let's go to the canteen."

"What day is today?" asked Mykhail. He was the last one to return from breakfast and his shirt bulged. Then he began to unload slabs of bread he had taken from the kitchen along with two apples. He looked over at Vasyl who was again stretched out in his bunk. "I suggest you do the same. Who knows what they will feed us on the boat."

"It is our last day in Europe," answered Vasyl.

"Did Gerta say when we would know if we passed the blood tests?" asked Stefan.

No one answered.

A few men farther down the line of beds spoke among themselves. Sunlight from the windows on the south side of the barracks streamed through the immaculately clean glass and lighted the opposite side of the room. It caught the smoke from a pipe as one man, sitting on his bed, lighted the tobacco. The smoke curled into the air and slowly spun in a gradually rising circle. Highlighted by the sun, it looked like a genie rising from a magic lamp.

"The sun's angle is low," Vasyl thought to himself. He had never owned a watch. Very few men in Protisne or Smil'nyk owned one. The only clock he had ever seen was the one in his father's house when he was young. He often wondered what had happened to it. Working in the fields, he had learned to tell the time of day by the position of the sun. Now, in late October, the sun is always low to the horizon. "It must be mid-morning," he thought.

"I wonder why it takes so long," Stefan added.

"Be patient. They are examining them under a very strong glass," said Danko. "It is called a microscope. That is what the nurse told me when she took my blood."

"Stefan. Go to Gerta's room and ask her," said Mykhail.

"Her door is closed," Stefan said.

"Then knock on it!"

He did.

"There's no answer," he said as he spun around to return to his bed.

Just then the front door to the dormitory opened and a smiling, slightly rotund Gerta Rubinsky entered. Puffing slightly, she said in a loud voice "Good news. Good news. I have good and bad news for you. The good news is that you all passed. You all are healthy. But, you will not be going to America tomorrow. The boat has trouble with one of its engines and repairs must be made before she can sail. They are not sure how long it will take but there is a rumor that it will be at least a week. In the meantime, you will be HAPAG's guests. But you cannot leave the village or you will have to redo the medical examinations."

The nine Rusnaks had never known what life was like with nothing to do for an entire week. It was spent playing cards or checkers in the dorm or playing pool in the Village's recreation room. No one knew how to play pool. Just hitting the ball around soon became boring so most of their time was spent in the dorm.

It wasn't until seven in the evening on November 5th when Gerta appeared in the dormitory. "You can board the ship tonight," she announced. "She is ready to sail. I have come to get you and to take you to the main mess hall to eat your last supper ashore for a while.

"Most of the other emigrants have eaten by now so we won't have to wait long," she said. "Bring all your bags because we will not come back here. After you eat, you will go directly through The Portal and onto the ferry. Do not forget anything."

It was already dark when she returned to get them. There was still a line in front of the entrance to the large mess hall when they got there. There were men, women and children, babies crying, and old people who needed help to walk.

There isn't a man in line without a beard, Vasyl said to himself, and they are all so long and black. None of his Rusnaks wore beards. He listened as they chatted among themselves in a language that was roughly familiar, but not every word. They must be Jews from Russia, he thought.

"Follow me," Gerta said and headed for a small door to the left of the main entrance.

"I have a special group," she said to a man just inside the door. He nodded his head. He had been through this routine before. Gerta took them to the front of the food line. There were some rumblings from the people already in line but the guard stopped them from moving ahead and let the Rusnaks start at the food trays.

Gerta ate with the group and kept them together because her job was not yet over.

"We go now, yes?" she said and the men followed her across the yard from the mess hall to the building with the huge clock. There were only a few people in the line to get into the embarkation center so she queued behind them. In a few minutes she was inside and said something to one of the attendants.

Along one wall was a series of elevated desks arranged in one continuous row. Each desk had an electric lamp with a green shade and behind the desk was a clerk in a HAPAG uniform. In front of the desk was a corral with a single line of benches facing the clerk. A guard controlled the gate into the corral behind the benches. When a clerk called a passenger to step up to their desk, the guard opened the gate and allowed another person to take the just vacated seat. Less than 20 passengers waited in a line outside the gate to be let in.

Gerta went to the guard at the gate, with her Rusnaks in line behind her. She said something to the guard and he let her in. She had previously gathered each man's *Schiffkarte* and handed them, along with a paper with the names of the Rusnaks, to the head clerk who sat at an empty desk elevated a foot above the others. He adjusted his *nez perce* glasses, read the list at least twice and checked it against each ticket. Seeming satisfied, he then pulled out a logbook that had CONSOLIDATED written on its spine and began entering the names.

"You have one German going to work in the mines?" he asked Gerta as he looked up, over his glasses and scanned the row of Rusnaks waiting at the gate as if to see whom it might be.

"No," she answered. "I don't think so. That may be the way Gruber spells Slavic names."

"We must correct that. The Americans are very fussy. Wasyl Nider, please come forward."

Vasyl was shocked. What is wrong? he said to himself as he stood silently. Maybe I will be stopped from going to America.

Gerta motioned for him to come to the desk.

"How do you spell your name?" the clerk. At first, Vasyl didn't answer.

"Ihren name? Ihren name?" She said without response then remembered. *"Meno? Meno?"*

Vasyl understood meno and then pulled out the piece of paper on which his priest had written his name in Polish: Wasyl Najda. The clerk made the correction.

"Okay," he said and nodded toward the exit-gate guard who was watching the clerk's every move.

The guard opened the gate and Gerta motioned for her entourage to follow her. She led them outside the building and onto the dock.

"We must wait here for the boat to arrive," she said to the men. "It will take you to the *Patricia*. Here are your tickets." She called each man's name and one by one they approached her and reclaimed their ticket.

The wait was less than half-an-hour. In the darkness, they watched the well-lighted ferry pull along the dock and stop about 200 feet away. It wasn't a large vessel, no more than a hundred feet long but it had double decks and thus a large passenger capacity. There were barricades around the dock that were already restraining hundreds of people waiting to get on board. Several HAPAG uniformed guards strained to keep the crowds in check. One turned around and waved to Gerta.

"Let's go to *Amerika*," she said. "Gather all your bags and follow me."

Chapter 16   At Last, The Crossing

Gerta led them to the barricade. The guard recognized her HAPAG uniform and opened the gate. Then she and nine Rusnaks passed through the opening to several ticket agents at the foot of an enclosed gangway that opened onto the ferryboat. Each man presented his ticket and walked down the gangway to the lower deck.

"Stay together," she said as she followed the last man onto the boat. The crowd, seeing the first passengers being allowed to board the ferry, became more aggressive and pushed on the barricades. The guards, however, with unleashed nightsticks, kept them in check.

The ride to the *Patricia* took no more than 15 minutes. Gerta led her men off the ferry onto a floating platform that was tied alongside the ship. A cold northwest November wind blew up the river and the men shivered in their light clothing. The air was filled with the smell of salt, something the Rusnaks had never experienced. They were amazed at the size of the ship. It towered like a mountain cliff before them as they looked up at her. Metal stairs with a chain railing ran alongside the ship's steel hull from the ship's deck down to the float. It clanged loudly as the float rocked out of unison with the ship.

"Be careful," she cautioned her Rusnaks, "the steps are probably wet. Hold on tight to the railing, we don't want to lose you after coming all this way."

Still another agent at the top of the stairs checked each man's ticket and said welcome aboard to each one. On deck, they huddled around Gerta as she spoke to a man wearing a white jacket and dark trousers, who had greeted her as she stepped onboard the ship.

"This is Wilhelm Kruse," she said. "He will take you to your quarters. He is the steward in charge of your section. This is as far as I go. Good luck and *bon voyage.*"

She turned and waited until several emigrants on the stairs came onboard. The agent at the bottom of the stairs temporarily stopped the line when he saw Gerta waiting to go down.

"Auf Wiedersehen," she turned and said to the Rusnaks, then disappeared down the stairs.

"Follow me," Kruse said and quickly passed through an open hatch. They followed him down five flights of stairs to their steerage level.

The Rusnaks immediately sensed that Kruse was physically different from them and not of Slavic heritage. He was tall, easily six feet, maybe more. His body was lanky, but not ungainly as he moved. His skin was lightly colored, and his face was sharp-featured, with high cheekbones, a straight, somewhat generous nose that ended in a point. His lips were pale, almost bluish and his eyes were colored gray-blue. His eyebrows were so lightly colored that they seemed to exist only in bright light. His blond hair was cropped short in the Prussian military style, like the doctor who examined them on the train at the border. He was a true example of a Caucasian Gentile, the archetypal Nordic type. It was amazing that he didn't speak Indo-Iranian.

Whenever he stood to address someone, he was stiff, ramrod straight, as if standing at attention. Because of his height, he was able to look down on most people imparting a superior attitude. His dark blue trousers were meticulously pressed and his white jacket, that of a head steward, was immaculately white and starched. He was in his late 20s and somewhere in his life had been in the military.

However, despite the overpowering bearing, he exhibited a friendly, though reserved attitude toward the Rusnaks. He was not at all condescending. Nearly three-and-a-half years ago, he had come aboard the Patricia on her maiden voyage to New York as an ordinary steward. After 37 crossings, he had risen to the rank of head steward and had most of the C Level passengers under his aegis.

"This will be your home for the next two weeks," he said. "If you need fresh air, you are permitted on the third-class promenade. It is located on either of the forward or aft well decks. We just came down from the aft well deck. When we are underway, you will find that is the best place to be out of the wind. Unlike first and second class promenades, there are no deck chairs or games there because this space is used to handle cargo when the ship is in port. You can sit where you find space, on the winches or on the lee of the air funnels."

The Patricia was a modern vessel and equipped as well as possible for ships of her time. She was the state-of-the-art ship, a steel-hulled vessel with a vertical bow, typical of her era that easily split the water before her, and a stern that featured a large, overhanging fantail. A solid, uninterrupted line of portals, nearly a hundred from stem to stern, dotted her sides just below the gunwales and marked the exterior of A Level. In dimensions, she was very similar to several other A.G. Vulcan-built vessels in the German fleet. She was 560 feet long, 62 feet wide and sported one, massive funnel and four in-line, extremely tall, cargo-loading masts. She was driven by two screws and designed to run at a service speed of 14 knots.

In her superstructure above the A-Level deck, she had 162 first class and 184-second class accommodations. Below decks, she had 2,143 third class or steerage accommodations. The definition of "steerage" changed in the second half of the 19th century as ship companies came to realize that their real profits were in numbers and on the third level below the promenade. At first, third class passenger accommodations were confined below decks to the after section of the boat, close to the engines and the steering gear. It was noisy, hot and extremely uncomfortable. But on ships like the *Patricia,* though still relegated to the third deck or lower, steerage expanded over almost all of that level, from above the engine room to the bow.

She was built in Stettin-on-the-Oder, specifically for the Hamburg-American Line and was launched on the 20th of February 1899 as a 13,023 gross ton vessel. After outfitting, the Patricia made her maiden voyage to New York on May 7, 1899.

By the time the Rusnaks borded her, four years later, she was already a well-used vessel, a workhorse of the HAPAG fleet. She was employed exclusively in the Hamburg-New York-Hamburg run and had logged 37 round-trip crossings. By the end of her service as a passenger liner in 1913, she would have made the round trip 96 times, or about ten a year; two weeks heading west and slightly less heading east.

The S.S. Patricia, Hamburg-American Line, used by Vasyl Najda in Nov. 1903 to arrive in America.

"I have never seen so much metal in my life," Mykhail said to Vasyl, and then turned to the others who were claiming bunks. "The ceilings are iron, the floors are iron, the walls are iron and even the steps are iron. Our beds are made of iron. Are we to sleep on these shallow iron trays?"

They were the first to arrive so they had their pick of bunk locations. The double bunks were arranged in clusters and the Rusnaks took one group close to the foot of the ladder (stairs) and a trio of metal tables that looked like iron picnic tables. They were welded to the deck. Each had a raised rim around its edges so that dishes didn't slip off when the ship heeled and rocked in rough weather. The tables were set, ready for breakfast. Plates were made of tin as well as the cups and bowls that would hold food. A tin water bucket on each table had a lid and the end of a dipper protruded from a hole in one edge.

"There's a blanket on each bunk and two cloth bags, one big and one small," said Vasyl as he examined a lower bunk he'd chosen. It will be hard sleeping on these bags."

Just then, Kruse came skipping down the stairs and overheard his complaints. "The blankets are yours to keep, a reminder or souvenir of HAPAG. They are figured in your fare. The big cloth bag, called a *palliasses,* is your mattress and the small one your pillow. There is fresh straw in the bin, over there," he pointed as he spoke. "Stuff it with as much straw as you like. On the last morning before disembarking, you will discard all your straw, through portholes on A-Deck, into the ocean."

As he spoke he worked his way over to one bulkhead that had a bulletin board mounted in a steel frame. From under his arm he took a roll of stiff paper signs and separated one from the others. He used thumbtacks, loose in his left jacket pocket, and secured the sign to the center of the board.

"Here is where all the important information for you will be posted. If you do not understand German, ask a steward and he will translate it for you. This collection of tables is where you will eat. There are three food galleys in third class. There are food stewards who will bring the meals to you and women who will clean the tables when a meal is over. It is too late now for supper, but breakfast is served at 7:00 o'clock, lunch at noon and supper a 6:00. Six passengers are served at each table. There are nine of you, so you may have to share one of the three tables with some of the other passengers.

"Down the center of this ship are a series of toilets. There are separate toilets for men and women. The men's toilets are marked with an H on the door and the women with a D. This ship is equipped with electric lights. You needn't worry yourself about them. They are controlled by the steward. They go on at 6:30 in the morning and are shut off at 10:00 in the evening. Lights in the toilets are always on.

"Every day, between 11:00 and noon, you must vacate this area while it is being cleaned. You can go topside to the third-class promenade on the two well decks. You are not to be in areas reserved for first- and second-class passengers.

"The ship has four doctors for 2,143 people, when it is full, not counting infants in arms. On this trip, the ship is full. If someone feels ill, sick bay is on the promenade level. There are two sick bays, one on the port and the other on the starboard side. When the doctors are not there, there is always a nurse. Their sleeping quarters are in sickbay. The ship sails tomorrow morning at 7:00. Does anyone have a question?"

As Kruse was speaking, other third-class passengers began pouring down the ladders jabbering in an assortment of tongues that would have rivaled the Tower of Babel. Their arms were loaded with all the possessions they owned. Children began running amuck once they reached the deck and their mothers yelled at them but it did little good. Luckily, the Rusnaks had a corner of the deck almost to themselves. They took their cotton bags to the straw bin and filled them until they bulged. After but one night on them, they would be back again to add more to insure they were well separated from the steel crib upon which they slept.

"I have done nothing today but I still feel tired," said Stefan, who occupied the bunk above Vasyl.

"Then go to sleep," said Mykhail, from the bottom bunk next to Vasyl. "Sleep now as much as you can, because once we leave Hamburg you may not be able to."

"What do you mean?"

"I mean you might be seasick for the next two weeks."

"Is that possible?"

"Go to sleep," Vasyl said while lying on his back with his hands crossed under the back of his head. "Your cousin never told me you talked so much."

It was not easy sleeping that first night on the *Patricia* because passengers continued to pour down the stairways until well after midnight. They seemed an endless horde; a stream of flowing, gibbering humanity that was both excited and confused.

There was not enough space onboard for all those currently waiting in Emigrant Village for a ship to America. And it was not beyond the agents, who were amiable to being bribed, to move some people ahead on the list. Those from the Austro-Hungarian Empire, however, seemed to have less trouble retaining their position, but the plethora of Jews seemed always on the bottom. However, they, too, could be moved up because agents knew that Jews from Russia and Rumania had sold their belongings and had money with them. The Slavs, on the other hand, were usually penniless but they had a built-in priority because of HAPAG's arrangements with Austrian officials and American mining and steel companies.

Monday was an inauspicious day for the emigrants' last look at the "Old Country." Most would never see it again. Many didn't care. Soon after eating breakfast, Vasyl's entire group went topside and was on the starboard side of the aft well deck. They lined the bulkhead as dozens more people clambered over the winches and hatch covers to find a place to stand or sit. A cold, wet northwest wind blew up the Elbe River. Mixed with it were flakes of snow that melted as soon as they touched anything, even the canvas coverings over the huge doors on the cargo hatches. It furiously flapped the pennants that were slung on thin, wire lines from mast to mast. The pungent aroma of salt water mixed with the sulfur-laden smoke from dozens of factory stacks and steel mills that lined the north shore of the river swept over the *S.S. Patricia.*

The ship's engines had been running at idle to maintain the generators ever since the first passengers arrived on Friday. Now, one could sense that they were running slightly faster. Sporadically, a large balloon of smoke would rise rapidly from the ship's only smokestack. The brisk wind would knock it down onto the deck and momentarily engulf the steerage passengers, leaving them coughing and scurrying to get out of its grasp.

During the night, two harbor tugs had come alongside the *Patricia* and through a series of lines they securely held the ship in their grip. At 7:00 sharp the ship's steam whistle blasted the air and every passenger on deck immediately covered their ears with their hands. At the same time, windlasses both forward and astern began retrieving the huge chains and the anchors that held the ship in position in the river. As the anchors were pulled into their hawsepipes, hosed and shackled, the tugs began turning the *Patricia* downriver, to the west. The crossing had started.

From a wing on the bridge, the harbor pilot, through a megaphone, directed the tugboat captains. As the ship came about, the wind now riled Vasyl and the others. It blew Vasyl's *shapka* off his head. Someone in the crowd caught it and returned it to him.

"You must secure your hat better than that," Simon Smolensky said as he handed it to Vasyl.

An astonished Vasyl Najda turned to see who was speaking to him.

"You made it," said Vasyl. "I didn't know you would be on this ship.

"Neither did I. It took what little money I had. Otherwise, I would still be waiting in The Village.

"Where are your friends?"

"They didn't have enough for a bribe and are waiting for the next ship. Maybe even this ship when it again returns. Who knows?"

The Elbe is tidal for 40 miles from Hamburg to Brunsbüttle on the north shore. From here it gradually widens into a large bay for the next 20 miles to Cuxhaven. After a few miles, the tugs released their hold on the *Patricia* and she slowly made her own way down the river. The captain favored the south shore and a half-mile off Cuxhaven she slowed, then stopped. Nearby, waiting, was a small ferry that eventually came alongside the stairway that was still in position outside the ship's port side.

The crew from the ferry tossed monkeyfists to the crew of the *Patricia* and they hauled heavier lines to the big ship and fastened the ferry to its side. When the ladder's elevation was secured, 30 more passengers left the ferry and scurried up the metal stairs, slowed only by the numerous bundles and handbags they carried. When they were onboard, someone onboard blew the ship's whistle and the lines were cast free.

Vasyl didn't leave the promenade until the Cuxhaven lighthouse was just a speck astern on the horizon.

"Let's go below," said Mykhail, "it is freezing up here."

As they dropped lower into the ship, they could hear the discordant sounds of people's voices and powerful engine blended together. It increased in loudness the farther down they went into the bowels of the ship.

"How will we be able to sleep tonight?" asked Vasyl.

It seemed that all 2,143 people in steerage were talking all at once. It must have been nervous anxiety that caused them to do so.

The Rusnaks occupied a space on the third-level deck that ran the entire length of the ship. It was located about a third of the ship's length forward of the twin, massive screws. The top third of each huge, bronze screw was always above the water. As each of the four blades, in turn, slapped the water upon reentry, they added to the rhythm of the ship. Along with the screws, the massive pistons of the two engines set up a vibration that could be felt through the feet of anyone standing on the steel deck above them. The rhythmic back-and-forth rocking of the ship, for now, was almost pleasant.

Vasyl, Mykhail and Stefan returned to their bunks. By mid-morning they could sleep no more and returned topside. The weather seemed to improve as the day wore on but the winds were still hard from the northwest. When added to the ship's 14 knots it was impossible to keep a cap on one's head.

"One good thing about this wind," said Mykhail, "all this fresh air makes one sleepy. I've had enough. Maybe they are serving food."

Throughout the evening, they could occasionally see lights on shore from the port side of the ship. They were still skirting the Netherlands coast when the lights went out in steerage. Only the red safety night-lights remained on. They were always on. As the men lay there, they could hear the band still playing in the first class salon. It came down through the fresh-air system with its huge funnels on deck, located just below the ballroom. That, too, lulled them to sleep. The darkness, however, did little to stop the numerous babies and young children from crying.

Just as Vasyl thought he was falling asleep, the lights in steerage were turned on. It was 6:30 the next morning.

I'm glad I am in a lower bunk, he thought to himself and turned away from the glaring bulb in the ceiling so the light could not reach him. Just as he was about to doze off, Stefan stepped on his bunk, shaking him, then thudded on the deck with his bare feet. There were disadvantages to being on the bottom bunk.

Stefan pulled on his trousers and ran barefooted to the second level deck where there were portholes in the passageway.

"The shore is close," he said after returning. "I thought we were going out into the ocean. Where are we?"

Just then a steward, carrying a collection of tin dishes, bumped against one of the benches and dropped them onto the table. If there was anyone still asleep, they weren't any longer. He overheard Stefan's question.

"We are in the middle of the Straits of Dover," he said. "France is 10 miles away on the port side and England 10 miles away on the starboard. Take a look. This is the last land you will see until we arrive off Long Island, just before New York."

Everyone who heard him scrambled for the portholes. Those who were dressed rushed up the stairs to the well deck.

"It is much warmer than yesterday," commented Mykhail. Soon we will be entering the Gulf Stream," he said with an air of authority.

"What is the Gulf Stream?" queried Vasyl.

Mykhail went on to tell him what a well-traveled steward had told him. How, for the first few days, the warm river in the Atlantic Ocean would send them into an almost tropical climate. But, it wouldn't last long, a day at the most, and after they crossed it, the cold, November winds would again blow down on the ship.

They crossed the Gulf Stream on the third day out, but instead of getting colder, the air became warm and moist. As the lights were turned on at 6:30 Sunday morning, Kruse seemed to gain a special delight by going through the Rusnak's area saying *tserkva, tserkva* with a German accent.

"Is there really going to be church services today?" Stefan asked as they ate breakfast. Mykhail asked one of the women who just placed on the table a tin bowl filled with hardboiled eggs.

"If Herr Kruse said there will be church service today, there will be......if the weather permits," she said.

"What has the weather to do with it?" Mykhail asked.

"They are held outside, on the loading deck, after breakfast," she said.

After eating, all the Rusnaks worked their way onto the open deck and milled about the air funnels that were supposed to bring fresh air below decks, but it never quite seemed to reach the steerage level. They hung around for nearly an hour. The air was pleasant and the sun warm. For the moment, it was as good a place to be. Any place was better than steerage, even though the

Passengers boarding the S.S. Patricia from a lighter (tender).

Immigrants huddled on the foredeck of the S.S. Patricia.

housekeeping crew had done a good, though fast job of cleaning the mess. At times, the air in steerage was so dense you could see it. The memory of what it had been for the last three days was enough to make many decide to try to sleep on the hold covers that night.

All of a sudden a priest, in long, black robes, stepped through the hatch. His long beard was as black as any the Jews wore. Around his neck, on a heavy silver chain, hung a cross with two horizontal and one diagonal bar. It swung forward as he stepped across the bottom of the hatch and caught the sun's rays, sparkling and dancing in the air.

"*Bozé moi!*" Vasyl said as he blessed himself with two fingers and the thumb joined at a point, touching first his forehead, then right shoulder and then the middle of his chest before bringing down his right hand.

"He is one of us, a Russian Orthodox priest!"

The other men quickly glanced where Vasyl was looking and blessed themselves in the same manner.

"Where has he come from? Where has he been the last few days?" asked Mykhail as the priest approached them.

"Being a man of God gives me no special advantages at sea," he said. "I've been seasick almost from the moment the *Patricia* lifted her anchor. Is there anyone among you who has served? I need help." Stefan immediately volunteered.

Being sensitive to the religious mix of the hundred or so emigrants who had gathered on the well deck, he delivered a service that seemed almost a-religious, neither Greek nor Roman Catholic, or even Orthodox. Vasyl saw Simon Smolensky sitting on the far side of the well deck, on the outside ladder that led to the half-deck that ended in the stern. As the priest led into a short Slavonic liturgy, out of respect, Smolensky removed his cap and watched.

For the next two days, the winds continued out of the southeast. During those two nights, Vasyl and several others took their straw-filled mattresses and gray blankets topside and were able to sleep on the hatch covers. It was the sudden chill that awoke them early Wednesday morning, before sunrise, and sent them scurrying bellow to the warmth of steerage. They had passed out of the Gulf Stream. It was as if someone had opened a gate and let them through. The winds slowly veered from the southeast, to south, then west and settled in the northwest, bringing down cold winds from the Arctic. For the rest of the week, the winds, though cold, were light to moderate and the *S.S. Patricia* rode well into them with a minimum of pitching or rolling. Though her chines were not especially hard they were adequate in these seas to keep the boat riding comfortably.

On the following Sunday, there were church services again on the after hold deck, but this time, the ship's chaplain held Lutheran services. Many attended and filled the deck. Maybe the sea had suddenly made believers of those onboard with doubts.

It wasn't until Monday morning that some of the passengers noticed the wind begin to back and settle into the southeast. By mid-morning, the sun disappeared behind clouds that thickened, darkened and lowered. Most noticeable was the wind that rose steadily in intensity the farther west they traveled. The *Patricia* responded and instead of the gently side-to-side rolling its swinging grew greater and greater. All at the same time she began to pitch forward and back and roll.

At times, the lip along the rim of the table wasn't high enough and the tin dishes cascaded onto the floor. The number of people sitting for lunch was sharply reduced and by late afternoon lines began to form outside the toilets.

A steward came around with a collection of buckets in his arms and began depositing them sporadically on the deck next to each table as he worked his way forward through steerage.

"For emergencies," he said as he dropped each bucket.

Fortunately, the thin, blue haze that seemed to dominate the ceiling in steerage for the past 11 days became a bit lighter. The number of pipes, even among the Rusnaks, were no longer being pulled out. Still, a few men among the Russian Jews next to the Rusnaks, insisted on smoking their cigars.

"What's the matter with you?" Mykhail yelled at Stefan. Stefan had slowed his eating as the others ate, slurping chicken noodle soup and chewing vigorously on the pieces of dark rye bread torn off a large loaf. Mykhail knew perfectly well what was wrong with Stefan who suddenly doubled up, clenching his stomach in writhing pain.

"Vasylij, the pail is closer to you," said Mykhail. "I think you better hand it to Stefan before something happens."

Nor did Vasyl, sitting opposite Mykhail, look too well. He was spooning the soup and trying to get down a piece of bread. After a moment or two of hesitation, he rose from the table. He leaped at the bucket, vomiting into it just in time.

A few minutes later, Vasyl was running up the stairs. Stefan was immediately behind him and Mykhail laughed at them as he followed to see what they would do. When they got to the top they found the hatch closed and Wilhelm Kruse, arms folded over his chest, looking out an open porthole just to the side of the hatch. When he heard the Rusnaks clamber up the stairs he turned.

"Where do you think you are going?" he asked

"I need fresh air," said Vasyl.

"I do, too," echoed Stefan.

"Find a porthole somewhere and stick you heads outside," he said sneeringly. "The captain doesn't want any passengers on the well deck. It is blowing too hard. Sparks just got a telegraph message from the *S.S. Pompeii. There is a late-season hurricane in the North Atlantic.*

"What is hurricane?" asked Vasyl.

In a tortuous manner that seemed to elicit delight, the tall, blond, crew-cut German explained it to the trio. He had been through several in the 10 years he had been in the shipping service, and ended it with.... "I'm still here."

"The winds are reaching gale force," he continued. "If we go towards its center, they will rise to more than 75 miles per hour; sometimes over a hundred miles. Can you comprehend what 75 miles per hour is?

"I didn't think so," he said answering his own question.

That evening, the *Patricia* met the hurricane. Fortunately, she was already north and west of its center. In its center, winds were churning the North Atlantic at 95 miles per hour. It was a Category 1 hurricane verging on rising to the next level of intensity. The *Patricia* caught its northwest edge and experienced only 77-mph winds which waned the father west she traveled. By noon on Tuesday, they had dropped to 50 mph and continued falling. In 1903, hurricanes were not awarded names. This one was simply identified as No. 8.

The S.S. Patricia, had been traveling at 14 knots both day and night, and was scheduled to arrive in New York on November 19th, possibly the 18th if she had good weather. She had 4,319 miles to cross. But for two days she bucked such fierce winds that her 14-knot speed was not even enough to maintain forward progress. On Wednesday, Nov. 18, the rain unexpectedly stopped at daybreak, the wind subsided, and the ship was again riding on an even keel.

Meals the day before were suspended because the galleys couldn't cook. If you could make it to the galley window, you could get bread and crackers and apple juice. The women and men in the housekeeping crew were almost as sick as were the passengers. It was dangerous to walk the decks in steerage without constantly holding onto bunks or tables because the deck was well lubricated with vomit. There was also a strong fecal aroma in the air because the troughs into which men and women defecated had backed up more than once in the last two days and there was no one able to clean them. Women with babies dared not attempt to make it to the toilets and accumulations of soiled rags were piled in convenient corners. And, they raunched.

The ordeal was magnified by the wailing of many Russian Jewish women in the row of bunks next to the Rusnaks. Every time the ship heaved and rolled they thought they were going to die, that the ship was about to sink. Almost in unison, like a chorus, they began crying and wailing, pleading to God. It caused their children to cry even louder and cling to their mothers. Everyone was vomiting, even babies on a teat.

The smells were becoming unbearable. The mixture of garlic and tobacco was bad enough but now the odors of disinfectants the maintenance women used seem to exacerbate the smells of everything that clung in the air in steerage. It burned the nostrils and made eyes water. The odor of discarded orange peels and overflowing toilets penetrated one's clothing, and worst of all, one's pillow and mattress. There seemed no escaping it.

"I can't stand it," Vasyl said. He rolled out of his bunk clutching his stomach, and managed to put on his shoes. "I'm going up. I don't care if Kruse is there with his stick."

When he got topside the hatch was unguarded. In fact, it was secured open in hopes that the foul air below decks would rise and escape outside. Moments later, Mykhail came out the hatch followed by Stefan. All the other Rusnaks were behind him and they lined the gunwale staring at the water that streaked past the hull in a steady, unbroken stream. Most stayed on top throughout the day. Only one or two dropped down looking for lunch, but there wasn't any.

"They said there would be only one meal today," said Yurko, "later on, but before supper would normally be served."

"I don't care," said Stefan. "I'll never eat again," he said clenching his stomach.

The air was cool, but not cold. Most of the men had returned to their bunks and came back with their gray blankets with the initials HAPAG on them.

Stefan did eat again, and so did the others. The next day was Thursday and in the morning Kruse posted a note on the billboard stating that the evening meal would be special, German delicacies and ice cream would be on the menu. None of the Rusnaks could imagine what ice cream could be.

The last day of the voyage was uneventful, except for the constant shuddering of the deck above the engines and above the big bronze screws at the transom that where turning at higher than service-speed RPMs. The captain had lost two days because of the hurricane. Even more important, but not spoken, was his reputation, and that of the service that HAPAG delivers, to always adhere to a printed schedule. Besides, he may have thought to himself, the price of coal is much cheaper in New Jersey than in Germany. The company could afford to burn a little more to live up to its image.

Chapter 17   The Arrival

"Vasyl, how long will you stand here looking at the statue? Kruse has given the order to empty the straw from our mattresses before the health inspectors come on board. That must be their boat now. Hurry!"

When they returned below with their empty sacks, Kruse was waiting for them. He stood against one of the tables near their bunks, holding a clipboard and pencil in one hand. From a box on the table he took a bunch of stiff pieces of white cardboard, roughly 3-inches square, that had a large number on it. Punched through a hole, fortified by a simple brass grommet, in the top corner was a large safety pin. He laid nine pieces, that had been numbered by a machine, from 17 to 25, on the table. In smaller type, above each number on each cardboard, was printed "List 30."

"When I call your name and number," he said, "take the number assigned you."

Vasyl's name was the last one called.

"Wasil Najda, List 30, Number 25.

"Men, take these and pin them on the left side of your outer garments."

Farther aft in steerage, other stewards were doing the same for their wards. Just then, there was a loud bang against the ship's outer bulkhead near where Kruse was standing.

"That is nothing," he said. "We are not sinking. That is the inspector's boat from the Health Inspection Station on Staten Island coming alongside. They will be down here after going through first and second class compartments. It won't take long. They will be here soon so stay in steerage. Do not go topside. In the meantime, gather all your belongings. Don't forget to take your HAPAG blankets, you paid for them," he again reminded them.

As he spoke two of the ship's crew were behind him assembling a pair of tripods capped with large reflectors with light bulbs. Farther aft in steerage, other crews were doing the same.

"I wonder what that is for?" Mykhail asked Vasyl.

"It is for the American inspectors to get a better look at you," Kruse answered.

Nearly an hour passed before they heard footsteps on the stairs coming their way. Three uniformed men appeared on the ladder. One is carrying a clipboard. If Kruse hadn't told them who they were, the Rusnaks would have taken them for military men. They wore Prussian blue colored military-style waistcoats clinched at the waist by broad belts and with collars that buttoned together under their chins. They had rank insignias on their shoulders. Their trousers were sharply pressed and their black shoes shone as if they were about to stand inspection. Only the red cross on the side of one man's shoulder hinted that health and not war was his venue. The other two were immigration inspectors and one had the ship's manifest on his clipboard.

"That's the longest it has taken us to check first and second class," said one. "This ship is really packed."

Behind them came several other trios of inspectors who would work their way in either direction in steerage.

When the two crewmen saw the approaching inspectors, they turned on the lights and Kruse told the passengers to line up according to their numbers.

"When you have passed, you will be given a Medical Inspection Card," the man carrying the clipboard said to the passenger. He appeared to be the leader of the trio. "Make sure you don't loose it. They will ask you for it on Ellis Island. Then, go topside and wait. Make sure you take all of your belongings.

"This is going to take a while," he said as he leaned over to one of the other inspectors. "There's more than two thousand on this manifest. We have Lists 26 to 30. Let's get started."

The man with the clipboard asked each person their name while the other two quickly looked over the individual. At best, it was only a cursory examination and unless you had something very visually apparent about yourself, you easily passed between the lights. It was probably more a corroboration of the manifest name and the data on it and connecting it with a live individual than a serious medical inspection. The inspectors felt no compunction to be more thorough because they knew that HAPAG doctors had examined all these people at least twice. HAPAG didn't want to incur the expense of taking them back home if the U.S. wouldn't let them land. All the Rusnaks passed but they saw another trio of inspectors add the names of several Russian Jews to a notebook.

"What is that they are doing?" Vasyl asked Kruse.

Kruse watched the other group for a few moments and saw, after an inspection, a notebook come out of the inspector's oversized blouse pocket and write something. "They will be detained for some reason and will go into a different line than you once you get to Ellis Island. Most will eventually get through, but some will make the trip back to Hamburg with me."

On deck, Vasyl and his eight countrymen formed a tightly knit group against an air funnel. His attention was caught by a noise above his head. He looked up at the forward mast and saw a large, yellow flag snapping violently in the brisk November wind. He looked ahead and saw another large passenger vessel at anchor. It, too, showed the yellow quarantine flag. He glanced astern, along the side of the *Patricia,* and behind her he saw two more ships. It would be a busy day at Ellis Island.

By noon, there wasn't a foot of empty space on the fordeck of the ship. Emigrants now turned immigrants were covering every space possible. The inspectors came out the hatch from below and forced their way to the ladder on the side of the ship that led down to their vessel. Almost immediately, the small boat blew a whistle as it pulled away. At the same instant, someone began lowering the yellow flag.

It was a signal for one of several government ferryboats to slip its lines on Ellis Island and head for the *S.S. Patricia.* Few of the emigrants noticed the move until the vessels were approaching the *Patricia.* What caught Vasyl's attention was the three-colored flag on the ferry's transom. It was the first time he had ever seen the Stars and Stripes. Behind it, a second ferry was also approaching the *Patricia.*

The ride to Ellis Island took no more than 15 minutes and Vasyl was impressed by the great number of boats, steam and sail, that were trading back and forth across the harbor. New York was a very busy place. He could even see Battery Park and the numerous tall buildings at the foot of Manhattan. He was about to say something to Mykhail when a commotion arose on the port side of the boat and everyone rushed to see what it was.

They were passing so close to the Statue of Liberty that they had to look up to see her torch. "It never misses," said the man at the helm in the ferry's wheelhouse. "It seems all those foreigners know about the statue."

"Don't cut it too close," said the skipper standing next to him with his arms crossed behind, "or we'll both be doing duty somewhere else. I know. It's worth it."

He smiled and reached for the horn's lanyard and pulled it, producing two sustained blasts followed by one short blast. He was telling the captain of the boat ahead of his that he was overtaking him on that captain's starboard side.

Vasyl suddenly noticed the huge size of the American flag that flew next to the statue. It was impressive.

The ferry had barely stopped its forward motion against the dock on Ellis Island when gangways started going over the side and deck hands began securing lines both fore and aft. It was easy to see that this procedure had been well-practiced innumerable times.

On the dock, men in uniforms with megaphones began directing people leaving the ferry. "Women to the left, this way," they yelled. "Men to the right, this way, no this way. Leave your luggage here. Leave it here."

Those with hand luggage were allowed to carry them into the building. Few immigrants understood what they were saying and other uniformed personnel physically guided them in the right direction. Those who still carried their suitcases where stopped and made to return to the mounting pile of bags. It was easy to understand why some were reluctant to give them up. They contained all their memories. But, they did.

"Stay together," Mykhail said as he turned around to the Rusnaks following him. They entered through three large arches with doors open. Ahead, on the second level, lay a set of wide, marble stairs that led to the Great Hall, and their first inspection. Up the middle of the stairs was a railing that separated women on the left and men on the right. At the bottom of the stairs, and at intervals along its edges, stood more uniformed men whose duty was to hurry the immigrants up the stairs, to almost make them run. At the top of the stairs stood four doctors, with chalk in their hands, and several aides who critically watched every immigrant. Each arrival was allowed four to five seconds of visual inspection.

The third man ahead of Mykhail was an elderly German. He moved quickly enough up the stairs but with a slight limp. When he reached the top, a doctor pulled him out and marked an "L" on the lapel of his coat. One of the aides shunted him into a large, caged enclosure.

There was method to this seemingly American madness. Taking the stairs at faster than normal speeds would immediately disclose some problems. If you limped, you got a L, if you were out of breathe, you got an H for heart or P for physical and lungs. If you had a swelling around your neck, you got a G for goiter. On the other side, women who were pregnant got PG. In the caged area the alphabetized immigrants were given more profound inspections.

All the Rusnaks passed and were held in a small group by an attendant who counted them. While waiting, Vasyl overheard the German who had been shunted to the cage telling the doctor *Krieg, Krieg,* and pulled up his trouser to reveal a scar from a war wound. The doctor erased the L on the German's coat. When there were 30 in Vasyl's group, the attendant motioned them to follow and he led them to benches in enclosures petitioned off by white-painted, waist-high pipes.

"Wait here until you are called."

The second test came after the men were told to form a single line. An interpreter asked Mykhail, who now was at the head of the line, a few questions. Language was a problem but the role of the interpreter was to further define the immigrants' state of health. He did this by asking each person questions and analyzing the responses and reactions. Can he hear? Is he alert? Does he respond readily? Does he appear dull-witted? Has he coughed during this interview?

Satisfied, he directs Mykhail to the right, to the next piped-off cubical and then turns and begins asking Stefan the same questions.

Vasyl is guided to a second doctor who specializes in contagious diseases. Opposite of the enclosure is another sectioned-off part with a curtain enclosure and physicians and nurses behind it and a guard at the entrance. When they were ready for another immigrant, the guard motioned Vasyl to move in.

Vasyl is ordered to drop his trousers. The doctor is looking for venereal diseases, skin diseases, parasitic infections and anything else he might happen onto.

Behind him is still another doctor, the most feared of all.

Vasyl approaches him and stops at a white line on the floor, as did the man before him. The doctor looks directly into his eyes as if he were trying to see into his head. Suddenly he puts his hand to Vasyl's forehead, abruptly pushes it back. With the other hand, he catches his right eyelid with the thumb and forefinger and rolls it backward to look under the eyelid. Then he pulls the lower lid down and out and examines it for a few seconds. He repeats the procedure with Vasyl's left eye. The doctor is looking for signs of trachoma, a chronic inflammation of the eye caused by a bacteria-like microorganism.

If someone is discovered with the disease they are held over at the island's hospital and treated. If they don't recover, they are returned to where they came. The next year, U.S. policy changed and these with infections were immediately returned without treatment.

"Okay," says the doctor. "Move on."

Behind the doctor is a nurse waiting with a basin of disinfectant and towels for the doctor. When Vasyl is finished, she asks him for his medical inspection card. Seeing that he doesn't understand her, she holds up a sample. It was the one the inspectors gave him on the *Patricia*. He digs into his pocket and gives it to her. She hands it to the doctor who is about to check another patient, turns, and then initials it. Vasyl returns it to his pocket. The nurse points him to the exit.

Vasyl is directed to a sectioned-off area with more enclosed benches. Most of the Great Hall is filled with similar enclosures. The noise from their babble fills the Great Hall, whose vaulted ceiling must be three stories tall. Stefan and then Mykhail join Vasyl and eventually his entire group.

"My eyes hurt," complains Stefan. "That doctor was rough. He would make a better butcher."

Vasyl is on the outside seat. A guard points to him and then to another section where a man is sitting behind a high desk with a guard in front. When he is ready for the next immigrant, he signals the guard and the guard picks the next person on a bench.

"Do you speak English?" the man at the desk asked Vasyl.

196

Vasyl looked at him with a puzzled expression.
"Where are you from? Your country?"
"Do you have a passport?"
"*Owstria*," Vasyl finally answered.

"I think this one's for you," the interrogator said and turned behind him to one of a dozen men at as many desks, in as many petitioned-off lines.

"Number 7," he said to Vasyl. "Go to Stall 7." Then he picked one of several cards on his desk, one with a large 7 printed on it and held it up to Vasyl, pointed to the 7 on the card and then the line with a "7" on its arch.

"What is your name," the nationality interpreter asked in Polish.

"I am not Polish," Vasyl answered. "I am Rusnak."
"My name is Vasyl Yurkovych Najda."
To Vasyl's surprise, he responded *po nashomu* to him.
"What do you do for a living?
"I am a farmer and a carpenter."
What is the name of the village where you were born?
"Protisne."
"Are you married?
"No.
"Do you have children?
"I told you I wasn't married.
"That isn't necessary.
"Have you any money? Let me see how much.
"Where are you going?"
"Pine Hill, Johnstown, Pennsylvania.
"Do you have a job there?
"I have a cousin who said there are many jobs in the mines."

"Have you ever been in prison?
"Can you read or write?
"Where is your Medical Inspection Card? Give it to me."

The interpreter pulled out another card, filled in Vasyl's name, signed it and then handed it back to Vasyl.

"This is your Entry Permit Card. Hold on to it. Don't loose it. It is your proof that you entered this country legally.
"Welcome to America!"

Vasyl waited outside the stall for Stefan, Mykhail and all the other Rusnaks. A half-hour later they were all together again.

"What's next?" asked Stefan. "Look. Over there. There are some of our bags. It took another half-hour to find them all.

"Now where?" asked someone.

A guard, sensing their confusion, came over and asked them where they were going. At the end of the hall were two exit doors that led to the railway halls, and between them was a set of stairs leading down. Above the left door was a large sign that said WEST. Above the right door, the sign read NEW ENGLAND. The stairs led down to the ferries that went to Manhattan or New Jersey.

"Johnstown." said Stefan.

"Johnstown, New York or Johnstown, Pennsylvania?"

"Yes. Yes. Johnstown, Pennsylvania."

"Go to the left, to WEST."

"Let us see if the Consolidated people in America are more dependable than those in Europe," a pessimistic Mykhail said as he led the Rusnaks through the left railway hall.

There were long queues formed in front of a dozen windows and immigrants filled the hall. Benches lined the sides of the large room and rows of benches were in the middle. Most of the benches were occupied or used to store luggage.

They walked around the perimeter of the room looking for someone or something that would say CONSOLIDATED.

"I found him," said Mykhail. "He is sleeping on the bench. See the sign he is sleeping against. It is CONSOLIDATED."

They gathered around him while he snoozed.

"We cannot wait until he wakes up," said Vasyl.

Stefan gently pushed on the man's shoulder while saying Johnstown, Johnstown."

The man jumped to a sitting position, rubbed his eyes and looked around. He knew what immigrant Rusnaks just off the boat looked like.

"I'm your man," he said, then looked up at the clock.

"I already have your train tickets.

"If we hurry you can catch the 9 o'clock to Pittsburgh.

"Follow me."

*Goodtown and surrounding mining communities
in Somerset County, southwestern Pennsylvania
circa 1910.*

Chapter 18   American Trains

No sooner had they found seats than the train began to move. Fatigued from the day's ordeal, the Rusnaks were immediately caught up in the train's monotonous rocking back and forth and sleep began to overtake a few of them. Steam hissed and spurted from leaky heater vents, through which pipes passed on the floor, and rose under the windows. The car's occupants had no control over the heat and it became unbearably warm.

"This morning," Stefan said to Mykhail and Vasyl, "as we were on the ship, I never would have believed that, on the same day, we would really be on our way to Johnstown."

Mykhail's head already bobbed back and forth, responding to the train's movements. He was on the verge of falling asleep. Without opening his eyes, he grabbed the jacket on his lap, rolled it into a pillow and lodged it against Vasyl's shoulder.

"My eye is still sore from that doctor," Mykhail said, still with his eyes closed. "He looked so long that I thought he was going to reject me. I was really worried as he kept looking and looking. For that instant, my future life hung in the balance. It was there, at that moment, that I could have gone back to Galicia or on to Johnstown. Honestly, I was frightened. Never before have I been at such a crossroads in my life. I felt helpless. There was nothing I could do about it. I don't know what I would have done if I was turned down."

"I, too, was upset when they pulled that Jewish woman out of line," said Vasyl. "Her children and husband had been passed but she wasn't. Can you imagine what it must be like for them to go on and she to be sent back. I cannot.

"What really worried me was the last inspector who wanted to know if I already had a job promised me. Remember Yurko, McDonald's translator? He told us that they had recently passed a law here against bringing in contract workers. In reality, that is what we are. They advanced us money to get here but we signed a paper agreeing to pay it back. That is a contract. Isn't it? Yurko told me to say that I was looking for a job, that I knew I could find one."

"Was that really worth worrying about?" Mykhail said. He had not really fallen asleep. "Do you think that last man would have sent you back? He was a Rusnak like us, though his dialect was a bit different. I think he was a Hutsul. Still, that's close enough. Go to sleep."

"Trains are faster in America," said Stefan, "and wider and longer."

The sun was just rising and its intense light, like an explosion, suddenly filled the railroad car as the train came out of a pass between two mountains.

"Don't you know? Haven't you heard," said Vasyl as he stood up and stretched his arms and legs, "that everything in America is bigger and better?"

"However, the trains also are dirtier."

Every time it made a turn, soot from the engine's billowing stack seemed to come through the cracks in the door and windows. The window next to Mykhail was a constant source of irritation. It rattled and would not close completely. He tried stuffing his train ticket into the crack. It helped for a while last night. But it had fallen out and the rattling wakened him at sunrise. He stood up to shake off some of the soot.

"They are also not made as well," Mykhail said, "especially as well as German trains."

"That's because everything here seems to be done in a hurry," said Vasyl.

"I'm hungry," said Stefan. "There is a place to get food, one or two cars ahead of ours. I see people coming back with coffee."

The dining car, three cars ahead of them, had a sandwich bar just inside the door. Behind the bar was a sign that read: "Rolls, 1¢, Pies 10¢. Half-Pie 5¢. Coffee 5¢ per cup. Milk, per pint 5¢, sandwich, ham or corned beef, each 7¢. Sausage and bread, each 13¢, 2 for

25¢. Soda water, ginger ale, or sarsaparilla, each, small 7¢. Smoking tobacco 10¢, cigars, each 5 and 10¢."

"Sir, what will you have," said a black waiter who returned to a position behind the counter after he cleared a table in the dining section.

The men looked at him then at each other in amazement. They had never seen a black person.

"Can't read English? Huh? I understand."

He read the list of items and their cost to them.

"How much is dollar?" asked Mykhail.

"New here, huh? On the way to the mills in Pittsburgh?" Then he noticed the note on Stefan's lapel.

"Oh! Coal miners.

"The money here is easy to understand.

"A dollar is worth a hundred pennies. A dollar can be either a paper bill or a coin like this," and he laid one on the counter to see. "Instead of counting out pennies, there is a half-dollar coin, like this." He added it to the counter. "Or, if something costs 25 cents you don't have to count out 25 pennies but instead you use a quarter-dollar, or, we just call it a quarter, or two bits. Let's not get into the bits part. Here is a dime or 10-cent piece. It is worth ten pennies. Next to the last, is a nickel. It gets its name because it is made of nickel. It is worth five cents. Then, there is the one-cent piece or penny.

"Now, what do you want. But first, do you have American money?"

"We have dollars," answered Vasyl.

"I want eggs but you do not have eggs on your list."

"You must sit at the table to get eggs," said the waiter.

They studied the menu as if they could read it.

"Give me two rolls, one coffee and pipe tobacco."

"That's 17 cents," said the waiter.

"Here is dollar," Vasyl said.

The waiter, imitating Vasyl's style of speaking, echoed him "Here is change." He then counted out the money on the counter then said, "Next."

They were uncertain about how to order food from a menu at the tables so they skipped lunch. The had heard stories of immigrants being cheated out of their money and they didn't trust the black man. Instead, they watched the Pennsylvania countryside slip past at 40 miles an hour.

"This land looks just like back home in Halych," said Stefan, "Same kind of hills. Same cold, winter look. We should feel at home here. Maybe not as much snow. But it's November. Maybe later in year."

"I think our home will be inside a black hole," responded Danko. "I don't think we will see much sun. What hours did McDonald say we work?"

"Nine, ten hours," answered Mykhail. "From six to five. We will never see the sun until late spring."

As the conductor passed by Stefan asked him the time.

"It is 3 o'clock."

"Three o'clock. Why are we not in Johnstown?"

"Remember? We got delayed early this morning and had to stop to take a cow off the front of the train.

"You should be there in 10 minutes. Get all your bags together."

The nine would-be miners left the train in Johnstown. New platforms were under construction causing the train to stop short of the station. The men got off the tracks and crossed onto the siding when they saw a man running toward them.

Out of breath, he asked, "Are you the guys looking for the Consolidated Mines in Pine Hill?

"Good. I am Patrick Kelly from the mines. Follow me. I got a telegram from New Jersey saying that you guys had arrived. I'm glad you made the 9 o'clock train. The wagon is on the side road."

It was an open wagon with a bench seat on each side facing inward and cribs across the seat backs to keep anyone from falling out. Two large, black horses pulled it.

"There's no cover on the wagon and it's getting cold," said the man from Consolidated. "I hope you have some heavier jackets or blankets. You're going to need them because we won't get to Pine Hill until well after dark. It's 30 miles away."

After taking a seat, each man dug into his duffel and pulled out a heavy, gray blanket with the letters HAPAG on it. The sun was already low on the horizon and would set in an hour. Before it did, clouds moved in from the west and obliterated its rays. It didn't matter; the sun's heat was only psychological in late November. At dusk, a light snow began falling and slowly got heavier as they traveled into the night. They stopped in Central City, about half way, and the driver found a diner that was still open.

"What is a diner?" the ever-curious Stefan asked.

It was near midnight when they arrived in Berlin.

"We are almost there. It's just down in the valley, two miles away at the most," said the driver.

In the darkness, they approached the mining community that was being constructed at Glen Norris, just below the crossroads village of Pine Hill. They could hear heavy engines running and other loud noises. For the moment, they had no idea what noises a working mine makes at night or during the day.

"Tonight, you will stay at the company's 'hotel'," said Kelly. "If you like it, it is $5 a month, meals included. That's about a week's pay. If you have friends or any relatives here, maybe you can stay with them. There are several married men and their wives maintain a boarding house. They cost between $3.50 and $4.00 a week. But they are cramped and you may have to share a room with four or five men. And, everyone snores.

Chapter 19   The Next Morning

"Stavai! Stavai Vasylko. "Will you sleep all day?"

"Stavai mi druh, mushish do roboty eteh."

"I have no work to go to, so why must I get up," Vasyl said as he began to sit up in bed. Then he saw him and they hugged furiously and kissed each other on the cheeks.

"My God, Paul, I hardly recognized you!" exclaimed Vasyl. "You have a beard and a moustache, one almost as long as our priest's."

"Why didn't you write me to tell me you were coming?" Paul Turko asked. "How is my father, and my mother?"

"You know I cannot write," answered Vasyl. "But I had the priest write you. I guess you didn't get my letter...did you?"

"No. But, I thought that maybe you learned something in the last year. How old are you now Vasylko? Twenty-three. Are you married? How is everything in the Old Country, in Protisne?"

"Why haven't you written?" Vasyl asked.

"My God, Vasylij, I work all the time. By Sunday I am so tired I cannot move. When would I have time to write, even if I knew how?"

"Don't you have a priest here who you can ask?" said Vasyl.

"We have no priest here. There aren't that many of us here. The mines are just opening. There are about 10 Rusnaks here. The rest, about 30, are Americans or Hungarians. When I came here last year, Ivan Khoma was the only one here. We're the first Hunkies."

"What are Hunkies?"

"That's what Americans call us. They think that we all are from Hungary. They don't know any better. They don't care to know. Some of the Americans in the mines are from around here. Farm boys or farmers who work the mines in winter. Most others come from Maryland where Consolidated has other mines. And, a few from West Virginia. They are the real Hunkies. Most of them are Magyars, from Hungary.

"When I came here the mines were just opening and owned by Pine Hill Coal Company. A man named Good, from Consolidated Mines, bought it just this year. Now they need all the miners they can get because they cannot get enough Americans to work in mines for what they pay. The Americans are leaving, a few every week. And 'Consol' just opened a new vein three days ago.

"Now, there are less than 10 Americans left. They won't work for the low wages Consol pays. Sure, it is low by American standards, but it is good by Halychyna standards.

"Come, I am boarding with Mrs. Dranchak. You remember her, don't you? She was a Pavuk, a cousin to your grandmother. I think she can find a bed for you in her house. There are five other Rusnaks boarding with her. It isn't as expensive as the 'Old Hotel'. Here they don't serve *halupki* or *perrohi*. You cannot get *kobasa* here. They have an Irish cook and all she can make is corned beef and *kapusta* (cabbage). She said that isn't an Irish dish. She said the Irish in America invented it because they don't have beef in Ireland. Come, we have steak and eggs for breakfast at Dranchak's.

With Turko was Mytro Antonishak, whom Vasyl knew in Europe. He, too, came over with Turko.

"This will be a big mine," Turko said as Vasyl dressed. "They have already built more houses here than there are miners. There are two mines on the right side of the creek and two more farther up the little valley. They are working on bringing up a second set of rail tracks into here from Pine Hill Station so they can haul out the coal. That is what they call the place where the spur starts. The little village of Pine Hill is on top of the hill above the mines. It is small, maybe 12 houses, a church and a store."

When they got downstairs in the Old Hotel, in a dining room next to the kitchen, several of the Rusnaks who had come over with Vasyl were already there. A large burley man with a clipboard in his hand, always the sign of authority, asked Vasyl his name.

"We are still missing two of your buddies," he said to Turko. "Go upstairs and look for them. I have something to say to all of them and I only want to say it once."

Turko was about to go up the stairs when Mykhail and Stefan appeared.

"Come down here," John Lynch ordered.

"Welcome to America," he said with a grin that lacked sincerity in any language. "It is payback time." He read off all the names and each man responded.

"I am John Lynch. I am the superintendent of these mines and you will be working for me. Before you do, there are a few rules you must learn.

"For now, we only have one shift, a day shift. The electricians are installing two new generators. It will be about two months before they go on line. The day shift begins at 6 in the morning and ends at 5 in the afternoon. That's 11 hours. When we get the second shift going, it will be nine hours long. You eat your lunch when you can. Your work six days a week and have Sundays off.

"You get paid by the weight of coal you load onto the cars. You push your filled car to the main line and a man with a mule will haul it to the scales. It takes four to five loads to make a ton. And, it will take most of you the full shift to load a ton. You get $1.15 a ton.

"You don't get cash but you get credit. The credit is maintained at the company store. If you stay at the 'hotel,' it costs you $5 a month for room and board. I suggest you find one of the married miners who takes in boarders or a house with a batch of bachelors who do their own cooking and washing. If you become a boarder, the rate is $2 a week for a bed. She prepares your meals and lunch. She puts all her food bills on a credit and at the end of the month the bill is divided by the number of people in her house. Your food part is deducted from your pay. Your boarding costs also are taken from your wages and paid to her, this way we know she is always getting paid before you get the money. The food bill averages about $2 or less.

"You will be given a pick, shovel and lamp on your first day of work. That's Monday, tomorrow. They are not free. Their costs will be taken out of your pay at a dollar a month. You will own them. Put your mark on them.

"You must buy all your food, tobacco, or whisky from the company store. If I find you have gone into Pine Hill or Berlin and bought food, I will deduct that amount from your pay. If you do it a second time, you will lose your job. If you lose your job for any reason, you also lose a place to sleep. All these houses are owned by Consolidated.

"I see from my list that McDonald has paid all of you for your ship's ticket and $25 'show-money' for customs. That, too, will be taken every month out of your pay at the rate of $2 a month. It used to be $1 but Consol's bookkeepers felt it was too long. If there is any money left over at the end of the month, we will save it for you. If we save it for you, we will pay you what the banks pay us, 3 percent in interest. Or, you can ask the clerk to pay you the remainder of what you make each week. If you do need cash for some reason, see the store manager and he will arrange it for you.

"I don't think this will happen for the first six months or so. 'Uncle' Jerry Smith, the clerk at the company store, will keep these records. It is available for you to see at any time. Are there any questions? Is there anything you don't understand?"

"What if someone gets too sick to work," Stefan asked.

"That's simple. No work, no pay. There is only one holiday. That is the 4th of July. You don't get paid for that day."

"I have two foremen. One will tell you Monday morning who you will work with and where."

"Lynch can be a bastard," Turko said as the three of them left the hotel, a converted house that was on the property when Isaiah Good bought the 2,000 acres in the little ho llow. "Keep out of his way if you can. Don't go to see him directly. If you do, the foreman will get pissed off and he can make it hard for you. If you don't like something, speak to the foreman first.

"Mrs. Dranchak," Turko yelled as he opened the front door to House No. 8, "I have a new Hunky for you to feed."

Another one of the Rusnaks, who was already in Pine Hill, two years ahead of Paul Turko, was Ivan Boburchak. He came over with his wife Anna and they now ran one of the boarding houses. He was also Mykhail's next-to-the-oldest brother and had a double house. He and Stefan moved in with him.

Chapter 20   Good Town the Mine Town

November 1903---Coal had been known to exist throughout Pennsylvania since pre-colonial times. There are two general types, bituminous or soft coal and anthracite or hard coal. Soft coal is found in southwestern Pennsylvania and used initially in households for heat and cooking because it is more volatile and can be ignited easily. It was readily exposed in numerous small valleys and hollows where stream erosion, over thousands of years, had cut through upper sedimentation layers and revealed seams of the "black gold."

In Somerset County, there were hundreds of places where it was exposed. It became a cottage industry for fortunate farmers who could use it to supplement their income. Farmers allowed others to back their wagons to the veins, load them, and on the way out, drop off a few dollars for a winter's supply of coal. But all that was about to change.

Andrew Carnegie should be called the father of the industrial revolution in America. The steel mills he built in the third quarter of the 19th century demanded to be fed voluminous amounts of coal and Henry Frick owned many of the coal mines that could supply their needs. They formed a partnership that affected every coal mine in western Pennsylvania. And, it seems that all rails led to Pittsburgh.

This demand for coal turned the numerous small, open lots of bankside mines into potential fortunes and mines began being developed everywhere a seam crept into the sunlight. One such place was Glen Norris Hollow less than two miles south of the farming community of Berlin in Somerset County. Buffalo Creek divides the township and has its beginnings just west of Berlin. After several name and size changes, it flows north into the Ohio River at Pittsburgh. But it was one nameless tributary, a mere trickle at best and just a mile in length, that over eons of time, eroded the land, created the hollow and exposed coal on both sides of Glen Norris Hollow. The stream starts at 2,300 feet, just below the crossroads community of Pine Hill. Even during its peak expansion in the late 1920s, Pine Hill never consisted of more than a dozen houses. From just below the community, the stream flows north, trickling into Buffalo Creek.

Realizing the enormous coal potential in the area after surveying the immediate townships, three local entrepreneurs, Isaiah Good, Norman Knepper and Daniel Zimmerman in 1899 bought the mineral rights to 2,200 acres of land. They paid Norman Hay and Solomon Coleman $13 an acre for Glen Norris. They did so just days before William T. Rainey of Berlin, also a coal speculator, could add Glen Norris to his already vast holding just to the north of the hollow.

The trio, led by Good, formed the Pine Hill Coal Company and Good was named vice president and general manager. They immediately and simultaneously began opening several exposed seams, built a tipple, company store and office, and "block" houses to be rented to miners. To get the coal out, they laid a spur line down the length of the creek to tracks at the bottom of the hollow owned by Buffalo Valley Rail Road Company. The junction became known as Pine Hill Station.

The next year, the coal company also donated, although somewhat reluctantly, a plot of land on the edge of the little stream for the Glen Norris Public School. It was pressured by the Brothersvalley Township that was required by state law to provide schooling for all children of school age. If history was correct, and would repeat itself, they anticipated the birth of many children in the fledgling mine town.

The new company's foremost problem was not money but manpower. Most of the first men to work in the mines were farmers and their sons from the immediate area. They worked in the mines during their off-season. They also drew men from the nearby villages of Berlin and Pine Hill, all within walking distance to the mine sites. While the flood of cheap labor from eastern and southern Europe had started as early as 1880, most of these men went to feed the steel mills around Pittsburgh and the mills and hard coal mines in northeast Pennsylvania and closer to the port of New York. At the end of the century, in the soft-coal country, their numbers were still only a trickle.

The first large number of alien miners, in the years 1890 to 1900, came from England, Wales, Scotland and Ireland but their domination lasted only a decade. Because they spoke English and many could read and write, they soon became disgruntled, like their brethren in the steel mills, with low pay and poor working conditions, and were able to move elsewhere into the mainstream of American society. The mine company owners realized that what they needed was a limitless labor force that couldn't speak English, could neither read nor write, who lacked more than an initial ambition, and who were accustomed to working hard for long periods for very little money. The mine and mill owners sent their agents abroad and appealed to people who had been oppressed for so many centuries that anything was better than what they would leave behind.

Good Town, named by the miners after Isaiah Good, as the settlement was soon to become known, was the perfect place to put this concept into practice. They would build a ghetto community isolated physically from other ethnic groups, especially Americans, create no need for them to communicate outside the site, force them to buy from company stores and live in company housing from which they could readily be evicted if they rebelled or struck. It thus would be easy for them to keep out unions and keep the pay low. It was low pay in producing coal that would eventually be turned into steel profits in Pittsburgh. Otherwise, Carnegie could not compete with English and German iron and steel producers. Good Town wasn't unique and the only such site. Dozens of other such isolated mining towns also evolved in western Pennsylvania.

Good Town, however, wasn't built in a vacuum even though the mine company tried to isolate its workers from the rest of the world. James Holderbaum was a Berlin dry goods merchant and Andrew Schlassnagle, owned a food store two doors from Holderbaum's store on Diamond Square. One day during its formation, they looked down on Good Town with concern. Berlin was a farming community and mining was new. These men watched with interest, from a field on the Hays farm, at the intense activity going on below in Glen Norris Hollow, as a mining town burgeoned.

"At first," said Schlassnagle, whose thoughts were recorded in a local newspaper, "I was all for it. But now I am not so sure. Last week I visited my brother in Meyersdale. He says the mines have hurt his business. Ever since the violent strike ended there a month ago, the mine companies are bringing in a new element to our area. Our American miners are slowly being pushed out, replaced by an element directly opposite of the 'come easy, go easy Americans'.

"The new element subsists on cheap food and spends little on clothing. A large portion of its earnings goes down into the boot until the wad is big enough to take them back to Europe to spend in their old age.

"The businessmen in Meyersdale were not prepared for the building of mining towns by the coal operators. Here, like in Meyersdale, the miners will have their own stores, schools and churches. This new town, Good Town they are already calling it, will take away business from Berlin and that's what I mean when I say the hardest knock is yet to come."

"I don't know," answered Holderbaum as they turned to walk back to their buggy tied to a fence on the road, "there has got to be some good down there for us."

"What good can come from an army of filthy Hunkies? They're worse than the Irish."

"Well," he answered, "at least they are not Catholics."

In 1900, only three alien immigrants worked in the Brothersvalley Township's expanding number of mines. The agents sent abroad to find more workers would offer them all kinds of incentives to help them cross the ocean. They flooded their minds with unrealistic ideals, pay and living conditions in America. It worked. By 1910, of the 600 people who then lived in Good Town, only a handful were classified as English and included the mine's management and maintenance personnel.

In June 1900, the Pine Hill Coal Company shipped its first coal. The next year it was absorbed through stock purchases by the larger Somerset Coal Company. On January 30, 1902, a constantly expanding and lucrative Good Town was bought for $300,000 by the interstate conglomerate Consolidated Coal Company.

When Vasyl Najda arrived in Good Town at the end of 1903 there may have been only a handful of Rusnaks in the mines, but there was an entire horde on his heels.

Chapter 21   Into the Ground...the Mines

Sunday passed all too quickly among the Rusnaks and was consumed by renewing old acquaintances and making a few new ones. The miners seemed like sponges ready to absorb anything that the new arrivals could tell them about their families, village conditions and events in the Old Country.

"I thought you would have been married by now to that little Mynkova girl. Kateryna, wasn't that her name?" said Turko.

"How is your brother Ivan?"

"He got married just before I came here. Married Juliana Lisko, a girl from Litowyschce and was living on her family's farm outside the village. My older brother Andrij now has two children, both girls. Life is still a struggle there. That is why I came here. Zellman just sold our farm to a Polak named Okonowski. You don't know him. He's from Lisko. He's a baker and turned a part of our house into a bakeshop. He won't make it. Everyone in Protisne is a baker. Beside, no one has money to buy bread when it is so easy to make. I think Zellman will get it back and make money in the deal. Hryec is still single and living with our Uncle Mykola in Sianok but he said he'd like to move back to Protisne and work for Uncle Andrij. Now that I'm gone, Andrij could use the help.

"The ship was packed with people. There were more than 2,000 immigrants on the boat with me. Most were Russian Jews. I feel sorry for the poor bastards. The Tsar is driving them out of Ukraine, out of Russia. He's holding one pogrom after another. We met four on the road from Litowyschce to Sianok. They had been walking for five weeks."

Good Town was a mining town, or mining "patch" as some called them, typical of many others built in southwestern Pennsylvania. All the houses looked the same. Like the ten already built, Dranchak's house was a two-storey duplex or double-block, or "block house" as the immigrants called them. They did look like square blocks but in reality were somewhat wider than deep. The widest section faced the path. A front porch extended the width of the house and one set of center steps lead from the dirt path to the porch. If the house was built on a steep slope, that rose behind it, as was usually the case, then it had a usable basement. Double basement doors opened under the porch. The outside was finished in clapboard siding and all initially lacked paint.

On the first floor, in the center, were two front doors, side by side, that led to each half-house. Stairs, just inside the doorway, led to the second floor. On the first floor were a kitchen, dining area and one large bedroom where the head of the house, his wife and often his growing family shared. Off one side of the kitchen was a utility room that served as food storage and washroom on Saturday nights. The top floor was divided into two large bedrooms and at times as many as eight beds occupied each bedroom.

A common door, if unlocked, communicated between the upstairs bedrooms on each side of the duplex. The kitchen door led into an outside shed where the miner's gear was kept. The shed door led to a privy that was 20 feet behind the house and was shared by both duplex occupants. About 30 feet farther up the hill was a hand-operated water pump. Its pipe went more than 50 feet below the surface. There was a common garden area in the back that was shared by several families. The houses were well built. Rusnaks had never before known such luxury or accommodations in a house.

It was snowing lightly Monday morning as Vasyl Najda followed Paul Turko up the path to the mine tipple and then to its entrance. In the dark, snow on the ground easily revealed the way and Vasyl could see the darkened figures of other men walking silently ahead of him and heard the low, muffled voices of those from behind. Only occasionally was the silence broken when someone coughed. A cold, bone-chilling wind swept up the hollow from the north and Vasyl shuddered as he pulled his new, dark blue denim jacket closer around his head. This was the last time it would ever look blue.

"One thing good about the mine," Turko said when he noticed what Vasyl had done, "there is no wind inside. And, the air gets warmer the deeper you go. This mine is new, still fairly shallow, so it is still cold until you get to your 'room.' This shaft was opened just seven months ago."

Robert Billings was already at the mine entrance and a few men had gathered about him. He was born in England where his father had been a miner. They had immigrated to the United States 30 years ago, when he was just an infant. Consolidated brought him here from one of their mines in Maryland and made him foreman of Lottie No. 2 Mine, named after Good's daughter. Above the entrance was a white sign with black letters that read "Lottie No. 2." Billings knew mining and he knew men, but he was just learning about Rusnaks.

"Turko," he said as he saw Paul approach the group. "You know enough English to help me. When I tell them their jobs, you make sure they understand. Ask each one if they know what they are to do. Okay?"

It was a few minutes before six when Billings glanced down the path lined with company houses. He saw it was empty of men and began to talk.

"We have nine new miners starting today. None of them have experience. I doubt any have ever been in a mine. Here, we work as two-man teams. Each pair is given a room where they work. I have split up experienced pairs so we can get these new men into mining coal as quickly as possible. I'm counting on you to teach the greenhorns.

"Here are the new teams."

He ignited his headlamp and dug a piece of crinkled paper from a grungy pocket that bore coal dust. When he came to Najda's name, he assigned him to Paul Turko. Just as he read the last name a shrill, high-pitched whistle blew. It startled the newcomers. It would quickly become their only clock and measure the important parts of the day for them. It blew at 6 a.m., noon and 5 p.m. No one wanted to hear it blow at any other time because that meant an accident.

"There's a bin just inside," Billings said and pointed toward the mine's main entrance. "Take a pick, shovel and light from it. They're yours. You will pay for them.

"Now, let's go dig some coal."

"Follow me," Paul said to Vasyl and led him into the hole in the earth.

"There are your tools. They are all the same. They are new. Before you put them on the Hryec over there," he pointed, "when the shift is over, make sure you have your initials on them. The headlight goes home with you.

"Here is the check board. I see that Billings already has your name and number on it."

On a large wooden board, painted white, were dozens of L-shaped brass hooks screwed into the wood. On each hook hung a dozen brass tags, the size of a quarter, called checks. All the checks on one hook had the same number. Next to Vasyl Najda's name was an 18.

"Take them all and keep them in your top pocket, the one with the button," Paul said. "When we fill a car, there is a hook on the car's side. That's where we put one of your or my hooks."

Turko stopped talking for a moment and took the lantern off his cap and lighted it. He showed Vasyl how to do the same and then they continued walking into the mine.

"Then we must push it to the main track heading. A mule driver will come along, hook it up and take it to the dock boss. The dock boss will check the car to see if we have loaded any slate with the coal. If its okay," he spoke as they slowly walked deeper into the mine toward their room, "he will mark the car and send it on to the weigh boss. If it's not okay, if he can get one or two buckets of slate from your car, he will call it 'dirty.' He will give you a couple days off, without pay, of course. Don't get a reputation for loading dirty coal otherwise they will always inspect your car very carefully.

"The weigh boss weighs your coal and then logs it in next to your name in his book.

"After it is weighed, a check boy gathers the checks and puts them back on the board next to your name and number.

"It may sound a little confusing now but you will know it all too well before the week is out.

"On second thought, leave your checks on the board. We will use mine because everything we weigh will be divided in two."

As they passed deeper into the mine's narrow corridors, sidetracks split off the main track and led to rooms occupied by other miners. Turko pointed out a series of chalk numbers written on a small wooden plaque mounted on a cross beam just at the entrance to each room.

"See that?" he pointed.

"On the board was 23/11/03.

"Don't go in that room, your room or any room that doesn't have today's date. That is today's date: 23 November 1903. Every day the correct day is also posted outside, on the check board. That chalk mark was made by the fire boss. He is in here every morning, well ahead of the miners, and goes into all the rooms and tests them for coal gas. If they are clean, he puts his day-mark on the board. If not, he gets the fans working until they are safe. Coal gas is very explosive. Working in mines is dangerous and coal gas is only one of the problems we face.

"Here is our room. See the mark? He has been here."

Turko led Vasyl about a hundred feet down the corridor that led to the room they would work. It was about 24 feet wide and almost as long.

At first Vasyl didn't notice the change as he walked behind Turko. Then he suddenly became aware that his heart was beating strongly. It seemed especially fast. Almost at the same time he began to sweat, a cold sweat that covered his forehead. He was being overcome by fear. He turned his head left and right and saw the beam of his light sweep from one wall to the other. The walls are getting closer and closer, he thought to himself. Suddenly, he realized he had stopped walking.

"Are you alright?" Paul asked as Vasyl saw his friend returning and put an arm over his shoulder.

Paul saw that Vasyl's breathing was rapid.

"What is happening to me?" Vasyl asked.

"Hold your breath. Slow down your breathing. Bend over and hold your head down," Paul said. He helped him bend over and forced down his head.

"Now breathe, but breath slowly."

In a few minutes, it was all over.

"Sensing that what happened had passed, Vasyl stood upright, inhaling slowly with large, long breaths and said, "I'm okay. I'm okay. What happened to me? Is there something wrong with me?"

"Don't feel special, it has happened to most of us, especially the first time we get deeper into a mine. It is a passing sensation, like the walls and ceiling are all closing in on you. It is all in your mind. You'll be okay. If it happens again, do what I just told you. After a while, you'll get used to being down here and it won't happen again.

Paul, too, knew the sensation but didn't know it was called claustrophobia. Being so tightly confined, and compounded by the engulfing darkness, was something none of the new miners had ever experienced, especially those who grew up in the wide open spaces of the mountains. For most, it occurred only a few times and then disappeared. For a very few it was on a clinical level that kept them from working in the mines, which maybe wasn't all that bad.

"The ceiling is called a roof and that side," Paul said as he pointed to the front wall, "is called the 'face.' It is where we will dig, following the vein of coal. It is not too thin, about 4 feet. That is why they like us Rusnaks to work these mines."

Paul and Vasyl, however, were anomalies at 5 feet 6 inches in height, most men averaged only 5 feet 2 inches.

"There is no work in here for big men. At times, the vein gets so thin, down to 2 feet, that we must lay on our sides to work.

"I 'shot' some coal last Wednesday and there is still enough on the floor to haul out. I figure it will take us two days to get it all loaded. Then, I will show you how to 'shoot' coal."

For the next two days Paul and Vasyl loaded coal. Big pieces were loaded by hand and smaller pieces and dust were shoveled. There was very little pick work needed on the face until the next day except when they uncovered chunks of coal that were too heavy to lift and had to be broken apart.

They loaded 11 cars on Monday but only 9 on Tuesday. Working the pick against the face of the room took more time. Only a small amount was on the floor when the quitting whistle blew at 5 o'clock. Vasyl had trouble with his "sunshine lamp" going out. That evening Paul showed him how to clean it. It burned a paraffin-like substance that produced a yellow light. It would be a few years before the brilliant white, carbide lamps were introduced in the mines.

"Today," said Turko as he and Vasyl entered their room on Wednesday morning, "we have to shoot down some coal. We knock down the loose coal from the roof, just below the slate that is on top of it. If we do it right, we cleanly separate the two, leaving the slate on the roof."

He then lay his "shooting bag" on the floor, against the room's face.

"First, we have to make a slot, a space in the roof between the slate and the coal with our picks so that the coal separates from the slate at that point. But before that, we have to support the slate roof with posts before we make the cut so it doesn't come down on us after the explosion. Get me two posts from the corridor and we will shim them in place.

"Now, about here," he pointed to a place on the roof with a tip of the pick, "we stamp around a bit with the pick point to rough up the spot. We must flatten it a bit and make a little pocket so the auger won't slide out but take a good bite in the top of the coal seam."

Satisfied, Turko, took a large hand auger with a 2-1/2-inch diameter bit, slanted it slightly upward, and slowly began to drill a hole in the relatively soft coal. When it had penetrated about 3.5 feet into the coal, he retrieved the bit. With the auger, he repeatedly removed all the loose coal from the hole until it was clean and smooth.

From his canvas shooting bag, he pulled out a large sheet of newspaper and laid it on the floor. Next, he took out a metal can, popped off its lid, then poured a mound of black powder onto the newspaper. He formed it into a row, then rolled the newspaper and powder in a diameter slightly less that the size of the hole. He crimped one end and tapped the sleeve lightly on the floor to move the powder to the bottom. Then he poured more powder into the sleeve until it was filled. He crimped the open end with several tight twists.

"We call this sleeve of powder a shot."

"How much powder do you use?" Vasyl asked.

"That depends on the way the seam looks attached to the slate. This one doesn't look real strong so I won't use too much. It is always better to use less than you think you need than too much. Too much is likely to bring down slate and you don't want that. If it's not enough, you can always shoot it again."

Turko slowly, gently fed the roll of black powder into the hole as far as it would go. Next, he inserted a foot-long copper needle, about a quarter-inch in diameter, into the center of the powder until it reached the end. With a tamping bar, having a flat copper end, so it couldn't create sparks, he began pushing, tamping the shot to the bottom of the hole. When it jammed, he gently tamped the needle until it penetrated the crimped end of the paper. It began traveling down the length of the shot to the bottom of the hole, at the same time also tamping the powder pushing it deeper into the back. When the needle reached the bottom, the tamping bar was pulled out, but the needle remained. From another can in his bag, Turko pulled out some river-bottom clay, mixed it with coal dust, and pushed it into the hole, beyond the free end of the needle and against the packed powder. This acted as a plug to keep the powder from falling out.

Black powder will only burn, not explode, unless it is ignited in a confined space. Turko began tamping the plug harder to compact the powder. When he felt it was as tightly packed as it could get, he began slowly twisting the copper needle to free it from the powder. When it spun freely in his fingertips, he slowly began pulling it out. When it was out, he returned to his bag and from a package he separated a long fuse, called a squib, from other fuses. It looked like a drinking straw filled with powder. He inserted it into the hole, twisting it and pushing it to the bottom of the hole the needle had created.

"That's it," Turko said.

"Vasylko, get back to the corridor, I don't want to lose you on your first shoot. Take the bag with you."

As Vasyl backed away, Paul took a box of wooden matches from the bag, hesitated for a few moments, and then looked back to see if his partner was in the corridor. Satisfied, he struck the match and yelled aloud "Fire! Fire! Fire!"

He waited a few moments and when no one responded, he lit the end of the squib that protruded from the hole. He ran back from the face, across the room and squatted next to Vasyl in the safety of the corridor.

"Don't look inside. You don't want to be hit by flying coal or slate."

It seemed like long minutes but probably it was less than 60 seconds when the black powder exploded. The gust of wind it created blew out Paul's lamp. He quickly relighted it using Vasyl's. The room was filled with billowing coal dust and took five minutes before it settled enough to see how well they had done. Almost automatically, the two men covered their mouths with their hands. Still, they began coughing.

"Let's get to work," Paul said as he pushed an empty car into the room. "It was a good shoot. It looks like it will take two or three days to load it all. I'll do a couple more shoots before I let you try one."

As they carried blocks of coal to the car Vasyl's mind temporarily slipped back to the day three years ago when he and Paul were harvesting hay above Protisne. It seemed another lifetime ago when they had last been together. His mind wandered and entertained him in the poorly-lighted room. It was easy to do. It was almost an out-of-body experience. He wondered what ever happened to Smolensky, the Jewish lawyer with whom he and the others shared a barn in Solina and then just a few days ago when he saw him again on the *S.S. Patricia.* Where had he gone? He wondered how the Rusnak from Litowyschce fared after returning to his village. Maybe he is better off that I am, he mused.

Vasyl began to settle down into a miner's routine. Each morning, at 4:30, Mrs. Dranchak would come upstairs and awaken her 12 boarders. Her own alarm was usually loud enough to awaken everyone in the household. By 5:00 everyone was down to the kitchen table where they worked through pork chops or steak with eggs and fried potatoes, homemade bread and lots of coffee. And oatmeal, always oatmeal. By 5:45, they were dressed in their miner's clothing, donned the knee-high rubber boots and checked their lamps to make sure they hadn't leaked oil. Fifteen minutes was usually more than enough to slog up the hill to the mine entrance. Usually, by the time the mine whistle blew they had their checks and were on the way to their rooms.

They placed their lunch pails with sandwiches Mrs. Dranchak had made and the coffee holders attached to the bottom of the pail, along the backside of their rooms. At 5:00 each afternoon, the mine whistle's shrill pitch reverberated into every room in the mine.

In the shed outside the kitchen, they left most of their outer mine clothing and washed in a series of basins set in a board on a shelf against the outside wall. If it was really cold and windy, sometimes the hot water, if Mrs. Dranchak had placed in the pail too soon, had skim ice. By 6:00, Mrs. Dranchak or her husband Peter would call the men down to eat. After eating, if it were too cold outside, they would sit in the front room and smoke their pipes, have a second cup of coffee and talk about the Old Country. By 9 o'clock, most were in bed.

For the first two weeks the routine was unbroken but on Friday night, December 4th, a fire broke out at the Penn-Marva Coal Company store in Rainey Town. "Red" Rainey Town, as it was known because all the dozen or so company houses built around the mine and store were painted a barn red, was less that a half-mile from Good Town. By the time the miners from Good Town got there to help fight the fire, the building had burned to the ground. It took with it the nearby house of Frank Coleman, superintendent of the Rainey Town mine. Mining there began a year before the Pine Hill Mines were open. There was a lesson to be learned from the Rainy Town fire but no one saw it.

Consolidated Coal had several mines in the immediate area in addition to Good Town. One was also in Rainey Town in addition to Coronet Coal and the Will Coal mines. It was while there, at the fire, that Turko, Vasyl, Mykhail and Stefan were talking to several immigrant miners from Galicia who heard that union miners there were planning to strike because of the low pay.

"It isn't us," said one of them. "It is the English and Welsh. We're in the union but only as bodies. They only talk to us when they need our numbers. But they are very unsatisfied with what we are getting paid. Nothing will come of it."

On December 15, just 10 days before Christmas miners in Rainey Town went on strike. Rusnaks, Hungarians and a few Italians there were forced to go out with them.

"Can this also happen here, in Good Town?" asked Stefan. He and Mykhail had come over to the Dranchak house after supper.

"I don't think so," said Turko. "There is no union here. If some English and Scots want to go out in sympathy, we do not have to go. It's the middle of winter and it's cold outside. I don't want to live in a tent until it's over."

The strike in Red Rainey Town lasted more than a year and the mines there lay idle all that time. The company had mines elsewhere in the area that were producing coal and felt no need to give in to the union's demands. It was a useless, ill-thoughtout and ill-planned strike.

Vasyl learned to shoot down a roof and got good at it. But 1904 was a disastrous year for the soft coal mine industry. A real depression saw even large conglomerates like Consolidated post meager earnings for their stockholders. However, miners in Good Town were able to work every day. One morning in late January, Billings read a notice to the miners who were interested in becoming citizens.

"I think I would like that," Vasyl said to Paul as they shoveled a new shoot. "There is nothing for me to return to the Old Country. I think I should stay here and become an American. My future lies here. Paul, is it very difficult?"

"You cannot," he answered. "You must be in this country for three years before you can apply for your 'first papers.' You have to be able to read the U.S. Constitution, or have parts of it read to you and understand what they mean because you will be asked a bunch of questions. And, you must be able to read and write, if not in English, then in your native tongue. You have to know who is president of the United States and..."

"I know that," interrupted Vasyl. "It is Theodore Roosevelt.

"...and the Governor of Pennsylvania and how laws are made in Washington and in Harrisburg."

"Maybe later," Vasyl answered.

In that year alone, 1904, more than 50 Rusnaks from the villages of Smil'nyk and Protisne emigrated to America looking for work. Of these, nearly two dozen found work in Good Town mines. The company continued building more houses but at a faster rate. They had discovered another vein of coal a few thousand yards above the two Lottie Mines and there was talk about beginning a collection of houses above Good Town. They even named it Upper Good Town, while it was still only an idea. It did, however, become a reality.

The biggest news in the mines in late May was the killing of three miners in Elklick, ten miles to the south, between the villages of Meyersdale and Garrett. Mine owners believed it was a good idea not to mix different alien miners. Those in Good Town were mostly Rusnaks; those in Macdonaldton, Slovaks and those in Garrett were Italian.

It seems that a bunch of "foreigners" became involved in a shootout and three were killed. There was a growing animosity between American store owners and aliens in Meyersdale because of what the coal company had done to their businesses. There was

225

also a growing enmity between the four immigrant nationalities from Great Britain, that banded together, and the Italians. The Somerset Coal Company had, early that year, hired a large number of Italians to replace striking English miners and moved them into the company houses near the mine.

According to a newspaper account, on a Sunday morning in May, an Italian named Lutini went onto the property of Dominick Bills, also a foreigner, also an Italian, to gather dandelions to make a salad. He was ordered off the property by Bills' young son. As he left, Lutini turned around and cursed the youngster. When the elder Bills got home, according to the newspaper account, he was told of the incident and went to Lutini's house to confront him. Bills was said to have told Lutini that he could gather all the dandelions he wanted but not to use curse words on his son.

Later that Sunday, Bills was riding past Lutini's house on a bicycle when someone, using a revolver, fired from the Lutini house. Bills was struck in the wrist. Bills ran into the house and was about to attack Lutini, who had drawn a stiletto. Lutini slashed Bills several times across his face. It appeared Bills had come prepared with his own revolver and shot Lutini in the chest killing him instantly.

Bills then ran to his brother's house. As his brother was bandaging his wounds the dead Lutini's brother appeared in the kitchen and shot Bills's brother in the leg. Bills ran out the back door to his own home and hid under the front porch. Lutini followed him and crawled under the porch where Bills was hiding and emptied six bullets into him. Lutini returned to his home, packed his clothes and disappeared. Bills' brother eventually died from the leg wound.

That same weekend, a prominent Garrett businessman was alleged to have been shot and killed by an Italian. But the man was never found.

Chapter 22   The Good Life in Good Town

Work in the Good Town mines was hard, the hours long and the pay poor. It was no wonder so many English, Scotch and Welch miners and their families began moving away. Vasyl had hoped to save enough money in the first year to send some to his brother John. They had agreed before he left that John would be the next to come to America. However, by the end of the first year, Vasyl had nothing put away. It took more than a year to repay the $60.50 advance on his ship's ticket and the "show" money. What advance was left was used getting his mine clothes, boots and a new carbide lamp. Occasionally, it was his turn to buy a bottle of brandy, at the company store. The money just seemed to dribble away. His only real luxury was a pouch of tobacco, one a week, and a new pipe.

Vasyl's only memento of the Old Country was a ceramic pipe. It had belonged to his father and before him his grandfather. It was probably his great grandfather's but he wasn't sure. When he would smoke it after dinner, the other Rusnaks would make fun of him about how old fashioned was his pipe. Almost all of them smoked pipes and, occasionally, a cigar. They, however, bought their pipes at the company store, corncobs for 5¢ each, and then later the coveted briar-headed "American" pipes.

Vasyl's pipe, when he smoked it, evoked memories of his past and the Old Country, his uncles and aunts and occasionally his father. He hardly remembered his mother. Then, there was Kateryna and he wondered what had become of her. The pipe seemed to rise in importance the longer he was in America. It would not have drawn much attention in Europe but in America it was an oddity. It consisted of a ceramic bowl that had on it a relief of the figure of a reclining man in a tricornered hat playing a balalaika. Below the figure was the date "1761." An ornate, hinged, perforated brass cap was fastened atop the bowl. The cap had become blackened with use and green with age. The carved bone mouthpiece was connected to the bend behind the bowl by a foot-long piece of cherry wood, with its dried, dark red bark still intact. A quarter-inch hole had been drilled through the entire length of the cherry shaft.

It was in perfect condition except for a chip taken out of the edge of the back of the ceramic bowl. That happened when someone had rummaged through their room in Berlin and thrown it aside while they were out to supper.

Another year passed and neither Vasyl, Stefan nor Mykhail had saved very much money. Frustration was overtaking them and their evening get-togethers were becoming more sullen and depressing. Memories of their old life in Europe were fading, replaced by the realties of working in a coal town. From their pasts, they now seemed to remember only their better experiences.

"Maybe it wasn't as bad there as we thought," Mykhail said one evening shortly after 'Russian' Christmas in.

"It was worse," said Peter Stanko, a new boarder and a miner new to Good Town. "I went back there in November to see my wife and family. Luckily we have no children. They have even less than when I left and I have been sending them a little every few months. I cannot believe my wife. She lives almost in rags and eats only potatoes and cabbage but she still refused to return with me to America. I think she is afraid of the ocean. She has been told so many bad stories of the crossing that she believes them all. When I came back, I left everything there I brought with me, except for the clothes on my back.

"I understand you have never had a strike here," Peter said. "That's why I came here, I've worked in the hardcoal mines in Wilkes-Barre. There, you work a few months and then you go on strike for a few months. I could not get ahead. Our mine was on strike so I went to Europe. After I got back, I found they settled, but I came here to work because it is more secure."

"What did they pay?" asked Vasyl.

"It is better than here," he answered. "Some pay 28 cents a car and a few pay 30 cents, or about $1.50 a ton.

"My God!" exclaimed Turko, "You can make $1.50 a day, maybe more. Our best is $1.25 a day. Just think," he said and turned to Vasyl. "In a week you could save $1.50 and $6 a month, and...in a year....$72. That is like being rich, a *bohatch*!"

Chapter 23   The Trip to Wilkes-Barre

Vasyl worked in the mines because he had to. He disliked it but seldom complained because he knew it would do no good. He sensed that his hope of buying a farm was fading. On Sundays, he would climb the hill behind the mines and walk through the company's fields of growing timothy and alfalfa. Consolidated maintained a farm to supply fresh foods for the company store. He would corner a calf and scratch its head. It reminded him of one his Uncle Andrij owned. He desperately wanted to be a farmer and a feeling of entrapment grew within him. His dislike for mines progressively intensified.

Vasyl Najda was a simple man with simple wants. However, at this point in his life, not a single one of them had been satisfied. He felt he had to do something about that. What Peter had said about Wilkes-Barre festered in Vasyl's mind. In the spring of '06, in early April, he decided he was going to go there to find a better job. To make more money…maybe to eventually buy a farm. And then, there was the promise he had made to bring over his brother John.

He skipped buying the brandy and tobacco and by the first of May he had accumulated enough money to take the train, and back again, if he didn't like the mines there. He walked to Berlin, took the bus to Johnstown and then the train to Harrisburg where he switched to a train that took him north to Wilkes-Barre.

He had stuffed his boots, mining clothes and light into a cardboard suitcase he secretly bought from George Gumbert at the Pine Hill store. In it he also added his old pipe and a few other worldly possessions. He left his pick and shovel with Mrs.

Dranchak, in case he should return. Mrs. Dranchak had baked him a loaf of rye bread and packed a few sticks of *kobasi*.

He walked 5 miles from the Wilkes-Barre train station to the mining town of Mill Creek, where Peter Stanko had worked and where he was told he could get a job. He got there just as the 5 o'clock mine whistle blew. He saw the men piling out of the mine located above town, and walking down the dirt road to their houses. It did look a little like Good Town, he thought.

He stopped one miner and asked if he knew where he might board. The man was from Smerek, about eight miles from Protisne. After some discussion, they realized they were once, for a few months, neighbors in Good Town. Volodymyr Kuzin told him to come with him; his house might have a bed.

"I have three," said Mike Rusyn. "You can take your pick. It is $6 a month that includes room, board and laundry. My wife likes to drink so I forbid alcohol at the table. If you must drink, keep it locked in your footlocker.

"Where are you working?"

"I just got here," Vasyl said. "I haven't had a chance to..."

"Are you a'?"

"No. I've been working in Good Town for three years, in the 'Consol' mines.

"Why are you here? Are they on strike."

"No. They don't pay well. I heard the mines here pay better."

"Good. They do. But you will find that mining hardcoal is a lot more work than soft coal. I will take you with me tomorrow and introduce you to the foreman at the Delaware Colliery where I work. They own several coal mines around here.

"What is your name again?"

The next day, Tuesday, at 6:00 a.m., Mike Rusyn took him to the mine.

"The superintendent doesn't get here until 8. Wait here. Tell him my name and that you're staying at my house and you need a job. Good Luck," he said and disappeared into the mine with the others.

John Hannity was a small man, even smaller in height than Vasyl. Vasyl had thought that all Irish were big, like McDonald. Hannity was not young, and though it had been many years since he loaded a car with coal, he was still in the mining business. He was a bit on the rotund side, his hair was pure white and his complexion was especially ruddy, almost red. Vasyl knew that a man who looks like this must like his liquor.

"I'll start you out breaking coal. I'm short under the tipple. If I see you can work, I'll eventually pair you with a miner and your own room."

That didn't set well with Vasyl. He was an experienced miner and a good shooter. Here, he was put with children and old men, separating and breaking coal before it went up the tipple. The only adults there were men crippled in the mines or alcoholics between binges. Despite this, he took a seat among a dozen teen-agers at the bottom of slanted bins breaking coal. By the end of the week, he was ready to quit. Friday afternoon, when Hannity happened by, Vasyl stopped breaking coal, rose out of his seat and approached Hannity.

The breaker boss yelled at him to get back...it wasn't quitting time.

He approached Hannity who turned to see why the breaker boss was yelling.

"What do you want, Hunky?" Hannity addressed Vasyl before he had a chance to speak.

Ten years earlier, almost every miner in Mill Creek was Irish. In the last decade, hordes of Rusnaks began arriving from Halychyna, gradually displacing almost all of the Irish. Hannity was a typical "Shanty" Irishman who emigrated from Ireland while he was just a teenager. He had come up through the mines and because of his own personal shortcomings had developed a great dislike for the Hunky foreigners who now dominated "his" town and "his" mines.

"I am an experienced miner," said Vasyl. "I was the best shooter in the Good Town mines. I left a better-paying job to come here. I cannot make money as a breaker. I am a miner."

"Not to me you ain't," Hannity snarled back. "If you don't like it, I can get a kid to replace you. All you goddamned Hunkies are alike. You come here, work a few years, and then you think you should be making what Americans make."

"Are you an American?" Vasyl asked.

Vasyl unknowingly hit a sore spot. Hannity had never bothered to take out citizenship papers. He was as much an alien as Vasyl.

"Get your ass back to the breaking bin or get out of here."

Vasyl turned and was about to walk down the road to the houses, then turned around and faced Hannity.

"You owe me money for a week's work."

"Pick it up Monday morning. It won't be much after your union dues are taken out."

"That Hannity is a putska," Rusyn said that evening after Vasyl told him what happened. "Don't worry. You can get a miner's job. There is another mine, the Pine Ridge Colliery just a half-mile up the road. Go there Monday."

Vasyl's head was hurting Sunday morning when Olenka Rusyn came upstairs to wake the men. They had a party among themselves in the upstairs room, celebrating Vasyl's quitting. Any event, no matter how insignificant, was enough to precipitate a party. Ironically, it was the only relief they found in their dismal existence.

"What's wrong with her?" Vasyl asked. "Today is Sunday. There is no work. There is no reason to get up so early."

"There is church," said Kuzin. "When is the last time you have been in a church?"

"You have a church here?" a surprised Vasyl asked.

"Yes," said Volodymyr.

"Bless yourself."

"Why?" asked Vasyl.

"Just bless yourself."

With three fingertips joined together, he quickly touched his forehead, then the center of his chest then his right shoulder and his chest again.

"Good! Fantastic! You are in luck. Ours is a pravo slavna, an Orthodox Church."

The return to the Orthodox version of Christianity was impossible for Rusnaks while in Europe because in every country in which they lived, the religion was established by that state and was both government sponsored and often financially supported. For

Rusnaks, there was only the Uniate version of Catholicism which many grudgingly and forcibly adopted over the past three centuries. That would change and was first accomplished in America. It was a Greek Catholic, an ordained Uniate priest, Alexis Toth, who came to America in1889 and who became instrumental in initiating the movement.

Toth was assigned a church in Minneapolis, but the Irish Catholic Archbishop John Ireland refused to recognize him as a legitimate priest because he, like all Greek Catholic clergy in Europe, was allowed to marry. Even though he was widowed by the time he arrived here, it made no difference. Ireland even went so far as to excommunicate him. In 1891, Toth and 365 parishioners made a monumental decision and went over to Orthodoxy. And, the only branch of Orthodoxy available to them was the Russian Orthodox Church. Tens of thousands of Rusnak émigrés went over with him and his followers. By 1914 he was hailed as the father of Orthodoxy in America. The movement was eventually carried back to Europe by returning immigrants and was met there with considerable opposition from both the Catholic Church and Catholic-oriented governments.

Vasyl walked with Volodymyr and his wife from "Irish Town," as it had been called for years by Americans because most of its inhabitants had been Irish, to the church in Miner's Mills. It was a new church, just three years old, and one of the first Orthodox Churches built in the United States.

"You will sit with us," Helenka told Vasyl as she led the way into the church. "Do not be like other Rusnak men," she added, "and sneak outside when the service is half-finished to have a smoke or a shot."

She entered a pew six rows from the front. The pews ahead were already filled, mostly by *babushka'd* women. After a few minutes, the service began and as the congregation stood up, he noticed the long blond, almost white hair of a young woman three pews ahead of him. For a moment, it looked familiar and reminded him of Kateryna. She was sitting with two other young women who also wore no *babushkas* over their heads, an indication that they were unmarried.

The custom is still with them, Vasyl said to himself, even in America.

When the tinkling of a little bell signaled the congregation to sit, the silver-haired girl turned slightly. Instantly, Vasyl's memory again flashed back to another time and another place...and another girl with long blonde hair.

He watched intensely as she put the back of her hand to cover her mouth as she whispered something and turned slightly toward the young women next to her.

Vasyl was dumbstruck.

Could it be true? It cannot be!

Half-way through the service, Vasyl could no longer contain himself and leaned toward Olenka Kuzin and asked who was that girl.

"Shush!" she said. "Be quiet!"

Services in Orthodox Churches notoriously last longer than in other churches and when the end approached those in the front row rose and one-by-one the people ahead went to the altar to take communion.

"It IS her," he said as she turned after kissing the icon and followed the others back to her pew. She kept her head down and eyes on the floor and never noticed Vasyl. He was the last person into his pew and thus the last to come out. People in the front row came out first and his line finally reached her. She turned and began walking up the aisle looking forward and then at the people on the sides. Her eyes suddenly met Vasyl's and for a moment time seemed to freeze, to stand still, as her mind fleetingly recalled images and raced through memories from the past. She realized it was Vasyl and softly screamed his name, then rushed forward and threw her arms about him and he his about her. Everyone in the church was watching.

"What are you doing here?" she said as she hung onto his arm outside the church, plying him with questions. Halya (Helenka, Olenka), taking it all in, was just steps behind them.

"You know this Rusnak?" she asked Kateryna.

"Of course you do. You must know him from the Old Country because he just got to 'Irish Town.' Wait 'till he tells you he just quit his job."

Halya loved to be the source of all information and was suddenly in her glory.

"Come," she said to Kateryna, "you will have Sunday dinner with us. You can talk on the way home. I have two chickens I have to get into the oven or the boarders will move elsewhere."

"I have been here since last July," Kateryna began. "My cousin Nadja and her father were coming here. You remember Nadja. She, too, is from Smil'nyk. She was in the wedding party for my cousin Helenka Salabaj.

"How is Stefan?"

"He still talks too much," Vasyl answered.

"Why didn't you write and tell me where you were?" Kateryna asked. "I thought you were going to Johnstown. I know some people there and they never heard of you or Stefan. We thought that maybe your ship sank. I never thought I would see you again. Still, I hoped."

"Johnstown was only the end of the train ride," Vasyl said. "From there, in a wagon, we went south to Pine Hill. To Good Town."

"I didn't know where you and he were.

"I have been in America since last July," Kateryna said again, "and I was hoping I would find you someday before it is too late."

"What do you mean, 'too late'?"

"There are more than 300 unmarried Rusnak miners here. Not counting Slovaks, Hungarians, Croats and Polaks. There are no more than a dozen young, unmarried women. Can you imagine how many times I have been proposed to? It is constant.

"I don't want to be a miner's wife. I want a life on a farm, like in the Old Country. Speaking of farms, have you bought one yet?"

"No," Vasyl answered. "Not yet, but I will. I agreed first to help my brother Ivan and Andrij come over. The *Schiffkarte* costs a lot of money. It took me a whole year of work to pay back the mine company for my ticket and mining tools. Money is not as easy to get here as we were told."

"How did you come over?"

"My Uncle Stefan decided that he had to come over to find work. There was none at home. Everyone is living from hand-to-mouth. His other brother Maksym was already a miner in Wilkes-Barre and wrote to Stefan saying he could easily find work here, either in the mines or on the railroad. He also said that his oldest daughter Nadja could find work in a boarding house or hotel.

He sent enough money for their ship ticket. When my Uncle Volodymyr, you know Volodymyr Salabaj, the blacksmith, heard Stefan was taking his daughter, he said he would give me an early wedding present, enough to buy a ticket. He is silly. He knew I had no intentions of getting married."

"How was your crossing?"

"The crossing was terrible. We had terrible weather. I swear the boat, most of the time, was going backwards to Europe rather than forward to America. I will not have to worry about ever going home because I will never, never get on a boat again. I think I was sick for most of the trip.

"It was supposed to take two weeks but we were a month on the water. It was an old boat, the *Rheatia*. It was a German boat out of Hamburg and had one smokestack that dirtied everything behind it. And the coal smelled strongly of sulfur and that smell came down the funnels into steerage. The other passengers had windows but we had only the stairs to the top. It was so old that it still had sails in front. They put them up and down, up and down, day and night, almost all of the time.

"Worst of all, there were more than a thousand people in steerage and it seemed almost everyone was seasick. There was vomit everywhere, babies constantly crying and that filthy cigar smoke always in the cabin. I had to sleep in a bed next to a woman who never washed in the entire month. It got so hot there that we spent most of the day, and many nights, on top sleeping in the open.

"When we walked out the exit at Ellis Island, there was a man there who was looking for hotel workers. He was from Passaic, in New Jersey, real close to Ellis Island. He said we could begin work the next day. I didn't have much money, maybe not quite enough to buy a train ticket to Wilkes-Barre. Nadja's father had enough but he found he, too, was short when he tried to buy her a ticket at the train office just outside the immigration building. We didn't know what we were going to do. The man was our only answer. She decided to stay with me and we went back and found him. The job also came with a room that we shared with four other young girls, Irish, who had been there for a few months.

"We worked for a week cleaning and emptying spittoons and bedpans. It was filthy work but we did it. Then the owner wanted us to work on Sunday. We don't work on Sundays, we told him. He said the Irish girls do. No Rusnaks work on that day. It is God's day.

"When we wouldn't work, he fired us. We made just enough money between us, and what Nadja had, to buy two train tickets. We got the next train to Wilkes-Barre and somehow found her father. We got another job, again in a hotel, really a big boarding house. We told the owner that we cannot work on Sundays because of our religion. He said he never works on Saturdays because of his religion. He is a Polish Jew from Lisko and said he understood. And, we don't have to empty spittoons. He has an old black man who does that. I never saw a black man before. Have you?

"I have been talking too much about myself. What have you done?

"Why are you here?

"I thought you told me you were going to...now I remember, Pine Hill. Is Pine Hill far away?

"Can we see Stefan today? Tell me. Tell me."

Before Vasyl could begin answering her multitude of questions, they reached the house. Kateryna still clung onto Vasyl's arm as they approached the front steps. The boarders who didn't go to church were sitting on the front porch, enjoying the first warm Sunday in a month and smoking their ever-present pipes.

"It looks like we should all go to church," said Bohdan Bluha. "Look what Najda has come back with."

All the men stood up as Kateryna climbed the steps behind Mrs. Rusyn. Vasyl reluctantly introduced her to the men he knew and some, who worked the night shift in the mine, he had never seen.

After dinner, they spent the afternoon together, mostly alone, as the miners went down the hill to Grogan's Emerald Bar in Irish Town. They were engrossed in conversation after the cold supper Mrs. Rusyn made for the boarders. It wasn't too well attended because several took advantage of Grogan's free barfoods.

It was late and Kateryna was getting ready to return to her boarding house where she worked, when Mrs. Rusyn came into the parlor.

Vasyl stood. He told her he wouldn't be needing a bed after that night.

"Are you moving into Kateryna's boarding house? You won't find the food there anywhere as good as mine."

"No, I'm returning to Pine Hill, to Good Town. And, Kateryna is going back with me. We plan to marry.

Chapter 24 Marriage to Kateryna in Good Town

Saturday June 9, 1906---It was a perfect day for a wedding. It was the kind of day upon which all weddings should be held. It bodes well for the future of the marrying couple. It was a warm, balmy, late spring day and the green fields above Good Town were lush and bucolic. The cattle on Hay's Farm, above the town were slowly, almost imperceptibly moving down the hill below Pine Hill. They were seeking out the sweeter grasses that grew along the small patch of woods that separated the farm from the mining community.

Three weeks earlier, Vasyl and Kateryna had been to St. Mary's Church in Windber, 20 miles away, and had arranged with Father Michael Balogh to perform the wedding. Because Rusnaks in Good Town had no church, once a month Father Balogh would come to the isolated mining town and say the Liturgy in private homes. This time, he came a day early for their wedding.

Because of the growing number of immigrants now working in their Good Town mines, Consolidated, in an attempt to keep miners from trekking to Berlin, Garrett or Meyersdale, began construction of a recreation hall. However, it would be months before it was completed.

"It would have been a nice place for the wedding," said Anna Kasper, "but still not as nice as a church. That is what we really need here, a church."

Kateryna had no trouble adjusting to life in Good Town. She was surprised to find one of her close girlfriends, Anna Kasper, also from Smil'nyk, now living there. Kasper's father had come over just six months earlier and brought his wife, two sons and Anna. Kateryna shared a bedroom with Anna until after the marriage.

Preparations for a wedding in Good Town were considerably austere when compared to the prenuptial activities that would have taken place in their home village. Kateryna had a simple white dress, one she brought from Europe. There were plenty of flowers on the immediate hills above the mines from which to create her wedding garland. Vasyl borrowed a jacket, white shirt and celluloid collar from Ivan Choma and was ready for the event.

The postnuptial activities, however, had special attention from everyone. Much of the cooking and baking began on Friday or the morning of the wedding. Everyone participated because everyone came. There was no special list of wedding guests because very few people here had more than one or two relatives living in the community. Anyone's wedding in Good Town was always open to everyone who wanted to come. Invitations were never contemplated. Though they came from many different villages in Europe, there was a sense of brotherhood they experienced only in America, one that wasn't possible among them in the Old Country. The sense of expatriation unknowingly bound them together. They never realized how much they all had in common until they came here.

The amount of beer, brandy and vodka stored in Paul Turko's house was enough to last for two or three days of celebration. And, it was not unusual for weddings to last that long, even after work on Mondays the celebrations seemed to be able to regenerate. Weddings were one of the very few social activities miners had opened to them. Another was funerals, and occasionally christenings. It was a true break from the long days of hard work in the bowels of Mother Earth. It was only natural that Paul Turko and Ivan Choma stand up for Vasyl and Anna Kasper and Natasha Lazorisin for Kateryna.

Immigrating with Rusnaks to America were many Gypsies. It was always possible to find a few here who would play at weddings as they did in Europe. Two miners brought their fiddles with them and by late afternoon the celebration was well underway and lasted into the next day. They halted only for Father Balogh's service and by noon on Sunday, they were again in full force.

Vasyl had no trouble getting his old job back, but this time he was now the senior miner of a new team with Nick Mohilchak, a man three years Vasyl's junior from Wolosate, about 12 miles farther upriver of Protisne on the Wolosatka River. Nor was John Lynch, the mine super hesitant about rehiring Vasyl. In fact, he was glad because the number of single men in his operation was growing disproportionately to the number of married miners who could take in boarders. The "Old Hotel" was full.

"I guess you'll be wanting a house of your own now, Wasco," he said, "now that you brought a woman back with you."

Wasco was the English variation of Vasyl to which many immigrants changed their names once they got here. It was also easier for the American's to pronounce. It evolved from Vasyl, to Wasyl, to Wasylko and then simply shortened by most Rusnaks to Wasko or Wasco.

"We have three more that were finished last week and are unoccupied. Numbers 18, 19 and 20. Take a look at each location and decide which you like best. Let me know because I think I have somebody for another one. As a wedding present, I'll give you two months free rent, plus the rest of June.

"I heard you didn't like working with hard coal."

Kateryna Najda liked the sound of her new name and kept repeating it as she sat on the edge of their bed Monday morning while brushing her hair. Vasyl had left for the mines two hours earlier. As she did, her mind was flooding with the many things she had to do that day, that week and even beyond. After their marriage, she immediately settled down to the task of turning Company House No. 20 into a home. Her experience in the commercial boarding house in Wilkes-Barre turned out to be quite helpful.

Finding boarders to offset the cost of renting the house was no problem. In fact, there was a waiting list. She picked from those she knew or whose villages were near to Smil'nyk in the Old Country. That wasn't difficult to do because McDonald had done his recruiting of that area very thoroughly. She knew two women now in Good Town from her village. One was her age and the other a few years older. They had been here just a year ahead of her but in deference to the older woman's age, Kateryna let them guide her in what she would need for furnishings to handle the task. The company store even sold single beds as well as the kind that could be turned into bunks and set one atop the other.

"Get that kind," the older woman, Mary Salabaj said with authority as she walked Kateryna through the nearby company store. "That way, if you want to have more boarders, the beds won't take up any more space. You just put on one top of the other. Like on the ship. Remember?"

"How can I ever forget," she said and blessed herself. She took Mary's advice not only because she was older but because their grandmothers were sisters. She really didn't have much choice.

In March of the following year (1907), their first child, a daughter, Mary was born. Vasyl had hoped for a son and they determined to try again as soon as possible. One day while shopping at the company store, that also served as an adjunct post office, "Uncle" Jerry, told her there was a letter from Europe for the Najdas. They had to wait until Sunday when the priest from Central City would be there to hold services in the new Recreation Hall before they could find out what it contained.

Very few Rusnaks, either in Europe or America, could read or write. However, there always was the one odd person who could. If you couldn't wait for a priest to write a letter for you or read one you got from Europe you could get help from the *pishmo* (letter) person. But, it wasn't cheap. They charged from 25 to 50 cents a letter either to write one or read one. Most often, life in Good Town was not lived at a hurried pace and they waited for the priest.

"Vasyl, it is from your brother Ivan," Father Fedorenko said as he read it. "He has written, or the priest in Litowyschce has written, that John bought a ticket to come to America. He will be leaving during the first week of September."

"Oh *Bozé*," Kateryna blurted out. "That is just a week away. He could be here any day. I have so much to do to get ready."

"Don't get so excited," Vasyl tried to calm her. "It takes two weeks to cross the ocean. He won't be here until late September."

It was Friday, September 13, and Vasyl was working in the Lottie No. 2 Mine. He and Mohilchak had just shot a part of the roof and the dust was still settling down when the day foreman walked down the corridor and called Vasyl's name. Paul Turko was in the room next to Vasyl and when he heard Vasyl's name called he, too, came out to see if there was any trouble.

"I have someone here for you," he shouted.

Vasyl and Turko both turned to see who it was and the light from their lamps caught his face.

"Ivan," Vasyl yelled and he ran to greet him. They hugged each other with vigor and kissed, as Rusnak brothers are wont to do. John was 33, six years older than his brother and a half-foot shorter. Turko, his long-time friend, also greeted him with a hug and a kiss.

"Come, let us go outside so I can get a better look at you," Vasyl said as he guided his brother out of the room.

"I will stay here and begin loading," Vasyl's partner said.

"I will be back in a short time," answered Vasyl.

Once in the sunlight, Vasyl stood back to look at his brother.

"It has been four years since I saw you, since I left Protisne. You haven't changed any."

"You have," John said, "you look more like one of the black men I saw on Ellis Island, than the brother I once had."

They laughed as Vasyl wiped the coal dust from his cheeks.

"I didn't expect you here this early."

"It was a fast ship, the *Kronprinzessin Cecile*. The steward said we were traveling at 23 knots. I don't know what that means but the ship did move fast. And, we had good weather all the way. Thank God," he said and blessed himself.

September 11, 1907 — Almost four years later, Ivan Najda, the oldest of the four brothers, born in 1874, was next to immigrate to America. He was 33 years old at the time and traveled on another German passenger vessel, the *S.S. Kronprinzessin Cecile* and shipped out of Bremen. He, too, traveled alone. He listed on the ship's Passenger List his last address as Litowiska (Lutowiska in Polish), a village about 5 miles downriver (north) on the Sian. He listed himself as married. His wife's name was Juliana. She lived in Litowiska. He could neither read nor write and listed his occupation as a farm laborer. He stated that he had never before been in the United States His nationality was entered as Ruthenian, a synonym for Rusnak (or Russniak). At the time he landed on Ellis Island, he had $10 in his pocket, a train ticket, all of which had been paid for by his brother Andrij Najda of Protisne, Galicia. He was 5'1" tall, fair complexion with brown hair and blue eyes.

"We left Bremen on September 3 and landed in New York on September 11th. It took just seven days after we left England and France. I was in three countries in two days. That is a miracle."

"Then you didn't go through Hamburg and Emigrant Village?

"No. I had to spend one night in Bremen and the next day we were let on the ship and it sailed the following morning."

"Did anyone from our village come with you?"

"No. There aren't many single men left in Protisne, Smil'nyk, or even Litowyschce where Juliana and I lived. Things are so bad there that I had to leave and find work. Will I have any trouble getting a job here?"

"Not at all. But, I must return to the mine to work with my partner. It is not fair to let him load the car alone.

"Our house is Number 20," he said to his brother and pointed down the path to where it stood. Kateryna is there and has been looking for you every day since we got your letter. I must work until 5 o'clock and will see you then."

There were more than the usual number of Friday night visitors to the Najda house that evening. Someone new from the Old Country is always a source of news. First the women came. Somehow the word was out and a half-dozen of them crowded Kateryna's kitchen as John held court while she tried to cook their supper.

By the time Vasyl arrived, they had gone back to their own houses with men and families of their own to serve. After supper, Paul Turko was the first to arrive. He had an unopened cognac bottle in his hand, a sure sign that he had seen "Uncle" Jerry. Then Mike and Alex Salabaj followed. Mike Boburchak and the Maruschak brothers arrived a few minutes after them, with a bottle of vodka and a handful of cigars.

It was well after midnight when Kateryna had enough and began to chase them home. Luckily Mary Salabaj came to get her husband because he could not have made it home alone. There had been many a Friday night, really Saturday mornings, when after being paid, that the gutters along the path in Good Town were filled with sleeping drunks who could not find their own homes or fell short of the trip. Many dove into the bottle to escape from the mines, even though it was always short-lived trip. Vasyl, almost a teetotaler, was still fairly sober and his brother had not had as much to drink as the other revelers because he was doing most of the talking.

Despite this, Vasyl had noticed a change in his brother's attitude toward him. It wasn't anything specific he could put his finger upon, but just the way he answered some of the questions he and the others asked him. It was a definite a shift in attitude Vasyl sensed by the night's end.

When they were finally alone, Vasyl, who was a candid person and always forthright, asked him if something was wrong. At first, Ivan was reluctant to answer him directly. Upon Vasyl's insistence he finally came forth.

"I would have come here sooner, but you did not keep your promise."

"What promise?

"To send back money for one of your brothers to follow you to America. It has been four years and we haven't received one koruna. Others in our village have received money but nothing from you. We figured that you abandoned us. We thought that you had become rich in this golden land and forgot where you had come from. You had become a *bohatch*."

"Look around you, Ivan. What do you see? Do you still think I am wealthy? Do you still believe what McDonald and others have told you of America that, like the calendars the mills and mines send back to the Old Country, that the streets are paved with gold?

"The only gold here is black. It is black gold that we mine. It is black dust that is getting in my lungs every day. The only black gold we own is in our lungs.

"They pay us only enough so that we can live here and work for them. The only extra change is spent on a bottle of whisky. We are trapped here almost as bad as we were in Europe. It took me more than a year to pay back what I owed Consolidated for the *Schiffkarte* and the $25 I had to have in my pocket to get off Ellis Island."

"Andrij had to sell a horse and some land to get enough money for me to buy the ticket to get here. You could have done that," said John.

"John, aren't you listening to what I have been telling you? We have no money. My only pleasure is a pouch of Red Man tobacco a week. "After I got here, I used what was left of the $25 to buy my pick, shovel and lantern. Then I needed boots because half the time we work in water above our ankles. I needed clothes to work in the mine. I couldn't wear the sheepskins I had in Europe.

"Then after Kateryna and I got married, we had to furnish this house. It came empty. If we were to make a few dollars a month, it would be from boarders. We had to buy beds and mattresses for them.

245

"Our daughter Mary was born here instead of the hospital in Somerset and we had to pay the doctor to come here and help the midwives because her birth was complicated.

"Ever since I got here, I have worked every day except Sundays from 6 in the morning to 5 or 6 in the afternoon. Do you know how much money I have been able to save?

"Kasha, get the jar," he ordered his wife.

Kateryna had been cleaning the kitchen and got the jar.

Totally out of character, Vasyl smashed it on the kitchen table and glass flew everywhere. This was the first time in her life that Kateryna saw her husband lose his temper. From among the shards he pulled out five dollars, mostly in coins.

"That is what I am worth. Do you want it? Take it!"

"I don't believe you," John said. He jumped up so quickly from the table that the chair he sat on fell backwards. He let it lay there and rushed out the front door, slamming it as he left.

"I cannot believe that was my brother," Vasyl said. "He has changed. He was never such a hot-head."

"Maybe it was the vodka speaking," Kateryna said.

"No. I don't think so."

The next morning, just after sunrise, John returned to the house. His valise was still in the front room. As he was walking out the front door with it, he heard someone behind him.

Kateryna was quietly walking down the stairs.

"You shouldn't do this," she whispered to him. "You are brothers. You are family, you should make up with each other.

"I know Vasyl is head-strong and you, too, have a temper. But make up or you will regret this all your life."

John looked at his sister-in-law for just a brief moment. Then turned, and quietly shut the door behind him. John had slept at Paul Turko's that night, on the living room sofa. Paul told him of two bachelors who had taken over a shanty behind the company's butcher shop and had made it livable, even in the winter. There was no rent required. John joined them.

Chapter 25   Good Town Fire in 1907

I doubt that a horrendous fire in a small, southwest Pennsylvania mining town, in the early 20th century, where several Rusnaks lost their lives, ever made the newspapers in New York or even in Pittsburgh. However, there might have been some mention of it by the priest in his weekly message to the congregation one Sunday at the Alexander Nevsky Church in Woods Run. Probably, Andrij Karas wasn't in church that day to hear it because he was working the day turn. But even if his wife, or wives of other Rusnak steel workers may have heard it, they paid little attention to it because none of them had yet heard of the Najdas and their *sushidka* (neighbors). Even it they did, it wouldn't have stirred them; because the steel workers had major problems of their own developing because of the more belligerent stance unions were trying to take.

But to the 400 or so people living in Good Town in 1907, it was an earth-shattering event. I remember my grandmother's repeated description of it, more than 40 years later. It must have had a grave impact on her.

"*Vasyl, stavai,*" yelled Kateryna from the kitchen.

"Get up! Can't you hear all the noise outside? I think there is a fire. I see lots of light and people yelling." She had gotten up a few minutes earlier when she thought she heard a loud bang outside that shook her house. It could have been one of the boarders falling out of bed, upstairs. It happens, especially when they are drunk. And some of them had been partying since the weekend wedding.

Vasyl sprang out of bed.

He would have been getting up in a few minutes to get ready to go to work. It was Monday and the weekend had offered a few days of escape from his depressing miner's life. Peter Levisky, from Stuposiany, in the Old Country, and Mary Hilczanska, one of Kateryna's girl friends from Smil'nyk, had gotten married on Saturday. Kateryna and Vasyl's friend Paul Turko had been witnesses at the event. It was a double celebration for most of the Rusnak miners now filling the company town because, the Thursday before, it had also been "Russian" New Year's (Jan. 14). Because of work, they couldn't celebrate until the weekend.

Vasyl grabbed his trousers and rushed to the window. He couldn't see outside because the window was covered in heavy frost.

"*Bozé mi!*" he exclaimed after he threw it open for a better look. "It is the Rezak house. The whole downstairs is on fire."

Nearly a foot of snow covered the ground in the hollow that contained Good Town and its surrounding mines. Vasyl was glad he had donned his knee-high work boots with the felt liners and his heavy coat. A brisk northwest wind blew up the valley. The Rezak house was just three houses up the line from the one the Najda's rented from the company. It was still dark but the growing fire began lighting up the other houses and the road.

When he got there, the Ohlers, who rented one half of the two-storey "block house" and the Rezak's the other half, had already pulled out some of their furniture. It was scattered haphazardly over the snow.

"I ran upstairs," Fritz Ohler said to the gathering crowd, "and tried to get them to open the locked door between our bedrooms, "but I got no answer. I could already feel the heat on the other side of the door and thought it would burn through at any moment.

"I ran downstairs and into the Rezak's side. They were awake and running out with their children. I ran upstairs, and got four of the Hunkies who were passed out on the floor and pulled them down the stairs before the flames engulfed the stairs. Goddamn it, they were really drunk. At first, I thought they were already dead. I could do no more."

The Rezaks lived in one first floor bedroom and kitchen. The fire had started in the back, in the attached shanty the miners use when they came in dirty from the mines. There, they hung their clothes, shoes, boots and hats with carbide lamps. Sometime during the early morning, the fire in the stove, that heated the entire house, had gone out. One of the miners had come downstairs to light it. It wouldn't start so he took kerosene, used for the house lamps, and poured it over the supposedly dead coals. In a drunken stupor, he was too generous. It was instantly ignited by coals, that were still alive, as he doused kerosene on them.

The fire spread quickly and in minutes had reached the shanty. It ignited some black powder the miners use to break coal seams. Someone must have brought his "shooting bag" from the mine. Black powder doesn't explode unless it is contained but only burns like kerosene. The combination was so volatile that it accelerated the flames and in minutes they reached the stairs.

Twelve boarders, all miners, all Rusnaks except one Italian, lived in the two upstairs bedrooms. Seven still remained there. People outside on the ground were helpless and could only yell to them. They threw snowballs at the windows in a futile attempt to arouse them. One man, clad only is his longjohns finally came to the window.

"The stairs are all on fire," he slurred his words as he yelled to the growing crowd below. "Someone get me a ladder."

"Wake up the other men," Vasyl yelled.

The man disappeared inside for a moment and then returned to the window. "I cannot. They won't wake up. They're too drunk."

"There are no ladders," someone in the crowd yelled. The heat became intense and he climbed out the window. He hung onto the sill for a moment, clad, only in his longjohns, as if to gain courage, before dropping to the ground. He writhed in pain as he tried to get up. He had broken a leg in the fall. Life was cheap at that price.

In 1907, there was no running water in Good Town. Nor had Consolidated Coal planned on a fire department. Nothing of this sort had happened in the company town's five-year history and the management at Consolidated felt no need for the extra expense. They should have learned from the Rainey Town fire, but to retrofit the houses, or even put in fire mains, would have cost money and cut into their profits.

The people below continued to yell but could do nothing else to save the men. One man came to the window, his clothes aflame, then fell backwards into the engulfing inferno. The fire rapidly grew in size and houses on each side caught fire. Most of their contents and all of the people in them were saved before they, too, were burned.

No one went to the mines that Monday.

"I cannot believe this has happened," Kateryna said to Vasyl as she sat at the kitchen table with both hands clasping a mug of tepid coffee. They were such a happy group. Do you knew who died?"

"There was Pietro Taglio, the Italian," Vasyl said. "Harry and John Cutor, John Rechis, Tony Rezak, Jacob Swimitiski, and Jacob Lipiski. They all left wives in Europe except Lipiski and Mike Cutor. Who will tell them what happened? Not the company. They don't care. They will just call for others to come over and take their places. Men's lives mean nothing to them. Good doesn't care. Maybe we should now call this Bad Town instead of Good Town."

"When the priest from Windber comes on Wednesday, we can ask him to write to their families," said Kateryna.

"Why is he coming?"

"Ivan Kohut and Maria Maruschak are getting married."

"On a Wednesday?"

"I think she is pregnant, that's why," said his wife. "I think it will be a quiet wedding. No celebrations, especially after today."

Chapter 26   A New Old Life in Vilag

It was a dichotomy, a contradiction of purposes.

At almost the same time the Najda half of my family was coming to America looking for a better life, the other half, the Karases, were returning to Europe for the same reason. Who was right and who was wrong? Could they both be right? Or worse, could they both be wrong? Looking at it from a perspective they could never know, I believe it was not so much them but the times that dictated what they could or had to do. It was within the limited sphere available to them in which they had to operate; within which they could make choices. Options were not open to them because they had little or no control of their destinies.

Late spring, 1907-- The place is again the mountaintop village of Vilag, exactly 24 miles, as the raven flies, southwest of Protisne. But the course to it from Protisne is all uphill half of the way until it crosses over the continental divide. The village is ensconced in a small bowl, just below the continental divide. The crest of the Carpathian Mountains behind it forms the border between Austrian-Polish Galicia and Austrian-Hungarian Slovakia. Vilag has been part of Hungary for nearly a millennium. Its people, however, haven't changed ethnically in those thousand years. Their isolation has kept them nearly homogenous. They are still very much the same Rusnaks they were when Halych was the provincial capital of Halychyna (Galicia) and all roads led to Kyiv. They still speak the same Lemko/Boyko dialect, as do those Rusnaks on the Galician side of the mountain chain.

Andrij Karas and his wife Zuzanna and their two American-born sons are returning to the village he had left 15 years ago to find work in America. Since they departed their ship in Bremen, it has been one succession of train rides after another, to Praha (Prague) and finally Humenné in eastern Slovakia. Ever since daybreak, when they left Humenné 24 miles to the south, the road north had climbed steadily in elevation, though imperceptibly, toward Vilag.

The monotony of the horse's gate and the bouncing of the buggy had lulled Andrij almost to sleep. It was now late in the afternoon as they rounded a turn in the leeward protection of a hillock, when the air suddenly turned colder. Andrij responded without opening his eyes by pulling the collar of his heavy overcoat snugly around the back of his head. Again comfortable, his thoughts began racing back to when he alone crossed the Atlantic. The ship ride from Bremen to New York had not been as bad as most claimed it would be. And the return trip was faster, the accommodations less crowded and better. But maybe, he thought, it was the eagerness to be returning home, to his parents, relatives and friends, and his own house, that made it seem quicker.

Caught up in his own building emotion, Andrij even surprised himself when he suddenly came fully awake and ordered the driver to stop the buggy. They had come to a slight pass between two towering hills that the muddy road shared with a small stream. He jumped down from the seat next to the driver and onto to the road, then walked a few feet ahead of the horse. His clean, new shoes became encased in mud. He didn't care.

Looking up the rising road, he could see a cluster of yellowish-brown thatched roofs. It was his village. It was Vilag. He could see the tall, red, masonry church where he and Zuska were married 16 years ago. It's steeple towered above all the houses. It was built on a prominent hillock more than 500 years ago. It was here where he was born 38 years ago. His house was just to the left, along the edge of a small stream.

Even though it was late spring, in the distance beyond the houses, above the fields and pastures, snowdrifts still lingered on the high peaks. Water ran haphazardly down the road and between wheel ruts created by other wagons. Though lilacs were blooming in Humenné, the trees here, at this higher elevation, were bare even of buds. It looked as if winter had left only yesterday. A chill wind continued to roll down from the mountains and through the pass in which he was standing. Without thinking, he again raised the large collar on his heavy overcoat to protect himself. It was cold.

Fifteen years earlier Andrij Karas had passed through these sentinel-like hills, but in the opposite direction. He remembered how red were Zuska's eyes from crying because he was leaving. She even said she feared she would never see him again; that he would never send for her. But he did. There were others in Pittsburgh who crossed with him, or who came before and after him, who didn't send for their wives.

For a moment he was lost in thoughts as he stared at his village and heard himself ask, "Have I done the right thing? Should we have stayed in America? He had still not resolved the contradiction in his mind. Maybe we will only stay here for a little while…a visit. Maybe longer, a year or two at most. Maybe Medveki won't sell me the woods and we will have to go back sooner.

Zuska had never been totally in favor of going to America to join Andrij. She was a woman of strong convictions even though she had seen little of the world before she, too, passed through these hills. Maybe she was too young to leave her family. She was only 17; he was 23 when they married in 1891. She was 21 when she agreed to make the crossing by herself. Though she could easily have found other women her age, who would have liked to have accompanied her, none had the money to do so.

It was Andrij's dream of owning the woods that fascinated Zuzanna. She loved it when he told her of his plans. It was one reason she decided to marry him. But there was no money to be made here by farming, or raising sheep, but there was good lumber in the woods below the border. However, the only money he could get his hands upon to buy the woods would be in America. Andrij had promised her it would only be for a few years, five at the most, just enough time to make the money he needed to buy the woods above his father's field.

"Andrij," yelled Zuzanna, "it's beginning to snow. Let's move on."

Jolted back to reality, he climbed onto the front seat and the driver snapped the reins on the horse's back.

The top of the Carpathian Mountains, just beyond the village fields, is both the continental divide and the old Polish-Hungarian border. When Andrij left, both were a part of the teetering Austro-

Hungarian Empire and its stability had gotten worse while they were away. The crest above the village in winter is often a frozen hell. Gale winds, saturated with snow, blow incessantly from the northwest building drifts in the lee that were often 30 or more feet deep. Even five feet of snow is not uncommon in the village. Temperatures seldom rise above freezing until late March. In summer, however, it is an alpine paradise and the memory of the cold seems lost after but a few warm, spring days.

Life in winter, however, is tolerable in the village because it lies in the lee of the mountains and faces the sun. Vilag sits in a small bowl just 3 miles south Vysoky Grün, a 2,969-foot peak atop the divide. The bowl was carved through eons of time, weather and water by the Vyrava that still begins as a trickle at the base of a snowfield. It is shallow and no more than 5-feet wide as it escapes through the pass where Andrij had momentarily stopped. It was enough water, however, to attract the first migrant Slavs who, in the 8th and 9th centuries, came over the mountains from Halychyna to build their homes and raise there sheep here.

However, not much grows well here.

"It grows only stones and trees, stones better than trees," Andrij's father Mykola would often say. Its soil is poor, too poor to raise wheat. Oats and barley do grow, but just barely. It is almost too poor even for subsistence farming and too poor to feed more than a few cows. Milk and cheese, at times, are brought up from Humenné to supplement what is produced here. Sheep somehow do find enough grass to survive so most villagers with land in the bowl are herdsmen.

A century earlier, when the population here was sparse, and when the trees--that cover its peaks and valleys like a green blanket--were first cut, the land was more productive. But decades of over-use have drained the soil of its minerals and left it nearly sterile. By the end of the 19th century, it had become a difficult place in which to make a living. Life became a constant struggle. Many Rusnak men would head south in late summer and fall to work as fieldhands on the large Hungarian farms on the more fertile lowlands. Now, as the land in the foothills and mountains is losing its productivity, it is an easy place to leave...and many did.

It was impossible to fully understand why Andrij Karas, his wife Zuska, and their sons Andrew and Steven, would have left Pittsburgh to return to Vilag. There were others who did stay and survived. It cannot be blamed totally on the financial debacle in New York. Even though life was extremely difficult for them in Verner and Woods Run, there was still hope in America. But here, there was none. Politically they were on the bottom of the ladder. Austrians were on top, followed by Hungarians, then Slovaks and finally the Rusnaks. Here they were, back again in Vilag, Andrij thought. We will just have to make the best of it.

Slovaks were hardly a step above Rusnaks. Even many of their countrymen, from the two western provinces of Slovakia, considered those Slovaks from the eastern province to be more Rusnak than Slovak. And, they discriminated against them accordingly. The difference that set the eastern Slovaks apart from their own countrymen was their dialect. Ironically, it was more closely akin to that of the Rusnaks. They had little trouble understanding each other's language. Some etymologists believe that they were originally Kyivian Rus who were changed as a Slovak political system was imposed upon them more than a thousand years ago, even before the Magyars arrived from the East. What now sets the eastern Slovaks uncompromisingly apart from the Rusnaks is Roman Catholicism, which came with Slovakia's expansion eastward.

The snow squall stopped almost as they entered the village. When they left Vilag, more than 800 people lived here. It boasted one church, two stores and one tavern. The few Hungarians and Slovaks who lived in the village attended the Greek Catholic Church with the Rusnaks, the major ethnic group. The two Gypsy families, when they felt the need, also attended the same church. The five Jewish families in Vilag alternated services on Saturdays between their houses.

Zuska reprimanded Andrew, 9 and Stefan, 6 for carrying on in the back of the buggy. "Stop it," she yelled again, "or you will scare the horse." The children were hungry and the long ride from Humenné had been cold and difficult. It was also wearing on Zuska.

"Andrij," Zuska shouted at her husband. "It will be dark in a few minutes. We must find a place for the driver to stay tonight."

Andrij knew his father's house was small and would not have enough room for his family and the driver.

"Maybe he can stay in my brother Paul's house. Or maybe my sister Mary's," he said.

"Do not worry about me," said Boris, the driver.. "I have slept in many a barn. However, I prefer clean hay instead of straw."

"A lot can pass in 15 years" Andrij thought to himself as they approached the outermost house in the village. "Stefan Baran's house hasn't changed," he said to Zuska. "I wonder what their son John is doing. There is no light inside."

"Maybe they don't live there anymore," said Zuska.

In the time Andrij had been away from his village, its population had dropped by nearly 250 people. Most of those who left were young men who would not inherit their father's house nor farm. Most, like Andrij, had emigrated to America to find work.

The road from Humenné bifurcates just as it enters the village and forms a large, triangle that is without houses in its center. Through the center of the triangle flows a small mountain stream that tumbles and turns as it escapes the village heading for the larger Vyrava River. Behind the triangle high on a steep hill is the Greek Catholic Church. St. Dymitriy. It is not a wooden church, typical of those constructed by Rusnaks on the north side of the continental divide, but a masonry church with a large foretower and the large nave behind it. It has but one tower and that is capped by a modified cupola that seems stretched as it rises high above the church and dominates everything in the village. It is painted a dull red.

St. Dymitriy is an old church constructed about the 16th century and the numerous graves of the Karas and Ivanco families dominate the graveyard on the right side and behind the church..

The creek tends to the left and most houses, in ancient times, like many villages elsewhere, are built along both sides of it for access to water. But in more recent times, as the road parallels the stream on its west side, houses have proliferated on both sides of the road. The road leads to the vast, open meadow between the village and the continental divide. When Andrij left to go to America, only three houses were on the opposite side of the road. Now, there were five. "Maybe the village is growing," he thought to himself as they passed through the triangle. "I wonder why?"

His father's house was the last one on the right, the highest one in a row of log houses which all looked pretty much alike. The road ended just beyond their house but continued as a cow-path that snaked back and forth in cutbacks as it rose in elevation toward the woods and disappeared deeper into the bowl.

"No one is outside," Andrij turned and spoke to his wife as he helped her with the boys.

"It's too cold to be outside," she answered. "It is still winter here. I wonder if they got our letter. Maybe they think we are still in Pittsburgh."

Andrij and the driver descended at the same time. Boris grabbed the halter on the horse and Andrij opened the half-gate that led to the house. There was a light inside and he could see a woman moving back and forth. It's my mother, he said to himself as he reached for the wooden door latch.

"*Sláva Isúsu Khristu!*" he said as he opened the door.

"*Sláva na viki!*" a startled Anna Karas automatically answered as she turned to see her son....a vision she had not witnessed in nearly 15 years. She dropped the pan in her hands and lunged toward him.

"Andrij, Andrij, Andrij," she said as the last words were muted by her kisses.

Just then, the back door of the kitchen swung open. Mykola had been in the barn feeding the animals. In the dim light of the single kerosene lamp, Andrij saw his father and rushed to greet him. Maybe it was the poor light, but his father seemed to have aged more than a 15 years of hard work would have caused. Mykola limped slightly as he rushed to greet his son. His father kissed him on the lips. His mustache and rough beard scratched Andrij's face.

I should have a mustache like my father, he thought. What a stupid thing to be thinking at a time like this.

He saw tears run down his father's cheeks and suddenly his vision, too, was blurred. He looks like an old man, Andrij thought. What have I missed of him in these years...what has he missed of me?

Suddenly, Mykola began coughing. He couldn't stop and Anna rushed to him with a cup of water. Finally, it subsided. Andrij knew something was wrong with his father.

Zuska, carrying Stefan came through the door.

"*Sláva Isúsu Khristu,*" she said as she entered the kitchen. Immediately behind her walked young Andrew who paused to close the door.

"Candles. Candles," Anna said. "I must see my grandchildren. Mykola, turn up the oil lamp." She feverishly pulled candles out of a cupboard drawer and began lighting them.

As she did, the front door again burst open and Mary and Peter Ivanco rushed into the room. Zuska turned and cried aloud, "Father, mother," and rushed to embrace them.

"The daylight was poor, but we thought it was you when you passed below our house," said Peter. "Why didn't you write and tell us you were coming home."

"We did," said Zuska," more than two months ago,"

"Oh well," he said, "you know how bad the mail always is getting to those who live on the top of the world."

Zuska's mother stepped back to better view her daughter.

"What has happened to my little Zuzanna?" she said as she rushed forward and embraced her again. "You left as a little girl and now you are woman, a mother.

"Where are they?" Zuska's mother Mary cried out, "Where are my little Americans?"

A few days later Andrij and his father walked throughout the village to renew his memories, searching the houses of his youth for people he knew and events they elicited. In many, there were only women and children. They had been left behind, waiting for their husbands or brothers to send the money needed for them to buy their passage to America. For some it came but for most it never arrived.

The village seemed to have worn badly since he departed. The road through the middle was worse than ever and the church in its center was badly in need of repairs. Opposite of his father's house, on the other side of the stream, he saw the crumbling remains of what had once been Volodymyr Karas's house. They were distant cousins, his mother told him in his youth, but they had all died long before Andrij was born, when cholera swept the village. Many people died at that time. He remembered how he and his brother and sister played in its crumbling remnants.

"Another store had opened in the triangle," said Mykola.

"It is owned by Polish Jews," he quickly pointed out. "They came over the mountains from Galicia. We go in there from time to time but they do not have much on their shelves. They are having a hard time of it. People here have very little money. Most of what they do have comes from America. You don't even need to exchange your dollars for *groschen*. In fact, they prefer dollars. You can buy more with them.

"Here is a new tavern," he said as they rounded the corner. "It is run by two Slovak brothers. More Slovaks are moving into our village. God only knows why. They seem to be the only ones making money. Shall we go in for a cognac?"

Ivan Charsky was a big man, with large hands and head to match. His unkempt, unruly hair made it look even larger than it was. His hands were rough and strong and you could tell that running a tavern wasn't his only business. Before moving to Vilag, he and his three brothers worked in the tin mines to the south. When the mines petered out, he made his move.

"The first drink is on me," Charsky said to Andrij. "Welcome back."

The word already was out.

"We have a brother, Mathew," Charsky said as he poured the brandy, "who is working in a shoe factory in Binghamton. Is Binghamton near Pittsburgh? Maybe you know him? Do you?

"Are you here for a visit or are you planning to stay?

"If you need a house, I have two that are for sale. Just let me or my brother Paul know. We will be glad to show them to you."

Andrij quickly came to realize as he walked the village with his father that one cannot go home again. It is true, like Tom Wolfe believes. You cannot because the moment you leave, home begins to change without your witnessing the changes. It stays the same only in your mind. And the longer you are away from home the greater are the changes. If you stay away too long, you will not recognize home when you do return. Home is really a fractional moment in time. It seems to stay the same while you are there but it really doesn't. The sensation is real because you and everything at home are changing together.

Andrij Karas learned this only too well.

Chapter 27   Spring in Vilag (1907)

It didn't take long for the entire village to know that Andrij and his family had returned to Vilag....and to stay. During the next two days, anyone with relatives in America, even if they were not in the Pittsburgh area, stopped by to ask if he knew anything about them. To Zuska's disappointment, her two best girl friends had gone to America but neither, according to their relatives, had gone farther west than Manhattan.

The first two days at home were an ordeal for Andrij because he wanted to see Zoltan Medveki and visitors were always at the door. When he was finally able to go to Medveki's house, his wife told him that he was away, on business in Kosicé, and didn't know when he would be home.

"He should have been here by now," she said, as she was closing the door. "He has probably taken up with some Slovak *kurva* and lost his money." The door slammed.

A few days later, Medveki was at Mykola Karas's door, asking to see Andrij. Zuska let him in.

"I will get him," she said, "Please sit down. He is back in the barn, helping his father."

A minute later, Andrij burst through the door of the kitchen that led from the barn.

He rushed to shake Medveki's hand as the older Hungarian rose to his feet. Then they embraced. He and Medveki had been more than casual friends. Andrij had often worked for him in his woods clearing deadfalls and pruning spruce trees. He loved the life in the woods but the jobs were always temporary, a week or two, here and there, and only when his help was needed.

Medveki was in his late 60s, a rotund, jovial man whose long hair was still pitch black. His large, handlebar moustache, however, showed signs of an impending color change. His heavy eyebrows made his black, deep-set eyes seem even darker. Medveki was no taller than Andrij, about 5-1/2 feet, maybe even slightly shorter. His plump hands felt soft to Andrij's as they greeted each other. A decade in the steel mills had hardened Andrij's hands beyond belief. Though they had lost a lot of their sensitivity to the heat in the mills, they were still able to measure a man's livelihood.

He has not worked hard to be able to grow so fat, Andrij thought to himself. What has he done right that I have not?

"You've changed, Andrij," Medveki said as he released his hand and stepped back for a better look. "America must have been good to you. You look trim and fit. But why did you return?"

"Because I missed seeing you," Andrij answered, "and your homemade *slivovitz.*"

"Seriously?"

"America was good to me and my family but I'd rather be a woodsman than a steelworker." Andrij mentioned nothing of the recession that was currently sweeping America.

"But you must have woods to be a woodsman. And, the demand for timber lately has been slow, so slow that I cannot hire you again to work in my woods."

"I don't want to work your woods, I want to buy them!"

Medveki was startled at the response. How could one of these Rusnaks ever get together enough money to buy my woods? he fleetingly thought as his eyes searched Andrij's face for a sign, a smile, or something that revealed that he wasn't serious.

"You are not joking? Are you? You would not make fun of this old Magyar? You want to buy my woods?" he said in long, drawn out words that revealed his mind was at work and his mouth was stalling for time to let the statement sink in.....to fathom its ramifications.

"Yes!"

"Do you have the money?"

"It depends upon how much you want. How many hectares are there?"

"More than a hundred. It would mean a lot of money."

"What is a lot of money?"

"I don't know now. Give me one or two days and I will tell you."

It didn't take Medveki that long to figure out what the 103 hectares (about 250 acres) of land was worth. By that afternoon he knew and sent his grandson Zolty to fetch Andrij.

"That didn't take long," Andrij said as he entered Medveki's house.

"Come. Sit down here," and he motioned to the kitchen table. There were two glasses and a bottle of Medveki's, village-renown, plum brandy on the table. "Let's have a little of my prune juice before we start."

He poured two generous amounts.

Zoltan lifted his glass to Andrij's and toasted in Rusnak, "*Na za drovya.*"

Andrij wasn't surprised. He knew that Zoltan knew the Rusnak toast. "To your health, too," Andrij answered.

"I will be honest with you," Zoltan started. "I haven't said anything to anyone but I have been thinking of selling my woods. There is still a great deal of timber there but I am getting too old to work it. And, all you young Rusnaks have gone to Amerika seeking your fortunes. There is not much help around nowadays and what there is, is afraid to work.

"I know it is worth more, but if you want it I will sell it to you, to you only, because you have always been honest with me and me with you. I want 5,000 korona!"

"What is a korona worth today?"

Neither of the men were quite sure but they figured it was about $800 American dollars. They would eventually go the bank in Humenné to be sure, Zoltan suggested.

"That is a fair price," Andrij said, then paused for a few minutes. Took a sip of the liquor. Zoltan did the same.

"I will buy it, but I have only 600 American dollars to spend. We can do this two ways. I can either buy three-quarters of your land or I can buy it all and owe you $200. As I sell the wood, I will pay you before I put a pfennig in my pocket."

Andrij could have paid for it all but he knew he had to hold some of his dollars in reserve. There would be new equipment he would need and other unpredictable costs to living again in Vilag.

"I prefer the latter," Medveki answered. "And, I will throw in the two horses and all the lumbering equipment I have."

Three days later, the two men rode Zoltan's two draft horses to Humenné, visited the bank and then consummated the deal in Shlomo Rudnik's office. They did not change the money into korunas because the dollar was worth more than the banks were able to pay. They celebrated with a few drinks, and then rode Andrij's two draft horses back to Vilag.

Spring is not the best time to begin harvesting trees anywhere in the world but there was a lot more work to be done before that could take place. Andrij spent May becoming familiar with almost every tree on his 103 hectors. He took young Andrew, as they called him in English, wherever he went. When Stefan cried to come along, he was told that he was still too young, "Next year."

A week after they had arrived, Zuska received a visit from Zuzanna Samandi. Since Zuska had gone to the United States, the Hungarian Government, prodded by Vienna and the Emperor, had built a lower level, grammar school in Vilag. Samandi, Hungarian, was one of a few Magyar families living there and was born in Vilag. She learned Rusnak as she grew up among the villagers and was as familiar with it as Hungarian. Her father was the postmaster and sent her to Budapest to be educated. She was the school's first teacher.

"How old are your boys?" she asked.

"Shouldn't Andrew be in school now?

"Did he go to school in America?

"That's good.

"I have room for him in my classes. We have two more months of school and he should be there. The government now mandates that all children in Vilag, and all of Hungary, regardless of their ethnic background or religion, must attend classes. There may be a little difficulty for him at first because all the classes are taught in Hungarian. That is also a government mandate. But, the children will learn fast. I have seen it with the other Rusnak youngsters.

"Stefan, didn't start school in Pittsburgh? Did he?

"Oh! He did. We can wait until the end of summer before he must go to school.

"By the way," she said and paused because she was hesitant to say next what she was required to say. "There is a law now in Hungary. If you do not send your children to school you will be fined."

"That sounds like a good law," Zuska said. "I wish it was so when I was growing up. The problem was that there were no schools here at that time."

Zuska looked at the younger Zuzanna and saw herself as she was a dozen years earlier. Her hair was long and dark brown. But, she didn't have Hungarian eyes. They were as blue as were hers. Somewhere in the past 1,000 years, their ancestors must have crossed. Even their first names were the same. She wondered what she would be doing here if she had never gone to America. Probably, she thought, she would have a half-dozen children by now.

"The law says that we can teach only in Hungarian," Zuzanna continued. "I don't know English. Do they speak Slovak as well as Rusnak?

"It doesn't matter. I speak both. Maybe, after a few years, they will also speak Hungarian or even German once they get in the sixth grade."

Andrew was disappointed when he came down from the woods with his father. The next day, he would have to go to school. It wouldn't be too bad. There were many Karases and Ivancos in the village, and more first and second cousins than he could imagine. In fact, Karases were one of the more numerous families in Vilag. They were so numerous that many of the men adopted their wives' last names, adding it to the end of theirs, to help identify each family. It was a custom followed in many small mountain villages where a few families made up the entire population.

Identity in the village could be a problem for outsiders because Rusnaks don't give their children middle names. For their middle name, male children automatically assume the name of their father and add -son to the end of it. Nor, is the variety of first names from which they may choose very great. Most were either Nicholas, John, Michael, George, Steven, Basil, Andrew, Alex or Paul with the occasional Harry and Gregory. These are their English equivalents.

Andrij learned from Samandi that the government maintained a forestry office in Humenné to help any foresters improve their tree stands and increase its yield. "He should visit them," she said. He did, and two weeks after the visit, the bureau sent two botanists, riding on horses, to help him survey his lot. They were surprised that a Rusnak owned a working forest. He learned much from them. He also saw the need for another horse, not one to pull logs, but one to ride his holdings and to get him back and forth to Humenné because that is where the lumber merchants were located. He wanted the kind the botanists had.

Three weeks after they had been there, Andrij was again in Humenné to visit lumber buyers. He came back with another horse and talked to Zuzanna about maybe soon getting a light buggy. With recommendations from the forestry bureau, about the size of his holdings, the lumber-buyers advanced him enough money against future sales, to buy the horse.

The next two years (1909-10) passed quickly and Andrij had cut enough lumber to pay Medveki all that he owed him. He even was able, from the last sale, to have money left over. He didn't have to touch the $150 dollars he had stored away for a "rainy day," as he used to tell his wife. He suddenly felt proud of himself. Now 40 years old, he may not have been able to fulfill all his ambitions, but finally he seemed to be on the way to attaining some of them.

One evening after supper, as he lighted his pipe and leaned back from the kitchen table with a mug of coffee in his hand, he told his father that the house is too small for all of them.

His father was taken aback. The shock caused him to start coughing and it took him several minutes to regain his breath. This worried Andrij. His coughing spells were becoming more frequent and were lasting longer.

"Maybe I should take you to Humenné to see a doctor."

"Are you planning to move?" Mykola (Nicholas) was finally able to ask him.

"No father, but we need more space. The house is too small, and we will have an addition to the family in a few months. Zuska is with child."

Mykola Karas was delighted with the news. Not only was his son not moving, but there would also be a baby again in the house.

"When?"

"About the end of May.

"I plan to add another room, if it is okay with you, off to the north side of the house. And, the barn must be expanded. The two draft horses are crowded and I hardly have room for the stallion. I will begin building in a month, if it has your approval."

"What can I do?"

"Go with me to see the doctor!"

Mykola didn't answer but got up from the table, when he saw Zuzanna enter the kitchen from one of the bedrooms and gave her an especially long-lasting hug. While still in his grasp, she said, "I guess Andrij has told you...but don't hug me too hard."

Two weeks later, Andrij and his father returned from Humenné. Mykola had tuberculosis and there was nothing the doctors could do. If they had seen him two years earlier, maybe even a year, they might have been able to help. But now there was nothing, nothing anyone could do but wait for the man to die.

"The disease has been the scourge of our people," Zuzanna said as he and Andrij sat around the table late in the evening. It was tuberculosis that took my father, and one of my uncles.

"My sister Maria was over today. She got a letter from Sam yesterday. They had another baby, a girl they named Anne. They see John Evans and his wife in church and when they go to his butcher shop in Woods Run. They said his business is doing well.

"Maybe we should have stayed!

Andrij and his young sons set up a sawmill in the woods and began selecting trees. Andrij's brother John was able to help because Andrij could now afford to pay him something and John wouldn't have to head down onto the plains and look for supplemental work as a farm hand. Andrij's sister Elena had married Mykhail (Michael) Ivanco. They had two sons before he went to Wilkes-Barre to work in the mines. The boys were now in their late teens and needed work. What money Mykhailo was sending back was barely enough to keep them alive.

The new bedroom was completed in late May, just in time for the birth of their daughter Zuzie, short for Zuzanna, on the 26th, 1909. She was born healthy but when she was six months old she developed an ear infection. The itinerant doctors never determined what caused it, but she seemed different after she recovered. She was less responsive to her mother. Everyone thought the worst. They feared she was retarded. Only years later, did a doctor discover that the early infection had damaged her ears and that she could hardly hear in either of them. They wouldn't accept her in school and it was difficult for her to learn even from her brothers Andrew and Stefan.

That following year, on January 28, Mykola Karas died. Because Andrij was the eldest son, he inherited the house and his father's field. His brother John, who was struggling to eke a living on his wife's family's farm, decided that there was no future for him in Vilag. One of their cousins was working in a shoe factory in Binghamton, New York. The pay was reputed to be good so he decided to emigrate with his entire family to the United States as soon as Andrij's barn was completed.

Chapter 28   The Impending War

The eight or so years after Andrij Karas returned to his beloved mountains and its woods were the happiest he and Zuska had ever known. For once in his life, and that of his family, they had enough food on the table, money for clothes, and even a surplus to be put away for the future. His sons were growing rapidly and while Stefan was still too young, Andrew was becoming an immeasurable aid to his father in the woodlot. He did worry about his daughter's hearing and her awkward ways but she seemed to be able to cope with it. Besides, there was nothing he or the doctors could do about it. He did wish that his father was still been alive to enjoy his success as a lumberman, but that was not to be. However, his world was about to change, to be shattered, torn asunder and left to Zuzanna to pick up the pieces, patch them together, and go forward with the dream of true emancipation for her family.

"While life has been good to us of late, these are not good times in the rest of the world," Zuska said one evening as she sat across the kitchen table from Andrij. It was their quite hour, their few moments together after their children were asleep. The children were in bed and his mother slumbered in a rocking chair next to the stove. He didn't look up but continued to write numbers in a ledger that was within the immediate scope of the lamp. The flickering flame from the lone kerosene lamp on the table cast bizarre shadows on the freshly whitewashed kitchen walls and ceiling.

Earlier that evening, Zuska had washed her long, light-brown hair. Now, unfettered, it cascaded over her shoulders. Admiringly, Andrij looked up and watched her as she moved about the room.

Occasionally, her hair mixed with her work. She was sewing a pair of his pants and from time to time glanced at him and smiled. There hadn't been much time lately for tenderness between them.

Little Zuzie, now six, had been playing a the corner of the kitchen and left her collection of corncob dolls strewn on the floor. Andrij had carved wooden heads for them and her mother made bonnets and dresses. Though she was only in her early 30s, Zuzanna looked closer to 50. The years of toil in Pittsburgh had aged her quickly and now her expanded household left her no time to herself.

Anna, her mother-in-law, seemed to have stopped caring about the lives around her after Mykola died. She sat in the rocker in the back of the room and endlessly rocked back and forth while staring, as if mesmerized, out the window, or at night, at the flickering yellow flame of the kerosene lamp. Her mind was surely somewhere else. Mykola had built the rocker more than 40 years ago, soon after they were married. Maybe she viewed it as a link to him.

When Andrij and Zuzanna first returned from America, Anna used to help with Andrew and Stefan. But now, she seemed to have lost interest in life, even in living. She contributed less and less as each day passed, even to the raising of little Zuzie, whom she once favored.

"I don't think you should buy Fetchko's woods," Zuska broke the silence. "Our woods are not making the money they did when we first bought the land. Things are suddenly, quickly changing. I don't like what I see ahead. The price the Hungarian buyers are giving us has fallen sharply in just a few months. It is now hardly worth the cutting. It is just as well that the woods now do not have a lot of mature trees to harvest."

"That is all true," he finally said as he looked away from the ledger toward his wife. "It is the uncertainty of the times. The Magyars, every week, are pushing the Austrians for more and more concessions. The dual monarchy is not working and most Hungarians want to be separated.

"The Czechs are no different. They, too, want their own country. Even across the border," he pointed to the north as he spoke, "the Poles are demanding more and more self-rule from the Austrians. Yesterday, I spoke to a Rusnak who had come through the pass in our woods. He said the Poles would not let our people there go to the new school in his village unless they admit they are

Polish. Nor will they let them marry unless they go to a Catholic or Uniate priest. Couples are now sneaking over here to find an Orthodox priest. Even Father Tidik admitted the other day that he had quietly married four Galician couples in the last two months. What is this world coming to?"

"That's why I say, don't buy Fetchko's woods, not at this time, maybe later. What little we have saved we may need to see us through this winter. If you put it into buying more woods, it would be years before they show a profit. No one is building in Hungary, the times are too uncertain."

"I know all this," Andrij answered, "and it has all been going through my mind for weeks. It is not woods I am thinking of buying. Our savings are dwindling just as we hold on to them. I am glad I didn't convert the last of the American dollars we saved. They are still holding their value. I checked at the bank the last time I was in Humenné looking for wood buyers. They are worth almost twice more than when we returned to Vilag.

"I have been thinking, the meadows below the woods still have good grass so I plan to buy more sheep. There is always a demand for wool and we can always butcher them or sell them alive. They take no feed and the barn is full of hay for the horses and enough to winter the sheep when the weather gets too bad for them outside."

"A bigger herd is just what Andrew and Stefan needed to keep them busy as the trees matured. Yes, I will go to Humenné tomorrow and take the boys with me. I don't know how long we will be gone."

The cattle merchants in Humenné had no sheep for sale but one knew of a Slovak in Koskovce, on the road back to Vilag, who might have some.

"No, I don't have any," said Pavel Hudak, "but my cousin in Zboiné has some, if he hasn't already sold them. I haven't seen him in more than a month. He doesn't live far from you. You shouldn't have any trouble buying from him."

"Karas, Karas, Karas," repeated Janos Madarash. "I was told years ago by my *Baba* that we have Karas relatives in Vilagy. I was there once or twice but there are so many Karases there that we didn't know which one it might be. You might even be my relative," he said to Andrij.

"That might be true," said Andrij, "but do you have any sheep for sale? I want to enlarge my flock."

"What! A Rusnak with money to buy sheep. You must be a Jew. Are you?"

"God forbid," Andrij said and blessed himself in the way of an Orthodox Christian. Janos smiled.

"To you, my brother, I am Ivan not Janos. Life is a bit easier around here for my family and me if I go by Jan instead of Ivan. The Magyars think it is too Russian. And, since the Russian Tsar sent troops to his cousin, the Austrian emperor, to put down the Hungarian revolt, being Russian here is not popular.

"Yes, I have nearly 30 head. The ewes are fat with lambs and they will almost double the number in a few months. But, I am in a predicament. I don't have enough hay to see them through the winter. The spring and summer here were dry and the grass was almost gone by the end of August. Do you have grass? Well, you're higher up and must get more rain than we do down here.

"Also, I want to go to America? Have you been there? You must not have. But if that were so, you wouldn't be back here, would you?"

"Don't believe everything you hear about America," said Andrij.

They easily struck a deal and it took Andrij and his sons less than a day to drive the sheep the 3 miles north to Vilag, through the village and to their farm. As they passed through the only road in the community, its residents came out to see who was driving sheep.

Young Michael Kalinich and his grandparents came to the fence along the road and counted the sheep as they passed. Andrij, on his stallion, tipped his hat to *Baba* Kalinich.

A few minutes later, she and the rest scurried back into their house. "*Bohatch, Karas bohatchi,*" she said.

"Are they really rich?" asked the youngster as his grandmother pulled him by his hand into the house.

A few days later, Andrij was in the small cemetery behind St. Dimytri's Church looking at the gravesite of his father. Even though it was late June, the grass was already tall on the grave. "It needs cutting," he said to himself. "Maybe I can tell Andrew or Stefan to do it. No. I should do it. I must come back and cut it, that is the least I can now do for him."

It was exactly five months, almost to the day, since he had died. A year after his father's death, Andrij would replace the small wooden cross he had made with a wire-framed cross he bought on a trip to Humenné. He wondered if his father would have been alive today if the doctors had discovered his sickness earlier. If it had been America, he was sure his father would still be with him.

"Life becomes more difficult by the day in Hungary," Andrij said to himself as he stared at the remnants of a mound. The woods have yielded almost no profit in the last year. "Thank God," he murmured, "that I bought the sheep. At least there is always a market for wool. Maybe we should go back to Pittsburgh, there seems to be no future here. And now, Zuska is three months with child. How will I feed the family? I cannot kill sheep or I will lose money. Life has suddenly again become a dilemma."

Chapter 29   Southward to Battle the Italians

Little did my grandfather know at that time that his future was not in his hands but in the soft, clean, perfumed and uncalloused hands of a few people in Wien (Vienna).

A youngster yelling aloud and repeating the same phrase over and over as she neared the church broke Andrij's thoughts. He turned around and saw that it was his daughter Zuzie running up the hill toward him. He saw her blue eyes and watched her flaxen hair bob as she approached. He also saw a fear in them that he had never seen before, and in someone so young. It puzzled him. Fleetingly, he wondered what was of such importance that could do this to her.

"Papa, Papa," she yelled from the side of the church. "The Duke is dead. The Duke is dead. "

"What do you mean?"

"Mama told me to come and tell you that the Duke is dead."

"What duke? Who is dead."

"I don't know," answered the six-year old. "Come home."

"It is the Austrian duke," said Zuska as Andrij entered the house. "Archduke Ferdinand, who was to be our next emperor, was assassinated in Sarajevo by a Serb. It happened a few days ago. Stefan Baran was in Humenné and heard the news. They say it will be war in a few weeks, maybe less. They say that Austria will be calling men from all over the empire, not just Austrians or Hungarians, but everyone to fight. They also say the Germans are pushing the Austrians to go to war and that Bulgaria and Turkey are joining the Central Axis Powers.

"Andrij," said Zuska, "this is not good. They say America will join the English and we might be fighting our relatives if they come to Europe to fight as Americans. I know the Hrinda's have a son in Pittsburgh who joined the American Army."

It didn't take long for the war to reach Vilag. A week after they had heard the news, on a Sunday morning, a man in a brown military uniform arrived in Vilag by auto. His car pulled up to the church where got out. With a clipboard in hand, his driver followed him and a third, a civilian, followed behind him.

The villagers had seen a Hungarian military uniform but this one was different, it was Austrian. As the people poured out of church the civilian, speaking in Slovak, told them not to go home, but to assemble in front of the church and wait. And, if they knew of any adult, especially male who wasn't in church, to send their children to get them.

A half-hour later, the military man, speaking in German, addressed what was the entire ambulatory population of Vilag. He spoke slowly and the civilian translated. Where he faltered, Zuzanna Samandi filled in, either in Rusnak or Slovak. He told them that Austrian troops had entered Sarajevo to punish the Serbs because the Serbs supported the assassination. And, that Russia, which supports Serbia, was joined by England and France in declaring war on the Central Powers.

The officer announced that all men, between the ages of 20 and 45 were to step forward and give their names to the man with the clipboard. And, that they were to report to Humenné, on July 4, in three days, (1914) for physical examinations. The army would send trucks that morning to take them to Humenné. Those men, who passed, were to be immediately conscripted into the Austro-Hungarian army to fight for the Emperor and their country.

"You have three days to get your affairs in order."

Before the war ended, three-quarters of the Austrian army would be composed of Slavs. It made many Austrian officers uncomfortable because these men all showed a reluctance to fight against Russians, soldiers who spoke a language very similar to theirs. Andrij fell into the group of men to be examined. He wouldn't be 46 until December. That night, as he and Zuska discussed what all this meant, Andrij suddenly laughed.

"What do you find funny to laugh about?" she asked.

"Just think," he answered, "if we were still in America, I would not have to go to the mill to work on July 4th. It is a holiday. There would be the company picnic, parades and the bosses would be passing out cigars. Here, I may go to my death to defend a country that isn't mine and though I was born here, as were my father, grandfather and his grandfather, and all my fathers before him, we are looked upon as aliens, aliens in our own land."

"What will happen to our sons?" Zuska asked. "What if the war goes on for a long time? Andrew is 15. In five years he will be 20. If the war goes on that long, they will drop the age and he could go in two or three years. Maybe we could send them back to America, to live with my brother or your cousin."

"Don't worry so much. They are saying that this will be a short war," answered Andrij, "that it will be over by Christmas."

"I pray to God it will," Zuska said and blessed herself.

It took two trucks to carry the 35 men to Humenné. The examinations were cursory at best and only four men made the return trip to Vilag. The next day, the soldiers who guarded the makeshift barracks, where the men from Vilag were quartered, could account for only 28 men. They were loaded onto two larger trucks with canvas shelters and driven southward for the entire day. They arrived at what was a hastily-built camp, surrounded by barbed wire and armed guards at the gate. It looked more like a field prison than a military training camp.

Their barracks were large, square tents with a pyramid-shaped dome. Inside were a dozen double bunk beds. The outside latrine was still being dug. After two weeks of drilling and small arms instructions, they were told they were ready for the front. During training, rumors of where they would be sent ran rampant through the conscripts as well as the staff. Most of the officers were Austrian with a few Hungarian noncoms. One Austrian sergeant told Andrij they didn't trust the Hungarians.

The new men were a mix of everyone from the polyglot empire, and composed of Austrians and Hungarians but most of the trainees in this camp were Czechs, Slovaks, Rusnaks, a few Ukrainians and even a few Poles. They had heard of the battles in France and were sure that that was where they were headed.

But after the men were loaded, the trucks headed in a southward direction as they left camp. After two days of driving, they never turned to the west. "If you were going to France," said an Austrian corporal who was in charge of every truckload of soldiers, "you would have been sent by train."

On the last day of their travel, an Austrian officer spoke to the men before they boarded their trucks. He told them, that they would be at the Serbian border by the end of the day.

The next day, as the men stepped from the truck, two men were handing out long-handled spades. "You will fight with these before you use your rifles." Each man took one and fell into line. There was no village or town to be seen. Instead, they were at the foothills of mountains that were larger than any they had ever seen in their region of the Carpathians. To the south, coming down through a pass, was a small river that meandered on the plain where they were bivouacked. It was no more than a hundred feet wide and so shallow that there were more exposed gravel bars than water surface.

"That river is the border between Austrian Empire and Serbia," said the officer who had addressed them earlier that day. "We have spies on the other side who informed us that the Serbs are amassing an army just beyond those hills," he pointed as he spoke. "They plan to cross this river within a few days. We will stop them here, and as more reinforcements arrive, we will drive them back. Some of you men will be detailed to string barbed wire across this line. Others will begin digging trenches, your homes for the next few weeks, until this war is over. So dig quickly and deeply for your own safety. Others will be gathering stones from the river, or from the hills just behind us."

The trenches Andrij and his group were assigned to dig were to be 4 feet wide and 5 feet deep. Digging trenches was safer than being one of those sent to the river to gather stones. The Italians, who had quickly been rushed to the aid of the Serbs, after the second day saw the Austrian activities and stationed snipers to harass the gatherers. When it became too dangerous to be along the river, the stone gatherers were sent to the fields in the rear to tear down stone walls. When these ran out, they were sent to a quarry.

It took the men less than a week to dig their assigned length of trench. Three times a day, an Austrian corporal would come along with a 5-foot long stick, and would measure their progress.

"Hurry up," he would yell at them if they seemed to lag behind. "It is your life that is in danger. The trenches will save you."

The finished trench would be 3 feet wide. The extra foot they were required to dig was to allow for stones to be placed in back to support the trench from caving in. It was the Austrian's idea of how trenches should be built. However, once the fighting began, the stones accounted for more deaths than the accuracy of Italian rifleman because of bullets ricocheting inside the trenches.

It began raining as the men started lining the back walls with stones. At the end of the day, many stones had slide out of position and kept cluttering the narrow trench and constantly had to be replaced. The men sloshed around in water above their ankles because the clay bottom wouldn't drain. No one had thought to line the bottom with duckboards and their only answer was a few bailing buckets that were eventually requisitioned from nearby town residents.

There was no where for the men to sleep, except standing up or leaning against a corner. It was forbidden for them to dig cubbies into the trench walls because one had collapsed during the first night from the excessive rain and several men almost died. They huddled together under oilcloths. It was an ill-equipped army the Austrians sent into the trenches. At each zigzag of the trench a small field kitchen was set up and the men sloshed through the water to get fed.

Halfway down the length on each trench, a small latrine area was cut into the back wall. It was too dangerous to climb outside the trench and build a latrine there. After the first week, water flooded the latrines and feces floated out into the trench almost every time a man sloshed by. It wasn't too bad at night because you couldn't see the floating turds but you could smell the urine. It was an unusually rainy July.

The spy reports were right. A week after (Aug. 1) they started digging their trenches, the Serbs and Italians moved mortars and light artillery into the low hills that lay just before the river and began bombarding the Austrian lines. It kept the Austrians in their trenches as Serb soldiers hurriedly built their own trenches on the opposite side of the river.

The small-arms fire was constant throughout the daylight periods and sporadic at night. However, at night, the mortars became more active. No one moved out of the trenches during the day, but at night, both armies sent out patrols and flares often caught them standing in the river that was now swollen from the rain. It was rising and began to pose a threat to the Austrian line. When selecting the position no one thought of a rising river.

There seemed no major push from either army. It was as if both sides were waiting for events to unfold on the Western Front and the various powers were using the time to hurriedly build their armies.

Andrij had been in his trench for three weeks (Aug. 21) and was expecting to be rotated to the back lines. It wasn't raining the day he awoke and felt as if he was on fire. It must have been the shivering that awakened him. How could he be shivering, he thought to himself, while his head felt on fire? And his head ached as if a bullet had banged his helmet. At first, when he tried to move, the muscles in his legs wouldn't respond. As he tried to stand erect, they screamed in pain. It was followed by aches in his lower back. But the pain in his shins was the worst.

It's standing in this damned water, he though to himself. Just the day before Yurko Ivanco, his cousin from Vilag, had complained of the same pains. He told this to his Austrian patrol leader. "Oh! You have only the flu," he answered. "Be a man. Bear with it. It will go away in a few days. There are others with the flu but no one is complaining."

That was a lie. The next day, the patrol leader experienced the same symptoms. Andrij saw him huddled against the stones, grabbing his stomach. Andrij passed him on the way to the latrine. As he did, he said to him, "Be a man!"

"Damn that Austrian," Andrij said to Ivanco, "he was right. I feel better today. The fever is gone. What about you?"

"I started to get better yesterday. The Austrians call it the 5-Day Fever."

All seemed to be getting better. It was good, because the Serbs began to intensify their fire. It was stupid to even try to look across the river because each time a head appeared above the trench a barrage of small fire followed.

Five days later Ivanco began to shiver again and the fever returned. By the next morning, stiff muscles followed. That day, Andrij, too, felt their return.

"Where are our replacements?" he asked the corporal as the Austrian walked the trenches inspecting his men.

"Soon. Soon," was all he could say. He had no idea.

Nearly eight out of every ten men in the trenches were exposed to what they thought was the flu. But when it began recurring every five days, after a five-day period of fevers and pain, the Austrians sent doctors to examine the men. They had no answer.

After four weeks (Aug. 28) in the trenches, a shivering corporal sloshed through the trenches telling the men to gather their gear and report to the rear trench. The replacements had come.

The rear trench ran perpendicular to the line trenches and was the entrance and exit to the maze. Andrij was burning up, felt dizzy and needed the support of the trench walls to move along. Three hundred yards later, they climbed the ladder onto the flat and were hurried to a high, stone wall where a truck waited for them. Milling about on one side were about 20 fresh troops who looked like Andrij and his companions did four weeks ago.

Andrij spent the next three weeks in a field hospital and life alternated between five days of fever and five days of debilitation where he could only eat with the aid of Slovene nurses who worked with the patients. Doctors did not know the exact cause of trench fever until after the end of the war when they discovered it was a blood-oriented disease transmitted by body lice. It wasn't until three years after the end of WW II that chlortetracycline had been discovered and could have been the cure. Many physicians suspected it somehow involved common body lice that infected almost everyone in the lines. The best they could do was to treat for the removal of lice with NCI, a combination of naphthalene, also called coal tar, creosote and iodoform, an iodine antiseptic.

"I have good news for you," a doctor appeared one day and said.

"Am I going to die?" Andrij asked. "You have a cure in that bottle in your hands?"

"Maybe, but that isn't it. You will be discharged tomorrow and sent home.

"That means I am going to die there?"

"No it doesn't. Trench Fever is seldom fatal."

It was late September when the truck carrying Andrij and Ivanco finally arrived in Vilag and pulled to a stop in front of Karas's house.

"Oh my God," Zuska screamed as she ran out the door and she saw two medics unload the stretcher carrying Andrij from the truck. "What have you done to my Andruska? He barely looks alive. Has he been shot? Is he wounded? Tell me!"

"I will get better," he said as she walked next to him as the medics carried him into the house. Her stomach was beginning to swell with child and she had difficulty leaning over to kiss him.

"The doctors said all I need is rest."

That wasn't true. While most men eventually survived trench fever, a small portion didn't. Most times, the recurring bouts stopped after about 12 cycles. Andrij's didn't. He seldom got out of bed and grew weaker and progressively more despondent with each day. His cousin, 10 years younger, did recover.

Zuska now spent more and more time alongside his bed, often just watching him as he slipped in and out of sleep. She began to neglect some of her house duties and, surprisingly, her mother-in-law picked up the slack.

Nowadays, Maria Hostina-Karas, Andrij's mother, always seemed to have tears in her eyes as she watched her son slowly slipping away from her. She looked especially forlorn, her daughter-in-law thought to herself, at night, just before bed. She would always undo her hair that was traditionally worn in a bun and let the long, gray strands fall over her shoulders. Zuska would silently watch her as she kneeled by her bed, facing a homemade wooden cross that hung on the wall, and said her prayers. Tears readily filled the old woman's eyes and ran down deep furrows in her ancient cheeks. Zuska eyes were also filled with tears. It was a sad time in the Karas household.

"You must speak in English, as much as you can...to Andrew and Stefan," Andrij said abruptly. His voice startled Zuska who herself was on the edge of sleep.

"But I am not very good in English," she apologized to him. "Maybe Pani Samandi will help them. I understand that she has been returning to the university each summer to study English. Who knows, she said once, she does it because maybe someday she will go to America."

"How old is Andrew now? Sixteen or 17?

"Don't let them take him into the army. He is an American.

"But aren't we fighting the Americans, or soon will be?" Zuska asked. "Then he will be an alien. What will happen to my boys?"

"It is a mixed up world," said Andrij. "If we loose, and I think we will, send the boys back to Pittsburgh as soon as you can. There is no future here for them now, or even after the war. I now realize that there never was. In a way, I was selfish. I wanted to return home and wanted them with me. That was natural, but that was not the way to freedom for them. We both should have thought more of their future rather than ours. It has been our mistake. Maybe my mistake.

"That's funny," he smiled. "I remember an Austrian officer telling us that it would all be over in a few weeks. I think it will take a few years, not weeks.

"There is a second thing you must promise me," Andrij said. "I learned many things while we were in America. The most important is the value of education. We were denied it in our youth but that must not happen to our sons. The Austrians have been better than the Magyars in the way we have been treated and even though we are at war, children must still be taught because they are the future.

"We Rusnaks are not a dumb people. But we are uneducated and unfamiliar with the ways of the world outside these mountains. I saw that clearly while we were in Pittsburgh. I never would have seen that if we remained here. Maybe some good did come of our trip to America.

"Promise me that you will make sure the boys do not quit school. No matter who wins, there will be school. Make sure they stay and learn. And when they go back to America they will not be the stupid Hunky that all our kind and I seem to have been.

"Promise me that Zuska and I can die in peace."

"I do," she said, "I promise you I will do all that I can to keep them in school. I promise."

Andrij's eyelids closed and his breathing slowed to an even, steady pace. The frown on his face disappeared. He fell asleep with his hand in hers. Tears filled her eyes and quickly overflowed.

The next morning, as Zuska was making breakfast and getting the boys ready for school, she heard Andrij cry out. She rushed to the room and heard him say he was hungry. It was the first time he had said that since he was brought home.

"What do you have to eat? Do you have any *studanenna*?

"It isn't cold enough to make pig's feet," she answered. "How about oatmeal instead?"

As she brought it to him, he tried to sit up in bed. Andrew and Stefan were behind her and helped prop the pillow behind their father's back.

"I had a dream last night," he said to Zuska. "I dreamed that you were carrying another boy. I was there watching him being born. You asked me what we should call him. I don't know why but I suddenly said 'Ivan'."

"Then that is what he will be named," said Zuska. "We both have brothers named Ivan. It is no coincidence."

Zuzanna knew of a neighbor who had killed a pig two days ago. Before supper, she went to their house and got two pig's feet from them. They still owed her money for a lamb they had bought from her in the spring. After dinner that night, she boiled pig's feet and before she went to bed, she went into the barn with the hot pot and several shallow bowls and set them where nothing could get to them. She placed the dishes on a bench and slowly poured the steaming broth into each dish until they were almost full. Then she ladled bits of boiled pork into each dish. By morning it would solidify into a jell if it got cold enough.

The first frost in the Carpathian Mountains was late that year. However, it occurred during the night Zuska set out the *studanenna*. She arose before the children and quietly tiptoed out of the room. Ever since Andrij had returned from the trenches, she slept with little Zuzie so he would not be disturbed.

She walked in her nightclothes to the outside toilet and noticed that the ground was white with frost. There will be *studanenna* for breakfast today, she said to herself as she crossed back to the house.

"Oh!" she said quietly as she brought her fingers to her lips, as if to muffle the cry. "The flowers are dead. The geraniums are gone until next spring. I must gather their roots today and hang them somewhere in the house where they will not freeze. Everything seems to be dying at once." She bit her lip as she uttered the phrase and hurried into the kitchen.

Baba Karas was already up and mixing a large pot of oatmeal. "*Baba*, don't bother," Zuska said to her mother-in-law after she came next to the diminutive woman and put one arm over her shoulder. "I made *studanenna* last night. Are the children up?"

She opened their door and saw them dressing and then closed it and went into Andrij's room. He lay quietly. Out of habit Zuska ran the palm of her hand over his forehead to see if he had a fever. She gasped!

His forehead was cold and had a strange feeling. She knew immediately what had happened. Her husband was dead. Andrij died during the night, along with everything outside. And a part of Zuska died as she stood there, silently, looking at his serene face. But, another part of him was especially active and kicked inside her. Two months later, on December 5th, 1914, an exceptionally heavy baby, Ivan Karas, was born.

A week later, when they were in church baptizing Ivan, a Russian patrol suddenly appeared in the village. The day before, a large force of Russian troops had poured through the pass in Ruske, just a few miles to the east. In the far off distance, there was the sound of gunfire. It had been going on sporadically for the last few days. Zuska half expected them to come through the pass on their land even though it was now overgrown and no more than a foot-and-horse trail.

The Russian patrol and its officer had come to Vilag looking for a site to establish fortifications. The officer entered the church while the christening was going on. He removed his cap and blessed himself and then approached the people gathered around the child.

"What is his name?" he asked

"Ivan. Ivan Andrijevich Karas," said his mother.

"Ivan Andrijevich Karas," he repeated. "That is a good Russian name he said as he looked into the child's blue eyes and blessed himself again.

"That is a good Rusnak name," Zuzanna corrected him.

Once outside, Lieutenant Andrij Velikanov, joined his patrol. It had been waiting for him at the top of the church steps. Several of the village men had gathered outside the church to see the Russians. He spoke to a few of the men, asking about the terrain. Later, the village men said, they were surprised by how easily they understood the officer. They had never heard "hard" Russian before.

Seeing no natural barriers that would facilitate a defense line, Velikanov dismissed the area. He moved south on the road to Humenné, to where the main force was located. His superior had already decided from information that was gathered that the Dukla Pass, farther west, would be the more contested area.

Chapter 30   Life in a Country Ghetto (1909-1920)

Ghettos are a natural phenomenon of immigration and the direct result of the movement of a large number of people from one geographic area to another. Ghettos have occurred everywhere in the world and it was easily predictable that they would also form in America. However, Good Town, and a handful of other mining towns in Pennsylvania, were unique ghettos for two reasons.

First, they were planned, created and executed by men whose ultimate and only goal was to make money. With their newly-found labor force now entrenched in the United States--and more available where these came from--the lives of these peoples were tightly, often ruthlessly controlled by coal-mining companies. To them, their inhabitants were no more than units of energy to be the manipulated by them. The inhabitants didn't have the slightest inkling of how or why this was being done. They all believed in the idea of economic emancipation, that they were being given an opportunity to better themselves. Once the immigrants were here, coal companies and steel mills did everything they could to keep them from achieving these idealistic goals because it was only under these conditions that a mining operation could produce a profit for its stockholders.

In doing so, their chief controlling factor was isolation. Unlike ghettos in large metropolitan areas where ethnically diverse peoples could and would eventually mingle, disperse and assimilate with others, and thus be considered a true melting pot, those in rural company towns were intentionally kept together as a unit and separate from outside populations. To achieve this goal, a company had to do everything it could to provide its workers with all the things they needed and thus give them no reason to wander out of town. Of course, this was only possible if the coal they were to dig was also in an isolated location, in rural parts of the country. Then, it would be possible, to a maximum degree, to keep immigrants from having social intercourse with people outside of the area.

This isolation was not as effective in Northeast Pennsylvania because of the proximity to several large metropolitan areas as it was in Southwestern Pennsylvania. Immigrants in northwestern Pennsylvania were assimilated into the American scheme of living sooner and at a faster rate than elsewhere. However, Southwestern Pennsylvania lacked really large cities, other than Pittsburgh, and this part of the state favored the mine owners.

This planned isolation was easily achieved at a time when individual transportation was difficult and communication was slow or nearly non-existent. It was also made easier by a people who didn't speak and who could neither read nor write English. Nor could they even read and write in their native language. The lack of such an uneducated labor force made the initial development of the steel industry, in places like Pittsburgh and Baltimore, take longer to reach its full potential than it might have with a better educated labor force. It was because the first immigrants to work the steel mills were literate. Most spoke the language because this force was composed of English, Welsh, Irish, Scotch and Germans. It wasn't until this group moved up the ladder within the industry, or moved to other industries, that the second large group of immigrant laborers from Europe, primarily Slavs and Italians, became eligible to give the steel industry the cheap, controlled labor it needed to maximize profits.

It was this massive labor force, composed of individuals who were denied even the basic education in their native languages in Austria, Hungary, Poland and Russia that made profitable mining a reality. These were a people familiar with hard work and who had for centuries been under the subjugation of an alien authority, either economical or political. In this case, the derogatory put-down phrase "dumb Hunky" wasn't too far from wrong.

By European standards at that time, the rural ghetto that mine companies created for the Rusnaks in Good Town wasn't such a bad place in which to live when compared to what their lives had been like in Europe. Everything they needed was here even though they were economic prisoners. However, any kind of freedom was something with which they, individually or as a group, were totally unfamiliar and thus they were not driven to attain.

Like most mill and company towns, the first immigrants who inhabited them were composed mostly of young men. Not many had the intention of staying more than a few years. They would stay long enough to earn enough money so that when they returned they could buy land to farm and support themselves. However, the longer they stayed the less was the likelihood that they would return. And when wives and young women began to follow these men to America, the return became even less likely.

The Najda's were typical of the growing number of families that now began to swell this mining community. The character of Good Town began to change as married men brought over their wives and older married men brought over their families, often with eligible young women.

In September 1908, a year after Kateryna's first daughter Mary was born, a second daughter, Anna was added to a growing household that now included five boarders. Two years later, almost to the month, Vasyl's first son Charley, alias Wasco, was born and their household expanded. When a new double-house was built in Upper Good Town by the mine company, Vasyl and Kateryna were given both sides to accommodate even more boarders.

A month later, Vasyl's oldest brother Andrij arrived from Europe. He had only been able to pay for his passage and left behind his wife Marie, and two young daughters. Andrij arrived August 10, 1910. He had just turned 34 and was four years older than Vasyl. Andrij was the shortest of the four brothers barely 5 feet tall, and the most outgoing. He had the same oval-shaped face as Vasyl and high cheekbones but had a larger, prominent jaw. Like Vasyl, a smile seemed his constant companion.

He arrive in America with two cousins, Ivan (John) Salabaj 36, and Salabaj's brother Yurko (George). They were on their way to see their brother Mykola (Nicholas) who also was a Good Town miner. When they arrived, they boarded with him and Andrij moved in with his brother Vasyl.

Late the following year, December 21, 1911, their youngest brother Hryec (Harry) landed in Manhattan. He, too, like John had traveled on the *S.S. Kronprinzessen Cecile* and made the crossing in just a week. John and Andy, as they were now called, had saved enough money between them to send Harry his passage. He was just 25 then, with blue eyes and light brown hair and still single, an unusual feat in a village now dominated by young, unmarried women. He, too, moved in with Vasyl. Only their sister Mary was left in Europe. Harry said, after he arrived, that he had not seen her in more than a year.

By now, Good Town had expanded to 70 houses and miners from Europe were still pouring in. Only eight were single-family houses. That year, during a windy, wintry night, the combined company store/post office burned. It was blamed on the pot-bellied stove. It was immediately rebuilt and restocked from another store the company owned in nearby Meyersdale. It was also the same year the Post Office Department decided to make multi-word towns into one-word towns. Goodtown and Pinehill did not escape the move.

Because John had a temper and Vasyl was headstrong, it took more than seven years before they truly reconciled. It was at Harry's wedding to Anna Drabish, from another Smil'nyk family, that left two of their older children behind when they emigrated. Kateryna had known her in Europe and was the matchmaker between her brother-in-law and Anna. It took place just before Kateryna had her fifth child, Catherine, in mid-October (1915).

John Najda's life had been complicated ever since he first arrived in America. On several occasions he had gotten the visiting priest from Central City to write a letter for him to his wife Juliana who had remained in Europe. After he had been here for two years, he even began sending her money so she could join him. Doing this was a chore for him because the only way to send money to Europe, at that time, was through a travel agency. He had to go to Somerset where an agent sold tickets for various steamship lines. The money orders were made by the lines and were as good as checks. In Europe, the dollars were converted to kronen, the coin of the realm in Austrian-controlled Galicia. A dollar was worth about 4 kronen at that time and would take care of a small family's needs for a week. It was amazing what even a quarter would then buy in Europe.

John finally had a letter written demanding that she come or he would come and get her and force her onto the ship. The money order accompanying the letter was for $164 or 800 kronen, more than enough to pay for a ship's ticket. It was a small fortune in Goodtown and a big fortune in Litowyschce.

It was four months before he finally got a reply. It wasn't from her but from a village priest in Litowyschce, 6 kilometers north of Protisne. He wrote that Juliana had died seven months earlier from a flu epidemic that swept several villages in the Beskid Mountains. It was so severe that few villages escaped its effects. Juliana never seemed to have fully regained her health after she lost her child in 1904. He was surprised and shocked that her family hadn't told him that she was sick again and, even worse, that she had died. A month later, he returned to Europe to see her grave and to get back his ticket money from her family. Her parents said they had used the money for her burial and to settle her accounts. Actually, the burial cost less than $5 and they never identified the accounts.

The first Sunday he was there he trucked up the hill to St. Michael's Church in Smil'nyk and saw Fenja (Fanny) Salabaj, a second or third cousin, in church. When he was still in Europe, it was she whom everyone thought he would eventually marry when the time came. She had never married and after a whirling week-long courtship, they were quickly married. John had his return ticket but not enough to buy one for Fanny. His demands for the money he sent to Juliana went unheeded by her parents and he had a ship to catch. He promised his new wife he would send her enough as soon as he could earn it, and maybe borrow some from his brothers.

It took John nearly a year to make the needed money and borrow what he could. Life did move at a slower pace in the America of that era. He sent it to her and expected her to arrive within a month or two. After a half-dozen letters and another year she said she, too, was afraid to cross the ocean by herself. In a rage typical of him, he quit his job, borrowed more money, then grabbed a train to New York and the first ship to Hamburg. He surprised her when he got to Smil'nyk and she, too, surprised him. She was fat with child. It had been two years since John had seen her. Even the night they were married, he claimed, he had not bedded her because of "women's problems". Disheartened, he returned immediately to Hamburg and got the next ship back to America. He would remain alone for the rest of his life.

"Your biggest mistake was sending money," Vasyl said when John returned. "You should have gone to the ticket office in Somerset and sent her a non-refundable ticket instead. You should have learned the first time. *Durak!*"

Because of the way the company had structured paying miners, the company store quickly became Goodtown's center of all non-mining or social activity. Very little cash was ever handled and life there was almost entirely on credit. With no refrigeration, not even iceboxes in the first years, almost every day the miner's women had to make a trip to the store and butcher shop as part of their routine. It was also a chance for them to see each other, discover what was new, who was pregnant, who had heard from Europe or who was fooling around with whom. It also contained the post office, their only link to Europe and while letters were infrequent, because people on either end could neither read nor write, it was now a means of sending what little money they made to relatives in *Starim Krayou*, the "Old Country."

"You cannot believe what I heard today," Kateryna said to her husband one night as he was readying for bed. "I just found out why John Kusinich has disappeared."

Kusinich was one of the few older men, near 50, who had come over from Europe. Three years earlier, he lost the lower half of his right leg in a mining accident. The company felt somewhat responsible for it and after they had him outfitted with a wooden leg in a Pittsburgh hospital, they gave him the job of running the breakers under the tipple. He oversaw a dozen or more boys who broke or cracked big chunks of coal into smaller pieces so they could go through the grading screens. He lived as one of a half-dozen boarders with the Boberka family in Gold Brick, a settlement with just a few new houses and two small mines owned by the Pine Hill Coal Company. It was located just a thousand yards above the Lottie No. 2 Mine, towards the crossroads of Pinehill.

"Two weeks ago," she continued, "when the sheriff, Wasco Boberka, and one of the mine foremen, went looking for Kusinich, he couldn't be found. When they got to the breakers under the tipple, he was gone. The boys said he was there when the work whistle blew but then went somewhere. Boberka and the sheriff went back to the boarding house and found Kusinich's trunk open and a few pieces of old clothing tossed aside. Everything else was gone. They went to Pine Hill Station and the clerk said he sold him a ticket on the next train to Johnstown. It wasn't due in for another two hours.

"They searched everywhere but no one found him. He just disappeared."

"Did he steal something?" asked Vasyl.

"Yes, I guess he kind of did," Kateryna chuckled.

"You know Boberka's 14-year old daughter Mary? The one that was sent to work for her cousin in Central City last week.

"Well, a few weeks ago her mother thought she was acting funny. Staying in bed, crying and acting sick. She finally got Mary to talk and they figured that she was pregnant. Can you imagine that, a 50-year old man, and with only one leg, making a 14-year old girl pregnant? *Bozéh mi*, what is this new world coming too?"

Vasyl then chuckled, "It sounds like he still had one good leg that worked. He must have left all his pay at the company store."

"No, he didn't," Kateryna knowingly answered. "They said that on that day his account was almost zero. He never left any balance but took it out every Friday."

"Maybe the rumor is right," said Vasyl.

"What rumor?"

"That he didn't trust the company store and kept all his money in his wooden leg."

Kusinich was never found though someone said that they saw an older man, later that day, jump on the train for Johnstown when it slowed at the grade near Beachdale. And, that the man limped.

It was shortly after that (1913) that there was a fire in the company store. It engulfed the entire building. The store as well as post office was lost. All the record books kept on each miner and their charges, as well as the monies due them, were lost. The company said it still had the weighboss's records but no miner was ever satisfied that his account was really as depleted as the company claimed.

After that, Clyde Ickes, a clerk at the store, suggested to each miner that he also keep a record of what they charged. It sounded good, but in reality none of them knew how to write. The store was immediately rebuilt, and "Uncle Jerry" as the miners called J.G. Smith, who had managed the Hull Mercantile Company Store since 1907, even expanded its size.

Company officials were sensing that the miners were beginning to see that there was life outside of Goodtown. They began taking counter measures to keep them at "home," first by building a recreation hall for them that featured three pool tables in its basement. They even leveled a part of the land next to it for a sandlot baseball field. Baseball was the rage in America at this time and each mine company supported a team composed of its miners.

Good players, Rusnak or not, were immediately recognized and other mine owners often tried to lure them to their mines to play for their teams by offering them better housing, better jobs and sometimes even better pay.

They also recognized that too many miners were going to Central City and Windber to get married or have their children baptized when churches in these towns couldn't send their priests to Goodtown. In an act of generosity, the company gave miners enough land for a church in Goodtown and even contributed $500 to its construction. The would-be parishioners formed a church committee and assessed themselves $15 for a single man and $25 for one with a family that went into a fund to build the church.

Construction of Sts. Peter & Paul Russian Orthodox Church was started in 1917. The following year, more than 200 Hunkies had their own Orthodox Church. Even though they all had been born into the Greek Catholic Church in Europe, they immediately embraced their ancestral Orthodox religion. Construction of the church was also aided by the Russian Mission to America. The Najda's sixth child, Andrew (1918) was born in April that year, just before the church was finished. He was the first child to be baptized in it.

Except for the mine work and its supervising personnel, Goodtown could have been any small, Rusnak town in southeast Poland. The close family ties that existed in these villages were easily duplicated in Goodtown. From the period 1904 to 1914, eight Salabajs immigrated from Protisne and Smil'nyk to Goodtown. Of course they were cousins of various degrees to the four Najda brothers. And from 1902 to 1913, a dozen Antonishaks, from the same two villages, also came to Pinehill, and Goodtown. And they, too, were cousins to the Najdas and the Salabajs.

There was Ivan Antonishak, one of Brian McDonald's first recruits, who, at 28, arrived in Pinehill in 1902, six months ahead of Vasyl Najda. Then came Piotr, Ivan Salabaj's brother-in-law, in 1904; Lucio in 1906; Stefan in 1911; the brothers Oleksa 18, and Iwan 17, came over together in 1912 on the *S.S. Comanello* through Rotterdam; Jenna, at 18 and the only girl, came over that same year, in November; Michael 30; and his cousin Fedio 26, came over together on Nov. 13, 1912 on the *S.S. Antwerp.* No one is sure when Vasyl Antonishak came over because he couldn't remember the date. Some say he wasn't all there. In 1904, more than 50 people, mostly men, abandoned Protisne and Smil'nyk to look for work in America. And, the majority, following my grandfather and his entourage came to Goodtown. It was a perfect example of string migrations.

Of all the Antonishaks who crossed the ocean, Michael was probably the most interesting. He died in America, on my grandfather's farm, in 1965, but his crossing in 1913 wasn't the first. His initial trip to Pinehill occurred in 1908 when he was 25, and then again in 1911. He would live frugally, save every cent he earned and then return. His motivation was a wife Pelageya (Pearl) and their son Mykola (Nicholas). When his money ran out the first time, and he could not find work in Europe, he trekked back to Pinehill. Two years later, he returned to Protisne and stayed another two years until that money, too, was gone. He knew, but the realization had to be constantly reinforced, that there was no way he could support his family with work in his or surrounding villages. He was torn by the inability to be in both places at once. America always loomed as the source for money after his initial trip here.

He was a restless, outgoing, friendly person, no more than 5-feet 2-inches tall and always thin, not skinny but wiry. He had a gift for gab and was a notorious storyteller. When that wasn't enough to retain the spotlight, he pulled out his fiddle and would play. At weddings and christenings, if he had a few drinks, he would dance at the same time he fiddled. Most thought his fiddling was as good as any Gypsy's. It was easy to see why he became known as "Mike the Fiddler."

He boarded almost all the time with his dual cousins Vasyl and Kateryna Najda. His mother was a Pavuk, as was Kateryna's mother. They were sisters and Mike's mother even delivered my grandmother. And he was a second cousin to Vasyl. It is an intricate family tree. Mike also had a penchant for travel and after a few years in the mines, he would go to Detroit to work for Henry Ford. Ford was offering unskilled workers $5 a day. That was big money and the enticement drew many miners to the Motor City. He had a cousin working there who paved the way. Making cars would sustain his interest for but a year or so and then he'd be back in Goodtown. He was always popular with children because his pockets, on a return trip, were filled with costume jewelry and trinkets. And, he always returned wearing a new suit. He was a dapper dresser when he wasn't in his mine clothing. He made the Detroit run three times before he finally settled in Goodtown for good.

Nor did he ever forgot his wife and child in Protisne and regularly sent money to them. The first few times, it was accompanied by a letter that Mary Najda, Vasyl's oldest daughter would write in Cyrillic, imploring his wife to come to America with his children. She refused and after a while the letters stopped, but the money didn't.

It was a big surprise in Goodtown one June day in 1911 when Brian McDonald showed up at the company store. It was almost like a homecoming. Probably close to 30 of the 600 men working there in the mines came to Pinehill through his efforts. The remaining men came as secondary effects of his recruiting. McDonald's efforts in recruiting miners was like someone siphoning gasoline from a car. Once he had enough people in the tube and flowing, the rest came without any more effort on his or his company's part.

"Are you still buying beer for Rusnaks in Dvernyk?" Vasyl asked McDonald the second night he was in town as the miners all gathered in the new recreation hall to greet him.

"No, Vasyl, that job ended in 1906. After that, Consolidated sent me back to Maryland, to the main office. After a year, I was made supervisor of a mine in West Virginia. Do any of you want to work for me there?" he said jokingly.

"I did my recruiting so well, that there was no need for me to continue getting more miners. You all took over doing that for me. By sending money and letters home, your relatives and friends realized that there was money to be made here and they came, slowly at first, then in larger numbers.

"Look at you, Vasyl. You already have two brothers here and I hear a third may be coming soon.

"I have all I can do to keep the mine going in West Virginia. Too bad they are not all Slavs like you guys. Most are Hungarians and they work hard and well, but they are not as easy to negotiate with. They are now talking about striking for higher wages. You guy's don't have that problem here, do you?"

The flood of immigrant labor ended abruptly in August 1914, when Germany declared war on France, and Great Britain, in turn, declared war on Germany. The great industry of transporting people from Europe to American stopped within a few weeks and some of Germany's grandest steamships were seized in foreign ports. They would later be used as war reparations and given to the Allies once the conflict was over.

The steerage trade was never resumed because the United States realized, during the war, that it no longer needed a cheap labor force for its factories, nor was one available to them. There were now enough Hunkies and their sons in America, at least for then.

Chapter 31   Destitute Times In Vilag and the Return to America

While the Najdas and other Rusnaks in America flourished, the Karases and Rusnaks in Europe suffered greatly because of the war that was supposed to end all wars forever.

Fighting in the Great War had come early to the Carpathian Mountains and one of the first battles was to control the Dukla Pass. The battle for the pass raged for three months in 1914 and it was estimated that nearly 1 million Russians and Austrians lost their lives. During the next three years, 1915-1918 the Austro-Hungarian Army pushed the line north, over the crest of the Carpathian Mountains, across most of Galicia and to what is now the Ukrainian border. Three major battles with the Russians took place in Limanova, Gorlice and Sianok; the latter, just a few miles from Protisne and only 50 miles from Vilag. Its reverberations were easily felt on both sides of the continental divide.

Nor was 1916 an auspicious time to even think of getting married, let alone to do so. But Andrew, Stefan's older brother, had had his eyes on Maria Chupik for a few years. "I don't think you should," Zuska told them when they approached her to endorse their marriage, "but it is really up to you. You are only 19 and Maria won't be 19 until the end of November. Can you even afford to think of marriage?"

"I can help you with *Baba* and little Ivan," said Maria. *Baba* Karas had long suffered from arthritis but had been able to cope with it. However, as she aged, it had become severe, almost debilitating. At times, she had trouble moving about without help and she was becoming more dependent upon her daughter-in-law. She was fast becoming an invalid.

"Wait until the war is over," Zuzanna said, maybe things will be different."

Love cannot wait. Reluctantly, Zuzanna agreed. Maria had already been spending more and more time in the Karas than at her family's house. *Baba*, as well as Zuzanna, were becoming dependent upon her.

They were married on October 21, three weeks before the war ended. At that time, there was no priest in the church in Vilag. They went to Vyrava, ten miles away, to be married by a civil clerk. Andrij's profession was listed as a *rolnik*, a peasant.

On November 12th, 1918, Czechoslovakia was supposed to become a nation composed of four ethnic groups, Czechs, Moravians, Slovaks and Rusnaks or Ruthenians, a Latinized name used by the League of Nations in lieu of Rusnaks. Those Rusnaks in Galicia were again denied their own nation and again forced into subjugation under Polish rule. Those Rusnaks who had been part of the Hungarian portion of the Austrian Empire were joined with the Slovaks and given recognition only as Ruthenians, in an artificially created troika, but with no political status. So much for the League's mandate of self-determination. The people of Vilag, along with many other eastern ex-Austrian villages were now considered Slovaks, or Czechs, whichever they preferred.

After the end of the war, times were difficult for everyone in Czechoslovakia, regardless of their ethnic backgrounds. The birth of a new country automatically meant the creation of new ties with all lands outside their domain. The economy was almost immediately plunged into a recession. People could not sell their products abroad nor could they buy from those countries that had the goods they needed. They had lost all economic channels because of the war, and being a new nation, reestablishing them would become a long, tedious effort that the peasants, more than anyone else in the nation, would have to endure.

Ever since her husband's death, Zuzanna Karas had taken over the management of the Karas holdings. I doubt that most other women in my grandmother's village, her peers, would have been able to do so. From her very beginnings as a youngster she seemed different, head-strong. Her father often warned that she would be difficult for any man to tame as a wife. Andrij never tried because he saw this aspect of her character as an aid to helping him achieve his goals. She exhibited a fortitude that was rare, uncommon among Rusnak women of her generation.

Her singular accomplishment of crossing the Atlantic to be with her husband, by herself, served only to fortify this feeling of strength in herself. And the boarding house she successfully managed in Verner was another measure of her success and a test of her character. After a sick Andrij returned from the battle front, as he lay dying in the bedroom, she was already preparing herself to carry on the duties not only of a new mother in the caring of three sons, a handicapped daughter, a daughter-in-law and an ailing mother-in-law. And adding to her responsibilities the investment they'd made from their toils in America in a woodlot and enlarged herd of sheep, she had a business as well as a household to run!

However, the woods were becoming a liability and non-productive. The taxes levied upon them by the new government were eating up any money they made on their sheep. The size of the flock rew rapidly and while grazing pastures for them was limited it was still sufficient. Fortunately, a large portion of the bowl below the mountain ridge was theirs and not the common property of the village and only their sheep now filled it. It was a moot question because few in the village had more than a handful of sheep. Besides, these wouldn't last long.

After Andrew's marriage, he took on a renewed and more intensive interest in the farm. Wolves had killed several sheep so he and Stefan built a hut at the lower edge of the woods, just above where the grassy basin began. When wolves were active and howling at night, the two would alternate evenings in the hut. From it, they could, with their two dogs, watch over the flock.

They had inherited their father's army rifle and in the first year shot a wolf. Stefan also shot a stag that year and provided them with a change from the mutton and chicken that made up most of their diet. Bears were also a problem but the dogs usually scared them off.

One day, Stefan had watched a wolf menace the flock but the dogs chased it off into the forest before he could get a shot at it. Intent on killing the wolf, he followed it into the woods. He was gone for most of the morning and when he returned to the hut, he saw his brother waiting for him.

"While you were hunting," he angrily chided his younger brother, "the wolf led you off. The rest of the pack came in and killed a lamb. There is almost nothing left of it. See," he said and held up a tattered, bloodied skin. In his rage, he didn't notice the blood on Stefan's hands and arms.

"When are you going to grow up and accept some responsibility?"

"Are you done?" Stefan asked. "If you are, I need help. Come with me and bring the rope from the hut."

"Where are we going?"

Stefan didn't answer but broke trail back into the woods.

He stopped for a moment to check his route, then turned a bit uphill and entered a small opening.

"My God!" Andrew exclaimed. "Did you shoot it?"

In the little clearing was a dead, large, wild boar. Even in death it look fearsome, frightening. It must have weighed more than 400 pounds. In the last half-hour, before Stefan returned to the hut to retrieve the rope, he had completed eviscerating the animal.

"I'm glad you're here," said Stefan. "I don't think I could have dragged it out by myself. Maybe we should get the horse.

"I think we will eat well for a while. I was tiring of mutton."

It seemed the more intense Andrew became in making a living as a herdsman, Stefan, now 18, was turning in the opposite direction. In many ways, Stefan was a contradiction of his brother. Where Andrij had dark brown hair, he had light brown, almost blond hair, and seemed to take more after his mother than father. His eyes were blue and Andrij's were hazel. Their dispositions also varied. Andrew was lean, serious, reserved, and reticent. Stefan was outgoing, boisterous, continually smiling, seldom serious and always joking.

All these features combined to make him extremely popular with the girls of the village. The fact that he was an American also seemed to have enhanced his stature. While the Karas's were not wealthy by most standards, the fact that they owned the most land and had the largest flock of sheep made Stefan the most eligible bachelor not only in Vilag but also in the surrounding villages.

In September 1919, Mary gave birth to a son they named Andrew Andrijovych, honoring his grandfather.

During the next three years, despite the expanding efforts of Andrij, life was slowly, gradually, almost imperceptibly, day-by-day, becoming a struggle for survival for everyone in the household.

It was compounded that summer when Maria gave birth to their second son Michael. There were no immediate solutions to the poverty that began to overtake their village and that of other surrounding villages.

One evening, after a meager supper of potatoes, cabbage and bread, Zuzanna Karas was about to face the inevitable. The entire family seemed to linger longer at the table, sensing that something was about to happen.

"Andrew, I think it is time for you to go back to America," Zuska told her son. "Your father knew how life here would become. He saw no future here for you or Stefan. The opportunities for you two now are no better here than when your father and I went to America. Before he died he made me promise that I would send you and Stefan back. All these years, I knew it would happen. In a way, I was selfish. I didn't want to give up either of you. I love you both very much. I knew it would happen but I kept putting it off. I didn't want to face reality. Times here are now so desperate that you must go. Andrew, what kind of life can you make here for your sons?

"Once you get settled in America, you can help us. Send money back to us like we sent to *Djido* (Grandfather Mykola) and *Baba* when we lived in Pittsburgh. I know it won't be easy. It wasn't easy for us. When you have made enough, you can send for your wife and children. There will be one mouth less to feed. Maybe then we can survive. And later, you can help your brother return to where he, too, belongs.

"To this end, I have slowly been setting aside some money so you can buy a ship ticket. It is only enough for one. Maybe not even that. That is why I decided that you should be the first to go."

"Why not send Stefan? He has no family here."

"Stefan is in his last year at the gymnasium. He must graduate. I wish you had. I can see that an education here does not do much for you. But in America, it will make a big difference. Besides, in America, I fear he would spend the money he makes faster than he could make it. He likes too much to have a good time, to drink with his friends. I know he is at that age when good times seem more important than anything else."

"That's not fair," Stefan interrupted.

"And there are many relatives now," she continued, "in America, in Pittsburgh, Ambridge, Berwick and Binghamton. No, you are the one we can depend upon. You will go!"

303

"*Mamo moia,* how can I leave my sons and Marysha? There is much work to do here. There are sheep to shear and tend. Stefan cannot do it alone."

"That will not last long," she said, "maybe a year or two and the sheep will be gone. Stefan can do it as well as you. If he needs help there are relatives who have no work. We are now living on old potatoes and cabbage heads that are so small it takes more than one to fill a pot. The country is in ruin. We cannot sell lumber. All we can sell are sheep and that will eventually end. No. It is not a choice. You must go to save us."

"She is right," Maria later said to her husband as they readied for bed. "People are leaving the village for America like rats fleeing a burning barn. Two men left last week. Ivan Popovych left. Mytro Baka left a week before him. Your cousin Paul Ivanco left a month ago. They have been out of work here for more than a year. I don't know why they waited so long. There is no work here nor down on the plains with the Hungarians. What will we do? Luckily I can still feed your Michael with my body, but how will I feed young Andrew?

"How is your English?" she asked.

"Stefan and I will practice, though he wasn't that old when we left the 9th Ward Public School in Woods Run. He was only six and in Grade 1. Mom and Pop always spoke 'Russian' at home so we didn't get a lot of practice outside the house. Most of our friends were Rusnaks so we didn't have to speak English, only in school. The Irish wouldn't even speak to us. They thought we were beneath them. And the Germans always spoke German among themselves and stuck together like flies on a cow platter.

"I will go, but not now. I will wait until the end of the year, when the hay is in and the sheep are shorn."

The next day, Andrew wrote to his uncle in Ambridge, located a dozen miles downriver of Verner, where he was born. He wrote about what his mother and he had decided and hoped he could find him a job. A month later, a letter arrived from Simon Karas. "Jobs were plentiful," he wrote, "and easy to get. I have one ready for you at the American Bridge Company." Also inside was a prepaid ticket for one-way passage from Bremen to New York.

"I was worried how I would get from here to Bremen," Andrew said to his mother and wife as they listened to him read.

"And the train fare from New York to Pittsburgh," his mother added. "It is not cheap. When I crossed the ocean in '96, the ship-ticket was $32. Now it is up to $198. What is the world coming to?"

His departure from Vilag was swift. It had to be or his mother and wife might not have let him go. He hesitated while hugging and kissing his two sons. He almost changed his mind. He embraced his brother Stefan and as they kissed he said, "Your turn will come. There is nothing here for you either."

It was early December when Andrew boarded the bus to Vyrava where he could catch the train to Prague. The next day, in Prague, he made his way to the American Embassy and there, in halting English, he told them he wanted to return to the United States. With the ship ticket his uncle had sent him was a certified copy of his birth certificate that was provided by Rev. Michael Fekula, the priest at the St. Alexander Nevsky Church in Woods Run. It took him several days to procure the passport.

He remembers thinking, as he rode the train into Germany, that he suddenly felt like a different person. It was a strange feeling that was brought on by the people and the flag, at the American embassy. He realized that he wasn't a Rusnak or a Slovak, or a Czech, but an American. And, he had a passport to prove it. He slipped his hand to his shirt pocket just to make sure it was still there and opened it up to look at it. It was the first picture he had ever seen of himself. He wasn't dreaming. He did feel guilty that Maria and his sons were left behind. And, he remembered his brother Stefan. "Maybe it was he who should have been on the train and not me," he again said to himself.

In Bremen, on 29 December Andrew Andrijovych Karas, the oldest son of Andrij Mykoliovych Karas, boarded the *S.S. George Washington* for his return to the United States. The ship was built in 1908 in Germany for HAPAG, and named *George Washington* as a public relations move. All immigrants knew of George Washington. After the Great War, it was given to the United States as part of the war reparations and the name remained unchanged. It became part of the United States Lines headquartered in New York.

It was a big ship, nearly 700 feet long, more than twice the size of the ship he crossed on from American to Europe with his parents and brother 16 years earlier.

It's funny, he thought to himself as he unloaded his bag in a third-class cabin, that I cannot remember that ship's name. I was eight or nine at the time, I should remember. Oh well, it doesn't really matter. Maybe I can't remember because deep inside I don't want to remember.

He did, however, remember how cramped it could have been. His parents took him below decks, into steerage, which on that ship was fourth class, to show him how they had crossed in 1892 and 1896, on other ships. There was great significance in what he saw. Steerage space eastbound had been temporarily converted to stalls and held hundreds of American cattle destined for German restaurants.

Now, he even had a porthole window in the compartment. It was fitted with four bunk beds but he was alone in this cabin. As he opened the small suitcase a bag of dried mushrooms fell out. On it, printed in Cyrillic, was "Simon" (Sam). His mother intended them for her brother. Among Rusnaks, dried mushrooms, *peepenkee*, are always the correct gift.

The trip was the greatest Christmas present Andrew had ever received. The S.S. *George Washington* landed in New York on Monday, January 7, 1924, "Russian" Christmas and pulled into a pier on Manhattan's west side. Twenty-four-year-old Andrew Karas showed his passport and the birth certificate, his uncle had obtained, to the immigration officer. His passport would have been enough. He passed through without incident. It was a far cry from what his father had to endure when he landed in New York 32 years earlier. Ellis Island was closed during the Great War and immigration into the United States was severely curtailed. Now entry by aliens was controlled by strict limits assigned each foreign country. Quotas were determined on what an immigrant might contribute to the United States and based on his or her education and skills. There was little or no call for uneducated laborers. How the world had turned in just a few years.

Two hours later, Andrew boarded a train in Penn Station for Pittsburgh. At Union Station in Pittsburgh he transferred to a local line and arrived in Ambridge just before midnight. There he found his relatives.

His uncle would take him into work in a few days and by the end of the week he had secured a job with the American Bridge Company. Andrew became a rivet catcher. The American Bridge company had eight plants located across the United States but its biggest was in Ambridge where they prefabricated sections of bridges that were eventually shipped to various sites. He was part of a four-man team. After the rivets were heated, they were thrown to a catcher who caught and then inserted them in pre-drilled holes. A third man placed a weigh behind the rivet head and held it tightly against the hole while on the other side a man with a pneumatic hammer pounded a new head on the protruding end of the rivet until it was fast against the metal.

It was a tedious job but paid well. After accumulating two months of pay he told his uncle that a room had become available at the Ambridge Towers, a four-storey boarding house run by the company, at reasonable rates, for single men. Besides, Sam's family was growing and six children already filled their modest apartment. And, there was another on the way.

During the first half of the year, strikes at the mills that produced the steel that American Bridge needed caused them to slow production and actually close for two months until the strike was settled. After paying his board, there were only pennies left. The first letters to his mother and brother were empty of dollars. It wasn't until six months after he arrived that the first money order arrived from Pittsburgh. It arrived just in time and was just enough to pay the increasing land tax.

Chapter 32   The Accident

Just 85 miles southwest of Ambridge, Pennsylvania, in a straight line, is the mining town of Goodtown. The mines there in the second decade of the 20th century were still fairly productive. Vasyl Najda's family, as were most families of Rusnak miners in the town, was rapidly expanding. The Great War had demanded lots of coal for the steel industries in Pittsburgh, as well as in Ohio and Maryland, and work had been good. But in the post-war era, the demand for coal was beginning to fall off.

It was a warm, hot, sultry August morning in 1920 and there would be no relief from it until he entered the mine. Vasyl Najda left the house in Gold Brick, adjacent to Goodtown, to where they had recently moved and walked the dusty, sandy, path uphill to the mine. It was an extension of the same road that he had now trekked for 17 years. He stopped a hundred feet from the house because he began coughing. He coughed so violently that he spat blood onto the sandy path. It was not the first time it had happened. So far, it hadn't happened very often but he knew what it was. Several miners, who had been there as long as he had, also had the same cough. It was the dreaded black lung.

Black lung is called the miner's disease and usually affects miners of hard coal but also those working in soft coal and graphite mines. When worked, hard coal produces more coal dust than soft coal and is more easily inhaled into the lungs. It is the smallest dust particles that become airborne, that enter the nose, mouth and throat when someone breathes in. They lodge in the air sacs that compose the lungs. In minute quantities, macrophages--blood cells that collect foreign particles--can carry them to places where they can be coughed out or swallowed. But as the amount of dust builds these special blood cells cannot accomplish their task. The dust buildup becomes permanently lodged and that reduces the miner's ability to breath. The result is emphysema and then chronic bronchitis. The lungs become marbled with the black residue and their ability to function progressively decreases. If continued long enough, the disability eventually leads to suffocation and death.

Just how bad the black lung becomes in an individual corresponds to the length of exposure. It can take anywhere from 10 to 20 years for even the first symptoms to begin to show. There is no reversal. And, the Rusnak's penchant for smoking tobacco hastens the effects. Strangely enough, Vasyl's brother Harry, who became miner only in 1911, was the first to show the signs.

I hope my son never has to go through this, Vasyl said to himself as he resumed the climb to the mine. He was referring to the birth of his seventh child, Michael, two days earlier. The disease had measurably slowed him in the past two years. Now, only 40, he looked 10 years older.

By the time the mine whistle blew, he had on all his gear and was halfway down the mine to his room. His partner was Steve Brus (Bruce), a Rusnak from outside the town of Sianok, who had worked with him for the past year. Bruce was already in the room and had pushed an empty car to its entrance.

"There's not much down, Vasyl," he said as he scanned the face and then the roof above it with the beam from his carbide lamp.

"I know. I figured we'd have to do a shoot sometime today. Let's clean the floor and then I'll find a spot."

Bruce could shoot a face or roof but Vasyl was said to have the touch. As Bruce shoveled coal on the floor, Vasyl ran his hands over the face, peeling off loose seams of coal until he found a sizable crack near the top.

This looks good, he said to himself, then went to the back of the room to get his 'shooting bag.'

How many times have I done this since I started with Paul Turko? he thought. I don't think I can count the number.

Twenty minutes later, he turned to Bruce and announced he was done. "Here, Steve," he said. "Take the bag and get behind the rib. Anyone around?"

"I don't see anyone."

Vasyl, like so many thousands of times he had done in the last 17 years, struck the match and yelled the perfunctory, "Fire! Fire! Fire!"

When no one answered he put the lighted match to the squib and ran back to the corridor where Bruce waited.

They waited and waited but no explosion followed. It should have ignited within 60 seconds. It didn't.

"Damn it," Vasyl said. "It's those new squibs Consol bought. They're cheaper and not as good.

"Maybe it was wet, from the moisture and humidity down here," Bruce suggested.

They waited another two minutes just to be sure,

Vasyl had just turned the corner to see what was wrong when the charge exploded. A fraction of time later, Vasyl screamed and his hands went up to his face and covered his left eye. The explosion had blown off his hat and lamp and coal dust engulfed them. When Bruce found him, he was on the floor writhing in agony. The light caught his partner's face. It was covered in blood.

Bruce helped him to his feet and holding together they ran up the mine to the opening. The foreman saw them coming out and rushed to see what had happened. When he saw Vasyl's bloody face he ran to get his car. He and Bruce rushed him to a doctor in Berlin. The doctor took a quick look at Vasyl's eye and immediately decided to take him to the hospital in Somerset.

"The eye looks bad," Dr. Evans said to Kateryna who was in the hallway outside the emergency room with her brother-in-law Andrij. "I have a call into a hospital in Pittsburgh.

The call came in a few minutes.

"Consolidated said to take him there as soon as we could. We will be going in a few minutes. Katie, I suggest you stay here. There is nothing you can do in Pittsburgh. A nurse is going with him in the ambulance and will stay with him during the operation. She will call me to let me know what happens. I will call the mine super. If it's too late, I'll drive down to Goodtown to see you."

Vasyl lost his left eye and spent the next four weeks in the hospital. Kateryna visited him but once because she had to maintain her boarders; they were now more important that ever. He stayed out of work for two months before the doctor felt he was able to go back to work. In a suspiciously benevolent and unprecedented gesture Consolidated waved his rent until he was able to work again.

Because the population of Rusnaks in Goodtown now numbered nearly a thousand and in effect dominated the workforce, and their Orthodox Church was beginning to act as a unifying force among the Slavic immigrants, Consolidated decided that it would placate its grumbling miners. It ceased mining operations at noon on Thursday, January 6, 1921, for Russian Christmas the next day and closed the mines until Monday. In an uncommon move; the miners would be paid for the Thursday and Friday they were off.

On Christmas Eve, Sviaty Vecher, or Holy Evening, the second most religious day of the Orthodox Church, that still held the Julian Calendar to be the correct one, all of the Najda brothers and their children gathered at Vasyl's house. It was a rare event that would never again be possible. It was Christmas Day when a horde of non-Lenten foods would be served. First, however, came the 2-hour Christmas Service in church.

It was late in the afternoon, when the four brothers and five boarders sat around the kitchen-living room smoking their pipes, that Andrij made his announcement. Paul Turko and Michael Boburchak had also dropped in. Some were glowing slightly from the whiskey that was brought out for this special occasion and it had loosened Andrij enough so that he could reveal his decision.

"I am going back to the Old Country," he said. "I have spent the last 10 Christmases away from my wife Maria and my two daughters. She will not come here, I know that. Like John's wife, she said she is afraid of the ocean. She has been keeping the house by herself and now she needs me, and I need her. This is no kind of life. I had not planned on staying this long but getting enough money saved, while sending some home when possible, has taken longer than I planned. I will work until the end of May and then I will go home.

"Vasyl, can you remember how beautiful the mountains around Protisne are in June?"

"Much like here," he answered.

"Yes, that is true. But here we spend so much time in the hole that we do not see what is outside. If I am to be poor all my life I might as well be poor outside, in the fields, on a farm, and with my wife and children.

"These are not good times to be in Halych (Galicia) and be a Rusnak," Turko interrupted. "I got a letter a few days ago from one of my brothers who said the Polish police are going around attacking Rusnak villages and shooting anyone they want. It has been like this ever since the Armistice was signed. The Poles are so vengeful that no Rusnak home is safe."

"Vasyl," asked Harry, as if to change the subject, "don't you, too, miss being a farmer? I thought that is what you wanted to be."

"That reminds me of an old saying," Vasyl answered. "Wish in one hand and shit in the other and see which one will come first."

The men roared in laughter, but they all knew there was a real element of truth in what he said.

"Maybe things will be different after the company settlement," said Boburchak.

"What settlement? What are you talking about?" asked Vasyl.

"Didn't Consolidated offer you a settlement for the accident, for the loss of your eye?" asked Boburchak.

"Do you think I am crazy to ask Consol for a settlement. I am lucky they gave me back my job. They have not charged me for rent while I couldn't work. They have been good to me."

"Good? That is bullshit," said Boburchak.

"No it isn't," retorted Vasyl. "The mines are petering out. You all can see that every day. The veins are getting thinner and we must go deeper. Pretty soon we will reach the end. Then what will we do? Find another mine? I haven't heard of a new mine opening in the last five years.

"Look at Raineytown. The mines there have shut down and they are even selling off the company houses for next to nothing. That is likely soon to be our future."

"Consol owns a mine near Clymer," said Mike. "I heard the story of a Rusnak there who lost a hand in an explosion and they paid him compensation. I know this to be true. I know the man. John Hrynko is his name."

"It might be different if we had a union here like the mines in Indiana County. Michael, do you think me crazy."

"No Vasyl, I think you are stupid," Michael answered. "Unions have nothing to do with it. It is a state law.

"They won't do anything to you if you seek compensation. There are laws in this country. It is not like back in Halych where the Poles did to us whatever they wanted. If Consol fired you now you could sue them. Go see a lawyer and ask him. Don't go to Hays in Berlin. He is working for Consol. Go see Peter Maruschak's son

313

in Somerset. He is a lawyer. He has helped a lot of Rusnaks get their first and second papers. I know he is young but he is smart. His father said he graduated from lawyer school just two years ago. He is one of us."

A month later, Vasyl found an excuse to go to Somerset. Peter Maruschak was going there to visit his son and he joined him on the bus ride. Basil Maruschak agreed with what Michael had told him and convinced Vasyl to let him file a suit on his behalf. The next week he filed one against Consolidated Mining Corporation in a Somerset Court. It was another two months before it was heard. In an abbreviated session, that took less then ten minutes, the judge ruled against Vasyl.

"This judge is prejudiced against Hunkies," Basil told Vasyl as they left the courtroom. "I will appeal this ruling in a state court in Pittsburgh, not here in Somerset County. There is too much coal money under the table here."

Nearly a year had passed since Vasyl brought suit against the company and his job was still not threatened. Consolidated had too much invested in Najda when they added up all his boarders. He was providing lodging for eight miners and they were all needed. And, their lawyers felt the court in Pittsburgh, that favored steel interests, would turn down the appeal, never hearing it.

Finally, Vasyl, his brother John and Basil Maruschak were sitting in the Pennsylvania Third District Court of Appeals in Pittsburgh waiting their turn for the case to come up before the appeals judge. There also were three other suits against Consolidated, all for injuries and damages that occurred on the job.

As they sat there, the Court Recorder read aloud the names on the docket to see if all were in attendance. When Najda versus Consolidated Mining Corporation was read, Maruschak stood up and was recognized. A few minutes later, someone from behind tapped Vasyl on the left shoulder. Before he could turn around to see who it was, the person asked, in Russian, "When was the last time you slept in a hay barn in Solina?"

Startled, while still sitting, Vasyl turned around. The man was on his left side. Since he could not see out of the left eye, he spun around to the other side and saw the man.

He stared at him for a long time without saying a word, nor did the man he looked at speak, though a broad grin was spreading across his bearded face.

"It looks like eye patches are now fashionable," he finally said to Vasyl. "You look like a pirate."

"Simon. Simon Smolensky." Vasyl said and then each violently shook the other's hand and hugged each other over the back of the seat.

"Vasyl. Vasyl Najda. Is it you? You have changed, more so than just for the patch. I don't think I would have recognized you if I had not heard your name. There are not many Rusnaks named Najda."

"I, too, would not have recognized you," said Vasyl. "You used to be so thin and your beard was so black. It has turned white and you have gained weight. It looks like America has been good to you."

"You would not have recognized my name," Smolensky said. "I have run into more Smolenskys in America than in all of Russia, Ukraine or Poland. They must have been great lovers at one time in Smolensk.

"But you, you don't look so good. What happened to your eye?"

Vasyl related the incident to him and Smolensky listened intently, like a lawyer building a case.

"What are you doing here?" Vasyl asked.

"I am still a lawyer. I spent the first few years studying American Law in New York. After I passed the bar examination there, my cousin invited me to join his law firm in Pittsburgh. The mills here are more negligent than the mines. It has been a good 18 years since I saw you last."

"What of the three friends who were traveling with you?

"I never saw them again after Emigrant Village. I know one was sent back to Russia because of his eyes. The others, I don't know.

"I have two compensation cases against U.S. Steel, men who were hurt on the job and now Carnegie is trying to get away without paying anything. I suppose your case against Consolidated concerns your eye."

Vasyl introduced him to Maruschak and they talked law for the next few minutes.

"I know this judge," Smolensky said, "I have been before him several times. Let me read your brief."

It took but a few minutes and Smolensky turned to Vasyl and then his lawyer and said, "Your claim is valid but not written

315

strongly enough. Consolidated has some good lawyers here and they will tear it apart.

"I think your approach is wrong. I was here a month ago and heard a case similar to yours, one, that involved the use of explosives in blasting coal."

Just then, the court clerk called Najda versus Consolidated Coal Mining. Maruschak rose and said, "Ready you honor."

"Wait," Smolensky said to Maruschak. "Ask for a 5-minute delay. I have an idea that I think will work; that will get the case immediately ended in Vasyl's favor."

The court granted a short delay.

"Let me argue the case for Vasyl," he asked Maruschak." I know what I am doing. Trust me Vasyl."

"I trust you, but I do not have any more money."

"This is the least I can do for a friend who has helped me. There is some loyalty in this world that transcends who we are, or from where we came or to whom we pray. I will gladly do it pro bono."

"At no cost? "Maruschak asked.

"At no cost," Simon Smolensky answered.

When the case was called, Smolensky argued that Consolidated Mining was breaking the law by allowing Vasyl Najda to shoot coal. He referred to a law passed by the Pennsylvania Legislature in early 1920 that required all mine blasting in the state be conducted by a certified and registered individual who had been qualified to handle explosives. Consolidated was aware of the law and disregarded it by allowing unqualified miners to do their own blasting, as they had in the past.

The court awarded Vasyl $1,000 in compensation and charged Consolidated with court costs.

"What will you do with all that money, my wealthy brother?" asked John as they sat next to each other on the bus ride back to Somerset.

"I don't have to think long about it," Vasyl said. "It is my ticket to be free of the mines. I will buy a farm; be it a small farm."

"In the Old Country?"

"No, here. My children are all Americans and I, too, will become an American. I will talk to Maruschak about my first papers. Peter, Maruschak's father, agreed with Vasyl. I think it is time that I, too, get my first papers.

Chapter 33   Father and Son Go Into the Mines

The year 1922 was a momentous one for the Najda Clan and was marked with many changes. That summer, in early August, a half-year since he announced his intentions, Andrij Najda returned to his family in Europe.

"It is time I go," he told his brothers one evening in Vasyl's house when John had come to visit.

"I know that Maria will not come here," he repeated himself as if to bolster his decision to return to Europe. "She is like John's wife and afraid of the ocean. She cannot understand how an iron ship can float. I am 46 years old, older than our father or grandfather ever lived. I have not seen my two girls in all that time. One is to be married later this year.

"I have missed a life with them. I have sent them money in these last 12 years and have been able to save some. Maybe I can buy a farm with it over there. I hear there are lots of farms for sale because so many men have left their villages to come to America.

"I will leave in two weeks."

There no longer was a need to travel to Johnstown or even Somerset or Meyersdale to catch a train. The coal companies had developed the tracks to Goodtown and now there was a small station in Raineytown, less than a quarter-mile from Goodtown. In those days, almost every coal train had at least one passenger car attached to it. It was taken off at Johnstown and transferred to the Main Line.

All of the Najdas walked to the Raineytown Station to see Andrij leave. He had no fancy clothing other than the one suit he wore to church. It was a bit frayed and had seen several years of

317

weddings, funerals and Sundays at church. Somewhere he had acquired an oval valise with running boards on the bottom and two mounted buckles that locked together when the valise was closed. It contained all the worldly possessions he had acquired in 12 years of working almost every day, six days a week and often added shifts.

"He told Kateryna he would miss her bread that he liked so and before they left that morning she presented him with an oversized load. She had been up before dawn and baked it. She wrapped it in a large dishtowel and tied the free ends together. In a jaunty air, he tossed it over his shoulder and boarded the train. Tears filled everyone's eyes. They all knew that there was no likelihood they would ever see each other again. Life can be bitter but they had all grown up with bitterness and were accustomed to its taste.

Vasyl seemed to cling to his brother longer than usual as if he knew he would never see him again. After they kissed, he grabbed his brother's right hand and clasped it in a hand shake. Andrij felt something in it. It was a crisp $100 bill. "What is this for?" he asked his brother with tear-filled eyes.

"I was not able to help buy you a ticket to come here" Vasyl said, "but now I can spare this to help you buy a farm a home."

"But it is too much," Andrij said.

"So I buy a farm a little bit smaller and maybe you can buy one a little bit bigger. *Ede z Boh!*"

Wasco, the Najda's first son, now 13, had become a disciplinary problem and refused to attend school. He preferred instead to run off to fish in Buffalo Creek with the Turko boys. The last time he did it, his father brought him home by pulling him by his ear. It was a technique that always got the Najda children's and occasionally my attention.

"Does anyone know what day this is?" Kateryna Najda asked her horde of seven children one evening, a few weeks after school had started. They were hanging around after supper because they had seen their mother, earlier in the day, making her fabulous hickory nut cake topped with maple icing. The kitchen table was full while 2-year-old Michael was in a corner crying, confined to a playpen his father made. He built it years ago, for Catherine when she was a baby, from wooden orange crates the company store had thrown out.

"It is Thursday," Anna said as she first passed a small plate to Wasco, her younger brother, then passed plates to others around the table.

"That's true," her mother said, "but it is also something else. It is a special day in our family. Today is September 21, 1922. What does that mean?"

"I know," said Mary, the oldest, who had just finished clearing the dinner plates and stacking them in the wooden dry sink. She had married Sam Philip in late May and they were having supper at her family's house. She returned to the table by way of the stove and picked up the coffeepot. She was pouring a cup for her father when she said, "It is Wasco's birthday."

"That's right," said his mother. "Does anyone know how old he is?" No one answered and finally she asked, "Wasco, how old are you?"

"I don't give a damn how old I am," he said as he reached for one of the square cut pieces of cake on a large plate in the middle of the table.

"He's 13," Anna yelled.

In a flash, his father, who was sitting next to him, slapped him across the back of his head. It sent the piece of cake flying across the table and onto the floor. One of two house cats beat it to the cake before anyone could lean over and pick it up. Wasco sprang back from the table, knocking over the chair, and clenched his fists as if ready to strike his father.

"You eat like a pig," his father said, "No one said you could take the cake. I don't like it when you swear. You have no respect for your mother or the rest of your family. Don't ever talk to her like that again!"

"Vasylko," said his wife in a compromising tone, "he didn't mean to be disrespectful. That is the way children are nowadays. He is your oldest son and he loves you. It is the Turko boy. He is a bad influence on Wasco. You should talk to Paul about him."

Vasyl didn't answer but glowered at her. The look was enough to tell her to be quiet.

"Get back into your chair," Vasyl ordered and Wasco reluctantly obeyed him.

"Your mother tells me that Miss Dickey was here Friday. She wanted to know why you have not been in school for the past three days. And, you skipped two days the week before. Why weren't you in school?"

"I hate school," Wasco blurted. "I hate it and I don't want to go. Mickey Turko doesn't have to go to school. Why do I have to go to school?"

"What would you do, spend the rest of your life fishing in the creek? You had off all summer. Wasn't that enough?"

"Why should I have to go to school when I don't want to?"

"Because by going to school and getting an education you can break the bonds that have me, and now you, chained to this kind of life. You are my first born son. Life can be different for you than it has been for me because you were born in America. You do not have to be judged by others or by what work your father does. You cannot know what that means but I do and that is why I have kept you in school. It is knowledge that gives a person control of their lives. Don't you see how the others, the Germans who have been here for a generation or two, in Pinehill or Berlin, how much better they live than we do? Doesn't their life look better, easier to you than ours? I know you are still young but hasn't God put some sense in your head by now? Have you had you eyes shut to the world around you as you are growing up?

"You go to school so you don't have to work all you life like I have done."

"I'm not going back...."

"Okay stupid. You don't have to go to school tomorrow. But tomorrow you will see the real world for the first time. You will see what lies ahead for you, for the rest of your life. Maybe that will make you change your mind!

"You will get up when I get up, at 5 o'clock, and you will go to work in the mine with me. You will load coal for me. From now on, if you want to fish it will have to be only on Sundays....and after church."

The next morning, Vasyl took Wasco into the mines. Like so many other immigrant sons, coal companies allowed the men to bring sons into their rooms to help load coal. At first, the only prerequisite was that they could do the work. Boys as young as 10 and 11 were in the mines helping their fathers load coal while they dug with pick and shovel. It meant more money and that bit could make the difference between just getting by and a satisfactory living. However, under intense pressure from child welfare groups, Pennsylvania passed a law in 1915 that required them to be at least 15 years old.

"He doesn't look 15," said the foreman.

"He is small for his age," rebutted Vasyl.

Since his eye injury, Vasyl now worked only with the pick and shovel and called in a certified shooter when the face of his room needed blasting. Consolidated had paid attention to the state law ever since Vasyl's accident. The coal veins in the Goodtown mines continued thinning and miners now were seldom able to work a full week. Coincidentally, the demand for coal was also declining as many factories and homes switched to oil-fired furnaces. Reacting to this, mine companies begin lowering the price they paid miners for a ton of coal. In response, unions were again actively recruiting and finding ready acceptance, even from the Hunkies.

Chapter 34   The Farm

In Goodtown, the Maruschaks, Vasyl and Anna, lived three houses up the road from the Najdas. It was really just a dirt path that occasionally saw a vehicle climb its steep grade when something heavy needed to be loaded or unloaded. They became close friends. They were from Caryn (Carynskie), a small village a half-dozen miles northwest of Protisne. When Anna Maruschak developed a complicated case of appendicitis, she had to be taken to a hospital in Maryland, south of Berlin, where she stayed for a week. Mary Najda took care of Anna's children while she was gone and made dinner for the boarders.

That is how Mary met a miner named Sam Philip and eventually married him. Sam was the son of Frank and Mary Pilip, and from the same village as the Maruschaks. The purser wrote his name as "Philip" on the ship's manifest. He didn't know, at the time, and later didn't bother to have it corrected. Besides, he believed it sounded more American than Pilip (Peell-leep). It did. Because they knew him in Europe, the Maruschak's readily took him in as a boarder. Of course, the other reason was money. Late in May, in 1922, Mary, Vasyl Najda's oldest daughter, now 16, married Sam.

The Najdas, like many other Rusnak families in Goodtown at this time, were undergoing subtle but long-lasting changes as their children matured. With Vasyl's diminished mining income the only sources for money now lay outside the mines. Reluctantly, Anna, at the behest of Vasyl, left school in the 6th grade and went to work keeping house for Dr. John Molineaux and his wife in Pinehill. Magdalena, the Najda's eighth child was born the first day of October in 1922.

Ever since the hearing in Pittsburgh, Vasyl had been looking for a farm to buy. With some of his compensation money, he bought a horse and buggy so that on days when there was no work he could scour the countryside looking for a farm. He found one, just 11 or so acres in size, but that was more than enough land to produce all the food the family would need and a surplus to sell and buy the things it couldn't produce. It was located less than 3 miles from Goodtown, and not far from Garrett. It even had a small stream, Swamp Creek, running through it. The two-storey house on the property was small, modest, but adequate.

Annie Snyder's husband had died two years earlier and she lived there alone, except for occasional visits from her adult children who lived in Berlin and Somerset. She wanted $1,500 for it but settled for $1,275. Vasyl still had the bulk of his settlement money and gave her $700. She agreed to a promissory note for the remainder.

"Today is a very important day in our lives," Vasyl said to his wife after the deed was registered at the courthouse in Somerset. Their lawyer was driving them back to Gold Brick, a cluster of company houses a thousand yards farther up the little valley of Glen Norris, above Goodtown. "It is also our daughter Magdalena's birthday."

"I know that only too well," Kateryna answered. "It was exactly three years ago today she was born. I had a difficult time with her. I swore she would be our last. But I guess God has ordained differently."

Four weeks later, on the first day of November, 1925, they vacated the company house in Gold Brick and moved to the farm.

Vasyl and Kateryna Najda stood next to each other in front of the unpainted barn located on a slight rise above the house. They looked across the small field, no more than a hundred yards long. On the other end, their older children were still unloading the contents of the open truck into the house. The wood-frame house looked old, older than its 50-year existence. The Snyders had let it fall into disrepair and the fields were overgrown. They did little farming on the land even when Annie's husband was alive.

"It has taken me 22 years to see my dream come true," he said. As he looked at the house his right arm reached around his wife's small shoulders. "There were times, in Protisne, and in the mines, when I thought this day would never come. In a way, if it weren't for the accident and the settlement, I would probably still be there. I have strange emotions," he said as they watched the activity at the house. "I feel happy and sad at the same time. I feel sad for my brothers and the other miners who will probably work in those black holes for the rest of their lives. They don't seem able to get ahead...no matter how hard or how long they work. McDonald was not as honest a man as we believed. But, we should have known better. It was our own fault because he really did give us a way out."

Vasyl was caught up in feelings he had long suppressed and then, unexpectedly, began coughing. A few minutes later, he spat on the ground and it was red with blood.

"Maybe this, too, will stop," his wife said with hope.

"Do you remember what I said at your cousin's wedding in Smil'nyk, that someday I would again be a farmer, like my father, like my grandfather and my fathers before them. Now I have a piece of land. It isn't big, but it is much bigger than my father's field. It is mine and no one can take it away from me, from us. It is funny," he said and smiled. "It was a Jew who took our farm away from us and it was a Jew who made it possible for me to be a farmer again. Life has strange twists to it.

"I know that I will die someday, and so will you. But it is my hope that this farm stays forever in our family and that all the Najdas can call it home."

He bent over and grasped a handful of dirt from the nearly frozen ground. He stood up, then let it slowly, gently sift though his fingers. Tears filled his eyes as he pulled his wife closer. She, too, hugged him.

"I do have one regret," Vasyl said to his wife as he continued to hold his arm around her shoulder. "The children will be changing schools, but that's not too bad. What I fear is that they will lose the chance to learn our language at the church school. Mary and Anna are pretty good, but Catherine and Nick are just getting started. That is a loss. It would be different if we could read and write, but it isn't. So, we must live with life as it is, not as we would like it to be."

Their thoughts were suddenly interrupted .

"Oh! I hear Rose Ann crying," Kateryna said and started for the house. "Kate is watching her. I must go see if anything is wrong." Rose Ann Nider, the ninth of ten children, was just six-months old.

Soon after the new church in Goodtown was consecrated in 1918, the priest who now lived among his parishioners in Goodtown began holding "Russian" classes for the miner's children. Each day after regular school, from 4 to 6 p.m., they would meet in a classroom in the basement of the church. Those youngsters between third grade and high school, or the eight grades, were expected to attend. However, neither Vasyl nor Kateryna could get Wasco to attend. After the move to the farm, the formal education in Rusnak for the other children also ended.

"A lot has happened in these years," Kateryna said. "I was just a child when you made me that promise. Now, we have a house filled with our children. The land looks so barren in the winter. I hope we can grow what we need. Look at this field. It has as many rocks in it as the fields back in Smil'nyk. Maybe more so. It is certain, that we will be able to gron stones.

"And children..." Vasyl said.

"I think we should wait a while before the next one," his wife interrupted. "I hear Magdalena crying. I must go."

Chapter 35   The Best Christmas of Their Lives

The Najdas move to the farm could not have been better timed. Work in the three dozen mines in Somerset County was dwindling as the demand for coal lessened. Correspondingly, the amount of coal available from the mines also lessened as the veins thinned and some died out completely. Working conditions also deteriorated as mine companies tried to retrieve the last remaining coal from the thinning veins. Compounding the problem was that the cost of retrieving a ton of coal became progressively more expensive the deeper the mines went.

But it was the lessening demand for coal that exacerbated the problem the greatest. In late March (1921) it caused the Brothers Valley Coal and the Berlin Coal companies to close all their operations. Only a few men, electricians, were still employed but only to keep the generators going and pumps running so the mines wouldn't flood. Their owners did this in hopes the mines would reopen if the demand increased. However, they had no idea when or if they would reopen. As a result, miners in Goodtown became scattered as they looked for mines still in operation in surrounding areas.

Much larger companies, like Consolidated, that had long-term contracts with steel mills in Pittsburgh, were able to maintain some of their operations but not at full activity. Consolidated and the Pine Hill Fuel companies were still running but working only two or three days a week. Some smaller mines were only working a day or two a week and many miners had not been paid in several weeks. To survive, mine companies, including Consolidated, began cutting wages. The cuts in pay had the miners angry. They had been struggling to make ends meet even before the decline in coal prices. It was not a good time to be either a miner or a mine owner.

It was under such conditions that Vasyl returned to work but only part-time. After moving to the farm, he spent most of the winter months plugging cracks in the house to keep out the ferocious winds that swept across the large open field to the north, and at times, through the old house. Wind had never been a problem in the little, protected valley in which Goodtown was imbedded. And, the company houses were well built so they resisted the cold. But it was different on the farm. Vasyl would also have to think about a new roof before another winter passed.

Despite these problems, that first Christmas on the farm was the most joyous Vasyl and Kateryna had known in America. Their family now numbered eight, four boys and four girls, the perfect size for a farm family. *Sviaty Vechir*, or Holy Supper, is one of the most sacred holidays of the Orthodox Church, surpassed only by Easter Sunday. It is tradition among Rusnaks that anyone who can make it home for that evening must do so.

Fortunately, Christmas Eve fell on a Friday, January 6, in 1922. The mine owners, because of the dwindling demand for coal, found no trouble not operating that day. Nor would they pay their miners for not working on that day as they had once before. Anna worked only half a day at the doctor's home and he drove her to the Najda farm from Pinehill in his new Ford Model T. Once home she, and her older sister Mary, began helping their mother prepare the great variety of dishes that would be served. They were all Lenten dishes because this was the last day of fasting. Vasyl's brother John arrived early in the day and took Vasyl's buggy to Goodtown to get their brother Harry and his wife Anna and their four children Anna, Mary, John and baby Michael.

Just before dark, Wasco and Nick were sent to the barn and returned with arms filled with hay. As was traditional in their parent's European villages on Christmas Eve, they spread it evenly on the long kitchen table and the smaller circular table in the dining room. Their mother then covered the tables with large tablecloths. It represented a manger scene in Bethlehem.

Two large candles, in heavy, pressed-glass holders, were placed on the kitchen table and one on the dining room table. When Vasyl thought all was ready, he led the family in a long prayer. All the children learned it in Rusnak and knew it by heart. When it was over, Anna, Harry's wife brought in from the kitchen pantry--

a cold-storage room—several, large, round loaves of *palinecha* (pa-lin-e-cha), a flat bread that had been baked earlier in the day.

"Before anyone can eat," Vasyl said, "we must feed bread to the animals in the stable as did Joseph, Christ's father on earth." The older youngsters knew the routine and had their coats on to accompany him to the barn. It was cold and blowing when they went out and snow blew into the kitchen while the door was open.

In preparation for the hike, Wasco had lighted the kerosene lantern and lead the way ahead of his father and Harry's children who wanted to see the horses, the cow and her new calf.

The two women and the older girls waited in the kitchen for their return. As soon as Wasco came though the door they began carrying dishes to the tables. No butter or dairy products, or meat appeared in their hands because of the restrictions. Whatever could be, was seasoned with olive oil and crisply-fried sautéed onions. The centerpiece on each table was the large loaf of flat bread, adorned on the sides, with piles of thinly-sliced pieces that would be dipped in a small dish of honey and poppy seeds.

Almost every meal, Lenten or not, contained cabbage, usually cooked or as sauerkraut that was prepared each fall and stored in large crocks in the cellar. And, always potatoes, usually first boiled then later fried until crispy brown in an onion-and-oil sauté, were in a place of prominence on both tables.

The Supper would not be complete without *peetpenky* (peet-pink-kee), mushrooms that Kateryna and her children had gathered throughout the fall wherever they could find them growing, usually under beech trees. Almost religiously and with tender regard they cleaned the fragile stems and tops then carefully strung them, with needle and thread, into large garlands. These were hung on nails on the ceiling above the kitchen stove until they were thoroughly dried. They were then taken apart and stored in large Mason jars, and when needed, were reconstituted.

There was canned corn and *gingarecha*, corn kernels that months earlier had been cut off the cobs and laid on large flat pans placed under the stove. They remained there for several days until they, too, were pronounced dried by Kateryna. They also were stored in large Mason jars in the pantry. And, they, too, were reconstituted in warm water whenever the meal called for corn.

Instead of the traditional herring that was used in Europe, or could only be acquired in America in fish markets in large coastal cities, the Rusnaks in Goodtown and its environs settled for canned sardines and canned Pacific salmon.

Another dish was heaped with a mound of steaming *pshenycha*, or boiled tan-colored grains of large wheat that popped their outer coverings as if pregnant. This was eaten with a coating of honey. There was always the Rusnak staple--*perrohi*--alias fritters. There were three kinds; those stuffed with mashed potatoes, others with sauerkraut and lastly those with small prunes. After molded into doughy triangles, these were boiled in water then pan-fried in oil and onions until lightly browned. At these feasts, they were eaten only with salt and pepper, maybe horseradish, both white and beet-stained. But on the following day, with Lent over, they were smothered in sour cream and covered with salt and pepper. There also were dishes of peas, carrots and lima beans.

And on each plate, one of the girls had diligently placed a few cloves of garlic. Everyone was expected to consume at least one piece. In front of each dish was a saltcellar into which the garlic clove was dipped after first being moistened by one's lips. A few minutes after the start of supper, the aroma of garlic would dominate the air in both rooms.

Though the children were already seated, waiting for Vasyl to return from the barn, not a morsel of food was ever touched. When he returned he took off his hat and coat and then came to his place at the head of the table. He crossed his hands, and for a moment looked around at the assembly and inside beamed with pride. "God has been good to us," he said

He paused exceptionally longer that Christmas and when no one rose, he cleared his throat. Harry, taking the hint, stood up and everyone else followed.

"*Otech nash.....*" he began the Lord's Prayer in Rusnak, and everyone followed him in his native tongue. As is always customary, before and after a prayer, everyone blessed themselves three times.

When it was over, he reached for the large *palinecha* and the long knife beside it. With the tip of the blade, he made the sign of the cross on its bottom and then placed the knife on the table and began breaking off pieces of bread. As he did, he ritually handed a piece to every child. On the other end of the table, Harry did the same.

"It is a sacrilege," he said as he did so, "to cut this bread at the Holy Supper. We must break bread, as did Christ, and hand it to our people at the table."

No one ever left the table not feeling overly stuffed.

When it was finished, Anna, Harry's wife came in with a big brown bag. Dipping her hand into it, she began throwing out an assortment of nuts around the floor. The children scurried to find them and loaded their pockets.

"It would have been nice to have gone to church tonight," Vasyl said as he and his brothers John and Harry sat around the table finishing the garlic the children had half-eaten.

"But it is too cold. It began snowing harder as I came from the barn. Besides, we couldn't all fit in the buggy. Our family has grown too large for that. We would need a hay wagon."

"We will all go tomorrow," Harry said.

"Yes, tomorrow," John echoed, "but in shifts."

"I wonder how Andy is doing in the Old Country?" Vasyl said as they sat around the big table. "We have not heard from him since he left in August. He said he was going to try to buy back our old house. I wonder if he did."

"I doubt if his wife would have left her mother's and father's place," Harry said.

"Mike Salabaj got a letter from his sister," added John. "She wrote that since the end of the war, the Poles again are in control of Galicia, and the Polish police are menacing our villages whenever they want. They killed three men a few months ago. For no reason at all. They did that just to show the Rusnaks who is in control. I cannot believe they would treat fellow Slavs like that. Are we not really brothers? We speak almost the same tongue. Our customs are almost the same. Are we not really the same people? Will they ever stop?"

"I think Rome is still behind all this," said Harry.

"I fear they are just beginning.

Part II The Next Generation Begins Its Moves

Chapter 36   The Umbilicus is Severed

Though the immigrants could not completely remove themselves from events in Europe, it was much easier and a natural occurrence for their children to begin weakening the bonds with their relatives in the Old Country. Now time, as well as distance, were thinning the attachments with them. There is no question that they sincerely empathized with what was happening in Galicia, Slovakia and all of Europe. It was, however, a world away from the immediate problems that beset them. But, it was the role of the next generation, whether they knew it or not, to begin the assimilation of their people into America society. It was a goal the Hunkies could neither imagine, nor hope to accomplish, if they could.

Anna Najda was a perfect example of the next generation. My mother never had any idea of the role she was about to play as a catalyst in the Najda family's move into the America society that existed beyond the venues of Goodtown. Her sister Mary, a year or so older, was thwarted in this goal, if she possessed it, because of her marriage at an early age, to foreign-born Sam Philip. She was almost immediately saddled with the responsibility of a family household and soon a large farm to manage with her husband.

Now that I look back with an overall perspective of the characteristics of a half-dozen of my nearest relatives, I can see that comparatively speaking, my mother was unique and vastly unlike her brothers, sisters or cousins. She reminded me, to some degree, of the independent nature of my grandmother Kateryna Mynko before she was married and the first few years afterwards. My grandmother's attitudes, values and motivation were reshaped first by the marriage, then the responsibilities of her expanding household that at times must have stifled her.

Though there were no genetic ties to link her and her characteristics with my paternal grandmother, Zuzanna Ivanco, had too many similarities in common with Kateryna Mynko to be accidental. Maybe it was the land, the environment and the subservient status of a women in their era that made them so similar. Or, maybe it was a distinct Rusnak characteristic that set these highland Slavs aside from other Slavs.

The most revealing characteristics that these two grandparents had in common, and they appeared early in the life of my mother as well, was their unabashed independence, self-esteem, self-assurance, discipline and dedication. In a way, these five characteristics are much alike and have much in common and are dependent and feed upon one another.

Anna had been born in the United States. But because of the planned isolation of her relatives and their friends by the mining company's interests in the construction of a ghetto community, it did not at first create a need in her to learn English or even a desire to do so. The few words her father had learned from the Americans working the mines, and repeated at home, were all she knew as a youngster.

The biggest source of English words for the Najdas and their children that were added to their vocabulary was when Anna and her sister Mary, and their mother visited the company store. "Uncle" Jerry and another clerk told them the English equivalents for bread, meat, milk or whatever fruits they bought. However, their retention at first was minimal because there was no need to use these few new words once they left the store.

Anna was perfectly capable of growing up in what could have been a village in Galicia rather than Pennsylvania. It wasn't until she turned six, in September 1914, that she was required by Pennsylvania State Law to attend first grade at the Glen Norris Public School. It was in this two-room schoolhouse, on the edge of Goodtown, where she suddenly became aware that people outside of her mining town really did speak a language other than the one she, her brothers and sisters, mother and father, aunts and uncles, and all the Rusnaks about her, spoke.

Her older sister Mary was the first to attend school and thus the first to be exposed to English on a grand scale. It was also her teacher, Miss Mary Dickey, who anglicized their last name to Nider.

She believed Najda too difficult for the little girls to spell and write. This is interesting, because "Nider" was the name Hans Gruber, the Austrian aid to McDonald, heard when he added Vasyl Najda's name to those going to America and Pine Hill. Ironically, Miss Dickey was also my Third Grade teacher when years later, after my father died, I went to live for two years with my grandparents.

Once in school, an extremely curious person, Anna was instantly motivated to learn. She had the slight advantage of not being the oldest girl in the family and, for a year or two, had fewer chores to perform. It was her father, however, who also spurred her on to do her studies well and to finish something once she began a task.

"It is English that will allow you to get ahead in America," he told them one night while the family still lived in Goodtown. "When I first came here, I thought I would only work for a few years, to make enough money to buy back our old family farm, or another farm in the Old Country. But I have not been able to do that. Things change and now I have a family too large to take back. I know that now. I may have to work all my life in the mines, until I die, because I cannot do anything else. You, Anna, will not be held back like I was. Your future is here and it begins with school. Learn well, because what you learn can never be taken from you, unlike land or money. With *rozum*, with brains, you can choose your own path."

That was really a strange exposition of my grandfather's philosophy toward women. He truly believed it was valid for his sons but felt education was not needed for a girl to be successful. But, when one considers the attitude of most men toward women at the turn of the 19th century, his thinking was not uncommon.

Anna continued in school until the sixth grade, when she was 12, in 1920. Disappointed, and to the chagrin of Miss Dickey, she was forced to quit and find work because of the family's financial straits. However, in 1920, a 6th grade education was considerably higher than most Rusnaks or even most rural Americans acquired. Hard times for the family, caused by the failing mines and then the accident to Vasyl's eye, made everyone look for ways to earn money. Luckily, she first found work nearby, in the Gumbert's General Store in Pinehill. She walked there and home each day. She held the job for several months until a doctor's wife in Pinehill had a difficult child delivery and needed help with her family. Anna was offered the job and moved in with them, just a few houses from the general store.

Her emancipation was the move to Pinehill, both at the general store and at the doctor's home. I have seen photograph's of my mother and her girlfriends at ages 14 to 22. I doubt that the *Sears Roebuck* catalog in those years carried such fashions but she and her contemporaries, all first generation women, the children of Hunkies, looked like they stepped out of *Vogue* or *Seventeen*. She was young, beautiful and chic. I cannot imagine that the chic part could or would have developed while down the hill in Goodtown.

Even after the move to the farm, what little money it produced from the sale of eggs and milk, and what Anna made at Pinehill, was just enough to keep the family alive. Vasyl decided that he would return to the mines to work part-time. Ironically, part-time was all that he and most of the other miners were now able to work. In late winter, whenever the snows were not too deep, long before dawn, he would harness his horse to the buggy. Accompanied by his son Wasco, they would drive the four miles to Goodtown. The horse remained inside the mine, in an underground corral dug out years ago, where mules had been kept before the mechanical versions were installed.

As spring arrived, Vasyl began plowing and planting, much the same as he did in Europe. Oftentimes, Kateryna was on the plow and Vasyl was forced to take the balking horse by its halter and vigorously lead it down a new furrow. He bought the workhorse from Harding Hays, a neighbor farmer, for next to nothing. The horse was old and probably had no more than a year, two at the most, of life in it. Because Vasyl's farm was small, only 11 acres, and half of it was in woods and pasture flanking Swamp Creek, the amount of work in three small fields that were tillable would not challenge the old horse.

Throughout the ensuing summer and fall, he commuted to the mines with his horse and buggy. At first, he was able to find work for two or three days a week, more if there was work, less if there wasn't. When not in the mines he would work his fields every day except Sundays. That was God's day, he would say.

Every Sunday all the Najda's would pile into the buggy and arrive in time for services in Goodtown's Sts. Peter & Paul Russian Orthodox Church. Vasyl and his brother Andrij, along with 16 other Rusnaks, founded the church. In a very real way to Vasyl, this church was the continuation of the church he started to build between Protisne and Smil'nyk. It represented a rebellion against Roman Catholic controls on the Greek Catholic Church his people had been forced to accept.

After two hours of Liturgy, and before heading back to the farm, the children were famished and couldn't wait to share dinner with the Maruschaks or Turkos. They had been their neighbors and close friends all the years they still lived in Goodtown.

"Did you hear what happened in Gold Brick on Wednesday?" Paul Turko asked Vasyl one Sunday, as they sat on the porch after Sunday dinner having a pipe. Gold Brick was the site of another mine just a short distance above Lottie. No 1. and the last place the Najdas lived in Goodtown.

"Did you know the Pine Hill Coal Company was going to give your room to the Bittner brothers from Berkeley Mills? Someone in the company said that you were not blasting it right, that there was more coal there than you thought there was."

"I suspected that they were going to do that," Vasyl said. "They didn't want to hire a blaster to come in and shoot the room. They didn't want to spend the money for him. They wanted me to do it. They were breaking the law. They knew it. I wouldn't do it."

"The reason they couldn't hire a blaster," said Paul, "because they were broke and didn't want to spend any money."

"Well, what happened?"

"When the two brothers didn't come out of Mine No 1. at 3:00 in the afternoon, like they were supposed to, the foreman went in to find them. He found the younger brother Ed, who was only 19, crushed and dead under a heavy fall of Hryec. The other, Harry, who was two years older, was also under the rocks but still alive. He died after they brought him to the top.

"It seems they did their own shooting and a whole layer of Hryec on the mine ceiling came down after they went in to begin shoveling. There was almost no coal that came down. It was all Hryec. All slate."

"I knew that the vein had petered out," said Vasyl. "They wouldn't believe me. The Bittners should have known better. They weren't greenhorns. They were young but they've been in the mines for six or seven years."

After that, Vasyl was more hesitant to go back into the mines. It was getting to be too dangerous. The money wasn't worth the risk. Nor was his health getting better even though he now spent less time breathing coal dust. The worst had already happened to his lungs and no amount of fresh air on the farm was going to clean them.

Wasco's share of the mine earnings came from his father's pay envelope. With nothing in Goodtown to spend it on he squirreled it away in a can he hid under a loose board in a huge, second floor bedroom that he shared with his brothers and sisters. Earlier that year, Yurko, the oldest Turko boy had been able to buy a used Model T and lauded it around Goodtown. He was not only first to learn to drive, but to buy a car. Wasco was envious.

It was an early December snowstorm that convinced Vasyl there had to be a better way to commute. During the buggy ride from the farm to the mine Vasyl and his son almost froze in the wind.

"Father," said Wasco as they unhitched the horse in the corral inside the mine, "I have saved nearly $200 and I want to buy a car. It is not enough money to buy a car but if you could lend me another $150, I could buy one. There is a one-year old Ford for sale in Berlin. I saw it a few days ago when I was with Yurko. I am now old enough to drive."

"No, I will not lend you the money," Vasyl said. Wasco was stunned. "But," said his father, "we will buy the car together. A horse and buggy is no way to travel in the winter."

The next weekday when they didn't work, Vasyl and his son went to Berlin. The banker didn't hesitate to lend him the money, especially with the farm as collateral.

The Najda's were now wealthy, or so it seemed to everyone else. Wasco, however, could only drive the car when his father was in it with him.

340

Chapter 37   A Winter Camping Out

A recession in the coal mines had been underway since 1922 and only worsened in the next few years. Consolidated's contracts with the Pittsburgh mills had ended. Every steel mill felt the effects of the prolonged industrial recession. In an attempt to avoid bankruptcy, Consolidated ordered a 25-cent cut, to be effective April 1, 1925, across the board in all their mines, for what they paid for a ton of coal. The miners were already struggling to survive the effects of several smaller cuts Consol had made and this would devastate them.

Though unions had tried to establish themselves for years in the Goodtown mines they had been unable to make progress. Even without a union to represent them, nearly 150 miners met one evening in mid-March, ironically in the company's recreation hall. They voted, to Consolidated's astonishment, not to accept the cut.

On April 1, Pennsylvania State Police along with Somerset County Sheriff's men, began evicting all the miners from company owned houses. Officials from the United Mine Workers of America heard of this and within days sent truckloads of surplus WW I army tents to aid the miners. The union even rented a farm field adjacent to the company farm and created a tent village.

The strike dragged on and the miners began to realize that the strike could be prolonged. Those miners with cars and who were able to find work elsewhere were able to survive. Several without cars began walking daily to Berlin and started working for the town repairing highways. Those who couldn't find mining work around Goodtown began looking for any kind of work, in other towns. Unskilled "American" labor in Berlin began to feel the competition for their jobs by a work force that would work for almost nothing, for subsistence wages.

Vasyl and his sons Wasco and Nick were haying the field above the barn when they saw a Ford stop in front of their house. They didn't recognize the vehicle and abandoned the field to came down to the house to see who it was.

Sam Philip, Vasyl's son-in-law and still a Goodtown miner, was with Vern Blaubough. Vasyl's brother John, or "Stritchko" (uncle) as his nieces and nephews called him, was out of work and had accompanied them for the car ride and the chance to see his brother. Blaubough was taking Philip to see the 200-acre farm adjacent to Vasyl's. It had been for sale for two years and Philip, too, was trying to escape the mines. They dropped off John and continued up the sandy road to look at the farm.

"Did you hear what some bastards did two nights ago in Goodtown?" John asked Vasyl.

"No. What happened?" Vasyl asked John.

"At night, some one put up a big, wooden cross in the field opposite where the miners have their tents. It was wrapped in rags soaked in kerosene. Then they set it on fire. There were about a dozen men in white robes and pointed hats dancing around the burning cross and yelling 'Hunky go home.'

"They had long pointed hoods over their heads and faces so you couldn't tell who they were. They had openings cut out for their eyes and mouths. Their hats made them look like dunces. They were," he said and paused. "They are so stupid they don't know how to make a Russian cross.

"Then the flames from the cross started to burn rows of dried hay in the field. The wind blew sparks everywhere. They couldn't put it out and it was headed fast for the superintendent's house and the school. They had to run into the tents and ask the miners to help put out the fire. Like *duraks*, they did. They should have let it burn."

The cross burning had no effect on the miners even though the Klan was active in Berlin and Meyersdale; even holding a parade in one town before they went by train to parade in Washington in August.

It wasn't the Klan that was driving out the miners but the lack of work. Gradually, one-by-one, miners and their families began abandoning Goodtown, never to return there to work. Those who stayed in the tents resisted going back to the mines until winter approached. The cold was too severe for families with children. After the first snow storm, the miners began to return to the mines and to their old houses.

Vasyl and his brothers survived. John had no children, but Harry and his wife had four by then and during the strike they moved in with Vasyl on the farm. In the fall, Harry found a job with a new mine that opened in Blackfield, a dozen miles from Goodtown. There, he was able to move into another company house. Vasyl was worried about his younger brother. He suffered from the black lung disease even more than Vasyl. He had contracted it after Vasyl but seemed more affected by it. Ironically, Harry worked the same mines, though he was the last of the four brothers to immigrate to America, but the coal dust seemed to bother him the most.

"Hryec, you smoke too much," Vasyl said to him one evening. "The company doctors in Somerset told me to stop or I would surely die. I haven't had a pipe in more than a year. You are never without one. Stop now Hryec or we will lose you. Sometimes you remind me of our father. I was young when he died but I remember how he would cough. You cough just like him."

"But he never worked in a mine," Harry answered.

"It doesn't matter, the cough was the same. Stop smoking or it will kill you faster than the coal dust!"

It was in August of the same year, in 1925, when Anna made her announcement. "I am quitting my job in the doctor's home at the end of the week," she told her father and mother as they sat around the long kitchen table after a Sunday supper. Anna, the Najdas' second child, was now almost 18 and had worked as a housekeeper for the doctor for the past two years. During the week, she lived with the family in Pinehill and came home weekends."

"What will you do?" asked her mother. "What will we do? You know we still owe money on the farm and even though Wasco and Nick go with your father to the mines, the mines are running out of coal. Your father said it wouldn't last much longer. They are only working one or two days a week, three if they're lucky."

"Why do you want to quit?" her father asked. "has the doctor and his wife put big ideas in your head?"

"No father. I hear there is more money to be made in the shoe factories in Binghamton. Anna Baka got a letter from Stanley Tataleba last week and he told her that everyone, men or women, are all paid the same. There is no man's strength needed to work there. It is piecework. I would get paid for each shoe I did. He said he makes between $20 and $25 every week. There already are several Goodtown families there.

"You know," she quickly added, "that Harry and Steve Bruce and their wives are leaving Goodtown. I saw them a week ago. Steve's wife Mary came to visit the doctor. She said I could go with them if I wanted. Baka's brother already has a house there. I could stay with them until I find my own place."

"If that is what you want to do," her father said, "I will not stop you. You are old enough to know what you are doing. Besides, you are strong-minded, like your mother. I learned a long time ago when to let you two do what you want."

It probably would not have made much difference even if Vasyl had tried to stop my mother. There is a unique independence among all the females in the Najda family. They seemed to have inherited this characteristic from their mother. It is a sex-linked trait. "It is the Mynko in you all," their father often said when they insisted on their own way. "I remember when I first met your mother," he would begin the oft-repeated event. It would now fall upon deaf ears. However, his evaluation of his wife and girls was correct. It was evident in them all, even as children, and Anna was the first to begin breaking away.

There was little future for her in Goodtown or the surrounding area. When she quit school to begin working in Gumbert's Store, then in Dr. Mollineaux's household, she took the first steps in the ensuing separation. If she stayed she could look forward to marrying a miner, usually several years older, one instilled with old-country ways, traditions and principles. She had already been exposed to too much of the world outside of Goodtown. The doctor's offer to adopt her when she was just 13 made her think of herself as a somewhat different person from her peers in the mining town. She would eventually prove that was true.

The move to Binghamton was the second step for Anna and while economics, like before, was the motivating factor there was also the latent desire to see the real world of which its existence had only been hinted at in her short lifetime.

Local Union #6212 of the United Mine Workers of America was formed in 1933. The Depression sounded the death knell for many Somerset County mines and workers began moving elsewhere. In Goodtown, the companies sold their houses and most were dismantled for their lumber. Not until WW II did life return temporarily to the mines and Goodtown. The Pine Hill Smokeless Coal Company bought all the mines and consolidated them into one, temporary operation.

Chapter 38   The Horsetraders

That same year that Anna Najda made her move to the big city to seek her future, the Karases on the south side of the Carpathian Mountains in Europe were about to face a crisis that would also drastically change their lives, or at least the life of my father, Stefan Karas.

The large vegetable garden upon which they depended each year--to see them through a winter--had produced but scant amounts of food. Their garden, like all the gardens and land around Vilag, had suffered a prolonged and unusually severe drought that began in 1924 and lasted into 1925. It might not have been as bad if the land had been more fertile to begin with, but more than 300 hundred years of tilling it without replenishments left very few minerals and nutrients. The loss of sustenance crops put a strain on what little food they had gathered for the impending winter. And, because of the poor rainfall and consequent lack of grass, the Karases lost nearly 40 sheep by the end of summer and were forced to begin selling off their remaining flock. Some went to a few villagers who were still receiving dwindling stipends from America and could buy a sheep or two, but most went to butchers in surrounding villages for a fraction of their worth.

It was a late summer morning and the sun was already shortening the days. Zuzanna sat in the rocking chair Andrij had built for her the first year that had returned from America and forlornly looked out the small glass panes at the struggling plants in the garden. The sun, as it slowly rose, crept down the hillside to the west as she measured its pace. Her fingers twinged and ached.

She massaged her hands, one against the other, seeking relief from the pain. The day before, she worked in the garden pulling weeds until it was almost dark. It seemed that weeds were the only plants to grow. The arthritis was getting worse.

We never should have come back, she said to herself as she gently rocked back and forth and twisted her hands. We should have stayed in Woods Run, like Helen and Sam. We could have moved to Ambridge when they did. Maybe it was nicer than in Verner. Who could have ever thought that life in these hills could become to difficult.

She heard Stefan moving about in his room. She hoped he would not wake his brother and sister. She needed a few more moments alone with herself. Then she heard *Baba* stirring.

The soil in these mountains had never been very productive, even when the first Rus began moving from the flatlands to the north into the dense forests that covered them. Even when the migrating Magyar hordes from the east separated them from their Slav brethren, eking a life here as a farmer was impossible. That was why they and the others kept to heading sheep for the first 200 hundred years or so, after the fearsome, war-like Magyar tribes arrived and settled on the lowlands. They bothered little with the Rusnaks who remained in the higher elevations. The core of the Carpathians remained inaccessible and did not attract the Hungarians.

But as their numbers swelled, and free land became scarce, they gradually began spreading north, displacing the unorganized Rusnaks, taking possession of these lands at will, without opposition. By the end of the 12th century, the sovereignty of a Hungarian king had been established. They built a two-city capital, developed a system of government and now had a standing army. And because of these achievements, for the past thousand years, Hungarians, their kings and their nobility had ruled the Rusnaks' lives.

As they expanded their realm into the mountains, that of the Rusnaks and other Slavs declined. That of the Rusnaks was easiest to manage because, unlike the other Slavs in the Carpathians, they had no leaders, no direction, no knowledge now even of who they were or who they had once been. Their dissolution as a nation, as a definable people, was complete.

This privileged position of Magyars in Rusnakia remained unchallenged until the end of the first World War. Huge stretches of forest were the personal property of titled Hungarian landowners; most were absentee-landlords who visited their Carpathian estates mainly to stalk bear, wild boar, deer and other game. These latter years of the 19th century were the heyday of Hungarian supremacy and they coined the slogan: *"Extra Hungaria non est vita, et si est vita, non est ita."*

While the small villages and hamlets retained their almost primitive, rustic Rusnak look, larger towns and small cities took on a distinctly Hungarian appearance. Their populations became very mixed but not with Rusnaks. Those in possession of power and position--officials, doctors, teachers, lawyers, judges, army and police officers, and members of the gentry--were mostly Magyars or Magyarised Jews. Even Magyar peasants, those who owned major farms in the lowlands of what was now often referred to as the Carpatho-Ukraine, were quite well off. The soil of this productive agricultural belt yielded a surplus of wheat, corn, fruit, vines and even tobacco. And, its lush meadows were well suited for cattle and horse breeding. Most Magyar farmers were able to hire Rusnak, Slovak and Polish peasants, really serfs, to work for them during their busy seasons.

This privileged life for the Magyars who controlled the Rusnaks and Slovaks came to an abrupt end in 1919 when this land was detached from Hungary and the days of Magyar supremacy were over. The Hungarian military, gendarmes and officials were gone,

Most absentee-landowners were forced to give up their estates for a financial compensation and property of the resident gentry was curtailed. However, farmers retained their thriving farms, and cattle and horse dealers carried on their profitable business

Overwhelmed by the task, the Czechs and Slovaks were slow to organize a new government and establish economic reforms and ties. It was such a shamble that Zuzanna Karas and her family now faced.

"Maybe we should try to sell some land," Stefan suggested to his mother as she laid a bowl of steaming oatmeal on the table before him. "It is doing nothing but eating away in taxes what little money we have been able to get from the sheep."

"I have asked about that," she answered, "but no one has money to buy land, especially land that cannot be farmed. Not even the Jews. And the lumber merchants in Humenné are no longer in business. The land is worthless. It has become a burden to us. Maybe your father and I should have stayed in America. He didn't really want to return. It was me who made him do so."

"No it wasn't," Stefan said. "It wasn't all that. I remember him saying that the mills had also shut down, that a depression was one of the reasons we came back to Vilag."

"Maybe so," she said as she blamed herself for their current misfortune. Her mind temporarily drifted back to Verner and Woods Run. "Maybe so. But if we really wanted to, we could have found some way to stay. My brother did."

By the end of spring, in 1925, the last of the sheep were sold and that money fed them until early winter.

"Stefan, take little Ivan with you and dig in the garden again. See if you can find any potatoes."

"But the ground is frozen," he said.

"Are you hungry?

"Then go and do as I say."

"I will go, too," said Maria, Stefan's sister-in-law. "The boys are crying. They are hungry."

"All we found was a horseradish," Stefan said and he held it up for his mother to see as he reentered the house. Behind him in the doorway was Ivan Chupik, Maria's father.

"*Slava Isusu Khristu,*" he said

"*Slava Bohu na viki,*" Zuska answered.

Mary ran to her father and hugged him.

"How are the boys?" he asked as he handed her a cloth bag. Inside were a dozen, small, green-skinned potatoes. In other years they would have been thrown away or fed to the pigs.

"These were to be my seed potatoes for next spring. But it is more important that they now are eaten. I can always find some, somewhere."

Late that winter, in February, (1926) Stefan found work among the Hungarians who still dominated the lands on the flat terrain south of the mountains. He went to work for a wealthy Austrian, Arnold Zeitmann, whose grandfather had been a count and acquired a vast estate near Michalovce while this land was still part of the Austrian Empire. Somehow, he had been able to hold on to it even after the Great War. Zeitmann specialized in breeding and raising horses, horses not for pulling plows or drawing wagons, but cavalry horses for the Austrian and Hungarian armies, and now the new Czech Army.

Stefan worked as a stable hand, feeding horses and mucking their stalls. He always had a penchant for horses and often rode the two his family had owned. He had learned to ride his father's stallion when he was but 10 and when he wasn't around would ride it bareback across the meadows, scattering the sheep.

When an incident occurred in the grooming of an uncontrollable yearling, Stefan's ability to calm the horse caught the eye and attention of Zeitmann and earned him a steady job with the Austrian. In addition to mucking, some of it was spent breaking-in horses to a saddle. Still, Zeitmann didn't pay Stefan what Hungarians, or even Slovaks, earned who worked for him doing the same jobs. Compared to the other ethnic groups around them, Rusnaks were always at the bottom of the social and pay scales, regardless of the kind of work they did. Despite this prejudice, he was able to bring home enough money to pay for food to keep the family going. What money his brother sent home was consumed by the steadily growing land taxes.

For two years after his arrival in the United States, Andrew led a monk's life. He intensely missed his wife and two sons and cached away every cent he could manage. When he had enough to send for them, he began looking for a place for them to live. He found a second floor apartment in a three-storey house on 312 First Street in Ambridge, and moved in. The next day, January 22, 1926, he went to the Ambridge National Bank where he had his savings. There a clerk, who was also an agent for the United States Lines, (banks did things like that in cities with large immigrant populations and were called "full-service" banks), purchased the ticket for him. It covered one full and two half-fares in Third Class for $265 and the train fare from Manhattan to Ambridge, First Class, for one full, one half and one free-fare, all for $24.63. Michael was only three and got the free ride.

It was a joyous letter, like a late, unexpected Christmas gift, that arrived on January 14, a day known among Rusnaks who followed the calendar of their fathers as "Little Christmas" or the Feast of Epiphany. Andrew sent them three ship tickets, one for his wife and two for their sons, and bid them come to America.

"Oh, how I would like to go right now," Maria said to her mother-in-law Zuzanna and Stefan, after she read them the letter. "But how will we get to Bremen? We don't even have enough money for bus fare to Vyrava or the train to Prague and Bremen."

"And, we will need passports. How do we get passports? We must find out how. I will ask the priest today, maybe he can tell us. It is different than when Zuska went over.

"I have an idea for the money," Stefan said.

"I will sell the stallion and the buggy. We don't need it anymore. The Jew who owns the *sklep* twice asked me if I wanted to sell him. Maybe now is the time."

Two days later, Stefan walked into Mendel Weisz's store. It looked bare, austere, with long, nearly-empty spaces on the shelves and two empty herring barrels against the counter. Scattered on the shelves were odd collections of canned and boxed dry foods. On the counter were several bags of dried mushrooms that were collected by people in Vilag, scrounging to make a few cents, and sold to the *sklep*.

Weisz saw Stefan look into one of the barrels and immediately responded. "If it is herring you want," I have a smaller barrel in the back. I just got it from Hamburg and haven't made a count. The price, however, has gone up. But tell me how many you want and maybe I can work out something."

"I don't want herring," Stefan said. "I was just curious to see the barrels empty."

"I am saving them for pickles. When the season comes in and they are ripe, I will make pickles. What do you want?"

"Do you remember, a few months ago, when you asked me if I was interested in selling my stallion and buggy?"

"Yes!"

"How much will you give me?"

"How much do you want?"

"I don't know, yet. I must find out what a horse and buggy are worth."

"I don't know either," said Weisz, "but it cannot be very much. Everything is cheaper now that it was. It is the recession."

"Then why is the herring now more expensive?"

"I don't know but I will give you a hundred koruna for the Hryec," said Weisz.

"If you don't know how much it is worth how can you then make me a realistic offer?"

"I'm willing to take a chance. Your family has always been good customers. You have always paid me on time. Your credit is good. I will take a chance."

"Maybe you would but I won't," answered Stefan. "Besides, we have never bought here on credit.

"If you are willing to accept a hundred koruna then it must be worth 200. Do you take me for a fool?" Stefan turned around abruptly, cut off the conversation. Letting his short temper get the best of the situation. He stormed out the door, letting it slam behind him.

As he did, he heard Weisz yell, "You will be back and I won't give you that much."

Esther, Weisz' rotund wife was in a back room and heard her husband yell. She came to the front and looked out the door window. "What did the *goy* want?"

"He wants to sell his horse and buggy," Mendel answered. "You know, the black horse that you admire so much."

"Oh!" she said, excited by the prospect. "It would be nice to have a good horse and a buggy instead of the wagon we must use to go visit my relatives in Zvala. Are you going to buy it?"

"We will have to wait and see."

The same day, an impulsive Stefan saddled the stallion and rode it to Humenné and saw three horse traders, two Jews and a Greek. "The horse and Hryec is worth about 140 to 160 koruna" the Greek told him. "But I have six horses and three rigs that I have been unable to sell. There is no money around nowadays. Life was better when the Magyars were here. If you can get some idiot to give you 100 for it, take it and run."

Three days later, Stefan again walked into Weisz's store.

"Seventy-five koruna and not a hair more," Weisz said before Stefan completely entered the store.

"It is worth 160 koruna. But I will take 150 for it."

They haggled for the next 15 minutes while Esther was outside petting and admiring the horse. It hurt Stefan to watch her because he realized that soon it no longer would be his. They finally settled at 120 koruna and 20 koruna in store credit.

They shook hands but as they did Weisz said, "But I cannot pay you now. This is a very slow time of year for me and you must wait two, maybe three months."

"I cannot wait that long. I need the money now. I will look elsewhere.

"When you pay me I will deliver the horse to you."

It was a slow business month and a slow year and by the end of February Weisz was still 30 koruna short. But, he had an idea and talked it over with his wife. He then went to the Karas house and asked for Stefan.

"I will make you a deal," Weisz said. "I will give you 30 koruna more, instead of 20, but in store credit, if you drive me to Zvala to see my wife's uncle. Besides, I want to drive the horse to see how he handles and ride in the buggy to see if it is in good condition."

"Why do you want to go to Zvala?"

"Someone there owes me money and I want to collect it so I can pay you for the horse."

The next morning Stefan harnessed *Tsar*, as his father had named him, to the buggy and stopped at Weisz's store to pick him up. There was a sign in the window "Closed Today."

Weisz saw him drive up and yelled to his wife. Well bundled, she came out and her husband was about to help her into the buggy.

"Wait," said Stefan as she began to climb, "you didn't ask if your wife could go. Her weight is an extra strain on the horse. It is a 40-kilometer ride both ways. And the hill into Zvala is long and steep. The horse will tire."

"Give the damned Rusnak 5 koruna more in store credit," she whispered to her husband. He offered it to Stefan.

"Okay, we go," agreed Stefan.

In Zvala, Weisz directed him through the village even though Stefan had been there before. They pulled up to another house that doubled as a store. In a few minutes a man, a Jew sporting a long black beard and black-brimmed hat came out onto the front steps. His wife was immediately behind him. She screamed with delight when she saw Esther. Esther jumped down without help from Mendel and embraced her Aunt Zelda.

"This will take a few minutes," Weisz said to Stefan. "My wife's uncle says there is water and some oats in the back. Go feed your horse while we talk."

"Uncle Aaron," he said after Stefan left, "I need a loan. Business has not been good. No one in Vilag seems to have money. I need 30 koruna so I can buy this Rusnak's horse and buggy. Esther has been after me for months to buy it. I will know no peace until I do."

"What? Mendel, does she think she is the Queen of Persia, that she should ride around the country in such a fine Hryec?

"When can I have it back?" Aaron asked.

"Done."

Late that day, as they arrived back in Vilag, Weisz told Stefan to come back to the store after supper and that they would settle the deal.

"And, I have written a note," Stefan said as he counted the money Weisz had just counted out and laid on the bare counter, "that I would like you to sign."

It was a note guaranteeing 31 koruna in store credit. Weisz read it and then balked.

"What is this for 31 koruna? I promised only 30. Why one koruna more?"

"That is what your uncle charged me for watering the horse and a small bag of oats."

"Are you sure that some part of you is not Jewish?" Weisz asked as he signed the note?

"I have it," Stefan said as he came through the door of his house. I have enough for the bus and train ride to Bremen. I even got him to throw in a bottle of vodka. His mother knew he didn't get it from Weisz's but she didn't challenge him. Weisz doesn't handle vodka with labels. He must have stopped at the tavern on the way home, she thought to herself. Oh well, what is done is done!

During the first week of March in 1927, Maria Karas and her sons Andrew and Michael were in Bremen. Ironically, the ship was the *S.S. George Washington,* the very ship her husband had boarded to return to the United States four years earlier.

Chapter 39 The Move to Binghamton

June, 1927--For the past two years, ever since Anna left Goodtown and Pinehill, she has been sending back most of the money she earned staining the bottoms of shoes in the Dunn & McCarthy Shoe Factory. She lived frugally and sent all she could but it was barely enough to keep them solvent. However, it was enough to pay off the farm as well as the car loan. But life was not all joy on the farm.

The black lung disease insidiously worsened even though Vasyl never complained. It continued to debilitate him even though he now worked only on the farm. He did so at the pace of an old man though he was just 48. His son Wasco helped him with some of the farm work but could only do it for one or two days a week, working the rest of the time first in one mine and then in another. In the end, Wasco contributed little to the family's income, especially if he stopped in a speakeasy in Berlin on his way home. Wasco and many of the miners were growing more reluctant to enter the mines because the incidence of cave-ins was rapidly increasing. Even the coal pillars, used to support the ceilings in the numerous rooms in a mine, were now being robbed just to get their coal. As a result, whole sections of mines were threatened and closed.

Nick, Wasco's younger brother, had just turned 15, but from the very beginning he never liked going into a mine to work and showed signs of claustrophobia. He was, after all, his father's son. His fears now were more than justified as the number of accidents, both fatal and serious, as well as minor, in the spent mines in Somerset County were rising appreciably. Finally, he adamantly refused to enter a mine and spent his time helping his father about the farm.

"God knows," he said, "there was more than enough to do around here for two or three men."

Vasyl's older brother John still scrounged around the several dwindling mines in the Berlin area and was able to make enough to survive as a bachelor. The only productive deep mines were two in Blackfield, a dozen miles east of Berlin, where Harry Najda now worked. They were not large operations, employing only 20 to 30 miners who worked three or four days a week. Here, it wasn't the shortage of coal that made short workweeks but the weak demand for coal that inversely slackened as the use of oil increased.

For five Rusnak families living in Goodtown, the situation finally became too difficult in the summer of 1927. They banded together and rented a boxcar that was sidetracked in Raineytown because the Pinehill Station was now closed. They loaded all their worldly possession into it and sent it off ahead of them to Binghamton. They hired a school bus and it took them all to Binghamton and a new life. There, in the TriCities area, that included Johnson City and Endicott, as well as Binghamton, was Endicott-Johnson, one of the largest shoe factories in the United States. Like the steel mills of Pittsburgh, it had an insatiable appetite for hordes of unskilled labor. The factories didn't discriminate between men or women when it came to jobs or pay. An energetic young woman could make as much as a brawny man.

Vasyl and his family were able to hold out longer because they were on the farm. While it produced enough food, and a surplus that could be sold, the future here looked bleak, especially for the maturing children. Mary, their oldest daughter and Sam Philip bought the farm next to Vasyl's but still lived in Goodtown where Sam was making some money working in the mines. In 1925, a son Samuel, and a year later Anna were born to them. They now had two children, and two boarders and were on their own as Sam continued to scrape a living from the coal remnants.

In the fall of '28, Vasyl and Kateryna, now with eight children living at home, faced the prospects of another winter in their deteriorating farmhouse. They didn't look forward to it. The house was badly in need of repairs when they bought it. There was no money from the mines to pay for the materials needed to repair it so the house continued to waste away.

"It is the chimney that is the worst of all," Vasyl said as he and Kateryna lay in bed one early October night, listening to the wind whistle through breaks in the ceiling. An unusually early storm dumped a half-foot of snow on the fields outside and a northwest wind howled through the cracks in the missing siding and left streaks of snow across the bare floor in their bedroom. It caused Kateryna to pull the cumbersome but extremely warm down-filled tick, the *peryna*, over her head.

"If the chimney was in better shape," Vasyl continued, "maybe we could make it through the winter. This morning, I found two bricks on the ground. I had Nick climb the roof to see where they had come from. He just touched the side of the chimney and three more fell. The mortar is washed out. The chimney must be rebuilt before we can really make a decent fire in the stove."

"We should have left this summer with the other families for Binghamton," said Kateryna. "The Salabajs say that all their children, except John the youngest, have jobs in the shoe factories."

"I don't know," said Vasyl. "We would have to rent a house or an apartment, a whole flat. Only Wasco is old enough to get a job. It is not like in the mines, here, where even Nick could work. The laws are stricter in New York."

"There would be three of us working," said Kateryna. "You and I could get jobs. And we can still count on Anna to help. "

"Maybe we could," he said, "but who will take care of Stephanie? She is just a year old."

"Huh! I have three daughters to help," answered Kateryna. "Kate is 13. Martha and Rose Ann are still too young. Kate could watch them. And, there is Andy and Mike. Boys can watch kids as well as girls."

The next day, Mary was on the farm visiting with her children Anna and Samuel. She complained to her mother how difficult it was getting to make ends meet in what little Sam was earning at the mines. Even the boarders were slow on paying.

"And, I worry about him every day," she said. "I think I would die if I heard the mine whistle blow if he wasn't home. Just yesterday, there was another cave-in in Lottie No. 2. Luckily, no one was hurt. But I think they are going to close the mine. That's what the rumor is.

"Sam and I have been talking about going to Binghamton. He doesn't want to be a miner all his life. He does it now only to make enough to pay off the farm. We are already falling behind in our mortgage payments. Worse, I don't know from where next week's food will come. Maybe the children and I will come to live with you for a while. I don't know what else to do."

Her mother then told her that she and her father had made a decision. They were going to close the farm. From the sale of the horse, two cows, a goat and four pigs, they would make enough to hire a truck and be able to move all their furniture and household goods to Binghamton.

"Let me talk to Sam," Mary said as she left that afternoon. "Maybe we will go with you."

The next day Sam and Mary were back on the farm. Two years earlier, Sam had bought a used Model T Ford. It allowed him to get around to the various mines in Somerset where he could work a day or two.

"Vasyl, we're going with you," Sam Philip said, "if it's okay with you and you can find room on the truck for some of our things. Some of the children can ride with us."

"Room, we can always find," he answered.

That day Mary wrote to Anna, telling her what their parents were doing and asked her to find a place for them and her family. Anna wrote back that houses were rare and expensive, that she would look for an apartment. Most of the Goodtowners were living close together in three or four, three-storey apartment buildings in the lower First Ward. These buildings offered the cheapest housing for them and they should plan on living in one of the flats.

Two week's later Dr. Molineaux arrived at the farm. "I got a phone call from Anna," he said as he walked into the Najda farmhouse. "She asked me to drive over and tell Vasyl that she found two apartments for you on Clinton Street, one right next to your cousins the Salabajs. She lives in the apartment above them and has two women boarders living with her. And, she found a smaller one on the third floor, next door, for Sam and Mary and their family. She has paid the rent on both starting the first of November. You should get there as soon as you can. They are vacant and you can move in anytime.

"And, she asked me to examine Vasyl, as long as I was here. She is concerned about his breathing."

Chapter 40   Ambridge-on-the-Ohio

It didn't take Marie Karas and her two sons very long to settle into their new surroundings. There were no such things as apartment buildings in Vilag and while she saw multi-storied buildings in Prague and Bremen, this was the first time in her life she was confronted with one in which she was going to live. Her first sight of it was startling, especially when Andrew announced, as they approached the building, that their apartment was on the second floor and that another Rusnak family lived on the third floor. There was even another apartment above that, in the roof's gables. It was smaller than the rest and was occupied by three bachelors.

The orange-brick building looked imposing. Every apartment, except the bachelor's, opened onto First Street and had a balcony/porch that looked south over the village, over the sprawling American Bridge Company buildings, and eventually over the Ohio River. Everyone in Ambridge worked for the American Bridge Company or in businesses that supported it and its huge work force.

As she and the children toured the nearly empty flat she was making mental notes of what she would need to turn this into a home. "We may not be able to get everything at once," Andrew cautioned. "But eventually we will. The work is steady and the pay is good."

"I saw three churches on the way from the train station. Which one was ours?"

"We no longer need to attend a Greek Catholic Church as we did back in Vilag," Andrij said. "My father, when he still lived in America, was one of a dozen men who found one of the earliest

Orthodox Churches in America. We have an Orthodox Church here in Ambridge but on some Sundays, we will go to his church. It is St. Alexander Nevsky Church in Woods Run. We can almost walk there or take the train; it is but ten minutes away.

"Our people have discovered that there are places to work around Pittsburgh other than the steel mills. Many came to Ambridge and found work with the American Bridge Company. My mother's family, the Ivancos (Evans) moved here early. I have half a dozen cousins here--two uncles, one a Karas and the other an Evans. You will feel almost like being back in Vilag with so many of them around.

"They also founded an Orthodox Church here, The Church of the Holy Ghost, which we will attend. It was built by money the founders raised from among all the Rusnaks living around here. Because they were able to, many of our people have returned to the religion of our ancestors. It was easy to do that in America, because there is no state religion here. Religion and the state are separated. It is written in the Constitution. Because of this, the government favors no religion over the others.

"But, there is still division among us. Some like the old ways in Vilag and say we are really Hungarians and they promote the Catholic Church. Some, especially those from Galicia, think we are closer to Ukrainians than any other people. After all, they say, our languages are so similar. Others favor the Russians and Russia has been actively courting Rusnaks in this country. The Tsar, when he was alive, even bought the bells for the church in Woods Run. He was hoping that we would be a force he could count on when Russia needed friends in America. But the communists ended all that. We are not Russian though our church is Russian Orthodox. It was the same as Ukrainian Orthodox but now there is no Ukraine because Russia absorbed it. Still, the people over there resist the Russians."

"Andrew," said his wife. "You have changed. You were never so concerned about our religion. Has something happened to you?"

"No Marysha, nothing has happened to me. Maybe it's because we never had a choice in Europe.

"But enough of this. We have to get settled and begin building our home."

Chapter 41   Lt. Stefan Karas of the 2nd Dragoons

The departure of Maria and her two sons from Zuzanna's table hardly made more food available. Instead of eight, there were still five mouths to feed but no one noticed a surfeit of food on their plates.

Again, the summer was dry in the Carpathians, almost without rain, just like the two previous summers had been. The once bountiful garden behind Stefan Karas's house grudgingly yielded just enough vegetables for his grandmother, mother, brother and sister and him. Twice, Zuska caught Mikey Ivanco and his brother stealing potatoes and chased them off. The third time she saw them she didn't go out. They were Ivancos, just like she was and were her cousin Anna Kundrat's grandchildren.

"Maybe his family needed it even more than we do," she said and turned from the window and wiped a tear from her eye. They had hoped for a surplus to be able to sell some vegetables and make enough to buy flour and sugar, but the drought made it impossible. The rains did come, but late that year in October and November, when they did no good. And that year the snows came earlier than they ever had or maybe their misery just made it feel that way.

A week after New Year's, Stefan rode one of their two draft horses to Humenné. Late that day, he returned in a car driven by the man to whom he sold the horse. In front of the house, he thanked him for the ride, and they shook hands again. The man departed leaving strange tracks in the snow. Automobiles were rare in Vilag, even in 1927.

"Here is enough money to see you through the winter," Stefan said as he emptied his pockets onto the kitchen table. "I was told we should spend it as soon as we can because its value is dropping every day. Go to the *sklep*. Buy all the canned food you can.

"There is something else I must tell you. There will be one less mouth to feed here after next week. I have joined the Czech Army. They have opened a new camp in Vranov, not far from Humenné. After a month, I was told I could come home on weekends.

However, it wasn't until the week before Easter, that Stefan came home the first time. He came by bus that now regularly ran once a day between Vilag, and several other villages against the top of the mountains, and Humenné. His great coat bulged at the pockets and his uniform was misshaped as he squeezed through the door. He emptied potatoes and onions from them and created a small heap on the kitchen table.

"Next week, there will be more. Here are a few korunas. The pay in the army isn't much but the food is good."

He didn't get a pass for "next week," but did for the week after.

"I won't be able to get home for two, maybe three months after this," he said. "The Czechs are sending me to officer-training school. I will get better pay. I also got paid last week. Here is more money to see you through these times." He emptied his pockets of more food and all his money.

Unknowingly, Stefan's character was changing. His mother sensed this but said noting for fear of calling attention to it. It was the first time her son seemed to put her and the family ahead of his own personal desires. Something must have stirred in the once flamboyant young man that had lain hidden, latent for most of his short life, until now. Maybe, Zuzanna thought to herself, with Andrew now in American, and his wife and boys with her, Stefan is finally assuming the role as the man in this house.

"Why you? Why are they sending you to school?" his mother asked. "You are not a Czech. You are not even a Slovak."

"Maybe that's why.

"It's because I graduated from school. Maybe it is because I can read and write Hungarian and Slovak and because I can speak English. Maybe it is because I can ride a horse. And, maybe because they found out I am an American. Who knows why? It is a chance to better our lot. That's why I am going."

It wasn't until mid-June that the Vilag bus carrying Warrant Officer Stefan Andrijovych Karas stopped at the fountain in the triangle opening in front of the church to unload its passengers. With him was another uniformed man, and two women with their *torbas* filled with canned food, and a priest.

Stefan and Janos Roby walked together up the road to the house. Roby was from Zvala, the next Rusnak village to the east, just a mile over the ridge to the next valley but nearly ten miles if you went by road.

Stefan was always a dapper dresser, even before he went into the service, though he really had anything dapper to wear. His brown uniform looked tailor made. It was because he'd put on a few pounds after leaving Vilag. It made him look good, robust.

He wore his field hat on a cocky angle and his gloves were neatly secured under his broad, leather belt. A small Czechoslovakia insignia, a lion in profile, made of shinny brass, adorned the left front side of his hat and attested that he was an officer. Two red insignias on his collar indicated his rank and the knee-high riding boots with spurs, but without wheels, revealed that he was a Dragoon, a member of the cavalry. The only thing missing was his sword and horse.

Lt. Stefan Karas (r.) of the 2nd Czechoslavakian Dragoons and Lt. Janos Roby.

Roby was an officer in the infantry. They had become friends while together in officer training school. He, too, was a Rusnak and that seemed to cement their friendship. Actually, his mother was a Rusnak and father a Slovak. Still, Stefan considered him more Rusnak than Slovak because they attended the Greek Catholic Church in Zvala.

Stefan's mother began crying when she saw him enter the kitchen. She kissed and hugged him feverishly.

"Why are you crying? You should be happy to see me."

"It is because you look so much like your father in that uniform. Maybe a little taller, but you look like him. And the uniform killed him. I worry about you if there is another war."

He introduced her to Roby and then to the rest of the family. His brother Ivan was duly impressed by his older brother and said he, too, wanted to be a dragoon when he was old enough. His sister Zuzie cried and hugged him and for the longest time would not let him go. *Baba* Karas had aged drastically in the few months Stefan had been away. She seemed confused by what was going on.

"We have a three-day pass," he said as things settled down in the house. "We have our final exams next week. After that, if we pass we will be line officers. Mother, you should see the fine horse I have. It is probably one I helped raise because they all came from Zeitmann's stables."

The following month, after graduating and being commissioned, Stefan went to Zvala with Janos to meet his family. It was there, at a church picnic that he met Natasha Hruschenko and immediately fell in love with her. She was 23, just two years younger than him, small, petite, almost fragile-like. Her hair was a light brown and she wore it long and straight, an indication that she was unmarried. Her blues eyes seemed appropriate for her alabaster-like complexion. And, she was the perfect coquette.

"How come a woman as pretty as you isn't married?" Stefan asked. "If you don't soon, in a few years you will be an old maid," he said teasingly.

"Maybe I haven't found anyone worth marrying.

"How come you aren't married?" she asked.

"I still have a long way to go. Besides, my enlistment won't be up for nearly two more years, in 1929. One cannot get married while in the military unless you are a senior officer. And even then,...

only with permission from Praha. And, maybe I, too, haven't found anyone I would like to marry."

That wasn't true. He immediately saw a potential in her. He would have liked to bed her that evening but he felt in no rush to do so. Here was a woman who challenged him and he liked rising to the occasion. She would not be as easy as some of the girls in Vilag. She might be worth waiting for, even marrying, he thought.

Any further thoughts of seducing her abruptly ended when her mother appeared. A women in her late 50s and with a voice that resembled a dying banshee. She disregarded her daughter's conversation with Stefan and rudely interrupted them, chiding her for not spending time with her. In seconds, Natasha was on her feet and following her mother. She looked back once to smile at Stefan and her mother caught her action and renewed the barrage of corrections.

Not to be outflanked by an old woman, Stefan watched intently where Natasha and her mother headed. They sat on a series of long, wooden benches to the left of a trio of Gypsy musicians who were slightly elevated on a wooden, box-like platform. He watched Natasha's mother as she clapped her hands to the beat of the accordion and two violins. Couples were getting together to dance on the well-trod earthen floor.

In a bold move, Stefan made his way through the crowd and approached Natasha and her mother. Natasha spotted him and braced herself. Her mother was deeply involved in a discussion with another elderly woman sitting immediately next to her and did not see Stefan approach.

He stopped immediately before her mother and stood erect, at attention. When she looked up and saw a handsome young soldier standing before her she was startled. Stefan bent over at the waist and extended his right hand to her. Before she could say anything, he asked the old lady if she would dance the *chardash* with him.

Suddenly flustered and embarrassed, she brought her hands to her lips and giggled in fright, in delight, almost like a schoolgirl.

"On no," she finally said. "I cannot dance. It has been years since I danced. My hip, you know."

"Then, *Pani Baba*, may I have the honor of dancing with your daughter?"

Without hesitating, she said yes and felt a wave of relief flood over her as the eyes of everyone around her suddenly shifted to her daughter.

Natasha rose and took Stefan's hand as they walked into the crowd of whirling dancers. In seconds, they were on the far side and momentarily out of the old woman's sight.

"You think you are pretty smart," Natasha said as she stared directly into Stefan's blue eyes. "You may have outwitted her for the moment, but she will have her way in the end. What would you have done if she said yes?"

"I would have danced with her, but I knew she wouldn't."

"How did you know that?"

"I watched the way she walked when she first rescued you from me. I saw her limp and didn't think she would have danced."

Natasha loved the attention Stefan laid upon her. He was so different, she thought, so different from the other young men of the village who are after her. I wonder how far he will try to go, she said to herself as she stared into his eyes. She saw no answer. He is different. They danced twice more when Jan interrupted them.

"Is it your turn, Janos?" Natasha coyly asked.

"No," he responded. "It is time for the bus. If we don't leave immediately, we will miss it."

Sunday evening, as they rode the bus back to Vranov, Jan kidded Stefan about his blatant fascination with Natasha.

"You can play," he said, "but you will get no where with her," he said. "Why do you think she is so old and not married. Most of the village girls are married by the time they are 18 or 19. Here, you're an old maid if you spend your 20th birthday alone. She is 23. Did she tell you that?"

"I could tell that," said Stefan.

"No you couldn't. There is no doubt that she is pretty. And there have been a lot of bucks after her ass. But she is saving it for a husband. I know her. I grew up with her. I don't think even being married to her would give you much advantage in bed.

"The problem is her mother. I think her father and brothers would like to see her go but her mother uses her as a crutch. She won't leave her mother and that's the main reason she is not married.

"Do you think you can break the chains?

369

"My advice to you is to see your Jewish girlfriend when you need some ass. After all, haven't you told me that Rachel is the best lover you have known?"

"So far," Stefan replied and was silent for most of the ride back, absorbing what his friend had just told him.

When they got back to the base they were given their assignments. Stefan was billeted to the 2nd Dragoon Regiment stationed in Milovice, about 25 miles northeast of the capital city of Praha (Prague). It was just being formed and filled with recruits from all over the country. His immediate superior was a Czech, a Major Anton Vladcek. Almost immediately, Stefan took a dislike to him, but didn't know why.

"I see from your file that you are an experienced horseman," Vladcek said when Stefan first reported to him. "Where did you learn to ride horses?"

"At home, on our farm," answered Stefan.

"Then all you know is riding draught horses?"

"No, we also had a stallion that I rode."

"Is that the extent of it?"

"No, I worked for Count Arnold Zeitmann. He raises horses for the military in Michalovce."

"What did you do there?"

"I groomed and broke horses.

"Oh I see," Vladcek exclaimed. "Is that why they call you 'The Cowboy'?"

"I wasn't aware of that name, Sir."

"I see from your record that you were not born here, but in Pittsburgh. Is that true?"

"Yes sir."

"Maybe that's why they call you the Cowboy, an American Cowboy. What are you, a Czech, Slovak or an American?"

"I am a Rusnak, Sir. Riding has been in my blood for generations, even though we may not always have had horses.

"How say you...in your blood for generations?"

"Yes sir. My great, great grandfather was a Cossack."

"He was then a common thief who rode a horse."

"No sir. He was a *hetman*, a general in the war against the Turks."

"He could not have been a very good general because I have never heard about him. What was his name?"

"Ivan. Ivan Karas, Sir. He was famous and there is an opera written about him and his exploits.

"I have never heard it."

"Then," said Stefan, "that is your loss."

"Dismissed!" yelled Vladcek.

Over the next few months, the animosity steadily grew between Stefan and Vladcek. He went out of his way to make tough assignments for Stefan and once, before his platoon, he dressed him down for an insignificant infraction by one of his troopers. This further infuriated Stefan. He had also been denied two weekend passes by Vladcek. On the last one, Stefan went over his head to get a pass. He claimed his grandmother was sick, which was true, and there was fear she was dying. He got it but Vladcek was enraged when he heard about it.

There is an old Rusnak saying that one black curly hair is stronger than the biggest draught horse. It is true. During the following year, Stefan made more trips to Zvala than to Vilag, at times, without Janos. His brother Andrew was now sending more money, not much more, but at least a few dollars every month. Some of it went to help Maria's mother and father. In Stefan's mind, that seemed to take some of the pressure off him to help his family.

If Stefan had remained in the cavalry as a warrant officer, he could have been discharged just after Christmas. But, he had to agree to two additional years of service after he received his commission, and that wasn't until the end of July, in 1929.

Near the end of November, Stefan managed a three-day pass and was in Zvala late on Friday. He was surprised and then dismayed when he knocked on Natasha's door and her mother answered.

"She is not here, she is with a friend...a girl friend in Ruske and won't be back until tomorrow. Go home," she said. "Go see your mother, your family. Leave me and Natasha alone."

Stefan never recalled Natasha speaking about a girlfriend in Ruske. But then again, he really didn't know all her friends. He walked towards the bus stop, to the store on the square where one could purchase tickets and find out when the next bus left. He had never been inside.

A women who had been in the back room finishing dinner, wiped her hands in her apron as she approached Stefan.

"When is the next bus to Vilag?" he asked.

"In about an hour. Do you want a ticket?"

She opened her ticket book and was ripping one off the page when she looked up at Stefan.

"Weren't you in here this afternoon?" she asked.

"Didn't I sell you one to Ruske? One for you and a girl? That Hruschenko woman?

"I could have sworn it was you. Well, anyway, it was another soldier.

Stefan 's mind raced like a locomotive on the ride to Vilag.

Who could she have gone to Ruske with? He asked himself. It couldn't be Janos. I just spoke with him a week ago. He was to be on maneuvers for the next three weeks. Besides, he has a girl friend. And, they are to be married after the maneuvers are over. He asked me to be his best man. It can't be him.

Maybe the woman was mistaken. But she couldn't have mistaken Natasha. What's going on?

His family was glad to see him even though he was unexpected. But Stefan always had the habit of arriving without notice. They never knew when he might be coming home. It was a quite, thoughtful weekend for him and on Sunday he left a few minutes early to catch the bus back to camp.

As he approached the building on the triangle in the center of the village, he saw in the back of the house, the buggy that belonged to him and his family at one time. It had been left outside. It was then that it dawned upon him that this was the back of Mendel Weisz's store. He walked to the barn in the back and heard a horse neighing. He opened the door and immediately recognized *Tsar*.

The horse immediately recognized Stefan and his voice as he scratched the horse's forehead and stroked its cheeks. *Tsar* looked as if he had not been groomed since Stefan sold him.

What terrible shape he is in, he thought to himself. I never realized that *Tsar* was such a beautiful horse.

It was at that moment that the door leading from the house to the barn burst open. Weisz stood in the doorway with an axe handle in his hand.

What are you doing? He yelled. What do you want here? Who are you?

As he approached the man, Weisz saw that it was no ordinary person standing with his arm around his horse. He recognized that it was a soldier.

As he got closer, Stefan let go of the horse.

"He could use some grooming," he said to the storekeeper.

"I have no time to waste on taking care of a horse, and ..." he responded.

"And too tight with your money to pay someone to do it for you," Stefan completed the sentence.

"Now I recognize you. Your uniform threw me off. You are Stefan, Stefan Karas. I hear you are now a big man in the army, an officer. Is that true?"

"I am an officer in the army," Stefan responded," but I wouldn't say that I am a big man. A lieutenant is the lowest officer rank.

"How has my horse been? Has he worn a path from here to your wife's aunt's house in Zvala?

"We have been there only twice since I bought the horse. It seems that my wife gets sick, her nose runs and her eyes water whenever she rides behind the horse. She cannot even go into the barn and I must clean the stables. I should not have bought the horse. Do you know anyone who wants to buy a horse and buggy? Cheap!"

"How much?"

"Because you are an old friend 200 koruna. For anyone else, 250."

"I though you said cheap. That is more than you paid me."

"It is not me, it is inflation. That is a cheap price."

"No. I don't think so," Stefan said as he walked out of the barn. As they spoke, he had heard the bus pull up to the stop in front of the house.

"I now get my horses free. The government gives them to me.

"Good-bye!"

Weisz didn't respond.

Two weeks later, in early December, Stefan got another pass. This time, Natasha was home and when he asked where she had been she never gave him a real answer.

"I cannot be with you all the time," she said. "I have other friends." Then she quickly amended it. "... other girl friends whom I like to see."

It was then that Stefan decided to make his move. He asked Natasha to marry him. "We can be married in the new Orthodox Church in Vilag. It isn't completed yet, but it would be fitting that the first *wedding there would be a Karas.*"

Then he told her why. Simon and John Ivanco, alias Evanses, Stefan's mother's brothers, had prospered in their businesses in Ambridge and they, along with many other Rusnaks now living around Ambridge, decided to raise funds and build a Russian Orthodox Church in their old village. It was started in the Spring of 1928 but wasn't finished until 1932.

"I would prefer the older church in Vilag," she said. "But, it doesn't matter. I cannot marry you."

St. Dymitriy The Great Martyr is the Greek Catholic Church in Vilag and was built more than 500 years ago. It began as an Orthodox Church but its parishioners were coerced into Catholicism by the wave of Polish-sponsored Uniatism that was sweeping over the mountains in the 16th and 17th centuries.

Disillusioned and searching for answers, Stefan went to Janos's house in the hopes he might be there that weekend. Janos's request for permission to marry had been denied so he and his girlfriend postponed the marriage until he was discharged.

"No, Janos did not come home this weekend. We haven't seen him for the past two months," said his mother, "We haven't received a letter.

"Do you need a place to sleep tonight?"

The next day, Natasha, in Stefan's presence, told her mother about the proposal. She went into a tirade. She berated her daughter for even thinking of marrying a Karas.

"I know that they are wealthy but that doesn't make any difference to me. I have heard talk about how he has seduced girls in Vilag," she said, "and maybe you. You cannot trust a soldier, especially an officer. They always have their way with women."

As Stefan stood silently next to Natasha, her mother adamantly refused to condone a wedding. It was a wedding only in Stefan's mind. He still believed that Natasha would change her mind. He failed to grasp what she had been telling him all along. He was unwilling to believe that she wouldn't marry him.

Stefan returned to base without a concession from Natasha. She is old enough to make her own decision, he thought to himself as he rode the bus back to camp. She does not need her mother's approval. There is something about her and her family that I do not understand. Maybe she had a boyfriend before I met her. But, she has never mentioned anyone.

Stefan was torn by frustration. He had always been in command of his life but now it hinged on two people, Natasha and Vladcek. Things were not going his way and that made him miserable. Two people, one whom he thought he loved and one whom he knew he hated were beginning to gain control of his life. He didn't know how to cope with that.

The following Wednesday, Stefan got a telegram that his grandmother had died the day before. She was on buried Friday and he didn't arrive until late that evening.

When he got there, his mother gave him a letter that had arrived a few days ago from his brother. Filled with grief, he set it aside and didn't open it until the following morning. It contained a ship's ticket for him to return to the United States and a copy of his baptismal certificate. Andrew and his uncle Simeon Evans had purchased the ticket for him. It also included a note that he could pay it back after he started working. Andrew also wrote that he had a job waiting for him with American Bridge and expected his brother would be returning to America almost as soon as he got the ticket. He was still under the impression that Stefan's military duty would be over just after Christmas. Stefan never told him of his commission.

When Stefan returned to camp, the orderly in his barracks said that Major Vladcek wanted to see him no matter the hour he returned.

"So you think you can go over my head whenever you want something," he said to Stefan as he entered his office. "That is one thing you will never do to me again."

"I had to," said Stefan. "My grandmother died and you were not available on the base when I got the telegram so I could not ask your permission for an emergency pass. I asked the duty officer. Wasn't that the correct procedure?"

Vladcek never answered him but rose and smashed his ever-present swagger stick on his desk. He had been thwarted again by the Rusnak and walked to the window and stared outside for a few moments. It took him a few minutes to regain his composure as Stefan stood at rigid attention before the desk.

Vladcek turned.

"I held a surprise inspection of the four platoons under your command. I was appalled at what I saw. Not one of them is ready for active duty. I will give you one week to shape them up. If you cannot do it, I will break your rank."

"There was nothing wrong with the state of readiness of my troopers," Stefan said to Michael Kosuth, his Slovak roommate, also an officer in the Dragoons.

"I know," he said, "but Vladcek doesn't care. He resents you for some reason, probably several reasons. He is not as good a horseman as you are and that's a start. I have watched him observe you as you rode in parade, and in the games, and I saw the reaction on his face. He resents a Rusnak rising above the station of his parents or ancestors. He knows of your ancestor's events and he dislikes you for that as well. And, that you speak Hungarian better than he does makes him feel inferior. Hungarians are still an influence, a factor in our lives. The old ways, even those we hated, at times are hard to dispel. Maybe you should better develop your Czech and really piss him off."

The next day Stefan had an inspection of his four platoons, their equipment, horses and personal lockers. There was nothing to improve upon. Despite this, he drilled his men each morning in the field. They were the regiment's sharpest units. Vladcek set the inspection for 9 a.m. Saturday morning. He meticulously inspected each man, his rifle, his kit and all the equipment on each horse.

"Be in my office at noon," was all he said to Stefan.

"Your platoons look worse than when I inspected them a week ago. You have not brought them to the standard set by this regiment. You have woefully neglected your duty as an officer and leader and are unfit to command troops. To that extent, you will appear before a regimental hearing Monday at 10 a.m. Dismissed."

A stunned Stefan Karas couldn't believe Vladcek would actually do this as the realization of the events that would follow were quickly dawning upon him. Later he later thought he shouldn't have been surprised by his superior's actions. That evening, he and Kosuth were in the officer's club. Both had a few drinks and Stefan was pondering his faith.

"I owe no allegiance to the Republic," he said. "It was created to solve political, not ethnic needs. At least you Slovaks got half a country after the Great War. It was supposed to be composed of three peoples not two. The Rusnaks, Ruthenians again, were dismissed. Maybe I really am an American at heart."

"What will you do?" asked Michael. "He will not let you resign because you have agreed to the extension. They want their money's worth out of your training. Let's have one more drink."

"No," said Stefan as he rose to leave. "I have had enough. I have a decision to make."

It was dark when he left the officer's club for the BOQ. Stefan saw a person approaching him, walking down the path before him. As he entered the bright cone of light cast by a lamp high on a utility pole Stefan saw it was Vladcek. For some unknown reason, both men stopped just a few feet from each other.

"Where's my salute?" Vladcek yelled at Stefan.

Stefan gathered himself together and was about to salute when Vladcek suddenly yelled: "You stupid Rusnak cowboy, you Cossack outlaw." Vladcek raised his swagger stick and was about to strike Stefan.

Stefan didn't know what had suddenly come over him. Instead of saluting he raised his left arm to ward off the blow and made a fist in his right hand. He punched Vladcek directly in the face. The major fell backwards onto the ground. Stefan rushed to pummel him again, but Vladcek didn't move. In one punch, he had knocked him out.

The few drinks he had blurred his senses. He panicked and temporarily was at a loss at to what to do next. He then gathered himself, grabbed Vladcek by the back of his collar and pulled him out of the scope of the light and against a hedge. He looked back and saw Vladcek's hat and swagger stick and rushed to get it. As he threw the hat on Vladcek's face he saw blood running from his nose and heard him moan.

"I should kill the son-of-a-bitch," he thought for a fleeting moment, then stopped.

Stefan rushed back to his room. His mind was filled with one thought. He knew he had to get out of there. He threw what civilian clothes he had into a small valise and what toiletry he owned. As he reached for the door to leave it flew open and Michael was standing there.

"Where are you going at this hour?"

He told him what he had done.

"I'm quitting."

"How much money do you have?" Kosuth asked.

"Not much."

Michael dug into his locker and pulled out a few bills and gave them to him. "This will get you as far as home, maybe more. Good luck."

They shook hands, then embraced for a moment.

"Good-bye," Michael said.

"Good-bye," Stefan answered.

Stefan hurried to the gate. Just as he approached it a truck came up from behind him and slowed. He knew the driver. The driver told him he was going to Prague for tomorrow's fresh produce.

Stefan climbed into the cab and the guard at the gate saluted him as they passed through.

"I have an emergency at home and must get there as quickly as possible," he told the driver. The concerned driver drove the 20 miles to the train station at a record pace. Stefan just caught the early train for Humenné and Uzhorod.

He arrived in Humenné just before the morning bus for Zvala was about to leave. He could not have timed it better. On the train, he had changed into his civilian clothes and arrived at Natasha's just before noon.

"Stefan," what are you doing here? Why aren't you wearing your uniform?" she said as he embraced and tried to kiss her. Stefan suddenly felt there was something wrong. She seemed almost to pull away from his embrace. Maybe it is that I startled her, he thought to himself.

"Stefan, there is something I must tell you," she said. "Something very, very important."

"First," he interrupted, "there is something I must tell you. Things are changing very rapidly."

Before he could begin, her mother appeared in the doorway. She had heard Natasha scream Stefan's name and came to see what was happening. Stefan took Natasha's hand and led her to the side of the house and out of earshot of the meddling old woman. Frantically, he told her most of the storey but not the fight.

"I have quit the army and am going to America. We can get married by the clerk in Humenné, but we must leave now. There is no time."

"Why is there no time?"

Stefan fumbled about in his mind and then came up with a plausible reason. "My brother sent me a ship ticket and it must be used in a few days or it will become void."

"No, I cannot. I keep telling you. Damn you. Don't you hear. Can't you understand what I am saying, what I have always been saying? I cannot leave my mother. Why can't you understand that? And maybe...and maybe I don't love you."

That brought Stefan to his senses. He suddenly, finally realized that there was no way he could convince her to go with him. After a few minutes he moved to kiss her good-bye. She turned her head and the kiss landed her cheek. That seemed so final on her part. She had just severed their relationship. It would be the last time he would ever see her. He walked to the bus stop, never turning to look back.

Have I been such a fool, such and idiot all this time? he thought. Yes, I have.

I cannot wait here until this afternoon to catch the bus, he said to himself as he began climbing the ridge that separated the parallel valleys that contain Zvala and Vilag to the west. It took him nearly three hours to reach the ridge above their pasture and the herder's hut he and his brother had built years ago. As he sat inside, catching his breath, below he saw a brown army vehicle wending its way up the road and pull into the triangle in Vilag. It stopped where two men were at the fountain, then continued on to his house. White PW (Military Police) letters was printed on its side. Two men and an officer climbed out and one knocked on the door.

The hunt had already started, he said to himself. They must have wired the station in Vranov and this vehicle was sent to locate me. They stayed in the house for nearly an hour and left just as the sun was setting. Stefan watched them drive to the edge of the village and pull off into a field and stop. He saw the officer get out and begin scanning the countryside through binoculars. When it became too dark to see, he returned to the vehicle and they drove south toward Vyrava.

It was close to midnight when Stefan slipped out of the hut and cautiously approached the house. The lights had gone out around 10 and the house was silent in the late December air. There was only a smattering of snow on the ground and Stefan avoided crossing it for fear of creating a silhouette and leaving tracks. The old draft horse heard him enter the barn and stomped its hoofs.

Slowly he opened the back door to the kitchen but a creaking hinge gave him away.

"Stefan, is that you?" his mother softly asked.

He told her the entire story.

"I could no longer take the harassment from the major. I cannot stay here tonight, I must get out of Czechoslovakia before they catch me."

"Where will you go? What will you do?"

"The border is just over the top of the hill. The old pass is abandoned, grown over. But I can travel through it. I know it like the back of my hand. I will take the old horse and sell it in Poland. There are always traders in Sianok and he should make it that far without any trouble. I won't push him. Besides, after the pass, it is all downhill.

"Go say good-bye to your brother and sister. I will pack you something for the road."

He startled his brother and sister and they were not fully awake when he hugged them and bid them good-bye. They embraced and kissed him, then followed him into the kitchen.

"Mother, I do not know what will happened to me or if I can ever again return, but know that I love you and my family.

"Go," she said, "they may be watching the house."

No one could see the tears in Zuzanna's eyes or the welling within her that she was stifling. If he didn't leave soon, she would break into crying.

In the dark, the old horse knew Stefan's touch as he put on a saddle. He walked the horse out the barn and led him up, though the pasture to the woods. A sliver of a moon hung low in the west but reflected enough light for him to lead the horse into the woods.

Just before entering, he turned back for a last look at Vilag. A few lights flickered in the village but other than that it was all dark.

The pass was still easy to find because the new trees were still small in comparison to the old growth and showed low in the horizon. It had never been a major crossing point and was usually used only by the people from Vilag who had relatives on the Polish side. Snaking his way through the brush, Stefan eventually came to a dilapidated wooden fence that marked the border between Czechoslovakia and Poland, between the edge of his property and some Pole, or maybe even a Rusnak, who owned the land on the other side. He had never met them. He had not been here recently because the lumber on their land was no longer profitable to harvest. The border and fence were the edge of his father's woods, the edge of a dream that started in Pittsburgh. The fence had been put up ten years ago by Poles to mark their reclaimed territory.

On the top of the continental divide, *Vysoky Grün* rose 902 meters to the west. On the right *Vierch na Lazem* rose 864 meters to the east. Remnants of an ancient, though now seldom used, footpath/horse trail still existed. It followed the west bank of the Magurycz stream toward two clusters of houses called Vola and Minchova. Stefan and his brother had once ventured here, into Poland, when they were teenagers and it was still part of the Austrian Empire.

Once the path led down hill, he mounted the horse. In a few minutes he was in an open alpine meadow. He avoided the bigger village of Smolnik on the Ostava River. By sunrise he had crossed over a height of land to pick up the road to Balihrod. By midmorning, he was in the village where he led the horse to the Hoczewka River. He let it drink in a place where the small river was free of ice.

Only a few people were moving about. Life in winter slows measurably in these foothill villages. From here he took the road north. By the end of the day he was on the outskirts of Lisko and found a wayside tavern. He had not eaten all day, except for a piece of bread and kobasa his mother had packed. Inside, there were several men seated among the few tables scattered next to the bar. One trio was feeling no pain.

As he listened, he was startled at first. He expected them to be speaking Polish but they were all Rusnaks and spoke the same as he did.

"Where you from?" one man blatantly asked Stefan as he rose to get another beer.

Stefan thought for a while and remembered a sign he saw. "Balihrod," he said.

"I lived there once," he said. "What is your name? Maybe I know your family."

"Baran," Stefan answered after wracking his brain. "Stefan Baran."

"I don't know it," the stranger answered, "but I only lived there for a few years when I was a small boy. Where are you going?"

"To Germany, to Bremen to look for work."

"I have a horse for sale. Do you know anyone who needs a strong draft horse?"

The tavern owner, behind the bar, overheard the conversation and interrupted. "My brother just lost his horse. He needs one for his farm."

They went outside and looked at the horse but it was too dark to see very much.

"I need to stable him and a place to sleep tonight." Stefan said.

"You can put him in the barn and I have a room above the tavern. I'll get my brother the first thing in the morning to look at your horse."

The innkeeper's brother bought the horse and the saddle that was an added bonus. That morning, Stefan caught the bus to Sianok and that afternoon, the train to Krakow and eventually Breslau. He arrived at the German border just before midnight. When asked for a passport all he could produce was his ship ticket and a copy of his baptismal certificate from St. Alexander Nevsky Church. The German customs officer felt the raised seal of the church on the document then went to the back of the train car where another agent was inspecting documents.

"This one has no passport," he said, "but he has proof of his citizenship. He is an American. What shall I do? Can I pass him?"

The second emigration officer looked over the church document and compared the names on the ship ticket against the certificate. "It's not worth all the extra paperwork. List him as an American, a transient, and put the stamp on his receipt part of the ship ticket."

A cold, late December wind blew across the docks in Bremen when Stefan got off the trolley. He asked directions to the United

States Lines. The office was at the base of a large pier, three piers down from the end of the trolley line. It was late in the day and the lights along the docks were already burning. It seemed deserted.

Inside the office, Stefan asked when the next ship to New York was leaving. A lone clerk was seated at a desk behind the counter and worked between two tall stacks of papers on the desk. He seemed surprised by someone's appearance in the office. The office was empty other than for them. Well-polished oak benches lined three walls of the waiting room. The bare, wooden floor must have seen hordes of people in its time because it was worn smooth except where knots resisted the footwear. In the center, a potbellied stove burned warmly and filled the room with its heat. Next to it was a half-pail of coal and in it a small, galvanized shovel.

"Do you have a ticket?" he asked as he rose from the desk.
"Let me see it.
"What is your nationality?
"Do you have proof?"
"The next vessel is the *S.S. Roosevelt*. She is now at the dock. She sails in three days, on Christmas Eve, and should be in New York next year, on January 2, 1929. Do you want to go on it? There is plenty of space in the third-class cabins. There are eight bunks in each cabin but you might be all alone on this crossing. Few people seem to travel during Christmas week."
"What can I do until she sails?" Stefan asked.
"Most passengers book a room in one of the nearby hotels."
"Can I go onboard until she sails? I have no money for a hotel?"
"No, that is not permitted." A few minutes of silence passed as the clerk continued to work on his documents. Then he looked up at Stefan.
"There is one possibility," said the clerk. "I know that the galley is short on help. If you want to work, I can make a call."
The clerk reached the galley office aboard the ship.
"You are in luck," he said after talking on the phone. "If they take you, you can work there until the ship leaves. But, I think they might want you for the entire voyage. If so, then you will be given free passage in exchange for the work. You can cash in your ticket and get its value...nearly 400 American dollars. Go up the stern gangway, there," he stood up and pointed through a window

in the office, "and tell the man at the top that you want to see Karl Schranz, in the galley."

"You look strong enough," Schranz said as he walked around sizing up Stefan. "Let me have your hands. They are soft. You say you are a farmer but your hands tell me that you have not been working on a farm."

"Not for three years," Stefan answered.

"I don't want to know why.

"Go to third class and find a bunk. Tomorrow we will be unloading fresh produce on the after-well deck. Be there at 7 sharp. You can come to the galley to eat breakfast. Follow me, I will show you the galley and the cabins."

"Can I working the whole trip?" Stefan asked He followed him below decks.

"First, we will see tomorrow how well you work. Is that all you have?" asked Schranz as he saw Stefan's small valise. "What are you running away from?" he smiled. He didn't wait for an answer but turned to enter the hatch and left.

Chapter 42   Galley Life

Stefan was not afraid of work. He had been accustomed to it all his life. It was just that he liked to avoid it whenever he could. However, in the confines of the galley and a dozen chefs who all believed they were his superiors, he couldn't avoid it. For the next two days he and two other men, Germans, unloaded huge pallets of produce lifted onto the afterdeck by the ship's cranes. Each box of fresh vegetables was then carried two levels below the afterdeck and stored in large, walk-in refrigerators. In cold-storage, he stacked sacks of potatoes 10 feet high.

He got the job for the duration of the trip.

Once the S.S. *Theodore Roosevelt* was underway his duties changed. Most of the time he peeled potatoes, trimmed cabbage and beets, or diced turnips. The passage was uneventful. Stefan only occasionally went topside for fresh air because it was a cold crossing. The weather moderated slightly as they crossed the Gulf Stream two days out of New York, but turned cold again as the crossed to the inside.

"Will you be going back with us?" Schranz asked Stefan as the ship lay in quarantine in New York Harbor. "I didn't think so. It was stupid even for me to ask."

In quarantine off Staten Island, the U.S. Customs Officials came on board with the harbor pilot. As the ship moved up the Hudson and began docking at the 51st Street Pier, first and second class passengers began queuing up to go ashore. An immigration officer had stationed himself and his two assistants at the head of the gangway. As each passenger approached they offered their passport and their names were checked against the ship's manifest provided by the shipping lines' officers.

When it came to a handful of third class passengers Stefan was at the end of the line with other members of the ship's crew. He offered him his baptismal paper and waited.

"Where's your passport?" he asked Stefan.

"I don't have one."

"What were you doing in Europe? Were you there on a visit?

"I was living there?"

"How long were you living there?"

Stefan quickly calculated the time in his mind and said, "Twenty-two years."

"Where do you live in the U.S.?" Then modified the question "Where are you're going in the U.S.?"

Stefan pulled out the envelope containing the ship ticket and showed the return address of his brother in Ambridge.

"I see from your baptism paper that you were born in Verner. Where is that?"

"That is in Pittsburgh."

"Where is Ambridge?"

"That is close to Pittsburgh, close to Verner and Woods Run."

"What's in Woods Run?"

"That is where the church is."

"Why did you go to Europe?"

"My father returned to his village in 1907 with me, my brother and mother.

"It is in Slovakia, now. It was a part of Hungary when they returned. After the war, it was no longer part of Austria-Hungary but became a part of Czechoslovakia.

"So you grew up in Europe?

"What did you do in Slovakia?

"My father was a forester until he died.

"How did he die?

"From a disease he caught in the trenches during the war."

"Is your brother still in Slovakia."

"No. He returned four years ago. This is his name on the letter. He sent me the tickets to return to the United States."

"I cannot find your name on the passenger list. And, you still have an unused ticket. Why did they not take it when you boarded the ship?"

"It was because I worked in the galley for my passage."

The immigration officer then studied the ship's manifest.

"Your name is not with the ship's crew. Are you a stowaway?"

"No. Call Karl Schranz, the galley chief, he will tell you."

"Please step aside, over there, while we confirm your story. Roberts," he said to one of his aids, "go below and see if you can find a Karl Schranz."

Fifteen minutes later, Roberts returned. "I was told that Schranz has gone ashore to buy provisions. However, two of the chiefs confirmed that a Stefan Karas worked in the galley during the passage."

When the last of the passengers going ashore cleared immigration, the officer recalled Stefan.

"We have a problem here," he said to Stefan "but I think we can get it cleared. Where did you last live in Slovakia? Were you a farmer or forester?"

"No, I was in the Czech Army."

"What? You were in the Czech Army!"

"Did you have permission from the U.S. Government to serve in a foreign army?"

"No."

"I'm sorry," Mr. Karas, "but if what you tell me is true, you have lost your American citizenship. You now must be treated as an alien. And, there is no quota for Slovaks to enter the United States at this time."

"But how can you do this to me? I am not a Slovak, but an American. You must let me enter the United States," pleaded Stefan. "What can I do?"

"I cannot let you enter without a visa. However, yours is a special case. I cannot rule in this matter. It is up to a federal judge. I will have to place you in detention unless you return to the ship and Europe. Wait here. I must go to the dock and make a phone call."

The immigration officer went down the gangway and entered the immigration field office near the base of the pier. He returned a half-hour later.

"It could be worse," he addressed Stefan. "There is a judge sitting in on a hearing here in two days. We will detain you in a cell we have in the downtown office until then. You will appear before the judge. In the meantime, I suggest you get a lawyer."

A few minutes later, two armed immigration officers appeared on the gangway and led Stefan in handcuffs to their patrol car. The cell wasn't all that bad. It wasn't much different from his cabin aboard the ship. A clerk in the office sent Andrew a telegram for Stefan. On the second day, Stefan appeared before a judge who questioned him even more intensely than the immigration officer.

"I understand the circumstances of your plight," said Judge Thomas Patrick Fagan. "But I cannot address the problem of your lost citizenship. I can see that you do not have enough time to mount a defense. However, I will grant you a 30-day visa and will forward this case on to the Federal District Court in Pittsburgh. You will receive a notice of the hearing at your brother's address. Is that where you will be staying? You're free to go," he said and pounded the gavel once.

"By the way," Judge Fagan unexpectedly said as Stephan turned and was about to leave, "Welcome to America."

Chapter 43   There's Little Harmony in Ambridge

Ambridge in 1929 was the epitome of a Pennsylvania company mill-town, but it wasn't always that way. In fact, its name wasn't always Ambridge but Economy, and it was called Harmonie before that. Economy, with its unique inhabitants who had a predilection for making money, was the perfect place for an aggressively expanding endeavor like the American Bridge Company to establish one of its largest bridge-building plants.

Economy was the child of Johann Georg Rapp, a weaver and vinetender, and a disillusioned German Lutheran who believed that religion and the state should be separate. His basic philosophy developed a following in the late 1700s and pit him at odds both with religious leaders and the German government. He decided that the freedom he and his people wanted could only be found in America.

In 1803 he purchased 4,000 acres along the Ohio River where the city of Ambridge now stands. His philosophy was based on hard work and a communal bond with God. The community grew to 46 families and two years later numbered 800 people who had emigrated from Germany specifically to join his group. Rapp separated his group from others in western Pennsylvania and created a communal society not only ideologically separate from other Pennsylvanians, but also physically, with a brick wall he built around the entire village. "Father" Rapp convinced his followers that they should combine all their worldly goods and live as one family, and together wait for the return of Christ. They believed it would occur within their lifetime and they formed the Harmonie Society and named the town they created Harmonie.

To enhance their chances of meeting Christ when He returned, they adopted a code of celibacy, believing that it would keep them more spiritually pure. Married couples were encouraged to live together as brothers and sisters. The only problem is this practice--without the continued addition of children and thus new members—was that the community would eventually self-destruct if Christ didn't return.

They eventually renamed their community Economy. The dedication to work made them wealthy beyond belief and the community, as it was dying, was also prospering in material riches. In 1905 the last member died, but before he did, most of their 4,000 acres were sold to American Bridge. The town was ceded to the State of Pennsylvania and in 1919 it was turned into a historical site and museum.

American Bridge expanded rapidly after it was established in Economy and made quick use of the lands the firm had purchased. It had a factory in Woods Run and when it built a new one in Economy, it moved its operations there and took with it any of its workers who wanted to move. They even changed the name of the burgeoning town, that quickly engulfed the old center, to Ambridge. American Bridge cashed in on the reputation they developed after building the locks for the Panama Canal and business boomed. They continued their rapid expansion of prefabrication bridges and this created a demand for a huge labor force.

The surge in immigration from Central Europe was halted in August 1914 by the onset of World War I. After the war, the flow of new immigrates was strongly curtailed by the U.S. Government when quotas were assigned to various countries and unskilled labor was not listed. However, there was a need for a huge labor force in Ambridge. This force already existed nearby in old sections of Pittsburgh, like Verner and Woods Run. It was the maturing second generation, the sons and daughters of Hunkies, who were now able to find ready and profitable employment outside the steel mills.

Economy became the "old section" of Ambridge and few second-generation Hunkies had the leisure time to stroll through its old, but perfectly preserved buildings. They had little or no interest in the old ways. Their generation was looking in the opposite direction.

"You shouldn't have told him that you were in the army," Andrew berated Stefan after dinner on his first evening in Ambridge.

"How was I to know that it mattered?" Stefan answered.

"We must find a lawyer to defend you," said Stefan's uncle Sam (Simeon) Evans. "They are not cheap but we cannot let you go back to Vilag."

Stefan was flattered by all the attention his brother and uncles and cousins were giving him. He was the center of a party the Evans gave a few days later and every relative, real or imagined, in the area was there. Everyone was eager of news from Vilag. Stefan was in a unique role. He was the first person in years to bring real news of their parents' "Old Country." Foremost among their questions was what role Hungarians now played after holding complete control over their Rusnak villages on the south slope of the Carpathian Mountains for nearly a thousand years.

"Their influence is still great," he said, "but their power is gone. The influence is not in their people or their government, but in what they have left behind, their schools, their legal system and how they administered the counties and villages. It is changing fast, but not the way we would like. Instead of Hungarians and Austrians, we are now dominated by Slovaks and the Slovaks by Czechs. I have no idea of what will become of it. The country is so poor nothing will happen there for a while."

Many of them knew that Stefan had joined the Czech Army but not even Stefan's brother knew that he had deserted. It was to become one of those deep secrets every family has tucked away somewhere in their closet with skeletons from the past.

Stefan was impressed the first Sunday he was in Ambridge by the size of the Russian Orthodox Church the Rusnaks had built. It would have towered high above the Greek Catholic church in Vilag. He told the priest that many of the Rusnaks in Vilag were becoming disenchanted with the Uniate church there and that word of many of the village's immigrants in America, who had returned to the Orthodox religion of their ancestors, was also influencing them. He told them of the progress of the construction of their church in Vilag.

After church Andrew asked Stefan if he would like to see where they were born and if he remembered anything of the old neighborhood and school. The thought fascinated Stefan and he jumped at the chance. He had heard his father and mother talk about the good times in Verner and occasionally the bad times. Stefan was only six when he left the United States so his memories were not as clear or as well defined as those of his older brother.

Andrew had purchased a used car from his cousins who had bought into an automobile franchise. Their father Sam, Stefan's uncle, had opened a car repair garage in Ambridge and as it expanded, becoming a dealer was a natural occurrence. Andrew needed a car to get to work because he had moved to the northeast edge of Ambridge and it was a dozen blocks to the plant where he worked as a riveter, and there was no public transportation available. He used the car primarily on weekends, and a trip to the old neighborhood was always an experience. Normally, he would have piled in his wife and two sons, but Marie had given birth to their third son Nicholas, just before "American" Christmas and she felt he was still too young to go out.

Stefan was startled by what he saw as the two of them drove down Beaver Street, turned onto Spruce and then Benton, the next block. Stefan remembered them as old, worn houses but filled with people and the streets flooded with children. And, there was always the dust and dirt from the blast furnaces but the Rusnak women were always sweeping the streets, the stoops to their houses and the back courtyards. There was always clean wash billowing on the lines in the courtyard and starched, lace curtains adorned all front windows of every Rusnak house. But now, all these were missing.

Verner had become a slum. Few houses were occupied. One could tell which house still had people because its windows were not shattered. Unemptied garbage cans spilled over into the streets and a wrecked car was on one sidewalk. It was stripped of everything moveable and sat on its chassis without wheels. Three black children were playing in it.

They pulled up to the corner of Benton and Spruce streets. Next to the corner house was Number 6 where he and his brother were born. They stopped for a moment. An old man, a lame steelworker with a cane, had fallen to the bottom of the stoop. He lay on the foyer floor with his back buttressed against the open doorway. A broken wine bottle was at his feet and the top of a pint liquor bottle dangled precariously from the shallow pocket of his great coat.

He was fast asleep, or drunk, in the afternoon sun. Stefan heard an old woman inside scream something to the man. She was a Rusnak. They were relics in what once had been a neighborhood teeming with life, filled to overflowing with Rusnaks, old and young men and women and children everywhere. All that now was left were worn-out men and women. The old man and the woman were those unfortunate enough not to have escaped. Maybe alcohol had kept him from making his *tysiach dolary*, his "thousand dollars." The man was old enough to have been Stefan's father...maybe older.

His is a life wasted, Stefan thought to himself.

"Want to go in?" Andrew asked.

"No," said Stefan. "Ours was only one in probably more than a dozen, maybe even two dozen families, who lived there since that house was built. Let me remember it inside as it once was. Let's go."

They drove toward Woods Run, past the Steel Car Company where their father had once worked. It had been closed for several years. Grass and stunted ailanthus trees grew along the entire chain-link fence and in cracks in the concrete. The office windows had been boarded up but someone pulled them down on one side. No one came around to repair them.

Woods Run, however, had resisted the influx of blacks. Those blacks who made it to Woods Run lived almost exclusively on one block, in two tenement, three-storey houses. One fronted on Petrosky Street and the other on Monhagen Street and their backyards opposed one another. One end was "Negro Row," as it was called, was on Ketchum Street exactly opposite of the St. Alexander Nevsky Church. The first blacks had been brought up the Mississippi from New Orleans and then the Ohio to Pittsburgh in the late 1800s. Andrew Carnegie had sent his emissaries south and nearly 60 of them were used to replace strikers locked out of the mills. They came, stayed and multiplied, but few if any prospered.

"Let's have a drink at the Men's Club," Andrij suggested.

Every church has its men's club, a social necessity. Many of the churches in Woods Run, which then numbered about a dozen, had men's fraternal organizations as a part of the church and its parish activities. The Ukrainians had one such club and Uniates had another. The Orthodox Russians, also Rusnaks, had the largest, maybe because it was the oldest. The Serbs and even Croats had one. They spoke a language so similar to the Rusnaks' that when they all were drunk one couldn't tell a man's ethnic composition. There were even two Slovak churches and they, too, had their Sokols and men's clubs.

Many of the bars, and there were a half dozen in Woods Run, all illegal because of Prohibition, were still run by Irish immigrants or their sons, although there were now one or two Hunky-run speakeasies. Fronting several of these places were pool halls but they didn't fool anyone as to their main function. All the bar owners resented the church clubs because they sold drinks at half the cost they charged, but there was little they could do about it. However, the attendance at the pubs was always better because almost all of the ethnic clubs forbade women. Girls, instead, flocked to the pubs and the young, viral second generation Slavs followed them.

Riding down Preble Avenue, just before they turned into Doer Street, Stefan saw a sign over an impressive-looking building. It was the Ohio Valley Bank. It caused him to remember the unused ship ticket he had been given by his brother and uncle. It was drawn on the same bank.

The Men's Bar at the Ukrainian Club was almost deserted when they entered it late in the afternoon. It was sterile-looking, with a long, dark, mahogany bar filling one side of the room, a dozen or so tables in the middle with chairs, and an empty stage on the side opposite the bar. The place smelled old and of stale beer. Sunlight entered three dirty windows on the south side and illuminated the cigar smoke, from three of the four card players. Smoke seemed to fill the room. Two young men sat at the bar drinking beer. Neither one would have been able to get into a speakeasy, not because of their age, but because their owners frowned on getting caught with kids drinking alcohol.

The club was also used for meetings, wedding receptions and occasional performances on the stage. They had one beer. Andrew suggested another place.

"How can you drink that stuff?" Stefan asked, "it tastes terrible, like piss."

"I guess you are used to drinking Czech Pilsner," his brother answered. "That is the best there is. It is home made. The Club is lucky they can serve that. Police don't bother them because it is a club, but it is still illegal. I don't know how they get away with it. There now are a few Hunkies on the police force. I guess they look the other way here. Prohibition has closed down all the American breweries, but I know where we can get bottled Canadian beer."

From the outside, as Andrew pulled the car alongside, Stefan could see that *The Blarney Stone* was crowded. The original sign had been whitewashed a few years ago to obscure the printing but it did a poor job of that. There were men and women talking in the opened double doorway that led inside. As they got out of the car they heard someone inside yell for them to close the door. It slammed shut before they could get in.

"Are we too late?" Stefan asked.

"Don't worry." Andrew knocked on the heavy, wooden door. A small window in the door slid open and a burley voice asked what they wanted.

"What do you think?"

A ruddy face appeared in the window and looked at Andrew, then his brother. A few seconds later, the door opened and they passed between two big men, each more than 6 feet tall.

It was a scene Stefan had never been exposed to.

The room was about 50 feet wide and 200 feet long. A single bar covered most of the length of the room on the side opposite the street. The wall behind the bar was fully mirrored but studded with empty shelves that at one time had contained rows of liquor bottles. Three large posters of scantily-clad women blocked parts of the mirrors. Whenever beer or liquor was needed, one of the four bartenders would reached under the bar and from a font filled the glasses. A half-dozen closed, heavily draped windows opened onto the street but you couldn't tell if it was day or night outside. Three huge ceiling fans did nothing but move the cigar- and cigarette-smoke laden air about the room. A sticky, brown residue seemed to cling to the surface of the ornate tin ceiling above the fans.

There was no room at the bar and all the tables and chairs were filled with men and women. Men and women stood two and three deep behind the bar. Stefan had never before seen a woman smoke a cigarette. He was astonished by one who sat on the edge of a table not more then 10 feet from him, talking to another women and two, seated men. Her hair was pitch black and cut in bangs, in a Pageboy style. Two, long strands of white, artificial pearls hung loosely from her neck. She sat with her legs crossed above the knees and her silk dress was pulled halfway up her thighs. Tan-colored stockings were rolled down to the tops of her knees. Her eyes were heavily covered in mascara and her lips were the brightest red imaginable. The blush painted on her cheeks made her look like a toy doll.

Her dress fitted tightly around her slim body and hid nothing. She wore no brassiere. Her breasts were full but not large and the silk material clung to her nipples. The dress was low cut and the top lined with fringe. As she leaned over the table to retrieve her drink, the tops of her breast were exposed.

She lifted the glass to her lips and revealed a small cigar in her fingers. As she sipped the drink she realized that Stefan was staring at her. She methodically took a puff on the cigar as she looked directly into his eyes and asked him in Rusnak. "What do you want? Haven't you ever seen a woman before?"

He couldn't believe she was a Rusnak.

He was stunned for a moment, then answered. "Never one like you. A puff on your cigar?" and he extended his hand to take it.

With the grace of a cat, she jumped off the table and came to him, cigar in her hand. She didn't give it to him but held it in her fingers and brought the butt to his lips and rested the palm of her hand against his chin. Her hands were warm and smelled of perfume. He drew on the cigar, held it for a moment, and then gently blew it in her face.

"You been in jail?"

"No. In the army."

"That is almost as bad. What do you think of my...cigar?" she asked.

"That's the sweetest cigar I ever smoked."

"What's your name?

"Stefan. What's yours?

"Oksana!"

"Is that Polish?

"Bite you lip," she said. "Are you a *durak*? It's as Rusnak as you can get."

"I know. I was only teasing."

"That was dumb, Hunky. Dumb!" she said and abruptly turned her shoulders to him and went back to the table.

"Let's get a drink," Andrew said as he grabbed his brother's arm and pulled him away from Oksana and toward the bar. "She is nothing but trouble."

"Welcome to America," Andrew said as he clicked shot glasses with Stefan and then washed it down with Canadian lager.

"What is that drink called?" he asked

"It's a boilermaker. No more or I won't be able to drive back to Ambridge."

As Stefan finished another beer he looked about the room. There were more than a hundred people and everyone was talking at once. Periodically, one of the bartenders would rewind the Victrola that sat at the end of the bar. The deep voice of a female jazz singer would then mix with the din. To Stefan, this was exciting beyond belief. Even Andrew was impressed. He seldom had been in a speakeasy and seldom drank except at weddings, christenings and funerals.

"I thought drinking alcohol was prohibited in America," Stefan said as he leaned backwards against an open space he finally had found at the bar.

"It is," Andrew answered. "All it takes is money. The police know it is here but all of them are getting paid to stay away. Money can get you anything in America. And, there is lots of money in America."

As Stefan leaned against the bar he was taken back by the sight of so many beautifully-dressed and stylized young, skinny women. Even when he and his army buddies went into Prague they had never seen such a scene.

"Andrew, she called me a Hunky. What is a Hunky? I remember some of the Irish kids in school calling me a Hunky but I forgot what it is."

"That is what they called our people. It is kinda like Hungarian because we all came originally from the Austro-Hungarian Empire. It is not meant as a compliment.

"Let's go," he said, "I must be up at 5:00 in morning and go to work. You can sleep in...for now."

Stefan was reluctant to leave but followed. As they passed Oksana spotted him and rose from the chair in which she had been sitting. She momentarily grabbed his hand and squeezed it, saying, "Come again, Stefan," as she drew out the pronunciation of his name.

"The foreman who said he would find you a job has taken a week off and won't be back until next Monday," Andrew said after he came home from work the next day. "We could go to the main office and apply for a job, but they are not doing much hiring at this time of the year. I think it best if we wait until he gets back and work through him."

Stefan didn't mind, he felt he could use a week of doing nothing. But, money was getting to be a problem. He had about $40 left from the sale of the old horse and he could see that that wouldn't last long here. Besides, he needed new clothing. He needed a new suit. "I look like I just got off the boat," he said to Maria one evening before going out.

"If you get bored hanging around the house," Andrew said, "you can walk through town. There is a lot to see because it is all new to you. Don't worry about the language. Most people here speak our language, or Slovak, some Polish. You will have no problem. Besides, your English isn't too bad. You seem to have remembered it quite well. You might want to go to Harmony, the Old Town. It is on the far side of Ambridge. It looks just like it did in 1907 when we left Verner."

Stefan was bored. He found Merchant Street, the main street in Ambridge and began walking west. He found his cousin's car dealership and stopped in to see Nicholas Evans and had a cup of coffee with him.

He walked two blocks farther west and saw the Ambridge National Bank and felt his vest pocket. The ticket was still there. He decided to go in. Inside, he asked a teller about steamship tickets and she directed him to a man behind a desk. He took the seat opposite the man.

"Where do you want to go?" the man asked.

"I don't want to go anywhere," he said. "I have an unused ticket and the ship's bursar told me I could get a refund. He handed the ticket to him.

The banker was also an agent representing the United States Lines, whose main office was in New York City. He looked it over and then separated the receipt part with the immigration inspector's stamp and handed it back to Stefan.

"You might want to hold onto this," he said. Then he pulled out a sheet of paper and on it began figuring the value of the ticket. It is $421.45. Do you want it as a check or cash?"

"Cash!"

Stefan felt like a new man as he walked out of the bank. His right pants pocket bulged with $5 and $20 bills. He felt rich.

Chapter 44 The Value of Citizenship

"Hear yea, hear yea, hear ye, all those who have business before the 5th Federal Circuit Court," cried the court clerk, "present yourselves before the bar and be heard by the Right Honorable Justice John G. Scarlisi."

Stefan Karas's case was fourth on the docket and it was mid-morning before the court called his name. His lawyer, George Brant, motioned for Stefan to stand up.

"Approach the bench," said Judge Scarlisi.

Stefan noted a slight accent in the judge's speech.

Judge Scarlisi pushed his reading glasses back on his nose and for the next few minutes reviewed the documents in a file folder with Stefan's name on it and in bold characters, CR#172909.

"Did you know you would loose your American citizenship if you served in a foreign army?" he asked Stefan.

"No, sir."

"I see you claim you were born in Verner, in the 9th Ward. Did you go to school here?"

"Yes. Kindergarten and part of the First Grade, sir."

"How old were you when your parents returned to Europe?

"I was 6. It was in 1907, sir."

"Why did they go back?"

"They said it was because of the market crash. My father was laid off. There was no work in Pittsburgh. Those who had some money returned to the Old Country, sir."

"You don't have to keep calling me sir. What was your rank?

"Second Lieutenant, sir."

"How long did you live in Vi.. Vila.. Vilag?"

"From 1907 until 1926, when I joined the army."

"Why did you join the army?"

"Because my family was starving."

"Where was your father?"

"He died in the trenches during the Great War."

"Did you live on a farm?"

"Yes."

"Couldn't you raise enough food to feed your family on a farm? How many were in your family?"

"There were five, counting myself, when I joined the army. There was my mother, my grandmother and a younger brother and sister. Our village was in the mountains and the soil was very poor and farming was very limited. We raised sheep and goats but had eaten them or sold them for money to buy other foods. There was a drought, for three years and not even enough grass for the sheep.

"You have a brother in the United States. Where does he live?"

"In Ambridge, sir. He returned to America but has a family of his own. What he could afford to send us just paid for the taxes on our land. The taxes were getting larger and larger."

"But why the army?"

"Because there was no work for Rusnaks. There, I was considered a Rusnak and not an American. But in the army I would get paid, not a lot, but enough to help buy some food. And when I came home on weekends I was able to fill my pockets and side bag with potatoes and vegetables. That is how we got by. Still, it was not enough. I decided that it was time that I returned to America. There was no future there for Rusnaks. We were a minority in our own land and discriminated against by the Czechs, Slovaks and Hungarians.

"How did you get the money to come here?"

"I sold our last horse and my brother sent me a ticket."

"Do you have a job here."

"Not yet, but I will next week. At American Bridge."

Scarlisi re-read some of the documents before him and then began scribbling some notes on the folder. Then he looked at Stefan for a long time. He looked directly into his eyes and he must have recognized something there of himself. He knew what famine had been like in Italy when he was a child.

"Raise you right hand," Scarlisi ordered Stefan, "and repeat after me. I pledge allegiance to the flag of United States of America and ......"

Chapter 45   Night Life In "Hunky Town USA"

Friday night arrived and Stefan asked his brother if they were going into Woods Run for a drink or two. "I cannot," Andrew said. "We are running behind on a bridge and I was asked to work Saturday. I cannot go out and drink then work the next day. Maybe I am getting too old." He was just 31 but that week he had already worked two hours overtime each day and was too tired to go out.

"That's okay," Stefan said. "Nick Evans said he wanted to come along with us if we did go out. I'll go out with him."

It was 3:00 in the morning when he got home. Stefan shared a bedroom with his nephews Andrew and Michael and woke them as he staggered into the room. Maria was up after the noise awakened her and Andrew was behind her.

Sunday morning Andrew tried to wake his brother for church but he refused to get up. They went without him.

"Monday, I will see the foreman about a job for you," Andrew said in a few terse words after they returned from church. Stefan was sullen and his head hurt. The bootleg booze may not have been the best.

"Wash you face," Maria told her brother-in-law as he came to the table for Sunday dinner. "You have lipstick all over it."

It had been quite an evening and Stefan badly needed the rest. It was just before daybreak that he finally got to sleep.

"He cannot fit you in this week," his brother said Monday after work. "But he said there is a good chance next week. There is a new order coming in and they will be putting together a new crew for that job. He said he thinks he can get you in then."

The order, however, was delayed for another two weeks Stefan sat idly waiting for something to happen. However, he didn't miss Friday and Saturday night in Woods Run and a new speakeasy that opened in Ambridge. Each night he returned home drunk or almost drunk. Stefan had now been in American for more than a month and still hadn't found a job.

A depressed Andrew came home Friday and found Stefan sitting in the living room in his undershirt, smoking a cigar and reading a newspaper.

"I have bad news," he said as he took off his coat and laid his lunch pail on the kitchen table. "We lost the contract for the new bridge and there won't be a new crew. The foreman said he couldn't get you a job now, maybe in two or three months, when the spring schedule starts."

That night, Stefan went out without even asking his brother if he wanted to go. The two Evans brothers pulled up in front of the house in a new red-colored Ford convertible and leaned on the horn until Stefan came out.

It was 4:00 in the morning when Stefan came home drunk, loud and unconcerned, and woke the family. Andrew stood in the doorway and watched as Stefan sat on the bed trying to untie his shoes, unable, he pulled one off and in anger threw it against the bedroom wall when he got it free.

"Stefan, you are my brother and I love you dearly, but this has got to stop. For the past two months you have disrupted our family. The boys are afraid to go to sleep on nights when they know you have gone out. I think it is time for you to find a place for yourself. I can help you. I know a few families who are taking in boarders and you can have a separate room."

About noon, Stefan awoke, dressed quickly and walked down Merchant Street until he came to a clothes shop. He bought a small suitcase and returned home. Silently, he packed what he owned, his new suit that was wrinkled and stained and new shoes. When he was done, he entered the kitchen where his brother and the boys were eating lunch.

"I'm leaving."

"Have you found a room?"

"There's no work here, why should I find a room here?"

"Where are you going?

"We have some cousins, some second cousins in Berwick and Wilkes-Barre. I will go there."

"Do you know where they live?"

"I will find them."

"Good-bye brother," Stefan said.

Andrew rose and hugged Stefan.

"Good-bye little guys. I am sorry I was such a noisy roommate."

He kissed Maria on the cheek and walked out the door.

That was the last time any of them would see my father alive.

Stefan located his relatives in Wilkes-Barre and they tried to find a job for him. Early March is not the time to be looking for work in Northeast Pennsylvania. The only work immediately available was in the coal mines. Stefan would have none of that. After two weeks of fruitless hunting and two "good" weekends, he took the advice of one woman he met. "There is lots of work in Binghamton," she said, "in New York, 70 miles away. Shoe factories there are always hiring. And, you need no experience, they teach you."

The next day, Stefan was on a bus to Binghamton. He knew he had a great uncle, John Karas, who lived in Binghamton. However, he had never met him. He hoped he could stay with him until he got a job. He knew John lived in the First Ward, across from a St. Michael's Greek Catholic Church. He also knew that the people who went to the church were Orthodox and many had come from the villages around Vilag. But when he got there and asked in a few houses, none of the people knew of him or the Karases. He went across the street to the church rectory. A cleaning woman said that she thought they moved to Lydia Street. The directions getting there were simple.

Susan Karas answered the door and was startled when Stefan asked to see his uncle.

"He is not here," she said.

"Where is he?" Stefan asked.

"He is on a hill above Glenwood Avenue, six feet in the ground."

"Who are you?"

"I am Stefan Karas, his nephew, from Pittsburgh and late of Vilag. My father was Andrij Karas and my mother is Zuzanna Ivancova-Karas."

She stood silent for a moment, letting what the young man had just said settle into her head.

"Your uncle died 11 years ago. He drank himself to death. Didn't anyone in the Old Country tell you?

"Huh! Some family.

"He left me with four children to raise.

"What do you want?"

After John Karas's death in 1918, his wife and four children moved from Clinton Street, across from the church, to Lydia Street, deeper into the First Ward. That is where Stefan found them in March 1929. His aunt offered Stefan a room until he could find one for himself. Three days later, he got a job at Endicott-Johnson Shoe Factory in Johnson City and after two weeks found a room for himself on Thorpe Street. He was glad to leave. He felt uneasy living with his uncle's wife and children. They were like strangers to him and there was no warmth in her. She seemed bitter about her years with his uncle.

The stock market's crash in October had little immediate effect upon the shoe industry. The firm's sales abroad were still strong and while companies here halted all new hiring there were no people laid off, for the time being.

Stefan settled into an easy life. Work consumed most of the week but on Friday and Saturday nights there was a plethora of speakeasies for him to discover. Prohibition worked fine in rural sections of America but in cities with large labor forces, it hardly functioned. And, on Sundays there was always church. It wasn't that Stefan was so serious about religion, though he dogmatically attended church because of the strict religious environment his mother and father had kept, both in Verner and in Vilag. It was the social aspect of the church that attracted him and he seldom missed a church dinner, dance or picnic. And, there were other Rusnak and Slovak churches in the First Ward and nearby Johnson City so that his social calendar seldom lacked events.

The phenomenon of the "Russia Day" picnics were unique to the Slavic communities in America during the second and third quarters of the 20th century. They arose as a desire by the émigrés to retain some of their cultural background and to continue it, or pass it on to their children. Such events occurred in Europe but with less frequency and fanfare. They also offered the aging immigrants an opportunity to see once more old acquaintances in settings other than in the church, especially those who didn't live in their neighborhoods. The were called "Russian Day" because most were organized and supported by Russian Orthodox churches.

Over the next year, he developed an expanding circle of people. He was outgoing and well-liked and easily made friends. Several were people he had known in Vilag or he had known their relatives who were still in the Old Country. These were automatic entries into the action.

The maturation of a Hunky's daughter Anna Najda to Anna Nider-Karas, from farm to factory

Chapter 46   The Ward....a New Place, a New Life, and a New Challenge

After the turn of the century, as the numbers of immigrants swelled in this small upstate-New York community, the First Ward in Binghamton became a unique place in America. "The Ward," as most residents who lived within its perimeters called it, is an area roughly 735 acres in size and located on a flat, river flood plain. It is bound on the east by the Chenango River, on the north by Mount Prospect and several nameless foothills of the Catskill Mountains, and on the south by the elevated tracks of the Lackawanna and Erie railroads. Its western edge is the boundary between Johnson City and Binghamton. There isn't even a sign on Clinton Street, the main east-west artery through The Ward, to tell you when you are about to leave one city and enter the other.

Even before the influx of Slavic emigrants, The Ward was composed of moderate-income houses that made up the blue-collar work force in this highly-industrialized and interdependent complex of three cities. In Binghamton and Johnson City, shoe factories paralleled the railroad tracks and work was not far from where their employees lived. Along lower (eastern) Clinton Street there were dozens of tenement houses. Several had originally been built as small, three storey hotels or boarding houses but were gradually modified as long-term housing for single occupants. However, few rooms were occupied by only one person. It was too costly for the immigrants.

Other buildings, mostly along Clinton Street, were designed and built to accommodate numerous boarders. As an added alternative, immigrant families rented many one- and two-storey wooden frame houses behind Clinton Street and several streets that paralleled the north side of Clinton up to the base of Mount Prospect. These houses were built in the center of the blocks that decades before had been the gardening areas behind the houses fronting on the main streets. Access was through driveways and alleys between buildings on the main streets. These houses also catered to boarders. Thus, places for single men or women to live in The Ward were never difficult to find.

Home owners and boarders in The Ward developed a symbiotic relationship with each other. A man with a family would buy a house but initially couldn't afford the mortgage payments on his own. He would immediately modify it, usually living in the basement with his small family, or the first or second level, and renting the other levels to immigrant families or a number of boarders. It was the only way both could afford to live during the early years of immigration. Eventually, as mortgages were paid off, or the immigrant amassed enough money, he would return it to a single-family dwelling, often driven by the need to accommodate his own increasing family size.

Before the turn of the century, and shortly thereafter, most houses were owned by Irish, German and English immigrants. Gradually, as their lot improved, they moved to other wards as newly-arrived immigrants readily sought one and two family, two-storey houses.

While of the émigrés to the First Ward began arriving as early as the turn of the century, the greater majority arrived after the Great War. Unlike the wave that preceded them before the war, they were not here to get rich and then return to the Old Country. Instead, they were dedicated to creating new lives for themselves as permanent settlers. Thus, care and property improvement were reflected in their houses and were improved over their previous owners. In a strange twist, property values improved rather than declined because of the immigrants who occupied them; a rare phenomenon in immigration scenarios. There was a pride in their homes in The Ward that never existed there before they arrived.

Opportunities for the Najdas, when they arrived *en masse* in Binghamton just before Christmas 1928, were almost limitless when compared to those in Berlin. Anna, in the meantime, had become but one of nearly 300 shoe operators in one vast room on the third floor of the four-storey Dunn & McCarthy Shoe Factory. It was located on the southern edge, just outside The Ward. There were four floors in the huge factory, not counting the basement. The din, created by nearly as many machines on each floor as there were workers, was almost deafening and easily heard well beyond the confines of the factory. Added to it was the constant chatter among the workers, mostly young women, as they talked incessantly among themselves to pass time in continuously repetitive manual jobs. Some were seated at their machines while others, because of the nature of their work, had to stand to perform their tasks.

Racks of shoes in various stages of completion were staged next to each operator. When that operator's special section in the production of a shoe was completed, it was his or her responsibility to move a new Hryec closer to the machine. There were boys on the floor whose primary job was to move racks from one operator to the next stage of shoe making but it seemed that they were seldom there when needed. Most women moved their own racks to make room for more shoes. They got paid by the piece and not by the hour and couldn't wait around for help.

The pace on the floors would have been too hectic, too trying a place for Anna's father to work. Anna was much like her mother and possessed an outgoing personality. She quickly made friends with everyone she met. While her tenure in the factory at that time was relatively short, her knowledge of making shoes and the various departments was well-founded by the time her family arrived. The day after they were in Binghamton she went to her supervisor and told him of her father's health, the black lung disease, and asked his advice about where in the factory he might find work. Later that afternoon, the foreman returned.

"Anna," he said, "I think I have a place for him. Unfortunately, it deals with coal but there is no dust involved. They could use a man in the boiler room. The furnaces are coal-fired but the coal is fed into the furnaces by large worm screws that lead from a hopper into the firebox. There are six boilers and there is a crew that maintains them. There is an opening there. What do you think?"

The next day Vasyl showed up, even with his miner's lunch bucket. There were three boiler-room crews composed of four men each, except on the day crew, that had six men. The crews worked three, eight-hour shifts. The foreman of the three crews, an Irishman, from the company's Massachusetts home plant, worked only the day shift. He seldom contributed to the physical aspects of maintaining the steam and heat. The remaining men were a polyglot of ethnic groups. Two were Rusnaks from Galicia, like Vasyl. Four men were Slovaks from Hungary but two of them spoke the same Rusnak, or Lemko/Boyko dialect as did Vasyl; another was a Czech, one a Syrian, two were Poles and two were second generation Germans.

Vasyl's work was not difficult. The only time anyone had to shovel coal was when the worm gear at the bottom of the coal hopper was jammed, unusually by a big piece of coal. This was rare because the pea-size coal had been screened before it was delivered. Other times it was a piece of wood or a branch that had become mixed with the coal when it was on the open railroad cars. However, the coal, if it became wet, occasionally would clump and not break apart. There was an alarm to tell the men on a shift that something had happened.

Most of their time was spent watching the gauges, making sure the system had enough water and pressure was maintained, and keeping the temperature in a range where steam was always being produced. Whenever the pressure would fall, and it wasn't because of something wrong in the boiler room, they would call one of the plumbers and he would have to locate the one leaky radiator in more than hundred or so in the massive plant. There was a plumber working every shift.

It was company policy to hold back a week before paying wages so it wasn't until the second Friday at Dunn's that Vasyl got his first pay. He couldn't believe it.

That night he stared at the small pile of bills and coins he emptied from the narrow, tan paper envelope that he was given by his foreman. "I made $3.60 just for sitting on my ass for a week," Vasyl said. "I cannot believe this. They pay me 9 cents an hour. If I work on the first night shift, I get 10 cents and hour and 11 cents if I work the last shift. Maybe there is gold in the streets in America. I have just been walking down the wrong road."

A few days after they arrived in Binghamton. Anna took her mother and sister Mary into work to find them work. Mary was immediately given a job in the Finishing Room. But her mother, after taking but one look at the factory floor, the noise, confusion and seeming bedlam, turned around and walked out.

"I could never work there," she said as she stormed off the floor, with Anna trailing behind. "It is all noise, all crazy-like. I, too, would be crazy at the end of the first day." She walked home alone because her daughter could not leave work. Kateryna was fascinated as she passed all the stores and spotted several speakeasies on Clinton Street.

"Mother," Anna said when she got home at 5 o'clock. "It isn't so bad working in the factory. Try it for a week. You will see."

"I already have a job," she quipped back smartly.

My grandmother had always possessed a sharp tongue. But for the moment it seemed dulled. My mother immediately noticed it.

"Mother," she asked, "you didn't? She knew of her mother's penchant for alcohol. Where did you get the money to buy a drink?"

"I saw John Hudak on Clinton Street, standing outside a hotel. He's from Smil'nyk. I haven't seen him in 20 years. He hasn't changed much. I would have recognized him anywhere. We were talking about the Old Country, about when we were kids. He invited me in for a drink. I only had one.

"Tomorrow morning, I go with my cousin Mary. I will work in the cigar factory with her. I need bus money. A ride is 5 cents but Mary said I could get 6 tokens for a quarter. Can you loan me a quarter?"

Catherine, the oldest of Anna's younger sisters, got a job cleaning houses with Mary Salabaj's daughter Mary, but the pay was hardly worth the effort. After three weeks, she and her cousin went to work with her mother and aunt in the cigar factory. They always needed women because of the dexterity of their fingers when rolling cigars. Wasco refused to work in the shoe factory but after a few weeks got a job separating metal at a junkyard. Nick lied about his age and got a job at Dunn's pushing shoe racks.

Andy hated watching the girls and his younger brother Mike. When the school sent a truant officer to visit them two weeks after they had arrived, and wondered why he and his brother and sister Martha were not in school, he was delighted.

"School is a hundred times better than watching baby sisters," he said after his first day in Daniel S. Dickinson Elementary School.

School, however, created a problem for the Najdas. Now, they were faced with what looked like a real predicament. They lost a babysitter. Anna, who now rose to a new role in the family--as their representative and connection with the people in Binghamton--came up with a solution. But before she broached it, she wisely first talked to her father's foreman and discovered he had a way out. He told her that one of the men on the 4 to 12 shift wanted to switch to days.

While Vasyl liked the 40 cents more a week he could now make, he wasn't that keen on babysitting his two daughters. But, it was a living. And, in the winter it was always warm in their flat or in the boiler room where he worked. For the moment, life was good to him and the rest of the Najdas.

On Sundays, the entire family walked the eight or ten blocks to St. Mary's Russian Orthodox Church on Baxter Street. It was part of the same church system as their church in Goodtown and they immediately felt welcomed and at home. Maybe it was also because they knew a large number people in the congregation, all transplanted Goodtowners. The church was still a very important part in the lives of the Najdas; Vasyl made sure of it. However, he had trouble getting Wasco to church. Pigheadedness among the Najdas, or Niders as they now were more commonly known, was not a trait restricted only to women.

It was at a Russian Day picnic, one Sunday in early June, at Bistrack's Farm that Anna Nider met Steve Karas. If you didn't know where you were, you could have sworn that it was a typical church celebration in the Old Country. There was even a trio of Gypsies, two violinists and an accordionist who knew and played all the Old Country songs. Their favorite, and that of the older women who were there, was "Lemko Wedding." They played it more than once. The older women almost automatically began singing the songs in the native language as the younger couples and their now grown children danced polkas and chardashes.

While the number of speakeasies, or "joints" as the immigrants called them, in the city were numerous and operated almost without restrictions, Prohibition was more respected at church functions. Many families made their own wine and it was tolerated at these events but there was always some young buck who had managed to bring a flask of whisky to these events.

While it was the young women who drew the young men to these events, for the now older immigrants it was also a chance to share their Old Country foods and renew acquaintances that had been established in theirs and nearby villages in Europe. And, there were always one or two "greenhorns" who recently had arrived from Europe. They were usually in the center of a crowd of old-timers who wanted to know what life was now like in the Old Country as they always referred to Europe.

Anna had never seen him before but was not unduly surprised when Stefan came up to her and asked her to dance a polka. Anna was attractive and never had a problem with suitors. Quite to the contrary. He thanked her when it was finished and she returned to a group of girls, many of whom with which she worked. She did notice a slight inflection in his English that was more European than American.

When the next dance started, he was again there and asked her to dance. When it was over, he asked her if she would like a drink, and he patted his breast pocket.

"I don't booze," she said, "but I would like a root beer."

As they danced, this time she spoke to him only in Rusnak. He answered correspondingly. Even his Rusnak is a bit different, but only in a few odd words, she thought to herself as he went for the drinks. She suddenly became more interested in him. He certainly is a Rusnak, she though to herself as she waited. His eyes are blue and his hair is almost blond. He looks like he takes care of himself. He has no belly like many of the men here. He could be a bit taller.

In the next half-hour she found out where he was from and all other things young people talk about when they first meet. His English was good, but even so, he spoke with the very slight accent. At first, she thought, he came over as a youngster and was still in the process of developing his English skills. She wondered aloud why she hadn't seen him in church or elsewhere. He told her he went to "St. Mike's," worked at EJ's, (Endicott-Johnson's) and had just returned from Vilag where he had lived for the past 20 years. He told her of his birth in Verner, "....outside of Pittsburgh," but little else.

The next Sunday, in her church, she saw Stefan.

"I thought you went to St. Michael's," she said afterwards as he waited for her just outside the door.

"It doesn't matter where I go to church, they are all the same."

Stefan's courtship of Anna during the next few months was intense.

Two weeks after their first encounter, St. Michael's Church was having a shared picnic with another Orthodox Church in

Scranton. The church hired a large bus and had no trouble filling it. Stefan convinced Anna to go with him but she didn't agree until her close friend Elsie Mohilchock and her boyfriend Charley Sauger also agreed to go. While in Scranton one of Stefan's cousins was at the picnic and he introduced Anna to her.

The following week, she had him over for Sunday supper and a chance to meet her family. At first, he was overwhelmed by the family's size. But, by the end of the evening, he had become everyone's friend. Everyone, except Vasyl. He seemed wary of him.

"There are too many unanswered questions," Vasyl said to his daughter after Stefan left their flat at 60 Clinton Street. "He is a man who has gotten around a lot, not just in the Old Country, but here. Why didn't he stay longer with his brother in Ambridge?"

After listening to her father, Anna realized that maybe her relationship with Stefan was moving at too fast a pace. During the next few months, and into the fall, she made a concerted effort to let it cool. He, too, seemed to have lost the intense interest he first showed in the pretty girl from an isolated mining town in southwestern Pennsylvania. He knew she liked him but she wasn't as quick to commit herself to him as other women he had known. And, the specter of Natasha back in Vilag must also have reared itself in his subconscious and knowingly or unknowingly inhibited him to some degree in pursuing another pretty face. Anna did date him occasionally but it was usually just a movie or a church social function. And when they did go out, it often was with one or two couples.

It was a winter wedding, in mid-January, in which they were both members of the wedding party, that things between them seemed to change. Maybe it was seeing her girlfriend marry that made her look at Stefan in a new light. She thought of him as a possible mate but never considered it seriously. She was just 23 and seemed to like the current state she was in. He was 28 and she knew he must have had experiences with other women. She liked her freedom but she also liked the novel idea of a husband.

Stefan had had several drinks and even Anna, who seldom drank alcohol, had more champagne than she realized. They both were feeling uninhibited when they got in the back seat of one of the usher's car and he drove them home. When Stefan began kissing her she responded. Fortunately, the drive home was only the length of Clinton Street and he walked her to the door.

That event seemed to accelerate their infatuation for each other and they were seen together at almost every church event, at almost every church. They were an item. Even though an engagement was never announced, there seemed little doubt that the two would soon marry.

One weekend evening after supper, Anna dropped down to her parents flat on the second floor. It was not an unusual event because she often spent evenings with her family and left her two roommates, who shared the rent with her, to themselves or their friends.

But that evening, she seemed excited. "What's wrong with you, Anna?" her mother asked.

She hesitated for a moment and when she knew her father was also listening she said: "He has asked me to marry him."

"Oh!" said her mother, "I think that is wonderful."

"I don't think so," said her father. "I don't like him. He is too smooth. No, don't marry him. Not now anyway. Wait a while until you can learn more about him."

"What do you think I have been doing all these months since I met him?" Answered Anna. "I think I know him well enough to marry him."

"I think he is nice," said Kateryna.

"What do you know about him?" Vasyl said sharply to his wife. "You like him because he brings you a little bottle of whisky once in a while."

"But I....."

"Shut up!" Vasyl said angrily to his wife.

"Anna, I forbid you to marry him."

Anna never expected her father's condemnation to be so severe. She hesitated for a moment and then began to cry. She covered her face with her hands as tears began to flow.

"But I love him," she said as she ran out the door and up to her apartment in the next building.

"What does she know of love?" Vasyl said to his wife.

"What did you know of love when we met in Smil'nyk?" Kateryna asked. "What did you know of love when you found me in Wilkes-Barre? She is as old now as you were then."

"Harrumph," was all Vasyl could say.

The next day she saw Stefan and told him of her father's decision.

"What will we do," she asked him. "We cannot wait too long."

At first, he wanted to wait another month to be sure. Anna had missed a period. After she told him of her father's decision, and began crying, Stefan made a quick decision.

"Next Friday, after work, we will go to Wilkes-Barre. You know I have relatives there. We can stay with them and get a marriage license on Saturday, and be married that same day."

They couldn't get the license on Saturday but stayed with my father's relatives until Monday. There were several Karases who had immigrated to the Scranton/Wilkes-Barre area. The following day they found a Justice of the Peace who married them. Vasyl did not happily receive the news when they got back to Binghamton but he was powerless to do anything. His only recourse was to shun her for a while but that didn't last more than a few weeks. After they were married, Anna decided to give up the apartment she shared with the two other girls and moved in with Stefan. However, his one-room proved too confining for them and after a month they regained Anna's old apartment and kept on the two girls as boarders.

It was a happy time for them, probably the happiest of their lives. Though, as I look back at it now, my mother spoke little of those times. It may have been the tragic events that were soon to follow that must have made that period too difficult to talk about, even years later to her children.

Spring seemed to come early in 1931 and balmy weather continued into a warm summer. The effects of the Depression were slowly making inroads on their activities and the activities of the friends, both married and single. One of their most enjoyable events were Sunday afternoon picnics along the banks of the Chenango River, about 2 miles above Binghamton. One of their friends had a Model A and getting as many as eight people in it at one time was a challenge but they always managed to do so. The external trunk on the back of the car acted as a cooler and after a stop at Cutler's Ice Company on Front Street, they headed upriver. And, my Aunt Kate's boyfriend at that time always had access to a case of Canadian beer.

Initially, life for them was simple and they were never at a loss for things to do. Despite the Depression and the shortage of money, church and group picnics, dances, weddings and christenings were always in the offing. However, as the Depression dragged on, Anna and Stefan, like so many other Americans in the early 1930s, saw many of these activities slowly diminish as expendable income gradually disappeared. As it did, they had two ways to escape the times; either the movies, which were still 5 cents, or the radio. My parents tried both but it was the radio that loomed larger as their prime entertainment. At that time, radios were still rare and a real luxury. During the 1930 federal census, the government questionnaire asked each person if they owned a radio. They used it as a gauge of a person's financial status. A radio was one of the first things they bought together after they were married.

In early fall Anna quit work at the shoe factory. Stefan insisted she do so. "I know it will be a boy," he said. "We cannot take any chances."

On slow nights, they would listen to popular bands playing on the radio. The only time Anna, who had become infatuated with swing music, couldn't listen to the radio was when there was a boxing match underway or news reports of John Dillinger's escapades.

It seems strange to us today that a criminal like Dillinger could become a hero. Dillinger became a folk hero to vast numbers of people during the Depression and they cheered him on every time he robbed a new bank. Most Americans did not look upon him and other bank robbers at that time as terrible criminals. He was often described as a Robin Hood when they discovered that he and other bank robbers took a particular delight in destroying all of the mortgage records when they a hit bank. Maybe he was a hero because he was doing what a lot of downtrodden people would have liked to have done.

Binghamtonians of that era were especially interested in boxing since one of their very own was Jack Sharkey. He was born in 1902 in Binghamton as Joseph Paul Zukaushas, the son of immigrant Lithuanians. He trained at times in a gym on Clinton Street, just a few doors down from were the Niders and Karases lived. When he decided to box professionally, his manager said he needed a better name for the posters. To accommodate him, he chose the names of his two favorite boxers, Jack, from Jack Dempsey and Sharkey, from Tom Sharkey.

My father was fascinated by boxing and oftentimes would be allowed to watch him spar in the gymnasium. Though ethnically Lithuanian he and his parents spoke Polish and my father was fluent

419

enough in it to speak to him and his father. My father was even able to bring my mother, who at first abhorred boxing, to watch some of the sparring events. She latter admitted that there was a certain attraction to the sport that she could not explain.

June 21, 1932 was a great day on Clinton Street, in fact all of Binghamton. It was the day Sharkey won a 15-round decision, in Yankee Stadium, against the German Max Schmeling. Two years earlier, Sharkey had lost a controversial decision to him.

Chapter 47   Good and Bad Times

Despite the easy money, Vasyl didn't like living in a city the size of Binghamton, or any city for that matter. He desperately wanted to return to being a farmer. He longed to get back to the small bit of the world that he now owned. He had been able to pay off the little debt that existed on its purchase and had been saving what he could. What Kateryna and their daughter Catherine made in the cigar factory went to pay for food and rent. Nick contributed his share but it was difficult getting his older brother Wasco to chip in. One was never sure of what he made in the junkyard because it was seldom seen. Too often it was spent or lost before he got home.

A few months after I was born, my grandfather announced he was going back to the farm. "I have enough money saved to put a new roof on the house," he told the family one Sunday afternoon around the traditional roast chicken dinner. "I will be going back in March or April, put a new roof on and get ready for spring plowing. I have enough to buy a horse and maybe two cows.

"By the end of summer, before school starts, you and the children can join me," Vasyl said. "It is good that you work as long as then," he addressed his wife, "because it will take a while to get the farm producing. "You three," he turned and addressed Wasco, Nick and Kate, "should decide if you want to move back to the farm. That decision is up to you. But Andy, Mike, Martha, Rose Ann and Stella are still too young to stay here and will be going back with mother."

At the end of March, Vasyl boarded the train and returned to Berlin and opened the farmhouse. It took Sam Philip, his son-in-law, another two years of working in the shoe factory before he, too, could return to his farm. Because it was adjacent to Vasyl's farm, he often walked over to the farm's colonial brick house to make sure all was well. Kateryna so missed her husband that in late June she boarded a train and returned to the farm for a visit. She was appalled at what she saw when she walked into the house.

Of course, it was bare of furniture, she expected that. It had all been taken to Binghamton when they moved three years earlier. She found Vasyl sleeping on a mattress cover that he had sewn shut after it was stuffed with straw.

"It is just like in the Old Country," he said apologetically when she chided him. "There, we never had more than straw to sleep upon."

When she returned to Binghamton she told the children of what she had seen. "If it was up to me," she said, "I would have stayed and made things better for him. But your father insists that we make as much money as we can, while we can. After we return to the farm we will go shopping for furniture."

It was the last week in August when Kateryna packed all she could manage and boarded the train to Johnstown with her children. Nick decided to stay behind and moved in with Anna. So did Catherine. Catherine remained in Binghamton with Anna until the following June. Then she, too, returned to the farm but only stayed for a year and returned to Binghamton.

Wasco said he had enough of the "big city," and longed for the country farm. No one believed him. There had been rumors that he owed some men money he had lost while playing cards. He must have figured that this was a good time to leave. The older children were all back in school in September. With the aid of Wasco, Andy and Mike the process of turning the farm back into a home moved at an accelerated pace. After the crops were harvested, in November young Wasco decided to return to the mines. It was the only work immediately available.

"I am too used to having money, at least some money in my pocket," he said to his father. "And, I cannot stay boarded up here on the farm. I need a car. I was talking to Uncle Harry (as he called Hryec). He said there is still some work in the mines where he works. I will go with him next week to see if I can get a job."

It was a mistake that years later would eventually lead to a bitter ending for Wasco. Even though he was just 22 years old, Wasco had developed breathing problems that were apparent even before he left the farm for Binghamton. He had worked in the mines long enough so that coal dust was now in his lungs.

For some miners, like John Najda, the effects of coal dust were minimal. He contracted it but it never developed beyond more than a slight cough. Vasyl's reaction to the black lung was somewhere between John's and Harry's. On the opposite end was Harry. Within two years of entering the mines, in 1913, he began to cough. For years it was little more than that but over the last decade grew progressively worse. When Wasco went to see him about mine work in Blackfield, where he now lived, a dozen miles west of Berlin, in Black Township, Harry could hardy hold a conversation without coughing during every sentence. It was frightening, especially when it was accompanied by blood. Still, it failed to discourage Wasco.

Wasco worked in Blackfield next to his uncle for a month when, unexpectedly, almost all the men in the mine were laid off. The costs of deep mining for coal were getting to be too expensive because of the depth at which it was now being sought. This, in combination with thinning seams of coal and constant flooding, was making the mines in Blackfield too costly for the company to turn a profit. The shareholders made the move to close the mines without any forewarning.

The layoff devastated Harry because it affected his ability to provide for his wife and now seven children, then ages four to 17. After a week or so, he was given work at the mine but only for a day or two. It consisted mostly of cleaning up wayward coal seams, vacant rooms and robbing the coal pillars. The latter was extremely dangerous work and many men refused to do it. Harry, however, didn't seem bothered by the threat. In fact, he once said to Vasyl that he might welcome it. There were weeks when he didn't work at all. Each day he would show up at the mine, never knowing if he would be sent in or sent home.

For Wasco, the layoff was a godsend. He now knew how to drive cars and trucks, and even learned how to operate a small crane when he worked in the junk yard in Binghamton. He almost immediately got a job just north of Berlin with a company that was using a new mining technique. It was called strip mining. He started by driving a large truck and hauling coal from the pit, a vast opening in the earth often 200 and 300 feet below the surrounding fields, where a steam shovel loaded coal onto the truck. He drove the truck a mile away to a railroad spur with a loading station. Here it was loaded by dumping it into coal cars. This was the beginning of an entirely new way to extract coal from the ground and became the venue of the second generation of coal miners, the sons of immigrants.

In the meantime, the first generation of immigrants in the coal fields of America was graying and dying. Dying from becoming old was natural and unavoidable but so many were dying from the coal dust inhaled in the mines that it was a near epidemic in some parts of the country. Dying from the black lung, however, was so miserable that it was not unusual for there to be one or two miner suicides a year in a county as small as Somerset. When the miners heard about it, or read about one in the newspapers, all were affected in some way. Too often, they knew the man or knew the village in Europe from where he came.

There were two primary causes that convinced a miner to take his life. One was ill health and the other was lack of work. Both were in play when Harry Nider showed up unexpectedly at his brother Vasyl's door a few days after "Russian" Christmas in January 1934.

"We missed seeing you in church." Vasyl said after his brother had entered the house and took off his hat, coat and gloves. "How did you get here?"

"There was a guy going to Meyersdale," said Harry. "I bummed a ride with him. We almost didn't make it in here. The wind is drifting the snow and in places it is nearly four feet deep."

"Sit down. Would you like some whiskey?" Vasyl seldom drank but always had a bottle in the house for such occasions. "What brings you here?" Vasyl asked.

"I am at my wits end," he said. He drank the whiskey shot in one gulp and slammed it on the table next to the bottle, expecting another. Vasyl hesitated.

"There is no work," he said and then began coughing. He rushed to the door and pulled it open and ran to the edge of the porch. Snow swirled into the house and in a second began to build a drift in the front room. Harry coughed, gagged and spit until the snow at the end of the porch showed signs of turning red. Finally, he quieted down and returned to the table as Vasyl closed the door behind him.

"Everyone is against me, even my wife," Harry said. "And, there are others. Two days ago I spent the night in the county jail in

Somerset. She called the sheriff and told them I had abandoned her and the children. Abandoned her, shit! What does she think I have been doing all these days when I'm not home, drinking or whoring around? She's crazy. Putting me in jail ain't going to put bread on the table. I've been looking for work, everywhere. Maybe I am too old," he said and then started coughing again.

He was only 45.

"Kash," Vasyl yelled, "bring me a Hryec."

His wife had been upstairs making beds and hadn't heard her brother-in-law arrive.

"Hryec, how are you?" she asked as soon as she saw him.

"Get him a Hryec or a towel," Vasyl yelled. "He is coughing badly and bringing up blood."

Kateryna disappeared in the kitchen and moments later came out with a clean dishtowel and a glass of water.

"Maybe you would like some tea instead?" she asked. "Hot tea always helps Vasylko when he starts that coughing. When was the last time you were to the doctor?"

"Going to the doctors is a waste of money and time. They tell me there is nothing they can do. Or anyone can do. It has gone too far. It is just a matter of time, they say, until I suffocate. That is how one dies from the black lung."

He wheezed as he gulped for air and then drank the glass of water.

"God damn it, give me another shot," he ordered his brother, then moved the glass closer to him. Vasyl poured another one.

Harry's hand trembled slightly as he brought the thick glass to his mouth. A small amount of whiskey spilled on his unshaven chin just before the rim touched his lips. Kateryna knew she wasn't wanted in the conversation and excused herself, saying she had work in the kitchen.

"Why did you spend a night in jail?" Vasyl asked after his wife was gone.

"She told them I wasn't home for three days and had abandoned them. They had no food, no money."

"Where did they find you?'

"I was in John's house, with his partners," he said and then gulped for air.

"They said I was drunk and they locked me up."

"Were you?

"I wish I was. I had only two, maybe three drinks. John didn't have much around. He never does."

"That's because he, too, drinks too much," said Vasyl. "If the black lung doesn't get him, the booze will. I don't know where he gets it but he seems to always have some around."

"He said he got it from Mrs. Sablich. She has a still in her basement that no one knows about."

Then he started coughing again.

"The next morning the stupid, son-of-a-bitch judge charged me with desertion and non-support. He ordered me to pay her $35 a month in support. Where the hell am I going to get $35? I've worked only four days in the month since they laid off everyone. I go there every day but they send me home.

"Everyone is ganging up on me. That bastard at the company store," he stopped for a moment to gain his breath, "he said I have lots of money saved but spend it only on booze. Mrs. Hudanych, who lives next to us, told my wife that she saw me with another women one night when I went up the hill to Berlin?

"I think a lot of all this is her fault. I think Hudanych is a witch and has given me the evil eye."

"Why don't you go and talk to the priest, maybe he can help," suggested his brother.

"He's no better than the rest. Everything I tell him gets back to Anna."

It was late when they finished talking and both men were tired. Harry had coaxed two more shots from Vasyl's bottle and sleep came easily. There was an imitation black leather sofa in the front room and he fell asleep there. It was drafty, next to the front door, so Kateryna brought down a pillow and two blankets from upstairs and covered him for the night. Vasyl banked the coal stove in the kitchen. Enough heat would flow from there into the front room to keep him warm.

Harry stayed with his brother for the entire week even though they tried to get him to go home to his family.

"Harry, you have to stop this," Vasyl finally said. "You have a wife and seven children at home. Anna cannot take care of them herself. When Wasco comes home from work this evening, we will take you home. I have an extra goat. I will slaughter it today and we will take it home for you so that your children have something to eat."

Harry didn't answer but sat sullenly at the kitchen table with his head and shoulders lowered and both hands clasped around a cup of black coffee that had grown cold.

Kateryna set about baking bread though Fridays were not the day she customarily bakes. She made four huge loaves. After they cooled, she wrapped them in cloth and put them in a clean bushel basket to take to Anna's.

That was the last time Kateryna would see her brother-in-law.

Vasyl accompanied his son as they drove Harry back to Blackfield. It was almost dark when they got there. Wasco carried the box of meat and his father brought in the basket of bread. Harry followed behind them but stopped at the base of the half-dozen stairs that led to the house's outside porch. He needed the pause to regain his breath. The others went up and entered the company house.

Anna began crying as they laid the food on the table. She grabbed her brother-in-law and hugged him for the longest time. The kids were glad to see their cousin Wasco. Harry finally came into the house and the children greeted him.

"Oh God," said Anna to Vasyl. "What am I to do? How long can we go on like this? Why has God forsaken us? How have we angered him?"

No answers were forthcoming.

Harry began coughing, not too badly, but he was also wheezing. His oldest daughter Mary, 17, found a clean Hryec and got a glass of water and took it to him. He refused both and disappeared into a bedroom."

"I worry about him," Vasyl said to Mary. "Hryec was talking crazy when he was with me. And, it wasn't the whiskey talking."

"I know," said Anna. "He thinks everyone is against him. Even me. Can you imagine that, he thinks I am against him. I have had too much to worry about just putting food in the children's mouths.

"I know it is hurting him...not just his lungs...but coming home each morning after going to the mine to see if he will work. Inside, it is tearing him apart.

"You know him. He has always been an independent man. He is frustrated because there is nothing he can do about the situation. He cannot find a job anywhere. The Depression has closed down many of the companies that would buy coal. But you know that. At least you were smart enough to buy a farm. You can always grow what you need and make ends meet until the times get better. This cannot last forever.

"Maybe he could cope with it if he wasn't so sick. There are times when he is afraid to go to sleep at night because he thinks he will stop breathing. He has trouble breathing when he lies down. I often wake up and find him asleep, sitting up in bed. Where is all this going?"

"Come on Pop," Wasco interrupted. "I don't want to get stuck in a snow bank after dark. It's still snowing pretty heavily."

Vasyl hugged Anna and then went to the bedroom. The room was dark except for a beam of light that came through the open door from the kitchen. Harry was sitting on the edge of the bed. Vasyl couldn't see him at first but heard him wheezing.

"Good-bye, Hryec," he said. "Will I see you in church on Sunday?"

His brother didn't answer. Vasyl stared at him for the longest time waiting for an answer. Finally, Harry, never lifting his head to see him, waved him off without speaking. Vasyl lingered a few moments longer, then slowly closed the door. He knew he would never see his brother alive again.

"I am afraid of what he might do," Vasyl said to his son as they drove though the blowing snow. "You should have come to the door and said good-bye to your uncle. Who knows when you might see him again."

Harry had a difficult weekend. The congestion in his lungs was rapidly getting worse and he hardly slept. He gasped almost continuously for air. He had difficulty putting on his shoes Monday morning at daybreak as he readied himself to go to the mines to see if there would be any work that day. Even if there was, he doubted he could do any work. He knew this. He no longer held out any hope of working because he had been disappointed so many times in the past weeks.

"It is over," he said to himself, "for some reason they just aren't telling me. Why are they against me at the mines? I have always been a good worker?"

"Where are you going father?" asked Harry's 14-year old son John as he watched him finish dressing."

"I am going to the mines, to the Enterprise Coal Company," he said. "I was told there might be work today in the Ponfeigh Coal Tipple.

"If I don't work, I will be back soon and kill myself. If I do work, I will kill myself in the evening."

Harry didn't bother to close the front door as he left the house. John closed the door and then ran to his mother to tell her what his father had said.

"Not today, Harry," the mine foreman said as he saw him approach. "We are the only two here. The mine is like a ghost town. I don't think it will open until this damned Depression is over. Save yourself a walk. Don't come tomorrow."

The foreman's statement did nothing but reinforce Harry's conviction of what he must do. He watched as the foreman disappeared into the office near the mine entrance then he walked to a small shack on the edge of the work area. He entered it and found an open box of dynamite. On the opposite side of the shack he found a fuse, some wire and a 12-volt dry cell battery and stuffed them in his pockets.

He returned home by 10:30 and went to the side of the house where a large log was still exposed above the drifting snow. He inserted the fuse into the dynamite, wired it and stuffed three sticks into his shirt. Then he buttoned his coat and lay on the log. He connected one wire to the battery terminal and was about to connect the other when he saw his daughter Mary open the door onto the back porch. She was on her way to the post office and about to go down the back stairs when she saw him on the log.

"Don't go," her father yelled to Mary when he saw her. "Wait until I die."

He touched the second wire to the battery. A shattering explosion deafened her ears and shook the windows in all the nearby houses.

About mid-afternoon, an unfamiliar car pulled up in front of Vasyl's farmhouse. It was the mine foreman. He told him what had happened. He took Vasyl to the site where Wasco was working and in Wasco's car they drove to Harry's house. Harry's wife was hysterical and all the children were in the kitchen, the younger one's were crying and the older ones were trying to adjust to what had happened.

As Vasyl and Wasco went outside to look at the site, a sheriff's car pulled up. The foreman had called them.

"There's nothing much we can do here," the deputy said. "But, you might want to gather him together."

Wasco found a cardboard box and he and his father gathered the scattered remains of Hryec Yurkovych Najda from the snow and trees.

Vasyl never fully recovered. "He was never quite the same after that," said his daughter Rose Anne.

Chapter 48   Life in a Depression City

For a while, life in Binghamton was pleasant but not easy for Anna and Steve, as my father now preferred to be called. The Depression and the ensuing scarcity of money were not only changing the way they lived, but the way everyone in Binghamton lived. It is true—that misery likes company—and they had gradually accumulated a group of close friends who were in similar situations. Most were Rusnaks whose parents had come over before the Great War and worked in the shoe factories. Others were children who came over at a very early age, grew up in Binghamton, and knew little of the Old Country except what they were told. And, there were growing numbers of "English," who were second and third generation Irish, English and Germans who had been assimilated a generation or two earlier. Binghamton had become a microcosm of the Eastern United States and its population was a mixture of recent Europeans and their decendents.

In order not to lay off and lose experienced shoe workers, as the Depression gradually deepened, both Dunn's and EJ's inaugurated a system where the factories stayed open five days a week but employees would work only four days a week, with staggered days off once a week. Most were happy to be able to work four days a week. Steve, for a few months was in a unique part of the shoe industry and was able to work a full week. However, in the fall that advantage ended and he was cut to four, sometimes only three days of work a week. On Friday's after work, when he worked Fridays, he and a couple of his buddies would stop for a drink or two at the speakeasy in the back of the Elm Hotel, on Clinton Street.

Anna didn't think much of it when this started, but became annoyed when he would miss supper. At first, he wasn't really drunk but she could sense that he had been drinking. That began to change as his return home in the evenings became later and later. It caused the first friction to occur in their marriage.

"I cannot understand how you can give your money to those guys running the joints," she said, "when we have just enough for food and rent. I have a mind to report them to the police."

"Don't be stupid Anna, the police are being paid to stay away. Do you think the backroom saloons would be open if they weren't? There are five…no six, on Clinton Street alone."

"I just don't think it is right that some should get rich while others struggle to keep their heads above water."

Two weeks later, on one of those weeks where Steve worked only the first three days of the week, they had their second quarrel. It was early Friday evening when Anna walked into the kitchen and saw Steve rummaging through the closet where she kept a scant amount of canned and bottled foods and cereal boxes. He had spent the afternoon playing cards in the basement of the church's recreation hall and someone must have brought a bottle.

"What do you want? What are you looking for?" Anna asked as Steve continued to ransack the closet.

"I know you keep it in here. I have seen you with the jar. Where is it?"

"Where is what? She asked even though she knew.

"Where is that damned jar with your change money? I need some money. I'm going back out and I am broke.

"Where are you keeping that jar?

"There isn't any. There isn't any jar."

"You're lying to me. I've seen you come to the closet and put money away. Damn you Anna, where is it?"

In frustration, Steve's temper flared as he grabbed a Mason jar filled with whole wheat and threw it against the floor. It shattered into hundreds of shards and wheat was everywhere. With the wheat was about five dollars of halves and quarters.

Steve immediately spotted it. He went down on his knees, picked the change from the wheat and glass, stood up, brushed himself off and then made for the door.

"Don't go!" Anna yelled. "Steve, don't go!"

He slammed the door and Anna heard his footsteps disappear down the two flights of stairs onto Clinton Street.

Anna sat at the kitchen table. For a few moments, she fought her emotions. Then, like a dam giving way, tears began to swell in her eyes and she began to sob. She suddenly realized that there was a side to her husband she had never quite seen before. She may have suspected it, but only now was it beginning to come out.

Suddenly, the door opened. At first she expected, hoped it might be Steve. It was one of the women boarders.

"What happened here?" she asked as she saw the mess on the floor." What was broken?

"My heart," was all Anna could say.

One Friday, early in December, Anna felt labor pains though the baby wasn't due for another two or three weeks. Again, Steve wasn't home. She became frantic near midnight and asked one of the women boarders to go look for him and tell him she thought she might have to go to the hospital.

He arrived so drunk that he had trouble standing up. Anna lit into him with a tirade that fell upon deaf ears as he passed out on the bed. The two boarding women took her to the hospital but returned within an hour. The pains were false, probably the result of something strenuous she did that day. However, the next morning Anna resumed her condemnation of his drinking and staying out. She did scare him and he agreed to quit drinking. He was home every day within an hour after work ended.

Anna sensed that time was revealing an aspect of her husband's character that she had not known. Maybe even he did not know it. Maybe it was the stress of hard times that was affecting him, she thought. While drinking, he began to develop an explosive temper that often frightened her. However, these characteristics seemed to disappear once he was "on the wagon"…a popular term that seemed invented for the Depression of the 1930s. Some individuals do change character after too much alcohol; some for the better, but most for the worst as their inhibitions break down. Unfortunately, from comments made later in life, my mother must have begun to reason that her husband belonged to the latter group.

Alcohol abuse was not unique to Steve Karas. Hardly a family existed in The Ward that wasn't affected by it. It was a sign of the times in the early 30s, a way to temporarily escape the worsening financial crisis in many families as factories continued to close and the unemployed labor force grew at a frightening rate. Binghamton, because it was a highly-industrialized city, seemed to be harder hit than other communities in the state. There was hardly a family untouched by the Depression and alcoholism now seemed more common among the immigrants and their now adult children. And, immigrants now constituted a large part of Binghamton's population.

Alcohol use had played a large role in the lives of the first immigrants who flooded the mills and the mines in the years 1890 to 1920. To many, it was their only relief to days on end of work, days 12 hours or more long. While its use was not excusable it was understandable. But the abuse of alcohol in the 30s had a different orientation among immigrants, especially Slavs. Maybe it was a backlash response to Prohibition. Because it was denied to them, maybe it was something they wanted to experience, that they needed, that was a requirement to truly becoming an American. After all, drinking was everywhere fashionable except among the prohibitionists, but it was the extent to which it was indulged among many of the Hunkies that made it devastating to the individual as well as their families.

During this period, drunken scenes were everywhere to be found in the First Ward and other wards in Binghamton, and other wards in all cities where a depressed people lived. While Prohibition ended in 1933, the Depression didn't. There wasn't a block along Clinton Street that didn't have a saloon after Prohibition died.

Just before "American" Christmas on St. Nicholas's saint's day, I was born. It was traditional among Rusnaks that a child born on a saint's day brought with it its own name, that of the saint. That was December 19th. I was the fourth child to be born in the third generation of Najda Rusnaks.

My mother's sister Mary already had three, a daughter and two sons. They occupied a small house behind the Clinton Street apartment where my mother and grandmother lived. My mother's mother, father and her brothers and sisters lived in the second floor apartment below her while the Salabajs, Kateryna's cousins, occupied the second floor flat in the apartment next to them. It was almost as if we lived in a close-knit village back in the Old Country.

For the year following their son's birth, life was again almost as happy for them as it had been just after they were married. Steve didn't return to the Friday night drinking bouts with his friends but he did overdo it at weddings and christenings. Two years later, in September, Anna gave birth to a daughter they named Anne.

Prohibition ended in April, in 1933 and Clinton Street suddenly came alive with bars, saloons, or "beer joints" as most of their First Ward customers called them and the notorious pool halls. The speakeasy in the back of the Elm Hotel moved its entrance to the front and its double doors were seldom closed.

One of Steve's close friends Frank Muha and his brothers, all from Vilag, who had bootlegged whiskey from Canada during Prohibition, and made gin in their bathtubs, opened a bar, the Sportsman's Bar, on Clinton Street. It was almost across from St. Michael's Church. On many Saturday afternoons, Steve and his friends would play cards in the Sportman's Bar until supper.

One of the attractions was the radio that seemed to always been on. Radios were rare at that time in The Ward, and very few homes had them. And though Steve and Anna had bought one soon after they were married, he now seemed to prefer to listen to one at the bar rather than at home. When Anna asked him why, he said that the reception there was better.

Radios were a standard part of every bar, much like television sets are today. Crowds in the bars, composed mostly of men, were especially large when fights were being broadcast, and especially so when Jack Sharkey was fighting. There was also a pool table in the back of the place but the cushions were so hard and warped, and the cloth so stained from spilled beer, that no one who played seriously would bother to cue the balls.

It was usually the loud church bells, announcing vespers, that announced their last drink before most family men went home to supper.

Chapter 49   The Beginning of The End

It was the first anniversary of the repeal of Prohibition that, in 1934, sparked a number of celebrations along Clinton Street. It was almost as if there was a big New Year's party, but in April. The Sportsman's Bar was not to be outdone and had even cut its prices in half for the event and advertised its free bar foods.

Steve tried to get Anna to go to the bar that night but she refused. She began to loathe his friends, feeling they were coming between her and her husband. She didn't like bars to begin with, even after they were married she only tolerated them because Steve was so insistent that they go out nights.

"How can I go?" she asked him. "How can I leave Anne? She is just six months old. I cannot leave her with someone."

"Then I will go by myself. All our friends will be there," he said.

"You mean all your friends will be there. I don't like Frank. I would never trust him. He is not your real friend. You think he is, just because you knew him in Europe. There are snakes in Europe just like there are snakes here. But, you cannot tell the difference. If you come home drunk I will go out the back door with the kids. You will never see us again!"

Steve slammed the door as he left.

He stopped first for a drink at Durkot's Bar & Grill. Mike Durkot had made bathtub gin throughout the Depression. When it was over, he had accumulated enough money to buy the building where my parents and relatives lived and opened the beer joint on the street floor.

It was past ten in the evening when he reached the Sportsman's Bar. It was filled with people, mostly men. Stagnant cigar and cigarette smoke filled the air even though the door was jammed open. A large floor fan in the back of the room hardly moved the air. It seemed everyone was talking, talking loudly, almost shouting. The half-price drinks were having their affect. A jukebox blared above the din and added to the confusion.

Frank Muha, a big man for a Rusnak, was behind the bar with two of his brothers. It took him a few minutes before he saw Steve. He came to the edge of the bar and reached over to shake Steve's hand. It was a big paw, appropriate for a big man. He stood 6-1/2 feet and easily weighed 250 pounds. The last 50 pounds were his belly that was especially fond of beer. His head was big, even unusually big for a big body. He was the kind of person you didn't want as an enemy.

"Steve," he said as he pulled him closer to the bar, "there's someone here I want you to meet. Come down to the other end." Steve made his way there as Frank passed behind his brothers.

Sitting at the end of the bar was a man about 35 years old. He was hunkered over a glass of beer and was twirling a cigar in his right hand. Steve couldn't quite see his face but there was something familiar about him. It may have been the way he was dressed. His clothes caught Steve's immediate attention. It was definitely a European cut and the lack of sideburns in the man's haircut revealed that it had been done in Europe.

"Recognize this guy?" Frank asked Steve as he made it to the end of the bar.

The man turned to Steve and looked at him. He stared at Steven and then a slight grin spread over the man's thin lips. His upper lip was almost hidden by a large mustache with handlebars. It immediately reminded Steve of the mustache his father used to have.

"Hello Stefan," the man said as he dropped his cigar in the ashtray and extended his hand.

At first, Steve didn't recognize him though he did looked familiar. Steve automatically shook the man's hand and peered into his eyes. They were as blue as his. His hand felt rough. He was a farmer, Steve thought to himself.

"You don't recognize me, do you?" he asked. "Though maybe you shouldn't. I never saw you that much. My brother and I were working in Budapest while you courted our sister. But you have even forgotten her, too. I hear you have found someone here, another Rusnak girl.

"I am Yurko Hruschenko. I was hoping to become your brother-in-law some day but my cousins here tell me you are now married and have two children. Is that true?"

"Who are your cousins?" Steve asked.

"All three bartenders. But I guess Frank never told you of his relatives in Zvala. Let's see, it has been five, maybe six years since you left Natasha. She has waited for you all this time to come back and marry her. Then his voice and attitude changed abruptly. The game he was playing with Steve suddenly ended,

"You son-of-a-bitch," Yurko yelled. It caused two men and a woman near them to turn to see what was the matter.

"You bastard. You said you would come back and get her. You were supposed to send her money to come and join you," he said. "You never wrote once. She was sick after you left. She was sick for months. She had your baby. A boy. Luckily for him he was stillborn."

"I never knew she was pregnant. She never told me," Steve said.

"How could she? She didn't know until you left," Yurko said as he raised his voice.

"I never touched her," Steve said. "I asked her to marry me. I said we could go to Humenné and get married but she refused. She said she would not leave her mother, that she depended upon her too much. I could never understand the strong bond between them though I believe she secretly hated her mother."

"You're lying. You're full of shit," Hruschenko said.

"I was puzzled by her behavior the day I left. She seemed cold to me, to be elsewhere, to be concerned about something else."

"You're lying, you bastard. I know why you were in such a hurry to leave. The Czech military police were at our house a week after you left. They were looking for you. They said you deserted the army."

"I won't deny that," Steve said. "I was in a fight with my superior officer. I thought I might have killed him or hurt him badly.

"But I didn't make your sister pregnant. I never fucked her. Now that I think of it, she acted differently toward me the last few times I visited her on passes. There must have been someone else, that's why she wouldn't marry me or go with me to America. She must have known she was pregnant. She knew I would know that I wasn't the father because I never fucked her. That's it. That was it all along."

Steve never saw it coming. Before he could react, Yurko's fist was in Steve's face and knocked him into the crowd. The people were so numerous behind him that he didn't fall to the floor but was caught by two men behind him. Yurko was about to come after Steve when Frank's big hand caught him by the shoulder and pulled him back.

He grabbed Yurko and pushed him into the back room. As he did, Frank caught the attention of one of his brothers, one who was almost as big, and told him to bring Karas to the back room. Frank opened the back door into the alley and pushed Yurko through the door. Frank's brother had Steve and together they shoved him into the alley.

"Finish this outside," Frank's brother said to him in a low voice. The crowd was so noisy that no one would have heard him even without the precaution. Frank still held Steve as Yurko landed another blow on Steve's jaw and then followed it up with two to the stomach. Frank let Steve fall on the brick path in the alley. As he did, he kicked Steve in the lower back. Steve lay there, semi-conscious, groaning and clasping his belly. Yurko was behind him and kicked him twice in the small of his back. Frank looked at Steve squirming on the bricks and then added another kick to the back where the kidney was located.

"Blood is always thicker than friendship," Frank said. "You know, Steve, I never really did like you. Your family always thought they were better than ours. You're not a big man here."

An hour later, Frank went back to the alley and Steve was still lying there, moaning but not dead.

"I think we better take him to the hospital," he said to his brothers. They drove their car around back, stuffed him into it, and then dropped him off at the emergency entrance. They told the attendant that they didn't know him, that he was drunk and must have been hit by a car crossing Clinton Street.

A doctor and nurse in the Emergency Room treated the scrapes on his face and nose and bandaged his head but kept him there for observation. The next morning, Steve took a cab home. Anna was flabbergasted when she saw him standing at the door.

"My God, Steve, what has happened to you?" she screamed.

"I was drinking last night and I guess I was crossing the street when a car hit me. I have been in the hospital until now."

Steve spent the next week in bed, recovering and felt he was good enough to return to work. His eyes were no longer swollen and his nose returned to normal. His job required that he stand at a machine while stitching shoes. By mid-afternoon, his lower back was engulfed in an excruciating pain. He stopped work and went to the factory's nurse's office. A nurse examined him and said he should immediately go the factory clinic. He had trouble urinating and was passing blood.

"Mr. Karas, your kidneys have been damaged," said a clinic doctor. I don't know how extensive. I'm sending you to City Hospital where they have more equipment. He was admitted and stayed there for three weeks. Through medication, his condition improved and he was released. However, he had to return once a week for continued monitoring. During the next three months, his condition seemed to improve and he even was talking about going back to work. The doctors forbade it.

The change was slow at first and urination again became difficult. The hospital began a weekly dialysis program. He felt fine immediately after each procedure but grew weaker and the pain increased daily as urine accumulated until the next visit. By mid-October, he grew so weak that he couldn't make the clinic visits and a doctor would visit him and do what he could.

The following is based on Anna Karas's description of events.

His son watched intently as Dr. Davis examined Steve Karas. The next day Nicholas had gathered together a few wooden clothespins and a small hose with an attachment that would fit on the nozzle of the spigot on the sink. His mother used it to fill hot water in the mobile wash tub and kept it under the sink when not in use. Nicholas retrieved it and wrapped it once around the back of his neck. He had the clothespins in his father's lunch bucket and found several Popsicle sticks he had been saving. Ten of them would get you a free Popsicle from LaTory's Ice Cream Store.

His mother had been in his father's bedroom, but left to get him water when the youngster, now nearly three years old, stopped in the doorway and knocked.

His father saw him standing there with the lunch pail in one hand and the filler tube draped behind his neck.

"Who is it," he said.

"This is Dr. Davis. I've come to see how you are today."

"Come in doctor," his father said, playing the game his son had initiated.

"How are you today, Steve?" he asked.

"I feel a little better," he said, "but I still have a pain in my side, here."

"Maybe I better take a look at it," Nicholas said and jumped onto the bed, next to his father.

He put the funnel end of the filler hose against his father's stomach and the other part near his ear. He listened for a while then pronounced. "I don't hear anything. You must be better." He climbed closer to his father and pulled one of the Popsicle sticks from the lunch bucket.

"Let me check your throat. Open your mouth," the boy ordered.

He pushed the tongue down with the stick and then appeared to be looking into his mouth.

"Say ahhh."

His father did so.

"It looks pretty good to me. Have you been taking your medicines?

"Good. I'll be back in a few days to see you again."

The boy gathered his instruments, jumped off the bed and then said good-bye.

As he ran into the other room Nicholas began laughing and yelling. "Mommy! Mommy! I fooled him. I fooled my daddy. He thinks I was Dr. Davis." Or, so I have been told.

Steve looked at Anna as she entered the bedroom. His eyes began to fill with tears. Anna took his hand and just then the baby began to cry.

"I must go and see what the trouble is," she said and tried to leave her husband's side but he held onto her hand. She really didn't have to. The baby was all right. She found it difficult, unnerving to watch him cry. Anna knew what was happening.

"Who knows," he finally brought himself around to speaking. "Maybe someday he will be a doctor. Anything is possible here. It is not like the Old Country."

Anna didn't answer but broke free and left.

Steve bit his lip as she left the room but didn't utter a sound.

"Steve, the doctor told him on the next visit." I guess you know what is happening.

"I'm dying," he said

"I wish we had the technology to give you two new kidneys, or at least one," said Davis. "I know that someday we will be able to do that. But for now, there isn't much we can do...except ease your pain."

"How long do I have to live?

"Two, maybe three weeks."

ditto

"Anna," Steve said to her as she sat on the edge of his bed after the doctor left. "I know I don't have long to live. I am sorry to leave you this way, with two children and no money. These are not good times. There is little money around. I know I drank too much and wasted our money on good times. It is too late to make amends.

"But you are close to your family. They will help you get through the days ahead. You are a strong-willed person. I wish I had been as strong as you, maybe things like this would not have happened. But, it is too late now.

"I wish my family had been closer. My brother Andrew must know that I am sick, dying, and he hasn't come to see me. We did not part on good terms. Maybe that is why. Maybe he is holding a grudge. I have another brother and sister in Europe. And my mother is still alive. Somehow, will you tell them what has happened to me? Tell my brother. I think he sends them money once in a while. He will tell them.

"I know that I have not been as good a husband or a father as I should have been. But it is too late to make things different. All I can leave you is my love. And, I love my son and daughter."

Steve's health began a rapid decline. He could no longer get out of bed to go to the toilet and had difficulty with the portable urinal. It was one evening during the first week of November that he called to her. She came, as she now so often had done, and sat on his bedside.

"Anna, I think it is time I go to the hospital," he said. "Call an ambulance. But first there is something I must say to you. I have been thinking of it these past few days. You are too young not to marry again. I think you should. But please, make sure the man loves you and loves my children. I worry for their future, a future that I should have had a hand in creating. My father and mother knew the value of being educated and passed it on to me. I cannot pass it on to my children because I have thought too much of my own needs. I figured that there was always time to worry about the children. Who could have known that this would happen? But you can. You are smart. Make sure they stay in school. School is what will separate them from others. It will give them the choice as to what they want to be in this world. You, nor I, really had choices.

"Now, call the ambulance. I don't want to die here...where they can see me."

Three days later, shortly after midnight on November 6, 1934, Stefan Andrijovich Karas died in his sleep. He was 32 years old. As was tradition then, his casket lay in their home for three days. On the last day Father Adelbert Bihary was there and gave the sermon. Then, six pallbearers, Bill Subik, Charles Sauger, Michael Woznic, George Spak, John Susko and John Nicholasko deftly managed to carry their heavy burden down two flights of narrow stairs to the waiting hearse.

The weather set the mood for his burial.

A light rain, mixed with large snowflakes, fell on two dozen people dressed in black who surrounded the casket that was supported above the grave. The site was at the bottom of the hill filled with other graves and markers on the lower edge of St. Michael's Cemetery. A small stream trickled noisily in a wooded ravine below the cemetery as the priest chanted over the casket. Anna sobbed intermittently and clung to her mother and was embraced by her sister Mary. Vasyl Najda, on the edge of the open grave, held his grandson Nicholas's hand.

"Djido, why are they putting my daddy into the ground?" he asked him.

"It is the way of life," he quietly answered. "We are born, we live and then we die. The body is placed in the ground, but the spirit, the soul, has already left the body. It is in Heaven with God."

"But I don't understand that," the boy said.

"Neither did I. Fifty years ago, I, too, watched my father being buried. It seems it was just the same kind of day, the same kind of place. I have been here before. You may not understand it now but you will as you get older."

Nicholas, with tears in his eyes, broke away and ran to his mother and clung to her coat.

The funeral director watched the priest. The moment Father Bihary finished, the director came to Anna and said, "It is time to lower the casket."

She nodded.

In a fleeting moment, Nicholas saw the funeral director tell the pallbearers to begin lowering the casket. He released his grip on his mother's coat and took three steps to the man and kicked him in the shin. The director was taken back for a moment.

"Why are you doing this to my daddy? Why are you putting him in the ground."

"I'm sorry, Sonny," the director said. "I know how this must seem to you. But I must do it."

A week later, Anna was at the kitchen table figuring out the cost of the funeral and what remained for her and her children to live on. Into three separate envelopes she placed what little cash she had and what the people at the wake had given her. The cemetery lot cost $36. Into another envelope she placed $440 for the funeral home. She had a mere $20 left.

That will not go far, she thought to herself.

Anne is now more than a year old. It is time for me to go back to work. I can leave her and Nickey with the Salabajs, or one of the girls boarding with me can watch them at other times.

Two young women still boarded with her and that was some income. If she could get her job back she could afford to pay her relatives something for babysitting. She wouldn't think of having them do it for nothing. A few days ago, Steve's foreman from EJs stopped by to see her. He said that they would find a place for her to work if she wanted that. She thought about it for a moment and thanked him. She said she would call him later.

These and other thoughts spun around in her head when she heard a heavy knock on the door.

"Yes," she said as she opened it and saw two men standing in front of her. "What do you want?"

"Are you Anna Karas?" the slightly shorter, younger man asked.

For a moment he looked vaguely familiar, then Anna quickly dismissed the thought. She had never seen him before, nor the other man.

"Yes.

"I am Andrew Karas, Steve's brother. This is Sam Evans, his uncle. We are from Ambridge.

"We only just heard of Steve's death," Andrew said. "I am sorry."

"Come in. Sit down," Anna said. "Can I get you anything?" Anne began to cry and she went to the bedroom and got her, holding her in her arms as they spoke.

The next few minutes were passed in obligatory chatter. Andrew seemed especially nervous as he spoke. He hesitated at his words, words that seemed to be pulled out almost one at a time.

"What do you want?" Anna finally broke the ice.

"We have been out of work for the past three months. The Depression has forced our plant to close. If it weren't for that, we would not have come here. We are broke. I have four children and a wife and there is no money coming in."

"That is sad," Anna said. "We are all in the same boat. But what can I do?"

"We made it possible for Steve to come here from Europe," Evans said. He was much older than her brother-in-law. Probably closer to her father's age.

"We bought him a ship ticket and sent it to him," added Andrew. "He was supposed to pay us back after he got a job here. It was $400."

"Did he?" Anna asked.

"No," they said almost in unison.

"Well, what do you want me to do?"

"We thought that maybe he had insurance and that you could pay us the money," Andrew said.

Anna thought about what he had said. Time seemed to pass ever so slowly as all this raced through her mind. It was no more than a minute or two and the silence began to affect the two men. They stirred restlessly in their seats.

Suddenly, Anna screamed out: "What kind of people are you? No wonder he never talked about you or went to see you.

"Do you know what it costs to bury someone?

"It cost me $440 for the funeral and $36 for the grave.

"He saved no money. He drank up his pay every Friday. He had no insurance.

"I have no job. Do you think the Depression is easier on me than on you?

"All he left me with are a bunch of bills and two children.

"Here, you want something of his. Take this baby," she said and offered Anne to Andrew, then Sam.

"I am sorry. Maybe we should not have come," Andrew said as they got up to leave.

"Yes, you should not have come," Anna echoed what he said as she slammed the door behind them. That was the last contact, the last Karas she would ever see or hear about.

The door had hardly been closed behind Andrew Karas and Sam Evans when Anna's son came into the kitchen.

"Who were those men, Mommy?" he asked.

"I really don't know," she answered without thinking. "I thought they were relatives but I guess they were not.

"It's getting late. Go take a bath while I put your sister to bed. Can you draw the water without me?"

"I'm a big boy. I can do that. I'm the man of the house now that Daddy is gone." It wasn't his idea. Someone had told him that.

Anna changed her daughter's diaper in the kitchen as she watched the water begin to heat up in the pot that contained Anne's bottle. She rushed over, turned it off before it go too warm and set it on the table next to her baby.

After a minute, she tested it. It seemed all right o her. She bundled up her six-month old and carried her to the crib in the bedroom where Nicholas also had a bed.

She stepped into the bathroom just as he was about to enter the tub.

"Did you try the water first?

She didn't wait for an answer but knelt down before the tub and pushed the water aside with her hand.

"It's too cold. Wait a minute."

Anna turned on the hot water and let it run into the tub as she pushed the water in a large circle to mix it with the cold. For a fleeting moment she was mesmerized, caught up in the slowly circling water. Her mind had drifted to a time when she, Steve and Nicholas, when he was just a year old, swam in the river on a hot August day. It was a riverside picnic and a few of her friends were there. It was a good time in their lives, she thought to herself. Suddenly, the water on her hand felt warm and reality rushed back at her. He was gone. There would be no more summer picnics, no more trips to the huge elms that bordered the river's banks.

When she was satisfied the tub water was warm enough she shut off the hot water and for a second ran the cold water to cool off the faucet.

"It's okay now," she said as she helped the three-year-old over the edge of the tub. The water level just capped his knees as he sat in the tub.

"I'm going into the front room. If you need anything call me."

She left the bathroom door ajar and went into the parlor. She felt an overpowering need to have time to herself; to put into perspective the recent event.

Most of the parlor furniture was still in the dining room. It was moved there to make room for the coffin. There was a chair near one of three large, double-hung, single-paned windows. She sat in it and aimlessly stared out the large window. The sun was just a few minutes from setting and its warmth still filled the room and illuminated the opposite walls. It caught the glass on a photo portrait that hung on the wall. It was of her husband. Anna had it made for his birthday in March. She stared at the photograph and tears began to form in the corners of her eyes. In minutes her eyes were flooded and she buried her face in her hands and sobbed uncontrollably.

The forlorn whistle of a train eased her back to reality. She looked out the closed window wiping her tears on an apron.

The view from the third storey apartment was always fascinating. It was the third-storey height that put the city in a different perspective for her. The view engulfed a great length of Clinton Street but was marred by a confusion of utility poles and wires. Below, people were moving about. It was a Friday night and Clinton Street, especially where the bars are located, is always busy.

She looked to her left and could see the Chenango River and where the railroad bridge crossed. The train station was just on the other side and trains entering the station always blew their whistles as they approached.

Suddenly the locomotive was exposed across the street as it passed between houses and a coal yard. It was a freight train and wasn't going to stop even though it slowed. It was long and heavy and the rumbling train shook the ground. She could feel its vibration even on the third floor of her apartment. It rattled the glasses in the kitchen cupboard. She wondered how people could live in the houses that were just a few feet from the tracks.

"Damn you Steve," she suddenly blurted. "Why did you do this to yourself? Why did you do this to me? Why, to the children?"

She began crying again, weeping more softly than before when her son suddenly appeared in the doorway wrapped in a large towel.

"Mommy, why are you crying?

"Is it because Daddy went to heaven?"

Anna ran to him, dropped to her knees and hugged him.

"Nickey, Nickey, Nickey, what are we going to do? How are we going to live? We have nothing."

She hugged him for a moment, rocking slowly back and forth with her head buried in the towel.

"That's not true," she said after a few moments on thinking. "We have each other. We have you and Annabelle and together we will find a way. God will see us through this terrible time in our lives."

Anna Karas now faced the greatest challenge of her short life. She had just turned 26, was the mother of two young children, saddled with the debts of burying her husband of just four years, without a job and in the height of a nationwide depression that offered no hope of an immediate end.

"I have my health," she said to herself that night as she tried to sleep...occasionally breaking into periods of sobbing. "My children are healthy and that counts. With God's help, we will see this through."

Though the offer from EJ's was especially generous in light of the scarcity of jobs at that time, Anna preferred to work at Dunn's because that is where all her friends worked. The employment office at Dunn's recognized her plight. She had developed a reputation as a good if not excellent worker before she quit to have her children. They were even able to make room for her in her old job, that of staining the bottoms of shoes. Like the other workers, they could only offer four days of work a week, but that didn't bother Anna when she was told. She was well aware of their Depression policy. It was still piecework and she could move as many shoes in four days as most other workers did in five.

I will have to be careful, however, she said to herself as she walked home from the factory. I cannot put in too many coupons for the racks of shoes I have finished or they will cut down on the price per shoe I am paid.

For the next five years, she played a game with the accounting department....turning in just enough coupons when work was slow so that each Friday she had a good, full pay envelope but not showing too much more than the others were making. Her foreman knew how she was working it, but he didn't mind. It made him look good as well.

Anna was still a young, beautiful woman. She was thin, outgoing, well-spoken and well-liked by everyone. It was only natural that suitors would begin arriving at her door. Several were men from the Old Country who were looking only for someone to create a home for them. She was well-versed in Old Country ways even though she had been born in America, and a generation after them. She had grown up among them in Goodtown. These men and their ways were not for her. They were not her ways. She now was truly uncaged, an emancipated woman.

After the hardship of the first few months, she found she was able to make ends meet without too much trouble if she watched her expenses. It gave her a sense of independence few women at that time enjoyed. She was not about to marry someone just to make his meals, do his washing and warm his bed at night. She had been down that road once and it had not been entirely pleasant.

Part III The Totally American Hunkies

Chapter 50   Growing Up On the Farm

After my father's death, almost every summer until I was a teenager, my mother took my sister and me to my grandparent's farm. For the first two weeks in early July, the entire factory was shut down. We looked forward almost as much to the train ride as we did to the life on the farm. We took it only to Johnstown because that was as close as passenger travel was possible to Berlin. In later years, when we were older, we were left on the farm until September, when school began for us.

I was small for my age and a rather healthy youngster, but at the ages of six and seven, each winter I would have a bout with bronchitis. Each year it got progressively worse and I was ill for longer periods of time. Finally, our family doctor suggested that maybe life in The Ward, in a highly industrial city like Binghamton, was not the healthiest place in which to grow up. This was during an era in America when tuberculosis was rampant. To combat it, New York State even established a public sanitarium in the Adirondacks where victims of the pulmonary disease could recuperate. He and many other physicians at that time believed that good, clean country or mountain air was the panacea for many of our ills. He suggested a year or two for me on the family farm.

While it was a traumatic move for my mother to part with her two children, she did it unhesitatingly. I can still vividly recall the parting scene. It is one experience I never want to duplicate. Life on the farm, however, became a unique experience for my sister Anne and me. I can now look back in that period of my life and see how it did a lot in shaping my future thinking and values.

That first summer was an adjustment to a new family atmosphere. It was one in which everyone, except my sister, was my boss. Immediately, there was my grandfather (*Djido*) my grandmother (*Baba*), my uncles Andy and Mike, and my aunts Martha, Rose Ann and Stella. Strangely, we were not treated so much as grandchildren or nephew and niece, but more as a continuation of one family, as being my grandparent's children following my youngest aunt, Aunt Stella. Maybe it was because she was only 4 years older than I that we were immediately integrated into the family.

We were also surrounded by an extended family. On the far side of a large field in front of the farmhouse, was my Uncle Sam's house and farm. His wife Mary, my mother's older sister, had three children, my cousins Sam, Anna and John. John was the youngest, two years older than I was. He became my closest friend. In a way, my Aunt Mary became my surrogate mother, when she had time.

In Macdonaldton, just outside Berlin, lived my Uncle Charley, a.k.a., Wasco, my mother's oldest brother, his wife Mary and my cousins Rose Ann and Phillip. We seldom saw my great uncle (Harry) Hryc's wife or his family after he died. For some reason they grew apart from the rest of us. I didn't know it at the time but they must have felt embarrassed by his suicide. There was no reason to feel such guilt. He was a victim of the mines, the times, and his own personal idiosyncrasies. The only true Hunkies in our extended family were my great uncle John, my grandfather's oldest brother, whom we all knew only as *Stritchko* (uncle) and Mike Antonishak, who was related to both my grandparents.

The family was so tightly knit that we could have been living in a village in the Carpathian highlands just as well as on a bucolic farm in southwestern Pennsylvania. I often asked my grandfather what the land was like where he grew up. He always answered, "Just like here, except maybe the hills are a bit taller, and in the background there was always the higher mountains." Life on the farm reflected the same closeness my relatives must have known in Europe. Whenever it began to fall short there were always holiday family get togethers to rejuvenate that unique, indescribable feeling of this sanguine unity, of the kinsmanship that only close relatives can evoke. Today, it is a rare experience among Americans.

I'm not claiming that bonds in Rusnak families are any greater or closer than in other families, but it did seem that way when I was growing up. Maybe it was because the shadows of their immigrant status were not that far behind and caused them to be more family-oriented that others I knew. Though unspoken, I could always sense its strength and existence. It was always there.

There was another factor that made my experiences on the farm so much more fulfilling, one that other first and second generation decendants of Slavic immigrants might never have had the chance to feel or experience. Through the numerous summer-long visits, the two or so years of living there, and the numerous short visits thereafter, I was able to become intimately familiar with the way my grandparents lived. Because it was a farm environment, I was able to experience their manner of living, which was no different from the way they lived or would have lived in Europe, as farmers, almost peasant farmers. Their methods of farming were strictly European because that was all my grandparents knew. I also sensed a difference between their farm and other farms about us when I visited neighbors. Most of my grandparent's farming was primitive in comparison. Some of this may have been caused by the lack of real income but I believe the real factor was their farming or peasant ethics and methods. It was done by hand while the more progressive American farmers around us were using more machinery and modern equipment as well as methods.

Other decendents of these Hunkies knew their parents and grandparents, who, too, had been farmers in Europe, but in America they knew them only as laborers who thrived in the artificial environment created in mill cities and mining town ghettos. My experience with my grandparents was so much broader.

My grandparents seldom spoke in English unless forced to. My grandfather understood more English than my grandmother. Most of the time, they spoke to me in Rusnak and I quickly leaned their language. It was not sophisticated and was the common language of peasants. When they talked to my five aunts and uncles, with whom my sister and I lived, it was often a combination of languages. They were always trying to help my grandparents expand their knowledge of English. I do remember their sense of embarrassment when an outsider would come to the house or they were shopping in nearby Meyersdale or Berlin and couldn't make themselves understood. One of my aunts was usually there to intervene.

I also recall, at these times, how understanding the locals were toward my grandparents, both the farmers around us and the merchants in town. Maybe it was because most of them were second and third generation descendents of German immigrants who still sensed that their roots extended to Europe. It may have occurred, but I never saw anyone exhibit any animosity toward the Najdas because they were foreign-born and couldn't speak the language.

But I do remember that when my grandparents spoke to my mother and Aunt Mary, it was almost always in Rusnak. I may contradict myself here, but it seems odd to me now, that I cannot remember exactly whether they spoke to me in their native tongue or in English. At first, I believe it was only in Rusnak. But later, I think it was in both languages. I had perfectly assimilated their language and spoke it without forethought.

My grandmother seemed especially fond of me in comparison to her other grandchildren. Maybe it is only because of my perspective that I sensed and believed this. But every once in a while, for no apparent reason, she would grab me, almost violently, hug me, and kiss me profusely. Passion is not a monopoly of the Latins. I think she may have felt sorry for me, that I was growing up without a father and she couldn't overcome her emotions. When we were alone, she would occasionally speak fondly of my father. My grandfather never mentioned him.

I can easily remember how embarrassed I felt at times when she hugged me in front of my aunts and uncles. She'd press me tightly against her ample bosom. She was just 5 feet tall and I was short for my age when I was young. I was no taller than her shoulders. At times I felt smothered.

Maybe I wasn't as unique to her as I led myself to believe. Maybe, in a way, she had the uncanny ability to make each one of her grandchildren feel that they were special, that we were her favorite at that moment. I did sense that she loved my sister Anne just as much. My grandmother was a cleaver person and had more control over events in the household than any of us were aware.

One of my chores was to keep the pail beside the stove full of coal. However, I always seemed to need to be reminded of my obligation. It wasn't a difficult chore though I did have to struggle hauling a full pail. The coal shed was next to the privy, just 50 feet from the back door. One afternoon in late September, the stove had gone out and my grandfather tried to restart it but needed kindling. That was stored in the cellar of the house whose only entrance was from the outside, around the back, and on the downhill side of the house.

I happened to be in the kitchen when I got the order to get kindling. I loved my grandfather and would do anything he asked. He was usually stern and reticent and I like that. But was also niggardly with his emotions. I even forgave him for the times when he pulled me by the ears when I didn't listen. Or, when after making mistakes, I was forced to kneel on dried peas he had scattered on the floor before a lithograph of Christ and recite *Otech Nas*, Our Father, in Rusnak.

Following his order, I ran around the house and saw that the large basement door was open. It always was open to keep the cellar dry. I dashed inside and was startled when I saw my grandmother there. It was obvious that I surprised her. She quickly adjusted the apron that she seemed always to wear. I even once asked her if she wore it to bed and was surprised by a slap on the back of my head from my grandfather.

"*Nikolaj*," she yelled as she saw me. "What do you want here?

"*Djido* sent me to get some kindling so that you have a fire to make supper." I began gathering an armful of kindling as she went outside. As I tried to pass her but she grabbed and hugged me."

The small pile of wood fell from my arms as she smothered me.

As I stood in her clutches I suddenly smelled something burning. I looked down and saw smoke rising between us. I drew back. She let me go as she, too, saw it.

"You're on fire *Baba*. Your apron is burning."

She looked down and immediately thrust her hand in the pocket and pulled out a lighted corncob pipe. She had stowed it there when she heard someone approaching. She quickly put it out and then smiled.

"*Nikolaj, sinu mi.* (Nicholas, my son), let us keep this our secret. If you don't tell on me, I'll bake you a cake...a hickory-nut cake with maple icing...you're favorite. Okay?"

My lips have been sealed until now.

Chapter 51   Growing up in The Ward

Looking back at it now, I guess, that in a loose way, The Ward in the mid-1930s, and into the '40s was a kind of a Slavic ghetto but very unlike the Goodtown ghetto. As a youngster growing up in it, neither my contemporaries nor I ever considered it as such, even if we knew what the word meant. We were bound together primarily by our schools and the daily contacts we made with each other. They included Daniel S. Dickinson and Woodrow Wilson schools that began as kindergartens and ended in the 9th grade. There was also a Catholic school, St. Cyril & Methodius, to which some, but not all, or even a majority of our Slovak and a few Polish friends attended. It ended at the 8th grade. Students there then joined us for a year at our schools until we all attended Binghamton Central High School. BCHS was not a central school like those in rural areas, but was designated Central because it was in the center of the city. There was also another high school at the north end of Binghamton, appropriately call North High School.

   We were also bound together by the churches we attended. There was St. Cyril & Methodius Catholic Church, St. Michael's Greek Catholic Church, that really functioned as an independent Orthodox Church, Holy Spirit Church, whose congregation in 1940 broke away from St. Michael's and continued as an Uniate Church, and St. Mary's Russian Orthodox Church. It was the latter church which my mother's family attended while they lived in Binghamton because it was the same kind of church they attended in Goodtown. However, after my mother's marriage, they attended my father's church, St. Michael's.

We also had our neighborhood groups. I refuse to call them gangs because they should not be construed as such and had none of the characteristics that today identify gangs. The Goodtowners who moved to Binghamton after the mines petered out tended to live together in The Ward around lower Clinton Street.

Even though we all knew that our relatives had come from Europe we always considered ourselves Americans. There was never even the slightest thought that we were anything else. Though most of my contemporaries understood the languages of their parents seldom did we ever use in our everyday conversations. That always seemed strange to me. Most of my friends should have been more familiar with their languages than I because they were first generation Hunkies. I was second. We seldom used the word Hunky to describe ourselves and usually only in jest. After all, we really were descendents of Hunkies and could not meet the exact criteria for the title.

From time to time we experienced forays into the rest of the city and its people, especially when our sports teams would play other junior high school teams. The great melting pot outside The Ward was the Boy's Club. Within The Ward, it was the Boy Scouts. This all changed when we daily left The Ward to attend high school classes. We discovered that there were large numbers of second and third generation kids with Irish and German backgrounds and a large number of first generation Italian kids. There were also several Italian families mixed among the Rusnaks living on Lower Clinton Street and even their children mixed easily with the Slavic groups. There were even scattered among us elements of English, Welsh and Scot backgrounds whose ancestors had been here for so many generations that they covertly considered themselves, at that time, a bit more American than we.

I don't believe any of us considered ourselves discriminated against by people outside the First Ward. However, there was only one close friend who did, but he had no basis for it. It was his unique problem and didn't affect us. In all, growing up in The Ward was an enjoyable experience. There's no doubt that we may have been lower on the financial scale that most others outside The Ward, but that never impinged upon us because there were too many of us all in the same boat.

Chapter 52   War Looms in the Old Country

Letters from Europe came more often during the 1930s than when Vasyl and his brothers first immigrated to America 30 or so years earlier. One reason was that education among the Rusnaks in the Carpathian Mountains, in both Poland and Slovakia, was now more widespread than when their parents were of school age. Both governments began to feel a moral obligation to educate their entire population even though they were ethnically diverse. Their motivation now was that they were competing for their minds as well as their bodies. They wanted the loyalty of their downtrodden for political support rather than their bodies just for labor and profit. Another reason was that communication mechanisms like mail, often delivered by airplanes or fast ships, between Rusnaks in America and Europe also improved.

It was the children of these and other emigrants who often attended church schools where they learned to read and write in Cyrillic script, the alphabet of the Rusnaks. Mary and Anna Nider were able to read and write in their parents' native language. The young people in Europe wrote to their relatives in America and in return they now received letters in languages other than English. All this amazed Vasyl Najda who was always sensitive to the fact that he could neither read nor write his native tongue, let alone English. He never had time for school in America but he insisted that his children did, at least the males. Despite thus, he still believed that it was a waste of time to educate a woman.

Rumors of German aggression in Austria and Czechoslovakia began to fill the airwaves during the evenings around the kitchen table as everyone listened to the radio. The only radio they had on the farm was battery operated because rural electrification had not yet reached the farm. I remember, when my sister and I spent the summer of 1938 there, whenever the batteries died, my uncles and aunts all piled into an automobile to listen to news on the car's radio. When friends from Goodtown would visit the farm, the impending war was the topic of concern and conversation. One rumor that had merit and eventually was partially put into effect was the registration of all aliens in the United States. There were millions of people who had come into the country since 1880 who never bothered to become citizens. As war clouds began to form over Europe, some long-time Americans were concerned about the loyalties of these millions of people.

"When I first came here, in 1903, I was going to apply for citizenship," one night several years after the Binghamton venture, Vasyl told his family as his children were busy around the kitchen table doing homework. He had just purchased a new lamp that burned white gas and had a mantle that lighted the room so bright it was almost as good as daylight, or that's what the kids thought.

"Why didn't you? What happened?" asked Rose Ann who was 13 and in her first year at Berlin Brothersvalley High School.

"I wanted to and I could have," said her father. "I was young then, 24 or 25, and you can learn better then....better than when you are old, like me, now."

"Oh Pop," said Andy, "you're not old. How old are you?"

"Let's see," he said. "I was born in 1880 and this is 1937. That would make me....make me....."

"You're 57, Dad," Rose Ann quipped. "She had already scribbled the figures on paper and had the answer.

"Maybe Dad is right," she turned to her two brothers and two sisters, who were sharing the large, round kitchen table. "Maybe you are too old Dad, to learn on your own. But we can all help. We don't want you being shipped back to the Old Country. But why didn't you become a citizen."

"It was my own fault. I didn't follow through.

"Like I said, it was in 1904 and I had been here for just a couple months. One morning before we went into the mine, Billings, the foreman, read an announcement he found in the Berlin newspaper asking any foreigners who wanted to become citizens to take the test. But Turko, you know, Paul Turko, he was here a few months ahead of me...maybe a whole year. I can't remember exactly now," he digressed. "He said I couldn't take the test, that I would have to be in this country at least three years before I could apply for my first papers.

"He said I'd have to be able read the U.S. Constitution, or have parts of it read to me and understand what they mean because you would be asked a bunch of questions. And, I must be able to read and write, if not in English, then in Rusnak. And, I'd have to know who is president of the United States and...and the Governor of Pennsylvania, and how laws are made in Washington and in Pennsylvania.

"By the time I had been here three years, your mother and I were married and you sister Mary was on the way. I didn't have time to attend English School and if I did, I was too tired after a day in the ground. I never did but now I wish I had. I always wanted to become a citizen. Others came here just to make money and then go home. I came here to find a new life and now I look around me and I see my new life in your faces, in your eyes. I am an American, but maybe not a legal American. I believe it is more important that you be an American in your mind and heart, not in what you say."

"I have an idea," Rose Ann said. "Tomorrow I will tell you."

"Where is Dad?" Rose Ann asked her mother the next day as she ran into he kitchen. She had just gotten home after walking and running the half-mile from the bus shanty.

"He is in the field, behind the barn."

Rose Ann ran out with her mother hollering at her at the open door that she should change her clothes.

Her father had the horse's reins over his shoulder and was steadying the handles on the plow and was about to start a new, single furrow in the field behind the barn. He stopped the horse when he saw her running toward him. At first, he thought something was wrong.

"Dad, Dad, I have good news. I talked with the Social Studies teacher and she said that the laws have changed since 1904. You don't have to be able to read or write but you must be able to answer a bunch of civic questions. She said that she would get me sample copies of the questions and answers.

"No," Vasyl said, "I cannot do it."

"Don't you want to become a citizen...an American...or are they just words you are saying?"

"I do, but how can I learn these things?"

Rose Ann paused for a moment. She was a smart young girl and excelled in school.

"I have a deal to make with you. I will tutor you, teach you all you need to know to pass the citizenship test. But, in return, you must buy me something. I saw a beautiful silk dress in Groff's Department Store in Berlin. If you pass the test you must buy me that dress. Okay?"

The next week, on March 6th, Wasco drove his father and Rose Ann to the courthouse in Somerset. There, they filed their father's Declaration of Intention, the "first papers" as they were popularly known among immigrants. And, that same evening, they began to study. It was amazing to watch and listen to the 57-year-old miner/farmer study to be an American.

Rose Ann had taken a monumental task upon her fragile shoulders but she was persistent and her father adamant in learning. Through rote, repetition and sudden bursts of enlightenment he began to learn what America was all about. It went well beyond just a place in which to live and earn a living.

With school out in June, Rose Ann grabbed her father every evening when he wasn't too tired from working in the fields and studied with him. It was hard, slow work and she couldn't get to him as often as she wanted. And there were times when Vasyl, in frustration, would throw his arms in the air and said he quit. But a few days later, with Rose Ann cajoling him, their heads were back together again.

A year and a half passed before Rose Ann felt her father was ready to take the test. It wasn't until August 4, 1939, that the trio again visited the Clerk of the Court of Common Appeals in Somerset. That day, they filed the "second papers" with the court, the Petition for Naturalization.

"This isn't too soon," Wasco said as they left Somerset and drove home. "I just read in the newspaper that Hitler is massing troops in Eastern Germany and Czechoslovakia and is getting ready to invade Poland."

Two months passed before they got a letter from the Court. The date was November 15. Late that afternoon, a white male of medium complexion, with blue eyes and black hair, and weighing 130 pound at 5 feet 6 inches in height, raised his right hand and followed Clerk Amos S. Mock in saying:

"I hereby declare on oath, that I absolutely and entirely renounce and abjure all allegiances and fidelity to any king, prince, potentate, state, or sovereignty, and particularly to the Republic of Poland of which I have heretofore been a subject; that I will support and defend the Constitution of the United States of America against all enemies, foreign and domestic; that I will bear true faith and allegiance to the same and that I take this obligation freely without any mental reservation or purpose of evasion: SO HELP ME GOD. In acknowledgement whereof I have hereunto affixed my signature."

In a scrawling signature, in a hand that was truly unfamiliar with holding a pen, he wrote: "Wasco* Nider."**

* Many Slavs whose first name was Vasyl, Wasyl in Polish, assumed the Americanized version as Wasco.

** His last name was changed to Nider by his daughter Mary's First Grade schoolteacher. Though the change was never legalized it became his name and that of his descendents.

"That was strange," Vasyl said as he, his wife and several sons and daughters left the Clerk's office.

"What was strange?" asked Rose Ann.

"I was never a subject of the Polish King nor ever swore allegiance to him. When I came over, Galicia and Protisne were part of Austria.

"So be it."

"Oh father," Rose Ann said as they were approaching the outskirts of Berlin. "You didn't forget, did you? There is one stop we must make."

Wasco, Rose Ann's brother knew what was about to happen and he pulled up the car in front of Groff's Clothing and Department store. Only Rose Ann and her father went in and in a few minutes they returned.

"That was a real bargain," Rose Ann said to her father.

"What, the $1.98 I paid for the red, silk dress?"

"No, the year and a half of tutoring for less than $2. But, father, I would have done it for nothing.

"How do you feel?" she asked.

"I feel like I will be 60 years old in two months."

"No, that's not what I mean. You know. What does it feel like to be a real American?"

"No different than before," he said. "I told you, I have been a real American ever since the day I got off the boat."

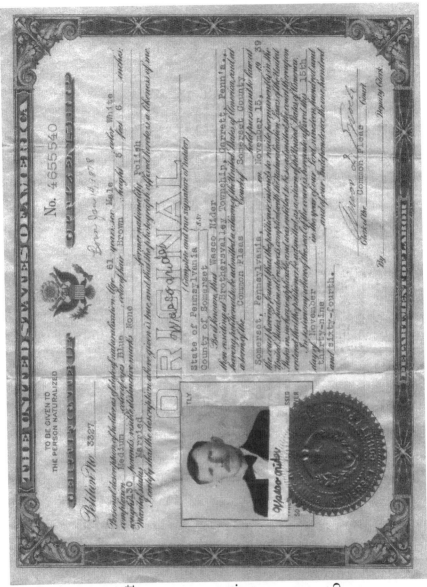

The hard-earned "Second Papers," the Citizenship Document awarded Vasyl Najda. His last name was changed by an elementary school teacher because she felt it was too difficult for his children to write. His first name Vasyl in Polish, is written as Wasyl and many other Rusnaks with that name saw it evolve in America to Wasylco or Wasilko and eventually Wasco.

Chapter 53   The War Years in Europe

After Hitler annexed Austria in March 1938, he began making territorial moves on contiguous areas of Czechoslovakia and Poland. The Allies urged the Czechs to cede these lands to appease him. They did but it didn't work. Immigrants in America became increasingly concerned about the fate of their relatives in Europe. A flood of letters, in both directions across the Atlantic, seemed to occur every time a new crisis arose. Just prior to the German invasion, Poles began a campaign of displacing Rusnaks in the southeast counties of the country. Hungary, in 1938, with Hitler's backing, regained several counties in extreme eastern Slovakia, actually the Carpathian-Rus Region, that possessed a dominant population of Rusnaks. To Rusnaks, it seemed the world was going backwards. It was!

Hitler and Stalin reached an agreement and signed the Molotov-Ribbentrop Non-aggression Treaty on August 23, 1939. It lasted until Hitler was ready to invade Russia in June 1941. Stalin signed it because he, too, needed time to build his forces. The Treaty reset the borders between the Soviet Union and Germany, again eliminating Poland, and based it on the Curzon Line proposed but not adopted after the end of WW I.

The Curzon Line was suggested as a demarcation between Poland and Soviet Ukraine-Russia. It was proposed during the Russo-Polish War of 1919–20 as a possible armistice line. British foreign secretary, Lord Curzon, made the suggestion to the Soviet government. Neither side accepted the Allied plan and the peace treaty (March 1921) gave Poland almost 52,000 square miles of land west of the Curzon Line and all of western Galicia. Stalin, in 1939, suddenly found it useful as a way of claiming more of western Ukraine. He and Hitler adopted it.

The Sian (*Shan*) River again became the border between the two factions. Germans occupied the lands south and west of the Sian and the Soviets the lands to the east and north. It had a devastating affect on villages along the Sian, especially my grandmother's village of Smil'nyk (Smolnik, Pol.). To exacerbate matters for the Rusnaks and Ukrainians, the Soviets immediately established an 800 meter wide (875-yard) no-man's land along their side. In this swath, for security reasons, they removed all structures of any kind and displaced the people who occupied this belt to areas in Soviet Ukraine. Except for the old church, they leveled the village of Smil'nyk. No one knew if the church Vasyl had worked upon had ever been finished. If it had, it, too, was leveled by the Soviets. However, the old church in Smil'nyk was left standing but was heavily damaged by the a-religious Bolsheviks. Fortunately for Protisne, for a while, most of that village was located on the German side of the river. Only those houses, most of which were built across the river, now on the Soviet side, from the village after WW I, were affected.

When Hitler moved into Bohemia in western Czechoslovakia, my father's youngest brother Ivan and many other young men in Vilag, who had earlier joined the Czech army as war clouds darkened, immediately went over in droves and joined the Soviets. The Germans so quickly overwhelmed the Czechs that they were at the Soviet Ukrainian border before the end of March in 1939. At first, the Germans came to the Rusnaks and Slovaks in the East as benevolent conquerors. But that didn't last long. The SS followed quickly on the heels of the army and took over political and economic control. They were looking for slave labor to work in German factories. As a result, many Rusnaks and Slovaks were shipped to Germany and never heard of again.

In Soviet Ukraine, some Rusnaks were given an option of where they were to be sent. Those who opted to go east, were settled around L'viv and as far south as Odessa. They were given jobs on farm collectives and, for a time until late in 1939, were able to move about in Soviet Ukraine.

Early in 1941, Jews and Gypsies began to disappear from the mountain villages on the Polish side of the Carpathian Mountains in German occupied Galicia. As the Germans completed building more concentration camps they turned their efforts southward and began activities in Slovakia and Hungary. Local people began hearing stories about death camps in Poland as rumors trickled south. They sounded so preposterous at first that no one believed them. "Even the German's couldn't be that cruel," they would say. But that, too, changed. In Vilag, a few young Jewish men and women began to disappear during the night. Some said they had gone over to the Russians to fight the Germans. That is partially true, but most knew where some of their neighbors were being sent.

One Sunday in Vilag, after services in the recently-finished Russian Orthodox Church, Father Vasyl Taschuck asked that the men and women in the congregation remain in church and that the young children be taken home by the older children.

The Orthodox Church was one of two Rusnak churches in Vilag and was relatively new. The older church, St. Dymitriy is a Greek Catholic or Uniate Church of the Byzantine Rite. It dated as far back as 1494 and began as a Rus-Orthodox Church. It and its congregation were converted to a Greek Catholic Church in 1597 as a result of the Union of Brest. The new church, however, was the culmination of the efforts of Sam and John Evans. They were cousins and were born in Vilag as Simeon and Ivan Ivanco and left the village in 1890s for the steel mills of Pittsburgh. My grandmother, Zuzanna Ivanco-Karas was Sam's sister. They quit working in the steel mills when the mills faltered in 1907 and eventually prospered as merchants and moved to the "suburbs" in the nearby city of Ambridge.

After building an Orthodox Church in Ambridge, they decided that one was also needed in Vilag. They donated most of the funds but raised additional monies from other Rusnaks in Ambridge and the surrounding area. Construction on the Vilag church began in 1928 and was completed four years later. It took that long because of the Depression in the United States. Father Taschuck took on the role as the church's first priest.

"This is an unusual meeting I have called," said Father Taschuk, "but these are unusual times. Once again the Germans are in our land and our lives and way of living are being threatened and changed daily. It is also your faith that is being challenged, your faith in mankind. God and the Christian morals we hold so dear are being taunted. We are being called upon and tested as true Christians.

"So far, we have suffered no more than some inconvenience though there were many among us who have been sent to Germany to work. But, I am sure that will eventually change. However, there are people in our midst, who are not Christians, who are suffering immeasurable pain at the hands of the *Schutzstaffel*, the SS. You all heard the German truck enter our village three nights ago. In the morning, four Jewish families disappeared. I think you all know where they went. And, I don't think they will be coming back.

"I know some of you don't like Jews; that you feel, that they as individuals, or as a group, have occasionally wronged you. I am not here to debate that question or even answer it. I am asking you all to look at them not as Jews but as other human beings whose lives are being snuffed out for no other reason than their religion. It is ironic, that we, the Germans and Jews all pray to the same god.

"We as Christians cannot morally condone what is being done in our midst, in our village. We can look aside and gain a moment of relief in that it is them and not us. But what kind of people are we if we choose that path? I was in Praha (Prague) two weeks ago and I saw men, women and children walking the streets with yellow Stars of David sewn on their clothing. It hasn't happened here but it is just a matter of time until it does. I find that appalling and you as Christians and moral people should also."

"But what can we do?" asked one young man in the audience. "We have never had our will or concerns addressed by the Austrians, Hungarians, or even the Slovaks. Do you think the Germans will listen to us? We are a powerless people."

"No we are not," answered the priest.

"The Germans are only now beginning to identify the Jews in Vilag and the neighboring villages. I have a plan, but we must act quickly before they develop their manifest of all Jews in our village."

"Let us hear it," an elderly woman asked as she stood up.

"We can baptize the Jews in Vilag, make them Christians, if only on paper, and then the SS won't send them to their death chambers."

The congregation was stunned for a moment as the thought sank deeper into their minds.

"What if we get caught?" another person finally spoke.

"That is always a risk. But, I think it is very unlikely. Right now, the Germans have no idea how many Jews live among us."

"But can we really fool them?" asked the young man. "I know that some Jews look just like us. Some have blue eyes and even blond hair. But others...one need but look at them and you can be sure they are Jews."

"That is true," answered the priest. "But there are always Jews converting to Christianity. Was not Christ a Jew? So were his disciples. So were Peter and Paul. One can be born a Jew but need not remain a Jew. This will take a commitment on your part, on everyone in the village. I don't want you to decide today, here or now. I want you to take the idea home with you and think about it. It is a monumental decision. We will meet again like this after services next Sunday. We cannot wait too long or the SS will develop its list. If any of you have questions about it, please come and see me during the week. I am always available to you."

"There could be a problem," said the young man. "What if none of the Jews want to give up their religion, to take part?"

"They will be Christians on paper only," said the priest. "They can still remain Jews in their hearts and minds."

There was another nighttime gathering in Vilag a few days later. It was the Altshulh family, who owned the food and dry-goods store in Vilag. Altshulh had six children and his wife's father living with them. Their disappearance seemed to strengthen the priest's appeal to the villagers to help.

"I was surprised this week," the priest said at the next meeting. "I was afraid that I would have been swamped with you coming to ask me questions about our plan. There wasn't a single person. I fear that my message last week did not reach your hearts. I did, however, have three visitors. They were Jews. You all know them. They have lived among us all their lives. They had heard about our discussion last week and wanted to know if it was true.

"I will prolong this no longer. I ask that you vote...vote with your hearts and conscience. All those who are **not** in favor of saving our village's Jews, raise their hands."

To the priest's utter astonishment, not a single person raised a hand. The priest looked up and blessed himself as he thanked God for the moral fiber of the Rusnaks in his village.

The inquisitive young man then rose and asked, "What do we do and how do we do it?"

"There are about 15 Jews left in our village," said the priest. I will contact the three who came to see me and ask them if they would like to be baptized. If they do, I will do the baptismal. But all of you will take part at one time or another. I will need three witnesses; one to be their godfather and the other their godmother. Your names will be entered in the church records along with their names. I will have to make some adjustments to the dates. The village clerk will then enter corresponding dates in the village's official records."

That week, in early 1941, Father Taschuk baptized all 15 Jews. When word about the Jews of Vilag spread to other villages, the number of Jews being baptized increased dramatically. The residents of Vilag, renamed Svetlice in 1939 by the Czechoslovak government in its efforts to remove as many traces of Hungarian influence as possible, almost to a person, became godparents. By the end of 1942, the priest had baptized more than 600 Jews. It might have gone on longer, but there were no more Jews remaining within the scope of his church and the people of Svetlice. They had all been sent to the concentration camps.

The people of Svetlice remained totally silent about what they had done. Because everyone had committed himself or herself to the events, and would implicate themselves if they spoke about it; no one ever talked. Three years after the war ended, Father Taschuk died and so did the story of what he and the villagers had accomplished. It would, however, be rediscovered.

In the fall of 1944 war again moved back to the Carpathian Mountains as Germans retreated under the pressure of Soviet troops. Not many buildings were spared in Svetlice. In the summer of that year, before fighting took place in the Dukla Pass, a strategic location about 60 miles west of Svetlice, the Germans were desperate for manpower in the bombed-out factories. They began an intense drive to gather every person possible in the area and send them to manufacturing plants in Germany and eastern Austria.

It was the young men and women who were shipped out first. Then, they raised the age to 50 and finally 60 as the Allies destroyed more and more of Germany's ability to produce war goods. Now, they would take even men and women over 60. One day in early June the Germans ordered everyone in the village of Svetlice out of their houses as soldiers stood guard. Anyone who looked too old to work, or was handicapped, was shot on the spot.

A German corporal stood outside 64-year-old Zuzanna Karas's house with a machine gun in his arms, at the ready, as an SS officer next to him ordered everyone inside to come out. There was only Zuzanna and her daughter in the house. Through the windows, the officer had seen them moving from one room to another. He began yelling at her, first in German, then in Russian. She refused to come out.

He cursed at the house and then took a hand grenade that was dangling from the corporal's belt. He pulled its pin as he looked inside the open door and a smile spread across his face. There stood a small, old woman, huddled against the far corner, pulling a shawl over her shoulders. She knew what was about to happen. She suddenly stood upright, stared into the eyes of the German and then a slight smile spread across her face. She blessed herself once, twice and was about to do it a third time when the German approached the door. He stopped at the threshold, lobbed the grenade into the kitchen and hurriedly stepped back.

It fell almost at Zuzanna's feet before it went off. Her body took the brunt of the explosion and protected her deaf 35-year old daughter Zuzanna who had crawled under the table behind her.

The officer looked inside, Nothing stirred. Satisfied that he had killed everyone, he moved to the next house along the slight stream and repeated the procedure.

Chapter 54   The War Years in America

War is never kind to anyone but to the Karases and Niders death's hand was lightly felt. In Europe, it took Zuzanna Karas. In America, only John Nider, Harry's oldest son, paid the ultimate price. He took part in the invasion of France on D-Day and was wounded. Eventually, he was shipped to a hospital in London to recover. A German buzz bomb scored a direct hit on the hospital. The toll was excessive and John Nider was among those killed. His cousin Mike Nider, Vasyl's son, served in the Navy in the Pacific Theater and Mike's older brother Andy evaded capture during the Battle of the Bulge in Europe.

Wasco went back to work at the strip mines. While his job was deemed important to the national war effort, it was his bout with black lung that kept him a civilian. His younger brother Nick was developing problems with his lower spine and though relatively mobile he was rejected from military service. However, he became a machinist, tool-and-die maker and he, too, was in a strategic war job.

Andy and Mike Karas both served in the Army in Europe. Mike, with his penchant for languages, was sent to the Army's Russian School and eventually served as a military interpreter. He was also the only one in the two families to take advantage of the GI Bill. After the service he got a degree in accounting but began studying for the priesthood. It was a sign of a family's social elevation in Europe to have at least one son join the clergy. If a family had no sons, a daughter turned nun had almost the same effect. It was one of the few ways a person could escape doing what his father and grandfather had done. It also worked, to a lesser degree, among immigrants in the United States.

Mike Karas's younger brother Nicholas, who was born in Ambridge, initially also had aspirations to the priesthood but changed his mind. He eventually became head of the Slavic Language Department at Bowling Green University in Ohio. John, Andrew Karas's youngest son, started out an insurance salesman. He and his wife Joanne, bought and operated a motel in Cocoa Beach, Florida. Concurrently, he attended college in Florida and eventually finished with a master's degree in business, which lead him to a job as a contract security manager for NASA.

Death worked in a different way for the second generation in America. It was the process of aging that began to take its toll of the immigrant generation. Slowly, one-by-one, the Hunkies began to fade from existence. Andrew Karas, Stefan's older brother and father of four sons in Ambridge developed cancer. He feared doctors more than death. When his two sons returned from the war and discovered his condition, they insisted he take action. However, it was too late and he died of the disease in 1949 at the age of 50.

John Najda, Vasyl's older brother, seemed to lead a charmed life as far as work in the mines was concerned. While Black Lung had struck him as well as his brothers, it seemed to have but little effect on his health. But alcohol, like it did for so many immigrants, was a problem. However, it wasn't cirrhosis of the liver that ended his life but a Ford automobile.

It was a warm Saturday evening on September 1, 1951 when John Najda and two of his drinking buddies climbed the hill from Goodtown and crossed a dozen farm fields taking the most direct route and entered Berlin from the south side. By this time, Goodtown was virtually a ghost town and fewer than a dozen families remained in the once bustling mining town. There was never a bar in the town and the company store had been shut down years ago. The closest bars were in Berlin. It was easily a 3-mile walk for them but in those days people in the country still did a lot of walking. Ex-Europeans were especially adept in that mode. Dry and thirsty, they immediately made for the closest and their favorite bar in the National Hotel on Main Street. It took most of the evening, drinking beer, to satiate their thirsts.

John, at the time, was 72. It had been a dozen years since he had worked for the Quality Coal Company. His living costs as a "bachelor" were minimal and through determined frugality he was always able to manage enough money from his Social Security check to be a regular patron at the bar. He also had another advantage. Verne Fischer, the husband of his niece Stephanie (Stella) Nider-Fisher tended bar there and probably bought him a drink or two when his money ran out.

It was near 10 in the evening, as the recounting went, when he and his friends staggered out of the bar onto Main Street. They gabbed for a moment on the sidewalk, when John unexpectedly decided to cross the street between two parked cars and never saw it coming. The Ford hit him, knocking him unconscious. The police took him to a doctor in town and called his nephew Andy, who lived in Meyersdale. The doctor told him that he needed to be in a hospital, immediately. Andy drove "Stritchko," to the nearest hospital, in Somerset. He died the next day without regaining consciousness.

John Najda left no one behind in Europe. His first wife Juliana had died while he was in America. His second wife, Fanny Salabaj, whom he abandoned after he returned to Europe to get her and found her pregnant with someone else's child, had died several years earlier.

"He was a nice man, I liked him, everyone liked him," Andy Nider said at his uncle's burial in the Pinehill Cemetery, just above Goodtown. "But his life seemed such a waste. We are all that he left behind to mourn him."

"All," was not that small when one considers the nephews and nieces and their children. The Najdas, Vasyl's and Harry's children, were a growing horde.

"It wasn't always that way," said Vasyl, his brother. "When he came to America in 1907, he was full of life, hope and expectations, like all of us. Ivan was just another Rusnak. A Ruthenian as we were called by outsiders, who knew nothing but farming. He was 33 when he got off the boat. Andy and I were here first and helped pave the way. Too bad he didn't learn from the mistakes we made. But who knew then? Maybe it was the women he chose who turned him into a single man. Maybe it was his temper."

"You have a temper, too, Pop," said Andy.

"And so do you." his father answered. "Maybe it is our curse in life. Maybe."

Vasyl must have been thinking of his own future, his own vulnerability as he stood and watched his brother's coffin being lowered into the ground. He had buried two brothers and had no idea what happened to the third. He was just two years younger than John, not much difference, but suffered from emphysema as well as the black lung. He was not in the best of health. He thought of his youngest brother. Hryec was now dead almost 20 years. No one knew what happened to Andrij who returned to Europe in 1922. He had never written after he left America.

Vasyl's health worsened during that fall. His coughing became more persistent and Kateryna often cried herself to sleep at night, sensing that her husband was slowly dying. The emphysema complicated his wheezing and coughing. He had greatly reduced his farming activity during the past year. His sons, Mike and Andy, married and working, one as a bulldozer and crane operator in a strip mine and the other is a steel fabricator building bridges and buildings. That fall, they brought in the remnant crops.

"I don't think I will plant any fields this spring," Vasyl said to his wife one morning at breakfast, just a few days after Russian Christmas. "I had a dream last night. I saw my brothers John and Harry. And then Jesus came to me. He said that I would soon be with them. I don't think I will be here to harvest another crop. The mines are finally catching up with me....and," he stopped, then started coughing.

It was near the end of March when the doctor from Meyersdale came to the farm to see Vasyl. Mike had been there on the weekend and saw his father's condition worsening. Only Kateryna and her cousin Mike Antonishak, who had now come to live with them, were in the house. After a cursory look at Vasyl, the doctor returned to the kitchen where the others were waiting.

"Kate, he hasn't long to live," he told Vasyl's wife. "If there is a priest who should be here, I think you should call him now."

Kateryna blessed herself and tears began to flow from her eyes. She pulled the *babushka* from her head and wiped the tears from her cheeks.

Sometime during the early morning, while it was still dark, Vasyl's soul escaped. His battered and worn body now lay motionless in the downstairs bedroom. Kateryna walked in, reached for his hand and felt the cold. She blessed herself three times and then walked into the kitchen. Her cousin was making a pot of coffee.

He looked up and watched her as she walked across the kitchen to the back wall and opened the face of the clock. She stopped the pendulum. The kitchen was silent for a moment.

"He is dead," she announced. "God has taken him like he said He would. He was 72. The same age as his brother John when he died."

It was March 1952, the 26th, when my grandfather died.

I would have been at his funeral but couldn't because I was in the St. Albans Naval Hospital when I got the telegram. It was during the Korean Conflict. I had seen him just a few months earlier and that placated my conscience. At the time, I was being transferred from Pensacola to Brooklyn to pick up the U.S.S. Pocono. It was being reactivated in the Brooklyn Navy Yard. It was the previous November when I got a few days leave. On the way north I stopped at The Farm to see my grandparents. My mother had written to me that *Djido* was getting worse and no one knew how long he would live.

I took a bus to Breezewood, on the Pennsylvania Turnpike, then hitchhiked west. I was at the turnpike entrance for no more than 5 minutes, with my thumb out, when a car stopped. Hitchhiking was easy in those days, especially if you were in uniform. Most often, it was an ex-serviceman who stopped and picked you up. After all, a big part of our population, only a half-dozen years earlier, was in some kind of uniform.

My grandfather, usually after a day of work, loved to sit at the stall entrance to the barn and look across the large garden patch that separated it from the house, no more than 75 yards away. It was on a slight rise and gave anyone sitting there an overview of the farm and the deep, verdant valley behind the house that was created over eons of time by Swamp Creek. Beyond the creek, our property ended and belonged to a man named Martini. His cattle were grazing on the large, semi-open pasture on the far side of the stream the day I arrived. I immediately went to the barn to greet him.

My grandfather had salvaged a kitchen chair, one without a back and it stayed outside the barn door in all weather. It had lost what varnish and stain it might once have possessed and now was a weathered light gray. I sat on the top rail of a wooden fence that encircled a small corral at the entrance to the barn.

"Neek," he would say the first half of Nikolaj, pronouncing it as a European would, "you remind me of Mike in your uniform."

My Uncle Mike had served a few years earlier in the Navy, in the Pacific Theater. When I joined the service, he gave me a non-regulation uniform, one with bell-bottoms and colorful dragons embroidered on the inside cuffs that were exposed when they were unbuttoned and folded back. You wore it that way only when you were far from the reach of the Shore Patrol.

"What do you plan to do with your life after the war?" he asked.

I was taken aback by the question.

My grandfather, though always close to my sister and me, had never asked me about what I would do or become. It was the first time he seemed to be addressing me as an adult. I'm sure it was the uniform and the knowledge that I could be killed in the service. It had been too short a period since he stopped worrying about his two sons.

"I don't know right now," I answered.

"I had hoped to go on to school, to college somewhere. I wanted to go right after high school but when I found out how much it cost, I was stopped. I thought that maybe I could work for a year or to, save some money, and then go to school. But I never figured there would be a war to interrupt my plans."

"I had hoped that one of my sons would go to college," my grandfather said. "I know Nick would have done something if he had. He was smart but we needed his pay to survive the Depression. When Wasco was younger, I tried to keep him in school but he was not one for school. I am disappointed that Andy and Mike never took advantage of the GI Bill. That would have made it possible. Maybe I didn't stress hard enough to them that education was the only way they could get ahead. I have tried to convince all of my sons, that education, knowledge, *znateh*, is the only way out. Knowledge lets you decide what your lives will be like. Without it, others will tell you what to do.

"Zellman got our house and farm because he had knowledge that we didn't have. I can still clearly remember what he said to me. I was about ten. One day he called me over and spoke to me in a way he had never before done. He did so as if I was his son. He had no children. I guess he felt sorry for me and my plight. Yes, he was a Jew, but he also was a religious man and may have felt guilty of what had happened to our family. It was he who told me of the value of education and what it can do.

"It is your way out of bondage," I remember him saying. "Jews have known bondage for ages. But knowledge has given us some degree of control over our lives. If you are smart, Vasyl," he said, "and I think you are, you should chase knowledge as if was a young, buxom girl."

"I knew what he said was true, but it was impossible for me or other Rusnaks to find teachers or schools in Europe. There were none for us. But here, it is all different.

"I had no education, but I was able to make it to American where one can find education. Maybe school isn't for everyone. But you, Nikolaj, I feel are different. Maybe it was because your father died when you were young that life created more of a challenge to you. I know your mother raised you well. I see she disciplines you just enough to keep you going straight but not so much to make you turn away from your own path.

"Nikolaj. Follow you own road. At times you may feel you have taken the wrong path but in the end you will see the wisdom that you now may not know you possess. God be with you," he said.

He rose from the chair and I jumped down from the fence. Unexpectedly and out-of-character, in an unusual show of emotion, he wrapped his arms around me and kissed me. He pulled apart for a second, then kissed me again. As he did, I saw tears in his eyes. He had seen his future and told me of mine.

My grandmother, Kateryna, held on for another 12 years. She and her cousin lived alone on the farm. Her daughter Mary, living on the farm next to her mother, paid more visits than before. So did her sons and daughters who lived in the surrounding towns. She died on October 18, 1964 at the age of 77. She died of complicated heart problems. She really died because she was tired of living, she was very old and worn out.

"Too bad," I remember saying to my Uncle Andy while at her funeral, "that we didn't get to know them even better than we did. Their lives were so involved with earning a living that we often forgot who they really were and where they came from. And we, too, have been so caught up in making a living and raising our children that we failed to ask the many questions of them that we should have. They have taken so much with them to their graves, things that we will never know and can only guess at."

Mike Antonishak died the following September and the last of the Najda generation of immigrants in America was now gone. He was the last Hunky in our family...or so we thought.

Chapter 55 The Educated Generation

For decades, most Americans believed that education was the panacea to our problems. It may have been based on the Chinese proverb, "Give a man a fish and he will eat for a day, but teach him to fish and he can feed himself." To a great degree, we still believe that education will solve many of the problems that have manifested themselves in our society. Our founding fathers believed that education was a solution and from the beginnings of this nation, public education has been at the forefront of our unique society. Was it they who planted the seed of this idea in our society?

What amazes me is that education as a solution to problems was also at the forefront in the thinking and actions of both my maternal and paternal grandparents. They, too, believed that education was the only way their children, and subsequent offspring, could break the yoke that fettered them in Europe. But how, and from where did they develop this concept? It surely wasn't through reading because neither of them, nor most of the others in their villages, could either read or write. It wasn't through exposure with outside contacts in Europe because their isolation in the mountain villages precluded this. And, if they did go out, none of the immediate European societies they could have met endorsed education for the masses. Nor could it have been because of exposure to others once they arrived in America because this concept was already well-entrenched in their thinking before they arrived on our shores.

The only answer is that it had to be an innate part of the human psyche. But if that is true, why didn't European societies embrace this idea? It must have been the environment in Europe in which it was trapped. In order to flourish, to grow or become active, it had to be planted in a democratic society, the kind the first immigrants established in America in the 17th century. Thus, it was not a phenomenon unique to Rusnak immigrants who arrived in America in the late 1800s and early 1900s. Whether knowingly or not, they, too, began to foster the role education would play in freeing them from the constrictions imposed upon them in the Old Country.

Like the generation that preceded them, the third generation of Najdas (Niders) and Karases had to wait for a war to end before they could begin to take their places in American society. The Korean War saw John Philip in the Army in Korea but with a safe return. Shortly after his return, his father Sam died of a heart attack. His older brother Samuel attended college on a football scholarship. But after two years, doctors detected that he, too, had heart problems. He quit college and returned to running the farm. Like his father, he, after but a few years, died of a heart attack. When John returned from the service, he took over running the large farm for his mother, found a wife, and began building his own family. John's sister Anna went to Washington during WW II and attended business school and eventually married a naval officer from her hometown.

I followed my uncle, Mike, into the Navy, but during the Korean Conflict, and spent part of my service in Europe. After being discharged, the modified Korean GI Bill allowed me to go to college. It was something I doubt I could have afforded on my own and forever feel indebted to my country for the opportunity. After that, I began the pursuit of a dream that was instilled in me at my father's bedside to become a doctor. When I was almost finished with my undergraduate studies I suddenly realized that that was not what I now wanted. An ardent naturalist, instead I earned a degree in biology and went on to graduate school.

While Vasyl Najda's early appreciation of education and what it could accomplish for a person failed to impress most of his children, I heard what he was saying. However, Nick, his second son and my uncle, did capture the idea. While he was forced into work during the Depression and never went beyond the 8th grade in school, he did impress upon his two daughters and me, just how important education would be to us. He decided to educate himself and enrolled in a correspondence course to become a machinist. He then went on to work as a highly-skilled tool-and-die maker.

However, it took a visit to my mother's factory to permanently implant the concept in me. My mother was on medication for a back problem, caused by decades of standing next to a shoe-buffing machine. One day in the late 40s, while I was in high school, she had forgotten to take her pills and her back bothered her greatly. The factory nurse called home and asked if I would bring them to Dunn's. Ironically, I had never been in the factory, though I'd seen it and EJ's, the shoe factory where my father had worked, but only from the outside. Unknowingly, I felt a certain foreboding about entering either of them.

I'll never forget how delighted my mother was when I arrived. She proudly introduced me to all the friends with whom she worked. I had often heard her mention them at home during the years as I was growing up. I was stunned by what I saw, the monotonous, boring, strenuous conditions under which she had to work to make a living. I had never realized the extent of the sacrifices she had willingly made on behalf of my sister and me.

As I walked home, images of what I had just seen raced through my mind. I thought to himself. For 30 years, my poor mother has had to stand up, in all that noise and confusion, and polish the bottoms of innumerable numbers of shoes to provide a home for us. I will never appreciate fully enough what she has done. Most important, I said to myself, I will never in my life work in conditions like that. If I am not smart enough to work where I want to, then I am dumb enough to work in places where I am told to.

There was an irony in my thinking that in later years came to fruition. Several of my close friends, friends with whom I had grown up in The Ward, after their stint in the services, went to work in Dunn's and EJs. I was utterly surprised that they would do that. The earlier visit to my mother's factory was one of the best things that could have happened to me at that age. Such motivation made future schooling so much easier.

"A good education is like an insurance policy," my Uncle Nick often said. "Once you have it, it can never be taken away from you. It is what you will build your future upon." He sounded a bit like my grandfather but was more eloquent. However, the message was the same.

Out of the 24 cousins of the third generation, half completed college and became professionals. It would have made Vasyl proud to see it happen. "Not bad for a bunch of Hunkies," he might have said.

I always had a penchant for writing, both in high school and college. It began in high school when I took journalism as my 12th grade elective for English. As part of the course, I was able to work as a copy boy on the Binghamton *Press*. I also learned photography and took most of the photographs for my high school yearbook. In college, I worked on its newspaper and edited the college yearbook. I was in my senior year, after I had decided that medicine wasn't for me, that I realized I could marry both my loves. I would be a science writer. I went on to graduate school and got a master's degree in journalism.

Soon after I entered college as a "Vet," and a student four years older than the freshmen around me, I got married. By then, I thought, I had seen the world and was ready to settle down. I married Shirley Elizabeth Hutton. After the honeymoon we returned to school, I as a student and she as a lawyer's secretary. It was her pay that saw us through some pretty lean times.

Seldom, however, is the path to one's goal a straight line.

I eventually got a job in New York City, on the staff of a major magazine. Located there, I was able to renew my friendship with Myron Surmach, whom I met while in the Navy. While in graduate school, Shirley and I had our first son. During that time in New York City, we had two more sons. However, the city seemed to stifle the naturalist in me. I broke free and for nearly a decade worked as a freelance magazine writer. My assignments took me all over the world but the demands of a growing family began weighing heavily on the need to travel.

When Cowles began the Suffolk *Sun*, a new daily newspaper on Long Island, I jumped at the chance to stay at home and stop traveling. I became its outdoors sports columnist. When the newspaper was folded three years later, I returned to freelancing for a short time, but my heart wasn't in it. Three growing sons are an irresistible attraction. Then I got an offer from *Newsday*, a major daily in New York, also as a columnist, and it gave me another chance to "work at home." However, during this period my science writing shifted more and more away from the technical academic world toward that of popular science, the naturalist and the outdoors.

I suddenly was as happy as the proverbial clam.

A modern map of the extreme southeast corner of Poland in Lesko County. Depicted here are the Rusnak villages of Protisne (Procisne in Polish), Smil'nyk (Smolnik) and Dvernyk (Dwernik). Note that Protisne today is a mere bus stop and not located on the Hluboki Creek the original site.

Part IV Roots

Chapter 56   The Journey Back to Where It All Began

Maybe it was a sense that I had no past beyond what I had known as a child growing up in Binghamton and my grandparents' farm in Pennsylvania, but there gradually began to grow within me a strange desire. My own history was too short. Maybe it is a natural phenomenon that occurs in all individuals as one matures, as one becomes cognizant of one's role in life or position in society. I began to look through the veil that had obscured who I was and where I had come from. I wanted to know. At first, it was the normal degree of curiosity of one's ancestry that is inherent in all of us.

My desire to know my ethnic past arose years before there was a national craving to discover one's roots. It began during the early 1950s while I was still in the Navy. I was a photographer's mate and was sent on a T.A.D. (Temporary Additional Duty) assignment to an amphibious unit attached to the 6th Fleet in the Mediterranean. It was on that cruise that I met Myron Surmach, a Rusnak from Manhattan. I envied him.

Surmach had always known who he was and from where his ancesters had come, primarily, because his father was alive and told him of them. His father, an immigrant, owned Surma's Ukrainian Book Store on Manhattan's Lower East Side, and had enriched his son with his memories of the Old Country. One evening onboard the *U.S.S Monrovia, APA-31*, as it cruised from Oran, on the North African coast toward Naples, its European homeport, we talked on the fantail of the ship. We had only recently met because the cruise had just begun and we had time to probe each other's backgrounds.

"I'm Russian," I responded to Surmach's questioning. Then, to support my claim, I began to spout the language I had learned as a youngster from my grandparents.

An amazed Surmach suddenly interrupted him. "You're not Russian. You're a Hunky, a Rusnak, just like I am."

"What do you mean, 'You're not Russian?' I asked.

"For years, my mother, aunts and uncles, and everyone around me, at church and at home, said we were Russian. We belonged to a Russian Orthodox Church. Doesn't that make me a Russian?"

"No," said Myron. "You're a Rusnak, just like me."

"I don't know if I should believe you," I said.

"Maybe you don't want to believe me," Myron said, "because it would change a lot of your thinking.

"The explanation is quite simple," he went on, "but it isn't really, if you know the background.

"Up until the 9th century, 879 A.D. to be exact, there was only one Christian church in the world. It was called the Universal or Catholic Christian Church. After the church incurred 'The Great Schism,' the Eastern part of Christianity became known as Greek Catholic Church because its center was in the Byzantine (Greek) capital of Constantinople. It was the Western part of the church, centered in Rome, that broke away, and became known as Roman Catholic. Because it was the old, or the original part of the Christian World, the Greek Catholics soon became know as the Orthodox or Eastern Orthodox. The term Greek Catholic began to fade but would re-emerge 600 years later to satisfy a Roman Catholic distinction it would create between the East and West.

"Two proselytizing Greek monks, Cyril and Methodius, were sent north from Constantinople to spread Christianity among the marauding Slavs, first into the Balkans, then farther north to the capital of Slavdom, which at that time was Kyiv. It was shortly after the Vikings arrived in that city and conquered its inhabitants that their leader Prince Volodymyr, believed that his pagan constituents needed a better, centralized religion. After meeting with representatives of several faiths, he chose Orthodoxy over Roman Catholicism, and even Jewism. He believed that the Orthodox form of Christianity better suited the temperament of his Slavic masses.

"Until the 16th century, Kyiv was the center of Eastern Slavs' world. But as the power of Kyivian Rus declined, that of Moscovy, in the province of Suzdal, increased. Both Ivan the Terrible and Peter the Great, two charismatic Russian tsars began to change the seat of Rus Orthodoxy from Kyiv to Moscow. It was another way of exhibiting dominance over Ukraine and Byelorussia, two of the three nations belonging to the group known as Eastern Slavs. However, western parts of the Province of Halych (Galicia), a part of Kyivian Rus, now came under Polish and Hungarian rule. In this new order, Kyivian Rus was now treated as a province of Moscovy, it was not known as Russia at that time, and the Ukrainian Orthodox Church in Kyiv was abolished. All Eastern Slavs now were considered Russian Orthodox.

"During the next 400 years, those Eastern Slavs now trapped in Poland and Hungary, without contact with the Russian Orthodox Church, were vulnerable to being coerced and eventually forced to accept the state-sponsored religion of these two Roman Catholic countries. However, the transformation was never totally completed and these Slavs adjusted to a modified version of their religion that allowed them to retain their religious rites but acknowledge the pope. The Church was then proclaimed as Greek Catholic. Primarily because all their rites were Byzantine or Eastern, they became known as Uniats, and eventually Greek Catholics, but they now differed from the original definition of Greek Catholic.

"After the Union of Brest in 1596, that's where the term Uniat comes from, after 600 years of being Orthodox Christians, they were required to sign over the titles of their churches, monasteries and religious possessions to Rome and acknowledge the pope as their spiritual leader. The Rusnaks' bishops had sold them out. The common people, the Rusnaks, had no choice. Not all Slavs in Poland and Hungary, however, were completely won over and remained in a limbo-like position, as independent Greek Catholics."

"Myron, you sound like you've given this explanation before."

"You're right. You wouldn't believe how many people come into my father's store looking for their heritage. And, my father is there to help them. I guess I've heard it so many times I have absorbed everything he has said.

"But, I'm not done.

"About the end of the 1800s, between 1885 and 1900, as many Rusnaks under Polish and Hungarian domination, and even some from Ukraine, immigrated to the United States and Canada, a movement began to grow, both in Europe and America, for a return to the religion of their ancestors. In the United States it was led by Father Alexis Toth and many Greek Catholics, under his inspiration, could now freely establish their Orthodox churches."

At that time, the United States was being recognized in Europe as a growing world power while the prospect of an all-engulfing war loomed on the horizon. To gain a favorable immigrant minority in United States, one that was rapidly growing in size, and one that might be able to influence U.S. policies toward Europe-- Poland, Hungary and Russia began to vie for their favor. All three nations tried to win over Rusnaks both in Europe and American. But the biggest attention was in America and the Russian Tsar Nicholas II established a well-financed effort and aided the return to Orthodoxy by sending Russian Orthodox priests to America to gain the Rusnaks as allies. He aided financially in building churches and even sent several churches the bells for their towers and had his government support the Russian Orthodox Mission to America.

As a result, Rusnaks, who originally had been Ukrainian Orthodox, could now attend an Orthodox Church in America. It didn't seem to make a difference that it was Russian Orthodox. At least they felt they had escaped the hand of the pope. "We were finally able to get the pope's hand out of our pockets," the converts used to say.

"While your grandfather was aware that he was a Rusnak," continued Myron, "and not a Russian, his children and grandchildren—your mother and father, your aunts and uncles— now attended a Russian Orthodox church and began to believe that they, too, were Russian. There was no one to tell them otherwise. That is why you and two generations began to believe that you were Russians."

"You know, Myron, I think you may be right," I finally said.

Startled by his long discourse, I only vaguely knew what a Hunky was because the term was seldom used in Binghamton, though it was prevalent in the Pennsylvania coal mines and steel mills of my grandfathers.

"I know what a Rusnak is," I said, "because that is what my grandfather always said he was. He used to differentiate between

Rusnaks and 'Rus-si-any.' The latter he referred to as 'Hard' Russians. I didn't know what the differences were or why 'hard' was used. I just accepted them, believing they were close, maybe even the same. I knew my grandparents were uneducated and thought that maybe they just didn't know better."

"The language you speak is that of the Lemkos, maybe some Boyko, as some portion of the Rusnaks are called today," Surmach said. "They are also called Rusyns and Ruthenians, but usually by others and not themselves. My father came from a village about a hundred miles farther east of your grandparents, along the ridge of the Carpathian Mountains and speaks a slightly different dialect. That's all it is, a dialect. And, between them, the people there speak still another variation of both called the Boyko dialect. It is all very similar and our people are grouped together as the *Horyschany*, highlanders or mountain people. That is what the lowlanders or Ukrainians call us. The language our fathers spoke was almost the same as was spoken throughout Ukraine more than a thousand years ago. Time and distance, and two political powers, Poland and Hungary, and then the Austrians separated them from other Ukrainians."

The seed had been planted in my mind but had to wait to mature until later in my life.

My military service time in Europe, and then a decade of bouncing around the Old Country as a freelance magazine writer, gave me a familiarity with the various countries in Europe that most Americans never had. It is a great aid now when I travel abroad. Ironically, I had never been to the places where either of my grandparents had lived. I hardly knew, at the time, where these were.

However, it was an exploratory trip to Poland, Hungary and Czechoslovakia, offered to the Washington Press Corps in 1978, that brought me back to Europe in a new capacity. I had already started digging into my past, interviewing various relatives, and recollecting the vague tales of the villages my Najda grandparents told me about. I even opened the Karas side of my history that had been sealed when my father died. All this, and with Surmach's help, and some old maps, allowed me to finally locate two villages. I decided I would visit them after the Press Corps schedule was finished to see if there were any relatives who might still be alive. I would skip Hungary because I had been to Budapest on several assignments and needed no fam (familiarization) tour at the time and instead sought my relative's Austrian villages that now were located in Slovakia and Poland.

In Warsaw, my wife Shirley and I rented a car, a Polish-made Fiat that in itself was a marvel, and headed south for the Dukla Pass through which we would enter Czechoslovakia. The border crossing should have taken but a few minutes. There were only a few cars ahead of us. When it came to our turn, the Polish guard examined the passports and then ordered us to pull over to one side. My wife was alarmed because it wasn't where the other cars had gone.

The guard ordered us out of the car and called to someone in the nearby office. Three men came out, dressed in similar customs personnel uniforms. A fourth followed who was dressed in a different uniform.

The three customs men began taking everything apart in the trunk looking everywhere possible. The suitcases were opened in the parking lot and the contents spread out on the tarmac. The fourth man asked for our passports and visas. He looked at them, then said "Journalista!" and disappeared with the documents into the office.

Satisfied that we had no contraband, the three guards returned to their office and the one who first stopped us told them through gestures and a few English words, that we could repack the suitcases and the car.

"What about our passports and visas?" I asked

"Must wait," the man said.

An hour later, he gave us the same answer.

Three hours later, he again gave us the same answer but added, "waiting for telephone from Warsaw."

Finally, after four hours of hanging around the car and the parking lot, the man who took the passports returned and gave them back.

"Sorry for delay," he said. "It was caused by delay in Warsaw office. Journalists are not usually welcomed here."

"But we are leaving Poland, not coming in," I said.

"Makes no difference. Your name is on the list in Warsaw and we cannot let you pass until there is approval from ministry. Lucky for you, the commissar said he met you and your wife at reception for press group in Warsaw.

"Is O.K., you go now. Go!"

I half expected a similar delay once we crossed into Czechoslovakia. It didn't happen. The customs man looked at our passports and asked us to wait a minute. He went inside, stamped the passports, handed them back, thanked us, then told us we could go.

It was a two-hour drive from Dukla to Humenné, the closest big town to Svetlice with a hotel. We found the Hotel Karpatia in the middle of the city and decided to check in before driving an hour or so north to the villages we sought. My wife felt uncomfortable giving up the passports to the hotel clerk, especially in a communist country, but that is usually the procedure in most countries, communistic or not. We were in the room, unpacking our bags, when there was a knock on the door.

"Oh no!" Shirl said jokingly, "it is probably the NKVD."

She didn't know how right she might have been.

I opened the door and a short, stocky man, probably in his mid-sixties and with disheveled hair greeted me in English. He needed a shave as well as a comb and was dressed in a poor-fitting suit that looked like it was constantly lived in. It was as messed as his hair.

"Hello Americans," he said in faltering English. "I was in lobby when you checked in. I could not help overhearing your conversation with desk clerk. I am Anton Drasnik. I have brother in Chicago. I was there once to visit him.

"I thought I might offer my services to you as friend," he said and broadly grinned as he offered his hand to me and made moves to push his way into the room.

I changed my position and blocked the door. It caught the man off guard.

"My wife," I said, "is changing her clothes. I don't think we need your services. We will only be here for a day."

"But," Drasnik said, "I can tell you where is best place to eat. Not here in hotel. I show you where to buy good souvenirs. Maybe you need to exchange money. I can get you a better rate than banks. Fifty percent more!"

"No," I said, "That's the black market and it is illegal."

"Not to worry," the man said.

"No." I repeated myself and slowly closed the door. "Thank you anyway."

"What was that all about?" my wife asked as she came out of the bathroom.

"I don't know. I'm not quite sure. But, one thing I'm sure about, I wouldn't let him exchange money for us. Dealing with the black market here is a crime and the easiest way communists have to justify getting you behind bars.

"Ready to go?"

When we got off the elevator, he was waiting for us in the lobby.

He got up and rushed us as we made for the front entrance.

"Pan Karas," he said and rolled the r's beyond need. "That is a fine Polish name."

"It isn't Polish," I said as my wife and I stepped outside.

"But you have Polish car. I see license."

"That's a rental. They were all out of Fords."

"I would like to be your guide, to take you through Humenné."

"Look," I stopped and must have shown signs of being irritated. The man quickly recognized the change. "We don't need a guide. We know where we are going."

"Ok. Ok," he said. "But, if you change mind, just ask hotel clerk for me. My name is Anton. He knows me."

"Ok, Anton. If we change our minds I'll call you."

Anton followed us to the car and opened the door for my wife. He saluted her and clicked his heels as she took the seat.

"Did you see that?" I asked her as we drove away. "Anton saluted you as if you were a superior officer. He did it automatically."

"Oh, he was just being polite," she said. "I'll bet everyone here has been in the military at one time or another."

"That's true," I said, "but I don't think his kind of military wore a uniform."

"The roads are well marked," I thought aloud. "Americans could learn something about road marking from Europeans, especially the Czechs."

The first town we were to explore was Zvala. My mother wasn't sure of the village my father told her he came from when he left Europe. It sounded like Z'vala but probably was Z'Vilag which means "from Vilag." We drove along the Crocha River to Snina then turned north and headed up into the mountains. We passed through Stacksin and Starina and came to a crossroads. The road to the left was to another Smolnik, the same name as the village in Galicia where my Najda grandparents were from. Smolnik is the Polish translation and spelling for Smil'nyk, as the Rusnaks knew them. The road to the right was to Zvala.

Excitement grew in both my wife and me as we saw the town sign on the road just before the village. It was small, maybe 25 houses. The road beyond ended at the base of a mountain. On the other side was Poland. We stopped an elderly couple walking down the only road in town and asked them if they knew of any Karases who lived in Zvala.

"Yes," the woman said, "just three houses away. I go get them for you."

An elderly man came out the door, followed by a woman, probably his wife, and we met in the road beside the car. Like the first couple, they, too, were old, probably in their '70s. It dawned on me that there seemed to be no one in the village but old people. Where were all the kids and young adults?

When I asked them if their name was Karas they said yes, but when I began naming my relatives who might live here I drew a blank. They were Karases, but not the right ones.

"Could this be the end of our journey?" I turned and said to my wife.

"I hope not," she answered, "we have come too far and too long to have it end so abruptly."

The man, a part of the first couple, came up to us and entered in a conversation with the Karases. He spoke so rapidly, and with a slightly different dialect, that I could not completely follow them. When it was over, the man turned to me and said that yes, at one time, there were several Karas families in the town. But years ago, they went to America and no one knows what happened to them.

Despair must have grown even more pronounced on my face and in my voice as I spoke to them in my Rusnak dialect.

"But," the man then said, "this may not be the right town. This Karas told me that there are more Karases who live in Svetlice. He is related somehow to them but doesn't know how because it has been so long since he visited there. He was just a young man when he was there last, before the war."

"It's not far away according to the map," I said to Shirl. "But we have to go all the way back to Humenné and then go north up another river valley. It's almost on the continental divide."

"It's too late now. It's getting dark," she said. "Let's go back to the hotel, get a good night's sleep and get an early start in the morning."

It was like a night in Hell.

We got back to the hotel after dark and found the restaurant closed. That evening, we had to settle for a box of cookies and a few candy bars that Shirl picked up in Warsaw. The night started out restfully but near midnight, all hell seemed to break loose. We were awakened by a lot of people yelling and cursing. It seems that a party was underway next door and the paper-thin walls didn't filter a bit of the sound.

I was going to yell at them and opened the door. The party had spilled into the hallway and three men were drinking, falling over themselves in a drunken stupor and yelling to people inside the room. One man sat on the floor with his back propped against the wall. I decided that the best course of action was to quickly shut the door and lock it.

"I think it is best that we stuff our ears with something," I said to my wife as I climbed back into bed, "and hope they don't come through the wall."

Moments later, someone began pounding on our door. I opened it and saw a drunk leaning against the frame with a bottle of vodka in one hand. I recognized him as one of those who had been in the hallway.

"He wants us to join the party," I said as he looked at my wife who was still in bed. It took me a few minutes to convince him that we were too tired. Just as I was closing the door, two young children ran down the hall chasing each other in a game.

The room didn't become quiet until near 4:00 in the morning.

My wife and I were awake at sunrise and dressed. We were surprised, that the small restaurant, off the hotel lobby, was open that early. We got the traditional eggs, bacon, potatoes and rye toast breakfasts.

Out of Humenné, the road north followed the Laborec River. Just beyond Koskovce, the river spun off a tributary, the Vyrava, and so did the road. A sign at the fork said that the right road led to Zbojné and Svetlice.

Months later I was able to confirm that my paternal grandparents were from Vilag, but in 1939, the Czech government, in an effort to reduce the Hungarian influence in Slovakia, changed the Hungarian name to Svetlice. I wasn't able to put together the connection between Zvala and Z' Vilag until we returned home. The Slavic word for candle has the same meaning as Vilag in Hungarian. It was the suggestion of the people from Zvala, that we met the day before, that we go to Svetlice to look for my relatives if any were still alive.

Just a kilometer from the village of Svetlice, the hills sharply narrowed on each side of the road. There was a small grotto-like structure just off the road, a chapel. It was about 10 feet off the road, about 5 feet tall, built of stone and covered on top by a two-sided slanting roof. It was surrounded by three linden trees that someone cut back regularly so as not to overwhelm the structure. It housed an iron Orthodox cross. I got out and took a picture of it.

As I stood outside the car for a moment, and looked through the pass to the village beyond, I was overcome by a strange feeling that I have never been able to explain. It was almost as if I had been in this spot before. It was *déjà vu* at its best. Gradually, I realized what it might have been. The hills concentrated everything into this 50-foot gap with just enough space for the road and the small stream to pass through from the mountains above. It was here that 75 years earlier, my grandfather and later my grandmother, passed through on their way to America. And it was through these earthen pillars that they returned ten years later with my father when he was 6 years old. It was also in the village above where my father lived until 1929 when he returned to America. Except for a quirk of fate, I, too, could have been born here.

We drove slowly through the one-street village and passed a building with the traditional European symbol for a post office, a curved horn. I guess postmen here toot twice rather than ring twice.

"This has got to be the best place to find out if there are any Karases in this town," I said.

"Yes," answered the postmistress in her tight-fitting postal uniform. She was a well-built woman, in her early 40s with short, blonde hair, a generous nose and exceptionally large breasts. There was plenty of space on her blouse for medals.

"Of course there are," she answered in a manner as if I should have known. "There are a half dozen. Who are you looking for?"

"I think I have an uncle and an aunt here. His name is Ivan and my aunt's name is Susan. Maybe my grandmother is still alive. Her name, too, is Susan."

"If he is from here, his name is now Jan and her name is Zuzanna.

"Were you not here before? Aren't you the one who is a priest?

"No, that must have been my cousin Michael."

"Did he not tell you your grandmother is dead, killed by the *Bosch* at the end of the war?"

"No," I said, "I've never met him."

"Petro," she yelled as she turned her head to someone in the room behind her. "Come here," she ordered.

"Take these Americans to see Jan Karas."

Ivan was outside his door, talking to an elderly couple when my wife, Petro and I pulled up to the house. The postal worker excused himself and left the car saying he would walk back, "It wasn't far."

I studied the man before me for a moment.

He had a round face accentuated by a crop of short-cut white hair. His blue eyes dazzled from under a wrinkled brow capped with a flurry of large, white eyebrows. He was about 5' 6" tall, a bit stocky, but no sign of fat. He wore a loose-fitting flannel shirt and wrinkled trousers that at one time had been a part of a dress suit.

As I got out of the car, he turned and looked away from the couple with whom he had been talking. A slight, polite smile spread across his face. He glanced down and saw the Polish license plate and said good day to me in Polish. I answered in Rusnak and the man's smiled broadened.

"Can I help you?" he asked.

"Yes," I said. "We're looking for Ivan Karas. The postmistress said he lives here. Are you Ivan Karas?"

"Who are you?" the man said as his smile suddenly disappeared.

I told him who I was. He stared at me for the longest time without speaking, then at my wife.

I stared back at him. He could be my uncle, I thought to myself. After all, I only know what my father looks like from a portrait photograph of him when he was 30 years old. I wonder what this man looked like when he was 30 years old. He could be, then again, most people in these mountains have many features in common. It's not like back home.

"Your father was my friend as well as my brother," the man finally spoke. "I was young, only….." he paused for a moment to think, "eleven when he left for America. We never heard from him after he left. We did get a letter from my brother Andrij that your father had died. He said that he left two children, a son and a daughter. You...you are the son?

"Come with me. It is just a short walk to her house. Your Aunt Zuzanna will be surprised. Don't be alarmed if she cries and carries on. She cries easily nowadays. That is how she makes up for her speech. She cannot talk well. She got sick when she was still a baby and it affected her hearing and speech. But she understands everything."

Just three houses away, Ivan walked off the road, opened a small gate and held it open for me and my wife to pass through. He was about to open the door when it opened from the inside. A short, stocky women in her late 50s, dressed in a somber-colored ankle-length dress and wearing a sweater and shawl over her shoulders walked out. An auburn-colored wig was held in place by the traditional *babushka*. Ivan later said she wore that when outside the house because she was embarrassed by the loss of some of her hair.

"I have someone here for you to meet," Ivan said to her.

She stepped out of the doorway and looked hard at me, then at my wife.

"Who are they?" she asked.

"Stefanovy!" was all Ivan said.

"Stefanovy? Which Stefan?"

"Your brother's son."

"You mean Stefan...the one who died in America?"

"Yes. His son Nikolaj and his wife Shirley."

It would be impossible to imagine what was fleeting through the poor woman's mind at that moment. Thoughts must have shot back to that day in December in 1929, when her brother hugged her and bid her good-bye before he disappeared into the cold, winter night.

For a moment she stared at me, hoping to see signs of her brother in my face. Suddenly, she lunged forward and embraced me.

The feeling and the moment were equally strange and explosive for me. Here was an elderly woman, one I had never seen before, vigorously hugging me. Here was my father's sister, the same flesh and blood as my father, and almost the same as mine. One does not deal easily or quickly with moments like this. One just lives them, savors them. They are so astounding that they cannot be explained, just experienced.

She did cry. She went on and hugged my wife as ferociously as she did me. Shirl, too, had tears in her eyes. How often does something like this happen in a family?

Ivan led us back to his house where he introduced me and my wife to Maria, his wife. His daughter, a Maria also, and her husband Stefan Kost were also there. They lived and worked in Prague and were here on vacation. The scene couldn't have been orchestrated any better by Hollywood. With them was their six-month-old-daughter, Zuzanna.

My uncle said he found it easier to live in Svetlice, among a growing number of Slovaks who now populated the old Rusnak village, if his name was Jan rather than Ivan. "Ivan sounded too Russian," he said, "and everyone hates the communist rule in this country. It doesn't matter that we are not Russians, they didn't understand the difference, maybe they didn't want to understand."

I asked about my grandmother. Zuzanna, who witnessed it, told me how a German had tossed a hand grenade into her house as they were retreating before the approaching Soviet Army.

"Later," said Ivan, "I will show you where she is buried. And, your grandfather, too."

I found it difficult at times to talk to my uncle and Maria in Rusnak because so many Slovak words had crept into their vocabulary. Talking to his daughter was even more difficult. They had been educated in what is essentially Slovak-speaking schools. And, in high school she and her husband learned Czech because it was the language you needed at the university and in the better paying jobs.

Ivan took me on a tour of the village and introduced me to some of the older residents as Stefanovich. Ironically, I had no difficulty understanding either them nor they me. Again, Rusnaks were now a minority in their own village and their language was slowly disappearing. As we walked about, every hour on the hour, loudspeakers mounted on every utility pole, blared a political message.

"How can you stand that?" I asked.

"Stand what?" Ivan asked.

"That constant communist indoctrination?"

"No one pays attention to it. We hardly notice it."

"See the big pasture above us?" he said as he pointed. "And, see all those big trees near the top. They are still called the Karas Woods by the old people in this village. They no longer belong to us. When the communists moved in here, after the war, they took all private property. They were supposed to compensate us and others who owned property here and elsewhere, but they never have. Now I have a little plot next to the house where I have a garden. But, it really isn't mine. They can take it away whenever they wish. Huh! Some system."

Ivan insisted that we stay a few days with them but settled for an overnight as I explained to them our tight schedule and flight back to New York. I didn't mention that we still had a village on the other side of the mountain to visit. It would have just complicated things.

Ivan told me of his tenuous years. In 1938, when Hitler politically moved into Czechoslovakia, he and several other men who had just turned 20, joined the Czechoslovak Army. When Hitler finally moved in with troops to secure the country as "an eastern province," most of the men in his division, composed primarily of Rusnaks, crossed into Soviet Ukraine and became part of the Red Army.

He survived the battle of Stalingrad and fought his way with the Soviets to Berlin. He was lucky to have fought so many years and to still be alive. He suffered only a fragment of shrapnel that was left near his spine as a reminder of what he had been through. He brought out the jacket to his dress suit. It was so completely filled with medals that there wasn't room for even one more. He told me, that because of his war record, he had received so much in compensation from the government that he was a rich man.

"Yes," he admitted. "I am rich but only because there is nothing here on which I can spend the money they give me. I can

507

ride the bus free, the trains and things like that. I get to lead the parade every May because no one else has as many medals as I have. That is one reason the communist postmistress sent Petro to show you where I live. She wouldn't do that for anyone else.

"Also," he said, "did you notice the pile of bricks on the side of my house? Each year, everyone who wants to build a house is given 100 bricks by the communists. You cannot build a house with 100 bricks so you must wait years until you have what you think is enough and then you start. For me, a 'hero first class,' it will take me half the time because I am given 200 each year."

"Do the people here like living under communist rule?" I asked.

"The women do more than the men."

"Why?"

"Because when someone paves the road in your village, the men can no longer bring dirt or mud into the house and a woman's job is made easier. And when someone puts pipes and water in your house, the women don't have to go outside in the middle of the night, especially in winter, to the privy to take a piss. Wouldn't you like someone who did that for you?"

Ivan coughed regularly throughout the night as he slept on a sofa in the kitchen. He and Maria had given up their bed for my wife and me and wouldn't take no for an answer. That is what a host does in this country unless they are rich and have more than one bedrppm. My cousin and husband slept in the room that had been hers when she lived at home.

The cough reminded me of his grandfather Najda's cough, but it was different. This was because of Ivan's smoking. A cigarette was in his hands almost all the time he was awake. The fore and middle fingers on his right hand were stained yellow from the nicotine deposited there by the strong tobacco used in the cigarettes. From time to time, he would reach for an inhaler and then pop a pill, an antihistamine.

"The pills work best," Ivan said, "but they are hard to find. I use them sparingly."

I took one of Ivan's empty prescription bottles and stowed it in my camera bag. I told him that I knew a doctor in New York who would write me another prescription and I would send them to him as soon as I returned.

The departure was anticlimactic.

"Everyone cried, even I had tears in my eyes and so did the worn old soldier. He kissed me on both cheeks then on my lips, as my grandfather and other close relatives did.

"Wait," Maria yelled, as I was about to start the car.

She ran into the house and almost immediately came out, carrying a filled plastic bag in her hand.

"You must take this," Ivan said.

"What is it?"

Ivan opened the bag.

Immediately I recognized the delicious, musty aroma of dried forest-picked mushrooms. It was the traditional gift one gives to someone beginning a journey.

"Salt," said Ivan, "I think you can find everywhere.

Chapter 57   The North Side of the Mountains

After we drove through Humenné, we made good time driving
west on the Czech highways. En route, we stopped for an hour to
view the numerous war memorials the Soviets had erected on both
the Czech and Polish sides of the border in the Dukla Pass. It had
been the scene of some severe fighting during the war...both wars.

Ironically, the same guard was on duty on the Polish side
and recognized the name and then my face. He called his superior
in the office. He came out, looked over the passports and visas and
waved us on.

"Thank God," my wife said as we continued the drive north.
The drive to the town of Dukla was relatively short. We then took
the road that headed east and moved through the county seats of
Sianok and Lisko in the very southeast corner of Poland. With new,
more detailed maps in hand, we began searching for the villages of
Smil'nyk, Protisne and Dvernyk. On the new maps, we discovered
that the names were changed to Polish and were now Smolnik and
Dwernyk, but Protisne was missing. These had to be the villages I
wanted because they were all in a line on the Sian (San in Polish)
River. However, on the latest maps we purchased in Poland, only
the village of Smolnik was listed.

"A whole village cannot disappear," I said to my wife as she
navigated, "can it?"

I was literate enough in Rusnak to carry on a conversation
with anyone we met and when that failed, three years of German
at the university would save me because it seemed that everyone
here spoke some degree of German. At first, I thought it might have
been because of the more than 200 years that this land had been

part of the Austrian Empire. Later, I was told, it was because of the German, not Austrian, occupation. I was disappointed, as we trekked east, because I had expected to meet more and more people with whom I could speak Rusnak, especially as we approached the cities of Sianok and Lisko. It was not to be. There was a dearth of Rusnaks in these lands.

As we drove from Lisko, the county's capital, I became aware that the number of people on the roads and in the small villages through which we passed was rapidly decreasing. We stopped one time to confirm directions with an elderly woman who was raking hay someone had cut along the side of the road.

"She looks almost exactly like my grandmother," I said to my wife. "She was short, not quite 5 feet, round, wore a *babushka* over her gray hair and even her facial features looked genetically familiar. I was amazed that I could so easily understand her reply.

"At last!" I thought.

"You are a Rusnak?" I asked.

"Oh! No!" she responded. "I am Polish. I was born here."

I didn't try to correct her or make her understand, though at the time I was unaware that she may have had a greater reason for not being a Rusnak other than maybe a poor childhood memory.

The road turned southeast toward our goals and rose steadily in elevation. Hills on each side grew smaller in height the farther up the road we traveled. From time to time we would see a fair-sized stream along the road and I assumed it was the Sian River. It has its source high atop the side of Halych Mountain, on the border where Poland, Slovakia and Ukraine meet. Field crops grew sparse as we traveled and larger patches of woods now dominated the landscape.

Finally we saw the sign DWERNIK.

In less than a minute we passed through it. It was no more than four or five houses and a bus stop.

"Where is the village?" I said aloud to myself. This is where my grandfather lived with a relative for a year or two when he was growing up. He was bounced around a lot. This is where his cousins, the Mohilchaks, came from. Oh, well. According to the map, Smolnik has to be just around the corner. There should be the village, then the road crosses the river and Protisne is on the other side. Just like my grandfather used to say."

In a few minutes of driving, we were at the river and the bridge. There was no Smolnik. There was a slight detour at the river as a construction crew was working on a new bridge that would cross the Sian. The summer must have been dry because there was only a trickle of water in what was a streambed that was about 100 feet wide.

I stopped the car and asked a man, with a hexagonal STOP & GO sign, where was Smolnik? He replied something in Polish. It wasn't a simple answer and I didn't understand.

Then I asked him where was Procisne. He pointed across the river to a small cluster of houses near the road. One, near the center, had a small sign with a Pilsner glass on it that hung slightly onto the road. We took the detour over the river and came to the sign, just before the cluster of houses.

About a dozen houses flanked the road. I sensed that something had changed. This isn't where the village of my grandfather was located, according to what he had told me. But, that was a long time ago and he could easily have forgotten. Or, I could have forgotten. It was supposed to be a hundred or so yards from the main road, along the banks of a small stream which here led into the Sian River, opposite Smil'nyk. I could see the little stream in the distance and only one small house, really a barn, stood by the river. There was the remnant of a sandy, dirt road that led from where we stood, down along the river, and to the barn.

"My God," I thought to myself. "What has happened to these villages. Maybe it was the last war. There were some battles fought near here, but I didn't recall reading or hearing of any being held here. It could even have been the first war because my grandparents had left this valley a dozen years before it started."

My wife and I were standing outside the car with the map spread on the hood when a middle-aged man in one of the nearby houses spotted us. I looked up for a moment when I heard a screen door slam and saw him approaching us. As he neared the car, I looked up and said "Good Day" in Rusnak.

"Good Day," the man answered in Polish.

"Is this Smolnik? Is it the same place as Smil'nyk?

"The man answered no to both questions, but pointed back across the river, to a hill above where the men were working on the bridge. The sides of the knob-like hill were planted in alfalfa and timothy, except for a rectangular cluster of trees that capped its top.

"What is your name?" I asked hoping it might be familiar. When the man hesitated to answer, I asked "Then, where are all the

Rusnaks? Where are the Najdas, the Salabajs, the Mynkos, and the Pavuks? Where are they all? Isn't this their village?"

The man suddenly looked quizzically at me, shrugged his shoulders and said, "Nie rozumie" and walked away.

"Shit," I said to my wife. "We've come all this way and there is no one here. What has happened here? I was hoping he might recognize one of the names."

It was then that I again looked back toward to where the men were working on the bridge. There tall grasses in the field above waved gently against the force of a light southwest breeze. Near the top, in the cluster of trees, I spotted a cross poking above the tree tops. It was a Christian cross but not an Orthodox cross. It bore only one horizontal bar.

"Well, I'll be damned," I said to my wife. "There it is. Right where my grandfather said it was. There is the church he had started to work on in 1903 when he was just a young man." Later, I discovered I was wrong. This was the church the people of both villages used.

We drove back across the bridge and parked alongside the road where a dirt path led up the hill to the church. From the top I could see where Protisne should have been, across the river and along both sides of a small stream that entered the Sian just downriver of the bridge. There was nothing there.

Smil'nyk, now Smolnik, should have surrounded the church. There was nothing left but the remnants of a crudely built concrete road over the top of the hill. It ran through the middle of the village and in front of the church. The road was constructed of 8-foot square blocks of poured concrete that had buckled and separated years ago, probably caused by frost heaves. It would have been a difficult obstacle course even for a Jeep. It looked like it hadn't seen a cart or car in more than 50 years.

Then in the distance, off the main road, where the village of Protisne should have been, I spotted a series of low-lying mounds. They stood out because the grass on them was a slightly different color and seemed a different variety. They puzzled me.

The church atop the hill in Smil'nyk was a typical wooden Rusnak church. Several years later, I discovered, that it was built in 1791 as a Greek Catholic church and renovated in 1921. It was abandoned after 1947 but in 1971 was renovated as a Roman Catholic Church. Because it had so few parishioners, in 1990, it was returned to the Rusnaks in the area as a Russian Orthodox Church.

Religion was so strong among Rusnaks that few villages, regardless of how small, went without a church. The cost of building a church was divided by the number of families in that community and nearby who would attend the church, then each one was assessed that amount. Thus, everyone became a "plank" owner and the people actually owned the church. Then they hired, and fired when they didn't like him, a priest. Orthodox Rusnaks felt allegiance to no one but God. This may also have contributed to the independent nature of many Rusnaks, especially when it came to religion.

Except for the stone foundations, their churches were built entirely of wood and always set on an east-west axis. Its construction was based on a tripartite design--sanctuary, nave and choir--each section was topped by its own cupola or pyramid. Each of the three sections of this church, that was once surrounded by the grass-thatched farmhouses of Smil'nyk, was topped by a large, shingle-covered, four-sided pyramid. The center section was wider and taller than those flanking it. Each pyramid was then topped by a small cupola. On top of each cupola was a three-member cross. In most other Rusnak churches, the front or choir third was often the highest. In some, the bell tower was atop the nave but others followed Ukrainian traditions and the bell was mounted in its own structure on the ground alongside the church. That was one way to avoid raising a heavy bell in a rural mountain environment.

Early Rusnak churches were extremely pragmatic and had no pews so attendees stood throughout the long services. Nor did they have wooden floors, like many of their houses. This was an expense they could do without unless the village was wealthier than most. The outside was covered in fir shingles, usually made on the spot if fir trees were available, or bought from villages in fir country with men who did little more than make and sell shingles. Usually they were left natural, unpainted that eventually gave the church an overall brown, somber, rustic look.

Rusnaks had developed a unique architecture in the construction of their wooden churches that is still reflected today in Slovakia, Poland, Ukraine and even in the Russian countryside. Wherever one has survived it is usually made into a historic site even though it may be in use. Its construction is unique and its shingle siding easily blended with the land and the forests from which it was built. Each church was a part of the people's character in that village and was shaped by the land and the environment of these mountain foothills.

This church looked like it had been rebuilt several times in the last 100 years. It had suffered the ravages of time, weather and probably wars. Only the foundation members on the stones looked old enough to have been handled by my grandfather. That created a doubt in my mind. My certainty that this was the church my grandfather had a hand in building began to falter.

"In a way, I'm glad my grandfather never returned to Europe to see this," I said to my wife. "It looks like the Rusnaks never raised enough money to finish it as an Orthodox Church. That's probably a Roman Catholic or Uniat Cross. The Uniats are Rusnaks who have accepted the pope."

" I know," she said, "you've told me that before.

"Maybe it's because all the Orthodox Rusnaks left and went to America to seek their fortunes."

"Maybe so," I answered.

There was a sign on the door, not written in Cyrillic but in Latin script. It was in Polish, announcing when services were held. Its name was St. Michael's Church. "Funny," I thought to myself, "I don't every remember my grandfather telling me the name of the church he was building. It probably didn't get a name until it was completed, until it was consecrated."

The front door was a poor fit and allowed anyone to see part of the inside. The church had a dirt floor and no pews.

"They still stand during service, like in the old days," I said. "It will be another four days before someone will be here. I'd like to see inside but we can't wait that long. We have to be in Prague on Sunday or we'll miss the flight home."

"Besides," said Shirl, "I don't know how long your mother can take watching the boys. We need to get home."

"She's tough," I answered. "Remember, Baba is a Hunky."

I jiggled the change in my front pocket. Among the Polish zloty I found a new Kennedy half-dollar. I pushed it through the crack in the front door with such force that it bounced across the wooden vestibule into the center of the church. It rolled in a tightening circle and fell when it lost momentum.

"God, what I wouldn't give to see the expression of the person's face who finds and wonders how it got there," I said.

This was in the late-70s when Americans visiting these villages was still extremely rare. It was only because of my press credentials that the Polish communists allowed the others and me into the country. They needed the tourist dollars. They needed any kind of dollars to bolster their fading economy. And, our side trip was not on our assigned communist host's travel itinerary that we were perfunctorily given. It made my wife nervous all the time that we were away from the body of American journalists.

"Let's go down and take a look at those rectangular mounds," I said. "They are where the village of Protisne should be."

At first, as we walked among them, neither my wife nor I could figure out what they were. Each one was about 15 feet wide and varied in length from 30 to 40 feet long. All rose to a level height about a foot above the surrounding ground. They were all laid out in a row-like pattern on both sides of the small creek that flowed into the Sian. Then, the realization of what I was looking at struck me.

"They are house foundations," I said to my wife. "I remember that few of the houses had wooden floors. Most were well-trodden earthen floors. This is where the village was, just like my grandfather explained. The houses were located on each side of a small creek they called Hluboki. It means deep."

"You better look here," Shirl said. She had wandered off in one direction just beyond the house mounds. "It looks like it was a cemetery," she said.

"My God, what happened here," I said in astonishment.

In great disarray were a dozen or so tombstones. A true count was impossible. Between them were mangled, iron and wire Orthodox crosses. On some stones, I could still read the Cyrillic writing.

"This was a Rusnak cemetery," I said. "This was a Rusnak village. This was Protisne.

"One of these mounds belonged to my grandfather's house. It looks as if someone came in here with a bulldozer and intentionally leveled the cemetery. It was completely leveled, but left uncovered, as some sort of reminder.

"I'll bet there are similar mounds along the river in Smil'nyk; and I bet that if we looked closely in the woods near Dvernyk, we'd find others."

"Who could have done such a thing? And why?" Shirl asked.

"Look," I said as I approached the farthest end of the rubble. "This is a larger mound than the rest."

Around its periphery were large stone slabs that must have been hauled from the river-bottom and used as a foundation. They were scattered in disarray and had been so long here that no one stone remained atop another.

"It must have been the old church where my great-grandparents attended," I said. "Maybe one of those crumpled grave markers belonged to my great-grandfather Yurko Najda. Wouldn't that be a kick if I could find that? But," after considering what I had just said, "I doubt it. They couldn't afford an iron cross, let alone a stone monument."

Reading a few of the broken monuments, I realized that all the stones were from a later date, and even found the year 1944 engraved on one stone. However, it was an intriguing thought, that somewhere in the ground before me were the remains of several generations of Najdas. It was a lot to grasp in a few moments of thought.

"It's getting late," I said to my wife. "I think that one of the buildings on the road below Smolnik is a tavern. Maybe it is an inn. It might be nice to stay in one."

"I don't know," she answered. "I wouldn't hesitate if they were like the country inns in England. But here, even churches have only dirt floors."

"Good day," I said in Polish to the man behind the bar in the tavern.

"Good day," he answered in Polish. "What do you want?"

I understood what he said but blurted out in English, "Two cold beers."

"Ah," said the bartender. "You English?"

"No, we're Americans."

The man was about my age, in his early 50s, with graying hair and a sanguine complexion that indicated he might have taken out some of his tavern's profits in beer.

He reached under the bar and with a pudgy hand placed two glass steins near the faucet that held the beer.

"Pilsner," he said with one hand on the faucet handle and the other holding the mouth of the stein against the spigot, waiting for an answer.

"Dobré," I said, and the man pulled the lever.

"You are Russian?" the bartender asked.

"Why?" I answered.

"You say dobré instead of *dobzheh* as in Polish.

"No. I am an American, but my grandfather lived here. He was a Rusnak and he built that church on the hill," I gestured in the direction of the church, "when he was a young man."

"Wait," the man said. "My English is no so good. But my son been to Chi-ka-go. He speaks good."

The man turned toward the stairs leading to rooms above the tavern and yelled for Stanislaw. A few minutes later a young man in his early 20s appeared and bounced down the stairs while asking his father what he wanted. His father told him and Stan turned to me and my wife,

"My name is Stanley," he said. "I lived in Chicago with my uncle and his family for four years. The last year, I attended a university there but ran out of money. I studied English here in school for five years before I went over. I hope I have not forgotten the English I learned."

His American was excellent.

"Yes, we have two guest rooms upstairs and both are vacant. Do you want one?" He told his father and he in turn yelled to his wife, or a woman who was in a room behind the bar. He told her there were guests and she immediately went upstairs to prepare a room.

"Do you serve meals here? I asked.

"Yes, but they are simple country meals. Our menu is very limited." Stanley turned to his father and asked what was available.

"We have ham tonight. Sliced ham that my father smoked in our own smokehouse. Of course, there are always potatoes and beans, green beans."

"Sounds okay to me," Shirley said. I, too, agreed.

"Do you work here for your father?" I asked.

"Only for a month or two during the summer. I am at the university in Krakow, a political science major. I just finished my third year and am home studying. I help out here and on my father's small farm.

"What are you doing here?" he asked me.

"I have come to see the place where my relatives were born and lived. My grandmother was from here, Smil'nyk, as it was called then. My grandfather lived across the river. He was born in Protisne. Now, it isn't even on the map, or even a bus stop. He also lived for a while in Dvernyk. But there is nothing there now. My relatives lived in several villages around here, some as far up the Sian, and others up the Wolosatka River to Wolosate.

"I was hoping to find the children of my great uncle Andrij Najda, or the Mynkos who were from here. My grandmother was from here; also, the Salabajs, the Antonishaks and the Pavuks. There are more, but there don't seem to be any Rusnaks living here. When they left for America, before the First World War, they inhabited all these villages.

"Was it the war that destroyed these villages?" I asked. "Was it the war that left no Rusnaks here? Where are they? Where have they gone?"

Stanley was slow in responding. I could see in his eyes and his facial features that he was having difficulty formulating a response.

"In a way," he said, hesitatingly, "it was a war. There are a few Rusnaks living here, now. They are slowly coming back?"

"Coming back. What do you mean...'coming back'?"

"It is a sad story. It is a story that many Poles are ashamed of. Even our government today still won't admit to what happened here. And, many ordinary Poles took part in it, but it was mostly the military, and the police...and the Russians, the Communist Russians and the Communist Poles."

I could sense that Stanley was getting a little heated; a little excited.

"I hardly know where to begin."

"We have the entire night to hear it," I said and looked around the tavern room. Two men, who had been drinking, got up and left as Stanley took a seat at the table with my wife and me. I sensed that Stanley seemed relieved after they were gone. His voice gained a decibel. He was concerned that they might hear what he was going to say.

Stanley was about to get started when his mother came through the kitchen door with plates, glasses and table settings in her hands and arms. Stanley got up and was about to leave us to eat alone when Shirl invited him to have supper with us.

Chapter 58   An Exchange of Populations

"The seeds of discontent between the Rus in western Galicia and Poles were sown in the 14th century," Stanley said after he came back from helping his mother clear the dinner table. "In 1340, in a desire to expand his kingdom eastward, Casimir the Great, King of Poland, wanted the land in the Rus province of Galicia, or Halychyna in Ukrainian. To do so, he backed a group of Rus boyars who were intent on finding a more generous benefactor as their leader. They assassinated Yuriy II, the last of the Romanovychi rulers of Galicia, then the western-most province of Rus, today's Ukraine.

"At that time, Galicia was ripe for the taking. It had been so devastated a hundred years earlier by the Mongol invasion that it was unable to recover. The Tatars killed the major portion of its population, its women and children were taken away into slavery, and its cities and villages were looted and burned. It was a depopulated land. That is when the church in Protisne was destroyed.

"It was an easy target for the Polish king, when our nation's southern and eastern borders with Galicia was the left bank of the Vistula River. But Nikolaj, you have to understand the times. Poland was then being pushed eastward by German princes who piecemeal were reclaiming land they had abandoned a few centuries earlier in their hasty migration south toward the Alps.

"Casimir simply annexed land on the other side of the river and moved soldiers into the decimated country without any organized opposition. He immediately arrested all the Rus nobles who survived in this half of the province and forced the remaining Rus peasants into serfdom. In reality, they were already the serfs of the few Rus noblemen who survived the Tatars. It was the way of the times, serfdom was everywhere in Europe," Stanley claimed.

"The greatest prize was the capture, almost without a battle, of the city of Krakow, then a major center of learning and commerce in Europe. He even made Krakow the capital of Poland," Stanley said. "Casimir then divided these annexed lands, the spoils of a one-sided war, among his noblemen, down to the lowest count, and even rewarded his military officers with newfound feudal fiefdoms. They existed unchallenged up until WW I. This land appropriation didn't take place all at once, but in increments, in stages over the ensuing centuries until stopped by the Soviets in 1939. Actually, this Polish stratagem didn't end until 1945.

"During all those years, even though these lands gradually became part of Poland, its inhabitants remained primarily Rusnaks. Among the Rusnaks lived Gypsies and large numbers of Jews. The latter were enticed by the Polish gentry to come from Germany to help establish a commercial system in Galicia and a management regimen for the new landlords. That's how their numbers came to dominate the larger villages and cities in Galicia. Also, a growing number of civil officials, of all ranks, were sent to Galicia from Warsaw to administer the regions for the kings who followed Casimir and finally for the government of the Polish Republic.

"From about 1850 and into the early 20th century all of Europe was going through pangs of ethnic identification and self-determination. In reality, that is what was proposed and executed at the peace table after World War I. Even the League of Nations, in 1920, had as it prime objective, the relocation of borders in Europe along ethnographic lines. In the end, it seemed that every ethnic group got something they asked for except the Ruthenians, as the League referred to Rusnaks, or Rusyns living in western Galicia and Slovakia. They were again returned to Poland."

"Stanley," I interrupted. "This is all interesting but what has it to do with the missing people here?"

"If you are to truly understand what happened here, you must know what events made this possible. Even today, most Poles outside of Galicia, are not aware of what took place here because our information is strictly controlled by the Polish communist government."

"You sound more like a Rusnak than a Pole," I said.

"Ethnicity has nothing to do with truth in history," Stanley responded.

"That's right," I rebutted. "But it does influence how you interpret what has happened in history."

"I didn't think it was apparent," Stanley said. "But if you must know, my mother is a Rusnak. She grew up in Lower Silesia and returned here in the late '50s as a teenager looking for her family's village. It was then she met my father who is all Polish. She knows a little Rusyn but the schools in Silesia were teaching only Polish. Not only was Rusyn not taught but also it was forbidden to be spoken in public. But, that is getting ahead of the story."

"Stan," I said, "you seem especially knowledgeable about the modern history of southeast Poland. Why? Is it your Rusnak half that is the motivation?"

"In a way that is part of it. The other is that I am in the throes of writing a paper. It is a very important paper. If it is accepted, I will earn a half-semester of credit and it will make me eligible for graduate work."

"It all started going wrong for Ukrainians in 1945 when Roosevelt and Churchill gave in to Stalin's demands for the resettlement of Poles living in Ukraine east of the Curzon Line, a new border, and the Ukrainians who suddenly found themselves living in Poland because of the new location of the border. They called it an 'exchange of populations.' But that, too, is getting a little ahead of it," Stanley said and paused momentarily.

"Ukrainian nationalism had been suppressed by the tsars for 300 years after they gained control of Kyiv. But, when Russia became part of the Soviet Union, the communists tried to eradicate Ukraine. Stalin, I believe, feared a Ukrainian revolt almost as much as he did Germany's plans for Russia. Between 1919 and 1941, he outright killed more the three-quarters of a million Ukrainians or sent them to Siberia where they disappeared. In the 1932-33 famine, he starved--some say 5 million and others 7 million--Ukrainians by taking all their food and sending it to Russia. He also knew that there were Ukrainians out of his immediate grasp, more than a million in Poland and Czechoslovakia. He wanted to get them all. He seemed to have an innate fear of Ukrainians someday rising internally and taking back their country.

"Stalin decided to totally eliminate Ukrainians in Eastern Galicia and Volhynia. After September 1939, Soviet troops and the NKVD began the slaughter of thousands of Ukrainians. Their actions were slowed, then stopped when Germany attacked the Soviet Union in June 1941. It is no wonder that some of the Ukrainians sought relief and help from the Germans. At first, the Germans, especially the military, seemed fair. Later that year, in a foolish move, the Germans, mostly the SS people, believed that Russia had been defeated. The result was that they suddenly changed their policy and introduced their own genocidal version called *Schrychhlichkeit*. It was a policy of terror and fright that the Kaiser invented during the first Great War. It was the systematic extermination of an entire ethnic group, the Ukrainians, from the Steppes. The Germans wanted the *chorny zemla*, the black earth, as much as the Russians, and now had a second opportunity to get it. It was a veritable breadbasket.

"The policy suddenly caused thousands of young Ukrainians to go underground. They formed the *Ukraianska Povstancha Armiya* or in English, the Ukrainian Insurgent Army. The UPA fought the Germans until the end of the war. Early in 1944, as the Soviets drove the Germans back and regained parts of eastern Poland, Stalin immediately revived his policy of eliminating Ukrainians and their dreams of becoming an independent nation. The UPA then turned and began fighting the communists.

"The USSR's first attempt to get the Ukrainians living in Poland to move to a Ukraine, controlled by Soviets, was a propaganda blitz asking them to voluntarily move east. They were promised free land and free farm machinery. But too many Ukrainians in Galicia remembered how Stalin had treated their countrymen east of the Curzon line just six years earlier. Very few of the 1,200,000 Ukrainians living in what had suddenly become Poland responded.

"Not a patient person, Stalin then used Marshal Malinovsky's 2nd Army, returning eastward after the war from Berlin, to gather up all the Ukrainians in Poland and move them forcibly into the Soviet Union. The onslaught began. But before it did, taking advantage of the army's movement, thousands of Ukrainians in the Malinovsky's army deserted as they moved eastward from Poland to their homeland in Ukraine. The deserters quickly joined the ranks of the UPA. The Soviet army, familiar with fighting on open battlefields and with heavy weapons and unlimited manpower, found it impossible to gain the upper hand against the UPA because they fought a guerilla-style war. At their height they numbered nearly 40,000 men.

"Stalin then used the Polish military, which he controlled with an iron grip, to take on the task. The Polish communists found it even more difficult to battle the UPA than the Soviets. The UPA forces even carried the battle against the Poles into western Galicia and were able for a time to control large parts of Galicia. They actually controlled and administered a triangular area defined roughly by the Dukla Pass, to Sianok and back into the mountains at the Lupkov Pass just north of Svetlice.

"Like all partisans, they owed much of their existence to local support. When this spilled over into western Galicia, into here, where we are now," Stanley emphasized by raising his voice and stomping one foot on the wooden floor, "it was Rusnaks, the Lemkos and the Boykos, who favored and supported them.

"At first, the Polish communists tried to duplicate what the Soviets had offered...a voluntary move. Communists here, like those in Russia, saw the UPA challenging their efforts and authority, but were unable to accomplish anything with the size of their forces stationed in the area even though it was fairly large. Chaos caused by the UPA among the Polish officers and their rank-and-file was so complete that the Soviets found it necessary to send in many Russian officers and NKVD personnel to reorganize the effort.

"In the summer of 1945, the Polish 8th Infantry was then sent here to defend the 'green border' as they called the wooded continental divide. Warsaw, now no longer fighting a German Army, was able to move a large force of soldiers into this corner of the country. They began a more determined effort to subdue and eliminate the UPA. Of course, they were under constant pressure from Uncle Joe. They were aided by the Soviet's NKVD. In fact, most of the officers leading the Poles, except for the very top brass, were Russians in Polish uniforms.

"The Soviets also encouraged marauding bands of 'Red Partisans' to form in Poland as well as in Ukraine. Their aim was to let these communist civilians terrorize and pillage these lands and wantonly destroy its people, burn their the villages and take the blame. The intent was also to make it more attractive for the inhabitants to move east. The Reds worked in unison with the local Polish police and the Polish secret police, the Internal Security Department, or the KBW.

"Those in the Polish government, as well as the military who were cognizant of their history, looked upon this as an opportunity to realize an ambition Casimir began 600 years ago, to finally remove all Rusnaks and Ukrainians from parts of Galicia that they now claimed as their land. For centuries, especially the latter two, the Polish ruling class was unwilling to give up its inherent plans to subjugate other peoples along its borders, especially Ukrainians. Too often, the Polish people were blamed for the greed of their royalty. The number of Polish counts even today, without a fiefdom, are as numerous as fleas on a dog's belly.

"The Polish army began to have limited success against the UPA as new recruits for the insurgent army, to replace those killed or captured, became difficult to find. The organization within the UPA also began to break down as their numbers dwindled. Most of their efforts now were relegated to hit-and-run tactics.

"It was then that segments of the UPA moved deeper into the forests of the Beskids for protection. These mountains were the perfect terrain for conducting guerrilla warfare against the Polish police and army units. Despite their renewed, intensified efforts, the police and army found it impossible to stamp out the UPA. They saw Rusnaks living in this region's numerous mountain villages as the major stumbling block to eradicating the UPA.

"The Polish communists then switched to a new tactic. They decided that they would make examples of several villages to influence the whole of 'Polish' Galicia. One such effort took place south of Sianok, the county seat just north of here. There was a large unit of Polish soldiers stationed there and led by Soviet officers. They started with Zavadka Morokhivska. Armed soldiers ringed the village. First, artillery bombarded it. As the villagers tried to flee outside the ring they were shot or bayoneted. After the shelling, the soldiers moved into the village, looting the houses, and holding people at bay inside the house. Any who resisted were immediately shot. When they were done, they began setting houses on fire. As the people inside ran out, they, too, were killed and many were thrown back into the blazing houses. Only three of the 70 houses in that village were left standing. The next day they did the same to Mokre, then Kamienne, Ratnawica and Wolica, and a few others whose names I cannot remember.

"Still, the stupid villagers remained in their homes and resisted any attempts to move them. I remember a piece I read somewhere that one old woman said that she would rather die where her ancestors had died for the last 1,000 years than be starved to death on some Soviet co-op in Ukraine. They immediately accommodated her. By 1947, two-thirds of the Lemko population, your Rusnaks, had been moved by communist authorities to Soviet Ukraine.

"Occasionally, the UPA came to the defense of a village in the Beskids that was about to be destroyed by the Polish army. But, after an initial encounter against such superior forces they usually melted into the surrounding woods.

"It wasn't until a small band of UPA fighters ran into a patrol unit of the Polish army and killed most of the men that all hell really broke loose in these mountains.

"I need a drink," Stanley said.

"It just happened," he continued after draining a stein of beer, "that among the dead in this brief, unplanned encounter was the Polish General Karol Swierczewski. He was kind of a hero to the army. In the 1930s, he fought with the communists in Spain and later in France during the war. He was known for being ruthless, brutal, and Stalin put him in charge of moving all Ukrainians out of Poland. The death of their hero at the hands of partisans so infuriated the Polish military that they fanatically pursued his plans to wage an all-out effort to rid the area of the UPA and all Rusnaks and Ukrainians. To do this, they then moved in several battalions from other parts of Poland.

"'Black Spring' is what the people, both Rusnaks and Poles called the spring of 1947.

"The Polish People's Army gave it the code name 'Operation Vistula'. Vistula is the river that was used as the original border to separate Poland and Galicia. I thought it was an odd choice. It must have reminded them of the border in the 14th century. I know no other reason. The main thrust of the operation was so thorough that it lasted only 27 days, from April 4 to the 31, as the official report stated. In reality, it continued on into mid summer before they felt they had fully accomplished their goal. When it was over, 273 villages in this region disappeared from the face of the earth. Only ashes and smoke remained. Protisne was but one of them. The Polish army, police, and Soviet 'advisors' had removed more than 150,000 remaining Rusnaks from these lands. There wasn't a live Rusnak in the entire area, that is how complete it was.

"The army swept these hills like a plague of locust. They knocked on every door and people were told they had 24 hours to get ready to move. But, even before the first day was over, some units were forcing thousands of Rusnaks onto the roads and herding them toward railroad cars waiting in several locations that took them to previous German territories in western and northern Poland. They were told that they could take only what they could carry.

"Not all of the Rusnaks in a few villages in southeastern Poland went to the west. For those from the village of Wolosate, it was a long foot-march to the East. For the elderly, sick and impaired, it was a death march to the border with Ukraine. Most of the old people never made it. Led by NKVD officers in Polish uniforms, they and Polish guards used the slightest excuse to bayonet or shoot someone. Children were no exception. The trail east was marked by a line of dead bodies. Those who did cross the border were lost in Soviet Ukraine.

"I once saw a photograph of the hordes of people leaving a village. I don't remember the village's name. It could have been Wolosate. The line extended as far as the eye could see. There were many carts, drawn by ox or by cows. The horses were confiscated years ago. The cows were eaten *en route*. People were loaded down with baskets and they labored to carry bundles made out of sheets that contained all their possessions. After a while, the sides of the roads became littered with what they could not carry. Most were women, old and young, many carrying children or babies. There were some men in the lines but none were young. Most men and older boys had long ago escaped into the hills or were killed in the war. Some had joined the UPA. It was a heart-wrenching photo.

"Over a million people were shipped west in boxcars. After the war, most of the German province of Silesia, that had an equal population of Poles and Germans, was given to Poland by the Allies. The Germans were given the option to leave voluntarily or they would be deported. Most willingly moved to Germany. Poland now had a large area that needed to be populated. Most Poles already living there immediately moved into the vacant German houses because they were often better built. Silesia was picked by the Poles because it was also as far away from Galicia as the Polish communists could disperse the Rusnaks.

"Operation Vistula was only the beginning for these people. The Polish intelligentsia came up with a unique plan—one of dilution and assimilation--to end forever the Rusnak problem in Poland. Those Rusnaks from Galicia were separated into units of one to three or four families and placed for settlement among indigenous Poles in Silesia. Their placement was designed so that they were always too far from other resettled Rusnaks and little opportunity for them to communicate with each other.

"Also, in their new location, their children attended Polish-only schools and were forbidden to speak Rusnak in public. Nor were they allowed to build their own churches, either Orthodox or Greek Catholic, but were forced to attend Roman Catholic churches if they felt the need to worship. Nor, could they form any organizations of their own. And, for more than a decade, they were not allowed to return to their native villages.

"Not only were the Rusnaks of the Beskids, Lemkos or Lemkivshchyna, moved to Lower Silesia, so were other Galician Ukrainians from Kholmschyna and Pidlasia. Some were shipped to Pomerania and the city of Danzig which was renamed Gdansk. By doing so, the Poles hoped that in time, these people would be assimilated into the Polish culture and loose their identity and no longer be a threat to the government's claim to Galicia. It certainly was a drastic way to remove all support for the UPA in Poland. Some UPA remnants attempted to reach Austria through Czechoslovakia, over the "green border," or crossed southeast into Soviet Ukraine.

"That is what happened to your grandfather's Galicia!"

He may not be Hodinko's Hungarian prince, who starved hundreds of Rusnaks in the village of Uzhhok, but this one was certainly among the privileged class in 1938 with a private hunting lodge and an estate dedicated to hunting and self-entertainment. (Margaret-White photo entitled: *Hungarian Landlord at Ease*).

Chapter 59   The Hermit of Wolosate

"Well Nicholas, now that you know why there are no Rusnaks running around in these hills to greet you, what are you going to do?" Stanley asked.

"You must be dry after a long story like that," I said. "Besides, the ham was a bit salty and I don't think the beer was enough, I need a cognac to dilute it. Will you join us?"

"Is the pope Catholic?" Stanley chuckled. "I picked that up in Chicago. Most people around here don't appreciate it."

"I know, he's Polish," I said.

"There are a few Rusnaks who have returned here from Lower Silesia, but not those sent to Soviet Ukraine or Siberia. The Polish government no longer seems to fear them, especially since the UPA is no longer in existence. Most who come back are young, seeking their villages. Some stay for a few days, cry a lot and then go back. If they wanted to buy back their own land, they would have to buy it from a Pole who has been resettled here, like my father. The government practically gave him the farm just so he would move here. Older Rusnaks who come back for a visit still remember their language but they are slowly disappearing. The young ones are now so Polish you can only tell they are Rusnaks by their last names.

"What were the names of your relatives who lived here? I know there are no Karases. But I do know a Karas in Krakow. He has a photo studio near the university."

"My grandmother was Kateryna Mynkova," I answered. "Her mother was a Pavuk and her cousins were Antonishaks and Salabajs. They lived here, in Smil'nyk. Sorry, I mean Smolnik as you call it in Polish. My grandfather's name was Vasyl Najda. There is a small river near Krakow that flows south into the Vistula that is named the Najda."

"Humm. Najda you say. That's interesting. Did they all go to America?"

"Yes. He had three brothers, Andrij, Ivan and Hryec."

"Are they all dead now...in America?"

"My grandfather is dead, and so are his brothers Ivan and Hryec. His oldest brother Andrij returned to Protisne in 1922. He had a wife and family here. No one has heard of him since they said good-bye at the train station in Goodtown."

"This is very interesting," said Stanley. "Have you ever been to Wolosate?"

"No," I answered, "but I know where it is. I have studied this region thoroughly but only from maps. It is on the Wolosatka River, a tributary to the Sian, about 10 miles farther up into the Beskids. It is not far from Halych Mountain, where the Sian starts."

"That is true," said Stanley. "Your knowledge of geography is good. Have you ever heard of the mystery of Wolosate? No. Good."

"Wolosate was one of the largest villages in this part of the Beskids, and had nearly 3,000 people in 1939, the last time a census was taken. But, when someone went up there in early summer in 1947, there wasn't a soul around and all the houses were burned and the farm animals gone. It was as if it had never existed, so thorough was its destruction."

"Was it part of the Vistula Operation?"

"Yes and no," Stanley said. "The truth eventually came out. Wolosate is just a few kilometers away from the Ukrainian border. What happened was that, at the end of June, in 1946, the Polish army surrounded the village, hundreds of infantrymen with bayonets on their rifles, like they did in other areas. But this time they didn't start shooting. Everyone was ordered out of their houses, not even given time to get a coat or shoes. They were force marched across the border. On the other side, the Soviets were waiting for them. The border was closed behind them, never reopened, and nothing was heard of them again.

"But that is not completely true. There is a man up there; we call him the Hermit of Wolosate. There are only three or four houses there now, all along the road, except for one small hut that is up a little path and built next to a spring. I have been there several times and have seen and spoken to him. He is an interesting old man and I think you too will find him very interesting...if I am right."

"What do you mean?" Shirley asked, "if you are right."

"You will have to determine that for yourself. Tomorrow morning, before you head for Praha, I think you should go up there and see him. It won't take long."

The next morning, after a traditional Beskid breakfast of bacon, eggs, mushrooms, potatoes, sausage, garlic and onions, Shirl and I bid Stanley and his parents good-bye, promising to stop for a moment on the way back.

From the inn where Protisne was supposed to be, the main road south into the mountains switches from following the Sian to following the Wolosatka River. The latter flows into the Sian a hundred yards upriver of Protisne. It is a stream about half the size of the Sian and begins in springs on the north side of Halych Mountain, 1,335 meters (4,390 feet) high. The one-lane, poorly-paved road soon turns into a gravel road and continually curves back-and-forth as it rises in elevation. Cultivated fields are rare and, where the forests of larch and spruce don't crowd the road, are replaced by open, marshy meadows.

Almost without warning, the road turned sharply west and entered a swampy, treeless clearing where two streams, one from the right and the other from the left, entered the Wolosatka. Just beyond them, a battered white and blue porcelain sign on a bus stop shanty read: USTRZYKI GORNI. The villagers who once lived here knew it as *Ustriky horiszni*.

At the bend, a rather unusually wide gravel road continued south on the left side of the river. There was no bridge across the stream but one was hardly needed. The gravelly streambed was almost dry and we easily forded the river to the road on the other side. The road paralleled the Wolosatka so we determined that this was the road to follow. From here, the road again narrowed and was relatively flat. Both road and stream ran southeast almost in a straight line. The Wolosatka was considerably smaller above its two tributaries. It wasn't long before the hillsides opened into a rather large, flat, almost treeless plain. The foothills were not especially high at this elevation and created a large, earthen bowl with the stream flowing through its middle.

"It's easy to imagine that 3,000 or more people could once have lived here," I said as I stopped the car on the road. We hadn't passed another vehicle ever since leaving Protisne so I wasn't worried about holding up traffic. There was a strange, eerie feeling in these mountains. They were uninhabited and devoid even of wildlife.

We got out to look around. At one time, in the village's early history, it was supposed to have been inhabited by mountain bandits but that activity was put to a stop when the Austrians gained control of the land. During the 17th and 18th centuries, when the people in this part of Galicia were under the heavy hand of the Polish *szlachta*, their gentry, their nobility, the village was said to have the right to protect runaway serfs. In the near distance, almost in the center of this plain, a hillock rose 50 or 60 feet above the valley floor. It, too, was topped by a ring of trees that once probably harbored a church.

It was just as Stanley had described. Near the base of the hillock were four houses whose front doors opened almost onto the road. It saved a lot of shoveling in the winter because this area is known for its heavy snowfall. A hundred yards above the last house, and 300 yards on the opposite side of the road and the stream, I spotted the little shack that Stanley said to locate.

It seemed as if a giant hand just stuck it into the side of the hill. Next to it, about 50 feet away, was obviously an outhouse. On the opposite side was a small springhouse. I could see a well-worn path to both destinations. From the main road, I could see an old man sitting in a rocking chair on a small, front porch. The door behind him into the house was open. Even from the road, I could hear the strains of an accordion playing a polka on a radio.

We walked over an almost dry streambed and up the steep path. The hike was occasionally made easier when one or two stairs were cut into the dirt and flat stones were added as steps.

"*Dzien dobry,*" I said in Polish as we reached a small, flat area just before the porch.

"*Dobré rano y dobriy den,*" the man answered in Rusnak and not Polish as I had erroneously anticipated.

The man was ancient.

He rocked slowly back and forth intently studying my wife and me. Our clothing was different and he must have immediately noticed that. He sat in the chair with his right hand on the top of a walking stick that, from its wear, had years ago been fashioned into a cane. He used it to keep the rocker in motion. His face was oval, chiseled, lean and filled with the wrinkles of time, exposure to weather, hard work and worry. His hair was long for the styles in this region but not for hippies in Greenwich Village. His lips were thin in accord with the rest of his features. However, his most noticeable feature was his light gray, almost blue eyes that seemed to pierce me as he stood in front of him.

His hands were gnarled and arthritic. Large veins stood out boldly in the back of the right hand that gripped a natural bend on the top of the cane. As he stared at us, a cat walked out of the house, mewed, then curled around one of his legs.

Finally, he spoke. "What do you want?" he asked in Rusnak.

Just as I was about to answer when an announcer on the radio station broke in and rattled off something in Polish but, about two decibels higher than the accordion music.

Irritated, the man struggled for an instant, then got up, moving surprisingly well once he was underway.

"Wait," he said, as he disappeared into the house. A minute later the radio went dead.

He returned to his rocker and shooed off the cat that had taken his seat.

Again, he asks, "What do you want?"

"Last night," we stayed at the inn in Smil'nyk and we were talking with the innkeeper's son Stanley. He said that we should come up here and speak to you, that we would find you and your story interesting."

"Stanley talks too much. It is his Polish half. But, you said you stayed in Smil'nyk, not Smolnik. Why?"

"Because that is the way my grandmother pronounced it.

"Where are you from?"

"America," I said.

"America. I used to live in America. Now I wish I had never left. I used to be a coal miner. You said your grandmother was from Smil'nyk? Come a little closer. I cannot hear as well as I used to. The damned hearing aid the state gave me is not worth putting in the ear.

"What was your grandmother's name?

"Mynko...Mynkova" I quickly corrected her name by adding the feminine possessive suffix appropriate for a female.

"There used to be a lot of Mynkos living here.

"What was her first name?

535

"Kateryna.

"Half the young girls from these villages were named Kateryna. When there were villages here. The other half were Annas or Marys.

"Why did you come here?"

"To see for myself what my grandfather had described for me so often. When I asked him what his farm looked like in Europe, he said it was just like the hills where his farm was in Pennsylvania."

"What was your grandfather's village?"

"He said he was born in Protisne, but also lived in Dvernyk, Stuposiany and even Litowyschce."

"Why did he live in so many places?"

"Because his mother died giving birth to his youngest brother, then a year later his father died and they lost the farm. He lived from time to time with different relatives."

At first, I wasn't sure. But as I spoke to him I saw a tear forming in one, then the other eye.

"I, too, was born in Protisne.

"What was your grandfather's name?" asked the old hermit.

"It was Vasyl Yurkovich Najda," I said.

"*Bozé miy,*" the old man gasped and immediately blessed himself. I knew this man was not a Pole because of the way he blessed himself. He was Orthodox; an old, old, very old Rusnak.

The man seemed to gasp for air for a moment and then said, "*Woda. Woda.* Inside. Get me water."

I rushed inside the one-room house and spotted an empty coffee cup on the table. Next to the sink was a bucket of clear water. I dipped the cup into it, spilling half of it in a hurry to get the water to the old man. On the other side of the room, that was no more than 12 by 20 feet, was a bed and above it a homemade Orthodox cross.

The hermit gulped down the water and after a minute or two his gasping stopped and his breathing returned to normal.

"Who are you?" he asked.

"My name," I said, "is Nikolaj Stefanovich Karas. My mother is Anna Najda, the second daughter of Vasyl and Kateryna-Mynkova Najda."

"Stand back, back in the sunlight," he ordered me. "Let me get a better look at you."

"After a few minutes of studying my face, he spoke. "You look more like your grandmother than grandfather."

"You knew them?"

"Yes, I knew them very well.

"My name is Andrij Yurkovich Najda. It was I who said good-bye to my family in Goodtown in the summer of '22. Your mother was just 14 and your Aunt Mary married Sam, Sam... I cannot remember his name. He was from...let me remember... Tsaryn, Carynskie, just a few kilometers from Dvernyk."

"This cannot be," I said as the math rushed quickly through my mind. "Everyone thought you were dead. No one heard from you after you left Goodtown."

"There was good reason," the old man said.

"My God, that would make you a hundred years old."

"A hundred and one," Andrij Najda corrected me.

"But tell me. Is Vasyl still alive? Kasha? Ivan? Hryec?"

It took me an hour to answer all his questions and tell my great uncle what had happened to Andrij's American part of his family. Tears streamed down the old man's face almost continuously and my wife kept giving him tissues from her purse until they were gone.

I couldn't believe how easy it was to talk to him in Rusnak. It was like again talking to my grandmother or grandfather, like when they were alive. I was swept by a strange feeling. It was pure Boyko dialect.

"Life can be cruel," he said after he seemed to digest most of what I told him. "Now, as I look back, it would have been better if I had stayed in Goodtown. I sent money to my wife. But she refused to come to America. She was afraid of crossing the ocean, especially with our two girls. So, I had to return to them."

"Now it's your turn," I said, "to tell me your story. "Tell me why you never wrote or got word to my grandfather, or others."

"I will," said Andrij, "but something first. My throat is dry." He again rose quickly for a century-old man. I heard him slamming a cupboard door and then the clinking of glass. In a few minutes, he emerged with a bottle and three small glasses, none of which were alike. The bottle had no label. He placed the glasses on the flat railing that surrounded the porch, then pulled a cork from the bottle with his teeth and filled the glasses with a bright, clear, crystalline fluid.

"What is it?" I asked.

"It is vodka. I know a woman in the hills here who makes her own. It is better than any Polish vodka you can buy."

He raised his glass and said, *"Na za dorovya."*

"Boh dast dorovya," I answered correctly instead of just repeating the toast "God gives health." My wife and I touched glasses with him. The glass held the equivalent of about two shots. My great uncle downed it in a gulp. It took me two, but my wife sipped.

"This is smooth," I said.

"This is the answer to my long life," Andrij said as he held up the glass, admiring it as if was an old friend. "One glass a day, no more or no less. It keeps the blood flowing in my veins and in my head. Now, my story.

"I was a fool to think that Protisne in 1922 would be much like it was in 1910 when I left," Andrij continued. "It wasn't long, just 12 years that I was away. But, at that time, at that age, it seemed much longer. What I didn't realize was that in those years much had changed in Europe. Of course, there was the Great War. I thought life had not been so bad here when I left but we have a leaning to remember the good and put the bad out of our heads. I thought, that with money in my pocket, it would be easier when I came back. The Austrians seemed fair even though they let the damned Poles govern us. They held the Polaks in check. All that changed after the war. Almost all of Galicia was given to the Poles.

"It wasn't the Polish people who made life for Rusnaks so bad, but there were some *putskas* among them. It was the government authorities...the police and the army units, they were the worst. The Great War ended in 1918 but there was still fighting here among the Czechs, Hungarians, Poles and Bolshevik Russians. Much of it was caused by the communists who tried to get hold of power in all these countries.

"Two years before I came back, the Poles here defeated the 'Rosiany'. It was the only time the Soviet Army lost a war and they were looking for revenge. As a result of that victory, Poland took western Ukraine and all of Galicia. The Poles made no differentiation between Rosiany (Russians) and Rusnaki even though they knew better. And when we speak *po nasimu*, in our native language, they said it was Russian.

"Before I returned in 1922, my wife Maria and my two girls were living with her mother and father, Yurko Lisko, in Stuposiany, just a few kilometers from Protisne. So, the first thing I did when I got back was look for a house with a good field so that I could farm. I felt rich. And, I was when compared to those around me. I had nearly a thousand dollars that I had saved while working in the mines. There were farms available, mostly owned by widows or abandoned women whose husbands went to America and died, either in the mines or the steel mills. And there were others whose husbands never wrote or sent money after they left. They were never coming back, especially if they found a younger woman in America. Why should they?

"Maria suggested that I look at our old farm, the one the Zellmans stole from us. I guess you heard that story from your grandfather. I went to look at it and was saddened by what I saw. Ihor Zellman had let the place fall into disrepair. He had put a porch on the front but other than that it looked like it did when I left...but older, neglected. He was a merchant and not a farmer and the house showed it. He had turned a part of it into a store before I left but the small sign was gone and the door shut. Later, I found out he sold it to a Polish baker. He had it for but a year or two and lost it because of poor business. Zellman held the mortgage and got the house back and the down payment.

"When I knocked, his wife Rebekah came to the door.

"What do you want?" she said in a nasty way. She never was nice. Ihor was okay."

"I want to see Ihor. Is he here?"

"Who are you?"

"I told her and she was surprised."

"Where have you been...to America?

"Ihor is dead," she finally said. "He died four years ago. He got the flu or something. By the time he saw a doctor, the doctor said it was too late. He left me with this monster of a house, a store and barn, and no money. The fields have not been cut in years, gone to seed. There are not many men left in the village to do that kind of work. Besides, they want too much. They have all gone to America where they have become rich.

"Are you rich?"

"Do you want to sell this place?" I asked.

"How much will you give me?"

"I didn't make an offer that day but spent the next week asking around at other farms. I went back and made an offer, a very low offer. I was struck dumb when she right away said yes. She didn't haggle. It was unlike her. She wanted to move out in a few days. After that, for the longest time, I couldn't believe that I would once again live in the house where I was born, where my father was born, where my grandfather was born and all my fathers before me. I would have paid her twice as much just to be able to do that.

"It took me a year to get the house back in condition, to remove the store front. My wife and daughters helped. Maria, my oldest daughter was now 16 and Anna 14. And, we now had another baby on the way. Life seemed good, almost too good. That was true.

"The Polish police had stationed one man in Protisne and as I worked on the house and barn he seemed to find real delight in harassing me. There was nothing for him to do here. There was no crime in our village, or other Rusnak villages. He was put here by the Poles just to show us who is boss. But he did it to others in the village as well so I didn't think it was unusual. He was a *putska*. He wasn't a young man, maybe in his late 30s and had been in the army, in the military police. He was arrogant and looked down on all of us. The village had no Poles living there at that time, just Rusnaks, about two dozen Jews, and a few Gypsies. There was only two or three Jewish families when I left. I guess they moved in as many of us went to America. We all seemed to get along, all except Stashko Kupinski, the policeman.

"I never knew it until it happened, but he had eyes for my oldest daughter. If I had known, maybe I could have prevented what had happened. On that day, I was working late, at the far end of the field above the house. I was cutting hay and had to get it all done because it looked like it would rain the next day. It was almost dark when I got back to the barn.

"As I got near, I heard noises, and then a woman yelling, and then screaming. It was my wife. I let the horse go and ran into the barn to see what was wrong. My daughter Maria was in the loft and crying. At the same time, my daughter Anna rushed into the barn from the house. I looked up and saw Maria with most of her clothing torn off. Then I saw Kupinski next to her, pulling up his pants. That bastard had raped my daughter. I was about to go up the ladder to the loft when I saw Anna rush to the base of the loft.

There was my wife, lying on the floor and not moving. Next to her was an empty pail of milk. It was my daughter Maria's chore to feed milk to the calf. Somehow it was spilled.

"Momma tried to stop him," Maria yelled when she saw me. "She climbed the ladder to the loft. She was fighting him and he pushed her backward. She fell off the loft."

"I saw it happen just as I came in," a frightened Anna screamed."

"Father, Father," Anna yelled, "Momma isn't moving."

"I ran to her and felt her neck. Blood was still coming from her ear and mouth. She looked like she landed on her head. She was dead. Her neck was broken.

"Kupinski jumped down from the last rung on the ladder and landed on his feet before me.

"He sneered at me and said, 'Damned Rusnak bitch'."

"I don't remember much of what happened after that. I know I lunged at him. He was bigger than me, I remember that. But I had strength that I never knew I possessed. I guess digging coal makes a man a lot stronger than being a soldier or policeman.

"My daughters said I killed him with my bare hands. I broke his neck. That seemed a fitting way for him to die."

"There was a trial. A joke. I was surprised they didn't hang me for killing a policeman. Or, that the policeman from Smil'nyk who came later that evening didn't shoot me on the spot. But his killing my wife and raping my daughter must have made the Polish magistrate in Sianok a bit sympathetic toward me.

"He asked me if I had anything to say before he sentenced me.

"Yes," I said. "You have taken my land, my sweat and my labor. You have taken my food, my religion and my identity and my dignity. Now, you have taken my wife and our unborn child. You have taken my daughter's virginity. You might as well take my life. What else is there left to take?

"He gave me life, life in prison. I spent 23 years there."

"How did you get out?" I asked, "Did they parole you?"

"Poles don't parole Rusnaks. Usually they die in prison long before their sentence is over. But I survived. You cannot imagine what I had to endure to survive. I was treated worse than an animal and kept on the edge of starvation for most of those years."

Chapter 60   Andrij Yurkovich Najda's Epic Journey

"But how did you get out?"

"One day, I heard a lot of shooting outside the prison in Sianok were I was jailed. There were no windows so I couldn't see what was happening. It lasted most of the day. It was, I think, in 1939. August I think. No, it was September. I remember that because it was so hot in the cells, even though it was dark. There was no fresh air.

"I was surprised that evening when a guard came around with food. It wasn't the Polish guard but a soldier, a Soviet soldier. I thought he might let us out, seeing that we were Rusnaks. He said that if he had his way, he would save the state the cost of feeding us and shoot us all on the spot. We feared he would do that. He was a Bolshevik. An atheist. The Soviets lasted about two years in Sianok and then were replaced two summers later, in 1941, by Germans. That's why I think it was in 1939.

"The Germans told us about the war and looked us over very well. They had a doctor inspect us. Those who had only been in prison for a few months must have still looked good. The Germans gathered them together and were sent to work somewhere in factories. Most of us were old and I guess there wasn't enough meat on us to be worth fattening and sending to Germany. I would have welcomed that, even if I died there. It was better than the prison. Anything was better. I even thought, from time to time, of taking my own life but I could never face Christ in Heaven if I did.

"Then the Poles were back. They were communists and treated us worse than the Russians. They made the Poles, who worked here when I first arrived, look like nurses. Then one day, near the time when the guards would bring the other prisoners and me our gruel, a man with a large ring of keys came down the line of cells and was opening each cell. Mine was the first one. He had on a strange uniform, a mixture of German pants and a Polish blouse. On his left arm he had a patch with a *triyzub* (a trident) on it. Another man, also with a mixed uniform and the same badge, was with him, but armed with a pistol.

"He came to my cell and asked me to bless myself. I thought he was going to kill me after I finished."

"*Pravo slavniy,*" he said and motioned me and the two in the cell next to me, who blessed themselves the same way as I did, to get out."

"Go! You're free. Go. Get out. Go where you want to."

"They were members of the UPA and had driven the Poles from Sianok and a large part of Galicia. That was in the fall of 1945, after the second 'Great War' was over. I was 68 years old. I was an old man. The *triyzub* was the symbol of the UPA. I didn't even know who or what they were at that time. Prison is not the best place to learn what is going on in the world, especially a Polish prison.

"I'll never forget the day I walked out of the prison. I had forgotten what fresh air smelled and tasted like. It was a cool, crisp day in early spring. There wasn't a cloud in the sky. It was so blue it hurt my eyes. And, the mountains to the south still had snow on their tops. Somewhere beyond them were my home and my people.

"I made my way back to Protisne and passed several burned-out villages before I got there. I saw many bodies along the way, both German and Russian. I saw a woman sitting along the road just south of Lutowiska and asked her what happened here. I remember how she looked at me. She didn't say anything but put her hand to her mouth and ran away. I thought I scared her. Maybe I looked too much like a dead man, all bones, a beard and long hair. Finally, I found a few who told me what had happened. The UPA had been fighting the Germans that year then, after the Germans surrendered and the war ended, they began defending Ukrainians against the Soviet Communists.

When I got to Protisne, I saw our old house was still standing but my daughters no longer lived there. It looked like no one had lived there for more than a year. There were still a few people in the village, mostly old people. I found a cousin, a Salabaj, an old woman who was crippled by a bomb the Russians had fired at a German position in the village. She told me that the Russians had already sent most of the people to Ukraine. They said a few who managed to sneak back told them that they were resettled somewhere around L'viv, in a village called Komarno. It was a cooperative farm on the banks of the Vereshica River, not far from the Dnister. I stayed with my cousin for two months, until I regained my health.

Then, I began search for my daughters. I walked to where Smil'nyk had been. I was told Russians leveled it in 1939 when the Sian, for a year-and-a-half, was made the border between the Soviet Union and Germany. Between them, they eliminated Poland.

"I met a group of partisans passing through Smil'nyk on their way to Ukraine to support units there. They helped me get to Horodok just this side of L'viv. During this short period the Soviets were forced back by the UPA. I searched every farm cooperative in the area but no one knew of my daughters. I couldn't find them. Some said there were other cooperatives farther east but were controlled by the Soviet Army.

Backed by troops returning from Germany, the Russians again were threatening L'viv. The partisans said they were going back to the mountains. The Russians were good fighters on the open fields but didn't do well fighting guerillas in the mountains.

One unit was ready to go so I went with them. They had captured a Russian truck with several cans of petrol (gasoline) and we drove to Sambir. The Russians were hot on our heels. Just before Sambir a Russian airplane spotted us and strafed the road. We took shelter in the ditches but the truck was blown up. The shells must have hit the petrol cans. We walked to Sambir. It was only 4 or 5 kilometers away.

At first the town seemed deserted and we wondered why. But soon found out. We were spotted by a Russian machine gun emplacement that began shooting at us. We all took cover in a garage. To our surprise inside we found a German staff auto. Its tank was full. The partisans with me decided to take out the machine gun nest. They passed through a back street and killed them with grenades. All was quiet after that. It must have been the only unit there.

The staff auto had an open top (canvas) and three rows of seats. There were nine of us and we filled the auto. I remember how pleasant the ride was as we got higher and higher into the mountains. For most of the way the mighty Dnister River was but a dwindling mountain stream. At the village of Strelki it turned to the west and disappeared as it reached for the top of the mountains, the continental divide.

Because of the greeting we got in Sambir, we approached the town of Turka with more caution. To our surprise, we met another group of UPA partisans. They had been there for two days and were being pursued by a Polish unit. We joined forces and I took part in a few skirmishes and helped kill a few Polish Reds (vigilantes) and a Polish policeman near Borinja.

"Our unit was made up of about 30 men and a few women. But staying alive was becoming more difficult each day. We were slowly loosing people and the Poles seemed to get stronger with the constant supply of fresh troops. The Polish army continued to hound us. We hid out in the Beskids Mountains for several weeks until they were gone. Like the Russians, who had first chased us into the mountains, the Poles didn't know how to defend against our hit-and-run way of fighting. When we found a Polish patrol on the move, we would suddenly appeared out of the woods, kill as many as possible and before they could call up more men, we disappeared back into the trees. Too bad for us, they were slowly learning. But they could replace their lost men but we couldn't.

"It is time to get out, to go farther to the top," said our leader, Stefan Hodinko. He was from Bristova, a village farther southeast in the Carpathians, a part of Ukraine. He had been a school teacher before he joined the Russian army. "Maybe we should go as far as Uzhhorod, on the other side of the mountains. Good! We go. We will head for Uzhhok Pass and there cross the divide."

"We all agreed that there was nothing more we could do here and uncovered the German auto. We had driven it off the road and into the woods and covered it with branches and leaves. It was well hidden. We didn't have enough petrol to make it to Uzhhorod, but the men figured we could ride most of the way.

"Besides," Hodinko said, "it's all downhill. And, we will pass through a sight you won't believe. I will tell you the whole story when we get to the village."

Uzhhok, in today's Carpatho-Ukraine may not be the highest village in the Carpathian Mountains inhabited by Rusnaks but it is close to the top at 564 meters (1,850 feet). Before the Treaty of Versailles, in January 1919, it was part of the Austro-Hungarian Empire. Actually, it was a coveted enclave of Hungary and the Magyars never really shared their Rusnak peasants with the Austrians. After the Treaty was signed, the League of Nations joined it to Bohemia, Moldavia and Slovakia as Carpathian-Ruthenia, as four nations bent of self-determination, and named them Czechoslovakia.

That was about as much recognition as Rusnaks ever got. Its self-determination was what the Czechs decided to give away. In 1939, when Hitler and Stalin needed time to build the forces in the impending second "Great War," Adolph gave it back to the Hungarians, who never really gave it up, as a reward for their joining the Axis Forces.

Even after it became part of the Czech Republic most of the land was still owned by wealthy Hungarians whose huge estates encompassed most of the alpine highlands and were used primarily as their private hunting grounds. One of Europe's greatest concentrations of wild boars, bears and wolves was in the area around Uzhhok.

"Before reaching Uzhhok," Andrij continued, "we drove through Uzhhok Pass. Just as we cleared the pass there was a road to the right and a sign in Polish pointing to Sanky (Sianki in Polish).

"My God," I remember thinking as I read the sign. "This is where the San River begins its life and runs past my front door in Smil'nyk.

"The pass was higher than the village. As we entered a narrowing of the surrounding mountaintops there was another sign. It said 889 meters. Even higher to the west was the top of another mountain. I forgot how much higher it was said to be.

"Out the other side of the pass was the village. It looked so peaceful and pretty in the sun. But that was deceiving. There were no people on the road, or in their houses or fields. There were not cattle or sheep on the grass that was a bright green. There were no dogs. There was no center to the village as in most *selos* (villages). The houses were lined up in rows on each side of the road for maybe 2 kilometers. Their white walls were as white as the fields of snow that still covered the tops of the surrounding peaks, even in late April. As in every mountain village, the fields were behind the houses and extend up to the snowfields. I will never forget the sight.

"It was strange that there were no people. I saw piles of cut wood stacked neatly outside the house walls. They had once been neatly piled but many had tumbled down and lay about the yards. Some of the house had no doors and those with glass windows had them smashed. The town was abandoned. Most of the high-pitched-roofs had holes in the thatching or the roofs were completely gone.

"What has happened here?" I asked Hodinko.

"He didn't answer but pulled the auto to the side of the road and stopped."

"It time for my story," he said, and began.

"Life in the tops of these mountains was always a struggle for those who lived here. Conditions were always primitive and it never seemed to change for them, no matter who was their master. Because of the strategic location of the pass as a gateway to the south this became a battleground between the Germans and the Russians. But war was not the main cause that turned Uzhhok into a ghost town. Its end began before war came here. It was not the result of what we see here but that of starvation.

"It began about 1930, or maybe a bit sooner, when the Czech government in Praha (Prague) was beginning to pay some attention to the wants of Slovaks and Ruthenians (alias Rusnaks) and were dividing many of the Austrian- and Hungarian-owned estates. It was like continued reparations for what the Germans and Hungarians had caused people here to suffer from the Great War.

"Uzhhok was never a village as we think of villages. But here in the mountains, the land shapes the village and most times there is a stream that runs through its center. As you can see Uzhhok is like that. At most it had two stores, a post office and three or four Rusnak churches. There were about 50 families with about 600 people who once lived here.

"You must also remember, that Czechoslovakia suffered more because of the war than most other nations because it was a new country without any established economy with the countries outside its borders. And inside, there were many 'aliens' who didn't like the settlements made at Versailles...most of all, were the Magyars (Hungarians).

"Having enough food for everyone in the new country was the biggest problem and starvation was everywhere but was worst in these mountains. Here the soil is poor and the growing seasons short because of its heights. But, it was made even worse by the actions of one Hungarian prince. I don't know his name, but he still owned many hectares of land around here.

"About seven or eight years ago, he was said to be hunting wild boar and was about to make a killing on an especially big pig. But when a bunch or Rusnaks marched across where he was waiting they scared the boar. They were gathering peepenkee (mushrooms). He was so infuriated by their presence that he decided they would never again disturb his sport. He was also angered because there were rumors that Praha was going to take away his lands and divide them among the peasants. He ordered his overseers, also Hungarians, never to give us work or food as long as his lands are part of Czechoslovakia.

"So began their starvation that ended in death for many people!"

"Why didn't they plant the fields behind their houses?" asked one man.

"They could," answered Hodinko, "if they had seed. It seems that had all eaten their seed potatoes years before just to have something to eat. They used the wheat seeds to bake their last loaves of bread after the potatoes were gone. Besides, summers here are too short to grow wheat."

"Why not oats," answered the questioning man." I know oats takes a shorter time to grow."

"That's true," said Hodinko. "But only horses and cows eat oats. You cannot make bread from oats."

"Then what did they do?" the man asked again.

"One of two things," answered Hodinko. "Some starved and are buried here, and the others tried to get out of these mountains. The sides of the road to Uzhhorod are marked with many crosses. Most of the people who started were already too starved to walk south. Don't count the crosses," he further advised, "because I hear it is bad luck."

"We slowly drove through the rest of the village," said Andrij, "and at its southern end saw a church in ruins. Behind the church it a field filled with unattended graves and white falling, crosses. They were all Rusnak crosses. No one had cut the grass for years and it looked forbidding. As we passed the church we blessed ourselves. I wondered when was the last time someone had prayed in the church. It made me start thinking of my future, what future I had left.

It made me decide that I was too old to run with the younger men. Besides Hodinko said his unit was going to be disbanded.

"I think it is time for me to go home," I said to Hodinko. "If it is time for me to die I would rather it be along the San.

"There were two others in our group, one from Lutowiska and another from Rabe. They were not much younger than me and both had served in the Russian army. They, too, decided to cross the border with me into Poland and follow the San home."

"In that case," said Hodinko, "I will drive you three back to the other side of the pass so you can take the road to Sjanky. It is less than a kilometer away. I don't think there are any Polish customs men waiting at the border. I will drive you there. If there are customs men there, we can answer their questions with our pistols."

"Just as we drove though to the other side of the pass, a land mine exploded under the left side of the auto and lifted us off the ground. As the auto was turning over I was thrown out of my seat and landed in a ditch. Hodinko and I were the only survivors. Hodinko had not been touched but I landed on my side and my shoulder was hurting."

"I don't know who planted the mine," Hodinko said as he brushed dirt from his face. I guess we missed it the first time across. There is a trenching tool in the trunk. Get it. We must bury our comrades.

"I have nothing waiting for me in Sjanky," said Hodinko when we were finished, "but I may still have someone in Bristova. Good luck," he said to me as we shook hands and kissed each other on the cheeks. "May God go with you. Good bye."

"The post on the border was unmanned and and pole-gate was up, in the open position. The guardhouse was rattled with bullet holes. A few feet beyond the barrier I saw a sign, written in German. Maybe it was left over from when the Austrians manned this checkpoint. *San Ursprung. Die Erhebung 1,028m*, it read, The Source of the San 1,028 meters (3,373 feet). It was a spring, the very source of the river that runs in front of my house. It sprang out of the earth about a hundred meters from the road. I walked to see it and filled my Polish canteen with Rusnak water."

Sjan, the river's name is not a wholly Slavic word. It is a word in the proto-Indo-European language; among which Keltic and Slavic peoples are members. It means a fast or rapid stream. In Keltic it means river. The fact that these mountains were once occupied by Kelts is supported by the discovery of Keltic tent rings in Trapcza on the Sjan, near Sjanok

Sjanky (Sianki in Polish) was not the typical Rusnak mountain village that is always built on both sides of a small alpine stream. This layout gives more people water closer to their houses. But here, most of its high-pitched, thatch-covered houses were located on the east side of the San River. The houses were ensconced in a shallow bowl surround by low-lying, gentle mountaintops whose peaks had been drastically honed by the last hemispheric glacier 60,000 years earlier. They have been freed of its heavy, icy mantle but a short 20,000 years ago. Like most of the villages along the north side of the Carpathian Mountains, an eastward extension of the Alps that disappear in Rumania, it was settled by Rus tribes that climbed from the lowlands to the north. As they cut their way upstream, they met scattered numbers of Kelts (Celts) who at one time, after the last glacier receded from Europe, were widespread north of the Alps from Rumania west to the British Isles. The soil was too poor for anything but subsistence gardens but rich enough for conifers. They had been cleared to expand the pasture lands for cattle and sheep.

Before the Great War started, Sjanky was populated by nearly 700 Rusnaks. Less than 500 survived, along with over a hundred Jews, after the war ended. In 1921, after the land was attached to Poland by the League of Nations, 224 Poles were counted in its population. In 1938 there were 176 houses in Sjanky inhabited by 724 Rusnaks, 137 Poles and 173 Jews. During the invasion of Poland in 1939, Sjanky was a part of Poland, and Polish forces tried to defend a line along the San River from Sept 6, 1939 until they were overwhelmed by German forces on September 12, 1939. On September 17, 1939, the Soviet Red Army invaded the eastern regions of Poland in cooperation with Germany. The Soviets were carrying out their part of the secret protocols of the Molotov-Ribbentrop Pact, which divided Eastern Europe into Nazi and Soviet spheres of influence. In the process, Sjanky was destroyed. However, on that date, Sjanky was incorporated into the Soviet Union and remain so until the Soviet Union collapsed in 1991 and became a part of the independent Ukraine.

Since then, it has again become a part of Poland. However, the border with Ukraine passes through the east part of the village and thus it is also a part of that nation.

By the end of WW II, there were no Rusnaks in Sanky, or Jews. What Rusnaks survived were sent to Ukraine, on the east side of the Curzon Line, the new Polish eastern border in an "exchange of populations" of Poles who had been on the east side and returned to Poland. The Jews died in the gas chambers.

During the height of the Rusnak occupation Sjanky contained four Greek Catholic churches, that had originally been in the Orthodox See, and one Lutheran church. But the real story is what transformation took place in Sjanky. It began in the late 1800s and early 1900s with affluent Hungarians, their nobility and their mountain estates. It was influenced first by the Polish nobility whose control waned in the Carpathians with the partition of Poland in 1772. Poland reappeared after it was recreated by the Treaty of Versailles in 1919. Much of it was built in the post-Victorian style but art deco crept in during the late 20s and throughout the '30s. It was its massive growth as a summer and winter recreation center for the elite, the archaic royalty of Europe and now its *novo riche*. There was a surge in the building of mansions and elegant hotels that must have stunned the primitive Rusnaks. By 1939 it was serviced by a first-class railroad and an elaborate train station. Pensions were everywhere available and elegant hotels hustled for clients. It contained spas and ski lifts, and even a gambling casino.

Since then, it has regained some of its importance as a summer resort but not even close to the scale it achieved before WW I I. Now nearly 500 Ukrainians populate the town. Its railroad has been rebuilt and it is again a stop on the L'viv-Uzhhorod line

"As a young man, before I went to America," said Andrij, "I had often heard of what the *sczlachectwo* (Polish royalty) had created in Sanky. I didn't believe it. I just couldn't imagine such things were possible until I was in America.

"As I walked down the road, along the little stream," Andrij continued, "I could see house foundations, places where big buildings had once been. Even parts of railroad track. But everything else was gone. There were still three churches in ruins and but looked abandoned. I guess the Germans and Russians ruined the place with their bombard ing the Poles. I was glad to leave the place.

"I walked south. Following the little used road to Beniowa and Bukowiec. The farther I went the more people I saw. They were all Rusnaks and they gave me bread and kobasi and I slept in their barns and drank from their wells. The route to Smil'nyk was much longer if I stayed along the San. I met two men in Bukowyj (Bukowiec in Polish) who were selling wood in front of what remained of the Villa Rubenstein. They said there was an easy trail that would take me over Halych Mountain. It follows a stream of the same name that rises from the mountain north side of the mountain, near its top. After that, it is an easy hike to the Wolosatka River. The Wolosatka re-enters the San just a kilometer above Protisne, my father's village.

"It was only 7 kilometers to the top of Halych Mountain but it took me a full week to make the climb. I guess they thought I was younger and stronger than I looked. Just before I reached the pass on the south side of Halych Mountain, I though I was about to be killed. The trail was almost covered with small, stunted pine trees and just before me I heard a horrible grunt. Then the brushy trees shook as the biggest bull I ever saw came running toward me. I blessed myself, thinking my end was to be here. Then it stopped and pawned the ground like bulls do before they charge. It was then that I realized it wasn't a bull. The hump on its back was too big and it was a dark brown. It was a bison, a mountain bison (buffalo). I fell to the ground and when I looked up it was gone."

The mountain is 1,333 meters high (4,373 feet).

"It was not all downhill," as the men from Bukowyj said. "It took me three days of walking fast to reach the headwaters of the Wolasatka River and another two days to reach the village of Wolosate," said Andrij. "We had relatives from Wolosate but I had never been there. I could go no farther. I was all used up when I reached it. As I sat on the roadside I was trying to decide what to do next. The village lay on one side of the road and the little river on the other. Beyond the river was a little house, no more than a hut, on the side of a hill. No one was in it. There were still people in the village. It was a big village. There were people walking on the road and after a while a couple, a man and a woman, approached me and asked what I was doing.

"I said I needed somewhere to sleep for the night and was too tired to walk over to the village. The woman said that the people who lived in the hut were sent to Siberia the year before (1945) because they had helped hide a UPA man. It was empty because it was too small for a family, so I moved in.

"All was quiet for a month and then one day a UPA runner came to Wolosate. He warned the people in the village that a large number of Polish soldiers were coming to burn the village. They were just a day away. From my perch here, I could see a few kilometers down the road. The next day, when I saw tanks on the road I figured I better get out. I ran into the woods, farther up the hill, where I couldn't be seen but could watch what was happening in the village below. I still had a pair of binoculars that I took off a dead Polish officer and a German rifle. With the glasses, I could see everything but couldn't believe my eyes. How could one Christian be so cruel to another Christian; that one Slav could be so cruel to his Slavic brother? They were like animals.

"I watched through my glasses, as a big, covered, troop transport truck pulled up the hill and stopped at the church, inside the grove of trees," he said as he pointed across the road to the stand of trees. "I saw them carry icons, candleholders, priest's garments and other things from the church and load them onto the truck. They had great trouble but were finally able to load the church's bell onto it. Then they set the church on fire. It didn't burn well at first, maybe because of its tin roof. Then the next day, while it was still smoldering, they threw incendiary grenades into it.

"I watched as one soldier crossed the stream then climbed the hill heading toward my little house. Not satisfied that there was no one inside he could shoot, he threw a torch into it. Then he turned around and went down the path and joined two other soldiers on the road. I could have picked them off with my Mauser. At the bottom of the hill, he turned around and saw that the torch must have gone out. In disgust, the idiot fired a few shots into the house and waved his fist at it.

"Lucky for me, I had a wash tub filled with water and had some clothes in it. The torch landed in the tub. God was with me.

"Look, there, there are the bullet holes," he said and pointed to the wall behind him.

"I feared for my life and spent three nights in the woods before believing it was safe to return to the house. The village was still smoldering when I got back and the smell was awful. It wasn't just wood and straw that had burned. No one was alive or moving in the village. I have been here ever since.

"A few years after the village was burned, a big truck came with three Polish families and all their belongings. They began to fix up three houses near the road, below me. There they are, you can still see them. Then a few months later, a Polish official from Sianok came to see them. They sent him up to my house. He was counting heads. He spoke to me and I answered him in Polish. I had learned enough Polish in prison so that he put me down in his ledger as a Polak. That is the only time I didn't mind being called a Polak.

"For a while, the Poles stationed border guards here and a few men with the Internal Security force. They were up here once, in the beginning, but left me alone. Then, the Poles declared this land a national park and for a while we had biologists and foresters climbing these hills. But I haven't seen them in some time.

"Once in a while a government person from Sianok comes here to check on the people. One time, one man brought back a thing for my ear so I could hear better. It never worked. After that, they left me alone. I think he kept coming back just to see if I was alive. Whenever he did, he left me a bag of batteries for my radio.

"Who could ever have imagined that my great nephew would someday discover me? Nikolaj, pour us another vodka. Today I will make an exception. I hope I can live long enough to empty the bottle.

"How full is it?"

Before my wife and I left Wolosate we found the woman who was making the homemade vodka. I bought six bottles at $1 a bottle and returned to say goodbye for my great uncle.

"Now, uncle," I said, "you must live long enough to finish these bottles."

"See, I told you it would be worth your while," Stanley said when we returned from Wolosate to say good-bye. "I knew you would be surprised. I figured that if he wasn't your relation, at least he was another Najda. They aren't all dead.

"Where are you going from here?"

"To Zakopane by this evening," I said, "to return this rental car. Then we catch a 10 o'clock train tonight for Prague. I guess it's an all-night ride."

"Too bad you don't take one in the morning. The train goes through some of the world's most beautiful mountains.

"Well, Nikolaj, did you find what you came looking for?"

I thought for a while before answering. The events of the past few days were so monumental that I had little time to absorb them or put them in a proper perspective.

"Yes and no," I finally said. "I never thought I would have to come here, this far from the coal mines, to find a live Hunky. But I did find some answers to a horde of questions that have been bouncing around in my mind for years. I would have liked to have found more relatives but I think I can live with what I did find. Most important of all, I found the ground from which my roots sprang and this has given me a firm link with the past.

"Stanley," I said as we walked out of the inn and were returning to the car, "will you do a favor for me? From time to time, will you look in on the old man? And, if he runs out of vodka here are two 20s. He will direct you to the woman who makes it up there."

"No problem," said Stan. "I know who she is. There are still a few secrets in these hills, but Zosia isn't one of them."

"Good luck," Stanley said as we pulled away.

"Good luck," I repeated. "Study hard."

The End

Appendix....

Who is a Rusnak?

Coming up with a definition of who are Rusnaks, Rusnyaks or Rus'naks, is not as easy as defining other ethnic groups. No one authority today seems to have established a universal or even widely-accepted definition. However, it behooves the reader to have some understanding as to who these people are before he or she delves into this book because the book is about them.

A working synonym for Rusnak might be the Rusnak/ Ukrainian word *Horyschany*, which translates into "those who live up or above." Up or above in this case refers to the Carpathian Mountains. They also might be called mountaineers and by some Americans, hillbillies because of the poverty in which they lived.

The Carpathian Mountains are an eastern extension of the Alps of central Europe, but older in their geological history and time and weather has made them less rugged. They begin by rising out of the Plains of Hungary just east of Vienna and Bratislava. They gently curve north in an arc through the extreme eastern part of the Czech Republic, across all of northern Slovakia and parts of southern Poland, through the southwest section of Ukraine, and end in northern Rumania.

In the 3rd and 4th centuries, Slavs who settled in the Prypit Marshes, between present-day Byelorussia and Ukraine, underwent a population explosion. Segments, primarily large tribes looking for new lands, began an outward migration in all directions except north from this center. One group moved south and west over these mountains. The forefront of this group went as far as the Adriatic.

They became the South Slavs or Yugoslavs (*Yuhoslavs*). Another segment went west and became the Western Slavs and today is composed of Poles, Czechs, Moravians, and those Slovaks in two western provinces of Slovakia.

Those who remained in the motherland became differentiated into Muscovites (Russians), who moved both northeast and east and Byelorussians (Belarus), who moved south of the Russians and between them and the Rus or Ukrainians. The latter group spread east and went father south, and extended their domain over the Carpathian's continental divide. It is this latter group, the most southerly element of the Rus, who became known as Rusnaks. They were physically separated from the Yugoslavs and their parent Ukrainians in the 9th century by the intrusion of Magyars (Hungarian tribes) who migrated west in several waves from Asia and settled in what today are the Plains of Hungary.

Those original Rus people (current-day Ukrainians) who settled in these mountains between the 8th and 9th centuries, later began identifying themselves as Rusnaks (as opposed to the remaining "flatland" Rus located to the north in Halychyna (Galicia). Their elevated domain might have been appropriately called Rusnakia. Still, they were a part of the Rus province of Galicia with Halych (Ivano-Frankivs'k) as its titular and initial capital, but L'viv as its cultural, economic and eventually its political capital. Halych was also the seat of Prince Danylo who commanded the entire province at the height of its existence. They occupied the foothills north and south, and all upper elevations of the Carpathian Mountains. Geographically, this area extended from about Zakopane in the west and along the Vistula River to Vatra Dorniy in the east, just south of today's Ukrainian/Rumanian border, and held sway over lands to the east as far as the shores of the Black Sea

Today, Rusnak occupation of this area has been greatly diminished by the encroachment of peoples who belong to the political entities that gained control of these lands. Large portions of the Rusnak populations were absorbed, assimilated into Polish, Slovak and Hungarian populations, where their ethnic identity was lost. Existing Rusnak populations were relegated only to the higher elevations and to the rural lands surrounding the largest villages, and most towns and a few cities. Over the course of the last 100 years, even many mountain Rusnaks lost their ethnic identity and have been assimilated into Czech, Slovak, Polish, Hungarian and Rumanian societies. Still, a core of ethnically, relatively pure Rusnaks lives in portions of Poland and Slovakia. Only in Ukraine, have they been able to maintain most of their language, customs, religion and traditions because this segment has not seen the intrusion of a foreign society, except possibly Soviet, and to a lesser degree, Russian.

Rusnaks--who became isolated from the Kevin Rus, and subsequently from the greater Ukrainian society by new political boundaries, and through time and distance—have seen their language evolve slight dialectic differences. Some of the outward causes for these variations were influenced by Polish, Hungarian and Austrian occupiers. Most, however, were the result of an internal evolution that is inherent in every language and occurs over a period of time. Three major dialects resulted. They are the Lemko dialect found in the westernmost part of the Carpathians; Boyko dialect spoken by people who are roughly separated from Lemkos by the Sian (San) River (pronounced Shan) and its numerous tributaries; and the Hutsal dialect, whose people occupy the eastern Carpathians that today is identified as the Carpatho-Ukraine. Those Boykos living in Ukraine often refer to themselves as *Verkhovyntsi,* or mountaineers or highlanders.

At times, the dialects of these three Ukrainian subcultures is so slight that one can hardly tell when one has moved from one area to another. The evolution of their speech, until most recently, was a natural phenomenon in these mountains where travel and communications had been sharply limited. They are about as different from each other as the microcosmic variations that develop in language between one village and the next one upriver. My maternal grandfather, Vasyl Najda, (pronounced Va-seal and Ni-da, long i) used to tell me that there was almost no difference in language between his village and the next. But, if he had reason to go three or four villages away, usually only upstream or downstream--the villages were almost all located along rivers-- that he was amazed when he discovered that the people there had slightly different words for the same object.

Ironically, it is in these people, in these isolated mountain villages, where the language, belief and some of the customs of the first Rus, have been preserved for nearly 1,000 years and are still closely akin to what they were before the turn of the 10th century.

Nor did, a hundred or more years ago, the villagers define themselves as Lemkos, Boykos or Hutzals. If you would ask any one of them who they were, their answer was almost always, "We are Rusnaks." They would also, almost vehemently follow with "We are not Russiany (Rus-si-an-y) or Moscovy, but Rusnaks." It is an ironic contradiction that many of the children of these immigrants to American began to identify themselves as Russians. That's another story and based on religion.

Today, many Rusnaks are grouped together under the term Lemko. To most Rusnaks, that term Lemko was unknown until World War II. In the early 1930s, the Polish government began to apply the ethnonym Lemko to these people, hoping their assimilation into the Polish population would be more rapid and easier than the Russian-sounding term Rusnak. This was especially so after the forced relocation of thousands of Rusnaks from southeastern to southwestern Poland, in post-WW II Lower Silesia, a German province before that war.

One major factor separates Rusnaks from their brother Slavs, be they other Ukrainians, Poles, Czechs, Slovaks or even Russians. It is the stern, challenging and unforgiving mountainous environment in which they lived and their character that evolved in this land. The daily hardships they endured just to survive in these mountains strongly influenced and gradually shaped their individualistic behavior. It created in them unique and separate characteristics that eventually differentiated them both physically and emotionally from other Slavs. More than a dozen centuries of living intimately in this demanding landscape molded their psyche, their behavior, and to some degree, their appearance.

Rusnaks are the most westerly of the Eastern Slavic Group that included Russians, Byelorussians, as well as Ukrainians. They began moving into these highlands in the 5th to 7th centuries because of their rapidly-expanding populations and at a time when these lands were sparsely occupied. In them, they found little or no resistance from the dwindling populations of indigenous Kelts. Unlike the more rugged and higher Alps to the west, the Carpathians are older and thus gentler. Eons of rain, snow, cold and heat, and leveling glaciers, have contributed to making them a more livable place, but still no less taxing to human habitation.

On the north side of the continental divide, scores of small streams grow rapidly in size as they drain downward into the Sian River. Near the mountain range's base, the Sian turns west along the foothills and eventually merges into the Vistula River to flow north into the Baltic Sea. When the first Slavs began moving into these mountains from the plains to the north, they were all heavily forested. The path into them was difficult and they chose the easiest route, along the banks of the numerous rivers, streams and finally trickles, as they pushed higher and farther into the mountains. Their goals were always to find new areas to graze their flocks of sheep. They were initially herders and not farmers.

Wherever rivers and streams created a fairly level flood plain, the migrants often stopped, cut away parts of the forest, built their log houses and grazed their sheep in the newly-created meadows. If the flood plain or valley was narrow, they built their high-pitched, thatch-covered houses at right angles to the streams. If they were expansive, they built their houses facing the streams. Seldom were houses ever built very far from water. Everything they needed to survive in this harsh landscape they drew from the water, the land and its forests. In their climb to higher elevations they unknowingly relegated themselves to the mountain's poorest soils and were hampered when their society changed from herders to farmers. By then, it was too late for them to return to the lowlands because others had gained control of them and their better soils.

To be able just to exist, from day to day, season to season, and year to year, all their energies were constantly directed toward securing shelter, food and clothing. That struggle left little time or energy for anything else. To satisfy these three needs, they occupied themselves with work from sunrise to sunset. If any one went unfulfilled, their very lives were threatened.

In their constant struggle for survival, the Rusnaks became a much closer part of their land than any of them could realize, or would admit if they knew. Their language, customs, fashions, values, myths, beliefs, and even religion, that originally was pantheistic, were all influenced, controlled and dominated by the mountainous environment.

That is what a Rusnak is. And, the highlands they inhabited are now under the political "aegis" of Poland, Slovakia and Ukraine, and might be called Rusnakia.

A word about the names of people and places in this book...

Many of the names, primarily first names, of people in this book, and the places where they lived, traveled and died, are written in several forms and several languages. One reason is that the spellings for their names often changed each time new conquerors gained their lands. To reduce confusion, the reader should be aware that in all the Slavic languages, as opposed to English and many Western European languages, names of individuals can have as many as half-a-dozen variations. This is often based on the persons gender, their age, or relation to the family and non-family members, and in both formal and informal situations. This is especially apparent in terms of endearment between parents and children and even among siblings and their extended families. It may make a language richer but it can be confusing to those unaccustomed to such approaches. I have not tried to keep them to a minimum because they give the reader an immediate sense of the relationship between these people. I hope I have written the prose in such a manner that inserted explanations are not needed.

The reader must also be aware that these people of the Carpathian Mountains, the Rusnaks, in the last thousand or so years, have been controlled by Tatars, Mongols, Hungarians, Poles, Lithuanians, Swedes, Austrians, Czechs, Slovaks, Germans and Russians. Each time a new authority took over controlling their lives, they often changed the names of the Rusnak villages and even the way the people's names were spelled and pronounced. The borders of their lands also fluctuated regularly between conquering nations. They introduced new words and new fashions that were at first foreign but eventually made their way into the Rusnak's everyday lives and vocabulary.

I have used their names and the names of their villages in the way they used them when they spoke among themselves regardless of how the dominating power at the time determined how they should be spelled or sounded. Thus, the village of my paternal grandparents was Vilagy or Vilagi, but Vilag in Hungarian. Today, on maps of Slovakia, it is Svetlice. And Smil'nyk, the village of my maternal grandmother, is now Smolnik on Polish maps.

Below are a few words with both versions. The left column is Rusnak the right column is today's version:

Halychyna	Galicia, on Polish maps
Protisne	Procisne
Smil'nyk	Smolnik
Sian River	San River
Lisko	Lesko
Sianok (Shee-yan-uk)	Sanok
Caryn (Tsaryn)	Carynskie (Tsar-in skyeh-i
Dvernyk	Dwernik
Vilag (Hungarian)	Svetice (Svet-lits-eh) in Slovak
Litowyshche	Lutowiska

After 1911 the U.S.P.O. also changed names.

Good Town	Goodtown
Pine Hill	Pinehill

Made in the USA
Middletown, DE
28 December 2020

30275892R00345